DREAMER

NATHAN BARRETT

This book is for any person who wakes each morning searching within themselves for a reason to go on as I have done many a morning, anyone who finds themselves lost in a world of dichotomous monotony, or any individual who questions only to fall into an unanswered abyss of unconsciousness. May you follow me, find yourself in dreams, and in turn make them reality. Once you conquer your dreams, you have conquered your world - a world of realized self and unlimited possibility.

This is for the Dreamers.

Part 1

The City

Chapter I
The End of the World Which Lives In Us
(Monopoly, Heroes, and a Cranberry Poison)

The first dream came to me when I was only ten years old. It has been many years since, but I remember it very vividly to this day. In this dream, I functioned just as if I was awake; I saw clearly and heard every sound. I felt my feet clinging to the rocky surface of the mountaintop. I could move my head as the wild wind whipped my hair back, threatening to whisk me away into the vast array of nothingness. In this moment, I continue to feel the winter on my skin. I can still hear the chaotic sound of destruction far below the mountain. The blinding orange glow of the flames is burned into my memory as I sit here today. Even at ten years old, I knew I had witnessed the end of everything.

I had feared the end of the world long before the first of the many lucidly terrifying dreams. I was raised in a rural town with few churches - chapels that preached an endless revelation and Armageddon. Therefore, my juvenile senses were perked and primed at every mention of the end. Weather forecasts weighed on my troubled my mind, and I feared a storm upon even a single cloud floating across a blue sky. I would cower under my bed as the cyclonic winds whistled and silently pray for another day. I was granted my wish - of sorts - until I was not. The end was not brought about by Mother Nature, but by mankind itself. What brought about the end was a question and the audacity to find an answer. Who do we answer to? Is it creed or commandment? Is it government? Or is it in the hands of whoever dares to take it? These are the questions to search within yourself for. You see, the end was not like it was in the beginning. Things became different. What used to be openly accepted was strictly forbidden. You may think me to be an insane fool - I did too at first. I had a difficult time adjusting to the new rules. Ever since the world ended, everything changed. Humanity went from an organized society to an anarchic unrest very quickly without explanation nor preparation. The world became so divided that the ground in which it stood upon ruptured, freeing the demons that it had hidden from for millennia to crawl out from the abyss it was founded upon. If it were not for a man named Jack King, we all would have perished in the uproar that we overcame. Under his wing, we - as one people - prevailed.

Jack King was our leader. He took all chances and sacrifices to restore order to the people that were left. He rid the new world of danger and risk by instilling fear into the hearts of all of us. Every soul bore witness to his ruthless leadership displayed through his ability to handle difficult situations with ease, along with his keen sense of superiority. I know I make him out to be some kind of hero, but do not let my empty words fool you, my friend. Jack King was not a force to be reckoned with nor underestimated. What could be seen was not everything anymore - at least not for people like me.

Allow me to provide a brief history of the situation. Things were normal for the longest time. People were entitled drunkards engulfed in their own graves of petty wars and minuscule day-to-day problems. The only thing you were entitled to was a coffin, and even that could be taken away. We walked the endless cycle of self-pity, always striving to be the greatest. Ancient inconsistencies only reiterated themselves, coming back stronger and in a new light. No one saw what mattered, and it took the world by surprise and storm. You see, it was never terrorists, natural disasters, or crime that threatened the human race. We are all the same until we find something different about us and it sets us apart and at odds. What happened was not about race, religion, or any other microscopic, divisive detail of life. It was what made life possible - the essence of difference. Difference was a cancer, and it was believed that what started as a cell could multiply and devour, and it did. It was always the unstated duty of the

5

government to eliminate problems within the human race, and it was in the shadow of their failure that brought about the downfall of the world. Or at least that was the story we were told. Nevertheless, capitalizing on the fear and desire of the public was always a necessary business.

People were so ignorant. Destroy what you cannot control. How juvenile. The only ones to survive were the people who heeded the warning - the ones who took it seriously instead of claiming it to be a hoax. There were quite a few of those in that time. Fortunately, my family took the news seriously, especially since it was pressed and hammered into the back of our minds for weeks. My father watched the news religiously any time international affairs or any type of terrorist situation was mentioned; he was a retired Lieutenant General of the Army, after all. I had been on the Earth for barely a decade, and all I could process at the time were tiny, inconsistent words and phrases such as "codes" and "numbers" among the frequent, short-tempered cursing. I remember watching the angry people on the television as my mother cooked dinner and my father stared dumbfounded and concerned into the empty faces of the news reporters, reading his ancient notebooks and writing down scribbles and gibberish across the yellow pages. Each day, their patience grew ever-thinner as times grew ever-darker, and I did not fully comprehend what was going on until years later. The tensions in both my home and the world around me only seemed to worsen, and my family had no choice but to take action. It is in the midst of chaos and the unknown that disaster and panic set in. I woke up one morning to find my family packing boxes and hauling them to the basement. After a long period of confusion, I ended up carrying bags and belongings down to the cellar. At ten years old, it was all a blur. There was no time for explanation of the matter; we hauled everything downstairs and locked ourselves down and away from the outside world. I did get one question answered, however. "Why are we down here, Dad?" I asked my father. "It's safe down

here, Noah," he replied. "We're gonna be down here for a while."
My ten-year-old patience was already wearing thin.

It was an adventure at first. I knew not what was going on, and it seemed almost fun to me. The basement was far from uncomfortable with its low ceiling and cozy setup. We had pulled the furniture downstairs, along with all of our food and most of our belongings. It was actually quite a warm and connected scene. We told stories and played board games. Monopoly was always my personal favorite - you had to make intelligent financial decisions and stay out of jail, which was the basic fundamental guideline and to our ever-changing world above. From the age of a small child I suffered horrid, violent migraines in which ended with a toilet full of vomit and an exhausted mind. I fought valiantly over the years to decipher the source, and I finally discovered it many years later. For so long I had blamed dehydration and eyesight for my pain, but I came to find that it was my anxious tendencies and unrelenting obsessions were the cause. I would worry myself to my knees and lose my stomach, and my concerns were never satisfied. I was a worrisome young chap from the beginning, and I relaxed upon the knowledge that everything was in order and together. I kept my colorful bills free of creases and in numerical order, lightest shade to darkest shade; my checkers were always laid out in a pattern and my cards were always straight. The experience was much like a clubhouse of sorts, and the family was together for the first real moment I had within my memory. Then the power was extinguished like a candle as the world had been - and just as mysteriously and never to return in its full light. It is in the hands of the situationally adept that are at an advantage upon disaster; cranberries fret not when the floodgates burst. We had been down in the cellar for a week at minimum, and the routine of entertaining ourselves was growing older and older as the monotonous days carried on. My mother lit candles and carefully arranged them around the room to get the best lighting. We heard a creak of a floorboard and a slamming of a door in the house above us one of the first nights in the basement. It was the first time I had ever been scared during our bunkering. There was nothing more terrifying than being silent enough so looters cannot hear you. I suppose desperate times call for desperate measures. The house was broken into at least three times in the first two weeks. My father kept a calendar in the table drawer we had brought down to the cellar. We had been down there just under three weeks before things took a drastic tumble for the worst.

The twenty-second of August of that year is one I shall never be able to forget, no matter how hard I may try. Our closest neighbors were at least ten miles in each direction, and the Nebraskan air was silent. The three weeks had felt like much longer to me. The facade of a playful escapade had dwindled to nothing but a boring stalemate and a feeling of being a prisoner. I remember hearing a deafening booming sound from outside. My parents and my brother, Jacob, had jumped up to listen to the noise, but they soon joined me back on the floor. I had hidden under the coffee table, being the youngest and quite the impressionable child. I remember dust flying everywhere as the house shook, along with the rest of the Earth. An intense heat filled the basement, smoldering the wood and forming sweat on my brow. I saw a blinding light through the locked cellar door above the steps ahead of me as I peered through my father's arm. We all huddled for protection - not that it protected us from the fear. The noise stopped soon after as the explosion died down. I later found out that the entire house had come down on the roof of the basement, trapping us down there; that was the first atomic bomb dropped on our region of the country. That was a frightening thought back then among quite a terrifying time in my childhood; perhaps that was where my juvenility ended. I later discovered the reality of what had happened, and the truth was far deeper than "going away for a while". For the first time in history, a homegrown terrorist organization had assassinated the President during one of the many distractive occurrences within the country, hacked into the government database during the uproar and confusion, and stolen nuclear launch codes to be released upon the American people and all humanity to end the world. I had no time for toys.

It was later relayed that it was the only bomb dropped on our direct vicinity; the experience was absolutely horrifying. I still heard distant bombings, which prompted a stop of the heart at first earshot. Noise was the least of our worries as time went on. As another few weeks passed in the nearly collapsed basement, our food supply quickly depleted. My mother began rationing our supplies carefully, but they were bound to run out eventually. And they did, sooner rather than later. What started as sandwiches dwindled to crackers, then eventually to crumbs. The sound of our rumbling stomachs was greater than any explosion above, and the fear of starvation was superior to the feeling of suffocating to death. We went another week living off of mere scraps, and life became even more miserable in the dusty and saturated cellar. My father had given up on his calendar dates, but we had spent somewhere close to a month and a half down in the cellar - give or take a week. Either way, it was far too long to spend cooped up in a dingy basement with an empty stomach and a barren imagination.

I honestly did believe that we would be down there forever, or at least until we died. Death was a distant concept at that age, and I knew next to nothing about it apart from the constant fear. I figured all of the rest of our belongings had been pillaged, along with everything else valuable to a weary and desperate traveler. When I heard a creaking of wooden boards and the crashing of debris, I wondered just what was above us and what was left of our home. Noises were monsters back then, and they created demons along with them. Whatever - or whoever - it was, cleared a path and opened the basement door. It had been quite some time since I had seen natural sunlight, therefore the sky above was blinding and headache-inducing.

"Anybody down here?" a loud voice called. My father shouted back, and the man descended the steps into the basement. He helped my father up, then my mother, my brother, and lastly, me. We climbed the stairs carefully due to our weak bodies and fragile bones and stepped out into quite a different scene. Our quaint little town was once a place of beauty, with its simple shops and decorative houses, but all that remained was pitch black ash and the smell of wooden smoke. I kicked through the rubble that was once our home as my mother began to cry heartbroken, terrified tears and my father consoled us all together. Our house, along with the rest of the town, the country, and the world, was completely destroyed. It was all gone, rendered to nothing but a smoky haze and an incredible sinking feeling.

Introductions were always constructed around a person like a stamp; they measured the amount of self-merit a person has within themselves and imprinted their existence upon you. The man introduced himself, shaking all of our hands. "My name is Jack King," he told us. "I've come to get you out of here." I did not get a decent look at him until we stood out in the setting sun. He was tall and dark-haired with jet black curly hair under a military cap, black goatee, and a few facial scars across his cheeks and forehead. He wore a brown hunter's jacket over a T-shirt, but not like a biker - rather like a soldier. He wore tan shorts to match his coat, and his hat even had a sandy hue. I could tell by the pins on his jacket that he was a leader - the guy who gave the orders. Any basic video game or set of action figures will teach you that. His muscles were firm and the man was a piece of meat - thick and tight in stature; this fellow did not miss a single day in the gym. From the top of his shiny hair to the bottom of his polished boots, Jack King was beyond intimidating, and he scared me to death. After all, I was halfway there already. As towering and juvenilely frightening as the man was, the most curious and intimidating factor of his appearance was his legs - or rather, his leg. His left leg was normal, tight and muscular in tone and complexion. But the other - the right - was prosthetic and metallic. I did not notice it at first, but as I saw him bend down to collect our bags, the top of his boot stood below a stump which led into a solid tinman calf. My young mind thought the stranger to be half robot; in my head, we were being rescued by Robo-Cop. Perhaps my method of coping was my imagination. Little did I know that that simple childlike freedom would soon be taken from me as well as all of the others.

I saw the color of the Hummer only in the light of the setting sun as I emerged from the broken basement one final time. It was a burnt orange hue, and it had the back cut out to form almost a truck bed frame. Across the bottom read **TEXAS EDITION**, and the tank vehicle stood far above climbing range. It was massive, and I was petrified with fear and anxiety. As my mother cried her eyes dry and my father hugged us until our arms were stiff, Jack King emerged from the basement hole with our belongings. He was incredibly strong; I could see his muscles even through his coat. Our bags had not even been unpacked; all they had done was sit in the corner of the basement for the entirety of our hibernation. After several trips on his part, he sat them down in front of the massive armored tank vehicle that I had stood appalled before as he labored with our bags. My father helped him load our suitcases into the back of the car, and Jack opened the doors for us like a chauffeur. Being the shortest, I needed a boost from my father to climb into the mountainous leather seat. The Hummer was huge, to say the least. It was much like a small room on wheels, complete with heated leather seats, a cooler, windows, and even a telephone. The windows were one-way glass; I could see out, but nobody could see in. My father quietly explained to us that it was military and government protocol. "Know something about military protocol, do you?" he shouted to my father from outside the vehicle. Jack climbed into the front seat and fired up the deafeningly loud engines. We started rolling over the debris like it was nothing, heading away from our home for the last time into a cloud of exhaust and uncertainty. "This ain't Mayberry anymore," the man said as we sped away from the shattered small town I had known all of my life.

I was only ten years old then, but I can still remember small pieces of what he told us. His voice was deep and overpowering, and his face was aged with stress. He started by making small talk with my parents, with the occasional joke intended toward my brother and I, as all adults do with small children. I could only gather a few details from what he said, but only one stuck with me. "This is the end of the world," he told my father, as they exchanged war stories from their time spent in the armed forces. Something like that is worth remembering, even for an innocent child like I was - although I could not begin to understand it. I listened in awe at my idol of a father's stories, as all children do. The terrain outside was heartbreaking and quite primitive. The rolling hills of our community were just that - hills. Nothing was left on them like chairs plucked from a beach and boulders thrown down a mountain. Trees and power lines were flattened along the road out of the homely town. The street was cracked and broken, making for a bumpy travel away from the wreckage; as a matter of fact, it was all wreckage. We seemed to drive for days on end as I twiddled my thumbs, eavesdropping on the conversation in the front seat. Children had a horrible knack to grow bored on borrowed information, and I was no different; I was utterly relieved when Jack King finally brought the vehicle to a stop. The windows in the car were tinted so dark that I could not see out clearly until my father opened the door and helped me to the ground. There was quite a change of scenery around us from the past destruction. I looked into the huge grassland valley in front of us, which harbored a small town with several buildings - much similar to the one I had called home and hell all in that previous decade. Mountains surrounded the site on three sides, with only one relatively safe and feasible route outward. Cranes and construction equipment drove throughout the prairie, moving materials and adding on to the community. It appeared to be the start of a city.

Upon our first hour of arrival to that strange and new place, we were greeted by several dozen soldiers who looked very similar to the man who had rescued us. I made the inference that the men were inferior to him, simply judging by the way they conducted themselves and gazed at him the way my family - as well as I - did. "Welcome to your new home," Jack said proudly. "That is, if you fine people would like to stay. The last city on Earth, and the start of the new world!" he exclaimed. "I have work on the other side of town, so these fine gentlemen will show you around. Once again, welcome." With that final statement, he climbed back into the Hummer and sped off down the dirt road into town, leaving my family and I alone with the group of soldiers.

Unfortunately, the team of soldiers was not as open, friendly, or charismatic as Jack was. They were kind, mind you, but brief and gruff in nature, and they acted with haste as if they were on a mission. They led us to a building on the outskirts of the growing town and ushered us inside. We were told that we were going to be given an examination, and after a few puzzled comments, they took my father back into the office. His absence left a feeling of vulnerability that was evident in my mother's eyes as she pulled my brother and I close as the soldiers guarded the door. I never cared for doctors. Too many of them in the world, in my opinion. I had a deathly fear of needles since birth, and my brother jumped on that opportunity upon every visit, even for a check-up. Naturally, I had a violent shaking fit upon the mention of the word "examination". That word always meant that an uncomfortable situation was on the way to a slimy and possibly stiff fruition. A minute later, my father emerged from the room once more. The military men took my mother back, then my brother, and finally - reluctantly - it was my turn. My brother came out holding his arm as if he had just been shot. He soon broke out into a hysterical laugh, and I whimpered like a whipped puppy. Upon every visit to the doctor's office prior to the end of the world, a check-up always consisted of a stethoscope, needles, and a monotonous ensemble of health-related questions. This was not the case in the new city. Behind closed doors, I saw none of the said items above. I could have sworn I was accompanied by at least five officers, but only two were present in the room with me. I was ushered into the room where nothing lay but a chair and table. The walls were parchment white and blank of character, and a glass of clear liquid sat on the table. The soldiers sat me down in the seat and handed me the cup, instructing me to drink. Nervous as all hell, I sipped the chilled contents and sat down the glass once more. "What do you taste? Water or wine?" the first soldier asked me. I thought to myself before answering. I had always been told not to lie, but what did I taste? I had never had wine; the only alcohol I had tasted was whiskey by accident, mind you. Even as a child, I had vowed never to drink. By circumstance, if you had two glasses of identical size and liquid, which contained apple juice and which held whiskey? That left only one option. "Water," I muttered in shaking, anxious fear. The two guards smiled at my childlike innocence. One looked me in the eyes before kneeling down to whisper in my ear. My heart raced with uncertainty, and I could not quite make out what he said. I did not know what in the world he was talking about as I asked him to speak up. He was apparently satisfied, and I was allowed to return to my family. My mind beat along with my heart as I pondered what the meaning was with curiosity, but my innocence was absent of audacity to search for an answer, and so I dismissed it.

I knew not what the strange liquid with two faces was until much later in my life. You see, the answer you choose was not the crucial extension of the subject - you had to drink it regardless of what you chose. I discovered later that once the cool liquid flowed down your throat and settled in your stomach, you had no memory of the joys and disasters of the previous world whatsoever, or more importantly, any sense or recognition of creativity in the slightest. Of course the melancholy basic layout was remembered, complete with its gray outline and whispering voice. Creativity created difference, difference brought about division, and with division came destruction. It was jaded behind a simple question: *What do you taste?* The liquid was also the cure to any and all disease. It was imperative to be consumed once daily in any form; once dissolved, any impurity and cancerous material in the bloodstream was eradicated to form a pure and holy blood content all throughout the human body. You see, there never was a cure to cancer, but a blanket remedy that purified the cell structure and filtered blood like water - a poison. Health was the epitome of the new world, and the city thrived on physical strength as well as all other forms of the word. In many ways it hindered the senses - sensitivity to light, sound, and smell. Upon drinking the liquid, one felt at ease and at peace with what lay before them - the reality of the world they perceived. Each household was given a gallon of the substance each week, and a small glass was to be ingested each morning. Drowned in the liquid, the city was a dull and comfortable haven free of creativity and perception. *Kill them all to kill a few.*

Medicine had always left a sour and bitter taste in my mouth and heart, and I loathed the idea of it. I would pour it down the drain, for I despised the process of taking medicine. Nothing short of a goddamn placebo. Fortunately, a pill form of the liquid was available and manufactured. I had a hard time dry-swallowing pills, but I learned to swallow the large grey liquid pill upon a summoning of saliva. I took one pill once a day and it kept the thoughts at bay, for drugs were better than acceptance. That was simply how the world always operated. Take a mouth full of pills and go about your day. The antidote - of a certain sort

\- created violent and intellectual visions that felt so much like reality that it could not be differentiated. It consumed the host like a parasite and formed a new and better world before us, smothering all idea of creativity with a negative and gruesome wrath. Violence was its own twisted peace, and so I saw the world before me in what I could never wish to create, but wanted so very desperately.

After the examination, we were led to a mess hall down the street. The smells of heavenly bliss surrounded the building, and I saw why on the inside. Every food you can think of sat on the the tables inside, teasing our empty stomachs like a carrot on a string. The soldiers allowed us to eat until we were full, and you can bet your life that we did. I think if my mother had not stopped me from eating then I would have spontaneously combusted into a puddle of soda and butter. Once we were done eating, the guards showed us to our sleeping quarters. They walked us to a fancy neighborhood, which was still being constructed back in those early days. We chose a house from what we were told was available and made our way inside, hauling our bags along with us. The guards left us idly by, and there was only one thing left to do that day. After a hot and rather lengthy shower, my brother and I departed to separate rooms. I left the door open that night to stay within earshot of my parents, for they were my only protection left in the world. I was trusting of this new man who had saved us, but I did not know where I was or why I was there. These questions reached out for answers, and I sought rest and escape from them. I was asleep as soon as my head hit the pillow, delving into what would take many years to settle.

Chapter II
The New Rules
(Friends, Family, and Fathers)

The second dream came to me nearly three years after the first. I was then thirteen years old, and my body had begun to change along with the city around me. The setting from the first dream was still present; that time, I was climbing down the extremely steep slope of the mountainside. Air was scarce, and my breathing was irregular and coagulated. My feet slipped multiple times, threatening to send me plummeting to my death. I somehow managed to keep my footing - barely. It seemed to take ages to get down the rocky cliffside. My heart skipped a beat with every stone that slid off of the surface into the valley below, my fear of heights clouding my mind like the dense fog surrounding me. I could finally see the ground after lowering myself down several thousand feet. In the valley below was an inferno. I saw the destroyed buildings and rubble of an old city, crackling and crumbling with flames. Wood popped and metal melted in the heat. I was utterly relieved when my feet hit the grass below, ending my terrifying journey down the mountainside. I could breathe again, and my heart began to beat regularly once more. It was warmer down there due to the extreme heat from the nearby wreckage. I was stricken with fear as the question of what to do next circled in my head as the reddish orange tails chased the destruction before me.

The flames climbed higher and higher up the city walls, swallowing bricks and smashing windows; its fiery tongue destroying everything in its path. The skyscrapers and structures came crashing down into the valley below. I barely heard the scream of a small child in the distance, that of a young boy in terror. His shrill voice pierced the city more than any flame could ever hope to. I looked around the scene frantically in search of him and saw him hanging from a split beam suspended a hundred feet in the air a short distance into the chaotic disaster. He was scared for his life, dazed and confused just as I was.

I laid eyes on a second person coming down the street, leaping over bursts of flames and sparks across the cobblestone and shouting a muffled name over and over again. The snarling of the flames and the thick smoke clouded every one of my senses, making it all too difficult to process the dream lucidly. In my confused state, I tripped over large chunks of concrete and the city rubble as I made my way into the wreckage to help in any way I could manage. Scalding embers singed my skin as I dodged falling debris. All I could gather was the sound of the struggling man and child. I imagined they must be father and son in the man's desperation to save the boy. I heard the sound of shouts over the smashing of glass. He grunted as he caught his son in his arms; the boy had come loose from the beam as the building staggered and creaked eerily, threatening to crash to the ground below. The skyscraper exploded into a thousand pieces, raining down on us. The pair barely escaped before they were crushed under the heavy debris. They ran toward the nearby bridge over the railroad tracks a few yards away. After the smoke had cleared and the rubble had settled, the father helped his son to his feet as they began to walk away hand-in-hand down the tracks. I watched in curiosity, and I was eager to follow, but something kept me frozen in place. The man turned his head to me for a second, and the last thing I saw was the bloody hole that was once his left eye.

I remember waking up drenched in an icy sweat. I brought my wrist across my forehead and wiped it on my t-shirt. I must have let out some form of shout in my restless sleep; my family filed into my room one by one to see what was the matter. My mother asked me what was wrong, and I told her it was just a bad dream. I shrugged it off, but my parents seemed much more concerned. I must have been a lot louder than I thought. My brother laughed and teased me as I expected and dreaded. After a few more awkward and uncomfortable seconds of being questioned and ridiculed, my family left the room and I fell back asleep. I had never felt so attached to a dream before. The man's bloody eye socket haunted me and the boy's scars were burned into my memory forevermore.

In those three long years, the conditions gained a sense of normality in our new home. I had spent my entire life in one of the smallest towns in the world, and I had a difficult time adjusting to life in a neighborhood. My backyard had always been acre upon acre, and I never went a night without being able to see the stars in the midnight sky. But change had taken over my life as well, and I had no choice but to adapt if I sought any sense of routine and comfortable regularity. I learned to accept the clouded sky above the streetlights and the sparsely-packed houses. We each unpacked our possessions little by little, even though we had indeed very little settling into the house as our uncertainty dwindled to a borrowed trust. Although it took a great deal of time, it became home just as our previous one had been.

There was always a certain dichotomy that one had to hold a full time job position in order to maintain enough lousy paper to fuel a comfortable life. In the city, this was only partially true. The city officials gave my parents jobs within the community. My father became a driver for the town officials, and my mother was assigned to be a record keeper for the city. Jack explained to her that a neat and organized record book was the essential key to management, and her background as a secretary for a well-known publisher sparked a keen interest in his mind. She was soon put in charge of population and expansion records in the town hall building across from the examination office, meeting with Jack King on a daily basis to discuss the statistics for that given day. My father spent twelve hours a day navigating the dirt roads and gravel pathways throughout the town, leaving early and getting home late. Jack believed that an occupation should be filled based on experience and talent as opposed to degree, and there was a consequence to be paid.

Within the city, the old world died along with its traditions and routines. The old world was full of too many people with the same name. How many Johns and Peters can there be? Jack King set out to change this. After all, a man named Jésus is often mistaken for Christ. There could be only one owner of a name, or more of a combination. If you were a Mark, you were the only Mark in the city. Your unique first name was paired with a singular last name per household. There was only one Johnson family within the walls, for example. How the name of *Willowby* fell upon my family, I did not know. But it worked, and I had forgotten my old name as the new one consumed me. It defined me - *Noah*. That name was then tattooed on your arm for eternity for everyone to see and recognize you by. The needles stung as much as my parents' objections did, but just as the needles were, they sunk and left their mark. First names were inked onto arms and last names were bore into spines. I remember the agony and terror all too vividly, but as I stare down at my arm today, the ink has all but faded - a painful reminder of who I will always be as well as I who I chose to be. Perhaps it is who I so desperately wish to forget. The first and last name has long been bloodied and bruised away, but although I am many, many years old, I am still kept prisoner by that goddamn jaded name - *Noah Willowby*. Perhaps it meant for a life full of sadness and despair.

Our government began as the small military unit, with Jack King as the benevolent despot of a leader. His group of soldiers doubled as police officers as well as city officials until we had enough qualified newcomers to fill those positions. To say that Jack ran a tight ship was a severe understatement - he was the definition of strict efficiency and sheer brutality. Nobody - soldier or citizen - bore any sign of laziness in his presence. He claimed that work had no essence of play, and from the look of the growing city around us, he seemed to be correct. Jack King was surrounded at a moment's notice by his twelve closest soldiers, which he referred to as his Disciples. The guards had no names and quite honestly no faces either; they wore thick metal masks and armor for maximum security for their Christ. Outside of the twelve elite, King had somewhat of a hundred soldiers under him as well for outposts and officer positions - men always looking for trouble.

Maxwell Wiseman was the most prominent and well-known armed guard on Jack King's force. Due to his prior history as a security guard in a past life, King tasked him with the area of the city marketplace as his preying ground in the beginning for weeding out anything that went against the city rules. Now, Maxwell was not as frightening as he is made out to be - at least outside of his mask and armor. He could carry on a conversation and make jokes as any other man could. But inside the metal suit of the city, he was a stickler for the rules and would punish as sadistically and accordingly. He was the ultimate theft prevention and punisher of everyday crime. He eventually worked his way into the direct line on Jack King, becoming none other than his right-hand man, an iron fist, and fingers of steel - all just as fearful as King himself, even if he kept it hidden.

The city was a metropolis, complete with skyscrapers, shops, and warehouses alike. Each sector of the city was built for majesty, absent of any dilapidation or desecration in the beginning. The center of the city was the place of all business and presentation, with the outer layers serving as both security as well as housing and development. Veterans and the elderly were housed in their own private, blissful wing, and business officials were given their choice of large, royal houses along the outskirts of the city. Common housing was laid out across the outer city in vast expanses, each home unique in construction and feel. There was no discrimination based on home, and therefore there were no labels to accommodate. Shelter came with service as food and protection did, and Jack King was a graceful and fair leader to those who earned and therefore deserved. The construction crew pieced together building after building, with streets and sidewalks snaking through the maze. A town square was designated with shops and important business locations alike. Skyscrapers touched the clouds as the years went on. The city was built upon the principle of earned equality, as previously mentioned many a time before. When the outlying houses were constructed as a form of wall around the town square, dormitories were built. Each room was nearly identical, as most houses were, and the single buildings full of hundreds of rooms allowed for a much more efficient use of space than sparse houses. Of course there was countryside and no one for miles if that lifestyle was chosen and preferred, and if earned, the choice was in the hand of the beholder. The work was fast and efficient with Jack King at the helm of continuation; he was an intimidating but effective leader. Under the condition that everyone obeyed orders and held their keep, no problems would arise. That was the number one rule in the new city. As long as everybody did their job and kept in order, nobody had to suffer. Where did that order put those unwillingly born into retardation and defect? The autistic and mentally deficient were given secluded, safe jobs where worry and limited focus can he harnessed. Jobs such as cooks and cleaners were given to those unfortunate beings, for Jack King was a fair and just leader when it came to squeezing fruition from every possible source of his city. Laziness was a famine - a societal disease and disability. It was contagious; it was in the water. It was everywhere to be found in the old world. Technology had sliced the knees and throats of mankind and weakened skill and created a fierce dichotomy and reliability upon extraneous creation. Jack King wielded labor with maximum yield and production, and technology was used for good as opposed to evil in the new city. Life was always about perspective. There was a certain amount of pity shivered onto ones that pinched pennies from couch cushions, but what did the ones who did not own a couch have to say as they were forced to beg? In the extinct way of life, the less fortunate plastic fork would drive on the way to work, passing the golf course where the silver spoon resided, but in the world of Jack King, everyone was the same - working for their place under him.

In the beginning of that place, the only fragment of an economy was sparse trading and loaning of sorts. As the base of the new society formed, markets were set up with booths and stands to formally and officially deal items. It worked much more smoothly than pocket swaps and owed debts. Money could make you dance or make you beg. It could make you humble or make you foolish. My father always told me to be the same person with a full pocket than an empty one. By the time I was old enough to understand that, all of the money in the world had been incinerated, and so the city thrived on a barter system. In the eyes of Jack King, this worked more efficiently than a currency system, and it was proven time and time again that he was correct. No one had the guts or the wits to oppose it. Who would? All food was free to those who worked. Citizens were issued vouchers for food, but Jack knew my family directly due to their line of work - which were government workers - and therefore I did not have to carry the voucher for my family. Anything else, however, had to be traded for something you deemed less valuable, which would then be traded for something else. It was a complete cycle. My mother would always give me an object to be traded for something I wanted. In her eyes, I was a fairly decent and well-behaved young man, and that was my reward. I would often trade it for candy or such wasteful juvenile desires. The barter system was amazingly productive. People worked or starved. Everyone was brought closer by trading. And lastly - but most importantly - nobody was judged based on occupation or a piece of green paper that meant absolutely nothing. This idea was most likely the greatest principle that Jack King had implemented. He had created a humane society, where people thrived as one, and regardless of how ruthless he was for his own order and class, it worked.

I had seen color my entire life, and I knew of the division it had presented in the old world. The city was different in a rarely positive manner. Jack King believed and instructed equality under his rule. As long as a man followed his leadership and provided for him, his color mattered not. Anyone willing to contribute and better the new world was accepted; anyone who disobeyed and laid down was slit from the throat of the beast. This was one of the many reasons why I looked up to him. Although the conditions were rather harsh, the fierce leader looked into a man's character as opposed to his skin. Color had wasted many years of progression, and Jack King extracted that division like an abscess. As twisted as his requisitions were, he had brought racial equality to the city. I was raised to judge by the content of character as opposed to the color of skin. One of my historical heroes taught me that. Perhaps this was the one thing I wanted to remember from my childhood and make a conscious effort to live by. After all, upbringing makes a person, not the color of skin. I would give the shirt off of my back to any man that deserved it. Things such as this made a person whole and just, and principle was found in realistic truth and moral. Close-mindedness was a societal disease, and it became frustrating to me quite quickly throughout my life the simply dense stupidity of mankind, and I sought to devote my existence to change it. And so I changed it, goddamnit. Another one of my heroes taught me to start with myself - the only thing I could actually change. On the contrary, characteristics that could be helped would either be suggested or forced upon. In the old world, there was such a thing as too much freedom. For example, the obese had every right to keep eating and worsening their condition. The morbidly obese would watch the frail and hungry through their television screen. The filthy rich would pass by the filthy poor in their lavish luxury cars while the elderly veterans down on their luck would sell newspapers for scraps. I told myself that this was a rather fucked-up caste system. I vowed to change it, but someone else took the opportunity before I was even old enough to think. How wrong was it that when a person of four-hundred pounds is next in line for more greasy, artery-clogging disgust that it is sold to them with pleasure and thanks? Trade eliminated that problem while money filtered the habits and desires of anyone with enough paper to value the drug. The economic system within the city eradicated unlimited want and encouraged work, chiseling at entitlement and abused freedom like a diamond sculpture of progress. The golden-bricked road was a simple one to follow - work and receive housing, food, and protection. Rebel and starve in the cold. It was really quite simple. Of course it was a change, but does force not encourage acceptance? In the eyes of Jack King, this was how it had to be. Food was distributed as seen fit based on numbers and weight. The topic was moaned about in the beginning, but in the end, help comes in both welcome and force. Was it not the duty of the strong to protect and better the weak, even if they did not see the purpose? In the eyes of Jack King as well as myself, it most certainly was. Judgement was clouded in the ancient structure. Skin color and sexuality had no directly proportional effect on obedience and loyalty, and so equality was truly born in the city. It mattered not who slept with who or the complexion of skin, but in the amount of compliance. It was in the distraction of a stereotype that a child plans an attack. A turned back is the best weapon, and as long as all heads were turned to King, one people rose and flourished. True wisdom came not with opportunity, but with denial. A fast car and an open road examples better disciple with control than with recklessness. King was the road, the car, and the driver. Of course he had utmost control.

The old world was simply full of too many people. Too many opinions. Too many places. Too little space and room to breathe. Perhaps we needed another plague, and it came not in the form of disease, but in the face of revolution. My father told me about such a thing as rush hour in the old world. It was a time where people all went to the same place at once - bumper-to-bumper traffic. It sounded miserable and like a recipe for an anxiety attack. After all, any time or place where society grouped together in large masses was a plea for disaster. And so Jack King changed this with an iron fist. There were city-wide dismissals and curfews within each hour - movement within the city was put at ease. Vehicles were hot-wired and brought to the city in convoys. Gasoline trucks were siphoned and hauled into the city, lined up inside a heavily-locked tanker while water was pumped and filtered inside underground tubes and pipelines. Vehicles for distribution were arrayed inside lots along the inner city, arranged by size, color, and value. Gasoline was rationed as it was imported across the walls and by earning; food and water was included in a household as long as it was deserved. Over the first years, there was no form of communication among the townspeople. Former electricians worked relentlessly to set up an electric current throughout the city, and after many hours of trial-and-error, it somehow prevailed. Power lines climbed into the sky like a forest of webs, the spider crawling in every corner with her many watchful eyes. In addition, a mail system was established to send and deliver mail across the city.

As far as laws went, anything that Jack King declared held steadfast. King had two simple, complex principles that were only deciphered long after they mattered no more: There was to be absolutely no creativity, and there was to be no God. No fiction, no thought, no creation. There was no music in the city - or at least any of public access. Sound was sometimes weaponized and used for punishment before an impending death would strike, but I knew not the sound of true music until many years later. The antidote given upon examination and each day after was mandatory, and it clouded the mind and heart - making for a dark and gray mindset and a robotic, monotonous lifestyle. Those who slipped through the cracks were punished severely, but whatever was the supposed cure for creativity filled the senses and created an acceptance and a custom of its own. In the eyes of Jack King, his law was supreme and above any holy creed. Murderous punishment was dependent upon intent - if a man needed to die, King would gladly feast his hands upon that blood. Serial murder was a celebrated offense, as if the perpetrator was a spider, eradicating the criminal scum like a guard. If one was aroused by murder, King would attempt to control that lust to his will as opposed to wasting a twisted talent. After all, King and his guards had been soldiers, killing for a general consensus and impossible dream of peace. So arose the question: Is murder a crime if it is reared for betterment? If a killer kills other killers, is he accountable? Of course not. In the old world, a young murderer would spend the rest of his life in prison, enjoying a gloriously free three meals a day and unlimited tax dollars on the backs of the blue-collared working man while veterans scrounged for food on the streets. I believed that anger could be channeled while the child molesters and woman beaters deserved a knife to the throat, and Jack King implemented this. They would answer to an omniscient, fair, just god upon their moment of bucket-kicking, but during their stay on earth, they answered to man. More specifically as far as the new world was concerned, they answered to Jack King. Rape was the deepest criminal sin - a bullet to the knees and a knife of castration. Corruption of women and children was the bane of the new city, for the old society had done enough damage to them. Stealing was permissible upon intent; after all, the absence of money had often led to the necessity of theft. Those who stole for the hunt were skilled and given a task, and the ignorant who allowed stealing were punished instead. Adultery was the fault of the individual, for the idea of the city was that of chasing a better variable. If one was unhappy, one was entitled to take another option and suffer his own consequences accordingly. Lies were soldiers, keeping peace like an omniscient being. Ignorance was peace, and the new laws fueled King's rule and took advantage of every ounce of good and evil to be found. Not a thing was wasted, and I admired his omniscience, for he was my God along with the rest of the city. Nobody was brave enough to oppose him. Jack was a United States Army General, after all. It came as no surprise when he declared that all laws be obeyed strictly. Consequences of crimes depended not on the severity of the evil itself, but in the amount of mistrust and disloyalty to his forces and rule. Crime was population control - only a necessity in the old world where overpopulation ran rampant. Relocation and thinning of the herd was necessary, and therefore there was crime. Not in the city of Jack King. Everyone was meant to walk the line and contribute. Or else if they chose the previous method of teaching, that would most certainty be arranged.

There was no prison - no time for quartering scoundrels and scum. Anyone who dared oppose the ruthless tyrant and his guards faced a sadistic punishment that made the wrongdoing balanced. Those found guilty of crimes were indicted and watched around the clock by a heavily-armed Disciple. There was no escape from that sentence. The perpetrator was then invited to the mansion of Jack King for a final meal of whatever they desired - a twisted adaptation of an old world practice. They were then executed by silence and sound in the town square the following morning in front of an unknowing crowd. Jack King had a rather unique style of execution. He could have easily hung wrongdoers like lights around the city or flogged their insides like a filleted fish. His force could have simply mowed them down like weeds with machine guns, but that did not instill enough fear for King and his sadistic tyranny. The most devilish of criminals were placed cross-legged in the town square with a bag over their head, holes cut out for the ears. Headphones were placed on them like earmuffs and music drowned out the outside world. The meaning of this was to cause so much anxiety within the human mind that a shot never had to be fired. The heart would stop in constant anticipation of a gunshot that never came. One dared not cross Jack King and his law. Hell or high water was always a decision, and most of the time it was made for you.

As far as gun control went in the city, it went two ways as well as one. There were always two options. Either every household had a weapon or none had any at all - only relying on the omniscient and all-powerful force of Jack King and his footsoldiers. This moral evolved as the city went on. At first, the rule of the King force would protect at all costs while weapons were gathered and supplied to every household. Once pulled together, safety was integrated into the neighborhoods and dormitories - watched overhead by the gods of security. It was always a choice. Safety as taken or safety as given. It was always up to you.

Healthcare and insurance was another goddamn travesty and comical misfire of society. *We'll sew you up and cure you for a price.* That was a fucking joke and a quite pitiful aspect of society. Jack King did away with it, as he did many other things. As long as someone worked and earned their opportunity to be healed, they would therefore be cared for. Drugs were outlawed as they always were, but perhaps King was a better enforcer. The world so desperately needed that - an involved god. After all, a drunken high spawned creativity, and that simply could not be.

Childbirth was frowned upon in the city just as it should have always been. How many children sat in foster homes awaiting a loving family that would never come? Was there a certain societal shame in raising a child of foreign bearers in the old world? Of course. But of course it sprouted from the ridicule and mocking of the society that had latched onto the people. One cancer. Abortion was outlawed. Every soul - born and unborn - had a job to do in the new world and was held accountable for their transgressions. The opinion of others was always heavier than that of self. Makeup was also frowned upon as it should have always been. King focused on the care of all people and omniscient justice. Woman needed but one face. Childcare was also a ridiculous concept. *Pay someone else to guard your child while you work and drink to the night's end.* This always brought a certain distance and disrespect with the upbringing of a spoiled child. There was no greater curse than a spoiled child who does not get their way. Christ, is that unnerving. The elderly portion of the population was and always will be just as fucking irritating in my eyes as the younger. Although I have long since joined them, I am not slow. I am not senile. And above all, I am not entitled. Am I mad? Why of course. There is and always will be a method to my madness, however.

King was an exemplary man of men, and a pedestalled lord of lords. He was a king - a true king. Things soon became nearly identical to how they were before all of the tragedy and disaster which had overtaken the world. We had laws, an economy, electricity, and many other necessities of modern lifestyle. Our new home was a slick-running machine, as silent and efficient as ever. We believed in it, trusted it, and relied on it, for it was the new way of life. The only way. If that was how the end of the world was destined to be, I was satisfied with how it ended up. Oh, how foolish I was.

Although I had lived in the city for three arduous years, it still did not feel like home - more like an extended vacation, as if we would someday return to our old lives. I pushed it to the back of my mind and dismissed it as a clouded truth, and after a while, I doubted the happening altogether. Perhaps it was the weak-mindedness of a child that accepted authority as a benevolent, omniscient figure and fell under the shadow like a spell. Jack King possessed that aura. He summed up to me his philosophy one day: "We all come out of the same hole and end up back in the same hole." Jack King would gladly shake the hand of anyone that would serve his ideology of a perfect world, and that was how it should have always been. Mankind had a nasty habit of focusing on micro-importance as opposed to true analysis of character. I never understood racial injustice - or the entire aspect of human dominance - to be quite honest. Was there a true white? In the face of immigration, we all come from somewhere. I was never a fan of the tiny bit of American history I had learned, but as I learned more, I became disgusted with the old world and wished away its memory. It was no question why Jack King wished to destroy it and start anew - to do right by mankind, no matter the cost. Perhaps he sought to restore true peace between one people under his rule; perhaps he hid his sadistic rule behind his kindness. I was only thirteen years old at the time, but I respected the man for far larger reason than he was an adult, contradicting the accepted theme of rebellion within my peers.

I have long since discovered that lifelong problems are either worsened by change or bettered by it. Change can either be a downward spiral or a stairwell to a better place. The city was the epitome of change - the ultimate staircase and spiral into an abyss. My mother was an abandoned woman from the beginning. She had a husband and two sons, but she was in many ways a lonely widow. Her father had left the family early on after an extensive stay in the Vietnam War, just as my other grandfather had died in. Nevertheless, both of my grandfathers were dead to me. My mother had a demeanor about her, not of search for pity, but of an expectancy of emotional abuse. No man had ever laid a finger on her, but their actions had ruined her mentality as she tried with all her might to raise my brother and I better. I understood it and made an internal promise to myself as well as her. My mother and I had our differences over the years, and she yelled at me far more times than my father. Perhaps we had two different mindsets. Was she wrong? In the moment, yes, but in the long run, I was always at fault. My father was just as much of a stranger to me as my mother. He was the face of hypocrisy; he would mock jealousy and then turn around to cause it. An arrogant, egotistical wash-up with an absence of talent or vice is destined for an angry life full of failure. I shared no physical attributes as well as attitude with him, and he had no apparent care for me apart from the art of dominance and control. In many ways he was no father of mine but a spot to fill a void in the absence of my mother's partnership. As far as I was concerned, I had no father and only a shell of a mother. Some children hate their fathers for their abusive treatment. Some children are beaten and molested by their fathers to the extent of a lifelong tortuous trauma. Many are neglected and abandoned at a juvenile age, only to grow up without a father as a guide and companion. But I, Noah Willowby, was abandoned and neglected in a much different way. My father was overprotective and terrified of the very idea of my harm. In other words, I never once mowed the grass, welded, or grilled. I would only watch my father and seek to chase his example, only to be let down and denied trial once more. I grew up not knowing how to fend for myself as a man, and therefore I was inept - inept and unprepared for the real world. "You've got your whole life to work, son," my father told me. I loved to work; I loved to be kept busy. My life had begun, and my fruit had begun to produce. I worked myself to death or damn near - mentally, at least. I would spend time with our childhood hound dog whenever I felt alone, but even he was taken from me. We could never keep a pet for long. Two weeks was normally the maximum amount of time a dog would bark in our household until we had to sell it again because of lack of time to care for it. We had a hound dog when I was a child named Diesel. My father built him a pen in the backyard, but he would dig under and escape. And so we gave the dog to my grandfather, in which from there he ran away forever. I hated dogs ever since. The barking turned my ears and the ugly faces needed a decent squishing. I missed Diesel every time I saw a dog, and so, like many other things, I pushed aside and delved into anger and hatred. I loved cats. No barking and they took care of their business inside - my kind of creature. In other words, if I could have had Diesel instead of my brother, by God, I would not even have to consider the offer. Barely seeing my father was better than not seeing him at all, and that is exactly what life was like while he spent eight years in the military from the time I was a newborn to just around two years before everything changed - always searching for something to replace his attention. I hated and resented him for that.

I am only inferring, but perhaps the start of the new city was a presentation of a golden opportunity for my mother as well as everyone else. Life had changed entirely, and chances were made available to those willing to take them. Was she unhappy with my father? I still cannot say. Perhaps she was only searching for a break in her routine she had chased for sixteen years. My mother worked alongside a man named Britton Chester. They became quick friends as he showed my mother a certain youthful perspective in and on life. My father was a hypocritical racist, and he hated a man based on skin color. For that, I wanted and wished his death in the end of our old world, for the new world as well as the new city became no place for hidden faces and discriminatory ideologies. Only one of equality and purpose could stand. My mother and Chester began spending time together as friends and nothing more, but in the eyes of my omniscient father, she had already been lost. He began to hate and degrade her with words and actions as the friendship continued. I had met Chester on many occasions to my mother's office, and he was a spectacular being of a man. He was a kind-hearted, comical, hard-working, honest addition to the city, and in the eyes of myself, my mother, and Jack King, Britton Chester was a fantastic addition to the city. However, in the eyes of my close-minded father, Chester was an African-American disease that must be treated and tried for his crimes based on born characteristic and traits. I would not become my father; I would become like Chester - an example to myself and others around me. One day, Britton disappeared into the depths of the city, only to be seen one time more. I sought to find him before it was too late.

I saw the epitome of my father's anger upon a rather ignorant decision on my brother's part. Can you just imagine that? The story goes rather like the three bears - cannot go under it or over it; must go through it. My father collected vintage military items along with his own modern equipment, most of which were given to him by my grandfather. I had never met him; he had died in the Vietnam War. His belongings were sent back to my father's family and split between him and my uncle for keepsakes and memories alike. Among the countless photographs of the Vietnamese landscape, my grandfather's uniform and civilian clothes were sent back to America. My father gained possession of the scorpion belt buckle that his father had worn in combat, and therefore he wore it every day as he drove around the city. The golden metallic buckle encased a dead scorpion in a glass dome in the middle oval, catching the light and wandering eyes for whoever came across my father. I admired it from the day I saw it for the first time, and I was disappointed the day I noticed it had disappeared. I never brought up its whereabouts, for circumstance brought it around once more. I heard the shouts of anger from the bathroom as I ran the razor across my face one night in my adolescence. I had noticed several things missing from the house, particularly my father's dog tags from his time in the Army. Once noticed, my father searched violently and sporadically to find them. As the details unfolded, I heard the angry shouting as my brother was shaken awake and questioned in a groggy and third-degree manner. "I didn't take your fucking shit!" I heard Jacob shout upstairs. One did not steal from my father, one was not right, and one was perfectly to blame. Jacob had stolen my father's dog tags and some articles of my mother's jewelry to offer to the Trader for cigarettes. He was beaten and taught a valuable lesson of who not to steal from. One cannot steal from a self-proclaimed God.

It took those three expansive years to finish the construction of the city. The population started small, with only a few hundred when we arrived. Soon enough, it was a bustling metropolis of thousands. Jack King led his crew of rough and tough soldiers out on supply runs, scavenging what was left to be useful. Each run generally resulted in a dozen new members of the community. At the start of the new city, supply runs were carried out nearly every day, but soon dwindled into once a week, then a month, and then, six long years later, the city was sealed off from the outside world. What would accompany it, I had no knowledge nor expectancy of.

After everything was settled there and the supply runs had long ceased, construction of the walls began. The initial idea was to seal the city off from the outside world, where danger and anarchy apparently still ran rampant. Every able-bodied man was called to work on the walls. Jack sent his crew to knock on doors to notify the men when they needed to report for duty. Naturally, no one argued with the barrel of an assault rifle. My father was gone from sunrise to sunset for just shy of a month. It was difficult for my mother to adjust at first, but the new routine set in quickly as time flew by. We all followed our regular schedule as the shadow of the fortress slowly and steadily climbed the horizon day by day. Each week, the wall had significantly improved. It evolved from a wooden frame to a steel barrier between survival and living. Whatever was beyond the gates, Jack King was terrified of and was willing to build walls to the heavens to keep it out.

My father made an entirely unexpected return. We knew the wall was nearly completed, but it was not quite ready to be sealed off. We heard an abrupt knock at the door one night and were deeply surprised to see our father back on early leave. Apparently, he had fallen a small distance off of the construction site and broken his left leg and was discharged for injury. My mother panicked as expected and worried her hair away and to gray, but after a long conversation with him, he convinced her not to pursue the city for compensation, as if there was any to give.

Jack lived by the moral that man was entitled to nothing, and it was in the best interest of every individual to take what was rightly theirs. He was given nothing but a pair of crutches for a short period, and he was satisfied with that particular turn of events. He had done his job until he could no longer perform his duties, and that basic military principle is what kept him alive in his time of immobility. No son wants to see his father incapacitated; even though it was not comical to the least extent, he always joked with us about how old he was getting. That was just the type of man he was - always finding the good in a bad situation. I guess that was what attracted my mother to him. Our family got used to my father's return as he resumed his job as a cab driver for the city. Fortunately, he drove right-footed, so his injury did not intervene with his job too much. My mother had the hardest time getting used to standing up straight around her slouched husband, prompting many a good laugh from my brother and I. We had an old hermit as the head of the house for about five months after while his leg healed.

I had horrible sleep apnea; I could never sleep the whole night through throughout my childhood and much of my life. It was only through the much later sedation that I could achieve a full night's rest. I would awaken in the early hours of morning and sneak to the kitchen for a snack and a drink of water, careful to avoid the creaky floorboards and devilish doorknobs. I could hear my father's snoring on many nights as I found my way to the refrigerator and cabinets in the downstairs kitchen. I could always name a different situation, even if I could not pinpoint what had changed. I pondered as I drank a combination of juice and medication as I knew it - my father's snoring. The loud and crackling rumble was vacant from my ears and the whole house, for that matter. I wondered in silence as the medicine came over me with fatigue, and I heard whispering in my mind as the door creaked open. I quickly ducked behind the counter and hid from who I assumed to be my father. Witness created an awkward scenario, even if no trouble ensued. My father stumbled into the kitchen - no clue of my presence. I knew his footsteps and breathing as he closed the door behind him. I heard him walk into the bedroom and close the door. I could smell perfume in the air.

Jacob and I were enrolled in the small but growing school system there. The old education system was a goddamn joke, a farce, and a social experiment by anyone's standards. Instead of monotonous book-learning, the instructors took a much different approach to what was needed to be taught. Children were taught to grow and harvest crops, and those of age would learn to drive, doctors and nurses taught modern medicine and first aid, and the soldiers ran strict sharp-shooting classes. Every subject taught would be a required skill some day in the eyes of Jack King, and the old education system became extinct. The school was full of hundreds of teenagers like myself, all going through the same evolution at different times. Many times I would sit in the back of the room in a daze, pencil in my ear to scratch an impossible itch. *How far could I scratch without hitting my brain?* It was a painful and rather shocking answer. My voice would crack along with my skin during those early years, and my thin frame made me scrawny and weak in the eyes of bullies. I had been picked on for as long as I could remember, especially by my brother. Jacob was four years older than I was, so I rarely saw him during the day, but he made up for my ridicule at home. Perhaps private humiliation is somewhat better than public.

There was a certain metamorphism of man - a certain contentment with misery. My parents worked factory and office jobs for their entire lives for the simple fact of income, for without it, life meant nothing in the old world. I sought to do what I loved for no pay at all, and that was my dream as well as my reality. My brother was nothing but an irresponsible, lazy, iconic figure of non-example. We were distant for many years, and I had lost nothing because of it. In many ways I was a single child that answered to a mindless permittance, and I was grateful for it. I realized something was missing much later, and I struggled to find it valiantly. My brother was a vile, volatile being full of anger and angst. He had taken our father's military absence at its worst and therefore had safeguards built on his heart like the mountainous walls around the city. I had heard my entire life that opposites attract, and Marisa proved that philosophy to be true. Marisa was my brother's girlfriend in the city - his one and only. As morally loose as his sense of humor and verbal ideology was, he would never dream of lying with another woman or harming a hair on the one he had. She came to the city with her family nearly a year after we had gotten settled in the new world. He met her at the city school in medical class, as surprising as it was. Jacob told me much later that the only reason he sat in the class was to be close to her, and I took it as the start of his emotional birth. She changed the way he thought and spoke, therefore morphing his actions into a more presentable display. She was naturally beautiful in every womanly possible way, and our parents never hesitated to let Jacob know how lucky he was. They loved her as a daughter, and I witnessed my brother change his hideous habits for her. However, alone, he was the face of miserable failure as our father was. A chip off the old block - the chopping block.

Teachers always went one of two ways - either you loved them or you hated them. There were always certain teachers that wanted to build a bond with a student - more of a friendship. Of course the school systems - old and new - were full of a general population of teachers that absolutely despised their students and their own miserable existence along with the pay that came along with it. I always believed that teachers should have been paid based on evaluation instead of a flat salary and tenure. For example, a magnificent, suitable teacher would make a magnificent, suitable salary while the ancient scum would be cast into the world of teaching religious commodities. My world systems teacher was most likely the best teacher I ever had. I took his class in the final months of the new school system, and he knew everything, for Christ's sake. Of course his only job was to educate myself and my peers on the old world governments and economic systems and how and why they failed, but his sense of humor and other advices were not required. He enjoyed his job, and he belonged. Of course my English teachers were always great because I enjoyed their classes, but something was missing from them. Literature was no longer created. It was only studied. *Forbidden.* This was also true for art. Punishable by death. *Treason.* Creativity was studied not for what it was, but for how it had brought about the end of the world.

The educational morale of the ancient world baffled me from the beginning. For example - dodgeball. *Be nice, you selfish little bastards. Here, smash each other in the face with these giant balls.* What a fucking farce that was. I hated dodgeball, along with every other school-related activity and participatory event. Sports were the bane of existence. Of course I played little league as a child; in fact, that is where I found my hatred for athletics. The coach wanted to transfer me to another team because I was not as proficient as the others, and so I quit. Was I wrong? Of course not. I came out ahead, goddamnit. From that day forward, I devoted my life to writing, and therefore found myself in pen and paper. Professional athletes were compensated millions for actions children carried out on playgrounds, and I received not a dime for my penniless written thoughts. But I was ahead; I was better. I won the ultimate game. For example, let us hold on just a fucking second and see if we can reason through a tiny percentile of societal mythology. The plural form of goose is geese. The plural form of moose is still moose. Not mooses, and certainly not meese. What bit of fucking sense does that make? Not a goddamn lick, but that is just the way it was. Contradictory, senseless, hypocritical madness. Meese was the proper term, goddamnit.

Can you erase the history of the old world? Of course not. I had obsessions and compulsions of my own, but I was relieved that a job of that magnitude was not mine. It would have been damn near fucking foolish, and Jack King was no fool. Instead of cutting it out entirely, he made it his agenda to warp it and use only the organs of the old world to his advantage. Bookkeepers were appointed to sort books that dealt with the old world and lock them away. How different was this from the old world? Perhaps censorship and selective teaching was one of the only things King adapted from the old world. In turn, I saw my opportunity and made it my agenda to achieve it. It was my dream. Dreams were channeled into creativity, and creativity brought about the progress of the old world. Any reference or discussion was castrated, decapitated, and flogged on the quarterdeck. In the mindset of Jack King, a question arose: Why worry oneself with the history of the old world? Its destruction was caused by creativity. Worry instead about building knowledge and growing roots in the reality of the new world. This ideology became a decree, and this declaration became law.

The school was where I met Sawyer Jennings, my first and best friend I made in the city. I had no problem making friends, but keeping them was a different game altogether. Perhaps they simply forgot about me. I was told I had an exclusive personality and opinion, and my peers headed in the opposite direction. As expected, children my age were juvenile and made poor decisions; however, I had to give them credit - at least they could make decisions. I was always distracted by other things - sex made up most of the teenage desire; some things never change. I could never make up my mind on any matter, and I lay awake undecided at the end of each day. I spent my free time reading instead of playing with the other children, the idea of furthering my mental stability surpassing the desire to sweat and bleed. I despised sports, and I kept to myself on most days. To most, I was a ghost. I sat in the far back corner of the classroom and tuned out the teacher. I knew it all from books and working ahead, and the rest fell in line with the common majority. The minority was a difference, and I was always the black sheep, the short straw, and the third side of the coin. Perhaps that was what drew Sawyer Jennings and I together. He was a troublemaker from my classes, always finding a way to get under the teachers' skin. Short to the tongue, he was always coming up with new, inventive ways to loophole his way out of mischief's path. Sawyer was far from a bully; he used his sharp wit in exchange for brute force as he got just about anything he had a sweet tooth for. Girls in our classes loved him; after all, he fit the image of a rebel. I saw in him the same thing I saw in my father and Jack King - the spirit of a leader. Someone else to call the shots. That was not me - I was a follower by nature. I hated confrontation. Maybe that was what he saw in me - someone to follow him. Sawyer dreamed of owning the world from the bottom to the top, complete with high hopes and an unmatchingly low work ethic, unfortunately. He was always changing his persona and endgame, and perhaps that was what kept the people coming to him. I was in the middle of *The Great Gatsby* when I met my best friend. I read the words as he approached me from behind, speaking them clearly as I gripped the book; I was used to the pages being torn from my fingers. "You must think I'm pretty dumb, don't you?" he said as I read the same phrase on the paper in front of me. I smiled as I stared at the ink on the page and replied to the boy I had formed a solid opinion on, which was then proven wrong. He continued before I could speak. "Perhaps I am, but I have a - almost a second sight, sometimes, that tells me what to do. Maybe you don't believe that," he knelt down. I closed the book and I turned to face him. "You're Noah, right?" he asked. I nodded and sat the book on the bench beside me. "What do you want with me, Sawyer?" I asked, rather suspicious. He laughed and pointed at the group of our classmates throwing a football back and forth; Sawyer was usually the star athlete in the field abroad. "They're a rotten crowd," he quoted my favorite work once more. "You're worth the whole damn bunch put together." With that, he sat down beside me and opened my book, unconsciously smearing dirt on the beautiful pages. I winced as I separated myself from it. "This sounds good. My mother loves Fitzgerald. Mind if I borrow it?" he asked. I turned to the dirty, rough-neck kid that had changed my mind about other children my age. I had not known if Sawyer could even read, much less understand the complex ideas of *Gatsby*. "Keep it."

Sawyer would then continue to split his time of recession between sports and reading with me, his blonde hair dripping with sweat as he ran over to the bench and hopped over the back. His friends would tease him as he picked up his lunch and walked past them to sit with me alone at the back of the room, but it did not bother him. He did not let the opinions of others get under his skin. He owned them, for Christ's sake. The old world revolved around laughs. How many laughs could someone get over on you? It did not matter how it affected the victim; in fact, they could go home at night and slit their wrists open like a fucking fish for all that was cared. If there was a joke to be had, it was feasted upon, and that would never change.

I soon found out that he lived only seven houses down from my family and I long before he knew my name. Once we became friends, there was no stopping our comradery. A trust was established, and we were as thick as thieves. We spent the hours after school joking and running around the neighborhood after girls, parting ways as the sun sank below the sky, only to meet up again the following morning. Each day I saw how different we were, and I could not help but ask myself *why*. Sawyer lived with his mother and stepfather on the lower side of the neighborhood. I later found out that he had several brothers before the city, but none of them of any account. His stepfather had none of the brothers as his own, and so he set out to own them and force his way into their lives, hence the division of a family. Victor was a middle-aged, middle-sized stock of a man. His short blonde hair cut every Monday gave him a rather shark-like appearance, and he matched the verbal-turned-mental composure of a stepfather in which I imagined. I believed Sawyer's stories simply from his stepfather's look. He was a man that looked like he beat and mistreated his family for the hell of it and was welcomed and had his hand shaken for it. There were always abusive men, and Victor Jennings wrote the book. Victor Jennings was a southern, loud-mouth impression of a man as well as the face of historical hatred and discrimination. The city was full of all walks of life and color of skin, and you cannot erase hatred and skin-deep difference. Not even if you happen to be Jack King, but he damn well tried. I never saw his mother as long as I or she lived, and I doubted her very existence. "Man, I seriously doubt you have a mother," I said to Sawyer one day. "Look, I never see her and you rarely talk about her. I'm convinced you made her up." Of course I would never throw that kind of judgement if I knew in fact that he had no maternal figure, but I knew she existed. "We just have no pictures together and she works the night shift in the markets," he replied. "Yeah, I get it, man. Whatever makes your sandwich. Whoever tucks you in at night," I winked at him. "That would be *your* mom," he winked right back. I punched him in the arm as we walked along the city sidewalk. "We used to do stuff all the time when I was little," he continued. "She was a nurse at the hospital for years until she retired. She would come to the school and do demonstrations and all kinds of cool shit," he smiled in reminiscence. I thought for a moment. "Sounds like a likely story," I punched his arm as we continued into the city. It was by circumstance that I confirmed her presence in Sawyer's life as well as mine.

As close as Sawyer and I became, I never saw his dick - mainly because he stayed balls-deep in any girl that dared and fared his way. My point being is that his dick must have been either covered in gold or cat nip for all of the pussy he was getting. He was a ladies' man lady's man. There was no girl in our school that had not felt the propensity of his morning wood or felt their own cum and blood run down their legs. Except for Valerie. She was mine. Sawyer spent most of his time out amongst the city, knowing people and chasing whatever he had set out to do for the time being, most usually pinpointing on a girl. It was natural for him to pursue female attention; after all, he had no mother as far as I knew. He had arrived in the city four weeks after the start of it all, or more so the end - one of the first to witness the uprising of the beautiful seed which was the city itself. By rights, he had in fact all rights to her. She was the definition of a queen and silently demanded the respect of Her Highness. Sawyer and I were walking home from school one day in the summer months and stopped at a bench outside of my neighborhood. I wiped the sweat from my hairline as I saw the girl but did not recognize her. Sawyer sat down and sighed as I stared at her quiet stride across the pavement. "Who is that?" I nodded in her direction as she turned the corner and headed into the town square. "That's Julia King," he said. "The Princess of the City, as we call her at school. She's the talk of the town and she doesn't even go to school with us. She's nothing special except a pretty girl." I sat down beside him as she faded from view. "I didn't know Mr. King had a daughter," I stated, still caught up in her aura. "Word is that he only lets her out of the house once a month," Sawyer continued. I was not sure whether I could not believe what he said or the notion that it would be another month before I would get the chance to see her again.

Sawyer and I would stroll through through the town square along the sidewalks of Main Street after school on some occasions. We grew up together in that place and watched the world around us change as we evolved along with it. Stores and shops opened for business week after week, trading posts and meeting places adjacent to the town hall and my mother's office building. Farmers grew their crops in the hundred acre expanse outside of the metropolis, still within the confines of the walls. One did not dare or fare going outside the walls. Fresh markets lined the street corners, offering a vast variety of fruits and vegetables. Sawyer took risks and enjoyed the idea of trouble speeding down the tracks at him, and he would exercise his bravery in every waking minute he could manage. We passed the neon array of apples and oranges one morning, the bright colors enticing us to snatch a single fruit from the neatly arranged basket. The desire was too much for Sawyer's weak self-discipline as he reached his hand into the wooden container. Before he could wrap his fingers around the apple, two hands clapped him on the shoulders and I stood back in shock of who it was. Jack King squeezed Sawyer's shoulders and asked him how he had been lately in a light and chirpy manner. "G-good, I g-guess," my best friend replied as fear and remorse glazed his pupils. He had long since dropped the apple, and Jack might not have even seen him grab it. He had, however. Jack released Sawyer and remained smiling. "Frederick!" he shouted to the shop owner. "You're just going to allow this young man to *steal* from you?" he grinned. Frederick Jones was the proudest shopkeeper in town with the most colorful arrangement of merchandise. His son was our age, and a spiteful little twat at that. Could we hold anything against him? Of course not. We were all rebellious, vengeful, angsty teenagers full of awkward misplacement. Frederick had not seen Sawyer; he had his back turned talking to other customers. He tried to answer as Jack raised his hand to stop him. "Maybe a repossession of product is necessary," he said sarcastically. With a simple swift movement, he snatched the axe from the back of his belt and cut the man's hand off, splattering blood across the baskets of fruit as the man shrieked in horror and pain. "You see, thievery isn't in the water, it's in the food," he walked away smiling, taking a bite out of the apple. "This is the one that spoiled the bunch!" he shouted. We were far too shocked to utter even the merest of sounds, and we hurried away as the shopkeeper was rushed to the hospital by several witnessing customers. Sawyer and I were scarred as well as the innocent bystanders as they stared blankly as the pool of blood dripping across the pavement, chasing them back into their homes and places of business.

I did not see Frederick Jones for months after the incident. Jack King had rendered him useless in the city, or at least without meaning to himself. Jones had always been a farmer and a shopkeeper, and one could not pick apples with one hand. When I finally saw Frederick, it was through his window as I passed on the sidewalk outside. His hand had been severed cleanly with the axe; Jack King had perhaps chopped wood for years. The stump was neatly cauterized, and Jones pulled the curtains to quickly upon my sight. Jack King had started something by his example - placing the blame on Sawyer. Who was to blame - the one who committed the crime or punished for it? Was rendering someone useless a form of murder? Was the death penalty not a form of murder? Knowingly taking the life or meaning of another was always murder to me, and so I questioned it. Nevertheless, Frederick Jones knew Jack King had punished him for Sawyer's crime, and I was an involuntary witness and accomplice.

It was within the newfound school system that I also befriended Topher and Klaus. Topher was tall and thin as a rail, as most children of our age were. He was indecisive as ever, changing his mindset and preference like a hairstyle. Much like Sawyer, he had a sweet tooth for women, and although the two rarely spoke, I was sure they shared many ex-girlfriends and lovers as the years went on. I had known Topher for a decent stretch of time before Klaus moved into the city, and he provided a rather foreign outlook to our friendship. Klaus was as stocky as a man can get without being chubby. He possessed a sort of gangster kingpin persona, always sporting exotic tennis shoes and jogger sweatpants. Topher and I always joked that he was going to be a drug lord one day, and from the smoke curling from his lips and the curve in his smile, he was already on the way. Topher was nearly the opposite in size and build. A tall, lanky fellow with a nose like the catacombs of France. As far as I was concerned, the only good things that came from France was their vanilla, fries, and hookers. Topher, Klaus and I would meet at one of their houses every now and again; my father did not care for either one of them particularly. It was rather comical and exemplative of his hypocrisy - he disliked their use and abuse of drugs, yet he took a particular liking to alcohol. Although I chose coffee, we all have a preference of buzz. He was more like Topher than I could ever be, and they looked at me as either a source of sound advice or a sheltered fool. As we grew older together, the pair of them pursued the shadowy acts such as drugs and sex like most other children our age. I was different - the friends I chose had often come from unfortunate childhoods and provided a different story than my own, leading to bad habits and smoke in the water in which I never dared to touch. I simply listened to stories and provided advice as to how I was raised and hoped it would help. Was I any better than them because my parents still shared a bed and I had not grown up hungry, beaten, and bruised? Of course not. I simply chased a different perspective on life, and I found it in the face of uncertainty. Perhaps there were always people who were so untrustworthy that you could depend on them for anything, and this was true of those two. I was the tip of our friend triangle - the two were so much alike and so different from myself. Opposites attract in every sense of the phrase, and we became a tight-knit group of companions from the time I met them. Where did Sawyer fit into this? Well, he was always more of a lone ranger than a man of dependability, and apart from myself, he had no other brethren counterpart. Although he was the center of so much attention, he kept to himself as we wandered the streets and sidewalks of our city. It was almost comical - perhaps Sawyer would have fit right in with our trio had he given them a chance. After all, him and Topher were like split personalities within the same being, and I longed to instill their minds together to form a perfect union of a friend. Pairs are better than groups, however, and I ran with Sawyer more than anyone. I had always had a best friend for a series of years and then they would silently fade into the background and forget my existence like a scar. I stopped chasing admirers, and so Sawyer found me.

"Can I ask you question?" Topher said to Klaus. "Go ahead, buddy," he nodded. "Are you dumb?" Topher asked. I laughed at the conversation between the two stooges. "Out of a city this size, complete with women of all walks and talks, you choose a girl named Delisha Cinnamon," he continued. Before Klaus could argue, Topher raised his hand in halting. "Let's break it down before you make excuses," he said. "Cinnamon is obviously a stripper name, and Delisha either sounds like the disease you're gonna get from her or the medicine you'll need to cure it." I was practically rolling with laughter. "I think she's great," Klaus said simply. "Follow me," Topher shook his head. We followed the skinny goof through the hallway and into the kitchen where he rummaged through the cabinets and shelves. He pulled a tube of ointment and a bottle of cinnamon out of the cupboard. He grabbed a cup and emptied the contents of the tube into it and dashed a hint of the reddish powder, spilling a great deal onto the counter. Mixing it with a spoon, he handed the concoction to Klaus. "What the fuck is this?" he asked in stunned curiosity. "I'm a wizard, Hairy," he joked. "Put that shit on your dick before you fuck her," he instructed with a straight face. "Have you seen me?" Klaus retorted. "I'm lucky to even *talk* to her. If she sees me doing that nasty fuck shit then it'll blow my chances entirely. And think of the rash I'm gonna get." Topher backed up and thought to himself. "That's the Pumpkin Spice Lube Special," he laughed. "It shall protect you." With that, he bent down, plugged one nostril, and proceeded to snort the remaining cinnamon off of the counter. As Klaus and I stood back in disbelief, Topher stood up and remained silent. "Goddamnit," he said calmly. "That was *chili powder*."

The kindest fellow I ever met went by the name of Strauss. His family came from German and Northern heritage - any trace of a Southern accent was far to be found. Strauss was a clumsy, oafish child at heart and I enjoyed his acquaintance. He was a hearty fellow and always had leftover food to share. The worst thing he ever did was wear his pants a bit low, but besides that, Strauss was a solid worker and dependable asset. He introduced me to another fellow named Joshua Peterson, who was the epitome of modern Einstein and professionalism. Peterson was the most political and sarcastic chap I ever met, and he was often overworked in the city due to his compliance and desire to please. A short, frail, blonde teenager with glasses was an easy target to place a job upon, no matter how weak his shoulders became. Strauss was a large diabetic, which made sense; that man would eat a piece of cake after a full meal for a snack in the middle of the day. I loved to eat as well, but my metabolism was high - mainly from pacing the goddamn house all day in my worries. Joshua was a pale hemophiliac, which explained while he kept to himself in the house all day. Peterson was a worrisome professional in whatever he strived for, quirky and obsessive as I was. He carried a pocket full of mints no matter the day or weather, and I always managed to swipe a few. He was the type of man that invented the television while men like Strauss drooled in front of it all day. I loved both men as my brothers, and they were true friends to me. As awkward as the two men were, they were quality gentlemen and reliable associates. Women were certainly missing out on those two. Nevertheless, Strauss and Joshua were the finest workers and most pleasant gentlemen I ever met, strictly opposing the character of Topher and Klaus. It was a societal shame- the purest and most honest people were often overlooked because they may have not been an eleven on the one-to-ten scale. There was always two ends of society, and these four men described the poles perfectly.

Chapter III
A Flower Sprout Named Valerie
(Cigarettes, Peach Candy, and Dog Shit Shoes)

It was in the time of adolescent forgetfulness and rebellion that my peers as well as myself began to wean themselves off of their demanded serum little by little as their parents had. I felt a false sense of safety despite the barbaric horror I had recently witnessed, but it was a protective safety as opposed to a peaceful one. I had seen the rules of the new city be observed, forgotten, and punished for, but is it not within human nature to follow that same path? I had seen these people follow their creative instincts and do their own will as opposed to King's as well as the horrible consequences that followed, and yet I chose to do the same. Slowly, my generation and those past began to remember things about the old world that were sworn off and banned from memory. How could this be? How could it be regulated? Was it voiced? Of course not. It was, and it was no question to be asked - aloud, anyways. One's mind is his own. No limits. No boundaries. A truly free world. After all, dependence creates withdrawal, and creation is one in itself. Nevertheless, absence of the medication in the bloodstream created mindless scenarios and violent hallucinations - ones I cannot even begin to understand even to this day. Pure and untapped creativity. True freedom. Perhaps there is such a thing as too much.

The adolescent mindset can basically be summarized into a single-statement philosophy: *Fuck or kill everything in sight.* It was in the core of a world full of change that I found the strangest emotions of my life. The day I discovered breasts was one of the greatest installments in my existence. Although the concept of vaginas baffled me and somewhat enticed me, I focused on the pair of welcoming teacups that every female possessed. Those bastards came in all shapes and sizes, and do not even mention the subject of nipples. *Why did males have them too, goddamnit? And if you cut them off, did they grow back?* Thinking back on it, I was truly an odd fucker, but who did not wonder the same things in their minds? I simply vocalized my curiosity. This was also a time in my life where I wondered how many testicles I had. Upon a slight squeeze and rummaging, I found that it was a dynamic duo. Hair was a strange and impending transformation, and I found myself running my fingers through it on many nights. *How could a two inch snake solidify into a six inch sword?* Teenage curiosity is a true wonder to behold.

It was in the time of lust for a certain woman that I clung to another in impossibility, just as was exampled to me. My luck can be best described as whatever omniscient being you believe in running a massive wooden train on me from the rear. In other words, if something could go wrong, it would. I was the zero-point-nine percent chance of getting ultimately fucked over. Forever and always. Was I cursed? Of course not. There simply always has to be a subject of misfortune, and it answered to the call of Noah Willowby. How much can you give without being taken? Is it better to ask or take? If you take and give back, are you a hero or a jaded villain? Hyde was always the product of Jekyll.

I was surrounded by peers of personas and substances new to me, exposed to backgrounds I never conceived, and immersed in a reconstruction of leadership and rule. I was confused by the new way of life as my perception became jaded. I saw my surroundings as examples through a hormonal and instinctual eye. As a minuscule piece in a world of transformation, I clung to whatever was presented to me, thrusted in my face, and appealed to my deepest desires. I had surrounded myself with ones who admired me, but I felt not an ounce of love upon my heart. Sawyer was the closest thing I had to a brother and Topher and Klaus were my escape from structure, but I had no object of lust. I had seen Julia King and I yearned for her acquaintance, but she was out of my reach as far as the stars were, and I could only stare and marvel at what could be. I had but an image in the back of my mind; I dismissed her existence over the years as it faded from my remembrance, for it was in the distraction of another that distant destinations disappear. My body was ravaged by change as I entered into the time of juvenile transformation. Innocence was replaced by curiosity and I chased it within my mind as I found it around me. I had seen the pasts of my peers and found no interest in their habits, but something deep within me was void of attention. I found the answer to this call in a single being of every detail in which satisfied my desires. This such being was Valerie Crowley.

Valerie was one of the first - if not the first - person I met with a total opposite childhood as I had. I had never gone hungry, been beaten, or been emotionally abused as she had, and so she had certain safeguards built around her personality that would not allow for enjoyment of most everyday routines. I had never had the gruesome responsibility of talking someone out of suicide before I met her, and let me be the first to say that that obligation is not one of honor or pride. I remember fearing the end of the world and the conclusion of my own existence, but my world changed in another light the first time I feared for someone else's life. One cannot save someone from themselves, only persuade them to wait for another time. I would be lying if I told you I had never sat and thought about women for the entirety of the day, but I have never had the nutsackery to chase one and make my thoughts reality. Valerie was the first. I cannot explain it - I felt such a connection with her. I sought to help her desperately, and so I brought it to life.

She was the summation of all of my teenage desires, whether they be anger, sex, or rebellion. I met her when I was fourteen years old - glued between the innocence of childhood and restricted from the freedom of adulthood. She was an outcast of society just as I was, cut out from the mainstream popularity. I had heard the crude humor and rumor about her; she was labeled with a positive and negative connotation as anyone and everyone is. She was known as *Velcro*, and I heard rumors that she was attracted to girls. That was my biggest fear - not for her loss, but for mine. She was not traditionally beautiful, but rather majestically adorable. I adored the way her ears curved and the way her nose wrinkled. I had always loved short hair and pale skin, and a fair body shape attracted me more than any curve. Her sense of fashion was rather odd by societal standard, and I was fortunate, for my sights were set on a description labeled barren and therefore outcast. I sat behind her on most days and stared at her vividly, lost in a world of curiosity and lust. That age called for a target of release, and Valerie Crowley was it for me, goddamnit. Disregarded by our peers due to her fuck-you attitude, she was all mine. I dreamt of her in silence in her presence before an introduction came to pass, and the idea I had was perfect. I studied her from the time I first saw her to the time we parted, and I knew just how to grab her attention. She would spend her free time writing letters to herself - she had a fascination with penmanship and stationary, just as I did reading and writing. There was something about a handwritten piece that carried a certain amount of care and sincerity. I would peer over her shoulder subtly as her pen curved around her letters, studying the way she wrote and applied pressure to the paper. I was immersed in her focus and lost my own as I took note of the way she darkened some words from her usual light and airy inscription. I wanted nothing more than for the letter to be addressed to me, and so I set out to bring that desire to fruition along with the rest.

I locked myself away in my room at night for a week and sat under the lamplight with pen and paper before me, struggling to arrange the perfect pattern of words across the page. I had peered into her mind of letters and knew what she wrote about: music, societal taboos, and sexual attraction. Her handwriting looked as if she held the pencil with two fingers instead of three;

she was left-handed, and her wrist dragged across the page as she wrote. Her letters were curved and etched like scripture, and I was mesmerized by it. I had to appeal to her open mind and heart, and the pen engrossed the paper, smearing ink and shaking my body as I delved into what I hoped would lead me to her. I always loved a rhyme. Over the course of seven days, I had constructed a masterpiece:

Valerie,

To what do I owe this musical concert of motion, desired and intended devotion. Wrought from the iron of gates constructed, write from the heart of society instructed. Witnessed death from behind your shoulder, brought to life by your hand and holder.

I folded the concise but meaningful letter and tucked it into her bag while she was not looking upon first chance. I waited for any form of response for days after, but to no recognition. I began to lose hope in her notice as I imagined her tearing the note to shreds and laughing tears onto the paper as it was shredded into sand. I eventually chose a different seat in frustration and embarrassment. My temperament in her presence became short-fused and hurried, for any stare in her direction brought shame and regret. I chewed my tongue and cheek until I tasted blood in anger and desire, and upon reaching into the front pocket of my backpack, I felt a slip of paper in my fingers. I pulled it from my bag and unfolded it, scouring the words as my heart skipped a beat in the opposite direction.

To whom it may concern,

Fuck off or I'll kill you.

I was taken aback by the words on the paper, and my heart sunk as my mind whirred with anxiety. Did she know it was me? She simply could not. She had not seen me, and no one knew of my lust for her. The other part of me wondered why she was so hostile to a stranger who meant well and desired her friendship and love. I found out within the next day as I overheard what had happened, and it fueled my anger for mankind beyond the edge of doubt or guilt. I caught a tiny drop of red on the corner of the paper which spoke more than her harsh words ever could.

I heard the whisperings of braggarts as I struggled to decipher the mysterious response. Patrick Jones was good friends with Topher and Klaus, and the three formed a rather impenetrable group of friends. Patrick hated Sawyer for what he had inadvertently done to his father, or rather caused the loss of his hand through a harsh parable of inattentiveness. And so I became an accessory to that hatred in his eyes. Patrick laughed and punched his cronies who I shared friendship with, absent of admiration, and I sought to find out what it was about. I waited for Patrick to leave as I approached the two. I asked what was the cause of laughter as they struggled to tell me with a straight face. They pointed to Valerie across the room and laughed a dry cackle as they told me what they had done. They explained to me in an apparently hysterical manner how they had taken a pair of velcro shoes and filled them with the droppings of their dogs, setting the disgusting joke on the front porch of her house. They giggled and dry-heaved as my demeanor remained silent and unmoved. I looked across at Valerie, who had taken notice of her mention. I stared into her eyes for the first time at that angle and silently expressed my apologies. She looked away quickly, gathered her belongings, and hurried out of the room. I walked away from the two heathens and mumbled under my breath exactly where I wanted to stick my shoes.

As I rushed home, I pondered writing another letter - that time, a detailed apology and desecration of my faux friends who had tainted the name of my love. But I did not make it home before she came back into my life, for she was sitting on the bench outside of my neighborhood. She held her head in her hands, and I could hear her breathing and cries of sobbing. I dropped my backpack to the sidewalk below and slowly walked over to her as not to startle her in her upset manner. I knelt down beside her as she raised up ever so slightly in my presence and quickly hid her face again. "What do *you* want?" she asked between sobs. I climbed to my feet once more and sat down next to her on the wooden frame. "To apologize for whatever they did to you," I said solemnly as if I did not know what they had done. "You can't change it," she added. I had a habit of apologizing for others' transgressions while worsening my own predicament all the more steadily. I could tell that it was going to be difficult. "But I can tell you that it won't happen again," I said. She looked up at me, tears streaming down her face. Seeing my queen in such a state set my heart on fire as well as my anger. I was willing to slit the throats of my own brothers to please her pretty face, and I accepted what I was about to suggest. "We can get back at them," I said, willing to wage war to satisfy her thirst for revenge. "I'll help you," I offered, as if my loyalties were not already clear. "You'd really do that?" she looked over at me and smiled a cracked, hidden smirk. "Of course," I returned the grin. I offered my hand to her face as she flinched away suddenly and quickly. She apologized as I wiped the tears from her eyes and shook her hand. "I'm Noah," I said. "Valerie Crowley," she replied, but I already knew that. Had she known my name all along as well? "But only you can call me Val Crowl. If you ever call me Velcro I'll slit your throat in your sleep." The voice was subsequent to the pen she used, and just as menacing. Sarcasm and challenge was a trait that ran in my family. "How will you know where I live?" I asked, deciding to take her threats as jokes. "Back house on the right," she replied. "Front bedroom." I was surprised and rather frightened at her knowledge, and I did not even have to question it. "I live in the middle house two streets over," she explained. She had studied me as I had studied her, and it was already a pleasure to do business with her, even if I had to lose a few friends of my own. The endgame was worth it. If the exposition was as magnificent as even to surpass my own expectations, I waited desperately for the climax.

And so we set out to do the deed - nearly the complete opposite of what I wanted to do with Valerie. We met each day after school for a week and laid out exactly what she wanted to do to my friends to exact her revenge. Was the situation a matter of betrayal? The quality of friends that Topher and Klaus were was not exactly pristine, and so I was willing to risk their trust if it meant I could get even an inch closer to Valerie. She really wanted to hurt Patrick, and in many ways I did too. Who would not want the bully's head under their bed? And so we set out to weaken the henchmen first. "What do you have in mind?" I asked her the next day we met. "I want to make them feel humiliation," she said through gritted teeth. I understood her anger; I had been the subject of ridicule since my unfortunate birth. Who had not felt humiliation and had their esteem stomped upon and spit on in finality? One could walk a perfect road and still trip over an uneven stone.

I met Valerie outside her window a week later upon the strike of midnight as we had planned in that fated set of seven days prior. She held a bottle of canola oil and a thick sack of disgusting dog droppings in her arms as she hoisted herself out of the window. "Let's serve up some shit," she said with a sly smile across her lips. We then hurried out of our neighborhood and down to the section of the city where the bastards called home, and we stepped quieter and quieter to their porches. Cloaked in shadows and driven by angry vengeance, we spread the oil across the wooden planks and lined up the canine feces along the steps and grass before them. Two more to go. I rang the doorbell, careful to avoid the trap as we sprinted away to the next house.

We continued our sick, twisted, vengeful ritual and continued to ring the bells as they echoed and drew bodies to doors and to angry, tricky reactions. As we sprinted away to our homes for the night and for a decent, satisfied rest, I could have sworn I heard a woman scream as she fell.

My heart was one large and vast while my mouth followed suit, shouting words and voices louder than life, but as I grew older and wiser, both receded into the shadows. I learned that silence was far louder than shouts, and I lived by it. Written word was always more powerful than spoken word, just as paper was to a handshake - superior. I had never had sex before, and I was ironically and comically nervous. What was human nature was dreaded and feared in my mind as I chose to brave the vast fantasy of sex. Perhaps I was worried that my equipment was not suitable for the job, or maybe that my newborn colt technique would not drip cum down a woman's legs, but I found myself mesmerized by women as I grew up. That was the time where teenagers wanted to fuck or kill everything in sight more than normal, and then came the moment to pursue the sexual experience with Valerie.

Valerie was a tough cookie to crack, to say the least. She would be distant one moment and then totally and completely involved the next. Perhaps I was the same way, and if we would have grown old together, I could imagine the possibility of losing our minds together. Perhaps we already had. She was the first person I had encountered that told me about the decline in the medicine, and I followed her example and its impression on me. In order to respond to her distance and random bouts of silence and topic discussion, I knew of no other way to cope by it match it. After all, my mind was riddled with torturous anxiety, worries, and thoughts of everything that crossed my troubled conscience. "What's your favorite candy?" I asked her out of the blue one day. "Peach rings," she responded with a blank look in her eye. My memory was impeccable and I stored away even our most minuscule conversations for later remembrance. To this day I still remember trading a piece of graveled limestone for a bag of sour peach candy.

"Where do you go when you miss school?" I had to ask her out of extraneous curiosity. "Different places," she replied blankly. "Sometimes when I feel small I climb trees out in the countryside. There's this one oak tree with a branch higher than the rest. I can see the entire city from that spot. It reminds me of how small I really am." I thought for a moment, and although I myself was a particular advocate for reverse psychology, I simply had to question her reasoning. "Doesn't that make it worse?" I asked her. "It depends on the day. I like to see the city a night. The lights remind me of how bad things can turn out good. That maybe one day we won't think the same way we do now." I was somewhat satisfied with her answer, but I struggled to follow with more questions. "Do you like to climb?" she asked with her usual sly, pink smile. "I hate heights," I said quickly and without a quiver. Her eyes glazed over with hurt and disappointment. "But, for you, I'll climb," I reached out to grab her hand. She took it in her own thin, frail fingers and tightened her grip as she stood up. "Let me show you."

And so we walked and talked through the city streets for seemingly hours as we made out way into the fading countryside that was the distance. The hustle and bustle quieted to a wavy whisper as the concrete turned to grass and the smell of hazy smoke drifted away to a breezy and open aroma of nature. She pulled her tennis shoes and socks off and bent her pale white toes into the soft earth that the dew had left for us the night before. "No shoes allowed," she whispered to me, urging me to take my shoes off. I tossed them besides hers and put my much larger feet on top of hers, comparing size. "I don't know, Valerie, size is relative," I laughed. "You thought you were gonna try to get out of climbing the tree," she giggled and smiled a true, beautiful smile. She had no worries in that moment, and she had found peace. I was eager to find it too.

"Foot to tree, hand to branch, foot to tree, hand to branch, foot to branch, pull, repeat," she said as she looked down at me from the highest point in the massive oak tree towering above me. Nervous as hell, I followed her instructions, slipping at first. After several terrified attempts, I pulled myself into the wide wooden branch and perched beside her as gracefully as I knew how. We turned as she pointed to what we had travelled there to see, and I paid no attention to the swift breeze that threatened all so mightily to whisk me over the edge. I brushed the hair out of my face as I smelled her perfume, yet I was focused on the cityscape before me. I could see every outline of the buildings and towers that had been built around us, all but shadowed by the walls miles behind us. "My god," I said quietly as I breathed the scene in. "Don't you feel just a little bit small?" she asked. And I did. We were nothing, but at the same time, we were everything.

That experience sparked many more after that. We would finish our school day and walk out to the tree in the countryside, sometimes climbing into the sky and others laying under the shade of the branches. We talked about everything under the sun and more, a bag of candy between us and a pack of cigarettes in her pocket. I had never smoked before I met her, but we shared many a smoke as it drifted away along with us. "Write me something, Noah," she said as she looked over to me under the tree one day. "What would you like?" I asked. "Something you won't get caught with," she followed. "If you got caught, I don't know what I'd do without you." I thought for a moment as I took her hand. "It would be worth the risk." With that, she pulled a weed out of the tree trunk behind our backs and handed it to me. "A penny for your troubles."

"What's your story?" I asked Valerie on the school bench one day. "You ever hear of Anne Frank?" she asked me. I had heard the name in history classes. She was a victim of omniscient rule, and so was Valerie. That I could piece together without her further explanation. History was taught thoroughly as not to repeat it, although the center theme of history was eradicated. The creativity that drove human interaction was eviscerated and sliced out like an abscess, and the new world was free of that cancer, or so it was thought to be free and proclaimed as. "Yeah, she was great," I said, attempting to compliment her. I had seen pictures of the girl and upon the thought of it, they favored quite a bit - both small and fragile as fresh clay. "She's my hero," Valerie said with a subtle smile. "I wrote her entire diary on my walls three times," she said. "I'll show you one day." I nodded in response and acceptance, hoping she would continue on. "My father killed himself when I was five," she started. "I imagine he couldn't put up with my mother. It's not that she's horrible; she just nags and nags the shit out of you about unnecessary shit. My clothes, my hair, my shoes, my face, my stuff, everything. You name it. I stay away from her as much as possible. I imagine she's just miserable and pathetic on the inside, but I can't help but blame her for my father's death. I never got the chance to know him. My mother married the first guy that showed her any attention. Probably because she got someone as an easy target to nag the shit out of beside me. He's rather abusive. My mother isn't abusively critically, but he is. He's violent and a drunk. He...um," she paused. "He'll get drunk and hit my mother and me. I watched him rape her once. Then he came for me," she finished, nearly tearing up. For the second time in my life, I felt true, warranted anger. I was undoubtedly in love with Valerie, and anyone who harmed her was my sworn Antichrist. I felt such a deep and dark pulse of violence within me, and I vowed to act upon it when the time was right. "I'm sorry," I said. Before she could turn, I cut her off. "I know that doesn't change anything, but I promise you, I will never let anyone hurt you ever again." She leaned against my shoulder as a tear soaked through my sleeve.

"What do you remember about your dad?" I asked her one night later as we lay beside each other. "He was in the Marines," she started. "He met my mom in high school and she followed him to the base where they lived while he served. He was active duty overseas for five years. He saw some nasty shit. He went hungry and was attacked more times than he could count. But what was fucked up was when he got home. It was in the safety of his own country - the one he had fought for - that he was killed in. Then my mother married Jason. Isn't it a shame? Good people die while the fucking scum walks the earth as a ruler." I squeezed her hand as it lay limp. "I agree."

When Valerie would have a bad day and become so depressed to the point of scarring her arms like a chalkboard along her name tattoo, I would attempt tiny victories in order to boost her morale and show her that someone cared far deeper than any cut. She craved detailed attention and loved the small things in life, and although she was in fact tiny herself, perhaps I did too. I would bring her things such as a piece of cake, a flower, or a notebook and she would smile and hug me for minutes on end. Was it a diamond ring or a much more valuable item as such? Of course not. Long after money had become extinct, actions still spoke louder than words or even the most paper in the world.

After a while, the question arose as to why I never went to her house and why she never came to mine. Her house was obviously out of the question, with her stepfather being the obvious culprit. But my family was decent enough and she asked why she could never come over. "This place is just so beautiful," I told her in faux confidence. She just nodded and smiled slightly and looked away. But deep within me, I was ashamed of my family for their hypocrisy and complacent judgement and for my brother's cruel verbal commentary. I would never dream of bringing her there or having her judged or picked apart in the slightest. Did I tell her this? Of course not. The truth would have hurt her too much. Little did I know that it drove a much higher wall between us than I could have ever imagined. She would put the pieces together sooner or later.

"Have you ever smelled your skin after a ladybug crawls on you? It's disgusting, yet it leaves its mark. It's beautiful." That was the kind of girl Valerie was. She was so observant and caring; tiny details of life were her foundation and scripture, and she lived by the forgotten truths of the old and new worlds in a daring and adventurous state of mind. We laid either in the tree or under it for many nights, arm-in-arm and hand-in-hand, yet we never contacted lips or bodies. Perhaps she could never bring herself to voluntarily be touched by a man. I heard her whimpers one night as my theory was proven to be correct, and I never felt right ever again. I pulled her over and looked at her tear-stained eyes. I could not see into them; perhaps we did not have that bond. "I have something to tell you," she whispered to me as I continued to hear her sobs. "What is it?" I asked as I struggled to make out words from her stifled cries. I wiped her eyes with my forefinger as she breathed heavily and spoke softly. "Topher raped me," she said. I did not need them to be repeated - those three words told me enough. I knew his character warranted those actions, but I was so consumed by anger in that moment. My legs began to sweat through my boxers as I ripped the covers off and sat up. Valerie sat up as well as tears streamed down her face once more in an angry embarrassment. "When did this happen?" I asked angrily. "Last Wednesday. He gave me something in my food. I was unconscious for about two hours. When I woke up, he was wasted and raping me. All I did was run. I didn't know what to do," she cried. "What were you doing over there?" I asked. "He told me he wanted to make up for what he did with the shoes." I was not angry at her, I was angry at Topher. He was supposed to be my friend, but he showed no action of friendship toward me as I did him. I knew he was a drug addict, even at such a young age because that was what was exampled to him. His intent may not have been malicious, but whatever he drugged Valerie with

63

wasted him to the point where he committed the unspeakable crime. In that moment, I imagined him cross-legged in the town square with the headphones on, waiting for me to pull the trigger. I would. I held Valerie until her cries stopped in fatigue, and I drifted off beside her in a fit of mental anger and premeditation.

Life was often like a bandage across a scabbed-over leg. Whether God or an omniscient being was reliant on the ripping of the bandage, things in my life had often been torn from me like teeth and nails from a prisoner of war. This pattern of fortune continued for the rest of my life and still continues to this day. Beginning when I was small child upon my birth, my unfortunate stroke of luck began, and it climaxed when Valerie Crowley passed away.

I had not seen her at school for three days before I began to worry. I knew she had missed over two-thirds of the school year due to ongoing medical problems and doctor's visits. She gave me a list of all the medicine she had been prescribed in her life and it easily took up a page of paper if not slightly more. She would usually miss five groups of two days a month to adjust to new medicine before facing the crowd. She had immense anxiety which led to violent depression, and I felt for her. When we were alone, I wanted to hold a lot more than just her body. I wanted to cradle her heart and soul and embrace her mind, allowing her to find peace and experience true happiness. I hoped that it would be me to take away her pain, and by God, I tried. What began as my lust for her transformed into passionate love, and perhaps that was the hardest thing to let go of once she passed on.

I found the letter in my room the hour before I discovered what had happened. My world ended that day as it had four years prior when I found her suicide note on my bed on that winter day. In my mind I knew exactly what it was, but in other ways I was oblivious as a deer in the headlights. I picked it up and ran my thumb over her familiar hand and began to read.

Noah,

I cannot begin to find the words to tell you this, but perhaps my hand can. I have told you time and time again the travesties that have haunted me and continue to haunt me to this day. I can no longer handle the guilt and blame for what has happened to me, and I want to thank you for all you have done for me. I want to apologize to you for my lack of affection and care toward you. My ability to love was stolen from me, yet you loved me with the deepest and truest love you knew how and I am forever grateful. Thank you for everything you have done for me. Although we must part, I will find you one day in the world of no disease and imbalance. I will find you, Noah Willowby. I love you. Goodbye, my love.

Val Crowl

I hit my knees and began to sob as I realized what the letter implied. My face hit the carpet beneath my legs and I collapsed. I banged my fists across the bed and pillows and floor - anything I could hit, I did. I was angry at myself. I was angry at the ones who had caused her so much harm. And above all, I was angry at her for how she felt and blamed herself. How could I be? Was that a selfish thought? Perhaps I deserved one. I pushed it aside as I thought about how she must have felt. Lower than dirt. Crowded with thoughts and emotions. I knew all too well the cancer of anxiety and depression as I once considered joining her in her demise. I could not. I had her death to avenge before my own. Perhaps that was the definition of true care and compassion called love.

I brought myself to my feet and snatched my coat from my chair and rushed out the door. I sprinted out the front door, knocking over my mother's beloved lamp in the process. My feet hit stairs and pavement as I nearly slipped and fell over my own feet. I ran as fast as I could down the street and turned the corner onto hers. I saw no car in her driveway; her mother did not work and her stepfather was more than likely out driving drunk God knows where. I knew her mother would be passed out asleep as she always was at five o'clock in the evening as the sun set below the city skyline. The shadow of the town square cast a pitch shadow across our neighborhood, blessing us with darkness before anyone else in the city. I had no time to knock and wait. I searched around for something heavy as my eyes set upon a garden stone in the front flower bed that her mother had so graciously set. I wrapped my hands around the cold stone and hurled the rock through Valerie's window. The glass shattered into a million loud, clattering pieces into a clean and neat hole. I climbed through the narrow window and ripped her curtains down.

I frantically searched around her room; she was nowhere to be found. I rushed into the hallway as I caught a glimpse of her sedated, defeated mother on the living room couch. The shattering of glass had not so much as stirred her. As much as I searched and rushed around the unfamiliar house, Valerie was nowhere to be found. I shouted in frustration as I heard her mother sit up and walk toward me. "What's going on, Noah?" Melissa Crowley asked me. "She's missing," I muttered between sighs and breaths. "She's tried this before but I never thought she actually would," she added as she started to cry too. She had lost hope as I had.

I walked quickly through the winding city streets and dodged the rush of people and cars as they headed home from work, making my way into the countryside. I broke out into a run as nothing stood in my path of finding Valerie as the answers that came along with it. I saw the shadow beside the trunk as I stomped the grass beneath my feet in a full sprint. She was apparently standing behind the tree waiting for me, and I ran as quickly as my body would allow. I rounded the tree and shouted in surprise at what I saw. There was Valerie Crowley, the love of my life, my best friend, and my other half, hanging from the tree where we had spent so much time together. I began to panic and lose my mind as I stared into her lifeless eyes. Tears flowed from mine as I reached around for something to cut the rope with. I pulled the belt buckle from around my waist and pulled back the leather, slicing through the tight strands with the metal place holder. I eased her body to the ground and pulled her hair out of her face and behind her ears. I pressed on her frail chest and breathed into her mouth, hoping that by some grace I would be able to save her. But there was no response.

I picked her up in my arms and began to run back into the city as fast as I could. Valerie weighed maybe a hundred and ten pounds, but it felt like a ton as my world began to crash down around me in a blinding and terrified panic. "Somebody help me!" I shouted as I rounded the concrete street and back into the city. People turned and looked at what was the matter, but none offered any assistance. I shouted curses and screams at the passersby as they at least parted from my path. I kicked open the doors of the hospital and screamed once more. A young nurse emerged from the office in just as much shock as I was. She then hurried two doctors out with a gurney and helped ease her onto the bed. "We'll do all we can," she promised me as they rushed her to the emergency wing. "Please bring her back," I whispered as the doors shut in my face.

As much as I would like to tell you that Valerie walked out of that hospital a few days later, I have made an internal promise to tell you nothing but the truth. Valerie Crowley remains nothing but a vivid and pure memory in the deep recesses of my mind, but I will never ever forget her for as long as I may live. When she passed, perhaps her lifelong depression drifted into me like the cigarettes I began to smoke in her honor, and my mental stability worsened all the more steadily. Habits carry memories, but they never bring the source back to fruition - no matter how many I smoked and put out on the same tree trunk we had spent so much time together under.

Valerie Crowley was buried four days later in the city cemetery with her family and friends surrounding her, as few and far between as they were. There were not even a dozen people in attendance, but the crowd felt empty. Tears hit the grass as they flowed through her cloudless eyes as they were closed and buried along with my other half and deepest love. I was never the same after she passed, and I still feel the pain to this day. The first flame never quite burns out, no matter how many time it is extinguished and pushed to the back of your mind. Topher did not slit her wrists or fill her throat with medication, but in many ways - if not all - did he cause her death. The dazed-minded addict had the nerve to attend her funeral. I caught a glimpse of him outside the graveyard following the burial, turning my stomach and boiling my blood like poison. I forced my hands into my pockets, burying my anger and my love as I walked over to him. "I didn't think funerals were your thing," I spoke shortly to him. "Can't beat a suicide," he replied. "A certain sadness follows it. I knew Velcro since we were just kids," he said. "You tortured her every day of her life, you miserable piece of shit," I grumbled through gritted teeth. "Hey, Noah," he raised his hand. "Funerals aren't a place for anger," he smiled before walking off. "I'm gonna kill you," I spat. He stopped in his tracks before continuing on. I saw Topher only one more time in my life before he joined Valerie in death.

Did my parents know I had stopped taking the medicine? Perhaps it was obvious. Rarely would they come into my bedroom to ensure I was still breathing, but they knew I was suffering after Valerie's death, and by the basic standards of parenting, they thought it kind to at least ask if I needed to talk. I did little but sleep and smoke for months after her passing, and my mother caught me on the rare instance that I was awake. She knocked quietly and came in, sitting down on the edge of the bed where I laid and thought. "How are you doing?" she asked consolingly. I shrugged as I thought of how to answer. "I know you're going through a rough time. I've never been there, so I can't offer you a solution, but I can at least help." I thanked her simply and abruptly, almost rushing her to leave before the obvious followed. "Maybe if you took the medicine, it would help. It would help you to forget," she said. "It doesn't help. Nothing helps," I cut her off. "I don't know what to tell you then," she replied. "I'm always here if you need to talk." With that, she was gone as she always had been and I was alone once more. "Don't smoke in the house either," she shouted. Perhaps I could not be helped. All I wanted was Valerie as I fell asleep into an empty and dreamless unconsciousness.

Valerie's last wish had set on my mind and heart for the longest while after her passing, and I had more than enough time to think and reflect on the possibility of bringing it to fruition. Would it bring her back? Of course not. But her legacy would continue through my motivation to please her - even if she could not see it come to fruition. Perhaps her spiritual ghost would smile at the finished product and watch over me for an eternity after. And so I sat at my desk - the very same place I had sat to write the very first letter to her - and uncapped a pen. With the turning to a clean page of the notebook I had given to her as a gift, I began to write, letting my deepest thoughts and opinions bleed onto the lines and onto the back of my hand. I found that pills and pencils carried the same high and were the same degree of drug. While my peers wasted themselves away on drink and substance, I used pens as needles and injected my thoughts and witnessings onto the paper before me. I became lost in it, for my drug of choice gave me a different life and world altogether in which I had seen. I became addicted to it and clung to literature for what was left of dear life. There were more than enough doctors and handymen, but where were the writers and artists? They had gone extinct, begging for resurrection like a forgotten savior. They had been destroyed - forced into the shadows. They would return once more; I was sure of it. And I would be on front lines. The notebook and pen stayed at the ready and on me at all times, tucked behind my belt and salivating for inspiration in which was thrusted through my life and newfound freedom.

To whomever may find this journal, this is your map of the new world. Was it I who brought about the end of mankind? Perhaps it was, for these words and scriptures sparked realizations that caused anarchy. This is a miscellaneous collection of my thoughts and ideas of society and where it all went wrong. If I had been found writing this, I would have surely been hung high and mighty on the Gideon horse or the wooden stake. May my words find a place in the world of yesterday, today, and tomorrow. May you also find a place in them.

Not a day past half a month following Valerie's death, her mother was found amongst an array of required medication bottles just as her daughter was. Perhaps Valerie was her only hope as I was for my mother, and without that light, her bulb burned out like an Alaskan candle. I saw Melissa Crowley three times in my whole life - once when she found me and Valerie in her room one morning and another time gardening out in her backyard. She was a rather petite, adorable woman as Valerie was, and my love received those genes honestly. Valerie was a domino, and the effect thereafter was that of repetition. Fire with fire, sadness with sadness, and destruction with more and more destruction. Following the death of the lovely mother and daughter who had cared for me but been taken away like splinters, I knew one thing for sure: Jason Crowley then lived alone. I knew my dominoes and the line in which they stood, and I knew what I had to do to force them to tumble.

I knocked on the door that I had used maybe one time on my visits to the Crowley household three times prior. I rapped in a serious pattern and waited for the only resident left to answer the door. The car sat in the driveway, and it was only a matter of time. Sure enough, he answered the door roughly and as seriously as I had knocked. "Oh, Noah," he wiped his eyes of a drunken sleep. "If you're bringing flowers, I'd rather have a new window," he snorted. "Come in," he opened the door further. I stepped inside to what was once a second home for me, yet it felt as strange as a cave then. "I'm sorry, Jason. I really am. If I could have done something, I would," I sympathized. "You did enough, Noah," he replied. We walked through the dark house and I saw just how much he had let it go and been hurting. Bottles cluttered the tables and floors and the walls smelled of ash and smoke. We walked to Valerie's room and he stopped to stare out the window. It had been taped over and half-assedly been swept up, large shards of glass still littering the carpet. Jason leaned against the wall and began to speak. I sat on the edge of Valerie's bed as the violent flashbacks overtook me. "I miss them more and more each day. This house is so empty. I loved them so much and it will never be the same again," he said through a drunk and stuttering tone. "Yeah," I said. "You have no one to mistreat and abuse. *You* killed them. This is on you," I said through gritted teeth. Jason did not turn around at first, but I heard his breathing. "*Excuse* me?" he said. He never turned around. I drove the largest shard of glass through the base of his skull, covering my hand in both of our bloods, leaving him to rot and suffer as he had done to me.

Chapter IV
A Visit From a Quartered Soldier
(Safeguards, Leg Stories, and Speeches)

Oh, hell. Where do I begin? It has always been a struggle for me to find a place to start a story and finish it, for a tale can continue on for eternity. Perhaps it starts with a word - a single, simple, omniscient, misunderstood, complacent word that blanketed war and peace like a leaf in autumn: freedom. It is often mistaken for entitlement, which is a societal sin. It was confused most of the time, and I struggled to understand it for the largest majority of my life. You had the freedom to say what you felt and also to cause as much pain as you could through words and actions - as long as you were comfortable with the consequences, that is. But what does a terminally ill being have to fear? Are they bound by conscience or fear of imprisonment? Of course not. Perhaps the most free being is of that misfortune, for they answer to no one and are tied down by nothing. With freedom comes fear. Freedom of thought leaked from the mind to the mouth and into the ears of an unwilling society like a well of pure, clear water. It was a tall glass of whiskey, and the outcome was sinisterly and similarly simpatico. You can have too much whiskey; you can get drunk off of it. It can make you do things that you would never do while bound by sobriety. Capitalize on speed and greed. For example, a car salesman sees a teenager come onto the lot. "Hey son, buy the car with five-hundred horses under the hood," he says. Kid buys the car. Kid gets pulled over going a hundred-and-twenty miles an hour. Ticket. Endless money. Wreck them, clean it up, and prepare for the next. Capitalization on speed and greed. Racing to be the best, no matter the road. Perhaps that is what brought about the end of the world - unlimited and untapped freedom.

My lifelong struggle with anxiety led me to fear and even run from confrontation - down to the very thought of a conversation. Jack King intimidated and frightened me with his very presence, but I remembered how I had chased Valerie despite the violent, tearing knot in my stomach. She was gone, and I could not spend my entire life mourning and running from the same things she had, so I set out to grow closer with what I feared most - namely Jack King, and I was terrified.

"How's it going, Mr. King?" I shouted to the man who ran the world as I staggered across the city sidewalk. "Noah! How are you, my friend?" he replied. Before I could squeeze out another word, he raised his hand. "My father was Mr. King. I was born Jack Ethan King. Please, call me Jack," he smiled behind his rectangular sunglasses. The sun glinted off of the frames, off of his metallic leg, and into my soul and I made the first of many handshakes with the very image of God himself. "Walk with me, Noah," he clapped me on the shoulder. My anxiety kicked into overdrive as we matched each other step-for-step. "How is school?" he asked me. "School is school, I guess," I replied sheepishly as he chucked. "You'll be learning to drive soon," he changed the subject. I nodded as I struggled to hold back a question. I usually lost those battles. "With all due respect, do you drive with the opposite keg?" I asked with instant regret. "Yes, indeed," he said. "You're probably wondering how I lost the leg," he followed. "It has crossed my mind," I returned. He paused for a moment as he struggled to think of how to word such a complex story. "The thing about the military is that you can never get out. I was in the Coast Guard for four years, then the Navy for eight. Then when I finally thought I was out, they roped me into contract shit overseas. If not for the end of the world, I would still be sniping kids with turbans and bombs overseas. As for the leg, I was in the wrong place at the wrong time. I was shot and got lead poisoning. It had to go." We walking in silence for a while as my mind and stomach whirred with confrontational anxiety. "How are the women treating you, Noah?" he laughed, one I could not match. "Kinda slow these days," I said quietly as I thought of Valerie. "You should try raising one. That's a job that's never slow." I laughed a fake laugh to lead into a possible mention of Julia. "She can't be that hard," I argued. "You'll have to meet her," he punched me in the arm. "I guess so," I slid in enthusiastically. With that, he clapped me on the shoulder one last time and turned the corner.

I love you. It was a beautiful praise of a phrase. It could heal wounds and mend a shattered heart. Yet it was weak. It was a temporary bond of no future value. Rarely did it stick, much like off-brand glue. It lasted until one party fucked up or over the other. Words were words, and I yearned to scream goddamnit in a church. I strived to piss off every fucking being with life left in them, because it was temporary. I would leave my mark.

I hated bright lights. Squinting to see led to many headaches in my childhood, and I was grateful for the city's gloomy and melancholy stature. Clouds covered the sky on most days and when the sun was naked in its rays, I chose to stay inside. I despised light and the heat it brought with it. My mind was a cold and dark place in which no one dared to traverse; my mind was partly a town square filled with shouting people of different opinions and volumes. Other times it was silent. I loved to clean - especially sweeping. I hated to dust, and my belongings were always cluttered, but I loved it that way. I was not obsessive about order, but about containment. Did I have all of my stuff? Did I forget anything? These were the questions that ran through my mind each and every day for years on end. You can worry your stomach to a violent rumble and shit into an endless bowl until your asshole is raw and bloody, but it does not change your worry nor take it away. I had a nasty nervous habit of biting the inside of my mouth and tongue until it bled, only to be cursed to repeat that action until I had a massive sore along my gums. The smell of blood was potent, but the taste was comforting and salty like tears. I was an utter and complete bundle of worry and obsession.

Life was always about addictions. Perhaps every being was addicted to something. Did it have to be drink or drugs? Of course not, goddamnit. Of course it could be, but there were always those who were addicted to slapboxing the dog shit out of their meat at least a dozen or so times a day. Overthinking was an involuntary addiction, this of which I suffered from for most of my life and still do to this day. Twitches and mannerisms were signs of a much deeper addiction, and a drug was not always a substance. Time was a drink, and I walked a buzzed existence for many years. Cigarettes would burn your lungs with a cancerous smoke and drink would drown your liver until it became poison, and yet we drank and puffed away like kings until we perished.

Sleep was a beautiful thing, and like many other pleasant aspects of existence, it had a jagged curse embedded within it. Dreams were a realm where anything could happen, and that did not always entail a positive outcome. Sleep was measured in depth, not time. If you slept eight restless hours and three deep, unconscious ones, which one would benefit you more? I found that a few short hours of complete rest resulted in a greater awakening than a lifetime of closed eyes. Sometimes in the subtle silence of the city I could hear voices in my head twisted into tunes and wrapped around rhythms.

The second time I ran into Jack King in the city, he was flying somewhat under the radar. I was used to seeing and expecting the massive orange Hummer; it was impossible to be missed. I would have completely passed over his presence had he not rolled down the window of the slate gray Range Rover and yelled to me. "Better be wearing sunscreen out here walking. You're getting all fucking red and shit, soldier!" he shouted. I laughed and waved as he sped off into the city. There was a white skull and crossbones on his rear license plate.

Perhaps the downfall of the world came with the accountancy or factoring in of a situation. Maybe it was the lack thereof. For example, you must factor in and account for traffic and accidents and the occasional funeral procession when you leave for a destination. Likewise, one must always account for outliers and impossibilities. Perhaps we did not. There was always a crack for the impossible to slip through. My life can be best described as violent bouts of crippling depression interrupted by sporadic pools of immense joy; perhaps it was the other way around. My childhood was one of picked scabs and migraines. I was raised on Andy Griffith and Spider-Man and I was content, but you see, this simply was not enough. I dreamed of books and songs, words and rhythms, and paper and sound. I wanted a world of my own that was not reality; I wanted to be taken away, but it was exampled to me that I had it all wrong - backwards, to be exact. I had to have myself taken from the world, and my dearest friend, I was. Can you imagine being so goddamn stressed out that you forget the original worry? My imagination was vast.

Society was a living, breathing hypocrisy. Spare the rod, spoil the child. Exploit the child and punish the predators that come knocking. Media was a disease. Coverage was a thousand bandages on a paper cut. A minor majority was always means for ruin. The more I looked around me, the more I saw how fucked up the world dichotomy was. I saw the church and how the people gathered to hear the minister - the flesh and bone being that spoke imperfect words about a perfect word. I turned on the television to see how views fueled the media, only to see celebrities and artists that caught sight of the drool from the lips of the peasants beneath them as I came to my omniscient conclusion. Man was god, and that gave me a good goddamn fighting chance. Perhaps I was lucky. I was born at such a time at the birth of the technological

76

age where I was able to know what a VHS tape was as well as a dinosaur television, and I was grateful for this. Experience is knowledge. Technology changed the world and weakened it while it also gave strength. Communication ruined social skills and abilities over-seeded the societal crop. Too much of a good thing is the downfall, and technology allowed creativity to fester like an open sore. This was how it happened - the end of time and the beginning of tyranny. Progress disgusted me over a certain extent. Woods were demolished, cut down, and burned to lay simmering asphalt and places of business to exchange currency. Money ran the whole goddamn world, and it disgusted me. Animals ran for their lives as their homes were destroyed - babies ripped from their mothers like an animalistic holocaust. But it was worth it for a few dollars in the eyes of man. Dollars were definition, and the world mattered not. Nature was taken advantage of and it exacted its revenge on its deceivers. I appreciated the immense beauty of life, and I was spared from the wrath of the elements. I would in turn exact my revenge on the world as they tortured me and ridiculed me. I would have my way with the women and slaughter the men who had mocked me and betrayed me. I would be king. I would be bound by no paper or creed. I would be God.

Even at my youngest age of thought, I knew that I was going to change the world. I was going to take the raw hatred and ridicule it offered and spit a heinous, vile poison into the face of society. I was going to erupt and disrupt the commodity and displace the common man. I was going to slit throats and wrists. I would become God. In the face of confrontation, I often pondered veiling myself in the shadows of pitch and losing myself to the evil thoughts within my mind. I pondered hiding my face and holding my adversaries at a weapon's distance, ripping the begs for mercy from their cracked, bloody lips. Other times I considered the taking of my own life. It was quite comical as well as wondrous. Even the ones that were different were even unique and set apart from each other. There was no true normal, no matter what the prerequisite may have been.

"Do you just own a used car lot?" I asked Jack King as he pulled up beside me in a silver Mercedes. The car was slick and shined, and the light bounced off of the metal and into his shiny black hair. "Something like that," he replied. "I've got two motorcycles I can't even fucking drive."

We were all victims of chance. The human race was a dichotomous allegory which alluded to that of random demise. If our fathers had rubbed one out the day before fucking our mothers, we would therefore be null and void in existence. On the other hand, if our mothers had bled one more egg, we would be just as lost in anti-reality as we were if we were born. I am the violent, calloused antithesis of man. The world was full of jaded hypocrites who gave the church a bad name and a horrible taste in my mouth. I turned away and found myself in the eyes and arms of omniscient, sinful power. I remember looking out among the ancient world lights and thinking to myself, 'In my lifetime, I will see you all die. The world will be mine.' You are either a proctor of evil or an imposter of good. There is no few, far, or in between. It is that simple. The simple human mind could simply not handle complex truth. It is that simple, and it was that complex - all in one ironic, contradictory lie. A fish logo on your back bumper did not make you wise or good, and the same went for slaughtering thousands in the name of a shadow. There was no good. Whether you were busting ass for pocket change or busting an ungodly obese nut in a white-collar cum office, there was no fulfillment, no good. It was only a matter of time. There was always an infinite amount of possibilities of how the world could have ended; there is an infinite amount of numbers between zero and one. There was always an infinite amount of possibilities of how a single scenario can play out. You can be the one that pulls the trigger, the one who gets shot, or the one that watches. So on and so forth.

Every being has regret. I believe that even mass murderers and rapists have regret. Could I have killed more? Could I have gotten away with it any longer? People like me regretted every waking decision they made. I would take a path and regret it. I would say the wrong adjective and regret it. I would make a choice and regret it, even if it was the tiny question of the other option lingering in my head for days and days until it left me. I was a walking, breathing apology, and I was sorry for it. Apologies were always a lie - a societal glue that made amends for any crime, no matter how minuscule or vast. Children were forced to apologize, and therefore they lost that regret when they grew old. No matter how sorry you were, it did not take away the pain of the wrongdoing. Only more pain can do that.

There were a million - a billion - possibilities of children that my mother could have given birth to, and yet my family - as well as the world - was cursed with me. The one-thousand-four-hundred-and-fifty-sixth sperm cell and the fifty-seven-thousand-ninety-eighth egg came together to form the societal savior of the world - Noah Motherfucking Willowby. Believe it or not, that middle name would have given me the same initials. Morgan had a quite different ring. I dreaded my societal exorcism, which would come many a time in my life.

A few weeks after my third encounter with him, Jack King made a surprise visit to our home. As expected, he was accompanied by a group of heavily armed soldiers. Fourteen was an estranged age - a time where I would stay awake all night and rely on the remains of my father's coffee to carry me through the next day. A time when change travelled through the veins of the city and into my own. A time of question upon every subject. A time of rebellion. *Difference.* The night was wearing thin, and the city full of tired inhabitants slowly drifted into their houses for the night. A quaint rap on the door startled me as my father limped over to answer it. The two men shook hands aggressively as old men do, I suppose. Once inside, my mother offered our guests coffee and other such refreshments. The security guards quietly declined, but Jack requested half-cream-half-sugar. My mother skittered off like a shaken squirrel and returned a moment later with his order, as if she lived to serve the one man who gave her true purpose.

After taking a satisfying sip, he asked how things had been for my parents at their jobs and how my father's leg was. They both put on their false attitudes with a twinge of inferiority and reverence in their voices, referring to their jobs as spectacular and grand - a privilege. King was known to disapprove of opposition or ungratefulness, and my parents took heed of this prenote. My mother reintroduced my brother and I, much to my disdain. I never cared for the spotlight nor thirst for any recognition. My brother loved it, on the contrary. Jack's face lit up as he recalled pulling us out of the rubble four short years prior. He went on about how we had grown and how manly we looked - the spitting images of our father. After the compliments ceased, he ushered me to sit by him on the couch as most authority figures tend to do, and with the exchange of a worried glance to my mother, I reluctantly took the empty seat beside him. He asked Jacob and I how school was treating us, and he looked to the man that had saved us years ago. He replied with the only thing I knew how to - a slight smile and a sarcastic comment. "The history book is a little *short*." Jack grimaced and looked down at him as my mother scolded him. "We're learning what *matters*, my boy," he smiled a faux grin. I hated confrontation; my mind was riddled with tendencies and inconsistencies as I was. My stomach turned as I myself grimaced inside as I prepared for the worst. Jack King was a sort of human building, towering above nearly everybody both in physical and mental stature, much like my father. He had a tightly bound ponytail running his dark hair down his spine in a neat arrangement. His goatee was shaved into a precise line along his jaw and cheek, casting a shadow along the run of his chin. His brown eyes were so deep with color; I felt his heavy spirit invading my mind like spilled coffee.

My arm lit up with fiery pain suddenly and soakingly. Jack King's facial expression changed drastically from delighted to concerned as he realized he had spilled the entirety of his coffee cup onto my arm. I definitely felt the pain, and I tried to scream, but something would not let me. My emotions were held prisoner in those dark, mocha-colored eyes. My father limped off into the kitchen as he hurried to get towels and ice. By the time he returned with a white cloth in hand, all traces of the accident were gone. My arm felt normal, and Jack's cup was full of mud-hued coffee as he sipped it gleefully. My family stood with a puzzled look on all of their faces, as did I. None of us knew what had just happened only moments prior. I sat silently on the couch beside the heroic, intimidating menace as my mother hurried off into the laundry room, embarrassed as her rosy cheeks and startled stature could be. It was truly a bizarre occurrence, and so we jumped on the first opportunity to change the subject in an awkward disarray and unsettled composure.

Jack sat upright as he drained the remainder of his coffee with a satisfying gulp. He told us about his upcoming speech on the Saturday of that week. Chills ran down my spine as the news of something exciting to look forward to fell upon us. The whole family was eager to get out of the house for once. All throughout that evening's conversation - no matter how much the subjects varied - I could not help but notice Jack King staring at me much more than normal. It seemed as though his eyes would be on mine every time they moved. His eyes were a parasitic abyss that latched onto mine like a leech out of water. He was fascinated with me for some reason unknown to me in that moment. As the night aged into the late hour, Jack called his crew of soldiers to start the vehicles and prepare for the return home. They all nodded to my parents, still remaining silent. Jack King thanked my mother for her hospitality and shook mine and brother's hands. They calmly and politely left our home as though they had never been there, leaving only a puddle of spilled coffee and a China cup to clatter to the ground.

On the night of Jack King's visit, I had the third and certainly most horrid of the dreams I had ever experienced. I was taken back to the burning city once again, just as I had been twice before. This time, I was the boy trapped under the rubble. The weight of the building felt as if the entire city was pinning me down, holding me prisoner as the flames threatened to swallow me up entirely. Seconds became millennia as the ominous wreckage crushed my bones like glass. My breathing became unsteady and dangerously slowed. Something as simple as taking in air became as difficult as moving the mountains that towered above me. I soon became desperate for my life and began to panic. I found myself screaming for help, just as I had heard the boy do before me in the previous dream.

My life flashed before my eyes as I struggled to keep my eyelids from collapsing. They were heavier than the burning building that kept me chained beneath its weight. Suddenly, I felt a cool, rough object grasp my hand. I strained my eyes to see only a few inches in front of me, and I saw that it was in fact another hand. It latched onto my arm and started to pull me out from underneath the wreckage. Both of us groaned and grunted as we struggled under the sheer weight of the building. There was no doubt in my mind that both of my legs were broken. Every inch that I was pulled forward felt like another bone was cracked and rendered numb. In reality, the pain would have been absolutely excruciating, but in the dream, I was merely numb from the waist down. The stranger finally broke us both free of the massive weight. He grabbed my shoulders and dragged me several yards away from the flaming scene. My vision slowly returned, and the sight of my mangled body was sickening. I quickly looked away, straight into the man's eyes. Half of his face was burnt and singed like beach sand, and his left eye was blackened and destroyed beyond repair. He displayed a tortured expression as he stared deep within my soul with his one intact eye. Blood dripped onto my arm, searing my skin just as the spilled coffee had done.

I jerked awake with an alarming start. My blood was warm and pumping through my veins vigorously. Sweat dripped down my face and neck, saturating my clothes. I leapt out of bed and grabbed ahold of my knees, ensuring that I had two working legs. Once again, I must have become violent in my sleep; soon after, my family surrounded me with curious faces once again. My brother continued his relentless teases as I was subject to every form of laughter and embarrassment that he knew how to dish out. My father wrapped his hand around Jacob's neck and sent him back to bed, and after a few whimpers on his part, he reluctantly left the room. Once he was gone, my parents began questioning me as to what was going on with me recently. I claimed the problem to be bad dreams again. Little did I know, that was the worst mistake I could have ever made.

Mankind always possessed the perfect formula for its own downfall. Was it in the hands of the imperfect swine created in God's own image? No, that was only the beginning. The human race was always built upon the principle of dominance and the perspective that came with it from the beginning to the end. What was a moment to man was the end for the ant under his boot. That is, until man became the ant. No one was ever safe, no matter the degree of security. There was always killing, there were always tragedies and disasters, and there was always destruction. Was there such a thing as born freedom? Of course not. A child can perish from the moment it inhales its first breath. Do we have a freedom from ridicule? From humiliation? From desecration? Of course not.

My friend, let me sum up the moral of the old world for you in just a few written lines. The old world was about capitalization. Capitalization on an idea or principle. Capitalization on the right point would make you good and goddamn rich. Think about it with me, my dear friend. Think back to the old world in which you live. Do you not capitalize on season? On holidays? On an image? The redneck style? The hood style? The rich? The poor? Capitalize on God once a week and twice a year. So many brands and ideas clashed together, making a corporation rich while the workers jacked themselves off and broke their backs with puny dollars and nothing but the smell of sweat and cum left to their name. Life was a constant cycle, with many examples of this truth. A bird would be smothered by tires, leaving a meal for the buzzards and vultures. A sweating glass would feed right back into the cup. There were no extraneous outliers - only those to feed the system again and again on an endless loop. All you needed in life was two fingers. With those two fingers you could make someone scream - in pleasure as well as pain - or make them bleed. They were your trigger, and if used correctly, the shot would be heard worldwide. It was all about making your mark, whether it be a bullet hole or a bloodstain. I would break free from the old monotony and be forced into a new enclosure like an animal. I would tear its heart out and forge cities of bones and a world cast from metallic flesh.

It took several days for the images within the dreams to fade from my mind, sticking with me as most nightmares will do. The school week dragged on as fast as a boulder rolls across a plateau; by the time Saturday finally drifted around, my family was more than eager to hear what Jack King had to say at the town assembly - myself especially. We got up that morning and ate a hearty breakfast of eggs and bacon. My mother cooked most of the time, occasionally switching nights with my father throughout the week. He prepared dinner quite a bit once he got back on his feet - rather literally - giving her a break and taking his position as a man back within our household. After finishing a glass of orange juice, we were rushed off to get ready. When my mother demanded something be done, there was no hesitation or question of the matter in fear of retaliation from my father. He had a relatively mild temperament, his military training disciplining him deep within, altering his quickness to react. My father had only yelled at me once in my life. The man was quick to fuss but slow to anger - my mother being the opposite. She was a woman of passive aggression, possessing the ability to guilt you nearly into slavery. "Have you been taking your medicine?" my mother asked me. "Yes," I lied. "Periodically throughout the day or are you trying to ration it out?" my father asked. "Yes," I lied again. They scoured and rolled their eyes as I walked toward the stairs. I had long since stopped taking the medicine. It was no cure, for it was merely sugar to me. It helped none, and I was all the better without it. I flushed it with the morning and hid it upon nightfall. It held me prisoner no longer, and I began to see the world for what it really was.

I changed from my pajamas to a pair of torn jeans and a dark t-shirt - that was simply my style. Grim colors made you a shadow, making it quite simple to fade into the background. City gatherings were treated as formally against anything else, so attire was generally expected as pleasant and respective. Jack King spoke out blatantly against church or anything even remotely of the sort, for he hated God or even the idea of anyone above his rule. After a brush of the teeth and a comb of the hair, I headed downstairs to impatiently wait on the rest of my family. My brother came down the stairs wearing his usual goody-two-shoes best, complete with one of our father's blazers and a pair of leather shoes more than cleanly polished. He always strived to be better than everybody else, especially me. He brushed past me down the stairs in his khakis, button-up shirt, and freshly slicked hair, shoving his hands into his pockets as he gave me a disgusted look. My parents soon followed close behind, both clad in their work attire, which were as casual as a black suit and a rose-red dress can be. We looked like an upper-class family with a dysfunctional youngest child - only the latter being true. The suit was a requirement of the job, a staple from my father's brief stint in the Secret Service, and the dress was a rather exploitable stereotype of an office secretary. The shoe polish was military grade.

My mother and father had a nasty knack for obsessing over their reputation. My brother was an obvious embarrassment, and perhaps the clothes I chose to wear merely added to that unnecessary attention. Was I a strange lad for wearing stripes and plaid? Black socks with blue pants? Ties with a t-shirt? Perhaps I was a bit odd, but it is in the face of oddity that creativity spawns. And so I was ridiculed and made to conform. Politics had always been humorous to me. There were always elections, debates, and media drama that brought about the mental decay of a sorrowful, pitiful generation. Just imagine how much our kind could have accomplished upon a system of agreement and cooperation. This is what Jack King sought to implement with his city-wide gatherings. Not only did technology weaken the human race, but difference of opinion created a herd of wild pussies and sorry bitches to cry dripping tears and rub lotion on their elbows like the entitled cunt that they were. In the matter of Jack King, he needed no vote and no upper hand. He was the upper hand, for Christ's sake. He was Christ in the new world in the metaphor of revelation. There was only man, and the only man was God - Jack King. Likewise, we gathered to listen, learn, and worship.

Being a personal chauffeur for Jack King and the city officials, my father had access to a top-of-the-line armored vehicle, one of the finest in the city. The brilliant shine on the metal attracted sightseers from all around, which mostly walked wherever they needed to go. Larger vehicles were hard to come by, as most of them were required by the city officials for supply runs and transports. We were very fortunate as we had always been, but in the city, fortune was nothing but null and void. Opportunity was earned and slaved for, and so we belonged. Somewhat ironically enough, a child's societal stature was determined by their parents' position, and therefore there will always be extraneous judgement. My father performed his job as his desire to please overtook him, opening all of our doors and ushering us all in before climbing into the massive driver's seat. The leather was brand new and the air smelled like fresh rubber. The starting of the engine echoed off of the walls of the garage. We reversed quickly and traversed into the heart of the city; the middle of the city was several dozen acres of buildings and an enormous meeting place where all of the city-wide gatherings took place in the town square. As we neared the chaotic rush of citizens, we hurried to park and join them around the stage in the open and full space. The people shouted and screamed with excitement as time grew near for Jack King's appearance, which was rare and celebrated. Several minutes passed as the remainder of the city filed into the town square, packing like sardines against each other to hear the message. An eruption of deafening screams and shouts followed the leader's arrival to the stage. He wrapped his fingers around the microphone and hushed the crowd strictly. He waved as the claps and cheers quieted to eventual silence. I can still remember his words to this day.

Like all things, his speech started minuscule and quiet, rising in intensity into a deafening roar, enveloped in screams and shouts from all around. "I would like to welcome you all to the first gathering in this stronghold," he began, his deep, gruff voice booming throughout the gathering place. More cheering climbed louder, but it was soon hushed once more. "It has taken three trips around a blinding, opposing sun to reach this moon we have conquered. We have all lost something and sacrificed a portion of ourselves to get to this place, but it has and will be replenished in its utter entirety and so much more with the completion of this metropolis. We have ceased supply runs and there is no source of life - whether it be material or human - outside of these walls. Over the course of the next three years, the walls will be sealed. Why such an extensive time period, you ask? We just waited three goddamn years to get here! But you see, progress is not measured in the time it takes to achieve it, but in the sheer perfection in the change that the progression makes. So I tell you, my fair people. This city will not be like the old world in any form. No, there is no division based on color, occupation, or status. There is no discrimination against any man. This a land of the new world - a world where you work or you die. You contribute or you are evicted. You obey or you kneel. In this three years, we are going to weed out the weak like a societal garden, my good people. Any sick weed or stray seed will be crushed by the metal and stone as the walls close on their children. There will be no weakness in this city, and I will ensure it. Under my rule, we will prevail. This is the new world, goddamnit!" More cheering erupted from the rear of the square at the announcement as he raised his voice. They loved this man for what he was telling them, yet I did not realize it in that moment or even years later until I connected and decoded his words. They cheered for eons on end because of one thing that he promised. They did not have to worry about anything, and everything was going to be provided for them. Food, protection, shelter, and any other common courtesy and luxury available in this kingdom. All they had to do was earn it. Weak links and frayed wires were going to be cut out and they only had one job to do, which was not to become one of them. It sounded so simple in that time, but his words carried a heavy burden and a weight of the world on tiny, thin, frail arms. His entire speech was a paradox and an impossible lie, but in that moment it was gospel. "WHAT BEGAN AS A DISASTER AND A BROKEN DREAM WAS FORGED INTO THIS MAGNIFICENT PLACE. THE WALLS AND BUILDINGS ARE SEALED WITH THE SWEAT AND

BLOOD OF OUR OUTCASTS." The crowd lost control for several minutes. "WE USED TO PUT OUR FAITH IN AN UNKNOWN FORCE, BUT NOW WE ARE SURE. I AM SURE. I AM GOD." That statement left the people in bewildered silence. "WE ARE ALL THAT IS LEFT! WE ARE STRONG! WE ARE THE NEW WORLD! THE FUTURE!" The cheers and shouts returned with an ungodly, deafening roar. "WITH ME AT THE HELM OF THIS SHIP, WE SHALL NOT SINK!"

Either that was the end of Jack King's speech or the crowd was too extraordinary riled up to continue. Despite the widespread joy and celebration of his speech, his words left me in a mental maze of the deepest thought. The city really was all that was left in the world. Something vastly evil had forced us into that stance of attack. *How bad could it be? What was Jack King capable of?* The crowd dispersed soon after the exit of our leader as we also pushed our way out of the tightly cramped town square. I felt the energy of the people around me, but I was numb at the same time. I did not know whether or not to feel safe in a walled-in city led by a determined tyrant as we were. I did not know how long the self-righteous facade of safety would hold. *How long would it take for the evil to eat through the steel like a cancerous rust and eradicate all that was left of the world?*

Chapter V
A Place in the New World
(Blinded Revenge, Dirty Jokes, and a Job To Do)

Indeed, it took three more years to prepare the city for "total isolation" and achieve the promises Jack had issued in his speech as he referred to our geographical secession from the rest of the world as. Life continued as usual after the gathering except for a boost of excitement in the hearts of the townspeople. The speech was a resolution - a scripture to live by at first and a loose reference as time went on. Labor and production was at an all-time high for weeks after, and the rest became a choice left up to those who made it. Most resumed the impressive quota, but a twitching thought in the back of my mind told me something was missing. I began to notice several people missing. They were people that faded into the background anyway, but when they disappeared completely, someone just had to notice. Perhaps that was my job - the way in which I earned my keep. I was destined to shed light on the mysterious happenings and theologies of a lost world. Once the city was sealed off, a sense of security spread throughout the townspeople. I was then sixteen years of age, an adult two years shy by the common definition and a grown man by the city standard. This was the age where every able-bodied newcomer of age was persuaded to join Jack King's military group of guards and officers. We were welcome to deny the request, of course, and that I did. Countless of my peers joined his force for the simple fact that they would be forced to earn their keep instead of what they thought was enough; after all, I had not noticed any of them going missing. Jack believed that no man should serve unless his heart was in the right place, and I agreed in totality. Oh so many people served for the fact of free housing and food for life, and perhaps this was carried on from the old world. The soldiers gave me a feeling of anxiety in my stomach and a feeling of inferiority in my heart. I would never become one of them. He believed there were two kinds of people - the ones who watch and the ones who are watched - the sheep and the shepherd. That life was not for me. I watched both parties from an omniscient view, for I was above them.

I had sat in church for the first ten years of my life as a mindless witness and formed my opinion when I came of pondering age. Did I belong there? Of course not. I would sit in the back row each week and plead with myself to kneel at the altar, with no answer within myself. Like any other, I heard the message for the hour and upon the car ride home, it had faded from my memory. I would plead with God for help, but as I turned on the news, I realized that He was preoccupied with the allowing of his followers to be slaughtered with no intervention from His holy hand. Did I abandon the idea of God? After years of struggling on my own, He abandoned me. I hated God, and so I became him. I had seen first hand the ant and the crumb and the mouse and the cheese. The ant will follow the crumb and become mush; the mouse will chase the cheese and lose its head. Ants would chase their animalistic instincts to the honey and become immersed and encased within it - trapped within their own desires. This was how it was with the human race - how it always was - and perhaps how it is destined to always be. I knew from what I had seen before me what capitalization on fear and desire was. Frighten people with the idea of eternal damnation and the plate becomes full. It was in the face of adversarial conflict that I discovered that peace was a nonexistent term. The largest word I ever came upon was almost; it showed either a great amount of skill or luck. There was always almost peace. Always is inversely similar to almost. Always is an infinite term until proven to be limited. Always provides immortality to a statement until it is cut open. Always is almost eternal. With so many denominations, how could a single god truly be served? Who was right? Who bowed

the right way and prayed the right way and called upon the right
name? God was a hypocritical myth to keep the unruly in line and
capitalize upon fear. I could have stumbled into a church and
massacred the entire congregation with no stir from the Almighty.
There was no Prince of Peace, for chaos was king. You see, there
was no god - only man who claimed that title. That such man was
Jack King, and there was fear.

Gregor McLindle was the face of the city's enemy moral. There were always people that heard rule and did the polar opposite to test the water, and this particular ocean was frigid and vast. Gregor was an artist and a musician - in secret, of course. I had heard the fantastical stories of his works from the children at school and the whispers of the adults in the town square. Their very mention of the man risked his existence, and like so many other times in the human sociology, selfish desires overpowered the greater good. My favorite author was not Poe or Hemingway. I was lost not in the works of King or Fitzgerald. My favorite author and poet was one that I had met, and it was Gregor McLindle. I kept his work secret, for it died with me. I remember the day very vividly that Gregor was captured and executed. He had built an underground bunker in his home on the east side of town in which he carried out his creativities. The convoy of soldiers could be heard and seen along the town square as they ran up his driveway and down his secret stairs to where he played his grand piano loudly and freely. Of course he was not expecting capture or even discovery, but society was his own downfall and he was content with it. I heard that he was ripped from the piano chair, his fingers abandoning the keys and his foot leaving the pedal untouched. The instrument was destroyed with an axe and set ablaze along with the rest of his home, and with that, Gregor McLindle dined with Jack King that night before being placed cross-legged in the town square the following morning. The headphones were placed over his ears, flowing quite possibly the same notes he was convicted of playing, and he was shot straight through his skull. Creativity and expressional freedom died that day, and the people of the city heeded the example of hypocrisy. I had heard Gregor McLindle speak but once as I had passed him by. His outgoing presence drew attention and fanatics from all around, which eventually led to his downfall. Jack King spoke to him once as he was placed in the town square to die. "You asked for this. It didn't have to be this way," King said to him as he was blindfolded. Gregor stirred. "When we surrender this world back to the birds, the birds won't want it," he spat through gritted teeth. Those were his last words - ones which no one ever forgot.

There was another far-fetched tale about a man which possessed money in the city. One cannot keep a riveting secret like that at bay for long, and the stranger ended up similar to an artist I once heard of but could never seem to name or recognize until long later in my life. The man's ears were supposedly cut off and hung on a necklace for him to constantly wear as a reminder of who to listen to. Man or money. King himself was currency, along with the opportunity that he provided.

There was a particular story which emerged from a rumor, bubbling from gossip and fortified by hearsay. There was a certain fairytale of sorts in the city - fairy tales had been outlawed due to their wild and vast creativity. Word was once the walls had been built and sealed off, two children had climbed over the wall and escaped the city. Some versions of the story told that they were brother and sister while others stated that they were teenage lovers. Their pictures were never posted anywhere as to not raise suspicion or take the hold Jack King had on the city, but there was an extreme caution and security along the wall as the search was carried out. I thought it to be a show as a child - a way to display the power of King. But as I grew older and learned of the story, I knew that they were on a strict order to find the mission's children. As far as I knew, they were never found.

God was either a violent, insecure coward or a malevolent failure; perhaps he was both. Parents who followed the rules and regulations of their book of choice mourned and begged their god to save their child from the cancer they were rotting away with, but no answer would come forth from above. Unfortunate things would always happen to the best of people with no answer or reasoning. The unchanging, monotonous sinners rubbed their hands together without punishment while the righteous and holy suffered the true hell. And to think that the cowardly failure was praised for His wrongdoings. He was celebrated by most in times of terrible need and holidays, but they would worship me forevermore. The world would fall upon my wrath - one way or another. Whether I would have to kill Father Time and fuck Mother Nature, I would rip the golden staff from the cold dead fingers of society. Perhaps the ultimate goal of life is to reach the epitome of silent judgement on others - to become so self-propelled that you are able to govern others. I so desperately loved that concept as I questioned and witnessed it. All repercussions considered, I kept silent and watched, waiting to take my place in the world as I lusted for unlimited power.

When I came of age, I was expected to take a committed, contributing job within the city. The general idea was to start at an entry-level position and move up to the top, mainly being in Jack King's direct line of officials. Naturally, I started at the bottom of the totem pole. The world could end a thousand times and people would still have a desire to shop. Markets lined the business district, and carts had been brought from the outside world shopping centers. The townspeople would enter the shops and leave their cart when they were done - sometimes in the strangest and most annoying of places, and so my job was to retrieve them. I enjoyed it, I really did. I got a job that allowed exercise and a feeling of completion. After all, I loved a sense of order, organization, and cleanliness. The city was my own and the weather was always fair as far as I was concerned. If you loved to do something that everyone else hated, you would always have a job and you never truly worked.

I worked with a disabled man named Alabaster Kingsley. Some called him Allah-Bastard in a comical humor, which lost blood and teeth for the religious reference. He was perhaps the smallest and frailest individual I had ever met. Alabaster had cerebral palsy, which rendered his voice to nothing but grunts and grumbles. If he could do our job, I knew that anyone could, although most fell short due to millennial laziness and entitlement. Forced to resort to sign language, he kept quiet and wrote letters for communication. Some said he had a stroke in his teens, but he had been that way since birth. I got to know the man although he had never spoken a verbal word to me, and he did the job just as well as I did with one hand. Through a hobble and a grumble, Kingsley was the toughest son of a bitch I ever knew. He could get away with just about anything, and rightfully so. Although I was royally pissed off at him most of the time, upon his forced retirement by his mother I missed the hell out of him. His mother watched his every move in an attempt to take care of him, and all of his earned opportunities became hers. He disappeared from my life, and I missed his own sort of voice and his written word. I never saw him again outside of the unconscious.

Perhaps the face of the American Dream was a gentleman named Leroy Hall. He was a country boy born and raised in Kentucky, hunting and fishing all of his life. He would sit on the street corner and smoke the day away in cigarettes as he worked for the electrical works of the city, telling me stories of the old world and his aging along with it. Hall was not the type to pursue a post-secondary education, but it is those people who had the best stories to tell and therefore the greatest existences. Leroy joined the Marines when he was twenty-one and traveled the world for eight years. He told me about how he had walked through the Last Supper quarters and seen Christ's tomb. They were nothing but rooms to me, but the stories were fantastical and I listened in awe. After the military, he worked as a death row guard at a prison in Nashville, Tennessee and explained deeply how he treated the inmates equally. He told me once that if a man looked forward to a piece of cake, then by God, he was going to get it. Hall told me that he was positive that if in the event of a prison riot, the prisoners would put him in a cell and protect him due to his fairness and treatment. Leroy told me he had met James Earl Ray, the man who had assassinated Martin Luther King, Jr. I knew little about that man until later in my life, but he became one of my heroes when I learned of his racial equality movement and peaceful protests against discrimination. It was a goddamn shame that men such as this could not exist in a cruel and everlastingly evil world. As legendary and down-home as Leroy Hall was, he had a dark side as all of us do. Perhaps his past and life of tragedy and hard work had twisted him. He had seen his best friend commit suicide before his eyes, and he had worked multiple jobs for years to feed his family. His discussion and treatment of women and other races was far from kind, and I struggled in my opinion of him. I kept my thoughts to myself as I listened to his stories in amazement, for he had lived. But in my heart I knew that he was the face of the old world and he could not exist in the world of Jack King.

"Come on, wind. Blow. Blow," he said one day as the young lady in the skirt walked by on a Sunday. "Look at those ass cheeks beatin' the hell out of each other. Fuck," he followed. I laughed as I turned away from the cigarette smoke he blew in her direction. She walked by without a stir or flinch, no knowledge of her verbal desecration. He stomped out his cigarette and looked at me with a laugh. "You ever seen two niggers kissing? It looks like two commode plungers sucking off one another." I smiled as it faded in rejection and disloyalty. "I've been all around the world, and one thing everyone has in common is chicken," he said. Leroy and his son made killer deer jerky, and they respected the wild more than anything. "We don't kill anything we won't eat," he said. It was a simple philosophy. Looking down at his bare wrist, he said, "It's damn near chicken time." He had forgotten his watch at home, revealing a bare tan line as white as Joshua Peterson's feet. Ten on a Sunday morning was always chicken time.

I knew of Roy Hall long before I met his father, but years later I made a close acquaintance with him and found that we had a lot in common as far as our childhoods went. I had never seen this pattern in any other family until I met his father. He was a skinny, goofy-looking bastard - much like myself and my other friends in that time. We shared many a good laugh as I did with his father in the later years. We worked in the same market when we came of age, and we had many stories to share and compare. He wanted nothing more than to join Jack King's army and serve his city as his father had done for the country in his early years. I loved the stories Leroy told, but I had no ambition to follow in his footsteps as a second son. I had the utmost respect for the military, but there was always a subtle, numbing regret within my heart for what my father had chosen over his family, what he had left us for, and what he had replaced us with. I vowed to never serve a man other than myself - no god, no tyrant, and no peer. I had seen first hand what that form of service could do to a being as well as a family, and I made another internal promise to myself to swear it off at all costs for the sake of myself and my sanity.

Leroy Hall loved to drink and have a good time, and sports always carried and sparked conversations. Although there were no professional sports in the new city, Leroy talked about the old world sports with his friends in the marketplace. One such friend was Richard Monthaven, a stockbroker and sports announcer in the old world. Very few people could out-drink and out-smoke Richard - not even Leroy Hall or Jack King. He had been smoking two packs of cigarettes a day for forty-five years and drinking a case of beer for at least that long. The two men loved sports, and they got along merrily. Richard Monthaven was a poet long before the city, and that memory leaked into his mind as he replaced his antidote with a beer and a smoke. He recited one of his poems from the heart rather eerily one day on the topic of how women will use and abuse you, and yet it made me want them even more.

There came a time after Alabaster had disappeared and Leroy Hall had retired that Joshua Peterson, Strauss, Topher, Klaus, Roy Hall, Sawyer, and myself all worked together in the city marketplace chasing carts like goddamn butterflies. Although Topher and Klaus did not last long and faded into the hidden lazy confines of the false productivity, they left the three brothers in the markets to carry out a fierce brotherhood. We were gods; we were lords of the parking lot. Joshua and I would exchange comical stories and historical topics while Strauss and I would discuss literature and speech techniques. I swear he could not write to save his life, and so I saved him rather literally multiple times over. I would scrap his work and simply start from scratch, contorting a masterpiece for him to take credit for. I minded not. Creation was my drug - in secret of utmost course. I remember talking to Strauss and warning him of his impending diabetic coma. It was the dead of summer and the outdoor work environment prompted a multitude of sweat drops and rivers from our bodies. He would sit down for break with his pie and chicken platter as Joshua and I stared at him in a rather soaked state of awe. "You're gonna die out here, brother," we joked. Was he selfish? Of course not. He was a jolly and generous soul. Of course we had to sample the food he dined on, however. There was plenty after all, for God's sake. He chewed and swallowed cheerfully as we went back to work. Someone has to take in order for someone to give.

Stephan and Hugh were two of the best managers in the town square shops where I worked for several years before moving to the library. When you are a part of something for a certain period of time, it becomes like a family. Contributing to society and making quality friends is a fantastic feeling inside. I felt many days like I mattered and meant something, much unlike my own home. When the city is a machine, you are a valid part and you have value. It was a beautiful process, and it worked. Stephan was homosexual, which was overlooked in the city and counted as important as a single hair. Close-minded, distracted minions of the old world worried themselves to gray and grave about whether or not someone was born gay, but at the end of the day, who gave a good goddamn? A perfect God would not create a being they hated. Or would they? Therefore, God was null, void, and nothing but a hole in the walls of the city. Those who worried about these matters ruined the wasted life they were given and therefore imperfect in the things they missed, and I found the key to life. Stephan once told me that what he did, as well as anyone else, behind closed doors was his business and did not in any way affect his outgoing life. Nevertheless, Stephan was married to a woman before and had a daughter around my age, and he loved the hell out of her. Stephan was one of the best and realest people I knew, and he deserved a lot more than rumors and a low title. He could have been Jack King if he wanted, but he was content, and everyone was content with him. Especially Jack King. They both knew their places, and peace was kept. Perhaps this was how it should have always been. So many times did sexuality and skin color jade human connections, and it saddened me. After all, it was the division of a people that brought about the end of the old world. Stephan taught me what people who discriminated missed out on, for he was a brilliant, hardworking man who knew just how to manage people and maximize efficiency while simultaneously being a friend and partner. His sense of humor was vast and flexible, and his outgoing opinion brought laughs from everyone he met.

When Stephan was not running half of the goddamn city marketplace singlehandedly, he was known by a much different name - *Tucson*. Sexual entertainers were once plentiful and dispersed, but the city had only two. Stephan was the male stripper by night, and a professional one at that. His signature outfit was that of a combination between the Monopoly Man and Colonel Sanders. His velvet coat and top hat with his faux cane set off a vintage vibe and therefore modernized the entertainment factor as he danced. Before the night was over, all that remained was the hat, the cane, and the eighteen inch cock he supposedly carried. Alongside Diamond, those two raised all kinds of hell and cocks. Word in the city was that Stephan was bit by a snake when he was four years old. The poison apparently made his dick grow to a magnificent size of eighteen motherfucking inches. Whether it was true or not, Stephan was a leader by nature in everything he did, and his dick was therefore the eighth wonder of the world. On the odd chance that he was not busting his own ass at his day job or busting other people's asses in the only nightclub in the city, Stephan loved to cook and read comic books as I did - in secret, of course. Comic books were rooted in creativity, and so we kept it hidden. Fiction was a crime, unless it be realistic fiction like *Gatsby*. That was simply a cover-up. This sparked many conversations between us; although he favored the opposite group of heroes that I did, we shared many a recipe over the years.

After two years in the city marketplace, Strauss got one of his friends hired - a young black fellow by the name of Johnny Wrongdoing. Perhaps the name was a nickname, or maybe it was the one society had given him. Johnny was run over by a car when he was an infant, and therefore he could not see clearly nor drive. This rendered him useless in some situations, but as far as working with me went, he was a master. Like myself, he was ridiculed and made a joke of due to his remarkable misshapen head while my nose and oily skin was the butt of most humor. He would carry on secret conversations of comic books with Stephan and I, and he found use in his interest and his job.

Stephan and Leroy Hall were a magnificent pair when they got together in communion. I got the exemplary pleasure of hearing their banter on multiple occasions. Although Stephan was gay, he had been married once to a woman in his early days. Leroy loved to "count wedgies", as he would put it. One day outside the market I sat with the two men, listening in on their conversation and laughing my ass off. "Spandex doesn't lie," Stephan said. "Yeah, poetry in motion," Leroy replied with a chuckle. He pointed to a young woman walking by in a poured-on appearing pair of pants. "Look at that wedgie," he said. "Looks like it's trying to eat itself out of there." Roy Hall made a societal living inside his father's shadow. Everyone knew of Leroy Hall and his wild stories and sense of humor. It made sense for him to be the spitting image of him - he was in fact Leroy Carroll Hall Junior. I dreamt of a son that I could call a junior - one to inherit my name. I yearned for a successful shadow for him to fall in. I could simply not put the cart before the horse. Or the lot, in our case.

Hugh was a common man to anyone else, but in the world of city commerce, he was the Everyman. He got along with anyone and was relatable. After all, the down-home country boy personality was the most sought after to me anyways. I possessed it and attracted it, and Hugh was a friend as well as a superior. He was what he referred to as an "automobilier creationist". Hugh Mosley would put large engines in lightweight sports cars and test them out on the open country roads on the outskirts of the city. "I could take King in that old Mustang any day," he boasted in confidence. He loved fast cars and set out to make them faster. He told me stories of Godspeed machines and incredible speed demons. "I want more power under the hood than God has in his hands," he said riskily. I understood this. To feel that speed and that power made you God. Either the speed or the mention could have gotten him killed, and it did. The mention of Jack King and a possible Mustang baffled and excited me. I drove myself mad to find out, for Mustangs were my favorite. Hugh's brother was Bobby Joe Mosley, the auto mechanic manager in the city markets. He had plenty of time to think up original jokes under hoods and cars alike, one of such as follows. *Why did the muffler quit working? It was exhausted.* Any and every automobile issue that arose was handled by B.J., and he was a king of mechanics while Hugh was the creator. Nevertheless, the Mosley brothers were a dynamic duo of the automobile industry in the city.

While Stephan told me stories of sales and his childhood, Hugh taught me about cars, which I loved, and we laughed about how he would love to do my job. Stephan said he would never do it, and he kept us in line in a comical manner. Hugh was my first manager there, but unfortunately he was not replaced by Stephan as I had wanted. A woman named Angela became my manager in my second year, and she was new and green as could he. A woman without people skills, I automatically connected with my coworkers better than she could. I worked in the area every day nearly, and I could make a better schedule than she could on the first day. Despite our unspoken differences, I chose to befriend her and she respected me as the best. I had been there the longest after Leroy Hall had retired, after all. I loved what I did, who I worked with, and the city I was a vital part of. Other managers were just as repulsive if not more so, such as Al and Phil, which I nicknamed Douchebag McGhee and Northside Pantywaist. Two men of chubby figures, neck beards, and unbelievably thick glasses, they stuck out like a sore on Diamond's face. They were the dynamic duo of abused authority and pointless tasks. These two were the perfect example of everything that should not be in a management position, and I will never forget the humor of Jack King punching the two men directly in the testicles for their corrupted sight. I despised them, and their clouded agendas eventually got them killed. Other more occasional friends consisted of those such as Jimmy Phillips and Ty Cornwall. Followers of managers such as Al and Phil, they picked up their negative characteristics - despite how much they were joking around. I hated that. I would rather be told the truth instead of being falsely crucified. Nevertheless, they would tell the truth and ask for details, although most of the time it was for my own humiliation.

On the strictly opposite end of the friend spectrum, Priscilla Ares was one of the sweetest and kindest friends I spent time with within the city marketplace as I worked day after day under the hot summer sun. When I first met her, I assumed she was my age with her thin frame and beautiful looks. After I discovered that she was married to a grade-A man named Johnny and had children, I settled for a friendship. I was never much of a homewrecker, no matter how far my mind wandered without the medication running through my veins. Priscilla had a sister named Mackie, and she was in fact my age and rather flirtatious. Priscilla told me that she had a boyfriend, which figures with my luck. It was when I found out through the grapevine that he was abusive and took advantage of her that my mind truly began to whir with a premeditated care. The city marketplace was full of "apprentice Traders" as opposed to cashiers, most of them being the rather attractive type. It was a sort of game to pursue them and capture their attention, which is rather difficult to do when you are a bundle of sweat and dirt, but a wink of the eye is all you need, my friend. I simply sought to help, even though there were always ulterior motives behind it. That family was my ideal form of true friendship - more like my own adopted family. We shared many a laugh together, and they came to my defense like a rhythm to the sweet lyrics of a song.

Germany Chester was Britton's daughter, and she was also an apprentice Trader. She was my age, and we had similar clothing style - seeking the eccentric and outstanding colors and patterns. Germany could sing - and that was a curse in the new world, my friend. She simply could not hold it in. We would meet in secret in the marketplace alleyways, and she would sing quietly as she tapped on the metal tables. Her rhythm was unmatched, and her words were pure and true as silver. I admired and longed to hear her sing forevermore, until one day she was heard by one of King's guards.

"That's cute," the officer said in a mocking admiral tone. When he pulled back his iron mask, I saw that it was none other than Maxwell Wiseman. I used to love music," he said as he brought his electric baton across her forehead, knocking her unconscious. I cowered in shock and fear as he turned his gaze to me. "Get the fuck out of here, kid," he said through gritted teeth. With a rock in my stomach and a pulling decision in my mouth, I hurried around the corner and in the direction of my house. I did not stop running until I was behind my bedroom door. It was only later that I discovered that her tongue had been cut out for her crimes, and she would never speak again - much less sing.

Like the world around me, I had ever-matured and become a fixture in the world I had discovered. My voice had long since deepened and my frail body had become solid, my jaw tightening and my eyes narrowing more and more with each day. I had grown taller and wiser in the ways of the world and my surroundings as I knew the city in its utmost familiarity. I felt as if the city knew me as well. More time was put into establishing a strong government, a flourishing economy, and a strengthened communication system. Crime was almost nonexistent when the city was in its beginning stages, but as the streets and sidewalks expanded, so did the crime rate. The military police officers brutally crushed any rebellion under Jack King's boot. There was no prison, no court, and no retribution. King himself was law - judge, jury, and executioner rolled into a single cycling machine of anger and debt. Protesters to the harsh and binding law were shot dead in that moment - King simply had no time for foolishness. It was a case of leaving a dead spider for all of its children to see; criminals caught on and kept their evil deeds in the shadows.

Holidays were a horrible time of year - an opposite opinion of the general public. There was no God to worship in the city, so Christmas was an extinct day and nothing but another day of work. God was nothing but a speed limit and a handrail. Those blinded and bound by a god knew no true freedom, and mass murderers and thieves answered to no one. Thanksgiving always baffled me as well. Lunchtime was about giving thanks for what you had and then after you emptied your bowels of grace, it was time to rush out to buy a few more inches of television. Human greed disgusted me, forever and always. Perhaps the richest part of society were the ones who begged outside of grocery stores. Ringing bells and a sad expression drew more money than any street hooker could hope to scrounge up. At the end of the day, a retired veteran looked forward to an impoverished lifestyle after their service, forever thanking the ones that owed the greatest debts. I was also thoroughly disgusted with the amount of people who would walk out of a public restroom without washing their hands. Society was a germ-infested petri-dish, and I was disgusted. Turn the world black and blue and leave a nasty scar for the next generation, haunting your descendants like a ghost of mistake. I am dead or damn near. Guilty as charged. Mary did not know. The greetings were not seasoned, the bells were not silver or jingling, and the night was far from silent. The years were never new. No one was ever saved. And by God, no one was ever fucking thankful. No matter what. New Year's resolutions were like popcorn-sized jokes - they would be hot for a moment and then pop. I always thought of it as New Years, new tears, but perhaps that was too melancholy and depressing for the human mind to process and understand - no matter how truthful it may have been. Nevertheless, fat people would flock to gyms, alcoholics would swear off drink, and smokers would get on the patch. Only for a moment, however. Then the tears would begin to flow once more. Merchandising was a trap. Name brand items were at least thirty percent more than the store brand, and often times all the lesser in quality. It is only those who searched for the best deal that truly won - for a personal price of whatever they chose to sacrifice.

    Sawyer's presence in the school was as well-known and custom as grass underfoot or air in the lungs. Each generation always needed a clown and facade of future success to utilize as an example for others, and Sawyer Jennings was the poster-boy for the idea of progress. Naturally, his absence was noticed just as much - if not greater - than his addition to the daily clockwork. Sawyer and I would meet outside of the school building after the day of learning was over - after his exploits with his other higher-dollar classmates, that is. My hand came in first but my heart was last. I felt forgotten as I waited on him - sometimes half an hour or more. It was his turn to be forgotten, and upon a three day hiatus of his appearance, I went looking for him.

    I had never been inside Sawyer's house; it was because of the stories that he told that I had a negative connotation of stepparents. His life gave me a perspective and a certain gratuity of my own. Although my father was far from perfect and a great deal jealous and assertive on most days, he was not an abusive drunk. Sawyer's stepfather was rumored to be verbally condescending and controlling; perhaps that explained why I had never seen his mother. Perhaps he kept her locked up in the house while he drank his sorrows and insecurities away. Sawyer told me he had been hit many a time in a drunken rage as well as watched his mother bleed and swell up like a thick bushel of grapes. I vowed to myself that if I were to ever get a stepparent, I would be sure to slit their throat if they were to outstretch their abuse to me or my family. My father was tolerable, but we rarely got along due to his absence in my life and internal need to govern my thoughts and actions. My mother was alone, and I felt for his mother as I had watched it happen before with my own.

I saw no car in the driveway; Victor was not home. I knocked on the front door several times, but there was no answer. I turned to leave solemnly with a strike of resentment as I descended the porch stairs, and the creaking of the door opening nearly escaped my mind. "Noah!" Sawyer shouted to me. I spun around and walked back to the base of the steps. "Where have you been?" I asked. Sawyer remained silent. I walked back up the stairs and stood face-to-face with my best friend. "What is it, man? We've been missing the hell out of you." He looked me in the eyes like a reluctant yet angry animal. "My mother was murdered," he said quietly and sternly. "What?" I asked in shock. "Sunday night," he followed. "Victor found her Monday morning. Her wrists were slashed and her throat was bruised like she was strangled." I thought for a moment; I was a newcomer to death, and I did not know how to respond. "Do you think it was a suicide?" I asked in a hushed and secretive tone. "No. As unhappy as she was, she would never leave me like that. That wasn't her." We kept silent for many moments as we leaned against the railing. "Do you think Victor did it?" I whispered to him, careful of volume. You could never be quite sure who was around in the shadow-like city of many monsters. "No," he replied. "He was distraught. He left Monday night and I haven't seen him since." I put my hand on his shoulder. "I'm sorry, brother. If you need to get out of this house, you know you can come with me," I offered. He smiled ever-so-slightly in appreciation. "Thanks, brother. I'll be alright. I need to be here. I have to find who did this." I turned to go once more. "You know where to find me if you need anything," I shouted in passing. "I don't think books will bring her back," he replied.

Four years after the death of Valerie Crowley, I was still just as driven and angry as I was on the day I had discovered her secret. Was I glad she told me? Of course I was. It gave me a purpose and goal - a means to release and avenge her death. I had not spoken to Topher but once in a friendly and hidden, sly manner since I had threatened him following my discovery, and I felt that the time was right to take action. I had been taught through the study of human history that it was indeed best to keep your friends close and your enemies closer, and that was how I planned to do it. I followed Topher after school and clapped him on the back. "My man Topher, what's up?" I said cheerfully as he whipped around in nervous anxiety. "Nothing much," he nearly stuttered. "We've gotta get together soon and do something, man," I said. "Yeah," he said distantly, as if he would rather be kicked in the ballsack by a horse than carry on a conversation with me. That was how he always was, though. He was raised that way. Belittling me to build his own throne. No more. The throne was mine. "Let me come over tomorrow night and we'll see if we can't get you into a game of Monopoly, man." He had always wanted to learn my skills and I desperately wanted him to, but he had more laziness than a bear in the winter months. I loved Monopoly, and I awaited his approval. "Sounds good," he said, his eyes red and hazy as he walked away.

With that, a night of schemes, and the next day, I walked up to his doorstep with a bag of two simple items and knocked three times. He came to the door forty-seven seconds later with a dazed look in his eyes as usual, and I stepped inside. We walked into the living room as he picked up several cans of energy drinks and tossed aside a pack of his father's cigarettes. "Set it up here, man," he said, nodding to the table. "I will," I replied coldly. "Bring me two glasses. I've got something you can't turn down." He rolled his eyes and huffed and puffed, walking into the kitchen and back as I folded through the paper money. That was all it ever was anyway. I laughed for more than one reason as I set the game up quickly. I pulled the tall glass bottle from my backpack. "What do you have for me? More of your dad's pussy juice?" he sneered in a narrow, joking tone. "Something you've never had before," I winked. "I made it myself." He laid down the two glasses as I poured the dark liquid into the cups. Tapping his glass with mine, I did not dare let the liquid enter my lips - only touch them. He emptied the glass and poured another. I sat mine down as he looked at me in wonder. I took my pawn and placed it on Boardwalk before moving his to the jail square.

I looked him in the eye and began to speak. "I know you raped Valerie Crowley four years ago. You drugged her and raped her while she was out. She was the love of my life and you took away her ability to love. You took her identity and security and shit on it. I want to look at your eyes when you die and know you feel remorse. You, my friend, just drank a combination of Jack Daniel's and rat poison." I heard the glass smash as he looked at me in utter shock and terror. His grimace changed from wonder to anger to pain. "You killed Jason Crowley," he spat. I stepped aside as he lunged toward me in a sick and poisoned attempt to kill, quite possibly the same volatility he had used on Valerie. He collapsed to the ground as the glass did and cut his chin on the shattered pieces. I turned his limp body over and watched the life drain from his eyes. I capped the bottle and walked out of the house, the pawns not moving and a feeling of immense, unsatisfied anger deep within my heart. As far as the city was concerned, Topher had had a heart attack or alcohol poisoning. But as for reality, Judgement Day had come at last.

Chapter VI
Through the River and Over the Woods
(Letters, Mustangs, and a King's Princess)

Becoming an adult was a multitude of emotion and gained freedom. It was a time much anticipated as well as dreaded. I had hated my family for much longer than that day I became a man, but that disposition only grew stronger. I had grown exhausted of my brother's laziness as I voiced my opinion, and yet it only drove a wedge in my family. I did not see my mother on that day, and I spent the entirety of the day away from that dreaded house. Why did I choose to come back? I was my mother's only hope, of course. That night was a cold and forgetful one as well as the first night I did not return home. I worked the following morning, and I drifted home to clean up the childhood behind me before I traversed forward and forever into the unknown. I yearned for it although I had tasted the freedom before. It was an acquired taste, and I searched for it inside the reality of the age. I knew my place in the family and I was content with it, for it was an outcast position.

It was within the coming of age that Sawyer and I decided to experience the city club scene for ourselves. After all, perhaps we needed to escape from the stresses of our lives for even the merest of moments. We slipped inside the door as the guards outside waved us through. The city street was quiet and dim, but the inside of the cozy club was far from dark and melancholy. Lights flashed as the crowd of people danced and cheered, crowded into two separate groups. I could hear the tapping of a cane against the wooden stage floor and I caught sight of the golden-lined mink coat that Diamond sported beside Tucson. By day, Stephan kept his hair folded into a neat and gelled arrangement, but by night, his hair fell into a messy and loose mop of a style as he spun and danced. He waved as he recognized me walk through the door; I remembered his joking invitations to the club as I came of age. As a matter of fact, I had not wanted to come at all. In that time, I was low from the years-long hull of depression and growing anxiety, and a crowded place of noise and lights was last on my list if desired destinations, but Sawyer had told me stories of Diamond's body and how it could bring any man to his knees. I wanted to stay on my feet, but I joined him anyway as I waved to Tucson and followed him to see Diamond. Her mink coat had long since come off, her pink bra barely supporting her perfect breasts. Smoke was blown into the crowd and my face, blocking my vision and senses as I lost myself in a compressed and unfamiliar place. She reached behind her back and let the material fall off in a teasing and flirty manner. As she stood there in her skimpy but matching thong, she reached down and pulled Sawyer onto the stage. Moments of shock passed by as she eventually led him backstage. I laughed as I fell to the back of the crowd and outside the door once more, back to where I could think. Little did I know that that was my curse in those days.

I collapsed onto the bench outside the club as I felt the pulse of the lights and the crowd inside my ears and along my neck. My head pounded with memory and thought as I held it in my hands. I had not gotten out much at all in the past several years; I had kept to myself in every meaning of the phrase since Valerie had passed away. There was simply no fun to be found and no joy to be sucked upon. I had fallen into a stifling and crippling bout of depressive motivation and began to write down my thoughts and transgressions onto paper in secret. If anyone were to find them, they would have lost their minds and locked mine away in a much more secure and safe place. I had lost my hope and patience with mankind and strived only to bring about hurt and pain onto the ones that had done so to me, for society had done that to me. But I had decided to return back out into the world that night, and I felt as out of place as I ever had.

Sawyer clamored out the door in a high and drunken state as he struggled to get his words and footing on the sidewalk. "How was it?" I asked him in a false tone of interest. "Deep, wide, and shaven," he mumbled simply. "I fit my entire goddamn head in that fucking thing," he said in his own amazement. We sat in an uncomfortable silence for a long while. "You're not gonna believe this, Noah," he whispered. "Two things actually." I looked over at him. "What's that?" I wondered. "Hit me with it." He struggled to manage words through violent laughter. "Tucson's dick really is eighteen inches long!" We both laughed hysterically as I put my thoughts on the back burner in my mind. "What's the other thing?" I eventually asked. "He had Mr. Broove backstage in a ... *taxing* position," he spoke slowly, followed by my successful chuckle. I always knew our world systems teacher was gay. I sought closure not for ridiculous purposes, but for the simple fact of knowing and being correct.

"I heard you guys having sex last night," Jacob said to our parents at breakfast one morning. I fell silent as my mother's face grew red. I had heard it too, but I had not the balls to bring it up - especially over oatmeal. "One day son, you'll wield the magic of the Willowby name," my father said before rubbing the dick of his sweatpants on the back of my brother's neck. I was disgusted and taken aback as Jacob was; perhaps he had learned to keep his sexually-aware tongue short. It was upon a rare and wild-card instance that our family had a swell time at the same time, and upon those random occurrences, I was content with my demise.

My brother and I established a schedule of chores and followed it religiously. The work kept us out of trouble and prevented fights between us. While he did the dishes and the bathroom cleaning, I took out the trash and got the morning mail. Jacob was convinced that he had been cheated, but I was satisfied with the division of labor. I loved to work and I carried an exceptional work ethic, as I had been told many a time. More and more chores were split between my brother and I as we grew older, and in the end, our parents did virtually nothing but their jobs by day, coming home to melt onto the leather furniture and become one with it while losing themselves in the television of ancient reruns, leaving Jacob and I alone in a much greater sense than absence of parenthood.

I would always arise early in the morning while my family and the rest of the city slept; it was in this habit that I found that the city around me - as well as the world - was mine. A week shy of five years after Jack King's speech, I got quite the quiet and quaint surprise one brisk and icy winter morning. I was then an adult in the eyes of my parents and worthy of more responsibility as they sat on the couch day after day as they rotted in front of the television. I left the house in my boxers and made the early and cold walk to the mailbox. Winter had threatened the city with a bitter, menacing vengeance. I loved the winter and appreciated it, for the summers where we lived were brutal as a child. My job was better than the mailman, I guess, seeing as how his shift ran at the crack of dawn - even in the dead of winter. He had no appreciation for his occupation, and therefore any merit he had fared a void of meaning, for he did not enjoy his profession. In my opinion, it was not worth either his time to deliver or mine to retrieve the occasional poster to advertise an upcoming event. They were always the talk of the town, but you see, King was creating jobs, filling spaces, and living up to an agenda that no one else could. The sliding door of the mail car woke me at every subsidization, and on that particular morning, all that awaited me at the end of the driveway was a single letter. I snatched it out and shut the mailbox, examining the envelope curiously. The letter was surprisingly addressed to me - from Jack King himself. I put it in my pocket to avoid suspicion from my family as I trekked back into the house and shut the door behind me, the heat enveloping my body like the excitement inside of me. My parents were in the kitchen; Jacob slumped down the stairs, still half asleep from the looks of it. He shoved past me into the kitchen and poured himself a bowl of cereal. I laughed at the bags under his eyes and his greasy hair; I suppose the walking dead needed breakfast as any other being so requires. I greeted my family and my father jumped on the subject of the mail, as he always had to have his morning paper with his coffee. "It makes it taste better," he told me. I told him that there was no mail and he cursed the mailman and continued to sip his supposed half-assed coffee. My mother offered me a plate of eggs and toast, but I quickly declined it and headed upstairs, eager to read the letter. As soon as I shut and locked my bedroom door, I pulled the letter from my coat pocket and sat down at my desk. I hastily tore open the envelope and analyzed the writing on the piece of paper inside:

Noah Willowby,

You have been cordially invited to my mansion to dine with me on the twentieth of this month. Whatever you do, do not inform your parents of this letter or your whereabouts on said date. If all goes as planned, we shall expect you at five 'o'clock this Saturday night. Bring the coffee!

Best intentions,
Jack King

I was confused by the letter - especially the last sentence. I blinked several times to make sure it was really written there, and it was. I shrugged it off and sat the letter down. As the feeling of oddity settled, excitement took its place. I knew the character of Jack King - one would have to lick the sweat from a thousand scrotums to get even remotely close to his home, and yet there I stood with a written invitation to dine at his table. No one was ever welcomed there unless of course they were set for execution the following day, and so set in the looming thought of *what the fuck did I do?* I never got invited anywhere, especially with anyone of importance. The highlight of my year - before the city, of course - was going out to eat once a month with my family. I was never invited to anything, much less anywhere like the dwelling of Jack King. To say that he lived in a house was a severe understatement; that was at least what he called it. It was not even a mansion - even that denied it justice. It was more similar to a goddamn castle. He had the place built on the stone overhang up on the mountaintop at the finish of the construction of the city. It could be seen from any point within the heavily-guarded haven. The stories towered above everything else in the city, belittling all others as he ruled from the heavens. Stone stairs ascended from the ground up to the porch, guarded by Maxwell Wiseman's elite force for protection. The home was complete with stained glass windows, massive stone columns, and brick porches. It was as royal and majestic as a home could be. It was meant for royalty; it was meant for a god.

I spent the majority of the rest of that day pacing my room and continuously peering out the window, planning my route to avoid detection in order to reach the mansion. *Do I skip the date? Tear up the letter? Hide myself away?* I easily spent hours mapping out a pathway through the city on paper which I tucked under my pillow for the ink to bleed into my mind, memorizing the route like a battle plan. Of course his home would have to be on the other side of the city - that was simply just my luck. I replayed it over and over in my mind, studying it like scripture and storing it in my heart for the date written on the note. I decided that I would tell my parents that I had a school project to research. That would definitely be believable, and it would get me to the library in the town square. I would then make my way to the subway station and take the train to the edge of the city, where I would walk through the woods to get to the gates of the mansion. On the back of the note, it said for me to show the letter to the guards at the gate. Under that, a strange emblem was etched into the paper. It was his initials formed into a set of praying hands. I was not surprised. Jack King wanted full control; he yearned and breathed to be worshipped.

I kept the letter and my plan a secret for the next few days, raising little suspicion to the source of my excitement. I was both nervous and exhilarated for my visit to the massive house on the hilltop. I did not know the purpose of the trip, but I worried not. Jack had always been kind enough to my family, but not hospitable enough to invite random strangers into his home to dine with him. The rough soldier was dominant and private, running the world from the shadows, making brief charismatic appearances of remembrance like a ghastly celebrity. He either wanted something from me or wanted me to get something from him. I kept my mind focused on other matters in order to pass the time until that Saturday afternoon finally rolled around.

I pulled on a pair of jeans and a button-up black shirt, as I would be able to blend into the night and my attire would be formal enough to fit in around the mansion. I pulled my broken brown boots on over my socks and combed my hair behind my ears. I had no desire for a uniform - I wanted the boots that the soldiers wore. I yearned for a pair of the slick, black military boots. I would never serve in the city's dark and twisted army just for the boots, however. With the letter tucked into my coat pocket, I set out the door and down the stairs to slip past my family.

A pang of nervousness and anxiety set into my stomach like a dissolving pill. My palms began sweating and shaking, not adding any nonchalance to my scheme. I felt my heart beat quicker and quicker, adrenaline pumping through my veins like water in a faucet. The stairs were never as noisy as on that evening; each step creaked under my shoes as I headed down into the kitchen. My mother had cooked dinner and Jacob was setting the table. He either wanted something as well or was paying off a debt for punishment. "Where are *you* going?" my father asked as I stepped into the kitchen, which smelled like my mother's delicious fried chicken. I always looked the man dead in the eyes when I spoke to him. He had a "common respect" between my brother and I. My mother claimed it to be a man or a military thing and dismissed it as something silly. If I had not been staring straight into his dark brown eyes, I would have missed something very peculiar. As I felt myself losing control of the situation and running out of possible answers, I saw a golden glint of light pass through my father's eyes. It was a millionth of an instant, but I witnessed it as plain as day. I dripped sweat on my mother's beloved carpet - a strict sin. I swear she loved a clean house more than my father on most days. "I have a school project to research at the library," I replied. "What about dinner?" she exclaimed. "I'm not that hungry," I said. "You haven't been eating much lately," my father chimed in. "He's gotta stay thin for that girl that's he's banging," Jacob joked. They both shot him a nasty glare and looked at me. "You always said school was most important," I told her, ignoring my brother. "I'm learning what *matters*," I followed, quoting what Jack King himself had recited years prior. She pondered that for a moment. "Very well. Go ahead. I'll wrap the leftovers." I said goodbye to them blatantly and slipped out through the front door. As I headed down the driveway with my jacket collar pulled up over my neck, I pondered what had just happened; I remembered the light in my father's eyes only moments ago. I brushed it off as a mirage and blamed it on the stress, excitement, and above all, the anxiety.

The portion of my plan that involved getting across town went relatively smooth. I traveled on foot through the neighborhood and through town as quickly as possible. I felt the tiny pinpricks of eyes staring at me from behind shop windows and curtains. The insect-like attention sent chills up my spine and sent me on my way that much quicker. I rounded the corner into the town square and followed my shadow under the street lamps. Most of the stores and businesses were closed for the day, and the skyscrapers of the city stood silently, also staring down at me from above. An eerie aura whispered through the dusk like a ghost.

The train station was most likely the filthiest place in the city, apart from the dump or sewer line. It was one of the final projects of the new world, and it was obvious that Jack King was ready for the city to be completed from all of the campaigning and advertising he had been doing. At that time, resources were low and corners were cut to make the wall as strong as possible. The walls were covered in moss and plant life, the floors were grimy and dirty, and the train cars were rough on the creaky rails. It was far from my first choice of transportation, but I could not exactly be chauffeured privately to the mansion gates. And so the subway it was.

Railway maintenance and construction jobs were given to either the homeless or the ones who refused to work. Jack King demanded that everyone contribute to his new society, and laziness was considered a crime. Crime was no answer, and the defiant citizens found that they could not argue with a gun in their face. Wrongdoers were sometimes given the choice and chance to work off their transgressions, and while the majority took advantage of this, the military force lost a number of bullets on the negative decisions of a mistakenly-entitled people. The logical ones were sometimes put to work in the subway station. Law-abiding citizens did not want dangerous or dirty jobs, so they were left to the lower end of society. The disgusting environment on top of the risky service made the subway a much less desirable place to be. The ticket master was - ironically enough - a biblically ancient man bald and worn with age. His head barely rose above the metal gate outside the train; he scowled at me as I handed him a pass. He nodded and unlocked the gate to let me through. I did not waste any time making my way toward the rickety train entrance.

The smell of sweat and wet dog hit me like a slap in the face as I stepped into the grimy and rancid subway car. The metal walls were dented on both the inside as well as the outside; the ceiling sagged and the floor was caked with dirt. I looked around the boxcar for a source of the stench, and I found in at the back of the train. A man sat with his back to the wall of the subway, slouched over with his head hanging to his chest. I could tell by his loud snoring that he was obviously asleep. The man was brown with dirt, his greasy hair matted with sweat and oil. His clothes were torn and tattered, and his shoes had many holes with no laces. Under the bench was a viscous-looking German shepherd, which was just as filthy as the man above. Upon sight of me, the dog barked ferociously and sat up with a snarling growl. I backed up slowly and scared, nearly ruining my favorite pants. I fucking *hated* dogs.

The dog's barking woke the man up swiftly and suddenly. He lifted his head and looked around, mimicking the dog's awareness. "Hush it, Half-Twenty!" he shouted. "I can't get an inkling of a fucking nap in around here with all that carrying on." The German shepherd whimpered and sat back down. The owner finally noticed me standing across the train. "Hey there, partner," he said. "Who the hell are you?" I walked toward him. "I'm Noah," I replied nervously as one does when they are uncomfortable and want nothing more than for the conversation to be over. "You're on the wrong ark, son." I looked around sheepishly. He smiled a disgusting smile and held out his filthy hand. I shook it softly and quickly. "What's your name?" I asked solemnly. "Arnold Matthews - but please don't call me that. Call me Luke."

Luke ushered me to take a seat. None of the seats were completely clean, but I chose one of the neatest ones and sat down. "Welcome to my train," he said proudly, arms outstretched in a displaying manner. "*Your* train?" I asked. "What makes it yours?" Luke smiled and leaned in, allowing the evening sunset to cast a shadow across the bridge of his nose. His eyes shone bright blue through the dirt surrounding them. One pupil was brown and the other was blue, casting an eerie glow across his saturated face. "Not one soul has travelled on this train since I took up shop here," he said. "Especially not the likes of *you*," he added, examining my shoes and clothes up to my hair and face. I must have looked like a million dollars compared to him. "I don't understand," I said. He leaned in closer. "Even after the world is over and there is none left to judge, there is still discrimination. Nobody wants to ride with old Luke. I reckon Half-Twenty puts the fear of God in 'em." He reached down and rubbed the dog's matted fur.

"I don't care who's train it is. It's the fastest way to get across town," I said, ignoring the knot in my stomach at the thought of an argument. He gave me a satisfied look. "Where you headed, son?" he asked, interested once again. I was not going to answer him at first; in fact, I pondered telling him that it was none of his goddamn business. What could the truth hurt? "Jack King's house," I said matter-of-factly. The man burst into hysterical laughter. He went on cackling and giggling for quite some time. Even his dog seemed to have a comical expression across his rancid, yellow, sharp teeth. He finally slowed his mouth to a wide grin and stared into my eyes. "You lookin' to die today, son?" he said softly. I was taken aback. "What do you mean?" I asked. He leaned in close - close enough for me to smell his rotting breath. "What Mr. High and Mighty can't control, he destroys," Luke stated. "Why would he invite me into his own home if he wanted to hurt me?" I wondered. "Keep your enemies closer; I believe that's the way the sayin' goes," he replied with another jaded grin. I was beginning to grow annoyed. That man wanted something.

"How do you know?" I asked the man. Luke leaned in closer than ever before and whispered in my ear. "Because he killed *me*." I was dumbfounded by the man's answer. I immediately doubted his reasoning, but the paranoia soon set in as it always did. *Was I talking to a ghost?* It simply could not be - that was foolishness. "What do you want from me?" I demanded.

He looked at me curiously. "Nothing but your safety," he grinned sarcastically as if offering it up as a question. I leaned back, convinced of his existence as an adult believes in the fucking boogeyman. "You're just a crazy old man." Luke now laughed wholeheartedly. "Don't I know it," he said. "It got me killed." Silence followed until more raspy, broken words leaked from his lips. "And for future reference, I *am* the fucking boogeyman." *He had read my mind.*

I decided to toy with him for a while. "Tell me the story then," I shot at him. Luke must have known what I was talking about. He resituated himself, sitting up straight and leaning in slightly. He cleared his throat and returned to his sly grin. "Your friend Mr. King found me on the road about a hundred miles outside of the city. Me and Half-Twenty were perfectly happy out there - nice and quiet. I argued with him for quite some time. The fucker won me over with a promise of food and water for myself and Half-Twenty. That old dog is all I got in the world. Been like a friend to me all these years. So I accepted. We didn't get by with a free pass, however. King said I would have to work, to pull my weight or some Communistic bullshit like that. I agreed once again. I told him I was a good carpenter, so he put me to work building houses for his officers. Everything went smooth for the longest time. We both kept our promises. Then it all went to hell. As you already know, Mr. King gets what he wants. He apparently didn't like the work I was doing, so he called me out on it. I defended my honor as he insulted me. That man has a hell of a temper on him. He got so mad he threw a punch right on the side of my nose. Hurt like a bitch, mind you. I threw one back, catching him across his left jaw. He reared back, pissed as a hornet. He pulled his gun and pointed it at me. Even the likes of me knows to respect a man with a weapon. King thought for a minute. His angry expression curved into a wicked grin, and he lowered the gun. Half-Twenty laid at my feet, taking a break from chasing goddamn butterflies or something. Jack King put a bullet straight through Twenty's skull right then and there. I exploded, throwing punches and kicking him where the sun don't *ever* shine. He was much bigger than me, of course. He grabbed my shoulders and tossed me across the yard like a tin can. I rolled several times on the grass, and when I sat up, he already had the gun against my temple. Before I could curse him one more time, I was laying there right beside Twenty. Nothing but two dead *dogs*. And as for you, don't you dare trust him. Don't you believe a word that comes from his evil tongue. Don't you make a deal with him. You do *one thing*. Put a bullet in him for me. He took everything from me, my whole family and all I had left. So I come here to haunt him. To never let him forget. You put a bullet in him for me, and I'll let you ride on my train."

With a tear from his eye and a blink from mine, Luke and Half-Twenty were gone. The only thing that lay in his place was a silver handgun. I pinched my arm several times to make certain that I was awake, and I was very much conscious. I still could not decide if Luke was real or just a fixation of my imagination. I knew that the gun was real as I turned it over in my fingers. I stared out the window for the rest of the journey, lost in the valleys and hills of the outskirts of the city and the surrounding countryside. I wondered if I would be dead before the night was over.

The train came to an abrupt halt at the subway station on the opposite side of the city. If I was not nervous before, I sure was then. It was ten minutes till five, and the shadow of Jack King's mansion covered the woods that led to the gates. The house had a certain aura that drew me closer, almost begging me to travel down the cobblestone pathway into the woods. I nodded to the ticketmaster as I climbed out of the train car and walked briskly toward the forest on the edge of town. The pathway was constructed of brown, sandy stones evenly placed in a neat pattern. Lampposts illuminated the forest enough to see and even gave it an eerie sense of comfort. The air was cooler as I made my way into the roofed forest over the driveway. Drops of dew fell onto my hair like tiny kisses from the evening. I heard insects chirping and buzzing around me, prohibiting silence. The castle above was obviously and omnisciently ominous, but the pathway was hidden enough to make it difficult to access. I exited the woods on the cobblestone roadway and faced the mountainous gates of the mansion. Two guards stood firm on either side of the gates, assault rifles in the ready position. I slowly approached them, studying them just as much as they did me. I had tucked the gun into my belt loop above my back pockets, so I carefully avoided it to pull out the strange invitation Jack had sent me. I handed it to the first guard while the other patted me down for any suspicious weapons. I immediately broke into an anxious sweat. The officer's hands patted my chest and legs and eventually my belt loop and pockets. As his hand touched the belt, the weight of the gun disappeared. "You're good to go," the soldier with the letter said. "He's good here too," the inspection guard replied. A pang of relief set through me as he handed me the letter and opened the gate. On the other side, I tucked the letter back in my pocket, right behind the gun. The stairway was ungodly wide and steep; there seemed to be a thousand steps from the bottom to the top of the hill. I reluctantly took the first flight slowly and worked up the stamina to tackle the rest. As I neared the top of the mountain, I looked out at the view from the highest point in the city. The sun was setting behind the skyscrapers, hiding and burying itself into the sands of time for yet another night. Light shone off of the buildings and streets and people throughout the town, illuminating the walls around the fortress, claiming us as its own. It was a masterpiece beyond compare.

I stepped off of the stairs and into what seemed to be the entryway to the mansion, but it looked much like a garden. The yard was easily several acres, clean cut in rows and lush with precision. The landscaping was full of beautiful flowers and plants; I could tell by my mother's memory that it had taken care and time to perfect. The house towered above the kingdom below, manicured by the perfect entrance. I followed the pathway through the gardens and onto the front porch. Two quartz beams supported the front end of the house, and the porch was white wood - flawless without scratches or dents. The front door was brown oak infused with stained glass. I was certainly out of place. I put my finger to the doorbell and out of nervousness, pressed it quickly and stood back. Nearly a minute passed before it creaked open. I expected to see the giant shadow of Jack King, but instead I saw a girl around my age answer the door.

She was royally and unrealistically beautiful - beautifully familiar. Yes, I had seen her before, but *where*, by God? Her long blonde hair stretched down to her shoulders; I drowned in the depth of the oceans in her blue eyes, and her skin was pale white with obvious time spent indoors. Her lips were curved and soft, and her voice was clear and pure as she greeted me. "Hi," she said. "You lost?" she followed. I immediately grew red in the face. "Jack King asked me to come here," I replied. She laughed a mesmerizing laugh. "Well you've come to the right place," she said. "And most people don't get lost behind heavily-guarded gates." We both laughed. "Your face is awfully red," she pointed out. "Stairs wear you out?" I shifted my footing. "Something like that," I replied. Before our conversation could advance any further, the shadow I had been waiting for arrived behind the girl. "Noah Willowby!" Jack King shouted in excitement. I nodded shyly in his presence. "Right on time," he said, glancing down at his metallic glass watch. I smiled as he invited me inside.

The interior of the mansion was just as the exterior suggested. Stone pillars held the ceiling upright, and the floors were oak hardwood; the walls were painted pearl white with stained glass windows. Cool air circulated the girl's sweet perfume, almost intoxicating. I could not help but stare at her blankly, lost in thought. "It appears you've met my daughter, Julia," Jack said, acknowledging the drool hanging out of the corner of my mouth. Yes, she *was* indeed familiar. I had seen her once years before. I never would have guessed that Jack had a daughter, or any children at all for that matter. How could any woman cope with a brute of a man such as Jack King? I came back to reality and nodded in realization. Julia turned and shook my hand. Her skin was soft; I took it in as Jack broke the awkward silence. "I'll go check on dinner. Julia, why don't you show Noah the grounds?" With that simple order, he turned down a dark hallway, leaving Julia and I alone in the parlor. I followed her as she went out a side door that led back outside to the gorgeous greenery. My stomach chased goddamn butterflies.

The side of the house was nearly identical to the front, full of color and shrubbery. Flowers were in rows along hedges and bushes, and the brisk air smelled of roses and honey. "It's beautiful," I said. "It's all mine," Julia replied. "You did *all* of this?" I said in disbelief as she blushed. "I've never seen you around town," I said. "I mean, I saw you once - about five years ago," I corrected myself. "It would surprise me if you had; I'm homeschooled by our butler, and I almost never leave the house," she replied. "Why?" I asked. "Dad never lets me leave the house," she said with a distant, exasperated expression. "I mean, I get to go into town once every month," she restated, mimicking my correctness. "He's *way* too overprotective." I smiled, empathizing with the feeling. "So how does it feel to be the Princess of the City?" I asked with a laugh. She grinned. "Well, it's not all honey and roses," she joked, staring at all the landscaping she had done all by herself. We both laughed for the longest time. It was when her smile faded that I knew there was a dark secret that I did not quite know yet.

"Dinner!" another voice shouted, waking me up from my mesmerization. A man in a suit went back into the house, but I could not see his face. I followed Julia back through the door and into the parlor. I immediately smelled a magnificent meal ready to feast upon. Jack King waited for me in the living room. Julia had went off into the kitchen with the stranger in the suit, leaving only Jack and I with the smell of her perfume in the air. I was nervous then more than ever - I had a connection with the girl of my dreams and was standing toe-to-toe with her father, who doubled and tripled as leader of the city and chief of everything that could make me disappear if the need were to arise.

"How are you, Noah?" Jack asked me. "I'm well, sir," I replied sheepishly once again. "Your manners are *extraordinary*," he stated. "You'll make a fine leader someday." Silence followed for what seemed like forever. "You might be wondering why I asked you here tonight," he said. "It *has* been weighing on my mind," I said with a smile. "I want to show you something, Noah," Jack said sternly. Butterflies raced throughout my body. That could have meant a million different things - from the barrel of a shotgun to the quickest way off the mountain.

I followed him through the same hallway that we had gone down previously; there were dozens of rooms up and down the hall. Eventually, separate hallways branched off of that one, with rooms and staircases and closets alike. The place was a goddamn labyrinth. I wondered what all the rooms were for, but I kept the thoughts private - much like all of the doors, which were closed. We came to what seemed like a grand staircase which appeared to be the middle of the house. There was a single black door at the top of the stairs, whereas all of the other doors were brown oak. I mimicked Jack's footsteps as we ascended the staircase. He turned the doorknob and I followed him inside; he shut the door behind us and I turned around to examine the room. There was a large window with a door that led out onto a porch that overlooked the city below. There was a bar counter across the room with a full rack of alcoholic beverages. Leather furniture sat in the middle of the room around a coffee table covered in paper and pens. A strange contraption sat in the corner of the cozy room, making a dripping sound with each second that passed.

"Welcome to the penthouse suite!" Jack exclaimed with his arms outstretched. "This is my escape, my getaway, my man cave," he laughed. He pointed to the leather couch across the room. "Make yourself comfortable, Noah," he said hospitably. I nervously took a seat with my arms crossed and studied Jack King. He rounded the bar counter and grabbed a bottle of whiskey. I expected him to pour himself a glass, but he sat down across from me with the bottle in his hand. Jack opened the cap and took a large gulp of the brown liquid. He gave me a satisfied look, full of thought. I seized the opportune silence to ask my question. "What is that?" I asked, pointing to the rustic machine in the corner as it whirred away. "That is the family *still*," he said openly, laughing. "My great-grandfather built it during Prohibition when alcohol was banned in the country. He ran his own secret bar, manufacturing all the booze he wanted and capitalizing on it. Imagine that, all the women you could ever *dream* of. Believe me, there was no easy-speaking back in *his* time," he winked. "He left it to my grandfather when he died and my father was born while his dad was in prison on a *moonshining* charge. My father was drunk off of its product almost all of my life. Now I drink from the same bottle, trying to do it *differently*. To be *better*. That's the poor man's rhetoric, after all," he finished. He held the bottle out to me in offering as I raised my hand in denial. "Come on, Noah, there's no age limit here," he joked. I shook my head again as he drank a second time. "I want to tell you my story, Noah," he said. I knew not what to say. "I've never told anybody." I was confused. "I have to tell one person my story and the things I have done in order to find closure. I worry myself to death about how people feel about me based on the things I have done. Things aren't always as they seem." He looked distant, as if he had never opened up to anybody in his entire life. "Then why would you tell *me*?" I said as respectfully as possible, wondering why he chose me to invite to dinner to tell me about his strange family heirloom. "You saw me chop a man's hand off, for Christ's sake," he joked. "In all seriousness, if one person understands me and how my mind operates, then I am satisfied. An *insurance* policy. Someone to answer the questions, asked and unanswered. So I choose *you*." I squinted in curiosity. "You're special, Noah," he said. I was not special by any means. I was only a boy from nowhere; my eyes were not blue and my skin was not pale. I was not Julia - the only specialty left in my eyes of existence.

After another swig of whiskey, he capped the bottle and sat it on the table in front of me. He sat up and looked at me with his hands folded on his lap as if he was in a business meeting. "This is my twisted, makeshift confession. I know what you're thinking," he pointed at me. "You don't think you're special. You think there are so many people who are better than you, richer than you, more powerful than you. I'm here to tell you that that is not true, Noah. These descriptors of worth are not based on detail, but on *will*. Not on circumstance, but on *determination*. I know this all too well because I was a victim of an unfortunate situation. I was *small* before all of this, much like you - both physically and mentally. Living in the shadow of an abusive father, no mother to comfort me. An only child of a drunk coward who took his anger out on me. I realized that he hated me because I was *different* than he was. My father beat me and burned me and tried to destroy me because I was not like him." He pulled up his coat sleeves to reveal burns on his arms among several tattoos. "I ran off to the military as soon as I could. I trained and pushed harder and harder to overcome that. Being a soldier taught me that I could be above what everybody thought and wanted of me. I could crush rebellion under my boot. Then the world began to change as it had been for *centuries*. The military was put in charge of dealing with this on a mass scale, but I was *above* them, goddamnit! They were a bunch of fucking pussies. Not I. No, I took control of weaponry and equipment because I was *bigger* than they were. I climbed the ranks until I had enough power to make a change. It's an *elementary* concept. I know how to deal with difference. Fucking destroy it, and that's exactly what I did. People dropped like flies. I had to make sacrifices. I lost my wife in the crossfire. It only fueled my hatred toward what had changed the world so. When I returned home, my father was living alone in the middle of nowhere, enjoying his prideful retirement. I put the old fuck out of his misery for many reasons. I got my daughter to safety and did what had to be done. The best way to destroy something is to reduce it to ash. I took it upon myself to find difference and destroy it. And you probably know the rest." I looked at him in almost comical laughter. "So you're telling me you were the one that killed the President and stole the nuclear codes? I'm sorry, Mr. King, but I don't believe you. I mean, don't get me wrong, you are an impressive man and a damn good leader, but a job like that is greater than one man." There were always those so entirely entrapped in their own persona that the only key to break away was to question it from the inside whilst also acting indifferent and in agreement. He laughed as he drank himself to an internal death, spouting more nonsense as his mouth and mind became two separate beings. Perhaps he was a silent man when sober, only drinking in front of people to unleash his mental entirety to an audience. I knew only *one* Jack King. "It is, indeed, my friend," he replied.

Jack took another drink of whiskey; I had no idea how much alcohol was running through his body in that moment, but it had to be a considerable amount. He was obviously heavily intoxicated, and I did not believe a word of his story. I looked at him pathetically. "What does this have to do with me?" I asked. He laughed for a moment, as if somewhat offended at the fact that upon the revelation of his secrets, they were spit and shit upon by the one person that would listen. "I took control of what's left of the world, Noah. I run it all. I made this world what it should have always been. I make decisions and I do what must be done. I've seen what I'm afraid of. I worry that this difference will penetrate our safety here. If it's not stopped, there will be nothing left. I need people I can trust to help me. Am I a *terrorist*? No. Am I *God*? No, I took over his position because He failed. A being pledged to help when called out to ignored my pleas, so I slit His throat and sprouted from His blood. Am I a *tyrant*? *Most definitely*. People will answer to your will if only you take it from them. I need *you* to help me," he finished.

I had heard little about this "difference". Nothing too specific, and I had no general idea of them. Nothing positive, mind you. I had no idea how to find them or even set them apart from ordinary people, much less capture them. He was an inherited drunk, after all, and the entire conversation was foolish, null, and void. My mind was made up. "I can't help you, Mr. King," I said softly. A disappointed expression spread across his face. "I was afraid you would say that," he replied. "It's okay, but I won't be responsible if you and your family are caught in the crossfire," he said, a tone of passive aggression taking over his somber excitement. I just nodded, hoping the conversation would be over soon, although my curiosity soon took over me. "What exactly is this *difference*?" I asked quickly before I could rethink it. After another chug of alcohol, Jack looked at me again, his eyes fluttering and his hair blowing in the breeze from the open window. "I wondered the same thing, my boy. I vowed to find out what made my father how he was and like he was and make sure that something as vile as his existence never would come to fruition in the world I made again. I did my research in government libraries and laboratories throughout my early adulthood in the military and formed my data into a stone truth. You see, the human brain only uses ten percent of its full capacity when fully awake. The other ninety-percent is used to develop *dreams*. Select few have access to their full one-hundred-percent capacity when fully awake, allowing them to make dreams reality. They're basically unstoppable. Too powerful for this world and they must be stopped. I have to take responsibility for that. That means they can't exist in this world. They're a poison to this existence - a *cancer*. And a cancer must be cut out. Utterly *obliterated*. I will most certainly kill every single last fucking one of them. I call them *Dreamers*." I still did not have a full grasp on the concept of these beings, and I did not believe him. Before I could respond, Jack finished the bottle of whiskey. "I can't keep my father out of my dreams. He was one of *them*. He haunts me like a ghost every night. He tortures me just as he did when I was a child. I can't take it anymore. He doesn't own me anymore. This is *my* world. *I* took it. And I'll be six feet under before I let him hurt me any longer. I need to kill all of these Dreamers except one. I will force them to bring my father out of the dreams so I call destroy him permanently."

Jack was obviously drunk - he simply had to be; the amount of nonsense he was spouting was impossibly unfeasible. The God-like shadow I had been under for years was then a child before me. "I'm sorry," I said unsympathetically. He gave me a blank expression in return. That poor man was a child in a man's body. Deep down, I truly felt sorry for him. He was driven to feel and say these awful things out of vengeance to his father, only to be a mirror image of him. "What did you want to show me?" I asked, changing the subject. Jack's face lit up. "Ah!" he said. I could definitely tell he was drunk in his time and voice. He got up and went out of the door that led to the porch, and I followed him out into the night. I could see the city lights from that one spot. Every building was easy to spot and make out from where I was standing. The glow was almost heavenly. Jack and I leaned up against the railing like two old friends. "I come out here whenever I'm stressed," he started. "I see how small my problems are compared to all of my accomplishments." He waved his hand over the city in presentation and grasp. "This is the real world, Noah. Destruction and rebirth. It's all mine. It could be yours too." That last statement struck curiously within me. "How?" I wondered. "If you help me eliminate the Dreamers, I will relinquish all of my power to you," he said. I was in utter disbelief. "If you help me get to my father, you will rule the world. Then it will be done." My answer remained the same. "I can't. I'm sorry," I told him. We stood in silence for quite a long time. The city light shone through a tear rolling down his face, but it did not fool me. That man's heart was pure evil - a selfish and unmitigated, vilified, and startled chunk of slime. Staring at the city below, I went into a peaceful state of mind and body as he had.

Jack eventually looked at me with his distorted drunken face; I barely noticed my vision change. Jack and I were sitting back in the lounge, and all of the lights were off. The moonlight reflected off of his eyes, giving his face an eerie shadow. "Are you a Dreamer, Noah Willowby?" he said through gritted teeth. I was confused beyond comprehension. "No," I uttered in confusion. Jack growled and reached for his knife. In one swift movement, he brought the blade through my hand and the table, pinning it there. My hand erupted in excruciating pain as blood spewed from the wound. I attempted to scream, but my voice was rendered silent. Jack asked the same question again. When he did not hear the answer he wanted, he reached for the whiskey bottle. He poured the remainder into my hand, the dark liquid running down the metal and into my wound, searing with unbearable, stinging pain. "ARE YOU A DREAMER, NOAH WILLOWBY?!" he shouted. "NO!" I screamed back. Jack threw his head back and laughed a maniacal laugh. "Very well, then." The scene changed once more. Jack and I were still in the lounge, in the same seats as before. The lights were on this time, and everything looked normal. Jack raised a cup of coffee to his lips, and he caught me staring at him as he downed it. The cup cracked, and boiling hot coffee spilled all over him. He showed no sign of pain; in fact, he just smiled that same wicked grin. Staring directly into my soul, he asked the same simple question, calmly that time. "Are you a Dreamer, Noah Willowby?"

"You didn't really think my own personal, unlimited supply of moonshine whiskey was all I have to offer, did you?" he asked me as I followed him through the expansive hallway behind the kitchen. The walls were lined with family pictures hung across the light brown paint. A woman stood beside Jack in most of the pictures, and I would have missed the curious painting if the light had not glinted off of his flask as he sipped the foul-smelling liquid. There was a thickly-smeared X over her face in each of her apparitions. I swallowed deeply and turned away from the ghastly photos. I struggled not to ask as I followed the idol of intimidation through the dim-lit hall to a portion of the house that smelled of motor oil. Jack pulled the metal door open for me as I stepped down onto the concrete floor of a massive garage. As large as the walls were, there was only one vehicle among the space for dozens. A thick grey tarp hung over the sides of the long-hooded vehicle, and I knew from my father's grease monkey hobbies that it was something worth keeping immaculate. "Surely you've driven a stick shift, right?" Jack asked me. "No sir," I replied. "He always told me if he taught me I would come home with the GT," I smiled, half embarrassed at my lack of ability to fill his expectation. His eyes lit up. "You're gonna love this," he said, gripping the corner of the tarp and ripping it off like a child on Christmas morning. It was then my turn to gaze. I had known from years of studying muscle cars what sat before me in all of its elegant beauty. "1969 Shelby GT500 Fastback Mustang," I said. He was proud, my knowledge outweighing my skill. "The epitome of American muscle," he grinned, presenting the car as if it was his most prized possession. "The only woman I need - besides Julia, of course," he added. I was preoccupied, peering into the window at the black leather seats. The windows were tinted pitch black behind the maroon redfire paint job. The car was pristine, and I was in love. "Go ahead, my boy. By all means. You've got a boner the size of Pinocchio's nose. Get in that car, goddamnit!" he shouted cheerfully, swigging more whiskey. I opened the door as carefully as I could manage and gently sunk into the leather. The car smelled of freshly-cleaned carpet and an oiled engine. I kept my feet away from the pedals - the extra one baffled me like trigonometry. My father made it out to be the devil's craft, and I feared it as so. Jack tapped me on the shoulder and handed me the key, for Christ's sake. I took it as my fingers shook against the cool metal. I slid it into the ignition and turned it just enough for the starter to turn over. The engine roared like a caged animal as the lights shone off of the far wall like blinding spotlights. Jack grinned as I did. I pulled the key out and sat back against the seat in silence. "I love it," I said. "That much is obvious," he retorted. "But do you want to *drive* it?" he asked. "I -..." I stuttered. "Come back sometime and I'll teach you," he invited. I smiled as I got out and shut the door ever-so-softly. "*Deal.*" He covered the beautiful beast with the tarp once more and escorted me out of the garage.

I followed Jack back through the maze that was the mansion and into the kitchen. We passed the library along the way - a magnificent, massive room lined with thousands of books. He must have noticed my keen eye as I stared into the lamp-lit room and nearly ran inside. "You're welcome to come borrow any of them whenever you like," he said, not even breaking his stride. The smell of delectable meat and vegetables was detectable from miles away. Julia helped the strange man in the suit carry dishes into the dining room, along with drink pitchers and bottles of wine. I finally got a good look at the man when Jack led me into the dining room. He was tall and the suit fit his small and wiry frame exactly. His dark hair was slicked back along his ears and he was clean shaven. His dark green eyes were like the soft grass that bordered the house outside. The only thing peculiar about him was the nasty and jagged scar along his left jaw. It would take a wide and sharp object to make that cut. I winced at the sight of it. "Noah, this is our butler, Sebastian," Jack introduced. I reached my hand out and shook Sebastian's hand firmly. "How are you,

134

sir?" he asked me in a light and friendly voice. I said very well and asked him the same. "I heard the car, sir," he continued. "Shall I hold another place for dinner?" Jack shook his head and clapped the butler on the back. "No, our guest has already arrived. Sebastian here is the finest chef in the world," Jack bragged. "The best teacher too," Julia added as she rolled her eyes. "I guess you saw the car," she coughed. I nodded in bliss. "The world isn't too big anymore," Sebastian argued. We all shared a good laugh to lighten the mood against a heavily-darkened statement. I later learned that Sebastian was a certified masseuse, a five-star chef, and a killer poker player. He had owned his own casino and restaurant service as well as hotels of his own, and the outdoor pool and indoor grounds was immaculately cleaned and maintained by the busybody butler. The race track outside stood straight and narrow across the back field fed by the massive garage, and the courtyard was gigantic. The King household was an empire, and rightfully so - as well as heavily-guarded so.

I pulled Julia's chair out for her and sat down beside her nervously, as expected. Jack took a seat at the head of the table, as also expected, and grabbed a knife to cut the meat. I shivered as soon as his fingers wrapped around it. Sebastian was the last to sit down. The amount of food he had prepared was unbelievable. I stared open-mouthed at the pot roast, vegetables, rolls, and drinks in front of me. "Dig in!" Jack declared. And we did. The food was so rich and full of flavor, I vowed to eat as slowly as possible as not to miss a single spice, as difficult and taxing as it was. Slowly but surely, my stomach filled up to maximum capacity. As the food disappeared, conversation arose. "Are you coming to the Jubilee next weekend?" Julia asked cheerfully. "What?" I asked politely, not knowing what she was referring to. Her father chimed in, unfortunately. I was looking forward to hearing her voice say just a few more words. "The Department of Trade is putting on a huge festival for the city," Jack said with a mouth full of potatoes. He chugged a glass of wine and refilled his glass.

"There's gonna be games and food and all sorts of fun shit to meet new people," he mocked. He had an odd sense of leadership, making fun of the old way of life while still enforcing the new one. It was not my business, however. "I told your dad about it," he finished. "He said you guys planned on coming out." I looked over at Julia. "There you go." We both laughed.

Already full, I brought out my second stomach for dessert. I feasted on cake and pie and all sorts of sweets. Julia kept hitting my leg with hers, seemingly on accident. I did not mind, but I knew something was going on. Every time I looked at her she would smile. I suppose that was her way of flirting. It was better than my method at least, and I doubted she had seen many men in her time. Perhaps that was my advantage; after all, ignorance is bliss as well as attraction. As the night grew old, I said my goodbyes to my hosts and made my way to the door. I shook Sebastian's hand once again and bragged on the delicious meal. Jack told me how much he enjoyed having me over for dinner and I replied that it was mutual; I was welcome back at any time. As they both made their way back into the house, Julia and I were left on the front porch. The silence combined with the chilly air, making for quite a peaceful night. "I guess I'll see you next weekend," I said. She smiled and grabbed my hand. She never said anything back. All she did was kiss me on the cheek lightly. We both smiled as I turned around. I heard the door shut behind her, leaving me to head back into the city lights all alone with only a cracked coffee cup and the smell of Julia's perfume. I pulled my coat tight against the winter cold, the stench of whiskey on my heels like a thousand shadows behind me.

Chapter VII
Unity Is (A) Key
(Answers, Hearts, and Too Much Grape Juice)

After the dinner at Jack King's house, my dreams only grew more severe in nature, violent like a hurricane and deeper than any vastly blue ocean. Instead of consisting merely of peculiar and rather odd visions, I began to form an emotional connection to accompany the physical aspect I had gathered from the first years of my life. I began to feel the terror and sadness of what I was witnessing. The core focus remained constant - the father and son were always the center of attention. I struggled to keep the images straight and in chronology at certain times. I knew what was real and what was fictitious, but the distinction between the two was beginning to grow increasingly more cloudy and hazy. Some nights I struggled to even think clearly as I awoke in a mass of sweat and bewilderment.

I knew of only one place to go for answers, even for possible hints at satisfaction for my burning curiosities - the conversational entangleship of Joshua Peterson. Each one of our meetings ended in a political discussion of the old world, and in turn the cause of the downfall of mankind. I knew he had studied and slaved over it, but political standpoint and opinion did not crumble the old society - the difference that accompanied it did. Nevertheless, I knew Joshua would have some degree of knowledge as to what kept me up at night. So I sought out one of the only men who had never been sought out by anyone.

The Peterson family was a nearly non-existent one - in fact, the only reason I knew he had a mother was by witness, and I had met his brother on my trips to the inner markets where he worked. I was always afraid to asked the dreaded question; I had heard no mention of a father like many times before, and in the case of Joshua Peterson, he had gone the deprived route as opposed to the violent one. Did he need a father to play catch with? Absolutely not. Joshua Peterson spent his time disassembling computers and reading science textbooks, and like me, he had no interest or time for sports - to play at least. Much like Leroy Hall and Richard Monthaven, he would talk about the ancient athletics for days on end to no care from me.

The first time I saw Joshua Peterson's sunglass contacts, I nearly ruined my perfectly good pants. They looked like something straight out of a horror film, which I could not place the definition of until years later. Joshua had always worn glasses, and upon his blackened pupils, I feared he had been possessed by a demon. "Jesus fuck!" I shouted at him as I jumped out of my skin. He pulled his bedroom door open and closed his eyes when I looked at him, opening them again when he turned the light on. "Relax, man," he grabbed my arm, not helping the instant terror. "They're only contacts," he reassured me. With that, he pressed his fingers to his eyeballs and the suction-cup lenses stuck to his skin. "New invention," he said. "Not that the sun ever gets bright enough around here anyway."

I rapped three times on his door before pausing for it to open. Miss Peterson was a frail, quaint woman full of kindness. The first time I had seen her, I believed her to be Joshua's sister. I was shocked when I was told that she was his mother - he had never mentioned her in passing conversation, and Joshua was more than capable of raising himself. The door opened quickly and the short, young woman welcomed me inside. "Joshua is in his room like always. I never know what he does in there," she joked. "Probably curing cancer or raising the dead," I returned comically. She returned to the living room as she waved me into the hallway.

"Let me in or I'll vote left, damnit!" I yelled across the door to Joshua. The door opened quickly to a bright grin, blonde hair, and glasses. I shook Joshua's hand as he widened the door to let me in. His room was layered with blueprints and spare electronics as he cleared off a chair for me to sit. Lists and notes lined his walls in thick ink, some crossed out and scribbled across. How Joshua was not a mental case, I did not know. "A threat like that must mean you're on urgent business," he said to me. "What can I do for you?" I sat down heavily in the chair and rotated across the room. "What do you know about nuclear codes?" I asked him, looking through the gap in my fingers as I held my head. "Are you talking about the end of the world?" he narrowed. I nodded in confirmation.

Joshua began to pace the small, comfortable room as he routinely did when he was about to educate or debate a sensitive topic in which he felt he was intelligently advanced in. "One of the most highly protected assets in the world," he started. "Set up where one can't take them alone." I sat up. "So you're saying it would have to be a group?" I asked. "Yes," he stammered. "And not just any group. It would be like breaking into Fort Knox inside the White House while every security guard and agent is firing at you," he analogized. "President has control," he said, "so you can see why I feel so strongly about who had control when the world went to shit." I stood up and began to pace as I thought through what I knew and what I was being told. "How would one retrieve them if the President had been assassinated?" I asked a final question. Joshua thought for a moment. "Distractions," he said coldly. I thought about what he had told me, and although it was highly unlikely, it was *possible*. I wondered still, and I had confirmation for my curiosity by the man who knew best. I decided to change the subject as not to arouse suspicion to my findings. I dared not example too much fascination in the old world.

"What are you up to these days, J.P.?" I asked friendly in transition. He hurried around the chair excitedly and folded up blueprints, uncovering a metal contraption that looked rather like a claw on a metal rod. "I've been researching and experimenting with prosthetics," he said, presenting the strange object with pride. "That's awesome, man," I said, not fully understanding how much time and effort he had put into it. He put it back down and unfolded the makeshift tarp back over it. "What about you?" he replied through the crumpling of notes and margins. "Doing a little research of my own," I said vaguely. "Explosives," I added as he nodded in approval. "Nice," he confided, reaching into his pocket and tossing me a mint. "You must be studying *politics*," he added. I rolled my eyes and shifted my sight to the walls lined with mathematical symbols and equations. "Have you cured yourself yet?" I asked. Perhaps he had found the cure to his sickness in his humor. He pointed to the wall opposite where I was looking. "That wall is dedicated to hemophilia study. You were looking at the amount of calories inside a waffle."

I remember the first time I recognized a shift in the dreams. That night, I had gone to bed earlier than usual. I told my family that I was feeling ill, which was a stretch of the truth. I wanted some alone time to think; I always enjoyed being alone and keeping to myself. I had grown so distant from my family that I had grown to despise them. My time was spent putting ink to paper or putting my head to a pillow - which oftentimes went hand-in-hand. I had kept a notebook recording of the dreams ever since I could remember them. I fell asleep as soon as my head hit the pillow, falling through the shadowy abyss that had become my storybook of nightmares. After what felt like an instant, I seemed to collect my thoughts and realized I was dreaming. I knew not a thing as to where I was except what I could make out around me; this was an entirely new scene. I was in the middle of a vast grassland, which could have easily been a valley or field of some sort. It was the middle of the night, the only light coming from the stars above and a dim light from a dilapidated house in the distance. I felt my feet connect with the soft grass as I staggered toward the broken-down shack. I heard a deep voice shouting from inside the home, and I immediately knew the source of it all.

All of my dreams revolved around that same father and son. I climbed the creaky stairs and faced the wood-split door. It amazed me how sound travels in dreams. The noise was muffled, as if my ears were covered by a pillow, but at the same time, it echoed on for eternity. Two deep voices shouted over each other, trying to outdo the other. I could not have easily knocked on the door; simply barging in was much simpler and avoided confrontation - which even in unconsciousness I loathed. Oddly, I never remember entering the building and I never remember coming across the pair. They ignored my entrance and entire existence as if I had never slipped into the room. I was drawn to them like a moth to a flame - like a bat to a street lamp. I was forced to witness the turmoil of that young boy - a torturous display of abuse as something within me stirred. I had seen it before; I had *felt* it before.

The images shifted as I passed through the doorway like a cloud. Once inside the eerie shack, I saw what I was being forced to witness. The father was challenging the boy - daring him, testing him, belittling him to the largest extent. I saw from the look in the boy's eyes that he felt worthless, like nothing in the eyes of his father. The boy was a teenager then. He had aged in the dreams in a matter of years as I had. His father had aged along with him - eight years graying the boy more than it did his father. They both wore angry expressions, especially the outraged man who was red with fiery anger. He shouted degrading insults at his son, only pushing the boy farther and farther over the edge. I saw the anger in the boy's eyes, the rage filling his pupils like crimson blood through an artery. The boy had had enough. He clenched his fist and brought it across his father's jaw. The man reared back in shock. He congratulated his son, giving off a false sense of accomplishment. He uppercutted his son twice, knocking him to the ground. Before the boy could climb to his feet, the man brought his boot to the boy's cheek, pinning him to the floor. He laughed before stomping his son's nose triumphantly. "Only one way you'll learn, son," he said through a muffled tone. A fire erupted in a nearby fireplace, casting dark shadows across the room. I saw that we were in a living room of some sort. The man tossed his son into the fire, and both of them disappeared - the fire being the only remaining figment of the dream. fire remained. There was always fire within the dreams, a constant theme of hell and destruction. I scanned the walls for a way to escape, but all I saw were shackles and chains lined along the grimy bricks and the spreading flames. I stared at the wall for a moment as I felt a rough hand on my shoulder and a familiar gravelly voice in my ear. "Only one way."

I jerked awake with a start. I despised the feeling of being startled; my heart was beating a thousand miles a minute. I had long since kept my childish shouts and cries for my mother within - no one came through my door to see what the matter was. I was never an admirer of the dark as the lamplight cast shadows across my cozy room. I shook as I wiped sweat on my shirt, the sheets binding my legs like shackles. I began to panic. I unwound my feet, managing to roll myself onto the floor rather painfully. I wiped my brow and sat up, shaking off the pain of landing on my arm. I calmly sat up against my bed on the floor with my arms across my knees, deep in thought. My mind raced with everything I had just seen. That endless puzzle desperately needed to be solved.

I opened my notebook and uncapped a pen, beginning to scribble my thoughts onto the paper. I wrote down all of what I knew - none of it which I believed. Jack King had told me that his father was a Dreamer. After Jack had killed him, his father haunted him because only ten-percent of him was dead - which was the human part - the part that kept him real. His father took over his son's dreams, wanting to finish what he had started. He must have wanted Jack to be like him so desperately he was willing to do anything. He became abusive and eventually drove Jack away to the military. Jack must have been so angry with his father and others like him, he wanted revenge and to put an eternal stop to it. He used all his might to train himself to be the best. After he had transformed into the monster that was the leader of our city, he returned home and killed his father, thinking it would get rid of him for good - only to be haunted every night by the ghost of his father. He could not stop people from dreaming, however. He could never hope to destroy the other ninety-percent. He built this city and collected all of the remaining survivors from the deadly worldwide attack that spawned that life, only to pick off the Dreamers one by one until it was finished. He needed the last Dreamer to go into the dream world and bring his father back so he could kill him once and for all. Jack wanted full control over all existence - both real and dream. The fact that he could not have it had driven him over the edge with both anger and fear. I believed only one part of the story - I believed that he had killed his father, but what he had spat to me in his drunken rampage about being responsible for the disaster was a lie. It was simply impossible and unrealistic. The images played through my mind like a horror movie, and my adrenaline pumped faster than ever. Sweat ran down my nose in anxiety and confusion as I closed the notebook along with my eyes and fell asleep on the floor. Foolishness was exhausting to decipher.

In the days that followed, my senses sharpened. I had to totally re-evaluate the way I lived my life, managing both my existence as well as the timeline of my dreams. I was subject to a mysterious host - whoever was haunting my dreams. My main focus was to defend against the biggest enemy - confusion. The week that followed my visit to Jack King's house was filled with excitement. The entire population had stomachs full of butterflies at the thought of the Jubilee that weekend; naturally, the days leading up to the festival dragged on and on endlessly. Day by day, the Department of Trade worked relentlessly to set up the town square for the festival event. I had to pass through the area each day, and as time went on, the place had been transformed into an arena, complete with lights and a stage and speakers all over the sidewalks. They really went all out, only causing more anticipation to get out of the melancholy routine of work and school to finally relax and let loose - to finally enjoy life rather than working like dogs to establish it. School trudged on and on like a horse-drawn carriage without the horse. Friday loomed like a distant dream until little by little, it became reality. The bell rang, sending the entire school into a chaotic uproar. Students erupted with cheers and shouts, much to the teachers' distaste. Their chastisement only made for more noise as the hallways and streets filled with anxious teenagers and young adults. I trudged along through the herd of wild heathens. I was never much of a vocal young lad; I usually kept quiet unless I was spoken to or was fighting with my brother. I was pushed and shoved and trampled; it did not startle me as much as when someone grabbed my arm and pulled me into a nearby alleyway.

In a slight panic, I turned around right into Julia. We were the only ones in the quiet alleyway. All of the noise of the outside world seemed to cease as I looked into her eyes. They were just like her father's. Not in color; Jack King's eyes were dark brown while Julia's were bright blue, but the two had the same depth, the same concern, and the same hint of a hidden secret behind the enticing color. "Hey there," she said quietly. "Hi," I smiled nervously. "What are you doing here?" I asked. Julia smiled. "Dad asked me to go to the market for peaches," she replied. I could not help but laugh at her ridiculous excuse. "What are you laughing at?" she exclaimed. "You come out of the orchard to get peaches?" I grinned curiously. She revealed a bag of slightly-orange pink fruit. We both laughed for a moment. "You thought I was kidding?" she giggled sheepishly. "I just wanted to say hello," she said. "So, hello!" she smiled. She really was a beautiful, detailed specimen. I thought everything about her was adorable, my crush for her becoming an infatuation of her laugh and voice. "Is that all?" I asked, stepping up to the plate a bit. She shook her head. "It looked like you needed a detour," she smirked. She turned around and pointed to a narrow street behind us. "That road should take you to the other side of Main Street." I thanked her with a smile. "Before you go," she added. She reached out her hand and took mine. When she let go, there was a small slip of paper between my fingers. I looked at her, halfway smiling myself, halfway wanting to stay there in the peace and quiet with Julia for a lifetime longer; perhaps I could have settled for even a mere moment longer. I turned around to head out of the alleyway when she said my name. A bright pink peach hit me square in the chest and busted all over my shirt, soaking my chest with cold fruit juice. Before I could laugh, Julia was gone. The alleyway was just another empty street.

I rushed home and clamored through the front door of my house, eager to read the note she had given me. My family was in the kitchen, my father and brother watching my mother cook dinner. They all turned around to look at me, unfortunately. "What happened to your shirt?" my mother shouted. "Spilled some water," I replied, shifting my weight to the other foot. My father inhaled. "Smells fruity," he said. "What did I tell you about him?" Jacob laughed, nudging my father in the ribs. I rolled my eyes and took off toward my bedroom, which had long since become my dimly lit cavern of excavation. "Don't you want dinner?" my mother yelled. I did not answer. My feet moved a mile a minute up to my room; I was far too anxious to eat. I burst into my quarters and slammed the door behind me. I tossed my backpack onto the floor and pulled the small piece of paper out of my pocket. Opening it up and flattening out the creases, I squinted my eyes to make out her thin handwriting.

"Meet me here at 7."
- J

My first thought was why she would go to the trouble of writing a note with such a small statement. I could not argue; I had something of hers - proof that she was real and not just a mere figment of my imagination. I loved the way she wrote a tiny heart inside the curve of her first initial. I put the slip of paper under my pillow, pulling off my shirt and throwing it across the room. I climbed into bed and pulled the blanket over me; the excitement of the Jubilee and spending it with Julia had drained my energy. As soon as my head hit the pillow, I felt the heat of the note beneath me. It breathed its spell into me as I drifted into the deep, dark hole of my subconscious.

I fell weightlessly until I saw light once again. The bright sunlight blinded me, unfamiliar as a stranger. All of my horrific dreams had taken place at night, hiding the mysterious faces like a shadowy mask. I opened my eyes, feeling my pupils dilate to acclimate to the lighting. Once my vision cleared, I looked around me, taking in the new surroundings - I was on a beach. I could hear the waves crashing in front of me; I could feel the warmth of the sand underneath me like soft, sifted flour. The squawking of seagulls above drowned out the peaceful sound of the water, circling the shore like vultures. I looked around for something to focus on, and I caught something in the distance. A girl emerged from the water a few yards in front of me. The sparkling ocean dripped off of her as she walked toward me. The salty wind whipped her hair back gracefully, revealing her beautiful features. With a curious second glance, I saw that the young woman was *Julia*. She smiled as she made her way closer to me, held back by the wind and the shifting sand. I smiled back as the birds circled overhead. They spiraled lower and lower as I began to stand up. The cyclonic wind of their wings knocked me back to the unstable ground. I covered my ears as they flew right above my head, the roaring of feathers deafening me. The flock of seagulls disappeared as Julia finally reached me. She latched onto my arm and pulled me to my feet. All sound in the dream was then silenced as Julia pulled me along with her out to the water. We reached the edge, but she still kept tugging at my arm. I tried to say something, but I could not. My mouth moved, but no sound emitted from my throat. Cool water rushed up to my knees, then my waist, then my chest. I was then yelling, screaming for her to stop, yet I could not pull away. The water enveloped us both, and I felt myself sinking. I looked around frantically for Julia, but she was nowhere to be found. I looked up and saw the reflection of the birds through the surface of the water. The sunlight dimmed darker and darker as my mouth and nose filled with saltwater. I was frozen in the heavy water, held captive beneath a thousand tons. I sunk lower and lower until everything went black as I felt myself slowly drown to death.

The dream shifted. I was in my bed, in my bedroom, and in my house. For a moment, I thought that I had woken up, but something still seemed unusual. I was still deaf to everything around me. I looked around my room, wondering what to do next. I turned around right into Julia, and I was terrified at the sight of her. What were once beautiful as the blue water that had filled my body were now pitch black holes. It struck fear deep within my mind. I rolled out of bed and onto the floor. She climbed across the bed and stared down at me emptily. She leapt across the floor, crawling onto me like a demon. I wriggled back across the carpet, but she pinned me to the ground. "Funny how what you think is beautiful can kill you, right?" she whispered like a snake. Her shrill tone echoed in my brain.

The dream shifted once more. I was in front of my mirror, staring at my reflection intensely. I flexed my muscles and gazed at my dark features, not recognizing what was supposed to be me. I looked so much older and worn. A wisp of smoke hardened into a figure in the mirror behind me. I looked behind me, and Julia wrapped her arms around me; she was beautiful once again. She rested her head against my back peacefully. I could feel her steady breathing against mine. When I looked back into the mirror, I did not recognize either of the people staring back me.

"Noah Morgan Willowby, you get up right now!" my mother shouted, knocking repeatedly on the door. I opened my eyes, climbing back into reality. "We're going to be late to the Jubilee!" I heard her footsteps retreat down the stairs. I turned over to face an alarm that read a quarter to seven. I leapt out of bed and pulled my shirt over my head. I looked in the mirror, combing my hair and making sure I looked and smelled good. I wanted to be sure I was as presentable as possible. Staring at my identical reflection, I halfway expected two warm arms to embrace me. Perhaps I had found one aspect of the dreams that was better than reality.

"Where you been, Sleeping Beauty?" Jacob mocked as I hurried down the stairs. I shot him an angry glance as he laughed. Our father was used to resolving conflict between his two sons, so he was quick to usher us out of the door and into the car. We climbed in and headed into town toward the flashing lights and cheering crowd. The Jubilee was talked up to be a grand event, and it surely lived up to that expectation. It was a celebration of the success and forthcoming of the city, after all. As we neared the town square, I could make out the stage through the waves of people, with Jack King making a speech to the roaring crowd. It looked as though the entire city had come out to the festival, and for good reason. The city really was a marvelous achievement in the new world. It *was* the new - and only - world.

My father parked the car, and we rushed to join the crowd. My parents loved to hear Jack King's speeches; they were mesmerized by his words, enveloped in them like his Disciples. I could care less what he had to say on that night - I had other things on my mind, beautiful, graceful, weightless things. His deep voice boomed throughout the massive town square, echoing off of the skyscrapers and out of the alleyways. All I heard was a blur of sound as excitement and anxiety rushed throughout my body. "I hate to leave so soon, but I have plans," Jacob said to our parents. His plans most likely consisted of getting shit-faced drunk with his friends, making him an even more pathetic waste of space than when he was sober. Could they argue or object? He was a grown man, after all. I often forgot I was as well. It was a subtle, forgotten truth with not many rewards in that time. I waited until he walked off to say something to my mother. "I'm going with him," I said. She gave her consent, probably because she thought my brother and I were going to actually do something together for once. We were never exactly the type of brothers that sat in the park on the weekends singing Kumbaya; we had never gotten along, usually because of the age difference between us - he was twenty-one and I was only eighteen. I was definitely more mature than he was, and I would much rather be with Julia than be around Jacob. I watched my brother disappear into the crowd as I pushed and shoved through the wall of people, eventually breaking through onto Main Street, which led to the school. I turned off onto a side road which took me in the direction of the alleyway where I had seen Julia only hours before. I came to the narrow stretch of road and walked between the buildings, but nothing awaited me but a slightly crushed peach.

I looked down at my watch, which read two minutes until seven; my plan was perfect. I grabbed the peach and hid behind the nearby dumpster. If Julia was anything like her father, she would be prompt - and she was. I heard her soft footsteps on the concrete almost two minutes later. I peeked out into the alleyway, and she had her back turned - even better. I softly tossed the wet fruit at the back of her shirt. It fell to the ground, leaving a patch of wet juice on her back. Julia gasped as I stepped out from behind the dumpster. She turned around to look at me in an amused state of surprise. Fuck, she was beautiful. Her blue eyes were hypnotizing; her hair gleamed with the setting sunlight. She wore a white button down shirt with black jeans, her pink tennis shoes explaining her light footsteps. That woman really was a masterpiece of perfection. "You got me," she laughed. I was glad she was not upset; she most likely had no clue that the juice had made her white shirt slightly see-through. Ignorance is surely bliss. I walked up to her, another joke in mind. "I love your *perfume*," I said, sniffing her. "*Peach*, is it?" We both laughed for a moment, jokingly punching each other in the arm. She looked up at me with a smirk. "Are you sure you'd rather spend the evening with me instead of joining the rest of the party?" she asked. "I'm not much of the party type," I replied. "That's what I was hoping you'd say," she smiled. "Which brings out the new question," I said, my turn to smirk. "What shall we do on this fine occasion?" I asked. Her brilliant eyes lit up. "I had something in mind," she said excitedly. "What's that?" I wondered. "Follow me," she winked. Was it a dream? I surely fucking hoped so.

Julia's personality was quite odd. She was flirtatious and open, but at times her demeanor would flip like a switch and she would go cold, empty of thought, and kept hidden by a secret I had not the slightest idea of. She was quick like that; I never knew what was next with her. One minute we were talking in an alleyway, and the next minute she was running around the corner of the building behind us. I followed as quickly as I could. The sound of cheering and festivities grew distant as we walked farther and farther away from the town square. I was familiar with the layout of the city to a certain extent; being the son of a government driver had its advantages, but as the buildings grew farther outside of my father's routes, I began to wonder where Julia was taking me. It became less of a game as I tried to keep up with her graceful pace. "Where are we going?" I shouted, half joking, half serious. "You'll see soon enough," she yelled back, in that same cheerful tone her father had. Streetlights illuminated the whole city until we neared the wall; my first impression was that we were going to leave the city. I grew uneasy, as that was strictly illegal. I was relieved when we took a sharp turn inward toward the business district. The dingy collection of buildings was a ghost town; all of the business associates were running the Jubilee. Julia and I were alone in the middle of the cold and empty cityscape. My nervousness soon returned despite her warm presence.

We came to a cobblestone building in the middle of the business district. I had neglected to notice it before, although it was easily one of the tallest skyscrapers in the city. As I studied the layout, the surrounding buildings almost hid it from view. It was also quite dilapidated compared to some of the more pristine buildings bordering it. The windows were cracked and foggy, covered in the same dirt and grime that clouded the run-down eyesore of a building. I was surprised that Jack King would allow such a disgusting mess in his precious city. Julia pulled a flashlight from her back pocket, which I had an excellent view of, mind you. I followed her up to the large metal doors as she hurried inside. She shone the bright beam around the dark interior, found the light system, and flipped on the switches. I was taken aback by what I saw. The inside of what appeared to be the dirtiest place in town was the most pristine and immaculate area I had ever laid eyes on. The floors were marble and the walls were solid tile - almost the opposite of the exterior. The air smelled like rubber, and warm air heated us up from the autumn wind outside. I had no idea what that place was.

"Well, what do you think?" she asked brightly. I looked around at the rows of military vehicles - almost identical to the one my father drove. There had to be at least three dozen of them, lined up like a car dealership - only without the dick-in-the-ass preppy salesmen. "What *is* this place?" I wondered in utter bewilderment. Julia did not answer. I followed her as she headed toward a flight of stairs across the marble lot. The stairwell was lined with the filthy windows, which dimmed the light to the outside world. The stairs were metal, lined with holes. I could see through to the first floor as we climbed higher and higher; I never was a fan of heights. The next floor was just as mind-boggling as the previous one. The second level appeared to be a warehouse, complete with shelves and crates and the whole nine yards. When I looked ahead at Julia, she was holding a crowbar. She walked over to the nearest crate and jimmied it open. Inside were dozens of machine guns. She handed me a crowbar from a nearby shelf. I just went along with whatever she was doing - whatever *mission* she was on. What she sought, I sought also.

We travelled around the storage facility, opening crates and examining the contents. I found an entire crate full of shotgun shells. Another one was stacked with machine gun magazines, arranged by the caliber. There were boxes of grenades, weapon attachments, and first aid kits. Anything that could be used in modern warfare could have been found in one of those wooden crates. Julia and I met up on the other side of the aisles; she was still oddly quiet. I followed her through another stairway, which led to another warehouse. There were levels upon levels of weapon storage. The amount of armor to be found was unbelievable. My legs soon grew tired as we weaved our way to the top of the skyscraper. A bright **EMERGENCY** sign buzzed brightly across the top floor of the building, and a ladder hung on the opposite wall between two crates across the room. I let Julia go first, for multiple unmentionable reasons. For one, I did not know what lay on the other side of the hatch in the ceiling.

I started up the ladder, as close behind Julia as I could get. She threw open the hatch, and we climbed out into the crisp air of the brisk autumn evening. The view was more spectacular than any weapon cache. I looked out upon the city - I could see everything from where we stood. We were on top of the city - on top of the *world*. We were higher than the mountains. There were no words to describe the beauty of the sunset below the beautiful city. The night was perfect; *that* was what Julia wanted to show me. "It's *amazing*!" I exclaimed. "Isn't it, though?" she replied. I could see every building, every light, and every soul from atop that building. My breath was stolen from me; I then relied on Julia and the open air to replenish it. "Better than any Jubilee?" Julia asked. I tried to answer her, but I was cut off. Not by words, but by lips. Julia's gentle hands wrapped around my head as she kissed me. In that moment, I forgot about the city and Jack King and the dreams. It was then only Julia and I on top of the city. She kissed me for what seemed like an eon, and trust me, I could not possibly begin to argue. She slowly pulled away, giving me a nervous look, as if she had done something wrong. "Definitely," I said with an embarrassed smile. Her look of uncertainty dissolved into an identical laugh. "What is this place, anyway?" I asked, shifting my glance out into the city far below. "I call it the Perch."

Julia and I spent that entire evening on that rooftop - or the Perch - as I soon began referring to it as. The moon climbed out of the fiery sunset like a newborn child, lighting up the large rooftop and illuminating Julia's beauty all the further. We talked and carried on conversation after conversation into late hours of the night. The rooftop was littered with lawn chairs, as peculiar as it was. We picked out two relatively close to the edge of the building, laid out under the millions of stars, and propped our feet up over the city. We exchanged stories in great detail. I had never been so interested in somebody. Julia had it rough - a lot more so than I did. Misery is always relative, and it sure does love company. I had always thought of myself as boring, but she listened nonetheless, catching on to every detail. It was a pleasant change for someone to actually care. I had not felt that since - well, you know.

"Tell me your story," she said. I looked over at her. "You first." She sighed jokingly and agreed. "It was hard, with my dad being in the military and all," she started. "My mom and I lived off the coast of Florida. Mom said it was the closest we could be to him without actually *fighting* the war *with* him. My dad was obsessive and compulsive, always distant and driven by rage. He never got along with my grandfather, and upon the rural mention of him, he would tell horror stories about the abuse he grew up in.

Dad put his work above anything else; I always thought he was trying to be better than what he was brought up in. Mom and I were always second place to whatever his latest craze was. The war *changed* him, as it does with anybody, I guess. Mom always told me stories of how he was when they first started dating and how much of a great man he was, but his job overseas had made him abusive and most of the time, a drunk. He hit Mom and I too many times to count, and his office was always littered with beer bottles. He would come home every few months for a couple weeks, but we rarely saw him. He was always working in his office or drinking, so Mom and I avoided him when he wasn't avoiding *us*. I always urged Mom to divorce him but she always said he would kill her. He always carried around a journal, always writing down notes and drawing little pictures. He always joked that it was his plan to take over the world. Mom stole it from his office one night, and Dad gave her a black eye when he found out. His final deployment before all of this was probably the longest. A week before he left, my grandfather died in a freak accident. Dad was so upset; I had never seen him cry. Dad never called, and he stayed overseas long after he was scheduled to return home. When he finally got back three months later, he was a mess. He told my mom and I to pack up all of our stuff and get ready to leave. The news was lit up with warnings to take cover. We were so confused. Dad, being with the military and all, knew exactly what to do. We moved into a military base in the middle of nowhere, which was safe as possible. I was confused most of the time, with my mom comforting me and Dad always rushing around the base. We were there for weeks until things calmed down. Dad filled us in on what happened; he told us all about the Dreamers and the plan and how it was for our own good. I understood it later in life. The Dreamers aren't meant for this world. Dad moved us into the middle of nowhere once again. He began ordering construction for this place, and slowly, it rose into the sky like an untold prophecy, like it was meant to be. Suddenly,

Dad became more like the boss, always giving out orders and taking control. This place seemed like a complete turn-around. That is, until my mom died. Dad came home one day from the sites in tears and in a rage. He said Mom had been killed by a Dreamer. We were both destroyed by it. My mother was my only friend. My *shelter* from Dad. Neither of us spoke much for the next few years as the city climbed higher and higher. We just lived as this place closed us in. After Mom was killed, Dad enforced harsh security officers to eliminate the Dreamers. He was driven, to say the least. He provided for me, but he never took care of me. At least not like Mom. He still drinks, but he hasn't hit me since she passed. I guess he felt sorry for how he treated her and stopped taking it out on me. I live alone in that huge house with the leader of this place. It should feel powerful, but it's empty. And lonely. I tend to the gardens. Flowers are my escape. Growth and decay and reformation. As much as I hate this ugly world we live in now, I can't hope to hide from it. I'm the flower of this city, and I'm wilting. And now I'm here, talking to you."

I was transfixed with emotion by her story, trembling to hear her misfortune. I contemplated telling her everything her father had told me, but something inside me told me that the time was not right. I stared into her eyes, tears balancing on the edge of her eyelids. She brushed them away, and the smallest fraction of a smile peeked out from her cheeks. "Your turn," she said, returning my stare. I reared back in a comical mock of a beginning. "Ah, where do I begin the lost tale of Shakespeare?" I said, prompting a brief laugh from Julia. I was glad I could cheer her up. "I was born and raised in Nebraska. There's perks of living in a fly-over state. It's quiet and peaceful. Lots of flowers," I winked. "But you can never help but feel...forgotten. The world can literally end and you would never know about it. It was my parents, my brother, and me. When the bombs hit, we took cover in our basement for months until your dad found us. He brought us here. As bad as his past is, he saved us. He saved people. That has to count for something."

Julia smiled, satisfied with the simplicity of my background. I tried the only thing that I knew how to, and that was to cheer her up. My only option was to build up her father, even though I knew what I had said was a clouded lie. The bell tower in the town square rang out twelve times, telling the city that midnight had struck. The loud ringing woke Julia and I up from our facade of a perfect evening. The time we had spent talking had spread out over five short hours. I could have easily spent five more, ten even. Time stood still whenever Julia was in the picture, but unfortunately, everything else continued spinning. I heard Jack King come back over the intercom system, thanking everyone for their attendance and dismissing them all back home. Julia and I stood up and stretched, reluctant to return to the lower buzz of the hectic city below us. We had enough excitement between us on that rooftop.

"My parents are gonna be worried about me," I rolled my eyes. Julia smiled. "So will Dad." We took one last look at the wondrous midnight sky above us and one last look down at the shining lights of the stronghold we both called home - on opposite ends of the spectrum. We descended the ladder back into the warehouse, along with the multiple levels of floors and stairs alike. We held hands as we ran through the armory and out into the chilly night air. She kissed me one final time and took off running through the alleyways once more. I followed as closely as I could, but I soon lost her. Her lips were still on mine as I came out into the town square into the huge crowd of people. I was full of excitement about my evening, and also with wonder about why Julia never said goodbye. I could not argue with her farewell, however. My lips were cold as ice but warm as a flame.

I soon found my parents on the sidewalk in front of the town hall, but my brother was nowhere to be found. He would probably be staggering into the house at three in the morning, with more than a few beers under his belt. I could tell that my parents had had a little more than enough to drink by the way they walked and talked, carrying themselves like drunkards. All I could make out was, "Have a good time?" I simply replied yes, with so much more implied meaning behind the word. The three of us swiftly made our way home. They waddled into their room as I ran up to my mine; the buzz of fulfillment had filled my mind and into the backs of my eyes. I was completely and wholeheartedly overcome with fatigue. I pulled my shirt over my head once more, which then smelled of peaches and roses, falling into bed. My eyes caught one last thing before they closed for the night. My desk lamp cast a dim glow off of the glass of my dresser mirror. Perhaps it was the brightest star in the night sky that never said goodbye.

Chapter VIII
Strange Happenings
(Highs and Lows, Strangers and Woes, and the Innocence I Chose)

Even after a considerable period of time following the Jubilee, the city retained a personality of certain carefree lightheartedness. It took a week and a hundred people to clean up the mess left behind by a generally buzzed group of people. Soon, Jack King had his precious city back in immaculate order. The Jubilee was the first city-wide festival; prior to that, celebration was frowned upon. Jack King always preached that there was work to be done, and if we wiped our brow after every drop of sweat, then there would not be any cloth left. He always motivated his people in twisted and harsh parables. Perhaps he only saw fit to take a break after everything was said and done. In hindsight, I knew that he was right. You can sleep when you die. The festival sparked a shockwave of pleasant emotions throughout the city and its people, rejuvenating souls like a laborious revival. There was not an upside-down smile to be found anywhere within the confines of the walls. Things ran smooth as clockwork, both in my home life and the continuation of the city. Life in that place had never been any better; I began to enjoy my time in the once strange metropolis. With my newfound relationship with Julia, the walls, the buildings, and the people all started to feel like home.

The second time I saw Luke aroused many questions within my mind. Where had he *gone*? The question pushed my mind further and further into curiosity until my legs followed suit, dragging me to the train station to find the man who had sparked so many of my ideas within my mind. The train station was dim-lit and dirty as usual, not a soul in sight except for the ghosts that followed me wherever I went in the city. "Looking for the man that chips the bricks out of these walls?" I heard from behind me. I spun around to find the man who I had come to find sitting in his chair, Half-Twenty curled up at his feet. "I've been looking for you," I said to him. "You might be the first," he said with a laugh. I walked over to him and sat down, not wanting to ride on the train he claimed as his own on that day. "Where did you go?" I asked him in utmost curiosity. "I had some reading to do. Coffee to drink," he said with another whiskery laugh. I assumed that the man was homeless, but his goatee was trimmed and kept clean as it was the last time I saw him. The only smell I detected was that of the cigarettes he puffed on. And so the question directed and forced itself from my mind to my lips. "Where do you live, Luke?" I asked, not meaning to pry or disrespect. He simply pointed at first and waved his arm around him to the filthy walls around me. "The train station is yours too?" I asked almost in shock. "It was there for the taking, and so I did," he explained. That was the very first lesson the man taught me.

And so I sat and talked to him for hours as the stranger became a close friend and adversary. He told me his story as I told him mine, and adult friends added a certain level of insight and perspective to my life, and the maturity drew me to people of an omniscient stature, such as Leroy Hall, Stephan, and Hugh. Luke grew up on a ranch in the Midwest, joined the Navy in the late 1960s, and spent his adult life in Alaska for seventeen years. He loved to cook and fish in Oregon despite the rain and cold, and he had stories for days. He told me he had four kids, sixteen grandchildren, and five great-grandchildren. I was amazed at his family tree, and he loved history. After all, he had helped shape it. He moved in with his daughter and paid her rent, which he later discovered that she was using for drug money. And so he set out on his own when Jack King found him and brought him into the city. He could not walk due to to swelling in his legs on top of the mesothelioma, diabetes, and lung cancer, and so Jack King let him govern the train station as his own. It was a sense of purpose when Luke turned down the mansion on the hill, and so Arnold Matthews became the man on the train, and he was a king of his own quiet, simple world. Through a few hours of conversation, I felt as if I knew the man more than I knew my own grandfather, and I was grateful for the city's blessing.

At first the dog had been mangy and filthy, but as I got to know Arnold, I looked beneath the dirt and grime and saw an innocent puppy that the dog really was on the inside. After all, only in dire situations are we forced to a growling anger. The night waged on and the moon lit fiery shadows across the train station walls. As I stood to leave, he told me one last joke. He would begin with a single pun which then led to stories, and then end with another joke to start off our next visit. "How do you tell which nurse is the head nurse in a high-end hospital?" he asked me with a smile. I thought to myself and asked the answer. "The one with the calluses on her knees," he laughed before he disappeared once more.

Oftentimes, my mother would send me into the inner city to scour the markets for items she had forgotten on her bi-weekly grocery shopping trips. She always seemed to catch me at the most inopportune times, which led to a rambling on of complaints on my part as well as hers. After my mother would win the argument - as any parent would - I would take the object she handed me and set out into the chilly air of the bustling city. It was the quiet Sunday morning after the Jubilee, and the night before had left my parents - as well as my brother - engulfed in a nasty state of hangover. My mother knocked on my bedroom door and eventually opened it, allowing me to get a good look at her sunken eyes and droopy demeanor. "I need grapes for a fruit salad for the business banquet at work on Monday. Do you mind running out to get some?" My first response was a slight chuckle. "Haven't you guys had *enough* grapes?" I joked. Her eyes sunk

160

even deeper into a glare, and I knew she had me beat. I decided that arguing would only ensue more trouble than I was already in for leaving my brother's side the previous night. Not for my sake, but his. I nodded and got up to get ready as she sulked out of my bedroom with heavy and exasperated steps. I pulled on my coat, drifted down the stairs, and set out for the markets.

The wind had been moderately picking up over the weeks prior to the Jubilee. Winter would soon flood into the city like an overflowing dam. I had never really minded the cold. After all, it fit the vibe of the city like a glove. Besides, that part of the country never really got too terribly hot; the highest temperature was at best in the mid-eighties. I pulled my hood over my hair as the breeze whipped it around. The whistling of the wind sang the song of the season as I rounded the neighborhood sign and headed further into the city. My eyes drifted from the quiet houses to the ominous buildings in the distance. I focused on the Perch, which stood above all of the other buildings - and everything else in the city, for that matter. If the city had anything, it was variety. The strict hierarchy that Jack King had placed within the walls stood true to even the layout of the metropolis. We lived in a place where you could have small neighborhoods and skyscrapers on the same side of town - as well as ruthless tyrants and bashful gardeners. I had never noticed the building before, but I knew of its presence then, and my mind was filled with thoughts of Julia. I lost my senses in the idea of her. My feet carried me along the road; I almost did not see the man I ran straight into.

He was unusually tall - I had to look up at him as Julia did me. He smelled of fresh cologne and looked as sharp as an arrow. The man was clean-shaven, well-groomed, and he seemed strangely familiar. I had felt this man's presence before. I stared up at his face, both of us stuck like a fly in molasses in the awkward silence. Time seemed to stop completely. I scoured his facial composition, searching for anything that linked him to anybody from my past. My eyes locked onto his, and I knew it. I

161

knew who he was, yet I could not quite pinpoint exactly. "I'm sorry, sir," I apologized. He smiled a jolly grin. "No quarrel," he said in a deep, booming voice. He brushed past me as I moved out of his way, and he headed in the opposite direction as I was. "Remember what I told you," I heard - nothing but a whisper in the wind.

I had been to the marketplace on more occasions than I could remember. After all, I worked outside the vast acres of merchandise, but I was closer than ever to the inside, memorizing the layout like the back of my hand. It was actually a cluster of stands and shops at least three blocks in size; anything you can name or possibly want could be found there. I knew the stores inside and out, mainly because I had done odd jobs in just about every shop I could think of. The farmer's market was always humid and packed with more people than should have been allowed in there for safety reasons. My main objective was always to get in and out as quickly as possible, and so I made my way over to the fruit section in a rather speedy fashion. I was in luck - the stands and aisles were practically empty. I examined the grapes with a careful eye, checking for mold or bugs. I placed several bushels of bright purple and green grapes into a plastic bag and made my way to the Trader.

As I made my way out of the vast maze of the fruit section, I walked straight into yet another person. I looked straight into Julia's eyes as I my heart began racing with the same speed which always ran in her presence. "Hey!" she shouted in her positive manner, which contradicted my natural negative energy. She looked down at the bag of grapes in my hand and laughed for a moment. "We always meet when fruit is involved." We both laughed. "I can partly understand peaches, but what in the world would you need grapes for?" she inquired. I shifted from one foot to the other. "My mom...," I started. I was cut off by another slight laugh. "I imagine they had enough grape juice last night." I nodded with a wild smile that matched hers. Julia and I seemed to always think alike. She followed me around the corner and stopped at the Trader's booth. The Trader was a very old man - ancient, by the looks of it. In fact, he was so elderly that his age could not be determined by first interpretation. The man was at least a hundred years old, but he most certainly did not fit the popular criteria. He walked with a straight back, with no help from a cane or walker. His silver hair was always slicked back, and his wrinkles sunk his minuscule eyes even smaller to the back of his head. He could always be seen in the same outfit, which was a pair of trousers, a blue shirt, and brown suspenders. A solid black top hat sat atop his head, coming to the brim of his brow and sending a shadow across his eyelids, which were covered by a yellow-glazed pair of reading glasses. The man was visually frightening; he was like looking at your future, death, and a zombie all within the same being. The children in the city avoided him in the market; they would attempt to steal items from the shelves, only to be sent back to the Trader by security, which was usually a duo of heavily armed guards hired by Jack King himself to keep theft to an exact nonexistence. The children would hand over their items to trade, and silently walk past the guards, missing fingers or teeth in exchange for their crimes. Legend told that the Trader kept a string of fingers around his belt, and so he terrified me. I had never heard him speak a word - as a matter of fact, no one had. The old man was practically an empty shell, taking people's items to trade and sending them along their way. That was his job and all he had to live for was a stolen candy bar and an entitled thief's pointer finger. Although I was then an adult, he still made me quite uneasy.

I searched around for the candy booth, but the aisle with the usual smiling teenager sporting the fake grin to cover up his misery, was not where it usual stood. Instead, an incredibly short old woman stood behind the counter of a florist stand. I bit my tongue as an idea popped into my head and smiled as I examined the bright colors and inhaled the light smells of the many flowers.

I found a bouquet of the brightest red roses I had ever seen. I slid the elderly woman the trinket my mother had given me to trade across the counter. It was most likely a gift my father had given her to cover up his affair with another woman. It meant nothing to both my mother nor myself. I handed the flowers to Julia, her rosy cheeks lighting up with spirit to match the flowers and her smile burning brighter than the roses she held. My mother had told me never to buy carnations, although I thought them to be prettier than roses. "Brighter than the sun," I said to her, lost in her eyes once again. "Just like you." I was no longer nervous or embarrassed around her. I had to express to her how I felt about her; it was so natural and felt so right. Julia and I stepped out into the open town square, where I could breathe once again and cool down despite my racing heart and adrenaline. She put the flowers in her other hand and laced her fingers through mine as we walked briskly through the city sidewalks, talking and breathing in the cool air. "How are things with you, after the festival and all?" I asked. "Usual," she replied with that same double-edged smile, rolling her eyes. I assumed she had been tending to her gardens and crying herself to sleep, isolated in every possible way to be felt. I decided then that I would be the one to change that. Things were certainly about to change in many, many ways.

Hours passed as we drifted around city blocks and through buildings as the sun lowered from morning to midday to afternoon. I enjoyed listening to her talk - regardless of topic or subject. Julia always appeared to be fascinated in what I had to say as well, no matter how boring and contradicting my stories were compared to hers. We both were so invested in each other with roots so deep and a love that both of us were so incredibly terrified to entertain. Above all, Julia and I were content in the new world. We had each other only, and that was enough to create a world all our own. Hand-in-hand, Julia and I rounded the corner by the library and subway station. She had hinted that she needed to be getting home, but it was obvious that she did not want to go, although it may have been more clear that I did not want her to go. Either way, the actual reality took over the reality we so desperately wished to be real, and we slowly made our way to the subway station. We came across a man sitting Indian-style on the bench in front of the library; he seemed as normal as a stranger can look. In fact, he was the *same* stranger I had bumped into earlier that morning. The man appeared to be middle-aged, with a dark coat and pants buttoned up tightly, bundled up for the chilly afternoon as we were. My mind told me that the scene was normal, but something whispered to me that something was not right. I could not help but stop dead in my tracks, Julia halting along with me.

What I saw was far from normal. Besides the stranger on the bench, we were the only other people in the quiet nook of the city. Julia stared at me as I stared at the man several dozen feet away. The wooden bench snapped at the base, the legs splintering in multiple directions. The stranger fell to the ground along with the seat, still in the cross-legged position. I was taken aback at the mysterious happening. The man sat there in silence for a moment; I realized his eyes were closed as I looked further ahead. They opened suddenly, both pupils as black as night. He levitated off of the bench, hovering several feet until he could outstretch his legs into the open air. His arms waved around, his fingers unclenching and stretching his entire body. The strange man was *flying*. I could not process the scene as I blinked in disbelief, my mind whirring like a machine with an oncoming jam. The gunshot rang out through the hollow cranny of the town square; up until that moment, the scene was like a silent movie. I viewed the occurrence in slow motion and in complete silence due to shock. I was woken up by the abrupt **PAP PAP** of an assault rifle. The man fell to the ground, dead as quickly as he had come alive. I had unconsciously put my arm in front of Julia as a defense mechanism, but she then pulled me into a nearby alleyway before the soldier saw us. We peeked around the corner to witness the rest of the scene from cover, hoping to a silent god that we had not been seen.

The soldier had emerged from the opposite direction we had. He lowered his weapon and swiftly approached the corpse with a careful edge in the stride of his step. He gazed down at the man he had murdered - shot down in cold blood - and made certain the stranger was dead. He then bent down, hoisted the man out of the rubble of the broken bench by his shoulders, and slammed him into the alleyway adjacent to the one we hid inside. The gunshot to the head had silenced him as well as blown half of his face off, but the officer continued, bringing the butt of the gun against the stranger's temple and nose time and time again. I could see the splatter of wet blood spray onto the soldier's face as he became satisfied with the inability to recognize his victim - his prey. Blood dripped onto the road as the soldier wiped his brow, strapped the assault rifle to his back, and dragged the limp corpse into the alley on the opposite side of the street. As far as he was concerned, no one had seen what he had just done, but we had. The image was frozen into our minds like frosted blood on the sidewalk before us. I could smell it, and I pulled Julia closer to shield her eyes from what she had just witnessed. It took several moments for the scene to resonate with me. My mouth gaped open in utter shock. I had never witnessed an innocent murder before, much less the grisly actions that had taken place moments before. I pulled Julia closer still, not only for her comfort, but also for mine. I looked into her blank expression of a strange familiarity - her usual sporty grin was gone. She was either mesmerized by it, or she had seen that sort of thing before.

"Let's follow him," she said softly. I had no time to question it before Julia pulled loose from my grasp, turning the corner and rushing across the street. I tossed the bag of grapes under a nearby dumpster and hurried to catch up with her. We stood over the puddle of crimson blood and slowly started down the trail the soldier had left into the dimly lit alleyway. We wandered through the labyrinth of the vast concrete hallways, the smell of the sewer lingering in our nostrils. It took what seemed like ages to follow the faded trail. The path was filled with obstacles and sharp turns. With the shadows of the buildings above, it was quite difficult to see where we were going; I ran into a multitude of dumpsters and brick walls. Our slow pace quickened to a brisk walk, then to a swift jog. The trail had nearly disappeared completely, and with the sunset approaching earlier that time of year, the bright orange sphere cast a glow through the hollow alleyway. Our legs soon wore out from the echoes of our footsteps, and we soon had to return to the humph of a dragging corpse. I wanted to give up, but the look of determination in Julia's eyes was motivation for me to help her reach her goals - no matter how strenuous or painful they were. It would be worth it just to satisfy her.

In a split second, Julia tackled me and rolled both of us under a dumpster. "Do not move," she whispered at a barely audible volume as the sewer runoff soaked into the back of my jacket, shirt, and eventually against my bare back skin. I cringed in disgust as I realized her motive; I looked under the dumpster and saw the pair of military boots come to a halt. God, I adored those goddamn boots. I *yearned* for them. The man who commanded them was a monster, however. We had clanged against the side of the dumpster on our way down, the sound echoing throughout the hollow alleyway. I heard the squeaking of wet shoes as the soldier spun around. He dropped the feet of the dead man as he searched around for the source of the noise. Julia tightened her grip on my chest as we both shook with nervousness and anxious fear. The soldier marched closer and closer to the dumpster, time slowing in the midst of our panic. I saw the palm of his hand snatch the handgun out of the holster around his waist. I heard the fear-striking click of the cocking of the hammer. I felt Julia's heart rate increase rapidly; she must have felt mine as well. As the officer inched closer and closer to our position, I prepared for the same death as the deceased stranger only a few yards away. The soldier pointed the gun at the dumpster and pulled the trigger. Blood splattered all over my face. I looked over at Julia and the identical red mask she now wore. The officer stopped in his tracks and laughed a cold, empty laugh. "Goddamn *rats*." He holstered his gun, picked up the body, and continued along his way, resuming his death march as our hearts stopped.

Relieved, Julia rolled off of me and we laid in the middle of the alley to catch our breath. "Holy shit," I said, exasperated and spitting rat guts out of my mouth. "Thanks for that," I whispered to her as she nodded. I had no time nor words to question further. I pulled my jacket off and wiped my face and neck clean - or as close as you can get without a mirror. I handed the coat to Julia, and after she did the same, we climbed to our feet. Putting the jacket back on, we followed the newly replenished blood trail out of the maze of alleyways. We walked out into the quiet, nearly empty evening in the city streets, standing on the curb as we watched the soldier from a fair distance. He was now dragging the body across the open street and to the other side. Once they reached the other side, the officer opened the door of the building and pulled the corpse inside. Julia and I just stood on the street corner, staring up at the Perch.

It took days to get the murder sequence out of my head. I dreamt about it over and over, always waking up in the middle of the night drenched in a frigid sweat. The basic dream evolved into something far worse with each night that passed. It was always somebody different getting shot through the temple. The scene was beyond horrific enough with the stranger, but the vast expanse of my subconscious transformed the original victim from a stranger to my father, then to my mother. My brother turned to Jack King. He morphed into Julia, which struck a heart-shattering awakening within me, complete with screams and further insanity and mistrust with each time I closed my eyes to rest. This psychotic torment lasted for weeks on end. At the conclusion of my sentence, it was *my* turn to die. I soon became afraid to sleep, and I would avoid it. I settled for a maximum of three hours every other day, and my face took on the ghastly detail of the Trader. Perhaps he had not slept in years; perhaps we suffered the same fate.

"Put the big scary one all the way to the floor," Jack began to teach me. The clutch pedal had a lot more room to fall than the gas and brake did, and no matter how long we practiced the routine together, I never could master the bicycle motion. The vintage beauty stalled and ground gears as we rolled across the open and wide driveway. There was nothing I could possibly hit there, fortunately. "I'll stick to the automatic," I told him, exasperated and frustrated. I was careful to avoid slamming the door, leaving Jack with the tarp as I walked toward the library - a place where I was a true master.

"Like a wise man once said, I too have a dream. A dream of a world without diversity and differences. A world without creativity and creation itself. A world without *dreams*, goddamnit. That is what this city is founded upon. And it shall be!" I looked at Jack solemnly. "Who said that?" I asked plainly and curiously. "Why, a King, of course," he smiled, a wicked grin overtaking his scars. "I can't pick one," I said to Jack as I paced the library walls and aisles full of thousands of books. "Take as many as you'd like," he told me. "I don't get near enough time to read anyway." I had to ask the keeper what he preferred. "What do you recommend?" Jack walked over to the S section and pulled a set of books out. "Ever heard of Sizemore?" I had only recently discovered poetry in Gregor McLindle. "When we surrender this world back to the birds, they will most *certainly* want this motherfucker," Jack spat as he left me alone with the tomb of books.

I followed him up the stairs and into his seemingly secret office we had shared a hardy and rather startling experience some number of months prior. "You know why the idea of God is a lie, Noah?" Jack asked me. I shrugged in forced ignorance as my eyes pleaded for an answer. "This fellow Jesus apparently went through his whole life without ever jacking off or fucking a woman. He surely never fucked a *man*. But he never found a wife. And that is a preached sadness, Noah. A man that finds no wife - that makes me cry. I see the way you look at my daughter and I surely approve of you. Who knows? Maybe you two will go the distance." I smiled as he clapped me on the back. "What was your wife like, Jack?" I asked him out of momentary curiosity and possible mistake. "She was - great," he paused. "I think I drove her away," his eyes trailed off in regret. Was he possible of regretting his vile actions? "I couldn't help myself, Noah. I couldn't. She would say things and I had to shoot them down. We could not agree, my boy. I'm not saying I was always right, but she came to defend the evils that brought about this chasm of depress. But she was *great*. She allowed for this rebirth. This *beauty*. The beauty that she was. And then she was gone. Inspiring it but not being able to enjoy it. And that I regret." Perhaps I saw a tear drip down behind his sunglasses as I clapped his shoulder that time. "All in good time, Jack. You did this. You built this place. These are *your* people. Keep your friends close. Keep your enemies closer." I had an unsettling suspicion that he was a suspect in his wife's disappearance. "What brought about the end of the world, Jack?" I asked. The leader of the city - and what seemed to be the world - and I were *bonding*. It was strange, yet satisfying. As if I had *leverage* - a place in the world in someone's eyes. Someone of *value*. "It was based on tits and sadness. Laxation and laziness. The great almighty Jehovah jerk-off session. The world ended, and so I took it as a bad omen from God. A sign that we were never supposed to inherit the earth at all. God had not jacked off in a long time, and things were well in the world. He got off on causing and witnessing misery. It was an *opportunity*. And so I took it. I was never too good at listening, as you can imagine. Only slaves and pussies listen. I served the world up a nice piping hot cup of ballsack tea and a side of shit and shoved it into the throat of the world. I live by three *simple* truths, Noah. Care to hear them?" Jack said in offering, as if he was not going to tell me *anyway*. "Go ahead," I waved. "Thou shalt not be a *bitch*. Thou shalt not be a *cunt*. And above all, thou shalt not be a *pussy*," he spoke. I laughed slightly. "I figured it would be four," I shot in his direction. "How do you figure?" I offered to him that time, "Thou shalt not be a *Dreamer*. King's coochie water." He grimaced and laughed, punching me in the arm. "I love the hell out of you, you little bastard."

When I would grow anxious and impatient with the pacing of the monotonous city lifestyle, I would traverse into the deep and quiet recess of the train station. Luke was more of a grandfather than I had ever had, and in fact, he was the only form of grandparent I knew. Arnold loved to cook as he fully described to me his recipes and spices, and upon our closer visits and longer stays, I got to see his kitchen and housing in the far rear of the station. Contrary to the filthy train car depot, his house was immaculate. The man needed not much space or many belongings to make it a home, and cooking in his house was an honor and a pleasure.

"You ever have pumpkin whiskey?" he asked me. "Can't say I have," I replied, grabbing onto his chair with one arm and kicking my feet up on the underlying support. "Well, you'll hollow out a pumpkin and fill it with beet sugar. You'll seal the top back on and store it in a dark and cool place until it gets real spongy, then you'll strain it. And boy, that pumpkin whiskey will kick your ass all over the room and then some." We both shared a laugh before he handed me the latest book he had finished. Arnold loved to read as I did, and we shared a lot of the same taste. He would read a book once and then give it to me to read. I vowed if I ever got a time where I could read a book in two days, I would. Perhaps he simply had more time than I did.

Joshua Peterson was a goddamn genius, to be quite honest. He was a survivalist by nature and an inventor by trade. His wrists were always portraying altered high-tech watches and his glasses were made from spare parts and one-way glass lenses. I was fascinated by his skill and entrepreneurship, and I watched in awe as he constructed magnificent objects. I often wondered how useful they could be if his talent was harnessed. His ingenuity could cure diseases and raise the dead if used in the right hands.

I had always loved the look and feel of sunglasses. Everyone I had looked up to in my life wore a pair of dark lenses over their eyes, and perhaps the secretive protection over their pupils is what supplied their power. Sunlight was the bane of my existence, and many times of squinting in the face of bright lights would cloud my mind with a horrible migraine. The city was a bright reflection of progress and the sun was a fiery ignition; I set my heart and mind on finding a pair of aviator sunglasses. My father had worn them in old photographs and Jack King was never seen without them. Sawyer could not be seen winking at women behind the thick lenses, and I yearned for a pair to set me apart from the rest of the world. With a pair of sunglasses, I would be powerful enough to change it. And so I searched market after market, shelf after shelf, and bin after bin, yet I could find not a size nor shape that enabled my inner personality, and upon the lost hope, an idea came to me. In the face of a forgotten inventor, I found power.

Did he tell me I was absurd? Did he laugh me out of the room? Absolutely not. Joshua Peterson knew all too well what it was like to be ridiculed and thought to be ridiculous. "I'll make it happen," he said to me when I brought the idea to him. "That's it?" I asked, almost in disbelief. "Of course, Noah. You're one of the few people that hasn't made me want to kill myself or others. I'd build anything for you, my friend." Perhaps kindness and friendship was power. Nevertheless, sunglasses were the face of strength and confidence.

Life continued on after what Julia and I had witnessed, becoming similarly sluggish and exhausted as I had. The terrible dreams had began to change the way I viewed the world around me. Everything, from the buildings to the people and even myself, started to take on a melancholy aura. We were the only ones that had witnessed the murder, and along with the secrecy of the hiding of the body, no suspicion was risen. On our walks around the city, we often saw the officer that had committed the crime. He always wore the grimace of a content yet tortured demeanor, as if the sick dog was proud of what he had done. We would identify his presence quickly and look away, doing our damnedest not to arouse suspicion or any slightest form of recognition. As hard as it was to place blame on the soldier, I had to accept that he was only following orders from a higher power.

"Does your dad ever let you drive his car?" I asked her one day. "I want to. But I could never master the goddamn stick shift," she laughed as I matched it. "I feel that. He tried to teach me but I got so damn pissed off I gave up," I replied with a laugh. "My dad let me drive the lawn mower when I was little, but he would never let me *mow* the grass. I almost knocked the grill over one day when we were grilling out. He was always *protective*. I never mowed the grass once. I never welded or sprayed wasps nests. So it surprised me when he taught me to drive. He's not patient like my mother is. But he put me on curvy ass roads in the rain at night. I guess we all have surprises," I smiled. "Yeah," she yawned as the sun began to set. "I never fucked with wasps either," we laughed. "What *did* you fuck with?" I asked, involved in the knowing of her childhood. "Dad was always gone. I remember the day he left for Iraq. I was a wreck. Mom and I would garden and cook together to get our minds off of him being gone. She was a sort of a best friend as well as a mother. I loved her to death," she nearly teared up. "My mother and I have *never* really been the idea of a perfect family. My father and brother have always driven a wedge between us. I haven't always treated her the best and how she deserves. Some nights it eats me alive. If only I could go back and behave myself as a child. I wouldn't cry one day. I wouldn't yell or cuss at her ever again if I could go back. We would bake brownies and cookies and enjoy each other's company instead of the other way around. I've made her life hell and I'm gonna have to live with that and pay for it one day. If only I could go back. I regret it each and every day. But we only get one chance. And I fucked it up." I wiped the several tears that leaked down my cheeks away and looked over at her as I held her other hand. "You say you and your mom cooked, huh?" I smiled through the emotional anguish I was boiling inside. "Yeah, but I always preferred baking. You know, brownies and cookies and stuff."

As slowly as the scarring of the scene had left us, it quickly made its sick return to our memory. Three weeks after the first murder had occurred, it happened again. Julia and I were making our way around the business district on a devilishly icy evening; winter had set upon the city and vowed not to leave for a vast eternity. Clad in coats, hoods, and gloves, we made our way out of the square hand in hand. Weather could not separate us - we had traversed around the cityscape in the pouring rain and sheets of sleet that never seemed to melt from the roadways, erasing any sign of a bloody shadow from the streets and sidewalks.

Hearing a commotion in a nearby alleyway, we nonchalantly stood behind the corner of the building to observe what was going on from a hidden perspective. Another one of Jack King's aggressive henchmen was shouting at a middle-aged farmer in overalls and a heavy winter coat, lying in the middle of the frozen concrete. An eerie blue light emitted from his eye sockets. As he sat up, I saw that his pupils were nothing but empty shells, red beads in the dim light. It was quite frightening; I squeezed Julia's hand tighter. Her return of pressure proved that our fear was mutual. The farmer climbed to his feet despite the yelling and cursing of the soldier, who now aimed the barrel of his assault rifle between the man's eyes. I felt the gust of wind as he levitated into the air, his limbs outstretched like a crucifixion, similar to the stranger in the previous odd occurrence. I flinched as the crack of the gunshot brought the man to the ground once more. The officer proceeded to beat the body to a pulp, seemingly to take out an inconceivable amount of anger. I could not comprehend why his differences would be against a common man such as a farmer. Once he was finished breaking his knuckles across the farmer's face in a bloody outrage, he dragged the seed-sower away into the night.

Julia and I were quick on the man's trail. Just as we had done the previous time, we weaved in and out of the alleyways, dodging dumpsters and massly confusing turns alike. We held back a short period to avoid a close-call confrontation such as before. I could not vouch for Julia, but I was positive that I was not exactly eager to be covered in vermin blood, or far worse - our own. Our hearts would beat and bleed as one. We found ourselves standing on the street corner under the Perch once again, witnessing the soldier drag the lifeless corpse through the heavy doors of the lifeless building. No one had seen, but we had.

The second occurrence was quite similar to the first, with each night warring with my mind, filling my subconscious with murderous scenes of the brutal end of my loved ones. Watching the sick continuation in slumber can be compared to being strapped to a hospital bed while having your fingernails and teeth ripped out, far more wicked than when I was awake. I then dreaded sleep more than waking up, which was certainly a quite miserable existence. I had an unsettling suspicion that that was not the end, and for once, I was not too pleased to be correct in my thoughts.

The third time was far more fantastical than the first and even the second. As unpleasant as an already brutal murder in the shadows can be was far more sickening when people begin to notice. Jack King had business dealings on the side of town easiest for Julia to slip out from under his careful eye at least three times every week. Her and I were walking up Main Street, as we usually would do nearly four times a week, when we heard the hustle and bustle of a crowd of seemingly excited people across the block. Dozens of bystanders gathered around one man in the middle of the street. The stranger stood beside a wooden crate of apples, most likely from the farmer's market close behind him on the outskirts of the town square. Once the group of people grew silent, the man stomped his foot hard on the asphalt beneath him. He repeated this action countless times, each step growing harder and harder, shaking the concrete beneath their feet. With each time he brought his foot down, a single apple rose into the air, circling him like a force field. By this time, Julia and I had entered the anxious crowd. The man waved his hands, and the array of apples copied the motion. The line of fruit arranged itself like bowling pins across the man's arms and shoulders, with the last one balancing on his head. The crowd cheered relentlessly, shouting their praise and worship at a magic act they had yet to see. They were mesmerized by it. Julia and I remained silent, for we had seen the act before, and we knew how it ended. There were always those like us - the unimpressed. The *accustomed*.

That time was different - there was then an audience larger than two hidden figures in the evening light. This time, it was broad daylight and high noon. The aftermath would not be easily hidden and forgotten. Regardless of the crowd, the repetitive motion that had always followed came to light. Just as quickly as the apples had found their place along the man's elongated body, they began exploding one by one from left to right. Bullets ripped each perfectly round piece of fruit down to its core, spitting the sweet juice and seeds onto the closest onlookers. Perhaps they were *confused*, or maybe the cheering had drowned out the gunfire. Julia and I heard nothing; our focus was on the man dressed in the black leather coat and the shiny boots heading toward the crowd. I had noticed the attire from across the street. The magnificent boots shed a beautiful light on the sleek leather coat I so yearned for. I expected the commonplace soldier to intervene behind the dreaded assault, but as the man came closer, I realized it was Jack King himself. Gripping his pistol, he aimed it at the last apple atop the man's head. The crowd soon hushed down to mere whispers; the stranger was in a daze just as we were. With highest military expertise, a final bullet penetrated the golden red apple, ricocheted into the silent city behind us. The stranger, who I recognized to be one of the most profitable store owners in the city, was the center of attention for another reason only moments ago - now the center of the entire city. Silent eons thumped past as Jack King stepped closer and closer to the man. The crowd parted as he walked right up to the shopkeeper. "Open your mouth," he whispered to the stranger, who now bore a terrified expression. The whispers echoed throughout the crisp air, possibly screams, like gunshots throughout a hollow core of an apple. I could not tell the difference anymore.

The townsfolk cannot quite recall exactly what happened that day on Main Street. Perhaps they *do*; they just would not tell you. Julia and I remember exactly what happened. The only detail they remember is the crowd being dispersed at once in an angry and violent array of shouts and orders, the rest a blank slate. Regardless of the other details, Julia and I knew what had happened. A man was murdered in cold blood by not only a ruthless tyrant, but the brightest and whitest face of the city - the son of every ruthless tyrant that had ever lived and died in and from power that feared strange happenings and acted out of rash fear. Julia knew her father had killed people in the line of his military duty, but she had never seen him commit those crimes, much less in an open and un-warlike scenario. She was scarred and warped in not only her mind, but her body soon followed an uncertain mistrusting pattern. She *hated* her father, but she had witnessed something that changed her entire view of him forever. We both were in utter shock and knew not how to deal with not only the brutality of the strange happenings, but also and more importantly the occurrences themselves. Our minds could not simply be wiped clean by ignorance and refusal to accept what we did not know. However, we could not answer what had begun to take place in the city, instead choosing to focus on the reality of the brutal murders following the differences.

Marisa had been transferred to the psychiatric ward following the recent incidents within the city. People began to see as I had and began to question. They began to create as they were destined to. One of her patients had slipped a scalpel into his belt from the upstairs wing and slashed her throat during an examination in a bloody and gruesome fashion. Jacob became as silent and empty as a coffin and closed off as her casket. He spoke no more and locked himself away, held prisoner by the images in his head of the only one who could love him for who he was - as twisted and jaded as his character had become. He took after our father in nearly every way without being the man himself. In many ways his throat was slit alongside hers, for he became a still and quiet picture of depressive solitude - a shadow, a ghost, and a bloody puddle in my life as his was consumed by the same cancer that had latched onto the city around us.

It was in the time of turmoil in the city that I lost my closest friend, Arnold. Not in death, but in disappearance. I felt a certain amount of emptiness in my life, which often brought me to

Arnold for freedom of mind and self. For the first time since my first visit, I heard my footsteps echo off of the crackled cobblestone and filthy tile walls. I knew Arnold enough to show myself into the kitchen and room in the back; after all, I had used the kitchen on many occasions. "Luke!" I yelled, hoping he would roll out of the back room in his wheelchair to surprise me. There was not a stir nor a noise. I immediately worried that something had happened to him, which quickly became one of my biggest fears. I had lost a great deal of people in my life in a short amount of time, many of which were my closest friends. Arnold was no different, but in many ways he was. I loved the old man and the appreciation I was able to give him and to show him. I was grateful for his friendship and for his leadership, for he was one of the greatest men I knew. No, he was the goddamn *greatest* man I knew. He *was* my grandfather, I decided. Not by blood, but by claim. If I could not find him, I would wait for him. I would repay his services to me. I knelt down to pet Half-Twenty as he whimpered in longing sadness at the whereabouts of his owner. I hugged the soft, clean puppy as I wondered as well.

Arnold could barely hobble from his bed to his wheelchair in the morning; sometimes the swelling in his legs would not even allow him to do that. He was on five different kinds of medication, most of which created nasty skin discoloration and sun sensitivity which was beneficial for him to live in such a dark and secluded environment. Upon his disappearance, I worried about his safety as well as his health. The wheelchair still sat beside the bed, which was his only means of transportation. My stomach ached in anxiety of his whereabouts, and I had to do something to impress his return. I looked around outside at the disgusting train station walls and dim-lit bulbs that hung along the tile. I had always loved to clean, and so I set out to finally pay back some of my respects to my true dear and closest friend in the city - my only true friend, apart from Julia, of course. I had never seen anyone put bumper stickers on the back of a wheelchair before I met Arnold. My favorite slogan of his was *'Keep honking, I'm reloading.'* His elderly humor gave me the motivation I required to overpower the childlike anxiety in my heart as I set out to bring back the one example I truly looked up to and admired without a clouded bias or force.

I searched inside his cabinets for the cleaning supplies that he was unable to use and sought to make good work of them. I found three large scrub brushes, two buckets, and five bottles of tile cleaner. Arnold had an array of light bulbs, all of which seemed like a visual fit for the mostly empty sockets outside of the boarding sanction only feet away - the barrier between cleanliness and filth. All day I scrubbed bucket after bucket full of gut-wrenching water stained with years of marred dirt and grime, a forgotten and lost sector of the city. After all, elderly veterans were always forgotten and lost in the old world, and perhaps Luke did not meet the standards of a human being set by Jack King, but rather a homeless bum. No matter the requisite, he was everything to me. I brushed the tiles back to their off-white glory and used a jar of paste to fill cracks and crevices, soaking the walls in cleaner and brushing them back to perfection. I used somewhere around thirty light bulbs to give the once malnourished train station a rather homely, cozy appearance to match Arnold's comfortable room in the far rear of the station. *Yellow light - never white. White is bright. Bright is absence of sight.*

Before the incident, Jack King was a needle in a haystack as far as the city was concerned. He was nowhere to be found in any nook and cranny of the vast labyrinth of streets, buildings, and people, for that matter. Julia always told me he stayed locked up in his office. She said he would never eat - just drinking himself away as he pondered stacks of notes and blueprints. Jack King had been a reclusive leader of the city, controlling every movement and shift from the shadows without showing his face more than was called for. After that day in the town square, however, Jack King made his presence known quite often among the rush of events within the city. As more and more murders and executions became public by both Jack King and his officers, watchdogs could be spotted on nearly every street corner. Jack would enforce his brutal laws as they were broken, with very little empathy towards anyone or anything. His henchmen were to act as he would, and they followed strict and subtle orders.

It was in the time of the attacks that I pondered the true definition of the Dreamers. Writers, artists, and thinkers had been murdered while soldiers, inventors, and farmers were left unscathed. *Ones who could make their dreams reality. We can not coexist with them.* Dreams were a catalyst - an awakening force that arose souls like dominoes; creativity was abstract - a last stand in hopes that someone would find it beautiful. Ones who had the ability to exercise that power could not coexist with the commonplace. I had always been normal, yet I found myself rather intrigued by the revolution around me.

I had seen the soldiers of the city snatch children from their beds as they colored by their instincts. I had seen heads bashed in as they thought freely as was natural. I had seen myself fall into hiding as I wondered and discovered the ways of the world as they could not be changed. I was an omniscient god from the shadows. No matter how many times the world was restarted, the same theme of hatred and discrimination could not be changed. No matter the city or the leader, the cash or the crop, or the god that was served. There was no god. Only myself, Jack King, and the terrible taint of the city as it breathed a poisonous smell. It was in the moments of subtle, silent passing that I heard the hypocrisies and double standards of the city officers. There was pure loyalty in the face and eyes of Jack King but upon his absence, there was angst and rebellion. Just as there *always* was. How many times did a police officer run a red light or speed down an empty highway? This was the moral of the human race, no matter the name or title. Jack King was the sun of the city. He was the heat, and upon his absence, there was frigid winter.

Victor was known to cause a racist uproar with his commentary and exemplary actions. I could hear the shouts and exclamations from my room as my family rushed to the windows to see the cause of the commotion. A crowd of people had gathered at the corner of the town hall, blocking our view altogether. My father told us to wait there as he rushed down the sidewalk to see what was the cause of the commotion. Crowds in those days usually meant someone was hurt or was about to be. Dire situations create creativity, and creativity was outlawed and punished. Hate sparked change and a certain fire within bystanders, and therefore creativity emerged. My father would watch and see what was the matter. He came back a short time later with an appalled expression upon his face. My mother and Jacob begged his response from his lips, and I fell silent in the background. For something to haunt my father, it had to be rather horrifying, as he has seen most everything that a man can witness without going mad. "Britton Chester is dead. Victor Jennings beat him to death in the town square," he finally spoke. With that, he walked out of the room and closed the bedroom door behind him. My mother began to sob; she had just lost her best friend. My father had always suspected something more between them, but it was sworn off by everyone except him. Jacob asked questions and was sent away as I watched my mother's tears hit the floor. So many tears of hers had hit the carpet under her in her lifetime. Sweat was no different than tears; it was always the same, just another form. A shadow, a ghost, and a puddle. She was fleeing and drowning in her own sadness. Therefore, I hurt for and with her. I later found out that Victor had fled upon the crowd gathering, and there was no body of Britton Chester to be found. Perhaps he was lost in the sea of tears.

This time period was the birth of a force without a face or name. True monsters were not men covered by sheets, but spirits wrapped in shadows. As matters within the city worsened and distrust became truth, propaganda arose. Did the artist show his face in his work? Did the writer show his passion in his memoirs? Did the thinker reveal the evidence behind his philosophy? Of course not. The author of the strange illustrations was a mystery inside of a mystery - a shell inside of a shadow. The first apparition came during the beginning riots and protests. There was an open wall outside of a furniture market in the town square that everyone passed by on a day-to-day commute. I walked to school one morning and came upon a crowd of people gathered before the alleyway. I struggled to see what the subject of interest was as I waited for the crowd to disperse. As they separated, I was left alone with the twisted mural on the brick wall before me. The once-cracked clay wall was then painted a faint sky blue, a colossal sun setting below the golden-etched horizon. The blue and yellow formed a magnificent pinkish purple shade, and the sunset marked much more than the end of a day. It was the end of an ideology, and I realized that as I stared into the beautiful desecration. I became lost in the colors, my soul and spirit bonded and blended inside the complex pigments. The next morning, a construction crew blasted out the wall with chisels and machinery, replacing it with brand new brickwork. The sculpture had been destroyed by the very philosophy that had created it.

Many times I saw Klaus's father parading around the city in his fancy red sports car that Klaus often was able to drive. I had not seen the man in weeks before I saw him one last time before he disappeared along with the city. I walked up to the car as the window rolled down and greeted the aging father. He looked rough and saddened, and I asked what was wrong. "Klaus is dead," he said plainly as a tear rolled down his face. "How?" I said, stifling my own sighs and depression. "Drugs. He was hit by a car," the man replied. I could only imagine Klaus getting wasted on LSD and walking in front of a car. Perhaps he thought he had seen Topher again and ran out to greet him.

"Where have you been?" I asked Luke in surprise and gratitude. "Hospital," he said solemnly. "Did they take care of the cancer?" I asked in hopeless faith. "They started my chemo," he said. "I see the hair," I said. "Oh no," he raised his hand. "I got bored," he laughed. Arnold had shaved his head out of boredom. That was one of the many reasons why I loved that motherfucker to death. "I came to visit. You've been gone six damn months," I said in humor. "I need a doorbell," he said. "Although I can't hear it." I would often have to repeat myself multiple times for him to hear me. He said he had gotten a rather nasty ear infection as a child and been rendered tone deaf. "My ex-wife told me I had selective hearing," he chuckled once more. I knew about that all too well. "What is your women situation like these days?" I joked with him one day. "As can be imagined," he replied vaguely. "The only thing that's gets hard these days is my *tongue*."

Being the supposed significant other of the leader's daughter, the increasing presence of Jack King made me constantly anxious - more than *normal*, of course. I would flinch and jump when anyone shouted or occasional gunfire could be heard in the vicinity. It was more of an anxious paranoia than any form of solid fear. Perhaps it was both. The idea of running into him while with his daughter nearly made me crawl out of my skin and head for the hills to search for a new one. As any dreaded flimsy wall of a fear tends to, mine came to an end the day it came true.

Ever since I had joined the King family and Sebastian - which was more of a broken household than any sort of structure - for a second visit that evening, I had not seen or heard from Jack King. His presence lived vicariously through Julia's stories and mentionings. She was an amazing storyteller. From what I collected, which was quite a bit due to her splendid description of detail, Julia King was a lot like her mother. I loved to listen to her talk about things, especially subjects she cared passionately for. In addition, tiny topics were made magical by her mesmerizing words as well.

Julia and I were eating lunch at the sandwich shop on Main Street when her father came through the door. I could tell by the way he carried himself and the way he casually looked over at us that he knew not of our presence. Perhaps he was merely an excellent actor. I had forgotten how tall and wide the man was; my philly cheesesteak started flowing the other way as soon as I saw him. The man behind the counter greeted him with a wave and ducked behind the liquor cabinet, returning with a bottle of whiskey in his hand. Jack waved him away as he pulled his silver flask from his coat pocket. As he turned to look at the menu on the back wall, he saw none other than yours truly on a lunch date with his missing, beautiful daughter.

"Noah Willowby, the man in charge!" he shouted. He had entirely forgotten about his order as he made his way over to our table. "Hi, sweetie," he said to Julia. As much as she appeared to be like her mother in nearly every way, I could not deny the resemblance between her and her father. The other customers in the restaurant looked at Jack in disdain for shouting in public, but he could care less. He *owned* the place, and every other place, for Christ's sake. Depending on who you asked, he might have even owned them. I hoped so desperately that that would be the end of the conversation - a mere hello. Switching my focus between Jack and Julia, I nodded my head awkwardly. I forced a happy, joking smile as Jack grinned at me like a lifelong friend. He shifted his focus to his daughter and resumed his smile. "What day is it, sweetheart?" he asked as if it was the most casual question in the world. There was so much emphasis behind it, as if her entire life depended on her answer. "It's November twenty-second. Friday," she answered. Jack nodded in remembrance and leaned against the table at ease. Punching me in the arm as a joke at first, he slowly knelt beside me and whispered something in my ear. Just above silence, I could barely make out the sound of his words. "Are you a Dreamer?" he shot at me. It caught me off guard. "What?" Julia asked. Jack King was gone, and Julia was questioning my blank, concerned stare. "Nothing," I shrugged as I blinked in my own hidden confusion. As I swallowed the rest of my sandwich, I caught a glimpse of the bloodstains on the street outside through the fogged-up glass beside us.

Julia and I grew closer and closer each time we encountered each other. I was crazy about her, which often lead to my questioning if what we had was real. As time marched on, I decided it was and that I *deserved* it, goddamnit. As far as a natural-occurring pattern goes, my life had been a rollercoaster of increasingly steeper dives and turnarounds, usually ending in an immense pool of vomit, and I was content with that. Some people are just not meant to have a pleasant life, and I had decided that it was I who would fill that position of a negative outlook. It suited me, and upon the happening of a positive change, it had to ambush me and incumb me like a parasite. I was in love with Julia King - I must admit that from the beginning. I had fallen in love with her the first time I had seen her, for she had become a dream in herself come to reality. If I was guaranteed an empty promise of the slightest possibility of happiness, I decided it was her. I also decided that it was time for her to meet *my* family. How could it be any worse than my encounter with her family? Besides, it was Julia's idea. She was on my case for weeks about meeting them. Her naive, open mind reached for the stars with that idea, but my family was the cloudiest night with an impending chance of rain. My mother was a seemingly passive aggressive woman upon first encounter, my father was a shry jackass, and my brother was the deepest part of that particular gene pool. I could only beat around the bush for so long, and the opportunity finally presented itself. I decided to face it and outstretch my hand in order to come to grips with it.

My mother immediately agreed to the idea as soon as I presented it to her. After all, get-togethers like that were right up her alley. She would harp at me about how selfish I was for never bringing her home and always taking advantage of her father's status, whatever the hell that insinuation was supposed to mean. Being the daughter of the definition of status had no benefits beside a shrouded connotation and the spark of rumors that were whispered to me throughout the years before I made her acquaintance. After several minutes of taking the most intense verbal damaging, she promised an extravagant meal to impress her, and we set the date for the coming Sunday afternoon. My father had no objection to the idea; he was getting a special occasion meal without having to take any names or fall off of a ten-foot wall, after all. On the contrary, Jacob had a field day once he found out. I had never been so brutally ribbed before in my life, and he could not hold a candle to my mother's light opinions. "When can Mom expect grandchildren?" he snorted. I had had enough banter from my brother. "Whenever you're sober enough to fuck some whore in the right hole," I said. He was more surprised than anything else, then anger set into his expression. Regardless, it shut him up. My father laughed hysterically as long as Jacob had his back turned. Perhaps I was right to say that while my mother was not in earshot.

Julia was delighted at the invitation. Sunday was once a day set aside for religious purposes, but that was long before the reign of Jack King. As you can most likely collect, Sunday had absolutely no trace nor a drop nor an ounce of religious mention in that place. It was just another day of work; there were no weekends in the city. Jack once said that the horse that stops for water never reaches the end of his journey, and the city continued to work in ignorant bliss like a silent machine. However, something about the first day of the week seemed even the slightest more still, as if the old way of life was on the tip of the tongue of a distant memory. I remembered it vaguely from my childhood so long ago. The people were more relaxed, trade was more scarce, and the city was just a little quieter on Sunday.

My mother kept her promise, as she always did. She seldom forgot anything - whether it be information or transgressions. Never had our house smelled so heavenly, filled with whiff after whiff of chicken, rice, vegetables, and fresh-baked bread. They may say a lot about my mother, but that woman could cook to meet anybody's standards. Her dessert could draw any soul in the city with a drooling tongue. Everything was finally falling together, at least for a moment. Despite the growing violent tension in the city around us, Julia and I grew together like soil and roots; perhaps that was what mattered most. I had just finished straightening my tie when the doorbell rang, following the previous shutting of an armored car door. It scared my already pounding heart out from behind my shirt pocket. My parents set the table as I came down the stairs to answer the door. I turned the knob as my breathing balanced out. The sight of her calmed me down immediately, just as it always did. Julia was a goddess whose presence demanded peace. Her long blonde hair fell just above the straps of her light dress, completed by a scarf wrapped around her shoulders. Her pale skin glowed radiantly in the dim light. Her eyes connected with mine, washing over them like ocean waves. She was absolutely stunning.

"Hi," she said softly, nervousness arraigning her voice. "Hi yourself," I attempted to hide my own anxiety. "You look good," she said, poking me awkwardly as she examined my outfit, which consisted of a tie, a tucked-in shirt, and shined shoes. My hair was neatly combed back with a little gel to keep it in place. My father told me I looked sharp. I valued his input despite my grudges against him - after all, we were far from spitting images of each other. As slick as I might have looked, I could never compare with Julia. "You always look good," I said, shooting a weak compliment in her direction, prompting that beautiful, quiet smile that captivated me every time I laid eyes on it. I invited her in by the hand and shut the door. I introduced Julia to my parents, and they spent several minutes getting to know her. I had never heard so many questions asked to any one person in my whole life. Fortunately, she answered each one as if it was the first. She was so patient and kind. From the look my parents gave her, I was positive that they approved of her. They admired her birth-given status in the shadow of her father - their king and their god. My brother sat slouched in the chair in the corner, his tie loose and his shirt untucked. He never took his eyes off of Julia's dress. Even though he was four years older than I was, I was much more mature and well-mannered in every way.

"I hope you like chicken," my mother said cheerfully. "It's my favorite!" Julia replied. We all casually made our way into the kitchen, drawn by the spectacular smells of the various foods. My mother shot me a strict glance, directing my hand to Julia's chair, as if I did not already know to pull it out for her anyway. My parents were undeniably strict, terrified of a marred reputation on their part. "How's your father?" mine asked Julia. "Oh, he's feeling sickly lately," she surprisingly replied. Jacob sat up. "Even the *immortal* get sick," he muttered in interruption before slouching back into the chair. "He says you're his best driver," she said, immediately winning over my father's blessing and changing an awkward topic. I had never seen my father blush before that moment. His graying beard grew just a little bit darker as he smiled, proud of the admiration of his work. Impressing Jack King was not a simple task by any means, and he thirsted for recognition and self-worth.

We all eventually sat down at the table to dine on the fantastic feast my mother had so graciously and tentatively prepared. Everyone stuffed themselves to the brim, as people tend to do in the face of anxiety of a new situation. Avoiding conversation was key to a settled stomach, and what began as piles of steaming food transitioned to stacks of empty plates. I barely had room room for dessert, but I always seemed to make room. My mother cleared the dinner plates and passed around smaller dishes for chess pie. My diabetic escapade ended when Jacob let out a monstrous burp. My mother slapped him on the back of the head with a spatula as my father cussed at him, prompting a laugh from Julia and I. Their reputation had just had its throat slit, and their rosy cheeks bore all the stops.

The night soon grew old as everyone's eyes threatened to close up as our mouths had done after the wondrous meal. Julia said goodbye to my parents and managed a slight mumble to my heathen of a brother - I was truly proud of her. I grabbed my coat as we stepped out into the chilly night air. My father offered to drive her home, but she politely declined, to both of our gratitudes. I imagine he wanted to have a beer with Jack King, or perhaps even get the honor of throwing his empty can away and wiping up his drool in gratitude for his tiny compliment. She perked up when I said I would walk her to the subway station; after a wonderful evening, it would end with some alone time between us.

Julia and I had little to say around the first few blocks - the union of our spirits spoke louder than any utterance. We walked along, hand-in-hand, just enjoying the cool breeze and the beautiful silence. She could have very simply called one of her security guards to retrieve her at a monent's notice, but perhaps the silence meant everything. She told me how she adored my family, which surprised me; I assumed my brother was grouped in there somewhere. Those were the only words spoken along the peaceful walk home. Once inside the subway, she kissed me and turned to go. I could tell something was bothering her, and the wounded stride in her step told me it had to do with going home. I knew she was unhappy living with her father. She always told me how lonely it was on our nearly everyday walks around the city.

Julia loved to get out of the house, and it warmed my heart to know that she wanted to be with me more than anything. At last, I finally *meant* something to someone, and I was eternally grateful that it was her. I watched as Julia turned the corner and boarded the train, then turned to go my separate way. I sometimes felt strange presences watching me in the dark; I slept with a desk lamp on, for crying out loud. It was a relatively short walk back home, but the constant feeling of being followed ultimately made my return feel like ages. No matter how quickly I walked, I could not shake the chills from the back of my neck nor the ghosts of the city on my heels.

That was just the way it was in the city - it would feel so normal, so *right*, and I would grow accustomed to it, only for the horrible dreams to return. The curse of my unconsciousness would then proceed to leak out into the roots of the city, spreading evil and terrible acts as a result of my faulty subconscious. As the dreams worsened and intensified, the city was always soon to follow. The dreams returned on the night that Julia joined my family for dinner. I witnessed things that felt so real, only to jerk awake into the puzzle of separating what was reality and what were strands of the torturous dreams. They would show me unnatural and sickening things; I saw mass murders, executions, and other unimaginable, inhumane acts of abomination. I had always heard people talk about dreams coming true as a *desirable* thing. Something that was *wanted*. I found out that nightmares also came true as well, for my very existence became one. What started as merely witnessing things, the dreams evolved into the disgusting deeds happening to me. It was one thing to watch others suffer; it was accompanied by its own emotions. Experiencing suffering firsthand was a completely separate being altogether. Over time, it felt like I was slowly losing feeling; I had become numb both in the dreams as well as reality. I was a slave in every aspect; I had simply lost control.

As the dreams intensified and became utterly unbearable, the chaos within the city was also spiraling out of control. The sparse executions slowly transitioned into groups of these strangers, then to crowds. All walks of life in the city were susceptible to this metaphorical disease. People of every race, gender, and occupation would simply disappear, never to be found again. Julia and I continued to spend time together walking around the city nearly every day around noon, which was when Jack King ventured into the city to make his rounds. School days were only three hours long; it was believed that school should accompany experience in our final year of education. After all, I had grown up in the new system, and as far as Jack King was concerned, I was ready to face his world. My peers hurried from the school building in a violent rush, but I shoved my way through the crowd for a *different* reason. Being with Julia evaporated the negative from my life as the sun does for the morning dew. Julia was my sun - the light of my life. Spending time with her alleviated the awful memories and constant mentality of it all. But as soon as the horrendous acts seemed to almost fade away and I would begin to forget, I was exposed to yet more destruction - both personally and within the city. I almost expected peculiar and gruesome things to happen, as they always had before. Once you witness the same thing repeat itself for an extensive period of time, you grow accustomed to it. My senses had become so keen and advanced that I no longer flinched at gunfire or explosions. I no longer blinked at any stray movement. I would feel no sympathy at screams or begging. I would just stare into space, cradled in my emotionally-void shell until it was all over. That time would not come soon enough; I had been emptied of all emotion. I was too far gone. Whether I was awake or asleep, I was subject to complete and utter destruction.

I scoured the marketplace for the finest ingredients two days prior to walking into the then-immaculate train station. I heard the squeaking of the wheelchair roll into view as I opened my arms in surprise. "What is all this?" Arnold said in surprise. "Time for dinner," I spoke simply. That evening, we prepared a masterpiece of a meal. Arnold spoke of his magnificent salsa recipe in which I was privileged to see prepared right before my eyes. The dark and dim kitchen smelled of onion and spice that night as we dried homemade tortilla chips and snacked on the perfected salsa appetizer in the cozy apartment-style home. Arnold also spoke of his love for omelets, and so he sautéed mushrooms and onions to mix into the massive six-egg pans. Whilst he mixed eggs and melted butter, I was occupied with the combining of heavy whipping cream and cream cheese. My stomach had an undying lust for Alfredo sauce, and I sought to perfect my own influential recipe. We were careful to make detailed notes of our recipes on a notebook set to the side as we cooked. I poured flour and eggs into a bowl and formed homemade egg noodles to mix in with the delicious sauce, and before long, we topped off an Italian main course with leftover mushrooms and onions. We sat around the cozy wooden table like a grandfather and grandson would and dined on the delicious homemade feast. We had a dessert of raspberry cream rolls and sipped on none other than Arnold's pumpkin whiskey. "Thank you, by that way," he said to me after a generous swig. "For what?" I had long forgotten. He pointed to the walls and smiled. I was appreciated as well as wanted, and at last, I had found *home*.

It was within the conversations with Stephan that he made me vow that upon a day off, I would bring him some of my homemade Alfredo sauce, and how could I let down the wielder of the eighth wonder of the world? I simply could not. I caught Stephan outside of the marketplace on his fought-for break and sat down the heated bowl before him. "There you go," I said. He picked up the fork and ate the entire contents before speaking a word. Looking up at me as he swallowed, he finally uttered a sound. "Be my cook," he said as he complimented the flavor and savor. "I would - if only you favored Marvel," we shared another laugh. He blew a cloud of smoke and handed me the bowl. "My recipe is better anyway."

Stephan told me about an object such as a scratch-off ticket in the old world. I had never heard of such a thing. He said that you would buy a dollar value ticket and upon a stricken luck of chance, you could win millions. This appalled me, mainly because paper meant nothing. *Paper to buy paper to win more paper.* Hugh explained to me in a rather pissed off manner about something known as a Roth IRA and how he had invested thousands a year since he was eighteen years old. He said that the world had ended right as he was about to cash it out and become a millionaire. He would then slam his fist on the ground in anger before pulling out a set of blueprints. "I would be in that mansion on the hill," he said to me. I had seen blueprints like that before with Joshua Peterson. His designs for a water-powered car appalled me. "You don't need money for that," I told him. "Only the right tools. I know a guy," I smiled.

I had pushed carts for nearly four years before an opportunity presented itself to me. There had been an opening of position in the library to destroy creative pieces of literature and copy historical and evidential works, and so I walked away from what I had known and loved for many years and took to what I had desired and wondered about. I later found out that I had met veterans, former musicians, and artist of all kinds. They were all hidden and jaded behind the mysterious medication that had overtaken the entire world in that city.

School shootings had always been a paradoxical topic to me. Sparse tragedies shed light on the fact that the portrait of the American dream had been tattered and torn somewhere amidst the bliss and destruction. In my head, we brought it upon ourselves. The old way of life thrived on the teachings of what to do in the event of an active shooter entering a structure and taking lives, and that was *enough* for a limited-minded society. But to me, I saw a void in the twisted instruction. What would we do in the event that the kid next to you pulled out a gun from his backpack and let everyone have it? What *could* be done? How do you prepare for that? And also, who is to blame? Of course, *psychopaths* are to blame for harming children, but in the event of a child harming another, who it to be put at fault? Is it within the realm of the parents' supervision and child-rearing? Is it in the hands of the *society* that causes it? Or could it possibly be the fault of the victim that brought it upon themselves? Lastly, is it such a horrible occurrence if children that did not need to grow up and reproduce only to spread more evil and hatred were the ones that were murdered? In my mind, if someone needed to die, then it was someone's right to take it upon themselves. You see, perhaps these questions are fated to be answered upon circumstance, and my dear friend, the blame is not so straightforward to place in the heat of the moment.

The school building was a massive brick campus with fields on two sides, woods on one, and an entrance to the street on the fourth. The system housed nearly fifteen-hundred children from age five to age eighteen, each third year complete with their own wing. The last wing was the largest - that of the final year students, which consisted of twisted hallways and stairwells with metal railings. The fields and ranges were available to each instructor as Jack King saw fit, and school was never dull or boring. Three hours a day were spent with your own age group learning real-life applicable skills. I loved to read and write, and so naturally, the library was my second home. Although I loved numbers and patterns, the only mathematics I pursued were tables of contents and directories. In my mind, I hated chapters because of the way they shattered the continuation of a story, and so numbers became obsolete to me. I spent my time lost in the library, organizing the thousands of books that had been salvaged from the old world. The librarian, an old crotchety lady in her late seventies or early hundreds, instructed me to collect and burn any piece of text that had to do with the creativity of the old world. As expected, I halfway obeyed and halfway dissented; I would collect the history literature and take it home with me to read late at night when the rest of the world went dark. If she ever found out, she would damn me to hell and Jack King would castrate me, but why on earth would they want to shroud a history such as the one of the previous system? As twisted and dark as it was, I loved history and kept it to myself as my own secret world in which I knew we had evolved from. It spoke of humanity as a whole, and no matter the minuscule sparks of morality, the greater part was a monstrous existence and in my opinion, it could and never would be corrected. It was always about being above another, and that was what put me above the rest of the world - *knowledge*.

I heard the banging of the handrails before any shots were fired. It echoed through the halls like bells in a steeple, and the whistling rang out like sirens as the world grew silent. The lights flickered as the first shots were fired into the ceiling, dust billowing around the corner as the wing went dark. I was up to my knees in stacks of books, organizing the letter M from *madame* to *mystery* when I heard the first shots echo through the hollow and silent library. I was no stranger to the sound, but I had never heard it within a building where escape can be limited. They startled me; I tripped over the surrounding books as I crept out of the aisle quietly and collectively, erasing all of my work for that morning. I peered around the corner and through the glass windows of the library wall, jumping once more as the second shots came closer. I heard another sound as I imagined the shooter coming closer - a ringing echo that resonated through the walls and vibrated up my spine like a bell striking noon. A cold, empty whistle accompanied the third shots as I saw a shadow come around the corner and stop under the glass dome rooftop of the commons level. I knew it was time for school to dismiss, but upon the sounds coming from the hallways, each wing seemed to remain on silent lockdown. The shooter had his back turned to me as I knelt down behind a shelf, my heart racing as I struggled to make out his identity. I could dissect a masculine walk through the thick leather pants and dark hood, an assault rifle gripped by an unshaking hand. He spun around in each direction and turned toward the library. Dark sunglasses covered his eyes below his bald head. He maneuvered his way forward into the adjacent hallway, and the tiny bit of testicle I had crawled into my throat as I cowered back below the shelf. I knew Julia would have wanted me to follow him despite the danger, but I could not do it alone. I kept my breathing silent as I heard his footsteps grow ever-so-further away and another array of shots get louder. I heard screams that time, and I knew silence was safety no longer. The slaughter continued for seemingly hours, shot after shot, scream after scream. I covered my ears in cowardice as I struggled to understand what was happening, and by the time the shooter ran out of bullets or targets and rushed out of the shattered glass door, it was too late.

I later heard through the shrouded grapevine that a student no older than myself had hidden his father's weapons in his bag and pulled them out in class and began shooting. The boy had slaughtered his entire class of thirteen witnesses before roaming the halls for his next victim. Some in classrooms adjacent said the thirteenth bullet was either for himself or the teacher, and some would say they heard her beg for her life as he chose her. When he could not find his next victim, he smashed the door and made his escape. There was no protection nor precaution for this happening in that world or the previous one, and it was the consequence of their ignorance upon the blood of their children. As I covered my ears for a silent eternity, something within me pulled me to my feet and followed the sound of footsteps. I shoved my way through the crowd as I struggled to see the scatter of the limp bodies lying amongst the bloodied tile floor beside the shattered window. As I looked down at their lifeless faces, I saw the ghastly distortions of Strauss and Joshua Peterson.

Following the incident, school became extinct altogether. The building was sealed shut and the campus became overgrown. I never saw the inside of the classroom, and groups of teenagers said the blood was never washed from the walls. The burial of the nearly twenty victims came as a violent and angry awakening as matters in the city began to worsen. I had lost my two purest friends, and a part of me had been also been fatally wounded. I cried that day for the first time with a legitimate reason, for theirs were the first deaths that impacted me personally as opposed to the reaction of my family's grief. It was in the human mind to find blame in anything but self, and I turned my eyes to a different source. As my peers pointed clean fingers at each other and vastly stretched conspiracies, I had *witnessed* that part of history. I had seen the shooter, and I had a terrible rumbling in my stomach at the very thought of my theory. I often passed Patrick Jones on the streets as he made his way past his father's old market, where a much older stain of blood lie. He was rumored to have had a brain tumor, and the surgeon required the shaving of his head for surgery. I had heard that the operation had failed and that the mass was too volatile to remove. I never told a soul what I had thought or what I had seen, but that awful trembling would make its return every time I placed him under the weapon and behind the disguise, coming for revenge on Sawyer.

As weeks passed, the city herself began changing. It was no longer a golden metropolis; it had shed its old skin and taken on a gray and gloomy hue. The streets and buildings seemed to crack and break down into an ancient crumble of dust. Even the air seemed to be a shadow of the people living within the monster of a city. The entire world was then a melancholy existence in every detail and aspect. There could be no prediction as to who would be the next head on the other side of the gun. Fear spread throughout the neighborhoods and apartment buildings, leaking into each and every house and dormitory and trickling into every mind and soul. People began hibernating in their homes like winter bears in a forest fire, hiding from the *animals* outside. Only the courageous or the foolish braved the dangerous streets. The question that had buried its head since the beginning of the city had begun to rear it once again - *safety*.

To make matters worse, shop owners and store clerks began to protest the barbaric means of crowd control within the city. They stood on street corners, shouting and attacking any officer that attempted to disperse them. The military officials no longer played games of catch with the children of the city, and neither did their fathers, for that matter. School was always taken for granted as not only a privilege, but also as an unknown necessity. To be quite honest, the makeshift teachers never taught me anything my books had not already spoken to me anyway. I had no problem with school being cancelled, but the absence of my brothers cut deeper than any bullet ever could. However, I started to put up a fight when my mother would no longer let me leave the house. She appointed my brother to keep me inside at all costs while her and my father were at work. That system lasted for about a week until my mother quit her job. She did not talk much about it - or rather, she really could not bring herself to. It affected her to an unbelievable extent. All I knew was that she was standing right next to the chief executive of her office building when he was shot in the head for opening the door with his mind. It had scarred my mother to the point where she would shake randomly and stutter her words. That sort of abnormal happening could have had a lot more severe effect on a woman of her stature; she was rather lucky she was not rendered dumb and mute. Regardless, I knew two things. The secretary was a government official. Jack King would go as far as to turn against his own people to eradicate whatever he was after. I also knew that my mother was weak-minded. I would usually think of myself as selfish, but that was before I had changed along with the city. She had seen absolutely nothing.

A week after the slaughter, I brought myself to Joshua's door and knocked slowly and solemnly. Inside my heart, I had wanted to come visit earlier, but I did not want to upset Miss Peterson any further than she had to have already been. The door opened and I was greeted by Shane, who welcomed me inside the dark and silent home. He was quiet and direct, pressing a finger to his lips. "She's been asleep for days," he whispered. "I won't be long, brother," I patted him on the back in empathy. "You're welcome to his things if you find anything of use to you. She hasn't been in there since it happened. I tried to sort through it, but I can't. Feel free to take whatever you want," he said before disappearing into the dim-lit kitchen and pouring a glass of the clear liquid, downing it in one drawl - forgetfulness washing over him once more.

I turned the doorknob and stepped inside the cramped and cluttered workspace that yearned for the presence of its master. I pulled the metal cord on the desk lamp and the yellow light cast shadows across the cozy room. I cleared a space off on the bed and sat down, taking in just how much Joshua had written and created. I folded the random notepads and blueprint folders aside and tossed miscellaneous screws and bolts into a box beside the bed. There was no way I could rummage through and organize the entire laboratory of sorts, and I began to lose myself in the scribbles and notations along the walls. The bombardment of ideas without a creator became too much for me, and I stood up to leave. As I reached for the lamp once more, I caught a glimpse of the design sketched under the light. Joshua was a driven and determined inventor. When he ran out of paper or pen, he would scratch his ideas into the wooden desk, especially vital changes or foundations he dared not forget. He told me his mother nearly ripped him a new asshole when she saw it, but her son's creativity and determination outweighed the marred piece of furniture.

I sat the stacks of papers on the bed and pulled the chair out to examine the design etched into the oak. There were notes scratched into the margin, labeling parts of the sketch like a diagram. *Fiberglass frame. Electrical wiring. Laser projection and cornea encasement. Knobs and dials for increased tint on left. Personal size and fitting on right.* I read the knife-work and put it all together; my hand became splintered as my fingers came to the edge of the desk. The desktop was *removable.* I lifted the heavy wood and placed it on the bed. Beneath lay a single object - the final invention of Joshua Peterson - my *sunglasses.* Sunglasses were a stretch; there were no lenses in the frames, for Christ's sake. I lifted the frame up and felt the light, sturdy material. The thin, dark sides felt almost like plastic; there were two knobs on either side in an even proportion, yet the lenses were empty. I was confused at first, but I rolled across the floor in the chair with the frame in hand and studied the design once more. I placed the empty glass behind my ears and over my eyes, looking down at the prehistoric-style writing. I turned the right dial first, and I felt the heat of the wiring inside the fiberglass case buzzing in my ears. I looked in the mirror atop the clouded dresser and the almost-glass lenses surrounded my eyes, though absent of color. A perfect fit. I turned the left dial that time, staring at the lamplight. I turned it all the way, and I could not see the rays. I rotated it to the middle position and pulled aside the drawn curtains, the horrid sunlight affecting me no longer. The creation was perfect, and I swore to cover my eyes when I avenged the death of the master who had crafted them.

Matters within the city grew ever worse, and I confided in Sawyer as a brother more than my own. Sneaking out was always his area of expertise, but had I not dared escape that house on the day of my best friends' murder, it would have swallowed me up and digested me. My mind circled with the things I had seen and heard, and I knew Sawyer had no place to go. He would roam the sidewalks and city streets to avoid his stepfather, yet he would not take up work within the city. There were always people who dreamed of success without wanting to sweat and bleed, and Sawyer Jennings was such an aspirer. He dreamt of shoes that never became worn and clothes that never became tattered and torn - things he had never had as a child and could then take for his own. I met up with him outside of our neighborhood, away from sight and earshot of my house along the rear of the development. The street was silent and the air was grim and smoggy, a smell of wet fur in the air. Sawyer stood nonchalantly on the other side of the street, hands in his pockets and back against the brickwork. I could only barely make out his characteristics as I whistled to him, announcing my presence. He looked blindly puzzled through the smoky fog and grinned as he stepped out into the street. I saw the shadow of the vehicle before I heard the horn; the driver had not lights on despite the necessary conditions. The steel front bumper collided with Sawyer's left hip, wishboning his body into a V-shape as he was thrown into the air. The scene before me slowed down as my heart beat faster and faster, adrenaline pumping like a train across a one-mile track. The truck did not stop as the wooden bed squeaked the shuddered, throwing apples across the street like abstract cannonballs. I knew whose truck it was - the prideful shop owner would not stop and face his crime, whether it be by chance or by premeditation. I heard the engine fade into the distant smoke as panic set in. I rushed to the limp and lifeless body of my best friend - the unlikely and impossible icon that had sought me out and shown me the world through an unbounded eye was dead. I beat on his chest in emotionally agony as I thought of Topher and Klaus - those two would have a list of drugs that would put Sawyer back on his feet right in that moment. But they were gone; all of them were dust. I laid in the middle of the street with him for seemingly hours. He had no family but his drunkard of a stepfather, and he would have cared as much about Sawyer's passing as Frederick Jones would have. I wiped my dreadful face and hoisted my closest companion over my shoulder, pulling him onto the sidewalk.

The only reason I wanted to leave the house was to see Julia. Being the daughter of the highest man on the totem pole, she had maximum security over her head. Jacob had the ego of a squadron of security guards, so Julia and I had somewhat of equal protection. Somehow, we both managed to sneak out and see each other, even if it was until one of us was caught and brought back to our prison. After a considerable amount of time, we did not even want to sneak out anymore. It was not worth the battered bruises Jacob would give me as a result of those that came from our father onto him. The city was too hostile of an environment, and absolutely nowhere was safe. Matters only grew more brutal as the walls around us closed in and tensions rose in every sort of fashion. If I was not awoken by the awful dreams, gunshots and explosions would pull me awake once again. The only part of the real world left was slowly evolving into an impossible nightmare - especially when my parents were taken away into the endless abyss of death that had swept over the city.

Chapter IX
The Inevitable Abyss
(The Ones Who Take, the Ones Who Fight, and the Ones Who Suffer It All)

Over the past few months, Julia had fully described to me the pain and anguish of losing a parent. I felt her heartbreak as I saw it in her eyes; however, nothing compared to the shattering feeling of experiencing it for myself and losing my own. Both of my parents were taken away from me at once in a sick sense of forced abandonment, as selfish as it may sound. I later found out that my parents were caught in the crossfire while risking a trip to the market. I constantly put the blame on my own head as various scenarios raced through my broken mind. *Maybe if they had not bought that for me, they would still be here.* I could not forgive myself for the selfishness that had taken over me and that the dreams had forced into me. It was absolutely devastating to live life after that. It was only my brother and I in that silent, haunted home. I realized that my home was not the four cracked walls I dwelled in nor the four massive walls that confined the city, but Julia in herself was my home in which I found safety and security. Jacob and I said not one word to one another. I rarely crossed his path, and he rarely crossed mine. It was easiest to mind our own businesses as we mourned and dealt with our own predicament separately. That was just how it seemed to us. We had never been able to work out anything in the past, and the death of our parents was not exactly an appealing moment to start.

Jacob and I barricaded ourselves in the house; we pushed the couch in front of the door and boarded up the windows from the inside. We made sure to stay in the middle of the house, from which little sound could escape into the whispering city. Our food supply was abundant, but we made sure to ration it properly amidst the depressive aura from the city that had leaked into the

204

home. It was a very watered-down version of life - only a drop of water running down the side of the glass, only to evaporate into nothing once again. I carried out the basic functions of life, but it was not because I was *trying* to live. If it had not been for Julia, I cannot be sure what would have stopped me from walking out into the city until I was freed from that life by a silver bullet. My brother and I hummed along to the sound of each other sobbing, passing time that refused to move along. Everything we had established and grown accustomed to was crumbling down once again, just as it had done before the city. Life always had a way of repeating itself. I honestly did not know how much longer I could hold on at that point. We took turns sleeping for hours at a time, but no matter how much I slept, I was always drained of energy and the will to go on. I began to lose weight and my skin became cold and light - much like the thin complexion of Julia. Perhaps anemia was contagious. I could feel my strength slowly deplete day by day. It seemed that the only peaceful thing that came was when the dreams stopped altogether. Sleep was then an escape from the nightmare of reality. I slept all the time, which was then nothing but slipping in and out of the endless, pitch black void. Life soon became repetitive and quite melancholy as it always had, an endless cycle in which I so pondered an infinite end.

I wrapped the belt through the waistline of my black pants and tucked my shirt inside the band. I wiped my eyes as I folded the collar down and pulled the socks onto my leg hair, stinging and pulling dozens like tears from heartstrings. I wrapped my fingers around the cold fiberglass frames of my sunglasses as I pulled the black jacket around my shoulders. The city was covered by clouds as it usually was, and I pressed the button on the side of the glasses anyway. It was a *dark* day, and I was alone. I would be as dark and clouded as the city was. That day was a melancholy blur, and it often pains me to reminisce upon it. Jacob and I matched our suits in a pitch black harmony, arms around each other's shoulders as we made our way from the house, to the sidewalk, and to the cemetery where several dozen others had gathered for the ceremony. I kept my head down as the diggers dug a deep ditch where the ghosts of my parents would struggle against the dirt for eternity. As the last shovel full of soil was tossed aside, the first digger nodded at me. It was time. Jacob and I each took an end of the first casket and lifted it into the first hole, setting it into the crevice like a nest. My mother was at rest at last, for she had finally found peace. My father had died in honor and protection, killed by his profession. He had found rest long ago outside of himself and his family, and even on that day, I resented him. I saw not the burial as tears streamed down my face for my mother.

My mind often created images in the dark as I slept, devoid of sleep and exhausted from my thoughts. I had left the window open in that time as the autumn air flowed into my bedroom, moving the curtains aside like ghosts as I sat up. My feet hit the floor as I reasoned that it had to be at least midnight if not after. Jacob slept on the couch downstairs, most likely intoxicated and unconscious beyond function. On that night I had awoken to the sound of scratching and limbs cracking. Once awake, I found it quite difficult to resume my rest, or whatever portion I could manage in that time. The thoughts and fear would seep into my mind like the changing season, and I was nothing but a falling leaf, subject to the relentless wind. The oak tree outside hung below my second story window, the limbs smacking the siding upon a storm. I remembered the many times Valerie would climb up the stair-step limbs and watch me sleep. My mind was as clouded, cramped, and cluttered as a November sky, a packed desk, or a miscellaneous trunk - shaken and taken by the wheel. My heart hurt with remorse and longing, and my head fell into my hands. I could no longer hear the faint rustling of the breeze outside as the demons of my past crept into my quarters as well as my soul.

I felt the noose around my neck as I jumped with start, ripped from my thoughts like tree bark from a wooden trunk. The material tightened, cutting off my breathing as I struggled to turn my head. The assailant gripped my shoulders and wrapped his fingers around my ears. I felt his forefingers reach for my eyes as I reached over my head in defense. I found his neck and squeezed, the release of mine coming slowly and steadily. I gasped as the attacker lost his balance as stumbled onto the floor, his grip bringing me with him. I rolled to my feet as he struggled to his, and I was taken aback at what I saw. *Sawyer Jennings* stood up and stared me in the eyes, a look of hatred and revenge in his glare. In his hand was my father's scorpion belt.

I shouted in agony as he brought it across my bare back. "What the fuck is going on, Sawyer?" I shouted at him. "I watched you die!" He ignored me in his angry state. "Do you know what this is?" he cracked the leather belt across my chest as I turned the face him. I winced at the sting of the whip, engrossed by angry confusion. "Do you know where this came from?!" he shouted angrily once more. I nodded as he slapped the tight leather against my collarbone and neck. I toppled over as he kicked my legs out from under me. "This belonged to your father. Do you know where I found it?" he sneered, putting his foot in my side. I felt the belt smack my ribs time and time again in his furious attack. "It was under my mother's bed. Covered in her blood!" My vision blurred as the pain became unbearable; I writhed across the floor to escape his wrath. There was no way what he was saying was truth. I knew my father had stepped out of his marriage before, but he would never harm a woman. Even from his grave, he would never dream of betraying his morals. He had been set up; I was sure of it. I raised my hand in an attention to stop the onslaught of whippings.

"It can't be, Sawyer!" I shouted as he continued to crack the belt. My skin began to welt and drip blood. "It is!" he shouted. "He took her from me!" There was no reasoning with an angered bull. I began to lose touch with consciousness as I gritted my teeth in agony. I blinked back steaming tears clouded with fury and desire to retaliate, but I could not escape. His attack was relentless, my blood splattering across my floor and my bed in which I could never inhabit again. My walls were bolstered with crimson drops as I yelped and cried in painful fatigue. I fell unconscious as I was whipped repeatedly by a lie and a lost friend.

Pain is something that is witnessed in dreams and felt when awake, and upon my wheeze of waking breath, I understood the true severity of what had happened the night before. My skin was covered in blisters and peeled skin; dried blood caked the majority of my chest and back. My breathing was unsteady and painful. My eyes were bruised and swollen and my lips were cracked and sore. I attempted to stand but collapsed once more onto my raw backside. I could not stand; I was rendered helpless as my vision grew dizzy and my head grew weak.

"You're kidding me!" I heard a woman's voice exclaim. "Who did this to you?" my mother asked. I managed to turn my head as she knelt down beside me. Her appearance was light and nearly transparent, but she was there, and that was enough. "Mom?" I asked, blinking back tears and weakness. "I'm here, sweetie," she put her hand to mine. I felt no touch; she was beyond my reach. I felt my eyes close in fatigue once more.

"Holy hell," I awoke to the girl speaking. "What happened to you?" she asked as my eyes struggled to focus on her. "Valerie," I whispered, all I could manage. "I'm here," she smiled softly. "I love you," she said, touching me with a ghostly hand. I blinked back a single tear - perhaps the very one that she lost that night. "Not enough," I replied as she faded from my sight. My mind went blank again; she could never touch me even when she was alive.

"Mother Of Christ. Noah!" I woke up with a start. Jacob staggered through my doorway and fell to my side. He felt my neck for a pulse and elevated my head. "What happened? Who did this?" he exasperated. I was able, but I did not speak. I could not think clearly in that moment, and I knew my brother would want blood. I could not decide what I wanted in that moment. I was a piece of meat ready to be cured. "Nevermind. Don't talk. Let's clean you up, buddy. Stay with me, now." Up until that moment, I had seen no indication that my brother cared for me. Perhaps it is in the moment of great distress that true emotions show. I drifted in and out of consciousness as Jacob lifted me from the floor and carried me down the stairs. I felt the leather of the couch beneath my back - a rather *stinging* reminder.

When I was finally able to stay awake for hours at a time, my wounds had been cleaned with antiseptic and bandaged with white cloth. I sat up and looked around the living room; Jacob sat in the chair across from me. He pointed at the table beside me. "Eat," he ordered, his tone binding his forceful nature to his newfound geniality. I sipped the glass of water, nearly dropping the cup from my nimble fingers. I chewed the crackers and felt the cheese melt in my mouth; I had not eaten in what felt like days. My energy had been expired, and had my brother not been there, I would have perished on the upstairs carpet like a stain.

"When did you become a doctor?" I tried to joke in a rather painful utterance of a cheerful wince. Jacob and I had never been close at all, and asking questions felt odd and awkward. I was closer to strangers than my own family, for Christ's sake. "Marisa tried to teach me. I never paid it much attention until after she was gone. I still have her books upstairs." I had seldom seen emotion in his eyes, but in that moment I saw tears stream down his face with no attempt to wipe, stop, or hinder them. I considered telling him about the apparition of our mother, but I feared it would sever our bond, never to be realized or repaired ever again. I pondered describing Valerie to him in order to empathize and grow closer to him, but the idea faded from my mind as she had left my life. "Rest," he said. "I've got some more reading to do."

Although the mental destruction of the dreams had halted, the chaos outside only grew darker. One of the few reasons I got out of bed was to peer through the crack in the wood at the source of the horrific gunshots and the echo of screams. The doors and windows were sealed, but there was one loose board in the living room where I could gaze into the world outside. I checked about once a day, and believe me, that was all I wanted or needed to see. Matters grew progressively worse each and every day. Unruly members of the community had painted explicit graffiti all over looted houses and businesses, all of which pronounced evil against Jack King and his force. Trash, belongings, and bodies littered the streets along the city. No one risked cleaning up the city anymore; it just got uglier and more hideous by the events that took place within her. The city was a living creature, controlled by the inhabitants as if they were the organs that functioned to bring life to her.

As the sounds and screams of the attacks came further away from the inner city and spread outward, the question of our safety arose. I knew that houses had been looted; people were desperate in that anarchic state. My father had a military-issued pistol in his dresser; this arose yet another question in my mind. *If he would have had that gun with him, would he still be here?* Those thoughts were torturous, more wrenching than any cut or wound. I found the handgun in his drawer and kept it hidden from my brother. It was in the immense silence that I heard the whisperings of all I had lost, and I realized that I had lost myself and everything that made up my miserable existence - my life entirely up to and including that moment. I fell asleep with my forefinger against the trigger, my arm going limp from my temple with sleep as I urged myself to squeeze it and release my suffering. Just as *she* had done. I let Jacob hold onto it after that difficult time. Emotional pain was already unbearable; the last thing I needed was self-inflicted bullet wounds - at least ones that were not fatal. I went quite a while without touching the gun, but matters only got *worse*, as you can most definitely imagine. We had determined that most of our neighborhood had either taken cover or been killed, and we survived by laying low and keeping quiet. Being silent in those days was neither a choice nor an option. I will never forget the night when a looter attempted to break into our house to try and steal what little we had left. It was the middle of the night, when a scuffling noise outside had jerked me awake. As quietly as I could, I stepped out into the hallway and crept down the stairs one at a time. The commotion had woken Jacob up as well, and I saw him crouched behind the couch in the den as I lowered myself down beside him. He looked over at me and signaled for me to hide. I laid flat against the carpet behind the couch, as excruciatingly painful as it was. The man outside was then rapping his fists on the door and demanding that we open it. My brother pulled the hammer on the gun back and slid it in between two boards against the door. With one final signal to cover my ears, he pulled the trigger. A loud thud was the last noise we heard that night. We did not have anymore problems - or close calls, as they often were - after that. Perhaps the lifeless corpse outside of our front door was not exactly a welcome mat. The gunfire tapered off to the west of our neighborhood, beyond any dangerous means to my brother and I. All that was left was the sound of silence and the constant anticipation of something to happen, which was louder than ever.

Our once plentiful food supply soon began to run low as weeks inched toward and endless month in our prison-like exile. We had dined normally at first, but as our cabinets became more empty, our stomachs soon followed as we started to ration whatever was left. The depression and mourning of our losses had affected our eating habits, and it was time for compensation. We regretted gorging the food in mourning, and the idea of a supply run loomed in our heads until it became a violent necessity. The electricity began acting strange as well, not aiding the already frightening feeling of isolation and the looming sensation of being preyed upon. The power never reached one-hundred percent capacity ever again, but the lights began to flicker and fade and disappear more than they ever had. Soon, all light vanished from our lives for good. The water was soon to follow. Without light and water, we resorted to flashlights and cleansing our bodies with soap and cleaning products that were supplied to us when we first arrived in the city. There was never any use for them until that time.

Boredom also set in - a tortuous killer. As we coped with our parents' deaths, the days slowed to a consistency of tree sap running down the rough bark - we simply had nothing to do but sit, cry, and rot in a lengthy sleep. One gets sick of listening to the sounds of destruction, so we settled for board games. Cards became our favorite; poker was basically a routine with us. I soon discovered that Jacob was not as horrid of a person as I had thought. We had never been close by any means, but perhaps the best things start with forced opportunities. After a lifetime of being strangers, we were finally *brothers*. The current situation soon modeled that of the times before the city, when our family had cowered in the basement of our old home. The process of making the best of the fear, doubt, and the unknowing of what would happen next accompanied the memories was somewhat pleasant. That is of course until we would notice the two empty voids out of the corners of our eyes.

You can only stay semi-occupied for so long, as well as simultaneously denying hunger and thirst. The distant idea of a supply run grew closer and closer, evolving into a temptation, and eventually to an inevitable, vital mission. One night after a lethal loss of poker on my part, we constructed a solid plan. We would sneak out the back door, cover each other on all sides, and weave in and out of the houses surrounding ours. Neighborhoods had disgusted me for lack of privacy, but in that dire time, the circumstances were grand. There simply had to be useful items that had yet to be looted; our survival depended on it. That statement is almost comical; we had always looked down upon and even feared looters. We had defended against them and now we would become them. That was the poor man's rhetoric.

Jacob made sure the gun was fully loaded as he filled his pockets with extra ammunition. I grabbed a trash bag, which would hopefully be full by the end of our trek. We both equipped ourselves with a sturdy conscience and a clear mind before unblocking the kitchen door. He slipped out first, quickly followed by me. It was a different world entirely outside of the silent safety of the house which had never been home, but more of a placeholder in the new world. Fences were knocked down, doors were kicked in, and windows were shattered. The once tranquil city had become a wasteland of destruction. I had not seen the sunlight in weeks, and neither had the city around us. The sky was plugged with thick, gray clouds and a hazy fog of smoke and acidic air. The only audible sound was that of squawking birds circling overhead - vultures watching us as we became them. The slight fear brought a pang of regret over me, and by the shaking of the gun in my brother's hand, I knew that the feeling was mutual. I had never known him to be a coward, but Marisa's death had left him numb and void of grip.

Our first stop was our next door neighbors, the Johnsons. They were the typical newly-wed lovey-dovey couple that had a tendency to leave their curtains open. Jacob liked to have a peek inside every now and then when they were in the bedroom. Mr. Johnson and my father had had many arguments over that topic. As we slowly policed the house, there was no sign of romantic behavior, or any movement or sign of life at all, for that matter.

The Johnsons were gone. They had apparently packed up everything and taken cover before their ideology of a perfect life had died along with them. They were smart, but we could not help but curse them due to their lack of supplies. All we could scrounge up were a few cans of soup, a bag of peanuts, and an immense supply of condoms. Disappointment comes with every mission, I suppose.

We had slightly better luck with the Duncans', our neighbors on the other side of our house. They were an elderly couple, and there was no sign of them either. They had most likely found their way into the city to a shelter. That is, if there even was one that existed in that twisted place. They evidently had not taken much with them, wherever they went, because their pantries were stocked with all kinds of goods. We loaded boxes of cakes, crackers, cereal, bottled water, and oddly, hemorrhoid cream, into the large trash bag. After all, we did not know how long we would be stuck in our house. The antibiotic never expired, and we just might have been there long enough to need it one day. I highly doubted my brother and I would live off of or live like the elderly couple we were stealing from, and I prepared to die with an empty ass.

We raided several other surrounding houses in the neighborhood until it nearly became easy. Petty crime is simple when it is justified. We would patrol the grounds, double check for residents, and then quickly load up anything useful we could find. The bag soon became heavy with cans of vegetables, bags of chips, fruit, medication, water, and other useful items for an unmeasurable amount of cover. The only difference between us and the seemingly selfish thieves of the community was that we left a few belongings for any other passing individual looking for something to eat. We knew the feeling of need for those things, and so we empathized by showing the slightest bit of sympathy while still protecting and serving ourselves. That was what people did best, after all - look out for self with little regard for others.

The great divide was the amount of sympathy you were willing to show without losing yourself in the process. Our plan had seemed to work, and in great victory, we set off to return to the house, our home, and our stronghold, if you will. It was the place we had worked so hard to fortify, had killed to protect, and had bonded to keep together for our parents' sake and legacy. Their two sons had at last gotten along and acted like the brothers they were, and yet it was too late to make any difference or change any transgression.

Just as we rounded our street corner, Jacob dropped like a sack of potatoes. Our father's gun clattered to the pavement with a clanging sound. Somebody grabbed me from behind, and I dropped the sack of supplies we had worked so hard and valiantly to collect. The stranger spun me around, and I came face to face with what we were up against - a band of thugs of about five men. They all carried heavy firearms, which barrels were evenly divided between Jacob and myself. One of the men had hit my brother in the side of the head with the butt of his rifle, and he was obviously unconscious a few feet away. The largest man had me in a headlock from behind. For the first time, I was truly alone. Physical danger is a lot like mental danger, with one of the thousands of made-up scenarios coming to fruition. This feeling had no compare with the artificial emotion of loneliness I had previously felt. I was in danger, and I was truly terrified.

"My, my, what do we have here?" one of the men said, motioning for one of his henchmen to examine the contents of the bag. "We don't want any trouble, kid. There's already enough people getting hurt around here. Just cooperate, and we'll be on our way." His raspy voice was unforgettable in my ears. All of the robbers were similar in their greasy and wild manner, clad in tattered clothes and voices that had clearly been smoking for years. They reeked of alcohol and tobacco; I could barely breathe, both of the stench, the fear, and the anxiety running through my mind. I would rather die than confront, and although I had already torn them apart in my thoughts, I considered letting them take the things we had fought for and leave empty-handed to avoid nervousness or imminent danger. "How about you tell us what's in that bag, kid," he said. I thought for a moment. "Hemorrhoid cream," I said sternly. The man laughed a cold, fake laugh. A moment later, he stopped abruptly and ran the end of the gun into my ribs. "Oh, boy, you're gonna need it." He growled with the intensity of a wild beast. I was shaking uncontrollably. The other thug left the bag alone and drew a switchblade from his pocket. He held the long, sharp blade against Jacob's limp neck. "How about now, boss?" the ringleader said coldly. My mind was a race of a thousand horses. Had this happened only a week before, perhaps I would have gutted him myself. But Jacob was the only family I had left. My heart beat out of my chest, and my mind was in fight or flight.

The looter with the knife convulsed suddenly. His head turned three-hundred-sixty degrees. I heard the snap like a tree branch in a silent forest. The blade rose and slit his own neck, spilling a flux of blood like a broken dam over the handle and onto the street where so much had been spilled before it. The two bystanders soon followed, collapsing to the ground as their hearts beat out of their chests as mine did. The man behind me released me as he went into a torrential fit of spasms and uncontrollable foaming at the mouth, hacking away as blood leaked down his chin. He moaned in agony as death claimed him as well. As his men were slaughtered before him, the leader backed away slowly, fear in his glossy eyes. He raised his hands in surrender, prepared to run away at any moment. I felt a sudden push behind me, as if something was lifted from my back pocket - I immediately thought it was another attacker. Before another second passed, the cool metal of my father's gun passed through my fingers, and a silver bullet passed through the last remaining robber's skull. In my adrenaline-crazed stupor, I proceeded to gather the bag of resources, threw it over my back, and dragged my brother's unconscious body into our fortress before anyone or anything else found a chink in our armor.

I am not entirely sure what brought me to the doorstep of Patrick Jones that day. Perhaps it was revenge; perhaps it was for a certain degree of closure, if there was even any to find. I had suck out the door early in the morning before Jacob could either accompany me or stop me, and I opened the door silently and slipped inside. If there was someone there, it would be only Patrick; the farm truck was not in the driveway. Perhaps he had taken it out as he had weeks prior, but I felt a certain answer that he was there. I eased into the kitchen with my gun drawn, peeking around the corner and into the living room. I saw the body lying on the floor, not a drop of blood on his face or chest. Bullets lay around him, expended on others as opposed to himself - just exactly the way he led his life. A bottle of whiskey was tipped across the table, dripping in a steady flow what Patrick had not ingested. He had either drank himself to death or his brain had hemorrhaged from the cancer. Either way, he got what was coming to him. I stared down at his lifeless corpse with not an ounce of remorse in my soul. I thought of Joshua and Strauss - how innocent and undeserving they were of death. They deserved to inherit the earth, and yet they had been taken by the very demons that had corrupted it.

I sat between my bed and dresser as I clutched the notebook and pencil for what I hoped would be the last time. I had felt the gun and knew my way around it like the back of my hand, and it had become another's hand against me as it pressured me and urged me to make a decision. I had - I wanted to live no longer. It was only a matter of time. I pressed the pencil against the last page in the notebook and began to write a plethora of truth and   lies:

To whomever may find this,

Most likely, Jacob will come across this letter. I want you to know that I thoroughly enjoyed these last few weeks with you, brother. I am sincerely sorry for the many years we lost to ignorance and distrust. Perhaps in the next life we will be true brothers. It is only a matter of time, brother. On the off chance that Julia discovers this letter, I want you to know that you are the only woman I ever truly cared for. Your father started something so pure and just here in this city, but his greed and creed has overtaken this place as it has me. I can be a part of it no longer. I am truly sorry to the both of you. It is only a matter of time. Goodbye.

Noah

I tore the page out of the spirals, threw the empty notebook across the room, folded the paper across my pillow, and collapsed in the chair with the gun drawn and my eyes closed.

"That's what I call a sharp turn of events," I heard her voice say. Was it Julia? Was it my mother? No, it was someone else. It was Valerie, goddamnit. I frantically searched around my bedroom in hopes that for a single instant she would be with me once more. "Remember how you felt when you found my note?" she asked, absent of body. I thought. "Would you do that to anyone else?" she pressed. "Would you do that to me?" I grew angry at the irony in her words. "What does it matter?!" I shouted at nothing. I heard her voice no longer.

"You know she's right," his voice said. Not my father, Jack King, or Sawyer. It was Klaus. "Besides, only pussies leave

notes," I heard the comical tint in his apparition. I was alone once more.

"Everything alright?" Jacob peered into my room. "Yeah," I mumbled, waving him away. I crumpled the paper and tossed it across the room.

Our newfound supply of goods we had collected lasted us a solid month after the attack. What had happened only made us more attentive and put us more on our guard. We were constantly paranoid that other groups of looters would attempt to steal our belongings, as if the supplies belonged to us in the first place. Had we not stolen them too? It was a constant cycle of anxiety and further protection. We had the house set up with more security than Jack King's mansion, booby traps and contraptions alike. As our resources shrunk yet again, the same inevitable urge to go out again fell upon us as five bullets loomed in our minds to either be distributed to others or ourselves. Fortunately, we did not have to.

One afternoon during a fiercely uninterrupted, furious game of blackjack, there was a knock at the door. In all reality, there had not been any sign or evidence of robbers since our last supply run, but the restlessness and possibility kept them in our vision and led us to expect the worst. Jacob could not have gotten his hands on the the gun any quicker. We looked at each other half-nervously, half-prepared to do what was needed. We knew what we had to do. We pushed the couch, along with the television stand and a footstool, out of the way. The wooden planks served as extra protection, but it hindered any sight out of the window as to who was outside. There was a second knock right before we opened the door. We had long since decided to shoot any threat on sight. Jacob slowly turned the lock, and as the door slowly opened, he lost all control - whatever he had left, that is.

He hit Jack King straight in the nose with the handle of the pistol, perhaps out of precaution, possibly out of rage. Had he seen Jack before he decked him? Did it matter? Who would be angry? He had failed to protect his precious city and had waged a civil war within those walls. Blood ran down his nose as he reared back in shock and a fit of rage of his own. Before he could react, Jacob ran the fireplace poker into his ribs, doing some serious damage apart from his nose. Catching his breath, my brother stared at Jack King, who recovered rather quickly. With a look of murder in his eyes, he grabbed Jacob by his shirt collar and cracked his knuckles against his collarbone. He head-butted him and kicked my brother square in the chest, knocking him back against the couch.

Jack King set his nose, ran his fingers across his ribs with a subtle grimace, and stepped inside. He looked at Jacob, who was slumped against the couch in defeat with a clear apologetic and fearful look on his face. "Thanks for the hospitable invitation, you piece of shit," he growled. A minute after the scuffle, he looked at me. "Hey, there, Noah." I nodded. "I brought someone you might want to see," he said through a slight smirk. He stepped aside, and Julia walked through the doorway. We both ran and embraced each other. It had almost been two months since I had laid eyes on her. *Had I forgotten about her in the mourning of my parents' deaths? Did it matter?* There was no way we could have gotten to each other. Once again, I was forgiven my transgressions by the city's graces. I must have been a sight, but she looked identical to the last time I saw her. She always had the same aura of joy and happiness behind a silent shadow that warmed my heart. You had to earn her good graces or you got an empty look of pity, for I had the only key. She kissed my cheek, and I checked for angry glances from her father. *Father.* It sounded so strange to ponder that word after losing my own. It brought back so many memories. I felt a few hot tears gather in the corner of my eyes, but I managed to blink them away. I forced myself to believe that they were tears of joy out of seeing Julia. And they were. I was forgiven once more.

I welcomed both of the newcomers into the house and hurried to shut the door. Before I could pull the couch back in front of it, Jack stopped me. "That won't be necessary," he said coldly, tapping his hand on the holster on his belt. After thinking on the matter for a minute, I did not trust Jack King to protect us. He had failed at protection. Calmly, I pushed the couch back into its place in front of the door, prompting a slight grin from Jack King. I wondered if he could sense my mistrust. "I wanted to visit sooner, but I've been busy *cleaning*," he said proudly, as if it was already spring and he had just gotten rid of his old belongings. Jacob giggled a sarcastic laugh in front of the fireplace, wiping blood from his jaw. Jack glared at him, ready to draw his gun and put a bullet in him like he had so many people in the city. Before the recent months, I would have encouraged him, but now, Jacob was my only remaining family member. I felt quite different about him than I had when my parents were alive. I wondered if everything had happened for a reason. To bring us *closer*. *Why did it have to be that way?* I put that question out of my mind; I was numb to it.

As if by some sadistic coincidence, Jack King spoke again. "I'm so terribly sorry about your parents. They were dear friends of mine for a very long time." I did not believe his apology for one minute. I remained silent, blinking back more tears as Julia ran her fingers up my arm, comforting me. Jacob did not buy it either, though he handled it much differently. "What the hell is going on?" he mumbled under his breath and behind tears. "Excuse me?" Jack asked. "WHAT IN THE NAME OF THIS GOD FORSAKEN CITY IS GOING ON?" my brother screamed. Tears were then flowing down his cheeks - angry, fiery tears. I had never seen him like that. He had always been passive aggressive and closed off. My whole family was that way; it was in our blood to be silently angry and plotting your death while smiling and shaking your hand. It was quite a change; he had buckled under the stress and pressure of everything. After all of that time, I thought it would have been *me*. After all, he knew nothing. "What do you mean?" Jack pushed. "Why are these people doing impossible things? Why is everybody dying? Why are your officers killing innocent people?" Everyone in the room was surprised at his outburst. Everybody except Jack King. He sat silently, waiting.

"This is what my workforce is trained to do," he started. "These 'people' you speak of are criminals. *Outlaws*. They must be stopped. These people are the same breed that brought about the end of the world so many years ago. The ones that have the ability to make dreams reality. Of course you have no idea because you're a simple-minded piece of shit. They do not belong here, just like you. Not in my city. But I need you here, Jacob Willowby. I'll be damned before I let this city fall." Jack sat calmly, staring at Jacob. "You're damned, alright. This city fell with the rest of the world. Let it die." Jack did not move a muscle. After a few moments, he continued. "We cannot capture them; they will escape imprisonment. We cannot plead to them; they will retaliate. My people are trained to eradicate them from this city to protect these innocent citizens. That is what it comes down to. Protection of this city. And I will kill every last one of them until she is safe." Jack remained still. "If it continues at this rate, there won't be any people left," Jacob shot. A wide smile spread across Jack King's face as he turned to me. "Even if you were the last one left, it would be worth it." He laughed a hysterical, crazy cackle. *"Are you a Dreamer, Noah Willowby?"* I had heard that phrase a thousand times before, both in reality and the dreams. I had accepted that it was not real, and that it only took a simple declination to bring back reality. *"No," I said calmly.* The dreams had stopped, and that was reality. Right before my eyes, right before my brother's eyes. *Julia's* eyes. Silence ensued for an eternity after.

"You boys are probably wondering why I came here," Jack said. Jacob and I nodded. "Not only to express my condolences for your parents, but Julia was driving me insane to come see you, Noah. But upon my visit to this area, I see that it is no longer safe here. Nowhere is safe right now. Temporarily, of course. I need to gather all of these people left as I did before. It is a cycle, and it worked before. A *refinery*." I finally spoke up. "It hasn't been for a long time." Jack nodded, halfway sympathetically. "I have come here to retrieve you boys," he said. "Retrieve us?" I inquired. "Others will live in shelters under my protection, but you boys are different. Yes, I want you two to come live with us in my mansion." Julia threw her arms around me. A sigh of relief escaped my body. I was going to live with Julia under the most heavily guarded location in the city. Was I a selfish bastard? Did we not deserve it? We had *slaved* for that city. "I am rounding up the remaining people and providing a shelter for them in the town square. But since I know your family personally, I'm sure we can find room for you in our home. After all, it *is* just us and Sebastian." Jack King winked at me; I remembered how massive the mansion was, and how kind Sebastian was. I was truly overwhelmed with excitement and relief, as well as regret and worry that I did not deserve what was being offered to me.

Jack instructed us to go get our belongings together, and even my brother heeded his suggestion. As openly selfish as he was, his silence expressed gratitude and reverence for the fact that he was being helped. Jacob went off to gather his things, and I climbed the stairs to my room. I remembered that my father had given me two of his backpacks from his Army days. He had only given them to me to keep safe and to use, that of which Jacob could not do. The bag smelled like dust and leather as I opened it up. I reminisced on old stories my father had told us about the backpacks. I zoned out as I lost myself in the memories. I silently folded my clothes, gathered my most valuable items, and packed everything inside the bag as images of my father dragging the bags through deserts and mountains and the things he carried on his journeys drifted through my mind. None of that mattered, however. He had died along with the old world he had fought for, and it meant nothing.

Lost in my thoughts, I neglected to hear Julia creep up the stairs after me. I jumped as I turned around to her standing in my doorway. "Were you watching me the whole time?" I laughed. "Yes. I like to watch you think," she replied. I teared up at the sound of her voice, which I had missed so terribly - quite possibly more than I knew myself. In the midst of my own strength, I was so very weak. Julia walked over to me and hugged me tightly, rubbing my back with her fingernails. I lost those precious tears into her shoulder.

We walked down the stairs, Julia leading the way. I heard Jack King and my brother arguing before we even turned the corner. I saw that Jacob had packed his belongings in an identical backpack as I had. In that same moment, I remembered that my father was a lying scoundrel and a miserable portrait of a man, and my cheerful memory of him died with the shadow of all of the lies he had ever told. Nevertheless, perhaps we had the same idea in order to keep our father's memory alive. Jack laughed in his direction. "What you got in there, dumbass?" he joked. Jacob glared. I pounced upon the opportunity for a joke. "Oh, he's quite the collector of Playboy magazines," I stated. I knew it was true, and his face turned red as we all shared a communal laugh, which was a welcomed lightening to the mood. My brother punched me in the arm as Jack led us out of the house. Jacob and I turned around to say one last goodbye to the house as we had known it before slamming the door abruptly, leaving our past worries on the other side.

Jack King had driven the same model car that he had driven on that day so many years ago, which brought back yet another flood of memories. Everything I was experiencing brought back a layer of mixed-emotional memories like knives and needles pinpricking the back of my neck. The armored car parked before us was undeniably the same exact one he had driven when he had rescued us from our old home the first time, nearly eight years prior at the time. Oh, the memories. *So young and naive, so much to learn.* Jack climbed in the driver's seat, cranked the engine, and after the rest of us climbed in and slammed the doors, we sped out of the ruins of the neighborhood we had called home for nearly a decade just as we had done the previous time.

Driving through the city was like watching Memory Lane be travelled by someone else - you cannot change anything; you are simply just along for the ride. Buildings were vandalized, shops were looted and destroyed, and bodies littered the sidewalks and alleyways. What was once a beautiful ray of hope and a symbolic beacon of light had become an echo of past destruction. History was repeating itself just as it had always done. The city looked and smelled of death - a moldy and rotted evil. The place of refuge and restoration Jack King - along with my parents - had worked so hard to preserve had long since become clouded and blinded. The entirely distorted man glowered his eyes and gritted his teeth. He had reluctantly let Jacob in the front seat I wanted to be in. The landscape was clearly affecting Jack King. He gripped the steering wheel tightly, his eyes back with Julia. The awful sights and horrible images of the fallen city faded into the back of my mind as she stroked and clasped my hand. Julia protected me more than anyone or anything else. She did not even know about the dreams; I had never told her, or anyone for that matter. She had saved me from myself; she was the only one that could truly keep me out of danger and self-destruction. As I focused on my love for Julia and the calming aura she washed over me, we neared the gates of the mansion. Jack King easily navigated through the brick pillars and iron fences and drove up the hill as the security guards quickly opened the gates to let us through. I wondered if all of the security was necessary, but I suppose Jack King had quite a few dissenters in those days. I had been there before; I had seen the marvelous layout of the mansion and grounds around it. It was now my brother's turn to gawk at the spectacular home of the once-great leader of the city. Visiting that land was once an honor, but now it was only a safe haven. The last safe place in the city.

The mansion seemed to be the only place in the city that had not changed even in the slightest manner. A simple idea like that was difficult to come by in those days. Our whole lives had been uprooted from underneath our feet; a peaceful place to settle down was a sight for sore eyes. We climbed the elaborate staircases as Jack led us to our rooms. There were plenty to choose from. I laughed at Jacob as he marveled at the wonderful artwork and sculptures hanging from the walls. "Don't break anything," Jack said to him, almost on command. After a brief laugh, my face grew very serious as I remembered the long labyrinth of empty hallways and the locked doors that were nearly begging to be explored. The curiousness called my name; I made a mental note to investigate the rooms upon first chance. Something about the vast expanse of open space within the mansion gave me a rather *horrible* feeling.

Jack King, as a gracious host, let us pick our own rooms. I chose the one closest to Julia's, which had a joint bathroom between the two. Jacob carried his stuff into the bedroom furthest back around the corner. Both rooms were complete with a mahogany bedroom suite, consisting of a king-size bed, dresser, nightstands on both sides, and a huge television in each room. Each individual bedroom was nearly identical, apart from Julia's, which was complete with her own decorations. The closest comparison for each room was a hotel suite, and I had to make sure I was not dreaming to be able to believe it. It was so difficult to believe that this fortunate occurrence had rescued me from all of the suffering. My life finally starting looking uphill, contrary to the valley that I had been traversing for so long. I could not help but doubt the reality of it all, and I constantly cast myself down as I did not deserve to be there. Perhaps the physical torture had come to an end, but the only thing keeping the emotional and mental anguish at bay was Julia.

Julia told me that dinner would be in a few hours and that I could clean up in the bathroom between our two bedrooms. I picked out my only other outfit for dinner and closed the bathroom door behind me. As you can imagine, every single component was fit for royalty. There was a massive bathtub, a large toilet, and a row of sinks. There were mirrors all over the walls, allowing for a three-hundred-sixty degree view. Vanities separated the sinks, and large-columned shower stalls stood in the corners of the bathroom. The air smelled of fresh linen, and it was a much welcome cleansing for me. I had not bathed in over a week, as far as I could count, so I grabbed a towel and turned the faucet to red. The hot water was perfect, once I figured out the confounded faucet setup. Nothing in that house was commonplace, down to the smallest detail. I let the refreshing shower wash away the memories of the past as I focused on what would come next in the events of the city. I scrubbed the dirt and blood off of me, getting completely clean. I wiped the slate clean, both physically and mentally. I knew I was changing. I had lost quite a bit of weight; I was even on the rather thin side, as my mother had said to me many times before her passing. My body had taken on a muscular tone after moving furniture and going on supply runs. It was as if my emotional stress had exercised my body. My face was changing as well. My facial features were deeper set than usual. My mother always said my eyes could move mountains; on the contrary, I felt as if I had climbed them and then been pushed off of them time and time again. I suppose the weeks of stress and worry had taken a toll on my appearance. I looked older; I *was* in every single way.

I soon snapped out of my emotional state and got dressed. I strapped a leather belt around my khaki pants; I needed it to keep them up. I buttoned up my shirt and combed my hair back behind my ears. It had gotten longer over the past few months. It was jet black and curling on the sides. It stayed in its place, giving me a sophisticated and tamed appearance, contrary to my prior demeanor. There was an array of razors and creams along the neat and organized shelves, and I chose the most familiar bottle I had seen my father use and went to work. I sheared the shadow from my jawline and chin, revealing a smooth and pale face. All color had vacated my body, and I still felt weak. I grabbed the remainder of my clothes and opened the door, leaning against the doorframe for support. Hunger had weakened me beyond belief, and not even a thorough cleansing can fulfill that. Julia was standing right outside the door, seemingly waiting on the bathroom. There was more than enough room. It was a pleasant surprise, although my empty stomach turned as I was startled. "You better not have used all the hot water," she joked. I laughed, enjoying this appearance and the closeness between us. She slid past me and shut the door, but not entirely. I could see into the bathroom through an inch of space. I stood outside the door, just as she did for me. I guarded the bathroom, waiting for her return.

Dinner was just as extravagant as I remembered. I had been hungry before, but then I literally was *starving*. Sebastian was delighted to see me again, and his outgoing personality certainly did some good for all of us. It was amazing how much a cheerful heart could do in a depressing situation. Jacob even seemed to be having a grandiose time. Sebastian performed his ritual of seating us and setting the table. As he brought out the food, the wild aroma of nourishment awakened our stomachs into a rumbling frenzy. We could hardly keep from diving into the plates as soon as they hit the table. After every dish was placed in an arrangement of savory flavor, Jack King dismissed us into the abyss of paradise. A home-cooked meal was a long-missed privilege. Jacob and I had struggled just to get water and basic food for so long. It made us appreciate the luxury, and as young men, we had a lot of catching up to do as far as eating goes. We had eaten canned goods for so long that things like roast chicken and pudding had become far from necessities. I had tasted the overwhelming goodness and savory flavor of the feast before, but the second time around was just as exciting. Jacob was a child in a candy store. Jack King only said one thing to him during dinner. "I wouldn't get too comfortable in that room, Jake," he taunted. My brother *hated* being called Jake; he took it as a personal insult. "You have two options, kid. You help me round up the rest of the people in this city and get them to safety, or you find shelter elsewhere. Let me know by morning." Jacob stayed silent, deep in thought. "You'll learn your place, you disrespectful bastard," Jack laughed through gritted teeth. I saw Jacob clench his fists. That was the end of the lighthearted feeling at the table, and my stomach rumbled for more. As Sebastian gathered the dishes and set them aside for a later cleaning, Jack said his farewell for the night and disappeared into the shadows, most likely upstairs into the loft where we had talked so many weeks ago. Jacob lugged his full belly up the stairs and shut himself up in his room for the night. I could have sworn I saw him carrying a bottle of Jack King's liquor up to his room. I suppose we all have our ways of relaxing. Julia and I were the last to walk up the stairs and go our separate ways. I hugged her again tightly and kissed her softly before hobbling into the unfamiliar room, weak that time with bliss as opposed to hunger. Was that not the way of the world? Some lived in luxury while others struggled just to survive. I had seen it, thought it, and lived it.

I unpacked all of my belongings from the backpacks I had brought. I unfolded clothes and placed them in the appropriate dresser drawers. I arranged my book and notebooks along the nightstands and pulled the curtains to. Just as I turned on the lamps and was about to climb into bed after a long and enjoyable day, there was a knock at the door. I pulled it open and there stood Julia with a sneaky smile on her face. "How long did you think it would take me to figure out you were standing outside the bathroom door spying on me?" she asked, suddenly serious. I felt my face get red and hot with fiery embarrassment. "I'm surprised you didn't notice me out there while *you* were in there," she said, relieving my embarrassment. She held out her hand, and I took it. She led me to her bedroom, which was customized and decorated in everything that reminded me of Julia. It was an impersonation of her exactly. It felt warm and inviting, just as Julia was. We spent the rest of the night talking and laughing until we fell asleep next to each other. It was a perfect end to a perfect day. *I could get used to this.*

Julia's body was thin and petite with just enough revealed skin and subtle flirtation to draw attention. I had seen Valerie naked many nights, but I had never felt her body against mine - at least in the way I had desired it to be. Julia was *different*. She was taller and built slightly differently in a more womanly manner. Her stomach was flatter and her chest was perkier, casting a shadow across her longer legs. Overcome with nervousness and situational anxiety marred with insecurities, her body released my worries. We laid together that night as I thought of Valerie and how much she deserved. What I could not give her. I slept not a wink that night as we lay there, exasperated and aroused. My mind was in a much different place - a much *different* world.

The sun shone through the large glass window across from the bed, illuminating Julia's golden hair as morning rose. We awakened to the pleasant sound of birds chirping in her gardens outside. The romantic scene was interrupted when we heard a knock at the door. Sebastian popped his head through the opening and walked in, his arms lined with trays of food and drinks. "I wondered if I would find you both here," he said, winking in my slightly embarrassed direction. He carefully arranged the end of the massive bed as if it was a breakfast table, told us to enjoy, and left. As most women do, Julia rambled on and on about how awful she must look. To be completely honest, she always looked stunning to me. She looked amazing in her pajamas, with her hair pulled back and no makeup on. I told her this time and time again, but to no avail. As I lifted my glass of orange juice, I noticed a small note on the underside of the cup. I pulled it off, examining it, but making sure Julia did not notice. I was shocked at the writing on the bottom of the glass.

'Enjoy!'
Jack

The next two weeks were like living in paradise. It definitely made up for the months of scavenging and living off of the bare minimum life had to offer. Jacob had chosen to work with Jack King as he relocated the people into the middle of the city. It was a more desirable option than finding somewhere else to live, I must admit. I hardly saw him, or Jack King, for that matter. They would arrive back at the mansion late at night and then be gone again as soon as morning came. Before Jacob started working with him, he had left our father's gun in my room and left me a note telling me to protect myself. I had put the gun under a bunch of miscellaneous books at the bottom of a drawer; I wanted to forget about it entirely. I did not need it there. Julia and I rarely slept apart in those days. We would switch between my room and hers, talking and laughing until we drifted off to sleep. The dreams had long since ceased, but that same burning question lurked around every corner. What had started as a dream had found its way into my reality. I calmly answered no every time.

Life in the mansion proved monotonous as time went on, but it was a pleasant repetition. It was the same basic routine every day. We would wake up, eat breakfast, spend the day playing games or tending to the garden with Sebastian, eat lunch, take a peaceful nap with the windows open, eat dinner, then return to bed, only to repeat the process the next day. As you can imagine, sex with Julia was an imminent thought to me, and it approached me like a train off of its tracks. It happened as naturally as I imagined it to be, and it became as routine as everything else. As similar as the days were, they were *never* boring. My life had changed for the better in those days, and I felt as if the universe has compensated me for my losses. Or perhaps that was a selfish thought. Did it matter? I did not care. I was alive then. I was happy. *I was a goddamn king.*

Jack King and my brother would always return home late, usually in the middle of the night when Julia and I had long since gone to bed. Sebastian said they were always dragging large bags into the house, but he had never had enough guts nor the nuts to inquire them about the contents. One night, during a magnificent dinner on Sebastian's part, we heard a noise outside. He was a master chef - it was hard to break our attention from the food. Part of me wondered where he was when Jacob and I were living off of crackers and soup. I was positive that Sebastian could have made a five-star meal out of something as simple as that. During the devouring of a savory pot roast and a furious discussion on chess strategies, Jacob and Jack King barged through the front door in the other room. They slammed the door and hurried into the dining room. Jack was hysterical; he was sweating and laughing and carrying on like a drunkard in a tavern. Jacob had a still expression. I knew he had to dislike the job he was basically forced to do without other option. He always looked uncomfortable. Who would not be? They sat down with a thud at the end of the table, prompting wild stares and mental questions from the rest of us.

"Finally!" Jack King shouted. He was grinning from ear to ear. I had never seen him that ecstatic before. He had always possessed a sadistic jolly about him, but this was much different. We took turns asking him what was going on, but he carried on about how long it had been and how hard he had worked. As his laughter died down, we pressed harder and harder, determined to get an answer. "I have finally collected them all," he said calmly, all traces of a smile eons away. Jacob coughed sarcastically, drawing attention to the apparent work he had done. With that, he took a swig from the flask in his coat pocket, took his shirt off, and flared his muscles wildly. As he headed for the master bedroom, the last thing we heard was, "City gathering first thing in the morning!" We stared at each other blankly, wondering what we had just witnessed. "He's been drinking," Jacob added. "Alcohol has no effect on him," Julia said. Sebastian and I pondered the topic for a moment. "Well, maybe he finally got drunk," he said with a childish grin. Jacob remained his silent, solemn expression. "Things are about to start changing." Such a tiny phrase meant so much in the long run as I think back.

The next morning came, along with many other things. Julia and I disentangled ourselves from each other as the sun awakened us once again. I experienced new sensations every time we were alone, and I was glad she was the first. After all, I could never find the girl nor the comfortability to lose myself to. Being with Julia always felt like a *dream* - the only pleasant dream I had ever had in my life. It felt so right and natural, and I was overcome with excitement, both for our future together as well as the future of the city. Everything seemed to be looking brighter at last.

We climbed out of bed, anxious for the meeting in the town square in only an hour's time. I walked into the bathroom, and as she had done so many times before, Julia followed right on my heels. We showered for half an hour, enjoying the warm water and soapy bubbles on each other. I most likely smelled like a girl, but as I weighed the balance, I concluded that it was well worth it. I suppose the people left did not have a "best" anymore, and even though I was fortunate, I settled for comfortability over vanity. I pulled on a pair of dark jeans and a black v-neck t-shirt, and I watched Julia put on a simple white dress. After combing my hair and waiting for Julia to do her makeup, we made our way swiftly downstairs for breakfast. She was most angelic in pajamas and a bare face, in my subtle and untapped opinion.

Sebastian had prepared a grand meal of pancakes and sausage. Topped off with fresh fruit from Julia's orchard, it served as a fantastic start to the day. Something felt different about that day. I could sense that it was going to be *life-changing*. I could *feel* it. Maybe, just *maybe*, matters within the city would finally regain a sense of normality. Jacob sat quietly at the end of table, enjoying his breakfast in a sweatshirt and jeans. Jack King came down the stairs with a fresh shave and a slick haircut. He wore a leather jacket over a black t-shirt, covering his scars and tattoos. His belt and holster loomed over his military pants and heavy boots. He looked like a new man, and not to mention, a new leader. The light shining through the kitchen window gleamed off of the gun on his hip. I remembered the gun upstairs in my drawer under all of those books. I regretted for a moment not taking it with me, just in case by some odds I would need it. The anxious feelings soon passed as I regained the excitement for the coming changes.

We finished breakfast as everyone complimented each other on our looks for the town meeting which would soon unfold. Once satisfied, Jack King led us out to the car in the driveway in front of the gardens. Sebastian was the only person in the city not required to attend the city gatherings. He stayed behind to prepare a lunch for us when we returned. Jack, complete with a buzzing smile and a victorious expression, sped through the security checkpoints, gates, and through the city until we reached the town square. Easily half the town had disappeared; what was once a huge crowd pushed back into the business district now barely filled up the space designed for such meetings in front of the stage. Jack King parked behind the town hall and escorted us into the audience. When I had attended the gatherings with my family, we had always been in the back. Being this close created an aura of *evolution* - I could feel a *change*. We were in the front row, and the silence of the crowd electrified me. Jack walked up onto the stage and addressed the crowd. He was speaking directly to us. Directly to *me*.

"WELCOME EVERYONE, TO THE BEGINNING OF A NEW ERA FOR THIS GREAT CITY," he began. I recalled the monstrous array of shouts and applause at the old meetings, but now they had been chopped down to a whisper. "YOU HAVE ALL BEEN BRAVE SOLDIERS IN THIS WAR FOR PEACE AND TRANQUILITY. WE HAVE OVERCOME THE DARK PAST THAT HAS THREATENED US ONCE AGAIN. THE DAYS OF SURVIVAL ARE OVER. WE CAN AT LAST GO BACK TO LIVING ONCE AGAIN." Still nothing above a brief hum of response. I saw the expression on Jack King's face from where I was standing; I was *that* close. "WE HAVE ERADICATED THE CANCER THAT HAS INVADED THIS CITY. IT IS NOW TIME FOR RECOVERY." That was just how it was in the city. It would feel so good and so right for so long and I would grow accustomed to it, and then it would change with the snap of a finger. Life in the city was like a festering blister that never quite went away. It would ache and ache until it got worse, erasing the pain of the past. "WE REBUILD!" Jack continued. "WE RECONSTRUCT THIS CITY BACK TO ITS FORMER GLORY. WE CLEANSE THE STREETS AND BURY OUR DEAD. WE TAKE BACK WHAT WE HAVE LOST, AND THIS TIME, WE MAKE IT STRONGER. WE MAKE IT LAST. FOREVER!"

Those were the last words I remember. The cheering seemed to seep out of the ground beneath us. It grew louder and louder until I could hear no longer. I clasped my hands over my ears and fell to the ground beside Julia. When I looked up again out of the shadows, everyone was gone. I stood up, immersed in the silence of the city. I stared up into the eyes of Jack King. It was only him and I in the city. The sun behind the monster of a man blinded me. Two guards marched behind me and bound my hands, forcing me to my knees and pushing my head down. The headphones were placed around my ears and I heard the music clearer than ever. I wondered in my mind if it was the same tune Gregor McLindle had been assassinated to. I wondered if it was the song in which Valerie had faded into death. I wondered if the melody had consumed my family and friends as they were taken from me. I had lost *everything* to that fucking song. In many ways I was ready to die, for I had nothing to live for except Julia. Although the townspeople had faded from my view, I could see the guards holding her back as she screamed through the cloudy haze. The blindfold was placed over my eyes as the song repeated. Finally, he broke the everlasting silence. *"Are you a Dreamer, Noah Willowby?"* he spoke through gritted teeth that time, his words emerging through the music with an angry scowl. Before I had a chance to answer, he drew his gun with a flick of his wrist and shot me in the head.

Part 2

The Dreams

Chapter X
Cast-away Castaway
(Beaches, Running For Something, and Working For Nothing)

I awoke instantly. As you can most likely infer, I was disoriented beyond an imaginable extent. Being shot in the core of your skull at point blank range tends to have that effect on a person. You may quite possibly be wondering why I was still alive at this point, but believe me, so was I. I was just as concerned, if not more so. I felt the burning torrent of crimson blood trickling down the bridge of my nose before I even opened my eyes. Upon summoning the entirety of my strength to pull my eyelids open, I was immediately blinded by the lethal rays of sunlight. I could feel the heat of the sun on my face as my eyes shut again. I mustered up what little strength I had to open them once more, but to no avail. So many questions raced through my mind as I vaguely attempted to decipher it all. I knew I was dead; I simply had to be. I was clearly not in the grim city any longer; the sun had not shown its face there in the longest time. Whether this was the Great Beyond or the Land of the Most High God called Heaven - which Jack King had fought so valiantly against - I was certain that this was not the end. The light was too bright and the heat was too intense for this to be a peaceful eternity - whether I was worthy of it or not.

When I first felt my body sink into the sand, I had no recollection of the city - or anything, for that matter. Jack King, my parents, and any memory of the city was as distant as the ocean's end before me. The memories returned in tiny doses upon mention and question. Others' curiosity sparked my own, and I remembered upon request. This was an ongoing struggle as I opened my eyes, born into a new and strange world as if I had become a child once more in a new world - reincarnated into yet another miserable and torturous existence. I brought my hand across my brow line, wiping the sweat from my forehead and brushing back my matted hair as I shielded my eyes from the deadly sunlight as I opened my eyes in one final attempt. It took a moment for my mind to adjust to the change in scenery, both physical and emotional. The wild confusion pounded upon my brain as my eyes strained to make out my surroundings. Quickly and all at once, I removed my hand, as if tearing off a bandage with the blink of an eye. The explosive beams of sunlight gleamed off of the ocean in front of me; I felt the sand beneath me as I ran my fingers through the billions of tiny grains. I turned my head to the slightest degree, prompting an awful aching sensation from my spine to the base of my skull. Blood dripped like iodine into the pools of water that had collected on the sand as the tide rushed in around me. I brushed the imprint of sand off of my clothes as I attempted to stand up. My legs turned to jelly, and I collapsed directly into the moist sand once more. The salty water stung my eyes and pierced my wounds like a thousand daggers, prompting a moan of agony and discomfort. I sat up, my head dizzy and my vision foggy. I climbed up one foot at a time; slowly and steadily, my second attempt was successful. I brushed the sand out of my hair as I stood up and processed the beach around me. Although the water caused much discomfort, it had managed to wash most of the blood from the wound. As a matter of fact, there was no actual point of exit - or entry, for that matter. Despite the excess of blood, there was no real injury to be seen.

Where was I? I had just been murdered, for God's sake. Why was I not dead? All of these questions came to mind as I thought of a plan of action. The city was nowhere near a beach - not even remotely or regionally close. I was surely very far from home, and the feeling of being lost soon set in. It surely was a frightful one - the one answer I did have. I looked around the island, taking in every detail I could. The vast and deeply blue ocean expanded forever, or so it seemed. The beach met the cool water in a clashing unison, echoing waves throughout my mind.

The sand continued for what I concluded to be a mile behind me until it faded into a dense jungle. All of a sudden, as I stared off into the gleam of light off of the water out in front of me, the thought of Julia rushed back to me. The sun reminded me of her soft, golden hair and the heat I felt in her presence. The crashing waves were a brilliant blue, the exact color of her eyes when she looked into mine. I had to get out of there. I had to get back to Julia, wherever she was, wherever I was, and however many miles there were between us. I simply had to.

Survival kicked in quickly and all of a sudden. The sun was sinking below the horizon oddly fast; I could practically feel the temperature dropping as the shadows elongated themselves along the beach. This place was mythically strange. I hoisted myself up over the tidal sand dune that the tide had piled up behind me. The monstrous wind blew tiny bits of gritty sand against my skin, stinging the pores on my arms and face. I trudged through the deep ocean of yellowish-white crystals, seemingly not moving even the slightest inch. My calves grew tired rather quickly; dying really is not the most ideal form of exercise. I knew from the past months in the city that exposure was a death sentence; I needed to find shelter as soon as possible. I scoured the flat terrain until I spotted the only possible place for even the inkling of a chance of avoiding the elements. There was a rocky cliffside that separated the beach from the dark jungle behind it; I had yet to notice it as I lay in the sand, but then again, it seemed to be my only option.

The cavern was damp, cold, and most definitely dark. It extended several yards until it exceeded my vision into the pitch black abyss. I put my hands to the walls, feeling for fissures that could quite possibly bring the entire structure crumbling down on top of me. The rough stone was dripping with runoff water from the jungle floor above me. The natural shelter seemed to be relatively secure, and I then knew the walls that would keep me safe during the night. The discreet hole in the cliffside was livable and I planned to fortify it. I returned to the beach through the one and only exit; I set out to gather a few supplies that the foreign environment had to offer. I gathered an array of palm leaves to line the cave floor; they could serve as both a sponge and a mattress. I dragged them to the cave entrance and returned to the line of palm trees at the foot of the jungle. There was an abundance of fallen limbs and dry bark that would serve as perfect delegates for a roaring fire. My calculations were nearly spot on. The bed of leaves was soft and surprisingly comfortable - or at least as pleasurable as a few minutes of backbreaking scavenging would allow. After several frustrating, blistering attempts, I eventually produced a spark from the grueling chore of rubbing sticks together. The flames cast wicked shadows up along the trickling walls of my makeshift shelter, and I fell asleep to the sound of crackling wood, the feeling of accomplishment, and the gnawing sensation of uncertainty.

The following morning brought a storm of counteraction to my previous satisfaction. I opened my eyes to face the open ocean once again. Looking around me in a dazed state of amazement, I knew that it was the exact same place I had awoken the day before. I dusted myself off, stood up, and climbed the sandy hill up onto the beach, shaking my head in confusion. I practically ran to the cave, my feet carrying me as fast as the shifting sand beneath them would permit. I arrived only to a greater amount of mental stupor - there was absolutely no trace of bedding or warmth that I had created the day before. I was somewhat angry amidst the curiosity as to where my hard-founded shelter had disappeared to. Instead of asking questions, I set out to collect supplies again. The sun had already risen halfway into the sky, and there was no time to waste standing around. I returned to the places I had scavenged the day prior, and they had not been touched. I resewed the bedding and rekindled the small fire that had kept me warm and dry the night before. By the time I finished retracing my steps of survival, I concluded that it must be at least midday; the blazing sun was nearly directly above the beach, warming the desert sand to a temperature that forbade being walked upon.

I loved to eat; I would eat anything besides vegetables and seafood. Of course there were exceptions; I would eat corn, green beans and potatoes in French fry or hash brown form. I would eat catfish, but like chicken, never off the bone. As you can imagine, I was not overly excited about eating crabs, but my stomach begged and pleaded for them. I was starving; I had not eaten in at least a day. I had no fishing pole to catch fish and no firearm or bow to hunt game; I had no means of catching food on the barren island. As I explored my brain for any trace of an idea, the rumbling of my stomach spoke to me. I knelt down to the edge of my green, waxy bedding and began peeling the strands off of the corners of the leaves. I then strung them together, tying the netting onto a long, narrow piece of firewood. After I had a makeshift net at my disposal, I dared the sizzling sand in the hopes of catching something to satisfy my yearning hunger. In the hours that followed, the small trap was teeming with beach crabs, all of them worth the singed skin and blisters on the bottoms of my feet. I piled log after log onto the fire to make it cook my meal even the slightest bit quicker. While the flames licked the wood, I impaled the crabs one by one onto another spare rod, much like the handle of the net I had used. I had built a fire pit so I could balance the kabab evenly across the fire. I had never been entirely fond of seafood, but in the most dire of circumstances, I would have settled for much less. I might have even acquired a certain likeness for them as my stomach filled to the brim. I drifted to sleep among a pile of crab shells and broken, charred wooden pieces.

Just as fate would have it - or *mine*, to say the least - I woke up on the beach. Again. In the same place. I was beyond irritated and flustered. I was fuming with anger at the fruitless work I had carried out twice - all for nothing. I leapt off of the sand and stormed off toward the cavern, which I knew would be empty. I came to the mouth of the cave, sweaty and red-faced; the air seemed to be getting hotter and thicker with the repetitive days that passed me by and ultimately left me stranded behind. The sand had most definitely grown more deadly with its fiery grains each day I had been there; perhaps it was merely my imagination. Much to my expectation, the hole was vacant. There was absolutely no sign of even the slightest notion of my existence within the cave - or anybody else's, for that matter. All of my work had been null and void. Even the food I had eaten the day before was gone from my body. I began to panic in an anxious worry and fruitless frustration. How could I refrain from starving to death if my full belly has been rendered empty within a matter of hours? I turned to face the ocean, attempting to catch a breath of relief from the slightest breeze. There was no use in collecting supplies that would only be gone the next day, and so I sat down, propped up against the rocks surrounding the hilltop that led to the jungle. I was unbelievably exhausted, exasperatingly hungry, and terribly frightened at the thought of slowly dying of starvation and heat stroke. I kicked my shoes off into the sand and pulled off my socks to allow the blisters I had built up to air out and fester in the salty and sandy breeze. The island air had changed drastically over the past few days - or however long I had been there. It was relatively cool when I arrived, but the heat grew gradually more intense and unbearable as the humidity suffocated me against the rocks. Even in my weak and fatigued state of mind, I could sense a storm coming.

I rested against the boulder all day, in and out of slumber and deafened by the grumble of my ever-aching stomach. The blistering heat and humidity sucked my breath away like an overbearing parasite. When I could take no more of the uncomfortable conditions, I pulled my sweat-drenched shirt over my head and tossed it into the sand near my feet. I searched the nearby ground for a jagged rock, and upon finding one that could do the job, I cut my jeans off at the knees. It was somewhat cooler, but the sunburns were ungodly. I was redder than a fresh-picked tomato by sunset. I was a half-naked savage, and it felt like I was continuously being pinched by a thousand crabs. Perhaps it was real, or it may have been the wicked sunburns; perhaps it was all an insane hallucination. The visions were mind-boggling. The blazing sun sucked the moisture out of me very quickly, and I could not hope to find fresh water. I did not eat either; mustering the energy was impossible. I drifted in and out of sleep the entire day. By the time the sun hid its face, I was whipped, tired, blistered, and starved. My outlying fears were commonplace - burning or being buried alive, being tortured, going blind, or dying a virgin, but it was in the core of fear that true terror arises, such as starving to death or being eaten by wild animals. These were my concerns on the island, and they were not so easy to talk a way out of or face. How long would I last on that terrible and fearful island?

I loved a routine. I rose at the same time each morning regardless of school, work, or even days I could have slept in. How could I waste precious time? I *hated* change, and this set me apart from the changing world in which I had just been ripped from. For the three days I had been on the island, I had never been pleased at the fact of waking up in the same place the following morning. My attitude about that factor turned around almost completely the day after I had hit rock bottom - rather literally, of course. My skin had its usual tan hue, my clothes were intact, and even though my stomach was empty, it was fuller than the day before. I was strangely relieved and even slightly pleased, and I had yet to even open my eyes. Upon the first flicker of my eyelids, I closed them back instantly. I hoped and silently prayed to whoever was listening that the scene would change. It was a horrific nightmare; the sky was pitch black, a magnificent cloud pattern stretching across the expanse of horizon. The gray wisps stirred like cream as they chased each other around the frightening sky. The wind roared like a thousand trains at once, whipping sand into my hair as it blew back and forth. I reared back against the sand dune behind me in a panicking terror. The hellish artwork of the frightening sky opened up, revealing a massive cyclone, constantly growing larger and larger right before my eyes. It was miles away, but I could see and hear it as if it was right in front of me. The waterspout threw hundreds of gallons of water in every direction. Sea spray stung my face as the storm grew closer and closer. However, I could not hope to move; I was paralyzed on that beach. As the violent tornado spun faster and faster, it only gained volume. The waves around it levitated into the air and circled the cyclone, only adding to the illustrious size and power of the storm. I could sit there dazed no longer. I jumped to my feet and rolled across the hill as quickly as I could. As I looked behind me, I witnessed just how large the monster had become. It easily covered a third of the sky, and the screeching and howling of the storm was deafening.

I kept my shoes on despite their sogginess. Wet shoes and sand naturally do not mix, and I nearly tripped multiple times. I sprinted as fast as I could in the opposite direction as the beach. I made for the cave at first, as it was the only safe place on the island that I knew of, and it had served as a comfortable replacement for a home during my stay there. My adrenaline was in rare form; I was moving a mile a minute. I halted and caught my breath at the rock wall, but the cave was not there. I was positive I was in the correct location, but there was no sign of an opening in the solid stone. I could practically *feel* the storm closing in - raindrops pounded my head, thunder crashed, and lightning flashed overhead, blinding me. The powerful winds nearly knocked me over as I searched for an alternative shelter. I rounded the corner of the jagged cliffside as the cyclone reached the beach. I was amazed by the sheer size and diameter of it, shaking off the bewilderment as I collected myself and made my way toward the jungle. I felt the sand hitting my body and legs like a million bullets. The wind snatched me with its snarling grasp; I felt its deadly grip as I dove into the treeline of the jungle; the storm was directly overhead. Everything went black.

When I opened my eyes again, all was quiet. Insects buzzed and sweat dripped down my forehead as I regained my senses and consciousness. I had been lying face-down on the moist jungle floor, unconscious to both my surroundings and the time I had been laying there for fate only knows how long. I wiped the muddy water from my face as I stood up and faced the beach through the thick forest of trees. The cyclone had dissipated; all that remained was the thunderclouds and an occasional flash of lightning. Looking through the overgrown shrubbery, the vines and twisted tree trunks shrouded my view of the beach as if the vast expanse of sand and salt had never been there at all. As I turned to face the massive strand of tangled jungle behind me, I was blinded by a lethal flash of lighting. The tree closest to me was split at the trunk. The hair on the back of my neck stood up as I smelled burning wood. I could feel the heat behind me, and I knew the tree had caught fire. As quick as the first, another strike of lightning exploded another tree next to me, that time in my direct view. The flames fought each other as they spread across the tightly packed vines and twigs surrounding me. As more bolts of light pounded the forest around me, surrounding me, I sprinted for the only gap I had as the blaze scattered in every direction. The faster my footsteps became, the more electricity surged through the jungle. Each crack of wood startled me, pushing me deeper and deeper into the depths of the dark forest. I caught sight of a hill up ahead, but I could not see what lay on the other side. It was the only way to go; I was trapped by the monstrous flames on every side but one, as if the elements were daring me to pick up my pace. As I got closer and closer to the mysterious mound of earth, not knowing whether a ditch or a canyon awaited me on the other side, a final bolt of lightning struck the heels of my shoes, sending me flying over the edge.

The curiosity as to what lay below the small cliff anticipated the fall. Even though the distance was only a few feet, it felt like minutes as I prepared for my sudden death. I landed hard on my shoulder in the dried out riverbed below. I rolled across the packed dirt and rock as I collected myself. I could see the light and feel the heat of the roaring fire only five feet above. I looked down at my arms, which were cut and scraped rather severely. I could not feel the pain, however; I was too surprised and shocked by what I saw. The blood trickling down my skin was *blue*, for Christ's sake. As the strange liquid leaked from my veins and onto my pants leg, I became extremely focused. It was far deeper than blood loss or any concussion. I was *mesmerized* by something. Something had control over me. What was it? And more crucially, where the fuck was I?

As quickly as the scene had become silent, I jumped to my feet as an explosion erupted above my head. The roaring fire seemed to be following me, searching for any trace of me as a watchdog sniffs out a vigilante. Sweat dripped down my brow as the flames singed them. I focused on the only open direction out of the riverbed. I hopped over uneven stones and rolled across flat boulders, feeling the tongues of the blaze licking the back of my neck as the storm pursued me. The monster raced faster and faster as I leapt across the treacherous ravine, praying to the heavens that I might not stumble. The riverbed circled downhill as the jungle dove deeper and deeper. The lower part of the stream still had a considerable amount of water in it; my feet splashed as I clung to the rough rocks beneath my feet and stuck in the inches of deep mud on the bottom. I could see only a few feet in front of me. The water got deeper and deeper and frothed as white as snow around the boulders. I ran and ran as the fire behind me finally took hold of me, burning my shirt. I felt my skin begin to blister and screamed in agony. Before I was completely cremated, my feet met a drop off, and I fell off the side of the hill into the gushing waterfall like the sweat and blood from my body.

My mind went blank as I hit the frigid water below; it was a relief, however. The searing burns and wounds were extinguished by the cool stream, replacing the pain with a slightly lesser evil. I had fallen off of a waterfall cliff several dozen feet overhead. The freezing water eased my burns and cuts, bringing relief over my entire body. This strange place was a struggle of pain and pleasure, and it was unfortunately unequal. As I pondered whether or not to resurface or just give up in that absurd extension of existence, I took in a breath. How entirely preposterous - I could breathe *underwater*, goddamnit. I looked up through the bubbling pool of water and saw the flames extinguish as they reached for me with a fiery palm. I was protected by the elemental force around me, and I was convinced that nature was always at war with itself. As my hearing ceased once again, I pushed myself to the surface and heard nothing but the peaceful addition of water to the pool around me. I climbed to the rocky riverbank and did just what I had done during my time on the beach. I laid against a rock and assessed what was going on. Only one question repeated through my mind then: *Where was I?*

I laid my clothes out on the rocks to dry in what little amount of sunlight broke through the thick jungle above. The air was solidly humid and miserable despite the arctic water, and I had to return to the river once more as not to suffocate. After they were dry enough to to wear with minimal annoyance, I began exploring the area around the stream. Believe me, it was much more enjoyable without a wild cyclone on my tail, and not to mention wet clothes clinging to me. I found vines full of ripe berries, which I picked by the dozen and gorged my empty stomach on. The palm leaves around the oasis had collected large amounts of fresh rainwater to wash them down with. I found a cane pole leaning against a tree, and judging by the eerie sounds of cracking branches and rustling leaves, I knew I might need it.

Life in the jungle was simply creepy and made me quite uneasy; my mind was haunted by what-ifs and imaginative shadows. The elements were ruthless beyond compare. Everything in my path was something to be tripped over, the air was hot and muggy, and every insect to be discovered resided within the forest, bringing with it their own unique dangers. The landscape was all but flat; the region was nothing but hills, valleys, and a few mountain chains. I was forced to scavenge for food and water along the way as I treaded mile after endless mile through the thick brush, and I was constantly fatigued.

Fortunately, the orthodox cycle of the resetting of days only pertained to the beach. I could not argue either, mind you. I do not know what I would do if I had to retrace every step through the dangerous jungle. It continued for miles, as did I. I would walk for hours on end and rest for a while, using my settling time to find food and water in order to keep moving. Luckily, supplies were plentiful in the area, almost as if the journey *begged* me to continue. It was a wager I could not hope to deny. I slept between tree roots and in caves, constructing and maintaining many small and weak fires along the way. Staying warm was not a problem, and I was grateful for it. The depth of night maintained a maximum of eighty degrees, and the soggy demeanor of the environment made it nearly impossible to start and keep a fire going. You could cut a hole in the intense humidity that was a flame's natural bane. I kept the minuscule flames in the corner of the caves, only to provide light. The jungle was far from friendly, and shadows were cast along the stone walls - shadows that had been following me since I had been there in that strange place. I had read fantastical stories illegally throughout my childhood, many of which consisted of island survival tales. Of course I *imagined* them, but I never once thought I would be part of one. I was the main character in the one I was living, and I did not know the ending. There was a certain inevitable fear in the island - the heat, the insects, or being devoured by jungle creatures. I bit down on the tongue of uncertainty and persisted forward down the mountain.

After a while, I pondered just how long I had been in that odd hysteria. After adding the days spent on the beach, I had been wandering through the vast expanse of endless jungle for ten long, grueling days. I was forced to scale one of the impossibly steep rock walls in order to get to the other side of the jungle, the classic tale of *cannot-go-around-it* proportions. With only the help of the cane pole staff I had found, I began the terrifying task of climbing the mountain. After hours of close calls and near-death experiences, I finally lowered my feet into the covered forest floor on the other side. There were far less trees in that section of the jungle, and I could smell the ocean once again. I had to be getting close to the end of the labyrinth.

That particular part of the island was much like the face of a man who could never grow a full beard. Some places were full of plant life, and others were smooth - nothing but roots and vines. My father could grow a full beard and as far as I was sure, the rest of my father's side of the family could. My maternal relatives could not, however. That was the gene that I received. I had begun shaving in the city years before the recent forthcoming of the end, and I kept that routine up until the death of my parents. Stubble had lined by chin and jawline, but my time in the jungle had expanded the length to a patchy, itchy shadow. There was no blade or stone sharp enough to makeshift a razor in that place, and so I scratched and rubbed my face until it bled a deep blue. My hair hung along my neck as it curled on the ends and fell with sweat and despair. They were gone - replaced by shadows. Not only had the aroma changed, but the temperature was much cooler and the air was filled with whispers. I could have sworn the jungle was haunted. Sometimes I convinced myself that the ghosts of my parents were watching over me, following me until I would join them. But as time went on, and as did I, I concluded that those voices were not those of my mother and father. These were the mutterings of a boy and girl, far too present and persistent to be my parents. They were long gone by then, quite possibly even worlds away.

Food was scarce there on the other side of the mountain. The vines full of berries had receded into the jungle behind me as the land turned to woods. The small leaves could not hold large amounts of water, and the air was much colder. Fortunately for me, the land was practically bone dry, and the fires I started there were much more efficient. Even in the change of circumstance, the land still provided for me. Perhaps my parents were looking out for me after all. It was in those frigid nights that the whispers grew louder, pounding my head like a blacksmith shapes weaponry. I stared into the fire all night long on my sixteenth night on the island. I did not sleep - I could not. I dreamt with my eyes open until day broke through the trees; I saw the beach in front of me for the first time in what I knew previously to be around a week. I stood up to run towards it, but I did not make it far. The whispers held me back like iron chains, and the fire grew higher and higher. The lack of food had made me hallucinatory, bending my reality - whatever was coined reality in those days, at least. At last, all went silent; all I could hear was the whispers getting closer.

I could take no more. I commanded my feet to carry me to the beach as fast as humanly possible. Something very heavy hit me with full force, sending me flying into a massive nearby tree. I was automatically disoriented as well as breathless. I smacked my head into the tree trunk by reflex and out of control. My vision was blurred and my brain pounded. Vines wrapped around the trunk of the tree, binding me to the rough bark. A thick root wound itself around my waist, locking my arms and legs to the tree. I had been captured and crucified. Something hard hit me in the face once more. I could feel the knuckles crack against the bridge of my nose. "Where you from, asshole?" a boy's voice demanded. Through my blurry eyes, I saw a girl attempt to pull him off of me. The boy only pushed her away, shoving her with full force. I did not reply - not out of spite, but out of confusion. I was far too disillusioned to wonder what had happened. The only thing running through my mind was the girl several feet behind my attacker. "The city," I finally muttered, though sputtering through blood and gritted teeth. "Who is in charge of this goddamn city?" the boy pushed rather charismatically. I could hardly breathe, much less speak; the vines tightened, cutting off my circulation from the throat as I struggled to think and answer. "Jack King," I uttered, barely audible with thought and voice. The boy released me, along with the root and vines that bounded me. I cluttered to the forest floor, breathing heavily and taking in air. "Well, holy shit," the stranger said through a thick cackle. "He's one of us."

Her apparition was cloudy at first through my dizzy vision, but as my eyes focused, I saw the Antichrist. She was angelically dark and a jaded woman - a symbol of everything I feared in that place on legs. Her hair was black and hung below her shoulders, cut along the back of her pale neck and face. Her eyes were green, almost hazel, and her nose was wrapped in freckles above her small, curved lips. She had an active shape about her, clad in her dark pants and tank top. I had seen it before. That *face*. That *style*. That *woman*. This internal question could not be as easily answered as the others could. The attacker ahead of her was a tall, lanky blonde with blue eyes behind dark aviator sunglasses and an angry force about him, as if he hated you upon first meeting. *Sunglasses. My sunglasses. Joshua. Strauss. Topher. Klaus.* He wore black shoes and a pair of dark jeans to match the woman, and his shirt was unbuttoned along his collar to allow his pulsing arteries to breathe. He seemed to be a ball of pent-up anger, and I had a large suspicion that I was the scapegoat and recipient of such violence.

The girl standing alongside the boy stepped over to me to make sure I was alright as I writhed across the wooden ground; I shoved her off with all the strength I could muster. She had not said a word since the pair had arrived. Instead, she maintained a steady scowl, hiding every ounce of caring that her actions could spare. Once she realized that I refused to let her near me, she joined her partner as he walked away from the tree. I laid on the ground for several seconds longer. I felt adrenaline pump through my veins; my breathing steadied back to normal and I climbed to my feet as silently and calmly as possible. I focused my eyes on the boy with his back turned to me as I snatched the cane pole from the base of the tree. I moved with the agility of a fox as I neared the tall, slender young man only several yards away. My footsteps were dead silent as I brought the splintering end of the stick across his right jaw. Both teenagers stopped in their tracks. I could see the shadow of liquid blood on the end of the rod, and I knew I had hit my mark. The boy shoved the girl aside once again as he turned around. I cringed as I saw what I had done to his face. His jaw was split from the corner of his mouth to the lobe of his ear. From the wound dripped deep blue blood, just as my arm had done days prior. I expected a hit like that to cripple him, but he only smiled a wicked grin. He ran his fingers along the cut, and the two pieces of flesh welded together once more. I was utterly shocked, and admittedly quite frightened at what might have happened next.

"Ain't that easy, pal," the boy laughed. "But you're lucky; you *almost* broke my sunglasses." He had a sadistic essence of charismatic arrogance about him, as if he indeed knew everything. As much as I hated to admit it, the man was not a stranger in that place like I was; he most definitely had the upper hand. The feeling of the unknown had always terrified me. Instead of retaliation, which is what I feared was next, he reached out his hand for me to shake it. Nervously, I took it in mine firmly but reluctantly. "I am Lucious Noy, and this is my sister, Felicia." His voice was cold as he awaited my name. "Noah Willowby," I returned lowly. As the feeling of uncertainty arose within me, it seemed that I had no other choice.

All introductions aside, the pair of teenagers turned and walked toward the beach about a mile away. It was implied that I follow, and I took hint of it quickly; I jogged to meet up with them. Curiosity had taken over my fear, and it filled my gut, replacing the shortness of breath and fueling my body with questions. "So who are you guys?" I asked, huffing and puffing, my house nearly blown down. "Who are *we*?" Lucious repeated. Regardless of the action or even questions directed at her, Felicia never spoke a word. She was quiet and quite mysterious; I made a silent vow to find out why. Perhaps her brother had cut her tongue out by mistake; he most likely would have enjoyed it nonetheless. "We're *scouts*," Lucious finally said, staring off into space. "For who?" I asked, pressing further. The boy laughed that villainous laugh once more. "So many questions for somebody that just tried to kill me - or *thought* he was, anyway." I became unsettled in the silence that followed. "No hard feelings," he broke. At last, Felicia finally said something. "We bring people back to the city." I was shocked at her powerfully quiet voice; that silent tone covered years of pain and suffering. "Jack King's city?" I wondered. "No, why would anybody in their right mind want to go back *there*?" she said, implying that my question was stupid. I pondered it for a moment; I was not throwing all of my eggs in one basket. "Well, it's either complicated or I'm not in my right mind." She did not say anything else; instead, she smiled the slightest curve of the mouth. "That's good enough for us," Lucious interrupted. "Who isn't out of their mind these days?" he joked. "Besides, there isn't a way back there anyway."

That subtle truth hit me like a tree to the chest. Memories came flooding back like the rapids over the cliff over which I had fallen. That place was a hallucination; all I could focus on was what was in front of me while the city lingered in the back of my mind. Not anymore; I remembered everything in that moment.

Julia was there. My imbecile of a *brother* was there. *Jack King* was there, destroying everything he had built with no challenge or forethought. "Am I *dead*?" I wondered out loud, almost uncontrollably. "Yes *and* no," Lucious replied sarcastically. "Only ten percent of your brain died back there; the other ninety lives here. Are you a Dreamer?" he asked. There was that burning question once more, yet it was no longer accompanied by a sneer and my name which I had grown to despise and resent. Every instance that I had been asked it flowed through my body like blue blood. "No," I returned angrily. "We'll find out soon enough," Felicia added. "We'd be damned if you weren't, and so would *you*," Lucious laughed. "How so?" I implored. "If you weren't, you wouldn't be *here*, kid. This is the dream world." He raised his hands to the sky as if to frame an imaginary picture. "Where all of your wildest dreams await you." He was brutally violent and sarcastic, casting a horrifying shadow of uncertainty of which I had not the slightest hint of.

I was not going to argue with those people; I knew I was not a Dreamer. I had seen such people back in the city. What they had done. That was not me. I was a vagrant caught in a mistake - simply a misunderstanding. Yes, that was what it was. Perhaps it was another dream, and I would soon wake up in the mansion again next to Julia - my only true home. That thought gave me hope; it was my wildest dream and striven hope. We walked onward toward the beach as Felicia looked over to her brother. "You know that's bullshit." I did not know whether she was talking to him or to me. It did not matter; her direction was enough.

The other side of the island was an exact duplicate of the opposite. This raised dozens of questions in my mind. "What *is* this place?" I wondered, not necessarily intended to be spoken aloud. "This is the Island of Lost Time," Lucious said matter-of-factly. "Time is *different* in this world. The island is the strongest point of time manipulation in existence. The day and night cycle are normal, but each day that passes, they will wake up much sooner or much later than just a single cycle. It's irritating, but with that combined with the crazy weather, new arrivals are bound to come right to us. Just like you, pal," he finished sarcastically. I was relieved that all of my hard work was not *entirely* fruitless. "How long do you *think* you've been here?" Felicia asked quietly. "Sixteen days," I replied. Her brother laughed coldly. "You've been here for a month, buddy," Lucious concluded with a chuckle. I was taken aback; time certainly was different there. The narcissistic teen seemed to read my mind. "Don't worry, you won't age here, Willie." Another cold laugh. I wondered just how long the two had been there, and I despised degrading nicknames. That was a new one on me, and yet it was the worst.

After another awkward silence, I decided to quench my thirsting questions. "What the hell happened to my camp?" I wondered out loud. Both newcomers laughed that time. "Time also moves *backwards* here." I ran my fingers through my sandy and dirty hair, dumbfounded once again. My hard work had been for nothing after all. "Can't we stop and rest a while?" I asked, exasperated both from physical and mental labor. Lucious pointed at the descending sunset over the expanse of ocean in front of us. "We have to get off this island before nightfall - that is, unless you want to make this journey all over again in a week or two." I felt nearly intimidated by his presence. I was no longer alone; I now had someone to answer to again. I did not know how I felt about that; that simple fact was somewhat comforting yet half-intimidating, pushing me into a corner in which there was no feasible way out. "How are we going to get off the island?" I inquired, awaiting a smart remark. "It'll be a *dream*, don't you worry," he retorted smoothly. I had known him for thirty minutes - or what I previously knew to be - and I already wanted to strangle him to death in an ungodly and grisly fashion.

We made our careful way down the rocky cliffside and regained our footing in the shifting sand below. Lucious led the way with Felicia on his heels and yours truly bringing up the rear. I honestly had no idea how we were going to pull it off both with the task and the time at hand. I was never much good at swimming, and the everlast fear of sharks loomed in the back of my mind like a black, cyclonic cloud. Lucious lined his toes up with the exact line where the sand met the sea. Our footprints filled with frothy water as the tide came in and receded again. He appeared to be doing an adequate amount of thinking, and I could tell it was getting to Felicia. I had seen that look before. "How are we going to do it, Luc?" she asked. I was surprised; I figured she would have been in on all the secrets of that mystic land. I knew and empathized her situational predicament; Jacob had treated me as if I was below him as well. Even the thought of him brought searing tears of anger and sadness to my eyes as I remembered the city and all I had left behind - all I had been ripped from.

He turned around and smiled at me. "Not afraid of the water, are we?" he mocked. He had certainly been inside my head, even the slightest of edges. He beckoned me forward as I met him at the crest of the oncoming waves. We were positioned at the exact distance where the water did not touch us, but we were immersed in it in its entirety. "How do you suggest we get off the island, Noah Willowby?" Once again, I remembered the city and the ongoing feeling of being talked down to. I really could not think straight at all whatsoever. Shaking my head and shrugging my shoulders, he stiffened his grimace. "Let me rephrase that," he corrected. "How do you *imagine* we get off this island?" he stated firmly. I thought as he studied my expression. "Look to your wildest dreams," he pushed, standing back beside his sister as I stared into the open water before me. I closed my eyes, searching for the tiniest idea. I could find nothing; I was forced to create one. "My, my, my. Good choice, kid!" I heard Lucious exclaim from behind my closed eyes. I felt his long, bony fingers clap me on the back as I saw the yacht before me; I could not believe it. "Not a Dreamer, huh?" Felicia remarked. One of them had done it; I was sure of it. This was a trick to win me over. I would not let them defeat me as everyone and everything else had. Lucious clapped his hands together cheerfully. "All aboard!" he mocked. As I reluctantly climbed up the ladder, I noticed the engravings to the right of the ladder rungs: *S.S Julia.*

Chapter XI
The Seven Seas
(Seasick, Seized, and Seeing Things)

To say that getting off of the island was a breeze is quite a humorous and ironic understatement. The wind had picked up drastically, reminding me of the storm that had passed who-knows-how many days prior. Needless to say, sea sickness set in rather quickly. The undying urge to get off of the island had transformed into the desperate need to get back to the shore. Lucious motioned for his sister to mount the ladder on the other side of the rather large boat. She scaled the steps quickly, overlooking the sea below. I was not nearly as graceful; I rolled across the deck and climbed to my feet quickly before Felicia could turn around. Lucious joined us on the ship, immediately kicking his inner pirate persona into high gear. He straightened his clothes and hurried over to the opposite side of the deck as the sun sunk lower and lower into the sky. He groaned as he pulled the anchor up above the railing and exhaled deeply. "Thanks for the help, asshole," he shot at me. I could not seem to understand his pre-emptive hatred for me. I studied him as he raised the sails, catching the upbeat wind almost instantly. Felicia and I watched in bewilderment as he spun the wooden wheel around, directing the ship out to sea. "Is he always this obnoxious?" I whispered to Felicia. "Pretty much," she replied.

The cyclonic wind rapidly pushed us off of the coast of the island. I watched as the large shore faded into a small dot in the distance and the unknown laid before me among the millions of gallons of salty water. "Do you think we're far enough away?" Felicia asked her brother. "I hope so," he sighed. "I would hate to do all that work *again*," he muttered in my direction. "Let's go see what our friend here brought us as far as lodging goes," he changed the subject. "I could use it." I knew he would not let it rest so easily. We filed down a large wooden staircase as the yacht sailed into the night. I brushed off the ridiculous accusations of my summoning of the boat. Hell, maybe it might even be comfortable.

Boy, was I correct. The lower deck of the ship was similar to a five-star lounge back in the city. I was so engulfed in the luxury of the yacht that the memories failed to overtake me. The sleeping quarters came equipped with three large bedrooms, along with their own generous bathroom and an open entertainment area with couches and a massive television screen in front of a long wooden bar counter along the far wall, complete with bar stools and card tables. Coincidentally, with a hint of strangeness and oddity, each room came fully equipped with the correct size and fit of clothing and accommodations for the individual. We all showered and changed clothes, getting our bearings after a very long travel, not even to mention my stay on the island prior. Once we had scrubbed the beach sand and ocean salt from our skin and rinsed it down the drain and back into the ocean where it belonged, the three of us eventually drifted into the entertainment area. Lucious flipped over the back of the couch and came to rest in a laid-back position. As I made my way over to sit down, he kicked his legs up into the open seats. "Sorry, pal," he muttered as his eyes closed. Felicia brushed past me and rolled her eyes at her buffoon of a brother. As she passed the couch, his eyes snapped open as he yelled, "Dinner!" Before I settled down from the jump, she held out a fishing pole to him and said, "Good luck tonight, sport," mocking his arrogant, domineering tone. The pair were most definitely siblings, and I would venture to say even closer - *twins*.

Once Lucious took the pole and climbed the stairs to the deck above, I was left alone with Felicia in the empty and silent bar; my stomach slowly tensed up with anxiety. "I apologize for my obnoxious brother," she said quietly. "He acts as though he is much older even though it's only by a few seconds." Her voice was crisp and sincere, as if she was comfortable and free from the oppression of her brother. She reminded me of Julia in many ways, even though the two were much different in seemingly every way. "Don't worry about it; I have one too," I replied with a slight smile and a roll of the eyes. "I can tell by the way you look at him," she said sternly. "You know what it feels like to be below someone." I could not argue, for she was right. It was as if she could read me. I wondered if she could see inside my head and dive into the swimming thoughts of the city, as well as the tightly oppressed silk web between myself and Jacob. Julia and her father. The city itself was in fact nothing but a struggle for power and control. The memories stung like distant pinpricks, and the way Felicia looked at me from across the bar counter told me that she knew everything that raced through my mind in the still and silent room. The waves splashed outside the porthole windows as she took in my invisible pain.

"Where are we headed?" I asked abruptly. I had no limitations there; Felicia was nowhere near as aggressive as her brother. The intimidation was no less - perhaps even more; she had that silent, omniscient demeanor about her. "The Promised Land," she said with a joking smile. I decided that she had the mockery trait rather than the vile anger. "What do you mean? Is this place *actually* Heaven?" I asked sheepishly, anxious that my previous assumptions might be correct. "You can rest easy, Noah, you're not dead. Far from it, actually. You are more alive now than you've ever been," she said as her eyes widened. "This is the dream world. You can have everything you desire here. This can be your 'Heaven' if you choose to *make* it that. There is freedom here; there is power. There are no limitations. All there is is the ability to unleash your magical power that you simply can't harness while you're awake," she rambled, explaining it all, as if it were that simple. I stopped her right then and there. "I don't have any *magical powers*," a tone of anger coming through my voice. "You just haven't realized them yet," Felicia argued matter-of-factly. "You people have made a mistake," I brushed her off rather abrasively, for I had heard it all many a time before. "We'll see," she replied enthusiastically sarcastic as the door creaked open. Lucious came bursting through the common room with an armful of fish. "We're eating good tonight, folks and jokes!" he hooped and hollered. "Did I interrupt something?" he asked with a false sense of care. "Just a little talk," Felicia answered, glancing at me, then back to Lucious. "Placing bets on your catch," I finished, my turn to be slightly comical and teasing. He grinned from ear to ear, somewhat evilly serious. "Never doubt me," he shot. Felicia shut the confrontation down immediately. "Okay, Luc, you caught them, but I bet you can't cook them," she said with a smile.

Beneath the almost bluish-blonde hair and impenetrable ego, Lucious Noy was an extraordinary chef when it came to fish-frying. My mother used to cook fish on occasion, but even her buttery fried salmon could not hold a flame to the heavenly spiced cod which then lay neatly sliced before us. The three of us dug in around the bar counter over the sound of waves crashing outside. There was not much conversation, fortunately. The fish kept our mouths busy and our stomachs occupied. It was the first real meal I had eaten since my arrival on the island. After weeks of eating berries and siphoning water, a hot plate of seafood really hit the spot - even though the smell made me want to vomit.

We soon finished our hearty feast, and I helped Felicia with the dishes behind the counter - of course with no help from Lucious. He just propped his feet up on the coffee table as he watched some dramatic romance movie across the room. As we scrubbed and dried the plates, Felicia bade us both goodnight and rounded the corner to her bedroom. The door clicked shut and several minutes - as awkward as they were - passed, signifying that she was most likely sound asleep, leaving me alone with the sniffling teenage boy across the room.

My mind whirred as a plan came to me. I would attempt to sneak around the corner and to my room without any confrontation. He had his back to me and was caught up in *The Fault In Our Stars*, after all. I was nearly there - only a few feet away - when Lucious clicked the television off. He hopped over the back of the sofa, landing on two feet as gracefully as any wild creature would. "Come here a minute, Noah," he said, sniffling. He wiped tears from his eyes, and he noticed me looking at him curiously. "Tell me why, man," he begged. I thought for a moment. "Why what?" I inquired. "Why would a sweet soul like Hazel Grace be subject to so much misfortune?" he sobbed, finishing his cries as he neared the bar counter which I had just cleaned. "How about a drink, shortstack?" he shot at me, returning to his usual hateful attitude. "No thanks," I replied as he took out a flask and emptied the contents into a shot glass he drew from under the counter. "How old are you?" I asked him, hoping for a straight answer. He thought for a second, pondering it, as if he did not know his own age. "Your guess is as good as mine," he said with a slight laugh. "Trying to figure it out is a hell of a headache." I remembered what he said about not aging there, and for once, I was *glad* about something in that strange place; I was more than happy to keep my hair and muscular figure. I dismissed the thoughts as I remembered the city and what I had to get back to. I would *not* get attached to this place or these people. I simply would not.

Lucious Noy stared into my eyes as he flipped the whiskey into his mouth, reading me just as his sister did. Maybe it was a thing with twins - so many similarities, yet so different. "Devil's piss," he muttered, wincing as he swallowed. It startled me when he smashed the glass on the counter in front of me, showering us with tiny shards of sharp dust. He staggered off to bed, mumbling something. "Could you get that?" I made out. "You don't mind, do you?" I grimaced with anger. His door shut as he laughed coldly. I finished wiping off the table in the silent and empty room and walked across the carpet to the counter. As I put the cloth to the wood, I studied each individual shard of wet glass. In each tiny speck I saw an apparition of Jack King. *I don't get drunk, son.*

The next morning was swell for Felicia and I. However, I cannot say the same for Lucious. I returned to the open common room after a good night's rest, only to hear pain-stricken groaning, along with multiple toilet flushes from his bathroom. Seafood and alcohol apparently were not the best combination while sailing the ocean blue - or anywhere, I would imagine. Felicia prepared eggs and bacon for the two of us for breakfast. She was an exemplary chef, must like her brother; it must have run in their family. Jacob and I could never cook anything as simple as toast without setting the house on fire or each other, to say the least. I must say, it felt good to be in the care of the cooks. We laughed and talked over the deliciously simple meal as the sunlight - the color matching that of our orange juice - shone through the portholes of the downstairs room. "Do you want to take a walk?" she asked with a shy smirk. "How could I refuse?" I returned a smile and followed her up the stairs, leaving the dishes for Lucious when he was a bit more presentable.

The sun was blinding as we climbed out of the dark and cozy dimness of the lounge below. There was a breathtaking cloud pattern up in the sky overhead; a snow-white, fluffy ring of clouds circled the sky for as far as the eye could see - something unreal and wild, something in between a hurricane and a cyclone. The cotton ball clouds danced around the sun like ballerinas in slow motion. The spectacular phenomenon cast pitch black shadows across the waves around us as dolphins slapped the bottom of the ship. Felicia and I propped ourselves up on the helm, taking it all in. I had not realized how large the ship was upon first sight until we began to pace the perimeter. Our footsteps made a pleasant clapping sound on the oak deck below us, similar to horseshoes on cobblestone. At our leisurely pace, we easily circled the railing of the ship for at least an hour, carrying on quite the lengthy conversation. We talked about nearly everything under the sun, or perhaps the strange cloud pattern above us, as if the heavens were keeping a keen eye on us. We got to know each other, everything about us. It had only been a day since we had met. Or had it been two? A *week*? I could not remember. Time had a strange way of moving on in that mysterious place, as I had found out all too suddenly and forgotten as such.

Felicia told me about the world around us in great detail. I absorbed it like the sunlight; I could feel it as the ways of the world in which I had been waterboarded into soaked into my skin and through my mind like saltwater. I became familiar with it as she explained the complex patterns and extraordinary events that took commonplace routine among the day-to-day basis. She apologized for her brother's boorish behavior, and I politely dismissed it nonchalantly, as if her hidden kindness evened his terrible behavior out in some strange equivocal way. She told me that her brother was nothing more than a self-obsessed drunk who had been exiled from the community to bring back lost people who appeared on the island. I saved my account of questions like a bank vault - secure and remembered like clockwork. I would get answers in due time, one way or another. Felicia told me that she had given up her job as an artist to accompany, as well as oversee, her brother as he ran wild throughout the dangerous world. "As big as my dreams are, family still comes first," she said, along with the first crack in her voice I had heard. That was a sign of weakness, as I had come to know it. I saw tears begin to well up in her green eyes like water in a valley. I floated down the river through my own eyes as I felt my emotions clutch. My family was gone, pardon Jacob, which hardly counted. *Julia* was my family, and in many ways, so was her father, as vile and evil as he turned out to be. *Shudders. Violent shaking. Mental trauma. Falling.* Felicia taught me that no matter how stressful and tense family gets, you have to support them no matter what. "Promise me you'll never give up on your brother," she said through a sob. I blinked back a few final tears. Odds were, I would never see them again. "I promise," I smiled, drying her tears as my own drained down my cheeks. It was an ever-empty promise.

Days on the eighth sea, in a certain sense, followed a certain routine, if you will. Felicia and I would take turns cooking breakfast, hers being the better of the two, followed by our morning walks. We would then spend hours playing cards, board games, watching movies, or just laying under the skyline above, talking the days and nights away, growing ever closer and closer. The evenings were always closed off at first, but as time moved either on or backwards, they were spent spilling stories over the corners of our lips like a fine wine. We were in another spiritual world. Time went nowhere, but it also travelled an unreal distance. Felicia and I bonded so strongly; we were inseparable. We rarely caught a glimpse of Lucious, and on the off chance we did, he was either drowning in a bottle of liquor or gawking at or mocking Felicia and I.

I really empathized with Felicia - I *felt* her. I saw and understood where she was coming from. I did not always need words to tell me; I could see the emotion etched into her solemn frown, hidden deep within her curved smile and blank, mossy eyes. Her road of struggle ran nearly parallel to mine. Lucious Noy was the spitting image of Jacob. The two could have been long lost brothers, for Christ's sake. Oppressed under the shadow of her brother, she had so much potential, yet she gave it up for someone who did not even deserve her presence - much less her help. I admired her willpower. However, our only dissimilarity was that I had *no* potential. I was no artist, no musician, and no poet. I was no Hemingway or Shakespeare as I had learned of before the end, and I was most certainly no Gregor McLindle. My only ability was that of misfortune, of remembrance, and of furthering. I kept marching on, numb to my surroundings. You have to keep moving forward to avoid being left behind, no matter how anchored you are; I never could stay in one place for long. In manys ways, she empathized with me too. I spilled everything to her. The city, my family, the voices in my head - all poured into the melting pot of our conversations. She cried at the story of my parents' death, as did I. I explained all about my dreams and Jack King. She smiled at that part. No words; I could read her expression like a book. "You belong here, Noah," she whispered convincingly. I left out only one part of my past as she took my hand in sorrow and comfort.

We had been on the ship for roughly ten days - in my book, at least - after leaving the beach. Ironically, they were the smoothest ten days of my life. I found myself happy and chipper, almost excited to wake up the next morning to do it all over again. The thing about routines is that you can get lost in them so easily. They are nature's greatest snare, and you will not even realize it. As all good patterns do, that one came to an end slowly but surely. Dark clouds circled the skyline for days prior before all hell broke loose. The storm had been ever-calmly brewing, but she was all but dormant the night she came. As the heavens raged with fury, the three of us battened down the hatches below deck in the lounge. The sound of rain and thunder was nearly deafening, and the winds shook the boat like a child's toy as he threw a tantrum. Speaking of children, Lucious had to add in his two cents, plus tax. "How annoying!" he shouted over the roaring noise outside the portholes. Looking at Felicia, he grinned from ear to ear. "Gee, sis, don't you wish there was something we could do to drown out this noise?" He then turned to me, his smile growing. I shrugged back as I always did. I wanted no part of Lucious's presence. He smelled of leather and cologne, with the obvious hint of alcohol on his breath. I got a nose full of the rancid air as he leaned down and got in my face, smile still glowing. I kept my solemn glare right into his hazel blue eyes. *Blonde hair and blue eyes. Julia. Tremors. Earthquakes.* "Make it stop, Noah," he whispered to me. I glared at him as he cackled with laughter.

"Plug your ears." I stood as still as a mouse. He laughed again. I caught the clench of his fist out of my peripheral vision. I felt pressure on my arms; I lost feeling as they went numb. They raised from my sides against my will; I was back on the tree when I first met those people. I was trapped. My fingers were extended; they stopped in my ears, plugging all noise. We were in immense and desperate silence. I saw him stop laughing, coming ever closer to me. "That's better," he said. I fell back as he released control of me. I hated Lucious with all of my being; I had to have control, however, for Felicia's sake. At least for myself, if no one else. I had to have me; it was the reason as well as the bane of my survival. "Bedtime," he smiled, downing the rest of his flask in his other hand. He nodded to his sister and disappeared into his bedroom and slammed the door. I glared at his shadow as he left. His aura disgusted me.

Once the thundering anger surging through my body subsided, I relaxed my tense muscles and walked over to Felicia, who had collapsed on the couch dramatically. I fell down beside her and ran my fingers up her arm. "Tell me something," I leaned over and said to her. "Anything," she replied, tickling my arm in return. "Why is Lucious the way he is? What happened to him?" I asked solemnly. I wanted to understand; I wanted to know why the hatred ran so deep within his heart for me. I felt her body go tense as she stood up and walked across the room to the kitchen. I followed her persistently as she poured herself a glass of juice. As she turned around to put it up, I took a gulp out of her cup. She whipped around right as I put it down. She looked mad, but it was the fake kind of mad. She broke out into laughter as her faux anger subsided, and I poured her some more as she eyed my stare. She saw me eye the bottle of wine on top of the fridge. "I don't drink," she said. *Those words. Knives.* She returned to her hilarious laughter as I did my best Lucious impression. We piled back onto the couch and settled in. The silence between us was not in her advantage. "You still didn't answer my question," I pushed. She finished her juice, sat the glass on the coffee table, and sighed. "Alright, if you really want to know," she said hesitantly. "I told you *my* story," I grinned as she neglected to return it. That was the first time that had happened; there are always boundaries. "He's always had a hard time," she started. "Dad was severely abusive, especially towards him. It was always a matter of who was the bigger man. Mom and I watched him grow up in anger. In a *shadow*. As he got older, he picked up Dad's bad habits. He started drinking and getting in fights with Dad. One day, he beat him within an inch of his life and told him to get out and never come back. That was two years before the bombings happened. We were caught in the attacks and all of us ended up on the island. Except Dad. He was nowhere to be found. We made our way to the new city, which we are headed to now. Mom raised us on her own, and you'll get to meet her soon enough. Even though Dad had been gone for years, Lucious was his clone. He was *worse*. He was violent and sporadic and volatile. It got so bad and commonplace that Mom banished him from the property. He can't go within a mile of our home. That *kills* him. I decided to give up my life to make sure he kept his. That's what I have to do. I have to live with that. He was then employed by our leader to find new Dreamers and bring them to the city. The factory of the future. Of human *destiny*. We're all Dreamers, our whole family. This is where Dreamers go to die. After they die. The ninety percentile, if you will. That's your story as well as mine, Noah Willowby. As well as Lucious. That's all that matters. Nothing else. You'll find out soon enough." It was like she knew my questions before I asked them and was prepared with an answer all the more readily. She analyzed me like I read her, just as I used to drink in page after page of my books. I still did not believe any of it, however.

By the end of her story, she was red-faced and teary-eyed. I sat up with her and put my arm around her to comfort her. She sobbed a bit into my shoulder as I kept her warm. Then the winter came, violent as a hurricane and sudden as a heart attack. "Boo hoo," Lucious craned as the door opened and he came limping out of his bedroom. "Poor little Lucious Noy, cast out just like his asshole of a father," his voice pitied. He dropped the act and laughed that same sarcastic, cold laugh he always did when he began to mock a situation. We stood up to face him, and we stared at the ghost behind us. His eyes were bloodshot as he stood there, shirtless with a pair of plaid pajama pants. He was so muscular, apparently from years of fighting and stress. He made his way over to the couch and grabbed my arm, flipping me over the back of the furniture. My arm exploded with pain, and his fist slid across my jaw. I heard Felicia squeal as I hit the ground hard. As he towered over me, I ran both of my legs into his torso, rolling him off of me. I climbed to my feet and bolted across the lounge. Once Lucious recovered from his blow, we made eye contact through a twenty-foot distance.

"Lucious, stop this! He has a right to know who we are!" she tried to reason. "Who the hell do you think you are, Felicia?!" he turned and barked at his sister. "Telling this scumbag all about us! You know good and goddamn well that you can't get close to the ones we find." Felicia stood up defiantly. "It's not a secret," she fought back. "You're just scared of it," she retorted. "I'm not." Lucious grew ever-more angry. I saw a red tint overcome his pupils as he glared at me; I could feel his fury. "Making me out to be some sort of charity case," he spit. He reached his hand out into the empty air, and a shot glass flew into his hand. Lucious examined the tiny glass vial for a moment, before chucking it across the room. It smashed against Felicia's left cheek as she attempted to dodge it, to no avail. I was disoriented at what had just happened; I was caught between a rock and a hard place. I made out the shape of the muscular teen making his way over to me then. He lifted his hand, and the once silent screeching of the storm outside returned, roaring as loudly and powerfully as it once had. With a flick of his wrist, the hatch opened up, along with the staircase, letting in vicious sea spray and the intense, blinding lightning flashes once more. I readied myself for more blows, but to my disillusion, he hoisted me over his back like an unconscious child ready for bed as we headed for the stairs. The next thing I remember was rolling across the sopping wet wood and the slapping of the downpour against my face. I was paralyzed; I could not move a single muscle. Lucious towered over me once again, that time with a sense of defeat as opposed to war. He knelt down, bringing his fist across my jaw. Again. And again. My vision clouded and my eyes rolled to the back of my head as blood mixed with the puddles below me. My limbs were numb, and I could not think straight. I knew what the visions were - my life was flashing before my eyes. I saw the final blow coming - the one that would end this misery. He stopped. He had beaten me within an inch of my life, just as he had apparently done to his father. Lucious paused to admire his work, standing back and smiling that wicked grin once again. Satisfied, he turned to face the roaring ocean behind him.

In the moments that followed, I regained my breath and my footing on the slippery deck. I limped quietly behind the captain's quarters and grasped the rope tied to the anchor on the wooden siding. I dragged the thick, heavy rope through the puddles and behind Lucious. I threw it around his neck in a sort of noose style, quickly and quietly, catching him off guard. I slammed my knuckles as hard as I could under his nose, cracking several bones. "You little prick," he said through clenched teeth. He glanced behind him as we neared the railing. He tried to return my blows, but I ducked, that time going for his feet. I hoisted him up by his knees and flipped him over the steel bars. The rope raced across the deck, tossing up a spray of salty mist. I heard a hard splash as the anchor clanked against the side of the boat. I backed away from the side of the ship, taking all that had just happened in abruptly. I leaned against the lifeboat rack, weak from the intense fighting. Every bone and muscular aches and throbbed from head to toe as I shook with spasms and surges of agonizing pain. As my vision faded slightly into the raging storm above, the flashes of lightning reflected off of something beneath my foot. I looked down to find the whiskey bottle by my leg. I bent down, somewhat painfully, and examined the bottle. It had to have been one of Lucious's from his brief moments of fresh air during his drinking sessions. I threw it into the ocean along with him as a sort of final goodbye. I collapsed against the wooden deck, water soaking through my jeans and washing the blood from my skin. Murder was never too far from my mind, as I had no conscience left - apart from how Felicia would react. Lucious deserved to die and he had been given every ounce of it I could muster, but Felicia would mourn. That thought murdered me in return.

I could see the bottle splash into the water below from where I sat. It sunk under the waves below me, just as its owner had. I took a slightly woozy note that bubbles were coming up out of the water. At first thought, I claimed it to be the downpour of heavy raindrops, but this was something far more *weighted*. The jet black water began to glow the color of whiskey, spreading for as far as I could see. The intense lightning above shone off of the golden, glittering water far below. The raindrops steamed and evaporated on contact; I was beyond captivated. I could see clearly through the pale waves, straight to the bottom. I could make out one creature in the vicious waves below me, and that was the bound and tied Lucious Noy rising to the top of the sea once again. The anchor broke the water and sailed through the air at an incredible speed right at me. It shattered the wooden wall behind me, sending splinters of wood against my soaking wet skin. It came inches away from decapitating me. There was not much of my brain present at that particular moment anyhow, yet I was grateful nonetheless and beyond terrified. What the hell was I dealing with? The rope wrapped itself around my waist, fastening me to the unmovable anchor behind me. The out-of-control psychopath was nowhere to be found, and I was far too weak to fight the handicaps. I craned my neck as far as they would allow to search for him, to no avail. The storm raged on continuously, but my mind went silent, blank and calm as the sea. I could feel the wind tickle my neck, sending drops of water down my skin. Voices whispered in my ear - *thousands* of them. *One of them. The same one. Over and over and over.* "*I am everywhere, Noah Willowby,*" he said, inside my own head. It was as if he was right in front of me, but I only saw the railing dripping water before me. The water below me took on its original pitch black hue. I clapped my hands over my ears for any sign of escape. There was none. *"Make it stop,"* he mocked himself. *The laugh.* I saw shadows to match each voice. *One shadow.* I screamed in agony as I struggled for control of myself. Before I lost consciousness, I saw Felicia instead of the shadows, coming out of the hatch across the deck. *"Hello, sister,"* I heard myself say, but it was not me. *That* was not me. *I was darkness.* Felicia pulled something from behind her back. "You'll thank me for this later, Noah," she said. She brought the empty whiskey bottle across my head.

In nearly every instance will I be completely and totally honest - rather blunt - surgically removing my true emotions rather than enveloping them in flowery dramatism. This shall be another such time - I felt like utter shit the following morning. My head was a jar of jelly, and my body was as weak as a newborn colt. It took several moments for my senses to return. I felt a warm hand put pressure on my forehead; I tilted my view ever-the-painful-slightest and was relieved that it was Felicia. Before my eyes had opened, I hoped to would that it would be my mother on the other side. Valerie. Julia. It was not, and so I settled. We were back inside the boat, down inside the common room and inside my bedroom, in my bed, wrapped warmly in all of my blankets and propped up on the totality of the pillows. I felt the rough cotton bandages around my wounds, covering them, but unfortunately not taking away the constant, throbbing pain. "Thank you," I said, cutting her off before she could say anything. "Good to see you finally awake," she smiled slightly. I did not smile in return; it was my turn to be distant and vague. "Where is he?" I uttered, changing the tone ever-so-suddenly. "He's...taken care of," she said, her smile fading that time. "How did I get down here?" I wondered with a painful chuckle. "Contrary to popular belief, you're a lot *heavier* than you look," she winked. I smiled as I felt my eyes begin to close again with fatigue. "Get some rest," she whispered, kissing my forehead gently. I wrapped my hand around hers so she could not leave - at least for another moment.

I was in and out as far as consciousness goes for at least two days - again, as far as *I* was concerned - following the seemingly fruitless attack. Felicia would sleep at the foot of the bed, as there was little floor space in the cramped corner room. We slept perpendicular under the pile of blankets and array of pillows. She had a certain comforting presence about her that I could not understand; however, I had no plan to argue with it. She took care of me, and as independent as I was and still am, perhaps I needed that at that given moment. "Where is he?" I wondered aloud one day in between dozing and a pre-coma. Perhaps it was a lost essence of my imagination - a pre-destined thought voiced aloud. There was silence after I grunted and winced the vague whisper. The silence that followed was more painful than the scheming aches deep within my body; I thought Felicia was gone. But as my eyes opened once more out of fear, I stared back into those eyes of hers. Her usual smile was as gone as I first believed her to be - nowhere to be found. "He cannot leave his room," she said bluntly, with no explanation. I was too focused on the throbbing in my ribs to even ponder what that meant. "He has plenty of food, water, and alcohol for the rest of this trip."

As therapeutic and beneficial as the prolonged rest had been for me, I knew I had to get back on my feet. I was never a believer in weakness, whether it be emotional or physical. As you can probably infer, that mindset entails quite a bit of pain - *definitely* physical. I fell several times before Felicia became my literal crutch to get to even the shortest of distances. Once I got to the couch in the lounge, to the bathroom, and eventually back to my room at night, I was well taken care of. She never returned back to her room during the remainder of the trip.

Life after the fight was one of recovery. With the idea and memory of Lucious Noy fading away day by day, the air was clearer and the days were as smooth as the waters beneath us. As I regained my strength as a baby bird does after being crushed, we began to walk the deck again. Once I got my momentum going and surpassed the hobbling stage, we could make it halfway around without taking a breather. As I stair-stepped my way back to health, I began helping Felicia with nearly everything. She was taken aback, as expected, of course. Most people in her life had passed her by with nothing more than a scoff. I would not join them. Over the course of the next thirty days, she became more affectionate toward me. Our walks around the deck were more meaningful, and she slowly inched her way beside me in that empty bed. When the nights were cool and the waters were calm, we would fall asleep together underneath the flashlight stars around the campfire moon. There were no more storms on that journey; the weather almost seemed to follow the pattern of the hostility among us. There were clear skies ahead of us, forever and always. Perhaps that place really was Heaven - or at least some twisted allegory of peace. I surely had an angel by my side. We had been aboard the ship for forty days when we finally saw light of our destination. During yet another starry night's sleep, Felicia shook me awake the following morning. Before I opened my eyes, I could hear the excitement in her voice. "We're *home*."

Felicia and I stood up from our chairs and set off across the wooden deck at a quick, excited, and somewhat groggy pace. The wind whipped the sail around and into place as we neared the shore in the distance. We climbed down the hatch and down the stairs, re-entering the warm and cozy entertainment room. It was quite a shame we had to leave that place. I had grown accustomed to it; it was a home of vacational sorts, complete with its cramped and cozy atmosphere. As all homes seem to end, we began packing our belongings as the ship inched closer to our much anticipated and unbeknownst destination. I watched Felicia round the corner and knock on the door to Lucious's room. "Pack your *shit*," she said, plainly and simply as a mother would. I knew that all too well, and so the memories flooded over me once more.

We watched out of the portholes in the common room as the distant beach grew closer and closer to the bottom of the boat. We soon ran ashore, sliding up the wet sand as smoothly and softly as we had sailed for such a long, extended, and captivating amount of time. Forty days to Noah Willowby may have very well been years to the Noy twins. I let down the ladder and hopped onto the deep and - as we found out - not very sturdy, sand beneath us. I shook like a snowman in the summertime as I got used and accustomed to land once again. It had been forever. On top of just waking up only an hour prior, getting your land legs should not be on anyone's morning itinerary. I helped Felicia down and she leaned on me as she got her balance. *'Where is he?'* I wondered to myself. "He'll be along a bit later," Felicia said, as if she could smell my curiosity.

We stood side-by-side as we took in the barren desert sand in front of us. I never intended to kill anyone's positive or over-exaggerative vibes, but that place surely did not fit Felicia's description. In fact, it looked exactly like where we had started from. *'This is the same goddamn island.'* I thought to myself. I could not help but laugh out loud. I put my hands on her shoulders as she looked at me curiously. "Tell me I didn't sail across an ocean for over a month, brave a storm, and get the fuck beaten out of me by your psycho brother just to end up on the same fucking regenerative cycle trap beach I met you guys on." My smile faded, and it surely did not spark one from her. "Watch it," she warned, calmly but collected - so *familiar*. I let go of her swiftly and passively. "This is the other side of the island," she said. I still did not understand. We had travelled across the island already and put an ocean's distance between it. "And before you ask a stupid question, yes, it is the same side. We had to sail around it to find the entrance to the city." Something I said had definitely set her off. "And you're wrong," she finished. "You sailed across the ocean for over three months. Every day here counts for three where you're from." She could sense my anxiety. "But don't worry; nobody ages here. You surely missed nothing." She walked around the sand in front of me, staring off into the distance. "When you have something this special, you have to hide it. It's taken as long as a hundred years for people to find their way back. We were relatively quick at it." She lost me somewhere near the beginning. A desert did not exactly scream, **"PARADISE THIS WAY, FOLKS!"**

"Show me this city, then," I insisted. "It's not that simple, Noah," she argued. There was always a catch, goddamnit. "You have to believe." Great. Perhaps we could catch a ride on the Polar Express along the way. "But I'm not a Dreamer," I said plainly, showing no sign of the disbelief behind the words. She rolled her eyes and trudged forward, away from me. "You have to believe, Noah Willowby," she said as she stomped away. "Even if you don't want any part of it." I stopped in my tracks as she spoke my name sternly and exasperated. "How? Show me," I said as I hurried to catch up to her. She stopped abruptly as I nearly ran into her. She turned to look me straight in the eyes. "What is in your wildest imagination?" she asked, extremely vague. "Imagine where you *think* we're going. *You're* in charge. *You* call the shots. *Picture* it, *feel* it, *make* it reality." I let that sink in. I had closed my eyes long before she started to speak, trying to create the place in which I had only heard about. Felicia's voice rolled through my ears like waves, laying out streets and buildings as high as the sky. I heard the city materialize brick by brick, steel plate by steel plate, and beam by beam behind closed eyes. The thoughts and ideas became blueprints as I put the people on the streets and the lights in the lampposts and skyscraper windows in their frames. The scene raced in my head as everything became supersonically fast, spinning and turning like a rollercoaster. Then it all came to a halt. I opened my eyes, almost expecting my city to be in front of me. But it was not. Only sand and Felicia remained. "See?" I said. "I did my best. That's all I've got. Nothing happened," I gave up. "Come with me," she said, rolling her eyes. "Where are we going now? *Oz*?" I laughed, making fun of myself as well as her, and also the whole make-believe bunch of nonsense that had become my life. I might as well get a few laughs out of it. "The entrance is over there," she corrected. I felt quite stupid as the color raced to my cheeks. I wanted to go home. I had gotten attached rather quickly and it vanished just as suddenly. I wanted my city, my house, and my Julia. It was what I had imagined, and only sand and the broken tears of dreams and hearts remained.

The heat on the beach was thick and intense, bringing sweat to our brows. The air shimmered as the tight, humid wind blew sand around into mountain-high dunes, and mirages of water surrounded us. I saw no entrance before us. "Look over there," Felicia said. I saw nothing. "In the middle of those sand dunes," she directed. Nothing again. "See how the air is sparkling a little?" she said in a teacher-like voice. Maybe I had to go back to the kindergarten level to know what the hell she was talking about. "It's a *gateway*." We neared the supposed entrance. The wind was intense around it; the air was cool as opposed to the humid air on the rest of the beach. It was freezing, to be exact. Lights shone through the bits of sand that circled the large entryway. It increased with energy as we got closer and closer. Nervous anxiety kicked in as I saw it with my own eyes. "Let's see what you've got for us," she said. "There better not be any fucking angels waiting for us with massages and bleached assholes," she warned, almost humorously. I had long since given up on the idea of that place being Heaven. I could use a massage though, mainly to calm my nerves. Hand in hand, we stepped through the sky and felt the ground vanish beneath our feet. I closed my eyes and hoped to God that it was not death. Another one bites the dust, goddamnit.

Chapter XII
A Place to Think
(Settling, Contentment, and Making a Decision)

Walking through the divide was like passing through a frigid waterfall; every inch of my body was refreshed and cooled down at least a dozen degrees. It was quite honestly the best feeling I had ever experienced. I was weightless and free - *truly* free, in a space-like and ice cold fashion. Hey, if that just so happened to be death, it definitely could have been a lot worse. Sure beat a gunshot to the fucking skull. No sir. I was even more amazed when I opened my eyes. The flat desert had fallen away to something unbelievable. Before Felicia and I, standing hand-in-hand, both enjoying the rebirthing experience of the portal, was a city. But do not let my mere words fool you, my friend; it was nothing like the cursed city of Jack King. Not in the least, slightest, grittiest bit. The metropolis which lay before us was constructed of pure *diamond*. Buildings, streets, sidewalks, and even the smiles of the people around us were glowing gloriously in the golden sunlight overhead. This new place was the polar opposite of Jack King's city. What was dark and gloomy was then bright and peaceful. This was *evolution*. This was exactly what I had imagined.

"Wow," I mumbled. That was all I could think to say. "This place is unreal," I said. "It's my dream world." There was a slight pause. "Should that make it any less *real*?" Felicia said, looking up at me convincingly. I smiled slightly. She was a smooth one, I can tell you that much. Our hands were still inseparable as we took everything in. We were in the middle of a crowd of people. The new silence of a fresh environment wore off and the hustle and bustle of noise took over. I glanced down and saw a manhole cover, also made of diamond. "It marks the very center of the city," Felicia said, barely audible through the loud hum of voices around us. She did not even look down. How did she know that? "It's also the gateway back to the island," she ended. I could not hear her.

There was so much to take in, and even that is a severe understatement. My eyes eventually adjusted to the bright shine of the fluorescent city. The air was cool but comfortable, and the noise eventually evened out to a rather soothing tone. It was background noise, as if everyone had a role to play, but not by force. Yes, by own creation. Felicia and I walked toward the nearest sidewalk across the street as a car swerved around the corner, heading right toward Felicia. I panicked, shouted and leapt from the pavement in front of her; there was nothing I could do. As the car raced at her torso, I prepared for the worst. I could utter no sound. As I plugged my ears and closed my eyes, the car passed straight through her. She joined me on the sidewalk as I picked my heart up out of the middle of the street.

"What the fuck -," I started but could not finish. "How did you -?" Again, there were no words. Felicia sighed an exasperated huff. "You have to *believe*, Noah. What did I *tell* you? Believe it, and it's already done." She brushed imaginary dust off of her shirt as she passed by me. What a show off. Much to my pleasure, I could actually finish my sentences the rest of the walk. "So everyone here is a Dreamer?" I asked. "Everyone except *you*," she said plainly and in a mocking tone. I stopped dead in my tracks, and she must have heard my footsteps stop like brakes on a wet road in the way she turned around to face me. "Just kidding," she laughed. I did not know anything about mood swings, but her attitude had most definitely took a turn for the better. I played along with her joke, however. "Then how am I here?" I said as she turned around to keep walking. "You don't believe yet, but you will," she answered. "You tell me," she shrugged. She started walking away as I pondered that question, as I have been furiously known to do.

My questions had left us at a verbal standstill; we walked for minutes - or perhaps hours in that land - without a word. I followed Felicia's brisk, light footsteps as quickly as I could. Word from the back of the line - the silvery light did wondrous things to her hair. The whole situation just did not seem real to me; perhaps I was satisfied with that. The old city was dark and depressing, apart from brief inconsistencies that allowed for a life of uncomfortable expectancy. Except for Julia. Oh, man. The memories hit me like a speeding car. I lost train my of thought, step, and balance. I fell to the concrete as my mind went blank. Felicia did not hear me fall; she kept walking; I was left behind. *Behind. Back. Trapped. Lost. Separated.* These were my thoughts from rock bottom. I climbed to my knees as I struggled to get control of myself. *What was this? What triggered this loss of control?* I had no earthly idea. My mouth gaped open as tears flooded my eyes from a deep, unknown dam within me. The old city was nothing but a distant, foggy memory, and Julia was the lighthouse. She was the *trigger*. That was what kept me rooted in that place. I figured it out much later, although it was an ironic and unappreciated truth.

I got my footing once again on the solid sidewalk right as the bright, blinding headlights rounded the corner. The car hit me head on, buckling my knees, rolling me across the hood, and sending me sprawling through the air against the alleyway wall several feet behind me. I groaned in excruciating, startled pain as Felicia screamed at the driver. As I gazed up from the sidewalk once again, I saw none other than Lucious Noy behind the wheel of the brand new cherry red Mustang. "Holy fuck - you didn't give him the believing soapbox lesson yet?" he barked at Felicia. She glared at her brother. "How did you get out of your room?" she demanded. Lucious laughed as he pushed his sunglasses back up over his eyes once more; I desperately missed mine. "You seem to forget that *anything* is possible here, sister dearest." He seemed preoccupied staring across the hood at the dent I had made. "Oh, you better believe you'll pay for that, buddy," he said. "In one way or another." I had gotten up by then. I gritted my teeth and bit my lip; there was no sense in fighting him. He was obviously stronger in both mind and body judging from the highlights of our last meeting. The aching bruises and scars that remained urged me to keep it quiet - for then, at least.

As Felicia and I stared at Lucious though the rolled down tinted window, he seemed to grow impatient. "Well, aren't you two going to get in? What are you waiting for? I'll burn in hell before I become a chauffeur." My turn to laugh. "You got that right," I muttered. I opened the backseat for Felicia and we climbed inside; the car smelled like leather and vanilla. As we closed the door, Lucious revved the engine loudly. However, the people around did not seem to notice. They minded their business as if they were in fact in their *own* dream world; I did not have time to buckle my seatbelt before I was awakened from mine. He turned the radio dial to a deep-bass rock song. The guitars wailed as the tires squealed around curbs and corners. I might have enjoyed the experience if my head had not made contact with the window rather hard upon pulling off. I heard a vague laugh through the ripping guitar solo.

As if I even needed to point it out, Lucious Noy was *not* a good driver. Ask the bruises up and down my body if you so happen to not believe me. If the road ahead of us did not conform to his every desire, he would have been responsible for dozens of deaths and thousands of dollars in property damage. I braced myself as he turned the corner violently to avoid smacking my temple with the window again. The combination of the engine and the music was deafening. We appeared to be leaving the city, or at least traveling to the outskirts. The silver glow of the city faded into grassy fields and farmland, and eventually, the cement faded into a dusty dirt road. I looked back at the distant outline of the city and gazed at the beauty. That place really was magnificent.

The car eventually turned into a driveway right off of the path. I was surprised we did not miss it going as fast as we were. The city was far out of sight and the long, winding driveway led to the only house I had seen for miles. Barns and silos lined the property among a plethora of farmland acres. Lucious brought the car to a slow halt as we crested the hill that nearly hid the house from sight. "Here you are," Lucious mumbled, as if something was tugging at his heartstrings and weighing heavily on his mind. I followed Felicia out of the backseat and into the dust cloud we had churned up. I looked back at him before I closed the tinted barrier of a door. He knew what I was thinking. Felicia grabbed my hand to pull me away gently. I kept my gaze at Lucious as he stared back at me. "There are some rules that you just can't break, kid," he said before I shut the door abruptly. I watched him pull out of the driveway and speed off into the distance until the roar of the engine was silent. That was the first and last time he spoke to me as an equal.

"What is this place?" I wondered aloud as we set our minds and feet towards the farmhouse in the distance. "My mother's house," Felicia said cheerfully, as if she was hiding something beneath her shy smile. "She created this place after Lucious killed our father and was banished." The slight curve slowly dropped downward as memories overtook her. It was hidden no more. "Lucious cannot cross this hill," she ended. She looked happy and sad at the same time, as if she was worried about her brother but content with her life with him as a jaded exclusion. "It's only Mom here. And the cat, of course." I stayed quiet as she figured out just what she was feeling. "Want to meet her?" she perked up. No, I absolutely did not. "Absolutely," I replied in the same cheerful, hidden tone. The dust settled beneath our feet only to get kicked up again with the next hill and curve we rounded. The long stretch of driveway led us to a set of creaky wooden stairs. The sides of the porch were walled-in by wooden lattice, which was quite the turn-on for the half dozen wood bees slapping the wooden posts. The sun was warm but the air was cool - a perfect hybrid of comfortable conditions. The farm was quite peaceful with all of its simple beauty as the sun lowered itself behind the right silo and middle barn. By rights it felt as if it should only be noon. Time was still an adjustment to be made, as was nearly everything in that new place.

The door creaked open several moments after Felicia knocked abruptly. I searched for a doorbell, but I found nothing. I might have just been trying to distract myself from the goddamn butterflies turning in my stomach. I usually was the epitome of the nervous type, and some things especially rendered me silent and shaky, such as meeting girls and their bearers. Perhaps mothers were better than fathers as far as the butterfly problem goes, however. I had a warped mind - that was an unnecessarily sick joke. I punished myself later for that statement. The short, plump woman that answered the door smiled at the sight of her daughter, but her grin grew even larger when she laid her eyes on me. She led us inside and closed the screen door behind us. "And who is this handsome young man, honey?" she asked cheerfully to her daughter. "Mom, this is Noah Willowby. He's new here." I shook her hand and automatically saw the resemblance between the two women. They bore extreme resemblance to each other both physically and orally; they were spitting images of one another in looks as well as their voices. The cheerful tone in their speech was almost as welcoming as their touch, and the family aura was a hospitable one. "Welcome, Noah. It's great to meet you. Are you a Dreamer?" she asked in the same chipper voice. It could not hope to mask the dark question. "Likewise, and no ma'am," I replied calmly. Her smile never wavered. "Very well," she shot back. "Come on into the kitchen. Dinner will be ready soon."

The area around the house had a calm, country feel to it. The breeze smelled of mown grass and plowed fields, and the house smelled of vanilla through the rustic halls and plain, simple furnishings. We followed the perky, wobbling woman through the narrow, dark hallway into a large and well-lit kitchen, which branched off into an ordinary dining room. My stomach lost Mrs. Noy at *dinner*; I had thought of nothing since she had uttered the word. The delicious smells helped none the more. "How long until dinner, Mom?" Felicia asked curiously. "About half an hour," she replied, her thoughts and spoons stirring. "I hope Noah isn't *too* starved," she added. "Oh, no ma'am," I lied quite painfully. "I'll give you a tour of the farm!" Felicia exclaimed. She scurried out the back door of the kitchen and into the screened-in sunroom as we clopped down the steps and into the shortly-clipped grass. The rear of the property was home to what appeared to be acres of woods. This tour could last a while - far longer than half of an unknown hour and an empty tank can hold. Great, a starving stomach *and* a load of exercise.

Julia would have loved it there. I stared at the neat and trimmed landscaping and thought of her gardens back in the city. I would often forget that place, dismissing it as a dark and distant memory. But when a tiny, minuscule element came across my senses, whether it be something I saw, smelled, or heard - mental or reality - the thoughts and memories would come trickling into my cranium like a leaking pipe. *A slit throat. Julia. Jacob. Jack King.* I dismissed it once again. I put on my butterfly mask once again. *My false persona. My fake smile.* "You can breathe here," Felicia said as we slowly strolled back towards the shade trees of the forest behind the house. "Yeah," I replied sarcastically, as if she was simply stating the obvious. "I mean *actually* breathe *actual* air. Clean, crisp, flowing air. You can think here. All because of the *actuality* of it all. We keep things simple out here. It's about the only place in this world good for anything, much less thinking." She smiled a satisfied smile, content with her little speech. I was content with it as well, for she was right. I could *breathe* there. The air was fresh and the aura was quiet, apart from a grumbling stomach here and there, that is - and certainly far more than a dingy, dirty city or even the pollution-free metropolis we had just left moments or hours ago. I did not know.

"Does he miss this?" I wondered aloud, referring to the Bad and Ugly portion of the Good, Bad, and Ugly. "I think he's gotten used to it," she replied. "He killed our father to protect his family. Lucious is a lot of things, but smart is among the list. He had to have known the consequences. Mom saw too many similarities between the two of them for him to stay, and she feared the worst, that maybe one day he might end up dead too. That quite possibly one of us might have had to do it. It was too much for her. She wanted to give him a new life. So he had to go find it. That's why I stepped up to watch after him. To make sure he didn't end up like Josh. And if somebody had to do it, it would be me. Not Mom. After everything, I wouldn't let her do that. I couldn't."

"Who's Josh?" I asked. "It's a long story," she shied away. I pointed toward the woods where we were headed as my stomach struggled its way back to the house. "We've got plenty of time," I provided. "Tell me the story," I said with a small, urging smile. I could tell she was uneasy, as if she needed to get this off of her mind. "Mom couldn't have kids. She gave up after her first husband left her. And the second. The third wasn't exactly a charm with Josh. Before she met him, she adopted me seven years prior. We lived alone in Kentucky. What a world that was. Then Mom met Josh and Lucious. Maybe it was out of pity, or the fact that he *knew* he could take advantage of her. I don't know. All I know is that I hated him. And Lucious. But I got to know him. He became a brother to me. He cared, underneath that hard shell. Soon after they married and we all moved in together, Josh's original nice-guy attitude wore off. He started drinking and hitting Mom. He had always beaten Lucious. Then me. We were all victims. All *slaves*. Then the bombings hit. The countryside was in shambles in a matter of hours as all the major cities were. We got caught directly in the middle of one. That's how we got here.

We found each other here. Josh was as much of a washed-up piece of *shit* as he ever was, if not more so. He took advantage of life here, and the temptations and the power took him over. He was still violently abusive. Lucious hit rock bottom one night and beat him to death with a liquor bottle. We kept it secret, but the pain attacked Lucious. After all Josh had done, he was still his father. Lucious became just like him, drinking and abusive and manipulative. Mom saw it coming and when it all came to a head, she kicked him out. I chose to go with him. She said I was always welcome here, but if he ever came past that hill, I would never be allowed back. Now we work as recruiters for the leader here." Her eyes were full of tears as her heart overflowed through her mouth of memories. I was right; she needed so desperately to get that out of her mind and into the thin wisps of air. Tears streamed down my cheeks as well; I hated to see her cry. "After all this time, why do you call him Dad?" I asked quietly, almost angry. "That was the first time. I didn't want you to feel sorry for me. I don't need anybody to feel sorry for me," she spit through gritted teeth. "Keep something in mind - he was *no* father of mine." "I don't feel sorry for you, Felicia," I said, pulling her close. "You don't need that. You're strong enough on your own."

We stopped to lean on a picket fence, resting from the little ways we had walked down the field. The fence posts overlooked the rolling hills and valleys behind us, combined with an extraordinary sunset. I had rarely seen true color in my life and much less appreciated it. I had a million questions after Felicia had told me her story. "How could you care about someone so cruel and vile that's isn't even *family*?" I asked. Jacob was the same way, and I had to pull together every ounce of strength I had to even attempt to tolerate him. I simply could not understand it even in the slightest. "Family isn't just blood, Noah. I don't have any blood family. Family is bonded through *love. Care. Compassion.*" I pondered that. "He's never shown compassion toward me," I muttered. "There wasn't a bond," she replied. "I guess he chooses who he cares about." I nodded. That made sense, and I definitely did not make the cut.

"What was the city like when you left it?" Felicia asked me. If what she was saying was correct, she had left the world when it was still a blissful paradise. If only it could have remained that way forevermore. "Just an inch shy of hell," I started vaguely. "I could have guessed that much," she rolled her eyes. "It was like a rope bound so tightly. Each string was so focused and concentrated. Then it began to *unravel*. Slowly at first and allowing time to adjust to change. Then it hit all at once. Things began to change slowly and then quickly. The human mind cannot process things it is not accustomed to. It was like seeing God, and it really was. It horrified them and terrified then. Fear creates a strict dichotomy and a divisive loyalty pattern. Two sides to every story, right? Two sides, and one is God; one is man. They cannot *coexist*. The city became the aftermath of God's return, in other words. God was always thought to be a just and righteous being. But he is a *jealous* being. There is no such thing as *coexistence*. Everyone yearned so desperately for the end of the world, and through that they missed that it was already over. Does that sum it up?" I finished abruptly and just as vaguely as I had started. She remained silent, apparently taken aback by what I had said. Perhaps I had surprised myself as well; my thoughts had become verbal for the first time in my life, and there was absolutely no return.

We had rested against the solid fence for several minutes in silence, nothing but our sighs, sobs, and breathing in the air. Talking about Lucious and Jack King did not exactly bring positive conversational ideas to mind. "Do you want to see the tree house?" she asked, her maternal, perky attitude returning once again. Her mood seemed to reset every few conversations, and it was confusing as well as slightly irritating. Curiosity soon took over, as I never had a treehouse as a kid. "Of course I do!" I said, mimicking her cheerful tone. "One condition…" she started.

I looked at her curiously. "Shoes off," she said with a smirk. "I want you to feel this place beneath your feet." How could I argue? I followed her lead as she slipped her sandals off. I took off my boots and socks and piled them with her shoes. "When I say go, take off running down the hill and through the field until you get to the woods," she said, that time nearly laughing. "Whatever you say," I returned. "On your mark, get set, GO!" she shouted over the sound of the wind whipping our hair back. She took off running down the slight slope and across the flat field below. I followed behind, only slower. After all, my energy levels were not exactly at full capacity. She stayed a few feet ahead of me across the soft grass the entire race. The dew was cool and soothing on the blisters I had acquired over the last few days; I felt exactly what she was feeling. *We were free. At long last.* I was mesmerized by the sound of her feet hitting the soft ground and the flow of her body as she ran. Felicia was stunning. She, in herself, was an element all her own. I did not and could not break my gaze or my stride until we hit the forest. And then she disappeared.

The woods were dimly shaded; the sunset shone through the tiny cracks in the forest roof with a quiet, quaint, and cozy lighting. Thick tree trunks surrounded me - only me. Felicia was nowhere to be found. I stayed still, with only the sound of my breathing and birds chirping overhead. Twigs snapped as squirrels scurried across logs; I flinched with every crack. I walked a little ways into the treeline, searching around every wooden pillar for any sign of Felicia. There was none. I came to a shallow ravine with a creek running through it; it appeared to be quite deep in a certain part. I peered over the edge to see if perhaps she had fallen in, but there was still no sign. I stood on the edge and thought for a moment as to where she might be. "Who you looking for, water boy?" I heard. I whipped around, finding nothing. "Up here!" I looked up above me. I saw the giant treehouse above us. How had I not noticed it before? There was no shadow and no indication.

Such a strange place that was. "How did you get up there?" I laughed. "I'll be down in a minute," she huffed. I watched her closely. She held a long rope, pulled it tight, and then jumped off the railing of the massive vessel above us. She swung down above the creek and let go right as she tackled me. We both went sprawling into the stream below.

The water was the perfect temperature, believe it or not. After the initial falling feeling subsided, I braced myself for the arctic cold and the brittle shock it entailed; there was nothing worse than freezing water upon surprise. The creek pool was at least a dozen feet deep; Felicia stayed latched onto me as we spiraled through the clear water. We surfaced as my hands found her waist. We pulled our hair behind each other's ears as we slid the water out of our eyes. "Thanks for that," I said as I spit out a few drops of water. "This place is *full* of surprises," she winked. "I'll remember that," I followed. We climbed out of the river by the bank and sopped to the ladder on the back of one of the trees. Felicia climbed up first, giving me quite a rather *wet* view from below. I climbed up close behind and tried not to slip and fall off the slippery rails. I was more than surprised when we entered the treehouse. Believe it or not, it was not treehouse-like at all. That place really was a miniature house up in the trees. It was one with the limbs, complete with a kitchen, bedroom, and bathroom. Roots ran through the walls like veins, and candles sat nestled in the thick trunk holders seemingly fashioned just for them. Felicia gave me a tour of the wooden castle up in the trees as the smell of pine cones and lumber circulated through the air. It was a rather cozy and comfortable place, as was every other location in that world had been.

After we had walked around the "ground floor", Felicia pointed to a staircase across the room; I would have missed it if she did not literally point it out. She pulled me along up the winding wooden steps that led even higher into the treetops. I was even more amazed at the sight of that. I do not know how I did not see the overlook from the ground; it could not be missed. But hey, this place was certainly full of mystery. The overhang was a large fenced-in porch which seemed to levitate on the tip-top of the trees. It allowed for a perfect, spectacular view of the entire property; every last field and barn could be seen and studied from the nest. Even the massive, shining city was visible, looming in the distance as a proper kingdom should. "Doesn't it just take your breath away?" Felicia admired. "Definitely," I said, leaning up against the railing. I was dumbfounded and entranced by the marvelous scenery. "Even though I've been up here a hundred times, it still feels like the first every time," she said, deep in the same trance as I was. I weighed what she had said and thought on it. I came to the realization that I had seen such a view once before. I remembered the same feeling as Julia and I stared over the edge of the Perch. *Falling. Crushing. Bleeding out. Memories.*

I turned around to face the farmhouse. It seemed like a thousand miles away, as did a million other things. The diamond city cast a faint shadow as the sun slipped beneath the distant skyscrapers miles and miles away. It seemed like ages since we had entered the city, since we had gotten to the farm, and since we had come to the treehouse. Hell, in that place, it probably had been ages ago. I could see the whole world from that one tiny place up in the sky. It gave me a bit of a God complex, as though I could see everything in all of creation. But I could not *control* it; it was not *mine*. "It's a great place to think," she said, staring into the distance just as I had been doing. "Tell me what's on your mind," she looked over at me, smiling. There was no use in shrugging it off or dismissing it; something really *was* bothering me. Ever since I had gotten on the island, the same thing had been eating at me like a mental and emotional cancer. Memories would hit me like bullets and my focus would leak out like blood from a punctured artery. The city was the gun, and Julia was the trigger. The emotions I felt were the bullets, putting hole after hole in me like a most-wanted target. I began to lose myself somewhere in between the two cities - the two worlds. I would soon lose my entire being and be nothing but a lifeless sack of bones and empty sockets. I trusted Felicia, and I could not hope to stop the feeling and the truth - the deep, down, dirty truth - from dripping out from my lips like the gallons of drool I would soon be standing in if I neglected to get it off of my mind and tongue.

I staggered back from the railing as the words attacked me, stammering my voice at first. So much was built up and I was so broken down. "I - I had a wife back in the city," I started. "Her name was Julia. I loved her. Now she's gone. Or I'm gone. I don't have a fucking clue but I don't understand it." Tears boiled in my eyes as I blinked them back. "Like every other goddamn thing I have. Or had," I continued. I was beyond angry and confused, fuming with emotion like a defective fire extinguisher. The anger fueled my heartbroken sadness as it poured out of me. "It's a cycle, all of it. Something gets taken, you get used to it, then it goes and changes again. Over and fucking over. This apocalypse. The old city. This new place. IS THIS EVEN REAL?!" I shouted at the top of my lungs, choosing Felicia as the involuntary target of my rage, which I regretted later. I did not possess a single, lonely care at the time. I was quite selfish when I was upset, but who could blame me? We all wear those shoes at one point or another. That was always the moral to the story of getting upset, after all. "All of the dreams. The constant changes. Not being able to tell what the fuck is real anymore. My family is dead. The undying, cancerous, fucking nuclear overbearing question of whether or not I'm a goddamn Dreamer or not. Which is definitely not. I AM NOT A DREAMER! I am normal, crazy, unstable, unlucky, unwanted Noah Willowby. That's all. That's the moral of the goddamn story. I'm a lost man trying to make sense of a lost fucking world. That's what's on *my* mind. That's *my* story."

My age-old struggle to hold back tears had been long lost. My face was searing as well as soaked as I leaned up against the railing once more. I distanced myself from Felicia as I stared into the distance just as I had done before I lost it. She had kept a calm and understanding expression the whole time; she knew what it felt like to so desperately *need* to get it out. She understood; she empathized. I knew not that she would comfort me, but boy, did I need it. I was raised by the principle that we did not always get what we wanted as it had been proven and experienced time and time again, but I was also taught that we often times went without what we needed as well. Perhaps I deserved distance and abandonment; it became more of a punishment than a desire. I waited for the touch that never came as we stood in silence. My face cooled down and my limbs relaxed. I dried my eyes and sat down on the porch, legs hanging out over the side. Felicia did, however, sit down next to me, situating cross-legged on the wooden deck-style floor. Perhaps she was waiting for me to calm down as I waited for her to calm me. Once again, another example of my blinded selfishness.

"I'm so sorry, Noah," she said vaguely, focusing on no single set-apart division of my ranting. I guess it covered the majority of all of it. *Sorry* was always half and half on whether or not it did the job; I have long come to discover that it depends on who the words come from. "I've lost it all, and I definitely know the pain of it all. I know the feeling of uncertainty and mistrust. But I can assure you that this *place* is real. *I* am real. And above all, *you* are real. I want you to *believe*, Noah Willowby," she finished, following up once again with her unspecific statements. She reached her hand out into mine and slid over closer to me. "The past is as dead as the old city. This is the future, and we can get it all back. Everything we've lost. Together. We just have to make the best of it," she said, that time with a teary-eyed hug on both of our parts. I could think of only one thing to say as I stared out into the distance - the only thing suitable to say in any difficult situation. "I'm sorry too."

What I am about to say may come as a bit of a shock to you, but as all things come to pass, surprises can sometimes provide you with exemplary knowledge in future situations. Whether you are running a marathon, playing baseball in the backyard, or hell, even putting the wood to the quiet girl that sits in the back of your English class, never - and I must repeat, *never* - yell on an empty stomach. All of the screaming and outflow of emotions had left me famished beyond any starvation standards previously mentioned. Felicia and I shared one last hug and pulled each other to our feet. "Dinner should be ready," she smiled, drying the last of her tears. Boy, my stomach perked up like a starving dog. It was my turn to go first down the stairs and then the ladder. I shall be completely honest with you; I hobbled as fast as I could across the sticks, stones, and grassy fields. That is, as quickly as my empty tank would allow. We slipped back into our shoes, which felt oddly uncomfortable and even a bit unnatural after being barefoot for who knows how long. The time for limping was over, and we briskly walked back to the farmhouse, the smell of fried chicken drawing us like an early-morning bird to the wormhole - as appetizing as can be.

Felicia showed me to the upstairs bathroom where I could freshen up; she closed the door on the way out as she made her way to her bathroom to do the same. The small bathroom matched the same rustic theme of the rest of the house, complete with a toilet with an ever-changing light in the bowl, shower stall, sink, and a cracked mirror among the wooden walls and chipped paint. I splashed water on my hair and face, taking notice of the newfound indentions in my facial structure, either from worry, sadness, fatigue, or perhaps a combination of all three. I repeated the process until I felt somewhat new, slicking my long, black hair behind my ears as I wiped my then deep-set eyes, which sat above two heavy bags directly underneath. My hair fell to the back of my neck, as messy as a lion's mane. I scrubbed the dirt from my brow and straightened everything out, looking as presentable as I possibly could. It amazes me what a little bit of water could do for my appearance. After that refreshment, I might have looked *halfway* presentable.

The three of us gathered around the old-fashioned dinner table, taking in the overwhelming smell of a home-cooked meal. It seemed like forever and a day since I had tasted my mother's cooking. Perhaps it *had* been; I could not even remember the last meal I had eaten that she had cooked. It could have very well been the same thing that lay before us then, but what did it matter? She was gone, and so was the city and world in which she had blossomed like a rose in Julia's garden, which had also been destroyed and ripped from me. It was of no *value* anymore. Hell, it was something I could not even manage to remember in its entirety; memories are often silent dreams and unstable explosives. They can go off at any given moment, and yet you will not go back. You will only see what was and what you want to see again. But you cannot. We sat down, and I waited for the go-signal to eat, as if some formal routine would be fulfilled as it had been in Jack King's mansion. Mrs. Noy stared at me as I gave the food a similar gaze, licking my lips in my head. "Dig in, Noah," she said with a laugh. "Go ahead and enjoy." She must not have gotten uptown much. On the other hand, I certainly did dig in as my stomach howled with gratitude. It was my first real meal there in that new land, apart from the amateur piddling around the ship kitchen and berry scavenging upon first arrival. Those times were distant happenings of childsay and survival. Our bellies became beasts as they groaned and seeped with appreciative gurgles; we finally began *living*.

Opposite of what I had expected, there were not many questions asked in my direction. Her mother asked a few basic questions, but Felicia answered them thoroughly as I wolfed down my food. Both women watched in awe as they made their way through the chicken at a moderate pace. I assumed Mrs. Noy understood from my appearance that I was not much for talking in those days; I nodded in approval and sported a slight smile every now and then, mostly when she exclaimed in surprise - whether it be positive or negative. I enjoyed the food to an unbelievable extent and in moderate silence, thanking both Noy women after. Felicia helped with the dishes after I offered and got politely turned down by her mother when I asked if I could do them. I stood at the island quietly, and thank whatever fictitious God they bowed to in that fantasy that made it a quick job. I am a firm believer than silence is more deadly than a serial killer, mostly because it is often hard to tell the difference between the two. Mrs. Noy whispered something to her daughter, which I unfortunately could not make out; I was quite nosey and *invasive* back in that time. Felicia turned to me, took my hand, and led me up the stairs as her mother dried the dishes with that same hospitable smile she seemed to have on constant tap. She flipped the hallway light switch as we climbed the stairs, illuminating the entire upstairs very dimly, just as the rest of the house was. It provided a particular cozy feel; I fell in love with the darkness as I always had before. Felicia led me into a large bedroom, obviously laid out for a man. The belongings in the room appeared to have not been touched for years; I smelled must and mold in the air. I knew it before she told me. "This is Lucious's old room," she said quietly. "It's all yours. You can sleep here; the clothes should be relatively the same size. Take a shower and meet me on the front porch," she finished with a smile. She then turned to leave, and I hurried as quickly as I could to the bathroom, grabbing the first clothing items I could get my hands on. Pleasing surprises usually lay behind the most common of smiles, and I hoped and begged that that propensity would remain true at least one more time.

The steaming hot water washed away the tread of that new place. The sand, the dirt, the sweat, the tears, and the blood all spiraled down the drain as the memories of the old city were cleansed from both my body and mind. Images flashed through my head as I closed my eyes to rinse myself of those chains. I saw *Julia*. I saw *Jack. Jacob. My parents. Sebastian's poker games.*

The Perch. The secret weapons cache. The mansion, the flowers, the many locked rooms. The entire city raced through my brain as the memories leaked out from my ears, down my chest, and around and around until they disappeared down the drain. I washed away all of the pain and suffering of the past. I shampooed my hair, pulling out burrs and tangles. I scrubbed my face and body of grime and stains. I breathed in and out, steadying and regaining my balance as I thought of what was to come. Perhaps this was a clean slate. Maybe this was a fresh start. I made a promise to myself to at least *try.*

I shut the water off and wrapped a towel around my body as I ran a comb through my hair. I found a ponytail holder and pulled it up into a bun atop my head. I dried my body and put on a pair of boxers before climbing into a pair of loose-fitting plaid pajama pants. I pulled a white tank top over my head, careful to avoid the deodorant I had not applied for what seemed like forever. I found a bottle of mediocre-smelling cologne and sprayed a few squirts across my chest - anything to help that horrid smell of experience and tread. It had been a considerably lengthy time since I had smelled even remotely *tolerable*; perhaps I had stopped caring long ago. Now I had a *reason.* I brought the towel across the fogged-up mirror and caught a surprising glimpse at my reflection. I was *unrecognizable,* even to myself. I had never had a ponytail before, but my long and growing hair called for it. I had gotten more muscular in that place; the tank top was form-fitting and comfortable against my chest and stomach. My veins protruded from my wrists and hands with a high metabolism that I had recently gained. I saw a grown man staring back at me that was so beyond unfamiliar that it was almost frightening, as if a stranger had stolen the slightest resemblance to my ancient being. I caught one last glimpse of the new, clean Noah Willowby and headed downstairs. I had nearly forgotten about what Felicia had said about the porch; I had been selfishly distracted. It was becoming a terrible habit of mine. *Forgetful. Lost in self.*

I hurried down the stairs to the pounding beat of my heart. I noticed Mrs. Noy curled up on the couch, nose and glasses deep in a book under the dim, yellow glow of the lamp on the table beside her. My goal was no contact, as if I could sneak past the woman in her own house. "Not so fast, Noah," she said right as I was about to round the corner. Her voice startled me as it broke the shrill silence I was trying so desperately to maintain. I was a large individual in height; how could I hope to simply creep through the house? As I recovered from my brief heart attack, my voice shook, much like the rest of me. "Y - yes ma'am?" I replied. "You're a very respecting and a very respective young man," she said with that same welcoming smile. I hoped that was as far as the conversation would go, but as you may have learned already, my hopes and dreams did not exactly line up with my destiny. "Thank you," I said, trying to sound confident as I inched my way toward the door. "Not everyone here is going to get to know you like we have, Noah," she said. I was confused. "I'm not sure what you mean, Miss," I said as respectfully as I could. She laughed, resuming what always seemed to come after that smile of hers. "What I'm saying is that you should look the part." I stood up straight; everyone had always told me to stand up straight. Mrs. Noy laughed again. "I see what Felicia sees in you," she said, almost blushing. There was a brief moment of silence, but it was loud with pounding hearts and colorful cheeks. "Let me clean you up," she said. I knew that was coming. I definitely was not in the mood for a sponge bath and a deep tissue massage - from a middle-aged woman and the mother of a beautiful woman who showed the slightest interest in me. "O - okay," I gave in. "Come with me," she put her hand on my shoulder. "Hope, by the way," she finished.

Mrs. Noy led me back up the stairs and into the bathroom, which had then cleared of the steam from my shower. She pulled a stool out from the closest and sat me down, facing the mirror. I let the sound of clinking metal tools fill the empty air for as long as it possibly could. Time always seem to move slower when you are nervous or in danger. "Thank you for dinner," I said awkwardly as she let my hair down out of the ponytail. "My pleasure," she replied, bearing so much resemblance to Felicia both in hospitality as well as facial features. "I'm sorry about your family," I followed, which was then followed by immediate silence; there was no answer. It was as if I had not spoken a word. I can imagine and understand that nobody wants to talk about their late family, no matter how pleasant of a person you are. Death is a black hole that sucks everyone in - eventually.

"You can call me Patricia," she said after a seeming age of nothing but snipping and clipping. I caught sight of each curl and strand of hair drop to the floor around me slowly out of my peripheral vision. After I could no longer see the edge of my hair out of the corner of my eyes, she ran scalding water over my face and lathered it down with shaving cream. The razor was branding hot as she slid it row by row down my cheeks, chin, and upper lip, erasing the stubble I had acquired from weeks of not shaving. Once done, Mrs. Noy washed my face and shampooed my hair, dried me off, and ran a handful of gel through my relatively short hair. She slicked every curl back behind my ears as it dried and solidified. With a finishing touch of aftershave and a cool towel, she stood up and rotated the stool so I could see myself in the mirror. "What do you think?" she exclaimed. "It's a lot lighter," I replied with a smile. She laughed once more. "Thank you, Mrs. Patricia," I said, my turn to smile. "You are more than welcome, Noah Willowby," she said with a final smile before leaving the bathroom. I took one last look in the mirror before I followed her. Just as I had cleansed myself of the old city and in fact, my old life, I said a solemn farewell to my past being - my *shell* - which had stared back at me only minutes before. I stepped across the pile of hair and shaving cream as I turned and walked away forevermore.

As I neared the front door, I heard the faint sound of *music* from the front porch. I had not heard the sweet sound of notes and rhythms but twice since I was ten years old, and my heart filled with guilt and the overbearing urge that I had sinned. Jack King did not own *that* world. I opened the screen door and joined Felicia out in the open and crisp air of the empty and flat countryside. She had also taken a shower, and was then sporting wet hair, blue pajamas, and an acoustic guitar. I smelled the roses before I even closed the door. She gazed up at me with a surprised and admiring look. "So that's what took you so long," she said with a laugh, nearly matching that of her mother. "How many showers did you take?" she asked, still laughing. "A couple. I had to make up for lost time," I said with a smile all my own. "I forgot to mention that my mom used to be a hair stylist," she blushed as blue as her pajamas. "I heard," I replied as I looked up at my new hairstyle and slick cheekbones, adjusting to the light and airy feel of cleanliness. I had not felt neat and collected in years.

Felicia strummed the guitar once more. I used to want so desperately to play, but could never get my hands on a guitar in the old city. They were outlawed, for Christ's sake. My minor talent could not hold a candle to what I was hearing then; she was just shy of professional. The chords and notes she picked brought my mind to ease, which was something very rare and extremely difficult to come by in those days. I sat down on the porch swing beside her, giving her enough arm room, but close enough so I could smell the roses, if you will. Something about the way she played gave me an overwhelming sense of peace, as if I knew everything was going to be alright. As if forgetting the past was not worth the amount of grief I had been giving myself. As if the moment was perfect, and it was. Because I *believed* it to be. Perhaps that was the moral and thematic beginning to my demise. She played for minutes on end, as I simply sat and listened, barely breathing for fear of interrupting the sweet sound of each string being plucked in a rhythmic melody. I could not help but stare at her as she focused on nothing but the guitar - the art of *forgetting*. It had been an eternity since I had heard real music - music that did not signal imminent danger or death.

As most people do when they realize they are being stared at and watched, she took notice and switched her focus to me out of the corner of her eye. She turned her head as she continued to play as if nothing had changed. I smiled in awe; something that minuscule meant talent to me. My teeth went from closed to open as Felicia let go of the guitar. My mind and senses had grown accustomed to eighteen years of *normal,* so you can imagine how shocked I was when the strings played themselves as if her fingers were still making love to them. The instrument levitated several feet above us and swung out into the yard under the maple tree above, illuminating the yard with the sound of the sweet music. Fireflies danced between the branches as if on command; perhaps they were. Felicia stood up and stretched; I was sure we were both quite fatigued after a long day. I could not seem to remember how the day started; only the exposition rang a bell to me. Perhaps that new world was designed to reset everything after a single day, allowing for a rebirth of beautiful creation with the following morning. I followed her as she rose and paced the porch, as if something was on her mind. "I think we're supposed to play follow the leader," she winked, implying the guitar's quite musical exit. The stars provided perfect light to see, that is, along the backsides of the fireflies buzzing in our ears. She reached her hand out and took mine as we slumped down the stairs and out into the yard. "You know the rule," she said with a wink. It usually took a moment for things to register with me, but that took effect immediately as I slipped my shoes off and felt the soft grass beneath my toes once more.

I took her other hand and waist as we slowly danced closely underneath the maple tree. We spun and breathed in slow motion; we had not anywhere else to be. Nothing on our minds or our hearts. It was quite silly, now that I think about it. We actually thought everything was going to be alright. Perhaps what meant so much to us was that it was alright for that moment. I have since learned to live in the moment instead of the past, so that is how I settle my stomach at night. We lived in slow motions for seemingly hours on end, and it was. The moon soon grew tired as the curve slipped behind the clouds, casting a dark shadow across the yard; the ballroom had struck the midnight hour. We agreed on one last dance as I whispered something in her ear, only inches away. "If this is the tale of two cities, this one *surely* wins." She only smiled, as she would often do with no answer. "This is just the beginning," she finally replied. "Why do we get to be happy, Felicia?" I wondered as we sat down on the porch steps. "We surely don't deserve it," I laughed, thinking and choosing not to dwell on the past which I had sworn off. Felicia sighed. "We don't; we are just the ones brave enough to demand it. And in this place, what you demand is what is promised." I was pleased with her answer. I had grown used to the reverence and honor of that place, and so I was ready to see it for myself.

My eyes threatened to close up for the night as we swayed back and forth in place on the steps below the house. I sent silent praises as she opened her mouth once more. "It's bedtime," she said with a laugh. "I didn't know we had one," I smiled, wasting what little energy I was running on. "I mean for you, Noah," she said with a false sense of seriousness in her voice. "You have a big day tomorrow." I was halfway worried and halfway excited; I simply could not decide what emotion to act on, as I often did. We retreated back into the house at a rather dizzy pace, nearly overcome with exhaustion and ecstasy. Mrs. Noy was fast asleep on the couch with the book across her chest. Felicia kissed her forehead and covered her up with the blanket at her feet. I followed her up the stairs and into my bedroom. I remember a kiss before she left, and that is all; my head hit the pillow and the rest is but a forced-away memory, whether it be by my choice or involuntary. I fell fast asleep to the sweet sound of the guitar and the glow of the moon as the stars took the floor once again.

The following morning came as it was invited and welcomed, contrary to being dreaded as all of the others before it had been. The bed was extremely comfortable, cozy in all of its king-size soft sheets, blankets, and pillows I had hid beneath for a decent stretch of ten hours or so. The quiet serenity of the farm provided excellent sleeping conditions. There was no alarm clock on the bedside table, for it would have been absolutely useless; in fact, I did not even set a time to awaken the night before. I would get up when I needed to. Or *wanted* to, goddamnit. If it was indeed *my* world, then the world would bend to *my* will. Perhaps I had been awoken in more ways than one. Shaking and fearful falling had always woken me into a terrified sweat many a night before. I had seen my fair share of aircraft carriers back in the old city; Jack King's army unit had a plethora of helicopters and jets on hand, stored in underground bunkers and hidden caves for emergencies. You very well may be wondering why my choice of topic has changed so drastically quick as it has since the beginning, but believe me when I say that I was just as surprised. Yes, I had a *much* different alarm clock that day. I felt it before I heard it; I heard it before I saw it. The bedroom shook like a blender as I heard the spinning roar of a massive engine outside. The glass panes rattled as I peeled the curtains back to see just what kind of beast awaited me outside. The helicarrier was at least triple the size of the monstrous fighter jets back in the old world and city as it hovered above the farmland outside the window. I had seen them scoping out the perimeter of the new metropolis upon our arrival. The size, sound, and surprise they created was far more advanced and futuristic than I was accustomed to - not to mention far more frightening when they shook you awake bright and early, terrifying you damn near half to death.

As I awoke to the sound of a thousand trains in my ears, shaking off the grogginess of sleep as the house shook violently, I leapt out of bed, my stomach sinking as I pulled a fresh set of clothes from the drawers across the room. I nearly tripped three times just trying to get dressed. If starting the day was this difficult, I could not imagine getting through the rest of it. I swept the ocean blue drapes completely open as I pulled my belt across my waist. I had been forced to make a few more holes along the leather strap following my time on the island. The grass was laid flat and colored white as snow from the intense wind of the gigantic aircraft as it touched down in one of the empty fields a ways away. The carrier cast a looming shadow all the way across the mile-wide gap between the house and the front wing, or so it seemed in all of its majesty. My body still shook and heard the noise ring through my ears long after the engines were shut off. At least my heart was able to settle for a moment.

As quickly as my stomach shooed away the butterflies once more, they flocked back inside as a knock at the door startled me. I paid it no mind at first; I focused out the window. I stammered nervously as I told them to come in. Felicia turned the knob and stepped into the room, joining me at the window. "What the hell is that thing?" I asked anxiously. "That would be your ride into the city," she said matter-of-factly. For a moment, I had settled on the fact that they had come to arrest me for trespassing where I did not belong, only to be brutally hung and gutted like a criminal. I had a terrible habit of overthinking and stressing about unnecessary scenarios, this one being no different. I would have much rather gone back to sleep, or even to dismiss the happenings as another anxious, nightmarish dream. But I had had none of the vicious, relentless dreams in that place. Only the memories. As sly and fox-like as she was, I chose not to argue. "Let's just hope they drive better than your brother," I said. For once, we both smiled at the same time. "Mom's got breakfast cooking," she said pointlessly; I could smell the bacon already.

I found an entire wardrobe of Lucious's clothes in the drawers and closet in the room. Contrary to our differences, we had the same size and style of clothing, much to my gratitude. I pulled on a pair of jeans as I walked away from the window, pulling the curtains to once more. I found a tight-fitting, black-collared t-shirt and pulled it over my head as I hurried to the bathroom to freshen up. Running cold water over my face, I buttoned a maroon and black plaid-style flannel over my clothes as a coat. I never operated well under pressure, and this was no exception. I knew the gigantic aircraft still lay outside and the plate of food awaited me on the table downstairs, but I rushed and hurried not. Fear brought uneasiness, uneasiness brought dread, and dread brought anxiety. I messed my hair up with the same bottle of hair gel and wiped the crust and oil from my eyes and face. I stared at myself for quite a while, forgetting what me if only for a moment's time. *Was I even the same person as I was so long ago?* I had not aged the first lick, but my travels had put miles on my ever-beating heart and deepened the wrinkles on my face as detailed as an omniscient caricature artist of a being would allow. My reflection shifted and shattered into images of my father, Jack King, then to Lucious, and eventually back to me before I even noticed a difference. Perhaps I was what these people had made me. *A tower. A building. Climbing ever higher and higher.* "What the f-," I stuttered this myself as I almost pulled the bedroom door shut. My *sunglasses* sat on the bedside table. *How did they get there? Had they been there all along?* I questioned not as I hesitantly tucked the device into the collar of my shirt and pulled the door to.

Felicia and her mother scrambled around the kitchen like eggs in a frying pan as I clopped down the stairs, returning to my anxious state. Mrs. Noy bade me a cheerful good morning with a gleaming smile. Some traits passed through generations like sand, and others like molasses. She told me to go ahead and have a seat; I surely did not hesitate. We dined on a breakfast of French toast, eggs, bacon, fruit, and coffee as the sun rose and broke through the window over the sink. I received puzzled looks as I chilled my coffee with ice as I always had, and I thanked them heartily by asking for seconds, scarfing the food down in a rush. I could not help but feel overwhelmed; I absolutely despised that feeling. Although I was in a hurry for no apparent reason, I was not rude. I was still forbidden to do the dishes, however. "The sunglasses are a nice touch, Noah," Felicia playfully shoved me out of the way with a wink and started showing off her cleaning skills. Women will be women - magnificently stubborn but goddamn beautiful - a true masterpiece of creation and my wildest dreams. "You've got a plane to catch," she winked as she finished drying the last of the plates. "Uh...where am I going exactly?" I stammered. "The helicopter outside will take you into the city and drop you off to meet our leader," Mrs. Noy chimed in. "And if you run into Lucious, tell him I said hi," Felicia whispered as she pushed me out the door and into the yard before she pulled it shut behind me. I was alone - just the helicopter and I across the yard. I pulled my sunglasses over my eyes and turned both knobs as I slowly made my way across the field.

Chapter XIII
The Man with the Patch
(Into the Air, Down the Hatch, and Through the Door)

'Helicopter' was an immense, vast, complete, and utter understatement. The carrier outside reminded me much of a spaceship, casting mental images of futuristic scenes I would often create as a child. I picked up my pace across the yard as I saw the group of uniformed soldiers hanging around outside the loading dock. They appeared to be drinking. Unlike the militia back in the old city, who wore the traditional U.S Army uniform, these soldiers wore all black. From the top of their short hair to their aviator sunglasses to their belts to their boots, they were pitch as night. These were the *elite*. Whether they be the elite fighters or elite drunkards, I would soon find out. "Looks like you woke up on the wrong side of the bed, little man," one of the soldiers said as I strolled up as least awkwardly as I possibly could. I could tell by that first comment, and in fact, the entire aura of those men, that just like Jack King and his army, this was yet another band of misfits. A Hispanic soldier in the back perked up and raised his hand. "You gotta be this tall to ride, ese," he laughed along with nearly all of the other soldiers. All except one cackled and punched each other in the arm. Who seemed to be the leader and myself kept silent, straight faces as we stared at each other.

The leader was tall, built, and professional as he stepped out from the crowd. He turned to face them and began to speak. "Our main objective is to deliver the subject to the center point of the city," he commanded with a stern salute. "There will be absolutely zero horseplay or bullshitting with said subject. God knows he's had enough of that already." His voice faded. I respected that man right off the bat. The rest of the crew did not as they busted out laughing, much to his annoyance. Mine as well.

The chief pressed a button on his watch, releasing the loading dock down onto the grass with a thud. The door was much like a drawbridge on a castle. He ordered the men on board and led me inside behind them. The air inside was crisp and cold, smelling of new furniture and engine exhaust as the door sealed shut once more. "Seats, ladies," he commanded as each one filed into their station and resumed their work positions. The pilot, which happened to be the Latino comedian from previous, started the engines back up once more. The trains were much quieter from the inside, much to my surprise - damn near silent.

The burly, solid, and compact man pulled me aside into a room I would have missed if it had not been by force. He closed the door and pressed the lighting buttons on his other wrist. The compartment was much like the goddamn Oval Office of the old world - large, quiet, and separated from everything. There was nothing in the room but a long wooden desk which stretched from wall to wall with chairs all around. "Sorry about that," he started. "I have to get a bit rough with those guys. A bunch of blasted assholes, the whole lot of them." We both smiled. "I'm Commander Logan Aaron," he said, shaking my hand firmly. "You have two first names?" I asked curiously. "I get that a lot," he chuckled. "This place is part time meeting place, part time silent room," he said proudly, outstretching his arms as if he was presenting the room to me. I ignored that. At least it was quiet. I had louder matters on my mind.

"Well, Commander, it sure is a great place you have here. It must be hard managing all of it," I started. He stopped me and started giggling like one of his cronies outside. "Wait a second, you don't think *I'm* the leader of this place, do you?" he laughed. "I'd be goddamned if I was," he followed. "My hair is still black you know." He was right; it matched the rest of his uniform. "Can you imagine running a place that is never solid? It's only what you make it. Talk about a fucking headache." He had one final laugh before returning my solemn smile. "In other words, call me

Logan," he said, back on my tolerance level. I took another deep and closer look around the room as Logan invited me to take a seat around the table. Although it was plain and professional, it held a certain depth. It was basic, ordinary, and seemingly normal - nothing of specialty or importance. In fact, the entire aircraft carrier was more like a portable office building than a military vehicle - boring, insufficient, and in dire need of something *more*. "My squad briefed me on your file," he said as he took the seat across from me. "I have a file?" I said in false curiosity. Logan stared back, taken somewhat by surprise. "Well, not an *actual* file. I have to sound the least bit professional to get on your level by where you come from." I admired Logan, for he was not too obnoxious to the point of aggression whilst also not taking anything too seriously, but he got the job done in due time. "So, how many more people know everything about me?" I shot, ending the light conversation. "You'd be surprised, Noah Willowby," he shot back with a sly smile. "I'm sorry all of that happened to you," he sympathized simply and solemnly. I nodded in appreciation and curiosity. "But that's over now. You can change all of that here. You can conquer your dreams here, Noah. No more heartache. No more loss." I smiled firmly. "That's not possible," I said as I stood up and began pacing the room. "Down to the last hair on your head," he laughed, joining me.

I walked around the table and back, putting distance between the two of us. I may have respected this man, but I absolutely did *not* trust him. I could not afford to trust anyone anymore. Logan walked over to a refrigerator that I quite honestly had not noticed as we had entered into the room. He cracked open a beer and took a swig. "Care for one?" he asked, swinging the bottle in my direction. "I don't drink," I said. "I know," he winked again. "No rules here," he said as he took his seat once again. *I had heard that before. I had been there. Memories. Knives.* He laughed a few moments after. "I think I've got something you *can't* turn down," he said coldly, as if he had known me my whole entire life. Logan reached into his jacket pocket and pulled out a thick box of cards. With a flick of his wrist, he sent the deck flying across the slick table surface. The top of the cardboard box had come undone, spilling all fifty-two individual cards across the wooden expanse in front of us. "Care for a game of cards, kid?" he said with a juvenile smile. He was right; that was an offer I simply could not refuse. All I did was nod, but he understood perfectly. "Do you believe in magic, Noah?" he cleared his throat. "No," I shook my head. "Well, do you believe in reality?" I stayed silent. He smirked matter-of-factly. He curled his fingers into a fist and brought it down onto the table with a thunderous crack. The cards whispered across the wood as if a breeze had awakened them. Some stacked while some folded as his grip tightened. The paper-thin slides built castles and buildings as they multiplied by the hundred - by the *thousands*. They danced around the table and piled up into dunes of sand as they chose another form. It *was* magical - not that I would admit the existence in that moment - but it was magical nonetheless. Their pace slowed as they became the original fifty-two card deck, and they assumed a neat and perfect stack in front of me once more. "You deal."

Logan and I played poker for what seemed like hours. Who knew? Once again, the element of time was stretched as far as it could be imagined. The game consisted of many flashbacks to my first poker game with Sebastian back in the old city. He had taught me everything he knew about the start of gambling, but it still was nowhere near enough to surpass the Commander's elite skills. I then remembered playing with Lucious on the boat. Even he was superior to me. I had a deep fascination with poker; I was so intrigued by the concept that you could start out with nothing and end up with everything and still win the game. It was a beautiful idea, even though I would always lose. Much like reality, I vowed - I *swore* - to myself, that I would win one day. *One day soon. One day so far away.* Once again, who knew? The Chief put me out of my misery and ended my suffering in every game we played. If we happened to be betting money somehow in the old world, I would be inept and he would be a millionaire. That is, if there was even a single unit of currency to be had. Besides humiliating defeat, the only thing I paid was extremely close attention to his techniques, just as I had done for my previous two opponents - both of which were gone. Fortunately and unfortunately, they were *gone*. Who had *really* won those games? Aaron remained silent for the majority of the time, excuse a few laughs and chuckles followed by a sigh and intense release of air. I tried my best - all I had been taught - but to no avail. I would have to use his own strategy against him. *Someday.* There was no chance I could win on the first match. "It's like war," he told me after. "I take yours little by little until you have nothing. Even in cards, nothing is fair."

"Commander, we're approaching Central Point," the pilot said over the intercom. The raspy static startled me as the silence was interrupted. It returned as Logan castrated me with cards one last miserable time. Logan pulled the cards back into the box and pocketed them as quickly as he could, returning to his former professional self. This particular professional just so happened to have had a few beers, all of which bottles had disappeared into the effects they had on him as he staggered over to the large, thick glass window across the room. *Had I noticed it before?* I simply could not remember. That whole world was a goddamn mind game. *A trick. A figment of the imagination.* I followed him closely as my jaw dropped at what I saw. The diamond city had looked massive when we had first arrived to that new place, but being one with it was simply indescribable. The shine, the glimmer, and the shadows of it all were amplified by a thousand percent. It was glorious, it was heavenly, and it was magnificent. The skyscrapers shattered the heavens, the glass was a mass of mirrors, and the rooftops were monstrous landing strips as big as Times Square of the old world. Or at least, that was a place that I had only heard of and had learned to compare them too. The hovercraft approached one building that stood out from the rest. Each building was pure diamond, but the target structure we were approaching was a deeper and more intricate style - a magnificent city penthouse. We slid in between each structure as gracefully as an eagle, taking in every last glitter of the city.

It took several minutes for the pilot to exact his initial landing point location. We ascended over the city and stared down at it as we neared and lowered over the building several hundred feet below us. We were mixed with the clouds as Logan hummed to himself, buzzing with, well, a *buzz*. I was sure he appreciated the shiny colors just as much as I did, just not at the same time and perhaps quite a great deal more. Even in his state, or any state, not appreciating something like that just had to be a sin. As we felt the craft sink like an elevator, Aaron turned to walk back toward the door, nearly tripping over himself. As we joined the rest of the crew back in the cockpit and operations quarters, I could feel the soft landing of the ship below us. Before he began to struggle with his watch to open the door, I grabbed his arm slightly. "What can you tell me about this leader?" I asked him timidly. "Don't worry, Noah," he said peacefully. "He's the nicest guy around." I could not put that much stock in what he said; I had become sure that *everyone* was nice when they were drunk off of their ass. He clapped me on the shoulder as he finally found the anti-lock button on his wrist. The crew looked up at us as we made our entrance seemingly out of nowhere. "Oh good, we thought we left you guys back at Old McDonald's," the pilot said. "It's a good thing we didn't though," he said, looking at me as he shut the engines off, sliding the side of his hand across his throat like a guillotine. The Chief gave him a woozy shot with his middle finger as he turned around to escort me out.

The door clanked down as it slowly descended into the rooftop several feet below. We walked down the steps as we adjusted to the air pressure that high up; it was easily the highest building in the city. Nervousness and anxiety kicked in as the wind tangled my hair up into tassels once again. "You're a good poker player, kid," he said, his voice almost sobering up. "But you're damn sure not the *best*." He giggled like a little kid, still highly intoxicated; I guess we all have ways of dealing with matters unknown to us. Perhaps cards and alcohol happened to be his; I know for a comforting, subtle fact that I had mine as well. "You'll want to go down that stairwell, through the door, then see the lady at the desk. Don't get too excited; this office worker keeps all the buttons up. She'll know who you are and why you're here. When you're ready to leave, just deal the cards." With that, Commander Logan Aaron staggered back into the helicopter as the bridge lifted once again. I stood back as the pilot started the engines, deafening me once again as it emitted intensely strong winds. I stared at the rapidly-spinning wings as the carrier disappeared across the sky once more. I looked around to find nothing but a stairwell, a door, and a deck of cards at my feet.

I straightened my hair and pushed my sunglasses up onto my eyes once more as I took in the layout of the rooftop. The altitude was jaw-dropping; I could see the entire city from that one pinpoint just as I had in the treehouse. The crisp wind stole my breath as I slowly and anxiously walked to the only exit off of the roof. Besides *jumping*, that is, which I also vaguely considered - if only for a moment. At a different point in my life, I just might have taken myself up on that offer, but not on that day; I was far too perplexed by the wonder of the city to simply *opt out*. Besides, who knows where I would end up? I had already found some sort of afterlife and still knew no god. I took the stairs one by one until I faced two metal-faced glass doors, which I pushed through and entered the building. Peaceful elevator music played throughout the entire penthouse, which gave the scene a rather surreal feeling. The cool, tranquilizing aura of the top floor cast a spell over me; I was hypnotized. Music was still a newfound memory at that moment - especially the soft and nonviolent type.

"Can I help you, sir?" an elderly woman behind me said. As I turned around to see her, the door was gone and a reception desk was in its place. How long had I been in a daze? It could not have been more than a few seconds. All I knew was that there was no way out. "I'm Noah Willowby," I said, still a bit shocked. The old lady lit up like a string of Christmas lights, which I had only snuck pictures of and heard about. All four-and-a-half-feet and a hundred-and-twenty pounds of her rushed around the counter and stood far below me. She got around pretty quick for her age. She bowed before shaking my hand, as if *worshipping* me; I was no god. Perhaps she was schizophrenic or suffered from dementia or Alzheimer's; maybe she had remembered the time she met Jesus, whoever the hell *he* was. I did not know; all I knew was that I was nowhere near worthy of the pedestal in which she had placed me on in that moment and action. "You can come with me, Mr. Willowby," she said softly, taking my arm. It was the first time I had been referred to by my father's name. *Baseball in the back yard. Driving through the countryside. Arguments. Car accidents.* Memories of my father flooded back as I walked in his shoes and took on his name. The woman led me to a set of elevator doors across from the desk. As awkward as it was, time elongated even further as we waited for the doors to open. She pressed the down button as she hummed do the soft jazz playing overhead. As the doors slid open, I saw that the shaft was empty as she gave me a shove - an impressive one at her age. I fell down a stone-cold crevice to the sound of elevator music.

Now, let us take a moment to examine the situation. As I mentioned sometime before, I would not have *jumped* off of the building. I did not seek death on that day, but you see, there is a defined difference in suicide and being agreeable when it comes your time to go. I was the latter. What was I trying to get back to? It was gone. And what was then would not be forever, and neither would I. So no, I would not have thrown myself down the empty elevator shaft. Certainly not. But you see, it was somewhat difficult to accept and face death when the soundtrack to your murder was Frank Sinatra. My time would have to give me a rain check. See, even death has to reschedule upon extraneous circumstance. A *Plan B*, if you will. I had to have been somewhere around *Plan S* by that point in my life.

I was beyond terrified, or at least as terrified as B.B. King would allow. They were some of my mother's favorites in my childhood, and I remembered names and melodies she would tell me about. Upon the first few feet of falling, I definitely gave the old bat her fair share of edgewise profanity. Falling is quite the strange feeling. I hated heights; I *despised* them. I was never a roller-coaster fanatic; in fact, I was the purse holder. The Perch was the only height I appreciated instead of feared, but then that was all nothing but a dead, distant memory. I flailed around like a raw pretzel as I got my bearings; I sailed through the endless elevator shaft as the chilling wind sucked my soul out through my nostrils. I somehow managed to glance through the gap in my legs to view the bottom of the ravine - there was *none*. Just black as the dim lights faded from yellow, then to orange, then to pitch, silent black. I floated through the dark silence as I embraced my apparent and imminent death; I was *content* with splashing into a pool of my own blood and guts. After all, I had reached adulthood, killed multiple people, had sex, and seen the damn near impossible. I was *ready*, and I accepted my fate - if there in fact had to be such a thing. I closed my eyes as the music stopped. It was long gone.

As you should know by now, I have always found it comical and quite magnificent how a predicament can change in a split second, especially when it is in your favor - as it rarely was for me. When I opened my eyes again, I was in a much different place. The pattern of my life seemed to be as follows - death would knock at the door, my eyes would close for the last time, and then I would be in a bright, new place. Perhaps it was life after life in my struggle to finally get it right. As I said before, I was no god, and surely no predecessor. I might have never gotten it *truly* right, but I was always given another chance, and for that, I was truly grateful. Or at least I was content. 'Come whatever may' had become the foundation of my mindset, and I was content with that subtle truth.

I was in a hallway of sorts, and much to my surprise, on my feet - both mentally and physically. I decided and had learned not to question, but to accept and move forward. It made the scheme of things much, much easier. Knowledge was sight, and a blind man I had become. The blind were wise, for they did not question, but concluded based on their other senses. The hall was lined with massive paned-glass windows, providing an excellent view of the city outside. I allowed myself to *wonder*, not question. It felt like I had fallen forever, and I was still extremely high up. My stomach turned as my mind whirred as I took in the glimmering shrine of the city once again. The sunshine was no match for the frigid temperature inside the sealed and plated glass. I shivered as my fear of heights culminated and slowly walked forward to the set of steel double doors several dozen meters ahead of me. The quick walk seemed to take years as I rushed to the end of the hallway. Anxiety pounded me like a hammer as I knocked and awaited anxiously what could have very well been my demise by my own worries. After all, we are our own undoing, unraveling, and our very own worst enemy.

The doors were pulled open by a quite peculiar looking gentleman. He was close to six-and-a-half feet tall with silver hair and an eyepatch. The man wore a pressed suit which smelled like cigars and cologne. All I noticed were his eyes, however. I had seen them before. *Somewhere.* As much as I wracked my brain, I simply could not place him. The one eye stared down at me as the doors opened the rest of the way, giving us a full, complete view of each other. "Well if it isn't Noah Willowby, the man of the hour," he said jolly and joyfully as images of a retired, exuberant lawyer Santa Claus passed through my brain. I never paid attention to *his* eyes. The man's voice was deep and raspy, all-knowing and benevolent as any older gentleman should be. "Welcome to my humble and gracious home," he welcomed me as I stepped inside.

The home was disproportionate to say the least, or at least metaphorically speaking. As I looked around me and we passed through the foyer of the penthouse, all I saw was an extensive amount of grace and a minimal portion of humility. This man had money, or at least whatever authority figured ruled the existence in that place. Money meant nothing anymore, but this man standing before me owned the world and he did not pay a goddamn dime for it. *He had earned it or took it.* I had yet to find out which, but I vowed to. There were so many windows; in fact, the entire apartment was *glass*. Transparent floors, walls, and ceilings masked by carpets and decorations and elegant chandeliers hanging above glinted their light off of the silver of the decor and the glimmer of his hair. *Apartment* was a severe understatement; *penthouse* did not even do that place justice in the justice. The home in which I was being led through was a *castle*, and a floating one at that. We stood on the heavens of the top floor of that new city, and I wondered just what hour I was the man of.

"My name is Peter King," he said, looking back to get my attention as he led me through the mansion. *Mansion.* The blinding light invaded my eyes and right to my mind as I had flashbacks of Jack King's mansion. *The rooms. Sebastian. The flowers. Sex with Julia. Julia. Jack King. The eyes. Those eyes.* That was where I had seen them before. I stopped in my tracks as we came into a massive open room in the middle of the house. "Holy shit," I muttered. He stopped as well and turned to me. "Excuse me?" he wondered in his same chipper tone. "You're his father," I said through surprised, shocked, and gritted teeth. "We need to talk, Noah Willowby," he said, his voice shifting to suggestive kindness. He motioned to a simple couch and coffee table in front of the gigantic glass window which overlooked the entire city, as well as the entire world. Everything glowed. Except those eyes. They were as dark as night.

The small, simple furniture did not fit the scene by *any* means. I made my way over to the leather couch nervously, still in shock at what the flashbacks had helped me realize. I did not believe Jack King's story upon first hearing, or at least not every detail. But then it was coming true right before my eyes before I could even remember it. I was horrified and confused beyond my own comprehension, and questions could do all but surface. Peter King swept around to the opposing couch and sat down as if he owned the place. 'The place' can be quite a large term. We were close then - only feet apart. Eye to eye. *Eyes to eye.* I noticed how his eyepatch curved around his head perfectly, allowing just enough room to let his braided hair run down his back. There were so many similarities between the two men - the eyes, the voice, the smell, the aura. The presence of evil; I smelled it in the air. Cigars and cologne masked whiskey and destruction as I stared back at the man who had made Jack King the man that he was. I struggled to trust either frontal kindness or past memories as I wondered nothing but the simple question of why.

"To answer your question, yes, I am his father," Peter said coldly, as if it troubled him to say it out loud. It was as if he had said he had terminal cancer - a truth not to be proud of but must be admitted nonetheless. "However," he continued, "my son and I are very different. I'm sure he told you a story, and I will do the same. But rest assured that what I tell you is *truth*. Let's see how they line up." I nodded blankly in approval. Peter King leaned up and put his elbows on his knees as he began his side of what had lingered in my mind day after day. "My son was always odd, above-average nutsack-crazy," he started. I heard his son's voice deep within the strange man's tone. "And not in the good, charismatic way. He spent his free time killing things, bullying the kids at school, and writing elaborate designs for inventions to take over the world. Eliza and I thought he would grow out of it, but he never did. It only got worse. Every so often I would try and talk to him, but he wouldn't let anybody get close. He was especially aggressive towards his mother…" Peter paused and ran his hand across his forehead, exasperated. His breathing roughened as he struggled to continue. Jack always wanted to go to the military; he *loved* the idea of fighting and leading an army. While he was away, I found his book of plans he kept as a teenager. He wrote *everything* in there, from blueprints to whatever was flowing through that machine mind of his. But what disturbed me most was what I found on the last page of that notebook: my son wanted to use the armed forces to destroy the world and then create his own from the ashes. When the Dreamers came into play, those *goddamn* Dreamers," he mocked, "we began writing letters to each other every week. I told him how I had found his plans and warned him to stay safe over there; these Dreamers could be dangerous. I knew I was one. My wife was one. I think Jack knew all along. He was so *angry* towards us, especially his mother. Jack was the only one in our family to be normal, to be *ordinary*. And it drove him crazy. He had to rely on what the world gave him instead of what he could do, which was nothing. He grew angrier and angrier over the course of those letters. He made threats and talked about how he was going to enslave all of us and have us killed in the most brutal of ways. His Commander found the letters and relieved him of his duty. Jack was imprisoned overseas for conspiracy to treason. Then the world ended. Our people had realized their full power and it was only a matter of time. My wife and I had taken cover in our home basement to ride it out. We knew death was imminent, and we welcomed it because of well, you know. On the day Eliza and I died, we heard a knock at the door. Nobody was above to answer it, but whoever it was kicked it in and rummaged through the house. The basement door opened and we stared back at the son we had raised and I saw the tortured little boy of mine be eaten

320

and devoured by the monster he had become. But he was *not* our son. Not him. He had never been. He killed his mother first. He made me watch. He blamed me for everything. I watched in terror and grace as he ripped her heart clean out of her chest. I knew I was soon to follow and would find her again in this place. Jack put the barrel of his pistol down my throat and pulled the trigger. I was the first Dreamer in this place. The diamonds thirsted for a ruler, and I was glad to oblige them. I knew not of what would come of this world and then I understood that it was mine. That it was whatever you wanted it to be. I came from the same curiosity and anger you suffer from now. I control everything here. My son plans to eradicate all the Dreamers in his world and mine. He knew not that once he murdered one there that they would end up here. We were only *obstacles*, things in his way. Now we wait on the back burner until he gets his real chance to end us for good. He knew by killing you that you would find your way here. He planned to have you bring me back to the real world so he could kill me. To kill you. To kill all of us. But when I die, all dreams die. All of the Dreamers. All that will remain will be his world, which is recognized as the real world. And that would be a sorry goddamn excuse for a life. A world without dreams. No sir. We cannot let this happen."

"What do you mean *we*?" I inquired. "Me. You. The Dreamers, of course," he replied matter-of-factly. "I'm not a Dreamer," I said, exhausted from yelling that response for eons past. "You would not be here if you weren't, Noah," Peter laughed as if I was inferior. Perhaps I was. "How did our stories line up?" he wondered. "He said you sent him to the military. And that you beat him. You're the reason for his scars. And you're the reason that his daughter is held captive there," I said through gritted teeth, not quite sure who I was angry at, only that I was angry. That was *enough*. "What of it?" Peter asked. "One of you is a goddamn liar," I spat. The old man chuckled. "I'll make you a deal, Noah," he said deeply. I widened my eyes and opened my ears. "Let me train you. Show you how to harness the power. Then you help me get back to the real world to kill my son. An even trade," he offered. I was done. I had lost everything; I had nothing left to lose. "Deal."

I had been asked the question so many times. It had become custom to hear it every so often, whether it be reality or in the deep recesses of my mind. Even that comparison had raised the question on most occasions. I had always denied all unnatural happenings, all chance of being a Dreamer. It had always resulted in me driving myself damn near insane at the end of the day when I lay awake at night. I now knew that I could be *trained*, and that I was right all along. I was not a Dreamer, but I had discovered that I could be one. *Did I want to?* I pondered the topic; I had never given it much thought. The idea of it was terrifyingly exciting, both of which put my stomach in a pretzel-like sex position. If this war of the worlds was going to be a living hell anyway, I might as well give it a try. What did I have to lose, after all? Only *myself*, and perhaps I was willing to risk that. All of the memories raged in my mind like a wild hurricane brewing, swirling with all of the stories I had been told. I vowed to find out what was truth in that existence for myself. I would become what I had feared and ran from for so long. I was in a corner, and a mighty small one it was. I had witnessed this false label for so long; it was time to finally be a part of it - to cut out the false faces and unveil the jaded masterpiece of a culprit.

"You can trust me, Noah," Peter said to me as he leaned in ever-so-closer. "This is a land of truth in which I have perfected every last goddamn frill. I will teach you everything; you will be all-powerful. Next to *me*, of course. Then we must use our knowledge to secure this place. To protect it from the outside. To save our own fucking skins." The old man sounded so *confident* in me. He might as well have put faith in a fucking snail. I could not help but remember my father's encouraging words. It amazed me how present ghosts could be. "When do we start?" I asked curiously, through a difficult silence of painful memory. "You go back to the Noy residence. Pack all of your belongings, you will live here for the entirety of your training. This will be your new home starting at noon tomorrow. When you're done with your training, you can choose whatever you want. Anything will be possible once it's over." Peter King talked about killing his own son as if it was childsplay. I had never seen such a hatred between blood before. My father and I had had our falling outs, but never threatening to our livelihood. It was usually Jacob and he that often went head-to-head. It was heartbreaking to hear those words of malice from the outside. It also led me to wonder how serious their battle for ideology must truly be, and far worse - what the two men were truly capable of.

Peter King bade me farewell and escorted me back through the hallway, that time with me in front and his hand on my shoulder. "Find something to drive you to *want* this, Noah," he said. "It won't work otherwise. It would be a false testimony." I repeated the words in my head as I thought of what would possibly settle my stomach and calm my nerves about that whole topic, but nothing came to mind. I retraced my steps through the lobby, said goodbye to the secretary, and walked through the final door once again. All of them had become linear once again, but I did not realize it until later; I was too distracted with other matters - such *strange* happenings. I wondered no more; I merely accepted for what was and what could be. *There was a way to get back to Julia. That was my driving force.*

The building must have been airtight apart from the quiet whisper of voices because the aircraft carrier sat just as it had upon my arrival; that sound could wake the dead. Logan Aaron leaned up against the chopper, puffing away at a cigar. "How'd it go, sport?" he asked cheerfully. I nodded in approval; words were damn near impossible to be heard over the roaring engines. He put out the cigar on his boot and pulled the door to the helicopter open once again. The rest of the crew carried on just as they had before, but I paid them no mind. Once again, my thoughts were in a much different place. Once in the secret room, we settled on a final game of poker - a sort of *tournament*. A contest on who was the *better* man. He won for then, but I vowed to best him; perhaps one day, long after my training was over and I had become a full-fledged mythical creature of the dream world, I just might take up poker-playing lessons.

She never said a word, but the subtle silence in her eyes told me that Felicia was devastated that I had to go away for a while. The most frightening and unsettling thought was that neither of us knew how long it would last. Long ago, I knew how long my father would have been gone, yet it still felt like an eternity; I could only imagine an unknown time away. It was quite difficult news to relay, but perhaps that would bring all of us together instead of the inconceivable wedge between us that would rear its ugly head if we did not go through with it. "I have to do this. I have to become a Dreamer," I said sweetly. "This is bigger than us." She walked away silently. The helicarrier drifted away until the next morning as Felicia and I came back into the farmhouse. I thought and hoped it would be my home - at least for a while. Perhaps someday it would be; it became a hope and a long-range dream. Mrs. Noy was delighted to see me again, and boy did she show it through the dinner she prepared for my last supper. *Oh god.* My choice of words never seems to fail me. We dined on a finely-basted turkey, vegetables, and an unbelievable array of desserts. It began to feel like the Thanksgiving from my childhoods before my belly was full. I remembered all in that moment, and the excitement combined with the anxiety made me whole.

My worrisome aura and topped-off stomach demanded a shower at the end of the day, and I was forced to oblige. I washed the wind-blown toxins from my body and mind and pulled on pajama pants. I flexed in the mirror, halfway admirable and halfway terrified of my reflection. As I opened the door to follow the steam out, I jumped as I saw Felicia standing against the hallway wall, clad in nothing but dark maroon underwear and socks to match. Felicia's face was the special hidden kind of beauty as I had seen before, but her body was hidden to the least extent. She often wore the low-cut shirts and tight pants, which is every young man's dream, but in that moment, I forgot the old world in my vast selfishness and was content with remaining there forever. Her stomach was flat down to her waist, her legs shaking in the cool air of the house and warmed by the steam of the shower. I smiled in amazement as I saw her wink in the dim light and reach her hand out to lead me to her bedroom, running her fingers along my bare chest. If it was going to feel like Thanksgiving, she sure felt the need to *give thanks* for my time in the Noy household. God bless and Godspeed. And on that night, I split my belonging between two women. I had sex for the second time in my life, and so I lost myself to a woman once more. For the first time since I had arrived in that place of mystery, I utterly and completely dismissed the idea of Julia. It was a selfish and vile action in which I paid for in all its entirety and still continue to to this day, although no matter how much I may attempt to, I still cannot forgive myself.

The next morning was refreshing, relaxing, and peaceful before I remembered it would be my last for an unknown period of time. I did not want to leave; I wondered if it was too late to back out of that whole training nonsense, but I convinced myself of the otherwise absurd decision as I stared at the one suitcase leaning against the door with what little I had in that new place. It meant so much to me, and regret and indecision soon warped my mind and whispered to me like ghosts of the past. We reluctantly got up, showered, and dressed each other before heading downstairs to the smell of pancakes. Mrs. Noy surely was a culinary genius in a simple country-style apron. Her breakfast was the second much-welcomed send off of that morning. I ate as slow as possible, as if the plate of syrup and butter was a sort of hourglass, but no amount of chewing could drown out the sound of the imminent engines in the backyard. The two women kissed me goodbye as I bade them farewell for their hospitality, one on the cheek and one on the lips. I promised I would be back soon; little did I know that I was about to find out what time really was in that place.

Chapter XIV
Who Is Thine Master?
(Believing is Seeing, Creating is Believing, and Fighting is Creating)

"Here he is, the early bird," Peter King said as he bade me welcome and good morning upon entering the then somewhat familiar door. I was not entirely sure he heard me come in; he certainly had not seen me as he had his back turned to the door. I stared through the hallway as I saw him standing at the window, gazing out into the city - *his* city. His deep, raspy voice bellowed through the narrow hall. The scenery inside the penthouse had evolved - or shall I say *devolved* - entirely. What lay inside the building the previous day had passed away; all that remained as far as I could see was the leather furniture and wooden coffee table facing the massive glass window. All sense of creativity and decoration was null and void. "Um, Peter, are you doing some redecorating?" I asked, wiping the rest of the grogginess from my eyes and wondering about the blank walls as well as the newfound void in my heart. "Don't come any closer," Peter ordered, his back still to me as I entered the massive, empty open room once again. I could not help but wonder what a *waste* the lack of decoration was. "I must make several things clear before we begin." I stopped in my tracks - frozen in the blank, dull room. "What is it?" I bellowed as my voice echoed off of the chandelier, walls, and off of the thick glass panes. The elegant chandelier was perhaps the most *luxurious* feature of the once beautiful interior design. "During these lessons, you will become a Dreamer little by little. It takes time. Do not be frustrated or angered by it. Let patience overwhelm you rather than the power. Do not become drunk on it as many before you have done. You and your human world know of that first hand. Do not be fooled by this place - it is full of danger and horror. You will be tested time and time again.

It will not be easy." I thought the old man was finished with his monotonous lecture, but he was not; in fact, it would not be over for a very long time after. "And lastly, there is no going back." His voice grew cold as I shivered; every hair on the back of my neck stood up to match the rest of my body, chilled by the frost of *evil* in the air. I mistook it for warmth as the sun rose over the tallest buildings outside the window. "If you cannot do these things, you might as well swallow a bullet, kid. Blow your goddamn brains out. This would be a better end than going back where you came from. If you can, however, come right on in and we shall get started." Although his back was turned, I could sense the wicked smile spread across his face. I chose to walk in anyway, leaving my entire existence behind like a shell and becoming enveloped in a new one.

I left my single, rather melancholy looking suitcase by the door where I dropped it. I had nothing in there that was worth keeping; none of it was actually mine, after all. "Are you hungry?" Peter asked me, his voice changing from solemn to chipper. Before I could respond, he rose his hand to stop me. "I know," he continued. "Patricia Noy cooks a hell of a meal, doesn't she?" he laughed as I nodded in agreement. "What's first?" I said, eager to begin - or perhaps eager to *end.* Maybe I was both. He smiled as elderly men often do before they respond, as if the younger generation is inferior to them; in this case I probably was. "There's no sense in rushing, Noah. I told you, it will take time. I know you have something to go back to, but let it be your hope. Let it *drive* you, you see. You will be back home soon enough." *Home.* What was home? There were several places that fit the title, but at the same time, none of them did. My home was found in people. *A person.* I could not decide which one; that truth haunted me for the rest of my life.

"But since you asked, we might as well jump right in. And you gave me the perfect starting place. All lessons begin with a story and end with a moral. A *theme.* What I'm about to tell you is the meaning of all of this. Come, let's sit." Peter led me to the simple leather furniture once again. He - along with his sly posture - settled into the chair as he sipped a cup of coffee, as the elderly portion of the human race is also known to do. I yearned for it as well. Coffee struck a sour note with me, however. I remembered a rather *heated* experience with the substance. I sat up, eager to hear what he had to say. "I want to tell you a little backstory about this place," he began. I nodded that I was listening and I prepared to take it in. "I was the very first Dreamer. The first man to bring dreams to reality. The normal are so goddamn *naive*. They thought I was a fucking *wizard*, for Christ's sake. I was forced into hiding. When Jack killed me - in cold blood, mind you - I found myself on a beach. A plain, normal, ordinary beach. I found my way to this place, this *fortress,* and fortified every goddamn inch of it. This is *my* dream. *My* home. *My* solidarity. All of those people down there are Dreamers too. You see, I found something I could not control. I uncovered the truth behind it all. Every single Dreamer has a 'twin', per say. Another being that links them to the natural world. When they arrive here, they find their way and hope to God they come across this twin, take them back to the real world, and take their place in the natural creation. They can choose to keep that said twin alive in order to have continuous travel between worlds. The only way to stay is to kill that person. That's why I have to train you, Noah. You have to find your twin and return to the natural world so I can bring Jack here and kill him so I can rule this place forever. See, Jack is *my* twin. It's an impossible mistake that I must control for all of our sakes."

I sat up along with him, breaking my stare out the window. "Let me get this straight," I asserted. "You want to use me to better yourself?" I inquired with quite a shot of attitude. "Not at all," he replied, straightening up. "I want to get you back to your wife and your brother." I stood up and walked over to the window, gazing down at the hundreds of people in the streets below. "It's an even trade!" he raised his voice. "It's the only way back for you, and I can make your world so much more *valuable.* If you help me save this place by saving myself, I will kill Jack and allow you to take his place. After all, you fit in perfectly there. This is simply a *vacation* for you. It's only a *dream,* Noah. Make this one a reality." I heard the words and considered them. "So you teach me, I capture my twin, we go back to the real world, kill Jack, and I become the leader? No thanks. What if I want to stay here?" I pondered out loud. I gave it not an ounce of forethought before the idea proceeded from my mouth like a cough; it was out before I even realized it. There was no way I could do that. I was in two different places. I had two lives, and I could only choose one. Peter seemed to read my mind. "You will simply have to make that choice when it presents itself. The deal is still the same." This man was selfish, arrogant, and vulgar just as his son was, but Peter King was *fair.* He was *just.* He provided an *option.* But he was still a King, and I had to watch my every move as well as his.

"By capture, I mean steal their ability to dream," he continued. When you can no longer dream, you must return to the real world or you will slowly waste away here. Find your twin, capture their ability to dream, and travel with them back to the real world to make that simple and difficult fucking choice. Then we secure this place and live out long eternal existences in Kingdom Come. This is the new Heaven, my Saint." *We* was a very, *very,* loose term. This was a one-man plan - and I knew *exactly* who it was. "How do we get back?" I asked my final question. Peter raised his hand to stop me. "That is a phenomenon in which you must witness first hand. And you surely fucking will, my son. Answers will come with your training. And on that sweet, lovely note, let us begin."

I could not believe that I had even *suggested* that. What in the name of sweet fucking Christ was I *thinking?* I was not; I decided on that truth early on. I will admit that. I could not coexist; I had to make a decision. *Sometime*. I would put it off as much as possible. My stomach did a dance of all routines. Giving up one life to live another. *But which one? Where did I belong?* I decided to listen to the words of Peter King when he promised answers among the training. I would let him be my guide. Not the light, but the teacher. The answer would present itself when I became what I was supposedly predestined to be.

Peter King walked over the to the smooth dark wooden coffee table and beckoned for me to follow. "Your training starts here," he said. "What do you see?" he pointed at the table. He then folded his hands in front of his waist gracefully. I examined the smooth, empty surface, scanning for anything I might have missed. I *knew* it was just a table; perhaps it was a trick question. I found nothing especially particular about it. "I see a table, sir," I replied sheepishly as he chuckled deeply. "I thought you would say that," he responded. "*Should* I see anything besides the table, sir?" I asked, eager to know the answer. I *wanted* to be this, and so I had to try. I gave it my all. "It's all up to you, Noah. You *choose* what you want to see and make it happen. Put it there. The first step to becoming a Dreamer is believing that you *can* do anything you set your mind to. If you *believe* it is possible, and you can picture it in front of you, then why shouldn't you be able to *put* it there? Make it happen. Right there in front of you."

The old man straightened his collar and rapped the table with his right knuckles. A pleasant, familiar smell wafted through the air. I looked down to find a plate stacked high with pancakes, topped with strawberries and whipped cream dripping with maple syrup - just what I had eaten for breakfast. "Do you believe what just happened?" he asked me before I had a chance to process it. I took a moment to take it all in. I *did* believe it, but at the same time I did not. I had witnessed it happen right before my very eyes. The same feeling I had felt every other time I had seen these extraordinary happenings flowed through my veins and clouded my senses. He noticed my silence and smiled. "Still hungry?" he joked. "I saw it happen," I started before he interrupted. "Yes, but did you *believe* it?" he nearly shouted. There was immediate silence, just as there had been on several occasions before. "None of this means *anything* if you don't fucking believe!" he shouted, exasperated and nearly bipolar, as if he was driven by anger or on a strict time limit.

In a blink of an eye, the dishes disappeared. "Let's try again," he said, his voice, attitude, and the entire room resetting. His apparent anger had vanished along with the sight and smell of the flapjacks. It all came back in the wind as he brought his fist down on the table; the force could have shook the entire building. As I flinched and looked back again, I saw a hand grenade rolling across the floor. With a flick of his wrist, the pin separated and flew across the room. I instantly began panicking, but I stood entirely still - paralyzed by anxiety and fear. I felt the grip of Peter's calming hand on my shoulder, holding me in place. I still feared the worst, but the old man's touch brought comfort to my unstable emotions. All ten thousand thoughts zipped around the room, exploding along with the grenade that never came. We stared at the explosive in slow motion, far past the expected detonation time. It *never* went off. I slowly relaxed my wincing expectations as he released my arm and settled back into his original mold. "Did you believe that it was going to explode?" he asked fervently. "I thought it was," I replied, my voice shaking from the leaving fear of my body. "I believed it was." I could tell by the look in his eyes that he was satisfied with my answer.

As the grenade vanished, Peter grabbed me by my shoulders, picking me up in the air. He was a very large man, and for his age, the man was damn surely strong. He brought me down face-first on the coffee table, nearly shattering the glass. My nose popped and cracked back into place as I rolled onto the floor in pain - enough to *anger* me. As I rolled back to my feet, I heard the click of a gun to my head. I stood up as he pressed it to the front of my forehead. "Do you believe that there is a bullet in here?" he asked me as sweat dripped down my brow line. I heard him pull the trigger, followed by another click of an empty barrel. He tossed the gun aside into nonexistence. "Don't *ever* do that again," I said through gritted teeth, rubbing my sore nose. "I have to *break* you, Noah. You have to *understand*. You have to *believe*." I growled at him, no words emitting from my lips. I was furious, frustrated, and above all, in the dark.

"Have you ever made anything happen, Noah?" he asked, nearly pleading with me. His voice chased the tonal crests and troughs as he practically *begged* me to believe. I was still heated from his previous attack on me, but I sighed in exasperation and came clean. "I've *seen* strange things. The dreams are always odd. At least they were in the old city; I don't dream here. But to answer your question, no, I *haven't* made anything happen." I leaned forward against the table as he pondered my answer, preparing himself to educate me on what was to come. It was in that moment that I remembered the coffee, my father's eyes, and the gun from long ago, yet I stayed silent. "That's because you are *living out* the dreams here, Noah. This *is* the dream. That's how you return to the real world. You steal your twin's ability to dream, you have to follow them through their dreams back to the real world, and then the decision is yours. I hope you're taking notes. Any questions so far?" he wondered out loud. I shook my head. "How do I find this twin?" I asked coldly. His face grew very serious, rather silent. "A twin is someone who has the same *dreams* as you. You have to find them in your dreams and take it. Find them, and you will find your answers."

"I have an idea," he smiled maniacally. "You seem to flourish in a *real* situation." That was all he said. I saw him pull the gun out of his pocket in a slick, quick motion. My vision went into slow motion. I heard the hammer cock back; this was *not* an empty barrel. I saw his wrist twist as he pointed the gun at me once more, this time his finger transferring to the trigger. I flinched and ducked under the table as he fired the first round into the middle of the wooden surface. I rolled under the other side as he pulled the hammer back once more. The second bullet ricocheted off of the apparently bulletproof windows and skittered across the floor. There was nowhere left for me to find cover. I winced as I heard the third and final cocking of the trigger. "This is the *only* way, Noah," he said solemnly. I am sure the old man would have pulled the trigger if there was even a gun in his hand of which trigger to pull. The gun had vanished. It was *gone* - along with all of the noise in the room for several long, heart-slowing moments.

"You just made that gun disappear, Noah," Peter said, breaking out into a smile. It rolled over in my mind as I climbed to my feet once again. Perhaps I did. No, that was *nonsense*. I had been running from all possibility of being a Dreamer that I had even turned the training away in my mind. If I believed - which I had just decided to do only moments prior - maybe I could become something *better*. Something *stronger*. Something more *powerful*. I simply nodded a coward's nod as he clapped quietly. That was the first real step of my training. Once I began to believe, no matter how slowly and surely, burden by burden was lifted off of my shoulders and out of my mind. The praise felt magnificent; this was the master congratulating the student - the *apprentice*. "Now it's your turn," he said proudly, clapping me on the shoulder. "What?" I inquired. Perhaps I had misunderstood him. "You've learned to believe, now it's time you started to *create*," he relied. I did not know the first of anything about that. I was fond of the "baby steps" method, and this child was growing up far too fast. I continued to look at the teacher with a puzzled expression. "Anything you think of can be created right in front of you," he said, not satisfying my curiosity. "You will need to start slowly - eyes closed and deep breaths - and little by little, it will become more natural. The more experienced you become, the faster and more skilled you will be." He motioned me over to his side of the table. I closed my eyes tightly as he squeezed my shoulder, delving into my inner thoughts as to what to create. My mind exploded into millennials of different possibilities, but only one was in order.

I opened my eyes to find the same handgun lying on the table, the handle facing me. I snatched it by the grip and pointed it straight at the face of Peter King. I placed the barrel into his one good eye and held it there. His hands slowly rose into the air in surrender. I knew he was fully capable of putting me in the ground, but something needed to be said, and I knew he would allow me get my point across. "Do *not* threaten my life again, or I promise you I will leave you completely blind for the rest of your fucking life." I warned him solemnly as my heart raced and thoughts grew cloudy. The gun vanished as quickly as it had appeared. I was so *close* to the man. I could smell his ancient breathing on my forehead as he laughed gravely. "You're a cold one, Noah Willowby," he said. "And a damn quick learner. I love it. That will be all for today. You've done *enough*." His voice travelled from threatening to prideful to melancholy all in the same endgame. I was done, at least for that day, and for that I was truly grateful. I was *exhausted*, for Christ's sake. *How long had we been at this?* I had surely lost track. *Time.* It was gone just as Peter King was. The old man was nowhere in sight as I turned and looked all around me.

I walked to the foyer and collected my one bag sitting lonely in the corner. I turned back and hoisted the surprisingly heavy suitcase back through the open training room and up the large stairwell. Upstairs was a decorational abscess, easily the size of another house. There were several more mosaic stained glass windows which matched the rest of the penthouse, of course. If the landscape was anything, it was consistent. I found my way to an abnormally small bedroom, or at least minuscule as far as the scale of the rest of the mansion went. Inside was a queen size bed, elegant but simple, an oak desk, plain and ordinary, and a rocking chair looking out into the vast city outside. The window beside it was foggy; you would have to stand right up on it to be able to see out of it. I remember passing a bathroom in the hallway and took note of it. *'It must be mundane as well'*, I imagined. There had to be a method to the madness of the simplicity of that place. I had an idea, and it went along the lines of the disapproval of the fact that I thought this would be the most extravagant place I would ever stay. It was nothing; I was used to my expectations being majorly let down. I would soon find out why that was. Either way, I was gracious for a place to sleep and an escape route if I ever was to need one. I thought to myself as I stared down the abyss that was the stories-high drop, suitcase tossed on the bed in deep thought. *Jesus fuck, it sure was a long way down.*

If not for the crinkling of paper I heard as I sat the duffel bag down on the bed, I would have completely missed the letter addressed to me. I moved the bag with a curious scowl across my lips as I straightened the edges to where the prim and proper penmanship was legible once again.

Noah,

By the time you read this, I strongly assume you have found your room. Sorry I had to make a quick exit; duty calls a lot more than you think. Make yourself at home; what is mine is yours. Above all, what you choose to create is yours as well. You can have everything you have ever dreamed of, Noah Willowby. With my teaching and training, you shall become whatever you seek to find. We will have a lesson everyday at dawn, but the training room is always open for you to practice anytime you please. If you need anything, I will NOT be available to you. It is the only way you will learn to create on your own. What I pass on to you will be far more than enough. You shall flourish like a wildfire under my wings. You will have all the privacy you need; it is only you and I here. You will see me during our sessions only.

The rest is yours. It is all yours, Noah Willowby.

-    *P.K.*

I laid the thin piece of paper in the rocking chair facing the window. It was present, but out of sight. Out of sight, still in mind. I took note of the words and stored them deep within the recesses of my mind. I felt the excitement, the anxiety, the stress, the worry, and the infinite amount of emotion that was truly there about the situation and future at hand. The letter triggered something within me; I *felt* the presence of Peter King in the room, saying those words, as the rocking chair leaned forward and squeaked backwards ever-so-slightly.

As much as I tried and as much as it irritated me, I could never tell time in that place. The time moved right along, but at the same time, it never seemed to move at all. My assumptions about Peter King shrouded my questions under a deep and heavy blanket in the back of my mind, tucked away, only to be pondered in the dead of night when the squeaking of the rocking chair kept me awake. Perhaps some questions are not provided answers, only thought. The thinking replaced the dreams in the new world.

It did not seem like I had trained for very long on that first day. Perhaps the clock sped up when I was learning. By rights and what I was used to, it felt as though it should merely be lunchtime, noon at the latest. But as I unpacked my things, I settled into the bedroom as the sun sank below the mountainous buildings outside of the unclear window. I enjoyed the peace, quiet, and privacy of the small and cozy room. I had always appreciated being alone, and that was the perfect place to think - warm, safe, and confined. Small spaces had never bothered me; in fact, I preferred a smaller enclosed environment. Keeps everything contained - never *trapped.* I laid back in the soft, comfortable bed over the blankets and rested my head on the goose down pillows. I fell asleep to the golden full moon and the buzz of the city below. No dreams - only blank and empty thoughts that filled the room as well as me.

'*Are you a Dreamer, Noah Willowby?*' I heard over and over, echoing through the tunnels of my unconscious mind. There were no images, only the faint whispers of the impervious question. My brain was a pitch black abyss in which I was held prisoner. This was no dream; this was the brutal reality - the sum-it-up of life. Of course, there were *always* the dreams that refused to end - the ones that bound you to the slimy brick walls of your own being. The depths of hell are indeed descended, deep inside each and every one of us. I jerked awake, cold sweat dripping down my brow. The light was still on, and for good measure. My heart raced like a wild mustang through my bare chest. I was almost *spooked. Frightened. Terrified.* The room was silent, yet I heard a noise coming from *somewhere.* My bare feet hit the carpeted floor as I ran my fingers through my hair, clearing my face of the sweat and oil of my intense and unsettled slumber. I was going to find where the noise was coming from. It echoed from somewhere in the mansion as the moonlight led the way.

On several occasions in the past as well as the following years, I found that the moon and stars provided a much more extensive amount of guidance than the sun could ever hope to perform. My travels through that strange place, whether it be the penthouse or the entire world itself - depending on your preference or personal interpretation - provides evidence to this. The gigantic glass panes were excellent carriers of the natural light; I swore if my father was there, he would have made multiple comments praising how much money he could save on electricity. Also, some memories choose to be Nazis, their cyanide draining your emotional sense of self and breath through tears. *Taking over.* The noise I heard was a single voice, not readable, not able to be made out. But it was calling my name, drawing me closer. I was enticed by curiosity, a feline with perhaps no lives left to spare. I proceeded nonetheless.

I descended the massive marble staircase, each step composed of slimy, grimy stones of the vertical chasm. My bare feet chilled with each frigid stair, sending shivers up my body like volts of electricity. The voice drew my hairs to their ends. The air was the chains, and I was bound to the room as I walked into the open training space. All that was present was the same simple leather furniture and glass coffee table in front of the elegant window. The midnight was frozen, frosted over the slick surface like dew on a countryside field. My nerves were twisted and turned like an arrest; I was a *prisoner*. "Are you a Dreamer, Noah Willowby?" I heard the voice loud and clear that time. It was raspy and deep, clear and creepy. *Chilling*. I spun around in desperate pursuit of the source of the mysterious whispering. *Nothing*. I cleared my mind as I heard it once more. I smashed my fist on the table and closed my fingertips around the trigger of the gun in my hand. I heard it again, and again, and again. I turned around in all directions, scanning all around the dimly lit arena. The ghosts had all come out to watch. The training room was a skeletal amphitheater. All around me was empty air, free of a single culprit.

Out of the corner of my eye, I saw a light coming from the window. More than the moonlight, more than a shadow, more than a faint whisper. This was not the overwhelming shine of the brilliant midnight, it was simple and subtle, peaceful and lonesome. I tucked the handgun into the waistband of my pajama pants as I slowly made my way to the thick glass window. I gazed far past the mountainous buildings, advertisement signs, and clusters of people, into the distant fields of and farms of the outskirts of that new city. I saw a bright, faint whisper of a light, quite possibly coming from a farmhouse in the countryside far away. All I could think of was a young woman dancing alone in the distance.

All throughout my childhood, adolescence, and young adulthood, I had been praised for my ability to learn quickly. This quality had benefited me all the way through elementary school and eventually the high school back in the old city. New topics came as easy as clockwork cake to me, and I had excelled in nearly everything with minimal challenge. The same was true for my training with Peter King. Although confusing and quite bewildering at times, I was a fast learner. However, knowledge is one thing and mastership is quite another. I began practicing what I had learned on the first day, which was the conjuring of various objects in a time of need. Before I knew it, I could summon nearly anything I could imagine at the flick of a wrist or the smash of a fist. The bedroom soon became cluttered with random miscellaneous items such as potatoes, hairdryers, and several handguns, which were always the default. The appearance of food was quite the privilege in the dead of night when peaceful sleep evaded me. To sum up the beginning stages of my practice routine, my room became cozily decorated with the trial and error of conjureship as almost a meditation temple. As I stared out the window and through the soul of the city, I could find an empty mind and a clear focus as I brought my minuscule fantasies to existence.

I reported to the training room at the bright and bushy-tailed, early, split crack of dawn, just as I was instructed to do. Peter was always accompanied by the smell of cigar smoke and the pitch patch over his eye. I did not mind getting up early; how could I argue with all the meantime I was getting to think and practice? Besides, I loved getting up early. The world was *mine* - especially *that* one. The bones that were thrown were easily retrievable. We spent the first few days practicing just as I had done on my own, and only with Peter, there was guidance. There was *supervision*. There was *judgement*. I could not help but feel inferior in the presence of my master of sorts. I tried to use my speedy progress to the best of my ability to impress him as well as move right along in the scheme of the curriculum, if you will.

I concluded that Peter King must have been relatively pleased with my advancement because whether I believed we would or not, we eventually began the second topic of my training. Something worthy of mentioning is as follows: The old man *never* spoke during my performance. He claimed he did not want to break my concentration. As wise as I assumed he was, I inferred the assumption that he wanted me to teach myself, in a sense, only with his guidelines and rules to shape it. I was accepting of that; Peter was no tyrant of the training room - more of a silent element. A whisper which carved authority into the brick walls of the hellish mental chasm that even *he* was a part of. Much to my surprise, on the fifth day of our quite repetitive sessions, Peter King finally spoke up. He hobbled down from the balcony beside the chandelier where he normally observed from and clapped me on the shoulder. The touch took me by surprise; I had just summoned a two-sided blade. When I looked down at my hands, I felt the weapon slip away into mere nothingness. "That will be all for step one," he said with a quiet, satisfied smile. I felt my face grow red with humility, success, and excitement for what may lay ahead.

"What is step two?" I asked. He grinned as if he read my mind; perhaps he *had*. It could not have been that difficult to assume. I had been doing the same thing for nearly a week in my mindset of time. "Step two is combat training," he said indignantly. "You've got the foundation for your house, the floor of your hut, and the basement of your mansion. You have a solid foundation - the emphasis of being a Dreamer. Now, like the building of a home, you must build upon that that principle. Use the art of creation for all purposes. Step two is the aggressive scenario. Weapons, blocking, deconstruction - there will *always* be a fight as far as dreams and reality are concerned. This is what separates the normal from the god-like. We are gods, Noah

Willowby. We are God himself." The mention of action excited me almost as much as being God did. It was the kind of excitement that lies deep within your stomach, churning and thumping to the beat of your mind. Being a god called for responsibility, leadership, and power. Some only seek power and live long enough to gain honor. I wanted no one under me; I simply wanted the *power*.

We gathered around the table as I looked to the old man for instruction. I had come across so many teachers and taken advice from so many young and old men and women, yet the teaching style of Peter King was so unique in its simple unreliant manner. He would give me a task, provide an example, and take a back seat as I completed it on *my* time with no rush and no pressure. There was understanding and guidance if desired, but I was alone in my training in the greatest sense of the word, and I progressed slowly but surely along the process in this way. It made the new experience rather enjoyable and alleviated much of the frustration that often accompanies new beginnings. Peter tapped the table before us as several weapons came into creation. I scanned my eyes over the machete, a shotgun, a pair of brass knuckles, and a wooden staff. As odd of a collection as it was, these various objects shifted the focus from firearms to melee weapons, which I was instructed that I would need more times than not. Not only was this a collection, but it must have been *his* collection. Like an assortment of fine chocolates, I had a sweet suspicion as to how I would learn hand-to-hand combat. I would have to *fight* Peter King. It would be as though defeating a ghost, something that you could not be sure existed, but at the same time you were positive. This phantom was in his opera house, and he was as sharp as they came. I saw Peter's rusty gray eyes blink a single flick, and the gear wrapped itself around his body. With the machete on his back, the shotgun on his shoulder, the brass knuckles on one fist and the other around the wooden staff, he was armed to the teeth. I could not help but feel *inferior* to him.

Weak. Like a child against his father. "You know what you have to do, Noah," he said. God could sense my anxiety. "Don't worry; I'll take it easy on you," he laughed coldly. "Let's begin."

"Let's say I was going for your eyes," Peter began. He brought his fist in slow motion toward my nose in the swinging position. The glare from the brass knuckles shifted upward toward my brow as he stopped it right outside the sockets of my eyes. "What could you use to deflect my attack?" he asked brightly. I scanned my brain for a valid answer. "Anything," I replied. His grin surely was bright. "Excellent, my boy, excellent, I say!" he exclaimed. I eventually settled on a piece of PVC pipe as Peter retracted his fist. He winked at me, signaling he was coming at me with full force this time. I saw his knuckles race toward me as I gripped the hard plastic in my left fist behind my back. I brought the rod down on his wrist in the true knick of time. The attack ended with the clattering of the brass knuckles hitting the ground. "Very good!" he exclaimed once more. "A true warrior, indeed." My blood simmered with pride as I turned the pipe over in my hands. "Now let's say I was coming at you from behind," he continued, moving right along in the quickest sense. He circled around me, observing my form and scanning me for any weak points. As I recollect, I imagine I had many a chink in my egotistical armor. I felt the wind of his unannounced kick and I spun around, bringing the PVC against the back of his legs, flipping him over backwards. He rolled over and climbed to his feet as I stood over him. "Careful with your old man of a teacher, my son," he laughed. I helped him up, my strength fading. *Old man and a son.* My father was heavy on my mind in those days as I looked to Peter King for guidance. He dusted himself off and caught his breath, as raspy and inconsistent as it was.

"Can I be honest with you about two things, Noah?" he asked as we both recuperated from the day's training. "Yes sir," I replied, eager to hear what degree of honesty what followed would be spun in. "I haven't seen anybody fight that well since I saw my son fight back in school," he said. He breathes heavily as I did the same. The memories of Jack and the stories I had heard replayed through my brain like a freight train. "What's the second thing?" I asked, changing the subject as quickly as I could. He smiled. "You're one tough son of a bitch." I grinned as well, wiping the look of disdain from my lips. "I've got a good teacher is all." *Smiles.* "Let's get back to work," he wheezed. *Crying.*

Over the course of my training with Peter King, the old man and I grew ever-so-closer each and every day and with all of the knowledge in which he imparted to me. The man appeared as though he could have been my grandfather, but Peter King soon took on the imagery of my father in that new world. Though separated and seemingly in another world, Mrs. Noy was my adoptive mother in that life as well. Separation and desperation are close acquaintances in this life and I fought off all thoughts of the Noys for the sake of my own sanity. I knew myself well enough to be sure of the fact that if I allowed myself to ponder on the subject for only a moment too long, I would surely lose my mentality. Perhaps losing your mind is far worse than losing your life, yet I intended to hold on to both for as long as I could bear it.

Words cannot consume my point when I tell you how amazing it felt to finally be a part of that mystery instead of staring through a foggy window from the outside. What I had feared for so long had become my livelihood, my bread and butter, and the rather literal reason I awoke each morning. What I had seen became what I was to accomplish, and the experience was that of an inauguration into a new world - which I knew all too well in the literal perspective. I craved the knowledge and the power that came with our lessons, and I found myself face to face with the clock, urging it to race against itself just as I had done. I had found that the impossible was indeed feasible if the essence was pushed far enough, and the amount of strength I had was immeasurable. "The second portion of combat training is learning *offense*," he said to me soon after. "With your deep taste in which you now possess in defense, you know where to go for, and most importantly, where to *avoid* striking. You know exactly where to aim and then divert to a lesser-known area. You have the blueprints to bring people to their knees. You simply have to choose *how* to do it." I had never been an involvement in machism, but the idea of overpowering another struck a deep-ringing bell in my ear.

"Let's see how you fare with attacking," he offered. His wide array of weapons had long since disappeared into the wisps of nonexistence as he stood before me in his suit, just as he always wore. A feeling of superiority was always present in the room, no matter how close the old man and I had grown along the way. I knew he was my *master*, and I knew I had a job to do and more importantly, a role to play. I was the student, and he was the teacher. Simple as that. Honestly, I felt uneasy about hunting Peter King in that particular portion of the training; I simply felt out of place. *Disrupting order.* Perhaps I was only worried about what *he* planned to bring to the table. "Give it a go," he teased. "Bring all you've got, Noah." Taunting was no stranger to me; I lived out my entire life until that point with an older brother. *Brother.* I shook the relapse off of my spine as I prepared myself for the task at hand. Peter stood several feet in front of me, his arms wide open in surrender, staring deep into my existence, awaiting my attack. *Did he already know what I had planned before I did?* I felt the slick but sure handle of a samurai sword in the palm of my hand as I tested the weight of the blade. He gazed at the silver as I brought it into view and across my shoulder. The teeth which filled his wide grin suggested that his calculations were perhaps correct.

I knew how to take a man down - any man, that is, in a very wide generalization. You go for the legs, of course. My father taught me that back in the city school when I was bullied. *'If you can get a man on his knees, he belongs to you,'* he told me. I never got around to test his theory; perhaps I was too frightened, but I feared nothing in that moment. I emerged from my thoughts as quick as a mirror as I swung the blade toward his legs. For a man in a suit, I must say that Peter King was rather *agile.* "Come on now, Noah," he laughed. I spun around before the words even left his lips, bringing the sword around to his stomach. He shifted to his side at the last atomic instant, leaving nothing but empty air as a target for me to slice through. My frustration in those days was rather similar to a fuse on an explosion - an *improvised* explosive. A homemade *toy* gone wrong. I felt my temper grow hotter and redder as I contemplated one last attack. I swung the blade around in circles as he cackled in amusement; I slid into a faux on his left and parried on his right, seconds before bringing the thin metal against his Adam's apple.

I watched in half awe, half satisfaction as I saw blue blood dripping down his neck. I had made a minimal cut - nothing lethal, but enough to bleed an extensive amount across his throat. I expected him to be angry, perhaps even *volatile*, but he simply smiled at me like a midnight fox. Peter waved his hand as the sword clattered across the training room, skittering across the marble pillars and stone tiles of the mansion. "Are you alright?" I asked nervously. "Of course, my boy," he laughed once again. "In fact, I've never been better." He wiped his hand across his chin and down into the wound as the tear repaired itself right before my eyes. "You healed yourself," I said in awe, this time complete. "Your training will give you all of your answers in due time, my student. But let me say this: to hurt me, you will have to try a lot harder than that." He smiled again, this time with a slight frown in the center. "That will be all for today. Excellent, my son. Excellency." I made my way to the bottom of the staircase as Peter King walked off in the opposite direction of the house. As my right foot tapped the first step, I heard a subtle but prominent clearing of a throat behind me. I turned around to face him. "Yes sir?" I asked, not even completely sure he was addressing me. "You are very talented, Noah. In fact, you are the most talented young man I have ever had the great honor of training. Once we complete your journey, you will make an exquisite leader in this place. This is your home. You belong *here*, Noah Willowby. I realize that now." I thought about what he had said; I became lost in his words. I knew by the crossing of the Ts and dotting of the Is that what he had suggested simply could not be. I had a great deal of courage, but not enough to break that news to the old man on that day. Before I turned around, I watched Peter King walk away from me, scratching his neck rather roughly. I had made God bleed, and perhaps he plotted revenge.

The following morning, I awoke somewhat sore from all of the sword swinging and parrying I had done the day before. I knew the day's training would consist of combat practice, and as whipped as the dreaded Hun was, I climbed out of bed and got dressed nonetheless. I dined on an elegant breakfast of my signature pancakes, and as I went to open the door to begin the day's contents, a slip of paper drifted against my bare feet:

Noah,

I could smell the pancakes. As I said before, you are a prize mule amidst a vast field of jackasses. I often compare our lessons to those of a mother bird teaching her chick to fly. Little by little, I will instill my knowledge in you in hopes that one day you will need me no longer. I have taught you the basics of combat and you have excelled brilliantly, so for the next week, whether it be my time or yours, I want you to train alone in the training room. Practicing both defense and offense, prepare for battle in your own way. Fly away, baby bird. One flap at a time.
P.K

As I found myself indeed alone in the massive and vacant training room that morning, I pondered which method of practice would best suit my needs. I remembered how Jack King's men used to kneel before him like machines, ready to accept orders and receive spontaneous bouts of attack at significantly less than a moment's notice. I decided on a particular *still* route of routine by summoning a row of like-size, featureless rubber dummies all in a row - a dozen of them. The number gave a twelve, a divisive four or three, each trading off either way it was separated. In other words, a dozen was a fantastic settlement.

Upon my frozen opponents' appearance, I relayed to choose my weapon for the day or even perhaps until I had perfected it, one by one until I could surpass my master and anyone else who would stand in my path. I made a halt in my train of thought as I diverted the thirst for power into my desire - my burning, churning, *obsessive* desire - to return to my unknown home. Although I was quite satisfied with my training and living quarters, I knew I was destined to be somewhere else. That decision was quite a deal more difficult than others. I settled on the samurai sword; I clutched the familiar blade in my left hand as I swung the lightweight handle around, taking several practice swings before bowing in front of my inattentive enemies. I began by poking and prodding at my targets, making tiny pores in the stiffly-materialed chests. Each dummy was identical, a middle-sized shapeless man with a hue of dirty white. The color of a latex glove, there was an absolute stillness about them. They knew no pain as I parried and regrouped down the line of toy soldiers. Soon each and every participant was defaced by scrapes and scratches as the metal pierced their thick rubber coating.

My breathing quickened as I increased my pace and striking up a bit. I switched to the task of heavying my blows, putting a significant amount of pressure into my attacks. I knew I had perfected the motion when the sword would create a gash in the rubber and remove itself cleanly as opposed to being trapped in the forming material, which happened rather too many times on behalf of my frustration. I spent the entire first day of combat practice defacing the dozen rubber dummies and dislodging the samurai sword from their chests as needed. I began the second day by returning to the wounded lineup of opponents the next morning. Sword in hand, I made my way down the line, beheading each dummy with the end of the silver blade. At first the end would get caught midway through and I would have to pull it from the seemingly stone rubber which was the neck of the frozen enemy. As I surpassed the fifth faceless man, I could get further through the thick material without coming to an abrupt stop. By the tenth, I could nearly break the impenetrable rubber coating in the very center. By the twelfth, the heads soared through the empty air like a bird set free. I breathed heavily as I sheathed the blade in the holder I had created for it across my back. I had grown quite fond of the weapon, and although I knew my training with it was nearly complete, I would without a doubt use it again. I knew its effectiveness and the swiftness in which I possessed as I gazed at the piles of rubber heads across the training room floor below me.

The third day brought far more than a single surprise with the rising sun. As I made my way down the stairs, I saw Peter King standing at the window, gazing down at his creation, before he even saw or heard me coming. "Goodmorning, Noah," he said in a monotone voice as he refused to break his stare, using that sixth sense he withheld to detect silent noises and nonexistent shadows. It was damn near impossible to sneak up on him. "I saw your work," his voice shifted with a smile I could *hear*, referring to the pile of manipulated rubber extremities strewn behind him just as I had left them. He tapped his fingers on the icy glass an inch away from his nose as he uttered his next words. "It's time for you to take it up a notch, my boy."

Peter never broke his focus as he peered out the window, his fingers never ceasing their constant tempo. The pieces of severed latex levitated back into place, solidifying in front of me one at a time. The then refurbished row of dummies healed like reptiles, forming a new militia of opponents. Only when they were back to their original state did Peter stop his oddities. He paced in front of me and the featureless figures as he crossed his arms. He stopped only centimeters away from their mouths; they were all the same height as Peter King, coincidentally enough. He breathed a cloud of crystallized breath into each one of the makeshift soldiers one by one. They all remained opaque and identical, but they all began to *move*. Yes, the warriors then had form, as void of shape as they were. The group of once frozen rubber dummies was a moving force of nature, as slow and basic as could be. "We won't give them swords just yet," Peter laughed. "Baby steps. You must begin with a moving target, as easy as these may be for now. But trust me, my boy, they will advance along with you." With the words whispering through the crowd of clustered soldiers, Peter King disappeared into the dozen blankly staring enemies I then had to face.

With Peter gone as quickly and surprisingly as he had appeared, I turned to face the awkward and slow-moving masses. The dozen bodies surrounded me, seeming like far more than the twelve original soldiers. I scanned each one, counting as I meditated my plan of attack, sword in hand as the army groaned like barbarians through their nonexistent mouths. There were indeed twelve present, but the space they enclosed me in made it at least double their numbers. As they closed in like a herd of the undead, I brought the blade through the neck of the closest dummy. The entire body fell to the floor, decapitated as a real soldier would have been. I swung the sword horizontally into the next shell, straight through the empty mass that should have been a brain had they had been human. I rotated and shifted my stance, taking out three with one blow. I was then surrounded by a row of lifeless bodies as the remaining circled me, their ranks lowered but their empty determination deepened. I brought the metal over my head and clinked it against the sixth and seventh parasite, execution style. I was forced to my knees by the enclosing half measure, only a foot of space between my advancing enemy and myself.

I sprung against the meaty legs of the closest member of the militia, bringing the sword through what would have been the chin. I flipped the eighth over my shoulder and put it out of its misery. The ninth and tenth fell hostage to a full circling of the blade through their even necks, the heads barely missing mine as I ducked under their eye level. Though progressing, my enemy was not one of advanced intelligence. The second to last rubber machine grabbed me with nearly lifeless hands, but enough to disarm me. It attempted to snatch the sword from my loosened grasp, but to a barely-escaped avail. I swung the blade from the ground up as the final enemy awaited his fate. I stood face-to-face with him - with *it*; as I looked closely, the figures were almost void of gender as well as any other figure. They were simply a shell given a moment of life. Just as *I* was. I limply brought the sword across its temple as I pierced the final skull. I dropped the sword as exhaustion overtook me. I joined the pile of rubber remains as I passed out. I spent the night on the training room floor, sleeping among the lifeless and the dead.

I awoke the next morning inside of a shadow. I opened my eyes into darkness as I looked around before up, taking in the abrupt fact that I had indeed passed out from exhaustion and slept on the pile of rubber dummies. I peered upward into Peter's one good eye as he smiled down at me. "Early bird catches the worm, I guess." I groaned and climbed to my feet, woozy after the night's imaginably uncomfortable sleep. "If you don't feel up to a lesson today, you've done well. You've earned a day off if you'd like one," he said to me. I wiped my eyes, not considering the subject. I had become *addicted* to the lessons and the practice sessions; I simply could not stop and take a drink of water. I was on a mission. I had something to take and somewhere I had to go, even if I had not decided what or where it was yet.

"No sir," I cut him off. "I'm on a roll. I want to keep going," I staggered. He nodded. "Very well," he smiled. "Which leads us right into our next lesson. I will need to teach you this sooner or later, and you have the perfect opportunity to learn it today." I thought of what it might be, but I settled on none of the ideas that came to mind. "And what is that?" I staggered, curious as a cat. "I haven't taught you how to *heal* yourself yet," he said. I had seen him do it on several occasions as well as Lucious but had never actually needed to myself. I imagined every scenario where I *would* need it, and braced myself to take in some useful information once again - as well as the expectation of excruciating pain.

I had picked up the samurai sword once again as I climbed to my feet. Peter took several steps back as I got my footing. Soon, we stood face-to-face several feet from each other, just as we had done nearly every day prior. "When you're ready..." he began, being nearly as charismatically dramatic as his son was so well known to be. I raised my eyebrows as a wicked smile ran across his face. "I want you to put the sword through my chest," he said blatantly and without waver. I was clearly taken aback; a sane individual - even *partially* sane -would never wish for pain such as he had. But I remembered where I was, who I was, and what I had seen, and I recollected that I had seen and heard *far* worse and this - judging by past trends - most likely was not the end of the peculiarity. I decided to trust his judgement as I swung the blade a few times before assuming the attacking stance.

"Are you sure about this, boss?" I asked quietly, making sure before I made a possibly grave and gruesome mistake. "Sure as a Sherlock shit," he said. His strange analogies almost made me smile, but I needed the utmost seriousness for my training to avoid flaw. I breathed heavily and sealed my eyes shut before bringing the sword quick, still, and hard through his ribcage. I felt contact and exit as the sword jutted through his shirt and out of his spine. I would have thought it was truly horrendous had I not been wondering when he had taken off his jacket. Peter was fast, agile, and above all, mysterious. I asked no questions; I only *wondered*. All he said was a single breath, soon followed by the same Grinch-like smile. It began small and emitted into an epiphany of brutality. An *enjoyment* of pain. I had seen the same smile before. I did not know where in that particular moment until much later.

I pulled the sword out as he motioned his hand toward me. I watched as blood dripped down the once smooth and shiny steel as thick ocean-colored liquid stained his buttons and chest. I waited in slow motion, expecting the old man to perhaps bleed out and die in front of me, with only one suspect to blame. I had a nasty habit of expecting the worst and anticipating it - almost *welcoming* it. I dropped the sword to the ground as I prepared to catch him if he were to fall, but he stood still as a mountain. Blood soaked through his shirt and down his stomach; then was to be the end if the end was as close as I believed it to be. There was a three-inch crevice where the sword had made a clean cut through his midsection, and blood trickled through it like a sub-level cavern. But it soon *stopped*. The faucet-like, deep-canyon colored liquid puddle on the floor rose and back into his shirt. What was there then ascended back to the wound and crawled inside like a snake. I could soon see through the hole against like a telescope downwind. Flesh and cloth repaired itself as he smiled brilliantly, arms wide open. Soon, there was no more wound, no more gash, no more blood, and no more sword. As if none of it had taken place at all. *Had it?* Or perhaps I had simply imagined it and stopped myself. Maybe I had killed him and been forever silenced by whatever punishment awaited me. I stared deep into his one eye, one thought crossing my mind. One question I dared not ask until the absolute, completely opportune moment. I hoped it would come before it slipped my conscience for good.

"Very well, Noah. Excellent," he congratulated me. "I should say the same to you, Peter. That was amazing." I relaxed my shoulders as I banished the nervous tension from my muscles and bones, which were not quite as complete as his were. "To heal, all you have to do is reverse the flow. Turn it upside down. Feel your inner power within you. Then make it whole again." I heard, but I did not understand. Many other questions now accompanied the first. He raised his hand as I opened my mouth to speak. "You will have plenty of time to learn and practice this. It takes time to master, but you will. Along with tomorrow's lesson. We will finish sword training, and I will be back here in the morning. As it turns out, *I'm* the one who needs the rest of the day off." I nodded to him as he limped away, breathing rather heavily. My exhaustion had subsided as I climbed the stairs and shut myself away in my bedroom - my new home - for a day of reading, practicing, thinking, remembering, and dreaming with my eyes wide open, wondering if there were perhaps some things that simply could not be healed - only mended for a short while.

I had made it a fresh habit to make it down to the training room before Peter in the mornings. I would sit in front of the massive window and watch the sun climb over the edges of the skyscrapers outside. As if I could *touch* it. As if I could *join* it up in the sky. I felt the warmth across my face as Peter would clear his throat, telling me it was time to get started for the day. He watched too, sometimes with me, sometimes from the balcony, and even from around the corner on occasion. Whether he was watching the sunrise or *me* is something I still cannot answer to this day, so I chose to leave it up to him, just as I did then. No matter what, Peter King was always there. Always present and always watching.

The next morning was far different and rather odd in an interrupted and vacant sense. Peter would surprise me by beating me to the punch down in the training room, and the following day was just that. I hopped the stairs like a jackrabbit as I wielded the sword on my back. I had begun to sleep with it on the bedside table for comfort. I knew I was proficient in something, and the sword gave me a reason to go on in a sense. I had grown used to it, and it had done the same to me. It was a part of me, and I was a part of it. The sword was *mine*, perhaps intro for the sole reason that I had declared it as my own. I had taken it as it had taken me. I saw something that shocked me quite a bit waiting for me down those stairs that morning. Peter had completely replaced my makeshift militia with a trained army - an *armed* army. I counted each - I could no longer refer to them as *dummies*; the soldiers which awaited me looked to be constructed of flesh and bone. Still with no features, they were identical in their utter simplicity. These were model beings, and as real as possible at that. Each one - I counted two dozen - all wielded massive swords at least twice the size of mine. I shuddered as I stared at the frozen statues, catching sight of Peter staring out the window across the room, watching the sunrise.

"You've got to be fucking kidding me, Peter!" I shouted across the room. "There's no way in hell I'll be able to win this." I heard his laugh echo through the monstrous, empty, and silent training room. "I'll tell you what, Noah," he said, not turning to me, not even breaking his stance or stare. "If you do win, with my guidance and coaching, of course, you owe me a favor if I am to need one," he said. "I'll be with you every step of the way," he added. I did not think about it at the time, and perhaps that was the greatest and bravest mistake I had ever - and would ever - make. There was simply no way I could beat the small army, as it rather was. I decided to give Peter the benefit of the doubt. "Deal," I said. He turned around and smiled to me, walking toward me. "Then let's begin, shall we?" He passed me by and breathed life into the now doubled army of seemingly massive soldiers. The glint of their metallic swords reflected off of the mountainous stained glass windows across the room. The faux men circled around me slowly, sluggishly, and without emotion. Peter stood off to the side, ready to coach me by and guide me to my apparent prophesied victory. I could not see that happening, but trust overtook me and I opened my mind to it nonetheless.

"You want to go after them one at a time, but always keep your eye on the whole as well. Focus on the offensive. *Become the enemy*." I chose my first target and clattered my blade against his, the blunt force pushing me backwards. I retreated my sword and swung for his legs, chopping through the skin and bone of its left kneecap. It toppled over as I kicked it in the temple and out of the way. My peripheral vision kept a close watch on the advancing adversaries as I prepared to take down the next one. I rotated to my left, decapitating one before performing an identical exercise on my right. The three deceased lined my feet like a sunken ground, like a marsh I had fallen prisoner to. I brought the sword across my shoulder and sliced the head from the severed body of the closest soldier behind me. I kicked the one in the front of me back several feet, clearing five feet in every direction around me. "You want to get as close as possible, but keep enough distance to protect yourself and provide yourself cover if needed," Peter shouted pridefully. They mirrored my swinging strategy, mocking me like robotic clones. The herd banded together to replace their dead and reinforce their strength, filling in the empty slots lifelessly. "Try to disarm them. The wrist can either be hit or twisted to trigger a release of the fingers. Try attacking them from behind and dropping their swords *for* them."

I sprung forward at the rubber warrior I had stunned to buy myself time only moments ago. When Peter would shout orders and advice, time would seem to stop, as if even the *elements* honored him. Perhaps it was merely my adrenaline. I skipped behind him, much quicker than it, and placed my sword behind his makeshift pit of his right arm and jammed the blade upward. My enemy's sword skittered across the tiled floor like clockwork. I decapitated the disarmed soldier and jumped back as I did the same to three others surrounding me. One in each direction, closing in as they approached the three foot mark, which was far too close by my standards as well as Peter's.

"Trick them, Noah. Take advantage of their ignorance and stupidity." I thought of a way to prey on their mindlessness. I slipped between two of them and back around the soldier on the right, slicing both of their wielding wrists and arms and putting the blade through their chests. The caveman-like machines were jumbled as my speed confused them; they stood dumbfounded as their primitively simple brains desperately attempted to comprehend that they had just been put on the ground, joining their monotonous brothers in practical death. "Walk among the dead, Noah! The shadow of death is only as large as the valley in which you walk!" Peter screamed over the *thuds* and *thumps* of the swords and lifeless bodies piling up around us. I weaved in between the maze of thinning soldiers, ducking under blades and shrugging off undead fingers as they tried to take me. None could master my ability; the pinnacle of puzzle was in my favor. Soon, only one soldier remained.

"This is the one, Noah," Peter said calmly, all noise subsiding. "He will mirror your exact movements; you will be fighting against yourself in a sense." I swung my sword as I kept a careful eye on the last walking soldier. Indeed, he swung his blade at the same tempo and path as I had, mirroring me exactly in both speed and agility. I brought my sword quick and fast against his as he blocked it exactly as I had done. The force was identically matching of mine in the tiniest degree of detail. I stepped back as he did the same, following my motions like a child. I planned my next attack in the moment in which I carried it out. I went for the head as I ducked to avoid being decapitated myself. Peter was right when he had said I was my own worst enemy, as anybody is. We simply cannot defeat *ourselves*.

The clash of metal had left scratch upon scratch on both of our weapons and bodies as blood dripped down both of us, no attack successful. I became fatigued and frustrated as Peter gazed at me intently, remaining silent during this stage of the fight. I decided on one final attempt before I would give up and admit defeat. I swung the sword one final time toward his legs, and as his blade matched mine, I leapt into the air with all the strength I could muster. The machine in which I was and had battled lost his head as I sliced its throat before his could touch mine. He clattered to the ground along with his weapon as I landed on my feet, my sword hitting the ground as well, disappearing among the dead. I was covered in blood, both mine and fake of the lifeless bodies I had waged war against. Against all odds except one, I had *one*, and I owed Peter a favor I silently hoped would slip his mind as it had mine.

"Outstanding, my son. Absolutely stellar," Peter said with so much pride I thought his voice would crack. The old man must have really been proud of me. I believed that my parents would have been proud of me as well; I had to hold on to that. I clung to it for dear life, for the memories and dreams of the past were indeed my life. Perhaps my mindless dreams were a prison and I was being held captive for a short while; perhaps I had just made my decision. I did not know which at the time. I felt alive and alert among the buzz of excitement and adrenaline as my body shook with so much emotion, all jumbled together like a cliffside explosion. I was humbled with the feeling of acceptance and accomplishment, and the aura of adorance and reverence was too enticing not to notice. "A true warrior indeed," Peter smiled slyly.

As I soon perfected the art of swordsmanship, Peter hinted at gun training as my next task. "You can slice through nearly anything, but a gun gives you the advantage of distance," he would say to me. Although I had begun with a pistol, I had soon grown *attached* to the sword. It had become my right hand upon every day. My *soulmate*. My *idol*. I decided to name it Julia; perhaps it was simply a way to torture myself. That was all life was - nothing but a simple decision of how much torment you will endure. Whether the decision is *yours* or not is yet another decision - a simple complex paradox. "It is indeed much fun to play Chinese Dojo for days on end, my boy, but gun training is much more effective when it comes to killing non-Dreamers," Peter started on the first morning of firearms lessons. "You already know that people use only ten percent of their brains in reality. The other ninety allows people like us to do what we do. The select few - the *chosen* people - have full access to their complete potential. With non-Dreamers, it is as easy as killing them and then they stay dead. But for people like us - the *Dreamers* - that is, is a lot more *tricky*. Believe it or not, you can commit mass murder with a goddamn *crowbar*. Guns just make it easier."

I contemplated what I had just heard. "One quick bullet is better than a bloody sword," he said to fill my silence. "I signed up to kill *one* person," I interrupted. Peter shifted from one foot to the other. "Just in case push comes to shove," he said, biting his tongue. With that, he whistled, summoning the same original twelve rubber dummies to formation before us. "You must be familiar with our friends here," Peter joked. "Are you kidding me?" I said. "They're my goddamn disciples." I laughed uneasily, still unsure about how I felt about the imminent possibility of taking lives for no apparent cause. That was senseless and unatoned murder. I put it out of my mind like a cigarette as I focused on the lesson. Whereas the row of rubber dummies had usually taken position across the room, they then stood towering in front of the window like innocent bystanders watching the sunset. The sun hid behind the nearest sky-clambering building outside, casting an ominous shadow throughout the training room. "Line up the sight with the forehead and pull the trigger," Peter said, his slightly smaller handgun in his right fist. He lifted the pistol and took out the first three targets on the right side toward the staircase. "You want smooth, quick accuracy," he instructed.

"One shot. You want to be able to shoot from every position and scenario. One shot. Let's see how you do."

I raised my pistol and took a crack shot, missing by several inches and skimming the left cheek before the bullet ricocheted off of the window behind the dummy. It took me a humiliating five more shots to finally put a silver cartridge through the forehead. It goes without saying that I needed a *lot* more practice. I would have been better off throwing the sword across the training room at each rubber target. "Slow at first. Take your time, assume your position, assert your aim, and then pull the trigger. That set of instructions will be slow at first, but it will get faster and faster as you begin to master a firearm." Let the records show that I *eventually* brought down the remaining eight targets, even if it did take me the rest of the day and a whole hell of a lot more ammunition. If the window behind the row of dummies was not bulletproof, the training room would have become quite drafty over the next few days. The brisk breeze brought a burning question from deep within my heart and soul. As Peter turned to clap me on the back, I spoke, "How did you lose your eye?" I asked abruptly. The question had been impaling my senses since the beginning, yet I had kept it contained until the frigid winter wind had ripped it from me like an organ. "Gunshot," he replied solemnly, and I was immediately remorseful at the idea that I had triggered some sort of post-traumatic, stress-filled war story. "I'm sorry, Peter," I apologized, but he raised his hand in acceptance. "I didn't mean to pry," I added. "Jack," he spoke simply. There was my answer.

"You have made magnificent progress these past few weeks, Noah," Peter said as the final cartridge clattered against the tile. It was obvious that he wanted to change the subject as he shifted from foot to foot once more uneasily. "I have to leave for a short while, but you can expect my return by the full moon. I have business to take care of across the city. So, in my absence, I want you to work on perfecting these first skills I have taught you in your *own* way. Upon my return, we will begin to conquer the really *spectacular* stuff," his eyes glowed. I told him that I would do just as he asked before he dismissed me. As of the following morning, I had the whole penthouse to myself until the dawn of the full moon.

The first morning in the mansion alone was quite *quiet*, to be completely straightforward. I halfway expected Peter King to be standing against the window in his dark-lined suit and his silver ponytail, gazing into the city like a prisoner behind bars. The frigid home was eerily silent, and for the first time since I had arrived there, I felt as if I was completely *alone* - free and clear of all supervision and bystanders. The feeling of being watched was vacant and completely absent. I was alone, and I was truly dedicated to my Dreamer training, although I could not quite figure out why in that moment. Was it because I was envious of the Dreamers I had seen? Was it because I wanted to be the man holding the shovel when Jack King was put in the ground? Could I not possibly live without Julia? She had been all that was on my silent mind for an agonizing while in that empty penthouse. The simple, complex thought of her engaged and energized my training, giving me a reason to fight and go on as she encouraged me to push onward. *That* was why I wanted to become a Dreamer, I decided. I *was* a Dreamer. As much as I hated to admit it, the only reason for it was to get back to Julia. My mind was made up and there was no hope of changing it - in that moment, of course. After all, I was always as indecisive as a cat before a car.

As I echoed down the cobble steps that morning, I remembered Peter's instructions on what I was to do. *To combine the first three lessons interchangeably.* My mind whirred away, conjuring up a way to go about that. I had to master all three to make a *fourth*, I decided. Summoning, swordsmanship, and firearms. Pondering each one, the only contestant which needed immediate work was the latter. I had the first two down pat, and there was my plan. I would perfect the art of the gun and then combine the prior. I laid out steps and stones like stairs to achieve this goal, with my watchman waxing in the northwest corner of the city outside the window. I was separated from it, only to witness. I was an *architect*, sketching mental blueprints in the air like a landscaper or a window washer, bringing each and every detail to life in order to free myself from overbearing and agonizing forethought. As the wisps of creativity spun bright blue through the cool air, I could not help but think back to my father's brief service on the construction sites back in the old city. His *injuries*. I could not help but wonder if what I had built would soon come crashing down on me as well, sacrificing me to the opposite choices and indecisions I had made.

I summoned the commonplace array of rubber dummies, plastered in front of the nearly blinding sun-sifting window like mallard ducks. The coffee table held the samurai sword and the handgun, awaiting my disposition and disposal. The feeling of authority and singularity was toe-bitingly exciting - nearly like *positive* anxiety if there ever was such a thing. Each day began as this - bright, early, and exciting as I inched my way closer to absolute perfection. My judge was an impossible-to-please jury and executioner as I used my free time to train harder and harder onward to impassable victory. The days pressed forward like bullets through rubber skulls and the shadow across the silky silver man in the moon up above as I soon surpassed the challenges of the pistol in my left fist. Three individual offenses soon became one as I created a system in which I could outsmart the then-moving targets. They went from still to silent, mirroring to silent, and - eventually in the final stages of firearm training - armed to silent. Each wave of attacks became a single advancement of war as I grew faster and faster in my abilities to change weapons and summon new defenses. I felt like a *warrior*, and from my reflection in the puddle of sweat on the floor at the end of each day told me I sure as hell looked like one too.

The nights in the open and free-flowing mansion-like penthouse were much different from normal in my lonely stay in those days. I slept on the couch in front of the window in the training room, watching the sunrises and sunsets each day and studying the increase in moonlight across the floor. My wandering mind studied the magnificent buildings and architecture of the city only windows away, often drifting abroad to the farms and open pastures lining the outskirts of the metropolis. My eyes fell from the mountain chain as far as they could see to the island shore opposite the hills. No matter where my head and wandering eyes took me, they always closed on the Noy house miles away, drifting me off to a peaceful sleep every night.

My childhood memories took much longer to return to me; the further back time went, the deeper and darker the dreams became. I remembered growing up in the Nebraskan countryside, only fences between the home of my family and my grandparents on the other side. I remembered the arguments between my brother and I and how we had grown closer as we had aged - especially toward the end. I remembered being scolded by my mother and spanked by my father when time and my actions warranted it. I remembered playing catch with my father and cousins for hours on end and watching television with my mother until another day of school came around. I recalled the long country road we traversed each day in our old blue car as my father worked the night shift - I saw him maybe twice a week during his time of service in the Army. Of course, all that awaited a Veteran in those days was a factory job. Before I could change the world, it was ripped from me. My family fell apart as the world did, and movement to the new city and world sparked a change and anger so deep within me that I nearly burst with anger. Then I found change and love and lust, and most importantly, *loss*. Then I lost *myself*. I found love again with a careful but blind eye and was ripped from her as well. There I sat in the training room all alone as I had perhaps been for my entire existence, and that was *my* theme and purpose. I decided and came to grips with that. I was a being of misfortune and poor luck, and most vitally, loss and destruction. My world was one of crushed dreams and shot-down, long-range desires - a world of dreams that ended not and a life of bittersweet love and purpose. I desired to read and write and play music. I knew I could not do this is in the dead and dying world in which I was birthed and bribed from. *Was I to stay or was I to go?* The age old question of self-pity.

The day-to-night cycle in that exotic world gave me hours worth of practice each day. As much as I loved to be training and furthering my journey along the beaten path of doubt and conquer, I soon grew tired of the same routine time and time again. My body bore definite signs of extreme exercise; my small amount of body fat I once wore had given way to a chiseled, muscular frame and focused definition along my chest and back. I had so much more *energy*; I was truly *alive*. I was physically and mentally toned and trained, and I was a completely different person in mind and body. Who knew what more transformation lay ahead? I studied the moon night after night, attempting to mark the exact day on which Peter would return. To be honest, I *missed* the old man. His smell of smoke and his elderly smile. His straight ponytail and pressed suit. His grandfather-like voice and teaching methods. I *loved* the old man, goddamnit; I cared for him as I would my own grandfather. I looked up to him as an example and I enjoyed his company and apprenticeship. I yearned for him to come through the front door of the spectacular home, the smell of a cigar wafting against the glass and into the wood once again. I counted ten days since he had departed, and much to my dismay, another three until he would return. If only the old man had taught me to speed *up* time. The following nights dragged on like a horse and carriage through the undriven snow, the white mist of frigid smoke absent from the house entirely. I could not hope and help but remember and think of Arnold - long, lost, and forgotten.

Although I had awaited the time for a week surpassed, I jolted as I heard the opening of the door. My training, both guided and self-taught, had advanced my senses and reactivity speed to the utmost degree. Upon the second echo of the *click* through the cave-like hallway, I felt the grip of the pistol slide into my grasp on instinct. I was starved for not only new lessons, but more of the stories I so hoped for the old man to tell. I was *devilishly* curious back in those times.

I had awoken that morning from a brief several hours of sleep; I was so anticipatory of my master's return that I could not beg the darkness to take me that entire night. Only when the sun had risen to the slightest did I fade away. I woke up in a daze as I heard the closing of the door, the sword lying on the table and the gun in my hand. I climbed to my feet quickly and hopped over the back of the couch. I knew who it was, and I had faced no adversity, but my training brought the firearm to me *involuntarily*. I wrapped my finger around the trigger as I neared the training room entrance with ease and attention. My nerves buzzed with anxiety, yet I marched onward. I could see the shadow dancing across the dimly-lit floor as the source made its way into the light.

"Easy there, partner," I shook Peter's dry, cracked hand as he clapped me on the back with his other in greeting. "My boy!" he exclaimed. "I missed you, my son," he said. I smiled as I slapped his shoulder; the man and I were nearly *friends*. The bond we had formed was like a father and son; we were *inseparable*. "Did you get your work done?" I asked, wiping what little sleep I had gotten from my eyes. "Indeed," he smiled that same crooked smile I had missed so dearly. "Did *you* get *your* work done?" he emphasized back to me. "Indeed," I mirrored, becoming a rubber dummy myself. "Now for the *real* magic," he smiled. We exchanged punched shoulders like friends, shook hands like father and son, and studied each other's brief pasts like a teacher and student as I recited and performed the exact routine I had followed for days on end. Peter King's eyes glazed over with the return of the smoke as my work bewildered him; the old man could not possibly have been more joyful, intrigued, or impressed.

It had seemed like forever since Peter and I had huddled around the wooden coffee table before a new lesson, and boy, was I glad to be back at it. But, as you have most likely gathered from the first half of my account, my luck would have nothing except yet another interruption. Yet again, I jumped at the knock of the huge set of double doors across the training room. As the gun became one with my hand once more - much to *his* bewilderment - Peter closed his fist as the doors creaked open, both of us scouring the shadowy doorway for the newcomer. I followed the old man across the smooth tile as our boots clapped in unison, each footstep echoing in the silent suspense. As we rounded the row of furniture, I laid eyes on Commander Logan Aaron for the first time in at least a month. He eyed the gun in my left hand moments before it disappeared to my will. "Well there, who is this young - Noah?" he stopped himself. "I didn't hardly recognize you!" he shouted through a painfully-forced smile as I shook his hand, wondering what exactly had brought him there. I oftentimes processed situations much later and only stared through them in the moment, this particular occurrence was no different. He greeted Peter with a slight bow as he closed the doors behind him, both of us awaiting the reason as to why he had come for the first time in what very well could have been *months*.

"What's the matter, Logan?" Peter asked gravelly, only moments before I would choose to break the silence. I eagerly awaited a response; my curiosity had been starved by Peter prior. Commander Aaron was the freshest face - as well as the only face - I had seen since I had arrived there at the King penthouse. The first to witness the outcome of my training who had not contributed to it; at the same time, so many had given offering to this. Everyone and everything had shed blood to bring this transformation about - from my childhood to my forced dichotomy to my silently musical murder. My thoughts flooded through my blank stare as I heard why the Commander had come, and it only brought more silence. "I bring bad news, I'm afraid," he started. "Someone has been murdered," he said stoically. He had most probably grown accustomed to experiencing death - as had I - but nothing could possibly have prepared me for what he would say next. "Who?" I asked, pushing past the barrier of my wonder and cutting Peter off mid-question - whether or not I had been invited to the conversation or not. Another *nasty* habit of mine. Logan was silent - quieter than Peter King - but no match for my urging stillness. "Patricia Noy," the soldier uttered; he had become the messenger - weighed down by the burdensome report of his duty. My stomach dropped as I did to my knees, and I could no longer hear or speak. The only movement allotted to me was the flow of silent tears down my face as I took in what I had just discovered. Mrs. Noy was *dead*. I did not know how or why yet, and perhaps I did not need to. I knew the short plump woman and I knew her children well enough by passing grace - one beautiful and one hideous. I had heard the stories and felt the pain; I *felt* the death as if it was my own. The identical suffering as my parents passing, I *remembered*. The woman had been a *mother* to me; she had taken me in, and then she was gone - crushed like a midnight firefly to burn and cast light no longer.

I immediately thought of how crushed Felicia must be; I had witnessed and been immersed in those emotions dozens of times over. I doubted Lucious even knew - or cared enough to - and I knew that Felicia was *alone*. A lonely loss is a *dangerous* one. Peter pulled me to my feet as I regained strength in my kneecaps. "It's going to be okay, my boy," he said to me, his words echoing through the cascades of my skull. My mind was empty and my eyes were broken. "Someone killed her and burned her house down last night," Logan said as Peter slapped his chest in disgrace. I was upset enough; Peter knew that. And then I wondered if Felicia was even still alive. *So many questions and not enough answers.* I was terrified of what might be - what *could* be. *Imaginable* situations. I assumed the worst as I nearly blacked out once again. Peter hoisted me up the rest of the way as Logan dared to speak again. "Come with me and I'll show you myself." I had already taken off into a full sprint toward the aircraft carrier on the rooftop before Peter could tuck his gun into his suit jacket. I felt mine appear on my hip before I had hit the ground.

Chapter XV
As the Willow Weeps
(Silence, Speech, and the Will to Go On)

I saw the billowing smoke long before we landed as I stared out of the frosty and foggy window of the carrier from inside the open conference room. For the first time since I had arrived, the hovercraft squad was silent. There was no sign of profane commentary or explicit remarks from any one of the hulking men. Perhaps it was the presence of Peter King - the city's leader - on board that kept their ruthless banter at bay. Or maybe it was the dire situation, the absolute need for professionalism, or just by the nick of possibility, they wanted to spare my feelings. Had they spoken a single out-of-line utterance, I would have cut the tongues and hearts from their bodies in a violent and gruesome exorcism. The pilot put the craft down in the open field beside the Noy house - or what was *left* of it. The once two-story farmhouse which cast a shadow across the countryside had now *become* the shadow, nothing but a pile of ashes, burning cinders, and an infinite amount of thick smoke. Logan had been telling the truth after all; no matter what, I could not hope to awaken from that nightmare. Peter had sat with me in the interrogation quarters, his hand on my shoulder and his lips as silent as my eyes were. As we touched down, he pulled my chair out and urged me to stand; my eyes were transfixed on the rubble of what I had called home for what was such a small period of time, but what had felt like much longer - an infinite lifetime. I could hear the cracklings of dying flames as Peter led me out of the room and rejoined the crew walking down the hatch. Guns at the ready and steady hand, they led us into the field and grounds around the foundation - all that was left. Peter had drawn his pistol as well, mine remaining several inches above my tailbone.

I could feel the heat radiating from the heap of ashes and the sound of crackling flames as I finally slipped my gun from my waistband. I rushed out into the front yard along with the battalion as we kept a safe distance from the fire. I scanned the surrounding area with my gun at the ready, hoping that the culprit of the murder and arson would show his cowardly self; I would surely end their sorrowful existence. In the ungodly heavy silence, I emptied my weapon one shot after another as I shouted in violent and volatile anger. I shrugged Peter's hand away as he attempted to console me. There was no movement as I glanced around the smoky air from left to right; I jolted and raised my gun to aim at the body that emerged from the fog. I laid eyes on the young woman as her features came into light, and I knew it was Felicia. She ran to me as I dropped my gun onto the matted and charred grass beneath my feet. She threw her arms around me as I hugged her tight, feeling her boiling tears soak through my jacket, into my shirt, and against my skin. I did my damndest to comfort her and she - we *both* - cried in a depressive harmony. *A melancholy rhythm.* I closed my eyes and felt the heat of the fire through her soft coat. I heard orders being shouted from outside my own self-involved and inflamed bubble; the crew moved out and surrounded the disaster scene, infiltrating the dilapidated wood piles and extracting the body of Patricia Noy. I watched from inside her embrace as Logan Aaron and his men carried the covered corpse out of the ashes and towards the helicarrier. I kept her eyes and ears covered as she sobbed, trying so desperately to find strength that never showed its ghastly, comforting face.

Felicia's tears poured to the beat of a song as mine kept rhythm - an *everlasting* song. The world went from an anarchic chaos to a benevolent silence as I comforted the distraught young woman - the spitting image of her mother. It was a *constant* reminder. As our song came to an end, I walked her over to join the aircraft pilots whose heads hung low as they took more than a moment's silence and more than a day's drink. Peter took back an instance of a heavy breath as Logan spoke up before he had a chance to. "Who would do this, Miss Felicia?" The question brought no suggestions to mind. "Some evil fucker," one of the crew members chimed in. Logan raised his hand in a commanding silence. "What do I do now?" she asked as her tears returned once again. "You're going to come stay with Noah and I," Peter spoke up; he had the *authority* to speak. Felicia nodded in subtle gratitude and acceptance as my stomach rattled in ever-so-slight excitement, although the time and setting may not have warranted it. Perhaps I was just *selfish*. With the silent skeleton crew and the dimly-lit future in front of us, we filed into the plane under Logan's keen eye of guidance. We lifted off as the house crashed and crumbled to the ground, smoldering and cindering into a smoke of memories and nothing.

The funeral for Patricia Noy was one of somber and melancholy stature. We flew out to the field beside the black mass of ash on the following cold and rainy Sunday morning; whether it was a Sunday or not mattered none - it *felt* like a Sunday, and that was enough. Life was never anything but a *feeling*, and death was no exception. The aircraft crew, Peter, Felicia, and I gathered among several other neighbors and farmers in the countryside. Commander Aaron - clad in his dress blues alongside the rest of his squad - had dug a grave for the casket to slide into after the service. I held Felicia tight as she cried; Peter held my shoulder as I shed tear after tear as well. The cold rain soaked us as we gathered around the casket to say our final goodbyes. I had known the sweet and hospitable woman for nearly a week on my time and yet she had felt like a mother to me. Time mattered not with feeling. The smell of soggy wood filled the air as songs were sung and speeches were given. The battalion of mime-like soldiers lowered the black oak box into the hole as I pulled Felicia closer. I knew she would not want to watch, and neither did I as Mrs. Noy was buried beside her flower garden. As I turned my head toward the apple trees in the distance, I could have sworn I caught a glimpse of a young blonde man in a suit leaning against his car, drying his own vengeful tears in a drink as his estranged mother was laid to rest.

It took several days for Felicia to even begin to function properly in Peter King's mansion in the clouds. As expected, she slept a lot and did not say nearly an utterance of a word. Peter and I tried to do all we could, but oftentimes that meant just letting her be. It is crazy how the best thing is doing nothing at all sometimes. She eventually lightened up and became accustomed to the new household, as exotic and different as it was from her small country cabin that she had known all of her life. I had been fired and forced into the same predicament many years prior, and so I empathized once more. Peter had more than enough rooms for her to choose from, and perhaps the elegant royalty vibe in which she deserved made her feel as though she was unworthy after all that had happened. She was wrong; she was a *princess* - a goddamn *queen*. If anyone deserved to waste away in the coattails of that mansion, it was surely Felicia Noy. Not me. Not anywhere close. As she settled in - as did I - the lonely apartment was more *full*, and it soon began to feel like *home*. Adjusting to having Felicia in the house was quite the transition, and not a miserable one by any means - more of getting used to her being there after it had been only Peter and I for so long. After so many nights of staring out windows and counting stars, I did not have to miss her anymore, for she was in the next room. I had to remind myself of that as I longed for her; she was then within reach. However, in so many ways was she present in body and absent in mind and emotion, and she had become a shell. Of course the thought also crossed my mind that her stay might cause distraction to my training; perhaps I did not mind. *Was I selfish for being grateful for her staying despite the circumstances that brought it about?* I most certainly was; I had decided that truth long ago. We can always pick what is truth, and selfishness is nothing but mere *survival*.

Peter and I had an in-depth discussion on the night of the funeral. Soon after we had arrived home, Felicia laid down for a miserable and empty slumber. I *resonated* with that; I remembered how long I had slept after my parents had passed away. I remembered and I certainly felt her pain. By the time she had collapsed on the bed, her pillows were tear-stained and she was fast asleep. I recalled the heat of the tears, the depth of the sleep, and certainly the flow of the anger through my veins. I *remembered*. I could tell by the rather gray and grim look in the old man's eye that he had known loss as well; I knew he would watch over Felicia as he had done for me. He then gave me the option to discontinue my training until Felicia regained a certain emotional strength to clear my worries away from my mind, and I humbly accepted. I knew I could help her along; after all, I had been in her shoes several times before. The soles were dirty and worn; after all, death was nothing but a hand-me-down.

The beginning of her stay was a thousand-piece puzzle, trying so valiantly to decipher the most effective way to mend her broken heart. She often slept the days away as I sat in the rocking chair in the corner of her room, guarding her and keeping watch over her as Lucious would likely never do. Jacob at least guided me in the most desperate times of need. I studied her restless sleep as I recalled the time after I had lost my parents. The cloudy sunset gave wake to her gloomy composure, spreading it throughout the home and dampening the air to a musty standstill. As all tragedies seem to have no end, the sky began to clear within the mansion's morale as Felicia came around. She began getting out of bed - later at first, and then on a routine. Her diminished appetite picked up from nibbles to as much as half a plate. Her frail, anemic aura soon regained its original glow as clouds scattered across the bedroom ceiling, around the chandeliers, and into every room, nook, and cranny of the house.

At first I had no words to say but a simple nod and an attitude of understanding, but sentences formed from sympathy, empathy, then to relatable stories as I worked my way back into Felicia's life. It seemed to soothe her restless soul. Pretty soon - little by little - Felicia Noy finally came back to me.

As the newcoming changes settled subtly and became routine parts of life over the following weeks, Peter slowly inched *his* way back into my life. The old man would drop hints in the things he said and the ways in which he said them; I had a keen eye for mystery. I caught on one night after the first dinner in which Felicia had joined us, and we discussed it as we had the discontinuation. Peter stopped me before bed that night, let Felicia climb the stairs and exit into her room, and we proceeded to meet alone in the empty and silent dining room. "She's faring well, don't you think?" Peter smiled happily. "Yessir," I replied, knowing exactly what he was getting at. "Are you ready to get back to it?" he asked, his smile never wavering. "I've seen fire in your eyes, Noah. I just can't decide whether it's your training or that girl upstairs." The old man nudged my arm. He was right, of course. I was ready to delve back into my journey, and having Felicia there with me made the flames climb even higher. My main focus had been her recovery, and then perhaps it was her turn to help me recover from weeks of relaxation. The desire to train had poked and prodded at my mind, and it was time to finish what we had started. "Yes," I said solemnly. "Excellent. We start tomorrow morning."

As most routines do, my training had become a habit, an addiction, and a pulse throughout my body - stored away and to be retrieved at a moment's yearning notice. Believe it or not, it was surprisingly easy to rise with the morning sun and descend the stairs at the crack of dawn. Once again, no matter how long it had been, Peter was always standing at the window in his smoky stupor - the smoke and fog and mist surrounding him like a mountainside. He would turn and smile at me when he heard me;

he knew I was coming. Putting his cigar out on the thick glass pane, he broke his gaze out into his city and came back down into his own *little* world which only had room for him and I. "Let's have a bit of recap," he said to me that morning. I nodded as I woke up the rest of the way, the remainder of the smoke filing past me and dissipating into the shadows. "I taught you to believe in the art, followed by summoning, then on to combat training. All fine and goddamn dandy. Now it's time for you to dwindle the physical spectrum and transfer it to the mental standpoint. I'll give it to you straight; you're in for a shitload of fucking headaches." He laughed a deep, raspy laugh. "It won't be easy, but I've seen you work, Noah. You're determined, smart, and strong. You are a leader. And a damn good one at that." I felt the heat of the compliment rise from my heart to my cheeks. "Once it's done, we will be on with the remainder of our mission." I accepted that, nearly positive that this would be the end - perhaps only the *start*.

"We will begin with flying," he started. The mention of that brought many comic images to my mind, sparking questions and triggering shivers down my spine. "How in the hell do you do that?" I wondered out loud, not sure if I meant to. Judging by the wicked smile across my master's glossy teeth, I convinced myself that I did. The rush of adrenaline brought back the very memories in which made me fall in love with my training. It was mesmerizing, exciting, and above all - stimulating. It was making me something *more* than what I was - or what I *believed* I was. I then understood that I could very well change it.

"It's actually quite easy," Peter grinned. I could not hear him, or maybe I had, but I was *distracted*. The smell of smoke caught my attention long before the sight of it did. The cloud of thick cigar smoke had made a full circle around the massive training room slowly, and it then floated into my nostrils, through my brain, and continued to my body. I was *consumed* by the icy tendrils, and as I tried to choke a cough, I was then *trapped*. "Look out the window; it helps," I heard the old man say. But he was *gone*. The smoke was gone as well, along with the smell, feel, and intensity of its consummation. I had been enticed, lead hook-line-and-sinker, and executed right there in that training room as my master had disappeared. I glanced around the room in every direction but the one that slipped my mind, and I heard the same frigid, rusty laugh from above. As I snapped my neck to see where he was, I looked upwards towards the chandelier. High above me, gripping the glimmering chains of the light fixture, was Peter King. As I clapped my hands in a false mocking congratulation, the old man weighed down beside me once more. "Teach me," I said, this time intending to mock his arctic tone and solid determination, attempting to hide my fervent excitement.

"First, you must clear your mind of everything -much like summoning - but this time instead of bringing things to life, you will be putting them away. Send all of your thoughts and inspirations into the wisps of nonexistence. You must become as light as a feather in your mind - not your body - for weight is not measured by physical stature, but by mental capability. You must be an endless cloud - a bird. You have to put it all aside and focus on *nothing*. This is the spawn of the headaches. Fair warning." I heard the message and took a shot at it. Indeed, it was difficult. *How could I focus on nothing? After all that had happened, all that I had been through, and all I had to think about?* "If you get dizzy, stop right the fuck then. I'm much too old to pick you up off the floor. If your brain becomes a hive of pissed off honeybees, smoke those motherfuckers. It's all about smoke. It's so goddamn *heavy*, but at the same time, it is nothing at all." I heard Jack King speak through his father; the word patterns and choice of analogies to explain things was so *similar*. It was a constant reminder of all I had to think about and what I simply could not *not* focus on. It was *impossible*. I was certainly quite a *heavy* person.

Over the course of the wild happenings of my life, I had learned to tuck certain instances away like sandbags at the bottom of an anchor. I soon learned to do the same with learning how to fly. I knew what I had to focus on and I knew what I wanted to forget, and all I had to do was get rid of it, if even for a moment. I started at the beginning and worked my way to the present, clearing my mind of all creation. I pounded and punched through city streets and strangers. I flashed and raced through buildings and rooms and houses and floors. I pushed and shoved through crowds at gatherings. I slashed and cut through the death and destruction which occupied the greatest portion of my life, causing a great pain to grow in the center of my head. I winced as I felt the cities collide and the barrier between them shift like sand underfoot. The headache grew as memories flashed through my mind one at a time. I forgot the faces and the smiles and the laughter and the good times and the bad times and the loss and the worries and the inconsistencies and the demands and the leaders and the followers and the Dreamers. It all stopped. There was *peace*. There was *silence*. My mind was as clear as the ocean abroad; my feet were as light as a feather. I was *floating*. I was *flying*.

Within the whirlwind of my thoughts, my feet had left the ground and my body had soared several feet into the air. As memories left and faded like smoke, I rose higher and higher, growing more and more weightless. My eyes closed and my features winced and closed tight, I felt the stress of the focus on nothing, and it threatened to slip with every breath. I heard through the pitch black silence of Peter clapping, this time in a non-mocking manner as I had done - he was *truly* proud. I had risen above, in more ways than just one. With the last echo, my eyes opened and I stared at the window, along with the smoky ghosts of my memories and I truly felt complete. I felt *independent* - free of arrogance, ignorance, and stupidity. I felt truly *powerful*. Perhaps it was the girl watching from the top of the staircase which was my power.

I was raised on childhood heroes. I read comic books and drew my own imaginative renditions. As I got older, I thirsted for that kind of power, and as the lessons progressed to be more like superpowers, it was quenched like a smoking fire. It gave me a feeling of omniscience, as if I were playing *God* - as if I *was* God. In the days prior to the next lesson, Peter had set up an obstacle course for me to practice flying. I had since learned how to balance using my body weight, and my cognitive feet-air coordination skills were put to the test as I flew over and under objects, around poles, and even through a simulated ring of fire. Needless to say, I had several bruises and two spottily-singed eyebrows. Felicia laughed and cheered me on from the balcony above. It was quite a heartwarming scene, even if it ended with cold compresses and looking like a purple Dalmatian.

"Mind control. Telekinesis." He had placed several objects in which I could not see on the table and took several steps back. He twitched his wrist ever so slightly, and a gun flew into his hand. With a flick of the opposing fingers, the clip withdrew from the weapon and upon wiggling his right thumb, it filled itself with bullets, closing again once more. He rotated his ankles, pivoted to face the window, and fired at the thick glass several yards away. But at the last second, the bullet stopped. It curved as Peter stared at it, void of blinking, and it smashed a statue's head feet away from Felicia, who watch the scene from the balcony above. He held his head and laughed. "Ouch." I smiled, eager to learn. "Once again, clear your head. Except this time, focus on the object you wish to control. Every piece of creation has a *soul*. Then bring it to your bidding and take over it. It's all about personal connection." I saw a throwing star on the table ahead and stared at it intently. I saw it flicker, but the thin sheet of metal clattered to the floor at the last second. "You must maintain that focus; don't lose sight of it. Practice makes *headaches*, my boy," Peter laughed. I already felt one coming on.

Before long, I could at last bring objects to me. Throwing stars, brooms, tactical knives, and even the bullets from an opponent's gun. He set up targets in every direction and level of expertise. I began using weapons and techniques I had yet to use, traversing more and more ground in my training. Believe it or not, a headache or two - or perhaps a dozen - were worth the extra mile of the journey.

"There is one more part of mind control," Peter told me days later. "Controlling *other people's* minds." I did not quite understand at first. The old man voided an explanation as he stared deep into my eyes like a scolded child. I had long since collected that he could read me like a novel in his vast library upstairs; I saw his pupils dilate ever-so-slightly. My senses and observations had heightened to almost terrifying lengths. I felt my eyes roll to the back of my head as I lost my balance and fell hard to the floor below, scraping my body on the thick rug under my feet. His hold on me soon released as I rolled back to feet. "That was unnecessary," I said, rubbing my elbows. "I feel you will seek revenge on that later," the old man chuckled.

"You must put yourself deep within your opponent's head. So deep that the only way out is to defeat them. You must *become* them. Become *lost* in them." The one-eyed man had long since lost *me* as his lessons became more and more vague as time went on. I struggled to understand in the end; I could tell this would be difficult as I ventured out on my own to find answers. "Study the person, know them, judge them. Then take control of them." I looked at him curiously, trying to follow his directions. "I'm a tough nut to crack, Noah," he laughed maniacally. And that he was. Peter King was a well-guarded walnut, and as you can most likely collect, no progress had been made by the end of that day. That is, if you discard the *headache*.

The next morning started off differently, however. Felicia watched me struggle from above, as she did every day. She was as silent as a fox, perched on the railing like a bird. She could have been meditating; she was always silent apart from laughing ever-so-often, and she rarely interrupted our lessons. If I am to be completely honest - which I have long since sworn to be - I oftentimes forgot she was there. I had had enough of the quandary; I was getting absolutely nowhere. I was beyond frustrated with so much tension built up inside me. I learned that anger can either be a blessing or a curse - determination or desolation. "GODDAMNIT!" I shouted out of rage. My head pounded to the beat of my heart as I let out my frustrations into the open and nearly empty training room. I was livid and flustered as a fatigued mule, and my face grew fiery with irritation. Felicia cleared her throat promptly, actually *startling* me. I turned around and she was right behind me. I put my head down in shame as I regretted displaying that amount of hostility in front of a lady. She smiled, putting her hand under my chin and lifting it off of my chest. She grabbed my hands in hers and looked across the room at Peter, who pretended to look away as he held back his laughter. "Perhaps I could help him," she half said, half asked. "I'm a little easier of a nut to crack."

"By all means," Peter smiled and looked away once more. He stood back, ready to help if needed, as Felicia took several steps back. She looked right into my eyes, lining up her corneas with mine. "You look so different," she whispered, barely audible, only for me to hear. I nodded silently, thinking only of her mother. From that distance, the two women were identical - one a shell and one a cocoon. Felicia was a kind of beautiful that could not be described - only felt through her kindness and personality once you broke through her shell-like coating and realized her true power. If I needed to focus for that task, she might just have been a far more difficult subject than Peter King.

"You know what to do, Noah," he coached from the sidelines. I stared back into the distant country roads that were her eyes, collecting every grain of dirt and every ripple of water that pulled me in with the tide. My emotions delved deep into her thoughts and memories. I felt her past and present in my body as I physically felt myself etched into her future. I dove into her inner peace as I swam through her desires and searched through her mindset. I slowly felt my mind grasp control of hers. I saw her pupils shrink into tiny beads as I saw her delicate frame twitch. I remembered the feeling of helplessness and loss I had felt when Peter had controlled me and I would not wish that on anyone, much less Felicia. I let go of the reigns immediately. "What are you doing?!" Peter shouted. "You almost had it!" I reared back to face him. "I will never do that again. I can't," I yelled back at him. "Not to her. Not to anybody. I swear it." That feeling - that memory - stuck with me like glue, like tree sap. "There is always a *price*, Noah. No matter what you do. You don't have to like it; you just have to *accept* it. You have to be able to do these things. No matter what. There will come a *time*. There will come a *choice*. You will have to choose between your life and someone else's. Your mind. Yourself. You have to be able to do this," the old man pushed. I stepped back, bewildered at what I had done; I simply could not let go. I could not forgive myself. Not after everything she had lost. Not again. "I'm sorry, Peter." I fell to my knees and resumed my thoughts, trapped inside my own mind once again. That is a prison in which I am more than content to serve my sentence.

I spent the rest of that day with Felicia. Peter presumed and respected that I needed the rest of the day to myself, and he retired to his quarters - wherever the hell they may have been - without a word. I laid on the floor for seemingly hours, tears streaming down my face as I recalled everything that had happened like a sick movie. I had hit rock bottom; I had reached my breaking point, and I did not know if I would ever make it back. Felicia helped me up the stairs and into my room. Behind closed doors, I laid down on the bed, exhausted and sore in every possible way. She plopped down next to me, as she had done times before. In that moment, everything faded away. I was there with Felicia, and I was *happy*. The tears had dried and the pain had lifted. We talked the night away until the sun gave way to the moon once again, hand-in-hand. The fluorescent moonlight cast wicked shadows across the cozy room as our conversations and stories faded to fatigue and sleepy theoretics. Butterflies danced across the walls as we joined them in song and rhythm.

"Everything is changing, Noah Willowby," she said quietly. The moon kept a constant spotlight on us as we faced the window next to the bed. "I think it's designed that way. The evolution of a situation. It all starts in one place and ends in another. And as it changes, it changes us as well," she continued. "What do you think?" she looked over at me curiously in the dark. "I think you've been around Peter too long," I laughed. "Be serious," she laughed as well. "I think," I started, "I couldn't have said it better myself." Her expression lowered to a solemn smile. "You've changed," she whispered, showing no indication if positive or negative. I knew I had changed both physically and mentally, and I like to believe I had accepted it. Still, I decided to give her the benefit of the doubt. "What do you mean?" I asked, blinking back sleep. "All of you," she began. "When I first met you, you were scared. You didn't know the slightest bit of anything. Here or there. You had known loss, but not accepted it. You became a man here. Your voice doesn't shake like it did, and neither does your body. Your face is worn and you're stronger now, in every sense of the word. It is quite beautiful to watch from the outside. Most people I see train usually fail or die trying. Because they simply cannot accept loss. But you, Noah Willowby, you are weak no more. You are not scared of anything. You are the epitome of change. And believe it or not, that is the one thing you cannot escape - even in your dreams. *Change*." Her speech was beautifully captivating down to every last detail, whisper, and word - even to the way she *spoke* each and every word struck a chord within me. I was exhausted, lost, and long surpassed. I was content, I was comfortable, and I was happy for the time being. I always knew - and even more so after I heard what Felicia had to say - that would change, sooner or later. And I would most certainly not be able to escape it. Before I could reply, all of the butterflies were asleep. I followed soon after, the light in which summons all life flickering away into the distance.

I woke up the following morning with my arms around her. It was *nice*. It felt *right* - the first thing that had in quite some time. I felt relaxed, safe, and most of all, rejuvenated. Perhaps I *had* changed after all. Certainly for the better, judging by the way I felt. I would not have dreamed of trading that feeling for anything. "Rise and shine!" I heard Peter shout. I wiped the sleep from my eyes, leapt out of bed, and hurried around the room in a panic, searching for the old irritating bastard as I had done so many times to my mother and father. "I give you a little time off and this is how you repay me?" he questioned through a wide grin as my groggy eyes fixed on him rocking in the chair in the corner by the window. By that time, Felicia had rolled over and brushed her hair back to see what the matter was. Peter looked satisfied - he had filled the role of alarm clock for the day. "Be up soon, my boy. We've got training to get back to!" With the next moment, the chair was rocking empty as it had before the old man had arrived - *snuck* in, that is. *Can you sneak into your own house?* I dared not be ungrateful.

"What was that?" Felicia asked me through a yawn. "Oh, nothing," I stuttered, "Just those damn birds," I came up with. I walked back over to the bed and kissed her forehead. "I have to meet Peter downstairs for training this morning," I said, slightly depressed. "Are you sure you're up to it?" she mumbled, already on her way back to sleep. "I'm sure," I replied through a smile she could not see, but one I was positive she could hear. I pulled my clothes on and closed the door before she started gently snoring once again. "You seem so familiar, as if I've known you damn near my whole life," I said to her one morning. "Makes sense," she mumbled. "I've been around damn near *forever*." I laughed and plopped down beside her on the bed. "How old is Peter?" I asked aloud one morning. She thought to herself. "I would say around a hundred-and-fifty years old, if I had to guess," she baffled me. "*Christ Jesus*," I mumbled. "He's the closest thing to it," she replied. I thought for a moment. "I know you may not want to talk about it," I started, putting my hand on her shoulder. "Don't, Noah," she flinched away. I stood up to leave her be. But I had to speak; I had to ask. I had to voice my curiosity. "Who do you think did it?" I asked blatantly. No answer. I walked away in regret and vengeance.

As close as I got and as much as I tried to get close to Peter, he always kept our conversations on the topic of the training. It drove him forward, and therefore it drove him mad. I was always pursuing deeper bonds and tighter friendships, and I was nearly always denied access to a furthered list of friends and companions. "With all due respect, Peter, the last time I played with fire, I lost half my eyebrows," I said sheepishly following his request for that day. "You're ready for elemental training," he had said to me prior. "I hope to Christ you don't mean chemistry elements - I failed that class back in the old city," I said. Peter smiled. "No, my boy, I mean the natural elements: fire, water, wind, and earth. You'll do exceptional, just as you have before. Eyebrows aren't your best feature anyhow," he finished with a joke. For an old man whose eyebrows had long turned silver, I was sure he was eager to make a sly stab in my direction.

Peter flicked his wrist, and with the smooth movement, a glass of water and a box of matches appeared on the coffee table before us. He willed the box to open and a dozen matches fell out, all lighting simultaneously with a single thought. With another wave of his hand, the flames lifted into the air. He brought the cup over, the water spilling out over the tabletop, but before it could reach the blaze below, he stopped the liquid in midair. With a final breath and a willing of mind, he unified the four elements together, extinguishing the flames and instilling order once again.

"Ta-da," he said, waving mocking jazz hands. "Creation was based off of balance, my boy," he said following his demonstration. Each one evens out another, no matter what the combination. You have to feel the *power* of the elements," he instructed. "Feel them, respect them, and know their destructive potential and harness it to your control. Become the *pain* they can cause and harness their beauty." His words rang through my ears like a constant throbbing as I thought and pondered my first and eager attempt. I focused on the box of matches, bringing the cardboard container open, spilling the contents of a couple dozen matchsticks. I imagined sparks and the first head took light, soon followed by the others. I became distracted as a draft drifted through the hollow room. The pile of lit matches skittered to the floor, engulfing the rug in flames below.

"Easy does it," Peter encouraged. "Remain *focused*," he edged as I began to panic. "Put it out with the water. Find a way," he suggested. I glanced down at the small puddle spread across the table in front of me. "There's not enough!" I shouted over the growing fire. "Make more," he said matter-of-factly, as if it was the simplest task in the world. I shifted frantically around the table as the flames lashed out at me and mocked my footing, singing more and more of the rug. I stared deeply at the glass of water below and watched it slowly fill again with water. I believed it to be my imagination as the cup ran over, spilling onto the table and eventually down like a waterfall over the blaze. Smoke filled the air as my heartbeat regulated once more, Peter clapping in time with Felicia, who had found her way out of bed as if the smell of burnt fabric matched that of bacon in the morning. It did *not*, in my opinion.

"Have you ever witnessed a tornado, my boy?" the old man asked me. "Yes sir, I'm originally from the heart of Tornado Alley. We had a basement more equipped for living than our own house." *The house. The basement. So long ago.* I pushed it away, as hard as it was to do so as Peter nodded. "Beautiful. But pretty goddamn destructive. The deadliest element in my opinion. You would think it would be fire, but you can *stop* fire. You can't stop *wind*. It is truly *free*. And freedom can sometimes destroy entire cities. Wind is the only element you can't see. Unless it is spinning dirt, of course. They all work together. *Creation.*" With that he placed several sheets of paper across the surface of the table, nearly covering it in white. I felt a slight breeze at first as he stood back and waved his hand, which soon evolved into an uncomfortable wind shear, whipping my hair around. The papers shifted slightly, then lifted up and began circling the cyclone. "In this case, it's not size that matters; it's control," he told me as he kept his hand steady. Closing his fist sparked an ear-shattering noise, the small twister he had conjured in place, tearing each sheet of paper into tiny slivers, then to shreds, then to dust as it only grew stronger, the powerful wind nearly knocking me over, my hands over my ears. Then it stopped abruptly, showering the room in the minute powder. Peter brushed off his suit jacket before he spoke. "Destruction. *Beautiful.*"

He reset the paper puzzle and stood back, signifying my turn. "Move your thoughts around in circles," he instructed. "Then make it reality. Put your own *spin* on it, per say," he smirked. I got bearing of my mind, shifting from memory to memory like foot to foot. I felt a breeze sway my shirt as I narrowed my movement, chills running down my spine. I continued quicker and quicker, memories and thoughts chasing each other like children on a playground. The paper lifted and spun around, spiraling around the room. "Bring them around and around again," Peter chimed in, nearly breaking my focus. I steepened my thoughts, stacking the paper. Intensifying my thoughts, I winced as the paper began to tear. The screeching of the wind shook the room as a cyclone of the same magnitude spun up and obliterated nearly every inch of the once fine parchment. It piled like sand and snow as the wind blew away, scattering like a cloudless day. "End of city," Peter muttered in congratulation.

"I've thoroughly enjoyed and been intrigued by my time with you, Noah, my boy," Peter said to me days later. "As much as I hope to drag on and wish to delay this, I'm afraid your training is coming to a close." I looked up at him in humble appreciation and subtle sadness. "I believe you're ready for the last two elements. The final lesson. The most powerful of them all." I thought for a moment. "What is it?" I asked him, anxious for the end, remembrant of the beginning, and mindful of the present. "Electricity," he replied after several moments of pacing, almost as if he struggled to find the words. "Very dangerous, very powerful," he warned. "You must use extreme caution and follow my exact instruction." I looked at him matter-of-factly. "Don't I always?" With that, the old man smiled humbly, as if something was bothering him. As a matter of fact, something very well was bothering *me*. Electricity was not even an element - or at least one that I knew of then. *How could it be more deadly than fire?* As close as Peter and I had become, we knew each other's thought process like our own. And it *was*.

"Imagine something so powerful that it ruled the world even before its discovery. Before its *invention*. Before its *creation*. Electricity isn't lights or power or charges - it is simply a spark. You ask yourself how it can be more lethal than that of fire, well let me tell you. You can be electrocuted in an instant while it takes minutes to burn at the stake. It's all about *suffering*, which may very well also be an element. I don't train you to torment, I train you on speed, on reaction. So trust me, my boy, this is a weapon you most certainly want to know how to turn the safety off of." The old man's voice had gone raspy and serious, all emotion blown away, smoked out, and shot into a million pieces. Peter paced the room, pondering an unknown situation subject in the vast expanse of his brilliant mind. He eventually reached a mysterious conclusion as he stopped dead in his tracks; I watched him work with the utmost reverence. He moved the furniture with his mind, out of sight. The training room was then as actually empty as it had felt on those cold, lonely nights. Perhaps I preferred it that way.

"Look at all of the electrical outlets in the room," he instructed finally. I found several on each wall, a dozen in total. "Electricity is a strange element," he said. "Much like water, it is always with you. But sometimes, it is simply *on tap.*" With the last word he outstretched his hand to the outlet across the room as sparks echoed off of his wrist, licking the air in the direction of the adjacent wall. He reached for the opposite outlet as the same reaction occurred. He brought the two charges together into a single rod of growing light, sparks flying in every direction. "Watch me very closely," he nearly shouted over the loud popping sensation. He seemed to stare at all of the sockets at once, all feeding power into the tightly-packed center of electricity in the middle of the room. It had gone from a rod to a ball to a globe-like sphere, growing ever-so-rapidly, taking on wattage and power like a wild monster. The popping turned to cracks and whips as it shot streams of bright white light in all directions. The licking electrical flames snaked up and down his appendages, wrapping around his torso like a suit of armor. His coattail blew back, as well as his silver ponytail. *All* of him was silver - his shoes, his clothes, his pupils. He was pure *electricity.* I heard the sound grow louder and louder as the lights grew to blinding heights. I could *feel* the raw power of the spectacular phenomenon.

As the evolution continued, he no longer needed his hands to maintain and control the electrical field. In fact, it was long *past* control. Peter shifted one hand to summon back the table, which held a large metal rod standing upright in the center. He released the power onto the metal surface with a shriek of agony. Perhaps it had gone *too* far. I was flabbergasted, backed up against the wall, diminished to a fascinated child - scared to death, but mesmerized nonetheless. There was an explosion of blinding blue and white light as the air simmered and popped like hot grease. The shockwave knocked me to the ground and the noise clapped my hands to my ears. My skin burned as I felt the power of the release. The walls shook and buzzed with energy as it searched for an escape, climbing higher and higher and around and around. There was *no* escape. It was as pent up in the training room as it was inside Peter.

I felt the low hull of the buzzing as the blue lightning emerged toward me. I could not see nor hear anything; I was utterly hypnotized by the light and sound of the electricity. It snaked up my arms and legs and around my head as I scooted back against the wall, unable to outrun the creature before me. It relentlessly continued coming, taking epicenter in my wrists. I started to shake with the sheer force of the power within me, rocking back and forth. I attempted to halt it, to no avail. It flowed all over my body, searing my clothes and tearing them in several places. The overhead lights flickered and imploded, washing darkness and glass to rain all over the room. The remaining voltage lifted me into the air, face-to-face with the metal rod only a dozen feet away. As my body could take no more, the final reaction sent me flying back hard against the wall, and the metal rod straight through the window opposite me, shattering it to nothing. For the first time since the lights had gone out, everything went black.

I awoke in my bed upstairs. How I got there, I did not discover until later. According to what I was told, the power surge had knocked Peter and I far past consciousness, leaving Felicia the only one sane in the house. The train-wreck scale of noise must have awoken her. I could not imagine what she found when she came downstairs - two barely-breathing bodies covered in cuts, bruises, and broken glass, a heavy breeze from the missing window whipping the blood-matted hair off of our brows. Peter was unconscious before I was - his fading out of the cycle transferred the power to me and that was what sparked the rest of the accident. The old man carried me upstairs to my room as Felicia cleaned blood from my face and pulled glass shards out of my skin. "Holy shit," I groaned as I rolled over in bed, still shaking from the surge of electricity. "I'm so sorry, Noah," Peter said to me as I came to fully. "I told you it was dangerous - I just didn't plan on making a mistake. And for that I am sorry. Take the rest of the day off. You deserve it, my boy. And tomorrow morning, we finish this. Your training. One more lesson. That is, if you're feeling up to it," he said. I opened my eyes the rest of the way. "Bright and early," I said. "One last time." And with that, the old man left the room with his sly smirk, leaving Felicia and I alone once again. I did not know if it was the remainder of the power exiting my body or sheer excitement - what always took over me in her presence.

She stared at me for what seemed like forever. "What?" I said after a while. "What happened to the old Noah Willowby?" she said, breaking into a laugh. "The kid that absolutely could *not* be a Dreamer because he was too *weak*." The last word hit me deep. "I'm right here," I replied, still stuck on it. "At least a part of me. When we change or learn things, we don't forget the time when we didn't, we simply build off of that and unify it. It is one." I heard my words and placed them on someone else. "You've been around Peter too long," she laughed again. "You get some rest, sweetheart. I have to go help Peter replace light bulbs. And judging by the size of that training room, there will be a whole damn lot of them." She half smiled and half winced as she left to follow her master as well as mine. Perhaps the old man had a hold on all of us in some way. Her kiss lingered on my forehead as she turned to walk out; I shortly drifted back to sleep as the rest of the power turned to full excitement and anxiety for the end - whether it be the end of the training, the end of all that I loved, or the end of me. What was to happen next frightened me because I was *unsure*. The thought of making a decision terrified me and made me sick. Like my master, I chose to run from it, delay it, and put it off for as long as I could possibly do so.

Out of all the time I had spent - or *would* spend - in that fantastical dream world, I only dreamt on one particular night. It was the night after the accident - or more like the *miscalculation*, as Peter put it. My body was thoroughly exhausted from being electrocuted a thousand-fold, and I still trembled like an old man with Parkinson's disease. It was a mighty restless sleep; I tossed, turned, and quivered all night long. It had been so long since I had last dreamed; I honestly believed I had forgotten *how*. They took me by surprise - by *ambush* - preventing me from even the hope of rest. I saw everyone I had been influenced by since the beginning of this long journey, whether it be a wild goose chase or a set-up - a trap that would lead to my assassination. I saw my parents, Jacob, Julia, Jack King, Sebastian, Felicia, Lucious, Commander Aaron, Mrs. Noy, and last but not least, the wrinkled silver face and ponytail of Peter King. The distant but familiar faces passed me by like speeding cars at midnight through an empty city. I saw mountains and forests and beaches and cities - everywhere I had been and traveled. I saw explosions and crying and shouting and war - everything I had seen and served witness to. I felt throbbing and pain and anguish. Sweat, blood, and tears ran all over me, covering me in slime and torment. My past *tortured* me. There it was - like a movie right in front of me. The memories had stripped me, chained me down, whipped me, beat me, and cast me down into the empty chasm of nothingness. The reigns were so tight - a life sentence, a death sentence, and no hope for release or mercy. Then I heard it - the same monotonous, repetitive, chilling voice I had heard so many times before and never forgotten. *His* voice. "Are you a Dreamer, Noah Willowby?" it asked me so lifelike I could have sworn he was in the bed beside me, whispering in my ear. It echoed throughout every tube and tunnel of my ear canals and through my brain over and over like a drug addiction - through every voice I had heard.

Everyone asked it time and time again, surrounding me like wild animals in a cage. All of my training rushed through my veins like electricity and raw power as I remembered who I was and who I had become. I was flooded with truth and acceptance of who I was and more importantly, *what* I was. And so I made my decision right then and there. "YES, GODDAMNIT!!! HERE I AM!!! KILL ME!!!" I shouted it at the top of my lungs for them all to hear. *Laughter*. And then my time came. I was *finished*.

I had not dreamt in eons, it seemed. I had long since forgotten the reality of the dreams - how *real* they felt. And they *were*. As I shouted deep within the recesses of my unconsciousness, I apparently had also bellowed out loud into the midnight silence, shattering it like the massive glass window down the cold cobble stairs. I woke up in a freezing sweat, shaking far more than ever before. My torn clothes were soaked and sticky as I leapt out from under the covers, pulling my shirt over my head and my pants down, standing in my boxers as I escaped the trap I had become ensnared in. Felicia barged through the door in dark gray pajamas, followed seconds later by Peter, dressed in a robe and slippers, his eyepatch and ponytail the only remnants of his superior masculinity in which he possessed in his regular attire. "What the hell is going on?" he shouted. "What's the matter, my boy?" he inquired, both of them wiping sleep from their eyes. I was immediately embarrassed and humiliated, feeling awful that I had woken them up - just as I had done to my family so long ago. They deserved to rest where I did not. Perhaps they could find peace in their sleep when I could not; I had long since become convinced of that truth. "The dreams," I muttered. "The goddamn dreams. They're back. It was fucking awful." I stared into space as the trauma remained. Peter shifted from one foot to the other as he dismissed Felicia. She argued and put up quite a fuss, making sure I was alright to the one-hundredth-percentile before she staggered back to her room.

"Sit down, my boy," he urged as soon as we were alone. I joined the old man at the edge of my bed. "Tell me what happened. What you saw," he said, his bewilderment turning to persistence. I did not want to relive it. "I saw everyone I've known and everywhere I've been all in one place. It was chaos. It was a goddamn zoo," I said simply. "It was a *city*." The wild look in Peter's eye released and relaxed as a smile spread across his shadowed lips, although I knew not what for as I waited for him to speak his mind - to give some form of guidance as to what had plagued my only hope for rest. "Good," he replied after a great deal of forethought. I reacted almost immediately. "Good?! This is the complete opposite of good. This is bad. This is fucking miserable," I nearly shouted, but stopped myself in fear of waking Felicia. "You don't understand, my boy," he said calmly. "The dreams return toward the end of your training, and slowly but surely, your twin will appear to you in your dreams. When you find them, when you pick them out of the crowd, you find them and take them out. That's the key. It's all a process. One big puzzle. And you, my good friend, have just found a corner piece," he joked. "Hold on a second," I interrupted. "This isn't going on any further. I won't sleep. I will not go back into those dreams. I can't take it." Peter laughed coldly. "Sooner or later, you must close your eyes. And that's when they will appear to you. Come out of the mix and grab you." With that, along with one more laugh or two, he left me alone in the night once again. I would *not* sleep. I refused - for as long as I could help it. And I helped it for about an hour; I was knocked out once more - against my will, mind you - as soon as I fought it off for the third time. My heavy eyes did not like that answer and took their own course of action. And action they did take; I fell into the dreams once again.

It was the same - the identical train of faces and places. Except this time, the ones who had died faded away into dust as I examined them, bound once again by the chains of unconsciousness. I watched my parents and Mrs. Noy disappear from my view as I screamed inside. I watched Sawyer and Topher and Klaus disintegrate into shadowy remains. I reached out as Joshua and Strauss were slaughtered in a gory and machismal manner. Those who deserved not were ripped from my mind and life as I watched helplessly as bullets pierced the skulls of the innocent and all-powerful Dreamers. The dreams were as real as reality ever was, and my heart shook when I saw these people again, for I hoped reality had become the dream and I would wake up into their presence once again. But I knew that simply could not be. I found myself awakening into silence and shock at the fact that my family was indeed deceased and I never would see them again but within the confines of the murderous dreams, staring at the ceiling in the silence. I was ready for the morning to come, bringing with it the end of my training, and I welcomed it without fear or anxiety. The dreams had returned with a vengeance, and revenge they would *surely* receive. Sooner or later. I was *terrified* to return to my unconscious.

"So tell me, Peter, what is this spectacular final lesson," I asked, full of various emotions and jaded sarcasm the next morning. I had changed into fresh clothes and taken a long, hot shower, cleansing my body of the sweat from the anguish of the dreams I had suffered and sacrificed the night before. I felt refreshed and confident to finish my training - something I had pursued for months over my stay with Peter King. As I blanked out and stared into space through the window across the room, I recalled the memories in which I had gained from my living in the mansion in the sky. And for the first time since the spark of excitement deep within my stomach, I finally felt despair at the thought of leaving. Peter strolled down the stairwell and marched in front of the window, breaking my constant and unbreaking stare through the glass. I could sense his approach long before I heard the clapping of his boots on the cobblestone steps. It took him a moment to respond, almost to the point of belief that he had not heard me. "Time," he spoke clearly. "What about it?" I asked, rather disappointed at his answer. Had some part of me hoped that we would be disarming explosives or perhaps setting some off? Absolutely. Did I hold on to that? Of course not. I accepted his response and tried my damndest to understand it.

"How to *control* it, of course," he said, perking my ears up in the slightest bit. "Now you're talking," I said. "Controlling things is our specialty," I followed. He smiled that strange smile of his once more. "Time is the most difficult thing you will learn to harness, Noah," he said emptily, as if a memory had led him down a road he did not want to return to. "More than electricity?" I stabbed, empty of emotion. I directed the insult at him as my muscles throbbed at the mention of the word. I did not hold it against him; it was a mere *mistake* - an *accident*. "Somewhat. Time is an entirely different breed of danger. It comes with a whole new set of rules." I saw in his eyes that he knew what he was doing, although I had a minor amount of difficulty trusting him. *Naturally*.

"Time is something you don't ever want to fuck with," he continued. "That is, unless she comes knocking on *your* door," he followed, always bringing in a considerable amount of sexual humor into our lessons to cloud the seriousness and severity of the content - much like his son was furiously known to do. It took our minds off of what the real cause was; it made it *childsplay*. "It is never a first thought, only a last resort. Only for life and death situations." I pondered those words. If time could *really* be controlled, maybe, just *maybe*, goddamnit, I could change what had happened to my family. What had happened to Mrs. Noy and Joshua and Strauss. That was most certainly *life or death*. Perhaps they would still be here; maybe the whole world would be. I dismissed it as a mere *hope*, but one that I did hold on to.

Peter handed me his gun. I had no idea how long he had had it outstretched to me as I swam through thoughts and emotions alike. He had cleared his throat, and before I could apologize, I was holding his pistol. "Shoot me in the head," he said as simply as saying hello. "Woah, are you sure about this?" I asked, going shaky and nervous. That was something you could not really come back from - *easily*, that is. "That could have... *shocking* repercussions," I said, stabbing even harder. *Was I angry?* No. I pushed it aside and focused on the weapon at hand - *in hand*. "Yes, damn it!" he exploded. His angry outbursts had become far more frequent. "Come on, it'll be fu -," he said, returning to his cheerful composure. As he shouted, I aimed the gun at his temple from several feet away. There was distance between the old man and I. Had he backed up? Had I fallen back? Before he could speak the last word, I pulled the trigger. I did not *like* being yelled at - not in the slightest. The bullet sped right at him, but at the last second, it stopped, resting on the one-inch gap between his rather bushy, gray eyebrows. Everything moved in slow motion. He reached up onto his face and snatched the bullet, rolling it in between his fingers. He aligned the path with the window across the room, which had recently been repaired, mind you. With the new course set, he released the time lapse. The silver bullet resumed its speed and collided with the window, sending a thin crack curving up the glass pane, lodged in the center. That was no ordinary gunshot; it was much faster and more powerful.

"How was it that strong?" I asked in utter bewilderment. "Time is strength, my boy," he replied, swallowing hard. "My turn?" I asked, almost *excitedly*. "No, no, no," he brushed off. "Your time will come, my son. Let the moment in which you need it be your example." I thought about that, rather disappointed. I concluded that after the accident, he did not want any more mistakes taking place - whether they be his or mine. Perhaps that was what had been on his mind for the longest time. It all made sense in that moment.

"FELICIA!" Peter shouted festively, his voice changing tones like a circus clown. In that moment and in that circumstance, Peter became Jack in both body and voice. Memories shuddered through mine as I flinched in realization. Felicia marched down the stairs quickly, most probably believing and fearing that something was the matter. "What is it, Peter? What happened? What's going on?" She was comically frantic. Peter clapped me on the back, congratulating me. "This young man has finished his training," he said proudly. It hit me right then; a warm feeling spread throughout my body. The sensation was not that of celebrations; I should have been *galant*, but I felt empty inside - *alone*. I stared into space once again as I was drowned in thought and overcome by mental anguish and anxiety. Something was not right. I knew what I had learned, but nothing of what was to come. There was a *chance* of returning home, but then again, where was *home*? I did not know where my home was any more than I knew who I was in both body and voice. I was torn between two cities and so many different people. I had evolved from a frightened child to a heavy-laden warrior - an uncanny transformation which demanded decision-making skills in which I had not learned. Ones in which only came with experience, and I had none. It would come; I was *promised*. But *when*? After I was long dead and impertinent to choose? I dismissed these thoughts, focusing on the work - the *job* - that needed to be done, though I knew nothing of it. *Yet.*

"Smile, my boy!" Peter demanded as I snapped back out of it, coming back to reality as if from a deep sleep. "What now?" I asked as if the answer would be immediate. "We drink!" he shouted, reminding me so much of his son. He circled the bar counter across the room and lifted a bottle of crimson red wine and a trio of wine glasses onto the table from below. He poured each one half full - a dainty amount of a short, celebratory buzz. He sipped his as Felicia followed. I stared at mine for a moment, getting lost once again in the thin blood in the glass inches below my chin. I caught sight of my reflection, then the apparitions of all those I had dreamed of passing through the coagulation of wine, spinning and circling around throughout the cocktail. With the ringing in my ears from the whispers of the ghosts around me, I lifted the glass to my mouth and downed every last drop. I slammed the glass down on the floor below hard, shattering it into a thousand pieces, along with the phantoms of my past, present, and future before me. The ringing subsided as I heard the smashing of glass crunching beneath my feet. I was alone in the training room once more.

Chapter XVI
The End of the Beginning
(Searching for Revenge, Acting on Anger, and the Bastard Betrayal)

It was in the days that followed that things began to change. Peter restored the training room to its former glory, complete with pristine furniture, royal sculptures, and even a fully reestablished window. I had become so accustomed to the bare walls and simple floors that it nearly appeared as a different world entirely. As matters also began to settle down after the completion of my training - the facade in which we had all shaped our lives around - Peter announced a meeting to form and gather a plan. Circling around the wooden coffee table - the epicenter of my training, the very place where I had learned all of the magical practices and lessons of becoming a Dreamer - I took an inscriptive look at what lay below. He had set aside pencils and pads of paper, along with city maps and blueprints across the table. Felicia and I sat on the couch beside the glassware opposite Peter in his infamous leather chair as he held his head in his hands. Rolling his fingers together strategically and clearing his throat before he spoke, the old man almost seemed anxious. He was far too mature for excitement; what he possessed was much *deeper*. His dream - his only hope - was about to come to fruition at *my* expense.

"Let's begin," he declared. "Where do we start?" I said, leaning back with my hands behind my head and around Felicia smoothly. I was anxious to continue this far-fetched mission, whatever it consisted of and wherever it would take us. "You have to first find your twin," he started. "They will show themselves to you in the dreams during this time." I nodded, remembering the mournful dreams, their sorrowful voices turning them to nightmares. "I'll help him," Felicia volunteered, clearly pleasing

Peter by his shiny yellow smile. "Swell," he grinned like a child. He was lost in his own thought; I could not read him as easily as he could read me. "What next?" I pushed. He sat back as well. "Once captured, you must take them through your past dreams to return to the real world. Felicia and I will follow. It's all about you, Noah. *You* are the key to all of this." I felt rather warm under all of the praise, as anybody would. I had no time for glory. That was *not* me. Warmth brings sweat, and sweat brings uncomfortability. *An unsettled desire and an unanswered question.*

"How do I do that, exactly?" I wondered out loud, not sure if I quite meant to or not. "There are two entrances and exits to this world," he resumed, rocking forward this time. "Either by ocean or by way of the mountains." The last word sent chills up my skin from nowhere as I recalled the ocean as well. *The island.* It all came back to me silently - the mountains, the wind, the burning city, the father and son I had witnessed. I replayed and relived it in the back of my mind as if years had been diminished to mere days, clear as a whistle and sound as a bell. By rights the memories should have been long forgotten, but that was not me by any means. No, forgetting was *far* from my strong suit - I remembered *everything*. It was both a blessing as well as a curse. "Mountains," I mumbled out of earshot, deep in memory.

"The other city lies just on the other side of the mountains," Peter continued. "From there, Felicia and I will leave you to find Jack. We will meet up where I can capture him, and then we get the hell out of there before the place crashes down on us. With Jack dead, his city will fall. We cannot survive there for long. Urgency is key." The serious sound of the setting was interrupted abruptly and all of a sudden. "Sounds exciting!" Felicia exclaimed in her usual sarcastic tone. Peter uncapped a marker and highlighted a route up to the mountain chain on the maps below. "We will go to the highest point of the hills," he said. "We will have to jump off." I was shocked. "What?" I asked, taken aback. "It's a time zone between reality and the dream world. Like a forcefield, just like what separates the island from this city," Felicia reassured me. I took a breath of relief; heights were the bane of my existence and the core of my nightmarish dreams. "Felicia and I will provide your protection over there," he said. "A quick operation. In and out," he promised. The adrenaline rush was unbelievable, although I was willing to wager a suicide for my own personal gain of peace.

"Before we leave, you must find your twin and take its ability to dream," Peter said. "They will show themselves to you in the dreams. Find them and bring them here. We leave that minute. Take the twin back to the real world and kill it. That's our free ride over there. Make quick work of it. No mess. A clean bullet," he dictated at both Felicia and I. He straightened the maps and dismissed us both, buttoning his coat as if as anxious as I was. "He's awfully worked up about this mission," Felicia said as we walked down the wide and empty hallway, staring out the windows through our peripheral vision. "I've never seen someone so eager to kill their own *son*, for Christ's sake," I followed. "As morbid as it may sound, it's a must for this place," she echoed. "We don't have to like it." I paused a moment. "He does," I murmured, barely audible. "It's for the good of this place, Noah. Dreamers are the superior race. The freedom of creativity is the most vital part of life. Taking that away is the ultimate sin." I nodded, my mouth empty of any structure or word.

It only occurred to me as we clattered down the front steps of the huge building that I had not been out of the mansion suite since my arrival following the funeral. The only contact with the outside world had been through the giant glass windows which allowed only mere, insignificant glimpses of the magnificent metropolis outside. With Felicia in the same living quarters, I could have died in there and known no desire to leave. However, the fresh air did feel marvelous on my paling skin as we stepped out onto the sidewalk and into the bustling and blissful chaos that was the diamond city. "How are we supposed to do this?" I asked nervously. I had wondered it since the idea had been instilled in me, but it had never made its way out into the open air until that moment. No reply; perhaps she had no answer as did I. I followed her to the bench against the building, a simple dark metal, along with the luminous shine seemingly *everything* in that city possessed. I sat down beside her, trying to grasp an answer as to what she was doing or the meaning of all of this. I could not help but feel exposed being out of the suite overhead. It was all I had known for however long I had been training there. I had grown *accustomed* to it. *Attached* to it.

"We sit and we watch," she finally replied. "We study each and every person, just as all of these people are doing. They are all searching for their twin, getting into people's heads, some losing themselves along the way." I had wondered why even in the dead of night, there were still hundreds of people crowding the streets, some with blank expressions, and others carrying on light and airy conversations. "How long have these people been here looking?" I could not help but wonder aloud. She pondered it as if she was uneasy to tell me. "Some weeks, some months. Some *years*." I did not have that kind of time. "Will you stay with me?" I asked her, knowing this could take some time. "Of course," she replied, slipping her hand in mine. Time was the one thing I did not have. It felt so strange sitting there, seemingly outside of my own body. Perhaps it was just the broken routine of being locked away in the mansion twelve stories above me.

There was an average of a dozen people crossing the street in front of us every five minutes. I stared at them like a watchful crane, analyzing their physique, searching for an angle to get inside. I collected their thoughts and dreams, just as I was taught to do. The headaches had long subsided; I had gotten so adapted to the routine of it by the end of that day that they no longer burdened me. Out of all of the people over the hours we sat in silence, no matter how short the time span may have seemed, not one stood out to me. I recognized not a single one from the newfound dreams. They were all the same in their misplaced irrelevancy. As the sun sank low over the cityscape and I could no longer make out the faces and memories of the ghosts before me, Felicia and I made the long and windy trek back into the castle of the golden city above.

As we approached the massive metal doors through the breeze of a hallway outside, we heard shouting and cursing from inside the penthouse suite. Felicia knocked loudly, curious as to what was the matter. The doors cascaded inward as we rushed inside to see only a gloomy glow in the training room; only the milky half-moon illuminated the old man. We found Peter on his knees tearing page after page out of a large leather-bound book before him in front of the window and shouting a thousand curses as he tore them to fiery shreds. His raspy, deep tone faded out as he reared back in anger as he realized our return. With his face still turned away from us, he spoke to us eerily from behind. "Any luck?" he asked, somewhat calmer. "No," Felicia whispered, almost *frightened* of his reaction. I heard the old man sigh in disappointment - *angry* disappointment - as he snarled and resumed his destroying of the text before him. "We try again in the morning," he shouted over the sound of the tearing and ripping of a thousand words, shouting a thousand curses throughout the night. I followed Felicia up the stairs rather hurriedly as Peter threw the leather binding against the window, a shell in the empty casket of a home - *his world* - that had *consumed* him. He shouted and cursed once more as he collapsed to the floor among the sea of ruined pages, words lost forever in the shredded sea of names.

The day after was somewhat different. There was no sign of Peter the next morning as we came downstairs, only scattered shards of broken leather and parchment. I did not aim to look for him, and as Felicia crept out the door before me, I knew she felt the same. We exited back into the noisy city through the hall and the flights of marble stairs. As I looked ahead on the sidewalk, the bench we had perched on the previous day was gone; I kept my questions at bay for once, attempting to gather answers for myself. "We need to find another place. They are not here," Felicia said, almost mystically. I followed her soft lead as we continued down the crackless emerald-hued concrete pavement. We paced streets and city blocks until we came to yet another silver bench. An entirely different group of people crossed the white and yellow lines before us - all of them the *same*, all of them *different*. I was not familiar with this environment even in the slightest. The numbers had grown to at least twenty-five people, bumping shoulders like mindless beings, all of them *searching*. I began my ritual of breaking into their minds, but I lost my touch as they walked ahead, faster and faster. Besides the feeling of being offset and unfamiliar, I felt nothing as I *too* became lost. Perhaps if not for Felicia, I would have been lost forever as well.

One of the first people I saw come across my view that struck a chord was a tiny rail of a man that reminded me of several people I vaguely reminisced on. I sorted the memoirs and memories into ages and faces as the figure had no exact identity in my mind. *Where had I seen the hobbling being before? Had it been in the mansion?* No. *Had it been in the forest?* No. It had been in the city. In the marketplace. Upon every work day for two years I had known that soul I saw before me then. A man of silence and cripple. I was gazing at the lost soul of Alabaster Kingsley. *Alabaster was a Dreamer.* Memories of his disappearance came flooding back like wisps of smoke through my mind. I imagined his silent and unspoken mystery of a death. His inability to fight back and speak up against the evils of the world. Perhaps he was where he *belonged*. A place that needed no words to express true self.

Then I laid eyes on someone else coming across the sidewalk that caught my rather *particular* eye. He wore a red and black checkered flannel over a printed t-shirt with jeans, towering nearly six-and-a-half feet tall. Smoke floated from his lips in colorful wisps along his salt and pepper hair. For only a moment, I thought I heard the piano keys he had died for. *Gregor.* I always knew *he* was a Dreamer, in a certain sense. This was where he belonged. *He* knew it, *I* knew it, and the *entire* city knew it under their shrouded veil of a mindset. In their eyes, he was better a murdered seed, but once planted in death, he was *truly* born and set free.

Then I saw the man. The one man I had never seen in my life, yet I knew from Adam in *all* entirety. I caught but *one* glimpse of him, and then he was gone. I saw *myself* in him, and so I lost myself in turn.

In those searching times I came across countless others such as Britton Chester, the man who had befriended and breathed a certain new life into my mother. Perhaps that was her last hope. I remember vividly the violent and discriminatory fashion in which he was murdered as well as those of the others I searched for with no source of satisfaction. I searched thoroughly and frantically through the countless crowd for the ghosts and souls of my parents. I saw them not in the crowd, no matter how hard I imagined them and called out to them within my heart and my own soul. I searched for Valerie Crowley, and I found nothing but an empty cask of a memory. I lost touch with the reality of the dreams and left the bench as I traversed into the crowd - I *became* the crowd. The noise, hustle, and bustle died down as I focused on each entity one at a time, searching their mind for any memory and link to what I knew and held true - what was now gone and lost forever. I found my way back and collapsed into a pile of hopeless and sleepless embers, only to return the next day for a deeper and more vital search. Only to return to the same depressive disappointment and denial.

The second day came to a slow and uneventful close as we made our way back to the suite. I could never again hope to shake the violent and free-flowing memories of those I had lost and some I had found once again. Up the stairs, through the hallway, and to the set of doors was an echoey venture as we neared the source of the wild chaotic sounds we caught wind of as we entered the building once more. Instead of her usual polite knock, Felicia pushed open the doors and hurried inside with me fervent on her heels. The shouting was louder this time and accompanied by thunderous thumps and whacks of wood splitting. The room lit only by the waxing moon, Peter flipped the furniture over piece by piece. The table was overturned and the couch whispered through the air like a feather. The chair smashed into pieces against the thick window overhead. Still no light, still back to us. "What about today?" he inquired through gritted teeth. "Nothing," Felicia muttered in another tone of fear. Peter brought his fist down against the marble pillar beside the stairwell; we jumped in startle as the marble cracked. We hurried up the stairs as he walked away from the chipped architecture. Peter just stared out the window, never to look back.

He was there the next morning. The furniture had been repaired and put back in its place as if his second outburst had never even been heard of or witnessed, but I remembered the horrible shouting and cursing. The ripping and tearing and flipping. I could not forget the old man and all of his anger, for reasons I not yet knew. He had always been patient and caring, for Christ's sake; he had to have been truly *desperate*. Peter stood with his hands behind his back as he gazed out the window calmly. Perhaps he had been there the entirety of the night, for it appeared as though he had not moved a single muscle. He was so deep in thought - so mesmerized, so *entranced* - that all he could do was stare out the window and simply ponder and search for what he could not find. He made no sound nor movement as we crept around him and out the door as silently as we could manage, fearful of our discovery.

"Where shall we waste our time today?" I joked rather impatiently as we closed the heavy iron doors behind us. "Patience, Noah," she urged. I was trying my best and I think she knew that. "I have an idea," she added. "I'm listening." She rolled her eyes as she had done a near million times before; that was her greatest trait, I suppose. The sarcasm, her attitude, and her quiet determination was her ultimate persona, and it was a magnificent one at that. "We need to get to the highest point in the city," she said, her eyes raising this time to the top of the skyscraper we had just stepped out of. "Right," I said. "But tell me we're not taking the stairs," I frowned. She shook her head and ran around the corner, leaving me in the drizzling rain and the smell of wet jewels and soaked sapphire. I followed on her heels around the side of the brick building into the alleyway behind in wonder and curiosity.

She stopped at a closed-in ladder, standing back to let me go first. I suppose she did not have time to be admired that day. I meant nothing by it. I scaled the rungs as quickly as I could, giving my fear of heights a swift arousal. I pulled myself up time and time again, not knowing where the top was in fear of looking down. If I was to fall, I would surely bring Felicia with me and tumble to my - *our* - death. Once atop the roof, I waited for Felicia to make her way up as she swept my hand out of the way; she needed no help. The panels were covered with gravel, a flat and sandy surface from weathering and time in the golden sun. Bits of tiny glass illuminated like silver sand, shrouding the entirety of the city in the same bright, blinding shine I had long since grown accustomed to. The square-like roof had only one escape route - the ladder - unless you count the obvious secondary option. This was indeed the highest point in the city aside from our supposed final destination of the distant mountains. I walked alongside her to near the edge of the rooftop, careful to avoid the metal carcass of the skyscraper below. Leaning over the brick barricade, I saw the entirety of the city and all it contained. It really *was* a dream, goddamnit. I could see over every building and into every crack and crevice of the landscape. I saw every person, every drifter, and every vagrant that wandered the streets below. I could feel their presence like an aura. Everything was at *my* command.

"How do you like it from God's view?" I spun around to see Peter strolling up behind us. How he got up there without us hearing him was beyond me, but I had witnessed stranger things. "This is *my* view," he said, not giving me time to answer. He joined us at the edge, admiring his creation as a painter does his masterpiece. The slickest breeze would have sent the frailing old man plummeting over the edge, but he remained still as a morning bird, ever-watchful. "Follow my example, my boy," he whispered so lowly I believed that brisk wind had come to take any of us away. He observed from the edge, fading into the background like a cat on a rainy day, sinking into the peripherals of the scene as if he himself was a grain of sand on the rooftop. I began analyzing the crowd of people stories below me as if they were face-to-face with me, only inches away as opposed to miles. I went from left to right, discarding the ordinary, unfamiliar ones into a group until none remained. I felt no special connection at all to *any* of them. In fact, I grew irritated and agitated at the fact that I felt nothing for these people. They were *below* me, goddamnit. I knew what I had to do and what I was searching for, yet I could not *grasp* it. *Could I feel hatred as a replacement for disempathy?* Peter stayed as silent as a starry night as once again the sun gave way to a heavy moon growing ever-so-larger in the midnight sky above. And when I looked over at him, he was gone. Time varied day by day, sometimes lasting ages and others mere minutes. Felicia and I descended the ladder, careful to avoid slipping into the chilly night air. We rounded the corner, climbed the stairs, and walked quickly through the hall, nervous and somewhat anxious as to what Peter would be destroying that night. As we neared the elegant doors once more, we saw that they were cracked open ever-so-slightly. The lamps were lit inside the training room, and we shut the doors behind us. Calling out to Peter and receiving not an inkling of a reply, we sat on the couch in the dim light alone. "Why can't I find it?" I wondered out loud to her, frustrated with myself, the past days' failure, and everything around me. All except for her. She grabbed my hand and ran her thumb along the inside of mine, comforting me. I felt my nerves settle and my blood flow evenly again. I asked the same question in multiple ways, trying to talk *myself* through it. When I looked down again, she was fast asleep peacefully against my arm. The poor girl must have been exhausted. She had followed my routine of minimal sleep and maximum awareness for at least a week as we scoured the city high and low in search of a wild goose. I felt the same caliber of fatigue, and it gnawed at me like a demon. I simply could not sleep until I found it. *Whatever* I was looking for.

I gathered her up in my arms as gently as I could as not to wake her. I climbed the stairs two at a time to avoid jarring her resting body more than I had to. Once in her bedroom, I laid her in bed, covered her with blankets, and kissed her forehead and she sighed a breath of unconscious slumber. I dared not lay beside her in fear of waking her, as much as I desired it. I simply could not rest until it was finished - whatever *it* may have been. I returned to the training room into the silent loneliness. I could not help but feel a chill at the thought of being alone. I *liked* it, but I was never really alone. Not anymore. I fell back onto the couch with the sly thought of sleep, but I fought it off like a wild animal. I studied the city lights stories below as I tucked away my worries for the day and finally found peace - as temporary as it may be. I would have nearly drifted off - in fact, I felt my eyelids droop like dilapidated rooftops. I would have been fast asleep if not for what caught my eye miles below.

I saw something glowing down in the city streets outside of the frigid and silent training room. It permeated my tired vision and pulled me awake like a speeding train. It could have been a flashlight at first, but it moved with a swiftness beyond batteries. Moving back and forth like a wisp rather than a light, it throbbed with blinding power - drawing me in, hypnotizing me, and enticing me. I focused on it as it captivated me, unallowing the deficit of attention. I was going to find out what it was - I could not help it nor fight it. I rose from the couch with a fatigued groan, pulled my coat on, and slipped out the door without a sound. I hurried down the stairs three at a time, still hypnotized by the strange and mysterious light in the street below. I opened the main door and stepped out into the quiet, empty city. The usual hustle and bustle had subsided - in fact, I saw not one other soul that night for the first time since my arrival. No cars buzzed by in the midnight hour. I was alone with the ghastly and ghostly glow yards away in the middle of what could have been the Main Street of that worldly city. I approached it slowly, unknowing of what it exactly was. *Was I scared of it?* Of course not. If anything, I would have been frightened by the dark. Much less a *light.* But those times had long passed; I feared *nothing.* I felt the heat and raw power of the orb now a dozen feet away. It spun and throbbed as I inched closer to it, squinting my eyes tighter and tighter as I approached it. As I came within falling distance, it danced onto the sidewalk, *teasing* me. *Testing* me. It radiated light like a silver sun and as fiery as the volcanic star itself, pulling me closer into it. I followed intently, captivated as it curved around the side of the apartment building and sped up the sidewalk towards the middle of the city. I broke into a full sprint to keep up with the ball of light, running like a wild animal, drafted by the power of it all. It came to a stop outside a short and hidden building a ways ahead. I saw it push its way inside the door, the trail of light fading as it illuminated my path. As if it *begged* me to follow it. As I made my way to the outside of the building, I saw that it was a *bar*. I huffed and sighed, pulling my coat tight as I opened the door, keeping an eye out for the crystal ball that had carried me thus far.

Much to my surprise, there was only one person in the bar - that being the bartender - his back turned to me as he dried shot glasses with a towel. I saw the light grow brighter out of the corner of my eye as it inched out from around the corner. It levitated as I turned to face it, before it rushing straight through the bartender. He dropped the glass as it shattered to the floor. Silence followed. I heard the laugh and instantly knew who it was. He swung the towel as he spun around to face me. "And what can I get you, kind sir," he mocked. I was standing face-to-face with Lucious Noy. I did not speak. "Come on, man, I haven't got all night, for Christ's sake," he laughed sarcastically, motioning to the invisible hubbub of customers. "The light," I said. "I was following it here." He took it in. "I bet you were. Shiny things do have a habit of attracting the *ignorant*." I cracked my jaw and clenched my fist. I was going to ask about it before he cut me off. "Word has it you're on a mission, my friend," he said. "Peter taught you to harness being a Dreamer, didn't he?" he sneered. "What a turn of events." He mocked me as he recalled the first time we had met. "Can't teach a blind man to see; can't teach a lame man to walk," he laughed. I felt a gun in my hand. "Put that away," he said as calmly as could be. "My mother is already dead," he muttered angrily. "You don't really think I killed her, do you?" I asked in a comical attempt to understand. "You're the only piece of this puzzle that doesn't fit. And now she's gone." He shed a single tear as dark as whiskey.

The tall, blonde young man hopped over the wooden counter of the dimly lit barroom, slapping me in the chest with the rag as if we were old friends. "I'll be honest with you, Noah Willowby," he said, close enough for me to smell his rotting breath. "I don't give a goddamn about whatever you're searching for, but I ask one thing," he started as my ears perked up, indicating I was listening. He stepped closer, putting his finger to my chest as he uttered his request slowly. "Leave my sister here." The order took him nine seconds to get it out, emphasis on every word. He *cared* about Felicia deep down, but he deserved her not. I popped my neck as he narrowed his eyes to mine. "She's going with us," I said with a face as straight as an arrow, finally owning my confrontation like a sore. He laughed calmly as if I had just told him a stale joke. "I wasn't asking," he said through gritted teeth. I saw his arm flinch and lunged in his direction. I pulled the pistol from my belt and fired at him, missed, the bullet shattering a bottle of liquor behind him. He raised his hand in a truce as he filed behind the counter calmly, grabbing a bottle of whiskey. He popped the cork and poured every last drop all over the counter, dripping onto the floor slowly. "Let's play a game, Noah," he smiled. "What do you have in mind?" I wondered out loud, not wanting to play games at all in the least bit. "I want to test your ability," he replied. "You've had your training, but hold me to this, you've had no *real* goddamn training. If I win, you leave Felicia with me. Deal?" With the final word, he sparked a flame on the tips of his fingers, ever-threatening to release it onto the alcohol only mere inches below. He whistled as he did a faux sneeze, smiling as he whispered, "Oops." He had not proposed a counter-offer if he were to *lose*.

Lucious pulled a small circular item from his pocket and turned it over in his hand. "Have you ever seen *money*, Noah?" he asked me. I *had*, but only when I was a child. I remained silent. I vaguely remembered the *controlling* currency as I saw it - the very thing that controlled the world and fueled the human race and all of its selfishness and greed. "Have you ever heard *music*?" he continued. Only several times; I remained silent once more. He tossed the coin into the air as it flipped and arced into the nearly ancient machine in the corner of the bar. As it slid gently into the slot, loud music began to play as it did in his car. *Violent memories.*

The roaring fire ignited instantly. I could smell the burning rum like gasoline in the small, shaded barroom. The floor beneath us erupted into flames, allowing only seconds to hop onto the bar stools several feet away. I saw Lucious leap onto the counter, slipping on the whiskey. I flew into the air above the heat, making my way over to him. I snatched his shirt collar where he had fallen and hoisted him onto the counter with me. *Face-to-face.* After a few seconds of a confused daze - whether I had saved him or merely played into his game, I was not sure - I tackled the frail shell of a man and threw him as forcefully as I could out the window. I saw him roll onto the street below after smashing through the thin glass pane. I decided to stay inside for a while and catch him by surprise. I saw him move outside the window, climbing to him feet and making his way to the sidewalk, peering inside to look for any sign of me. I saw the flames climb up the counter and and surround the wine rack, bracing myself for the explosion. I felt the heat and vibration of the noise as the building fell around me. I dove out the window, careful to avoid the jagged edge of the deadly glass as the stories above me came crashing down. I ducked into the alleyway as he covered his eyes from the smoke billowing from the only hole in the blaze. He was *blinded.* The second explosion had knocked the wind out of him as he held his stomach in agony.

I rolled back to my feet as I landed back on solid ground once more. I circled the wounded man as he searched for any sign of me, not backing down from the wreckage as much as it was hurting him. He wanted to watch me burn. I put him in a headlock and flipped him onto the cold asphalt below. Before he could react, I placed my heel on his throat. My hostile foe was reduced to nothing but a cough. "Game over," I said, whistling. Mockery was an explosion of pain all its own; God knows I had been humiliated all of my life. "Not today," he mumbled raspily. He straightened out his fingers, sending a wave of hot air at me, knocking me off of him. He struggled to his feet as we switched places on the street, the only two people in the city outside the smoldering city block. I felt his fist against my face hit after hit. Time after time. I tasted blood and spit when I could out of the corner of my mouth. I felt the world close in as I saw black - nothing but pitch *black* everywhere in every direction. I was covered in my own blood as I was nearly beaten to death, pinned to the concrete. I tasted the hot alcohol through my nostrils; the city had taken on a smell of ash. It was nothing but a flame, and mine was about to be blown out. I balled my fists and felt the rush of power within me, as minute and tiny as it was. The flames snaked out of the window, across the pavement, up my arms, and into my body as I felt the warmth and searing heat in my soul. Each movement was a throbbing pain - an *expedition*. I released the tension in my palms as I winced under the power of my enemy. It took all I had, every ounce. Every last drop. With the explosion of power from within me, Lucious flew dozens of feet down the road toward the middle of the city. I could see the sewer manhole cover from where I lay through the only jaded bloody vision I could muster.

It was only him and I. Nobody else. The city was silent; I had long since lost my hearing. I could barely see, barely breath, and barely stand. Lucious had rolled at least half a dozen yards on bare concrete, both of our clothing torn and burned from the fight. I saw his body remain lifeless as I limped toward him from the smoky fire. He turned over as I neared him; I stomped as hard as I could on his nose. A man who despised me for no apparent reason other than I had taken away his sister - his only life support other than the hatred he breathed in and lived by like a code - I could finally make him hurt as he had done me. I kicked him in the ribs as he wheezed for air, a final breath to sustain at least one more blow on me. I could not allow it, for it would surely kill me. He raised his fist as I pinned it to the manhole cover. He grabbed ahold of my calf and knocked my leg out from under me; I fell onto the street below once more. I did not have the strength to rise a second time. I laid there for the longest time as he struggled to his feet. He stood over me, blood dripping onto my torn pants leg from his nose. I had clearly broken it, along with his arm and quite possibly his collar bone. He winced with every step as he stood to claim victory over me. I could not allow it; it would surely kill me.

"No one will ever take her away from me," he said slowly through an agonizing breath. I barely heard his whispers. "You're wrong," I uttered. "It's not her who needs to leave you; it's you that needs to leave her," I said through gritted teeth, flinching as he raised his leg to stamp out the last breath I could muster. I summed up the very last blast of energy through my veins and let him have it. The force of the wave struck him square in the chest and sent him head over heels backwards into the vast abyss of nothingness. What once was an orb hovering over the manhole cover had become a wall of wisps and spiraling blue spirits chasing each other in circles, evaporating the body of Lucious Noy, disappearing him into the frigid night air. I was alone in the dying midnight, quickly passing away with it. I am quite surely positive that I blacked out several times over the course of the hours I laid there on the frozen asphalt. As I came to and groaned through the miserable moments of brief consciousness, I swear I saw yet another light emerge from the invisible line which marked the division between the real and dream worlds. Each time I would close my eyes, it would await my return, floating toward me, closer and closer. Calling my name. I reached my hand out to it as if to *catch* it, the only movement I could bear. The orb radiated energy through my body, rejuvenating my bones and muscles to health once more. I sat up on the concrete with a breath of frozen air, the first one of the night that had not tormented me. Upon touching the strange new light, it became ever-so-familiar to me as I realized what had happened. Lucious Noy was my twin, and I had just taken his ability to dream.

I turned around and sprinted back to the castle of a mansion, following the sidewalk back to the building, marching the stairs two at a time and rushing through the hallway once more. I pulled the penthouse doors open with my mind, still high and driven from the fight that had gone down seemingly *hours* ago, though it had been only mere *minutes*. I heard the smashing of glass and shouting from the end of the hallway before I even entered the complex. "STOP!" I bellowed, not in my own tone - instead a deep and forceful bellow. He was smashing bottle after bottle of his own private liquor collection before the bar counter in the back of the room. Sweet-smelling whiskey sprayed everywhere as he hurled the final bottle at my head. I caught it with my mind and sent it whizzing against his head, knocking him to the ground. I made my way around the counter, furious with his volatile and borderline-psychotic behavior late into the night. "What is your goddamn problem?" I shot at him. He looked up at me with his one yellow eye and golden teeth. "It's taking too fucking long!" he shouted back. "You should have found it by now!" I brought my foot to his mouth, hushing him. "It was Lucious Noy," I said softly as Felicia slept upstairs. He was silent as I removed my foot from his jaw. "I saw a light down in the city and I followed it," I started. "Lucious was there and he tried to kill me. Like he wanted me to *prove* myself. I pushed him across the boundary and he disappeared. He's gone. But he left an orb in the street. It found me." By the time I had finished my rather concise account of what had happened, Peter was already back on his feet. "This is magnificent," he started to pace, this time excited as opposed to hostile. "You took it a step further, my boy!" he shouted, grabbing and shaking my shoulders in joy. I shushed him on account of Felicia, but his voice grew louder. "We don't even have to take the little angry shit back with us! He's already there!" That thought had never occurred to me until that moment. This time I took Peter by the shoulders, as taller and broader as they were. "*You* listen to *me* now," I ordered. "*She* does not find out about this," I said slowly so he understood through his fit of joyous rage. Perhaps the old man truly was a psychopath. However, he was not a *monster*. A harmless hermit, at best - an emotional vagrant. His son had become the true criminal - the endless pit of all evil. And *I* was the *monster*.

"We leave first thing in the morning," Peter spoke once more. "That gives us three hours to get ready," he followed. Perhaps what had happened minutes ago truly had been hours prior. I will *never* understand time in that constant cycle of a dream. "Tell Felicia right now. Wake her," he demanded, returning to his prior aura of control. I looked back at the old man with the twinkle in his eye one more time before heading upstairs. "I think you already took care of that for me," I said, exchanging a final smile with the man. It might quite possibly have been our last pleasant memory together. I climbed the stairs slowly as Peter rushed me from below. His thin lips curved into a wicked grin as I turned around and barged in the bedroom. I shook Felicia as I pondered what to say in a fervent panic. "What?" she uttered as she came to. "I found my twin. I killed it. We have to leave in a little while. You have to get up," I said as politely as I could manage without breaking into tears as the thought of her finding out exactly who it was. "Who was it?" she asked drowsily, rubbing sleep from her eyes. By the time she asked the question, I had already left the bedroom, closed the door to mine, and fell to the ground in angry, hidden tears as the clock began ticking.

I awoke with an hour to pack all of the stuff I had acquired in the new city into the tiny suitcase from the Noy house. I packed what I could like a puzzle and broke the rest into a thousand pieces, losing myself in the memories of that place. I brought my bag down the stairs and helped Felicia with hers, taking one last look at the room we had shared so many nights in. We came down the stairs to find Peter pacing the training room, mumbling to himself. Being the only one to return, he had nothing to pack and a whole hell of a lot of time on his hands. He spun around to see us with a bright eye and an ushered spring in his step, eager to start *his* journey - or perhaps to *end* it. "Ready?" he asked cheerfully. We nodded in unison. "Excellent," he replied. "Let's go!" it seemed unbelievably *rushed*. There was apparently no time for formal goodbyes. "Right now?" Felicia wondered, probably still exhausted from the sleepless night before. I know I was, but I could not sleep to find true rest - only to remain consciously dormant for a spell. Peter led us out the door as if we were simply going out for ice cream as opposed to leading a murder mission on his son. We left the training room in a careful hurry, avoiding broken glass and puddles of wine. "Are you going to miss us, Peter?" Felicia asked cheerfully. "Of course," he replied. "What will you do with all the spare time?" I followed. "I have a bit of cleaning to do," he joked. The doors slammed shut, quite possibly the last time I would step foot in the glorious training room. "How are we going to get to the other side of town?" Felicia asked in that same blissful tone. "Your brother loaned us his car," Peter chuckled. That was such a sick game to play. Sure enough, we exited the penthouse building to face Lucious Noy's Mustang glimmering in the morning sunlight.

Bags inside and us as well, Peter fired up the engine and roared smoke, speeding off the curb and into the bare minimum traffic. We passed places I had seen, but so many places I never wanted to see again. I had never been so glad to be going so goddamn fast - nobody paid any mind to the smoking rubble of the barroom across the street. Felicia took my hand in the backseat and squeezed it tightly. I *knew* she knew something was wrong, and I was *terrified* of it. My stomach sunk as she spoke. "When we get back there, I'll help you find your wife," she whispered. I was caught off guard. "Why?" I asked, bewildered. "She made you happy; I want to see that again," she replied. We sat in an endless silence the rest of the way; my mind knew not just as my heart did - a constant example.

The massive skyscrapers passed us by along with the cars and people of the dream world city. The car raced through the outskirts of town, tearing through the countryside. We passed trees and wildlife - the unfamiliar mediums to the urban hell we had served for so long. I was hypnotized by the childhood memory of pine needles as we were immersed in the smell of the forest. The air grew ever chillier as we neared the mountain range. It was a blur, a fairy tale coming true - one beauty and two *beasts*. Peter brought the car to a stop at the base of the rocky cliff. We all got out and stared up at the plateau stories above us. "We fly from here," Peter said. "Don't worry, I'll come back for your things once we reach the top." Felicia and I clasped hands once more as we rose into the air together. We flew upward, leaving Peter King in our shadows as we fulfilled yet another fairy tale. She was my Tinkerbell. We whizzed around rocky cliffs and through caverns as we approached the top of the frigid rock meters above us. The rush of wind picked us up as we landed on the flat surface of the mountaintop. Peter was nowhere to be found as we looked around for him intently. It was just her and I atop the windy cliff miles above the landscape; the car was merely a dot as we stared over the edge. We spun around as we laughed and danced, forgetting the severity of the explicit mission - if only for a moment. I pondered what she had said. Felicia made me happy as Julia did. The two had strikingly different ways of doing that to me; I was truly at a crossroads. Then she asked the dreaded question. "You never told me who your twin was," she smirked. "Who was it?" she asked in an ironically cheerful voice. I saw a shadow out of the corner of my eye as the questions overtook me in a fervent and dominating fashion.

Peter landed smoothly beside Felicia. I saw him pull something from behind his back. He had knocked her unconscious with a large rock before I could even blink. "No!" I shouted as I dove toward her side as she laid on the rocky surface, taken aback by the quick and volatile moment. "You were wrong, Noah," he spat. "Lucious was never your twin," he shouted. "PETER!" I shouted at him, lunging away from Felicia to attack him in a fit of rage. "Wh - where is my brother?" she asked sleepily, disoriented from the bloody gash on her forehead. Peter flipped me on my back on the solid concrete-like ground. My heart sunk; this was the feeling I had felt as I had searched. "It was always Felicia," he said, drawing his gun. "No!" I shouted again. I raised my hand to stop him, reaching for my gun in return. He balled his hand into a fist, kicking it away from my grasp. My mind roared of things I could possibly do. It drew a blank as he straightened his fingers out quickly. The blast of freezing air knocked me closer and closer to the edge of the cliff. I heard the shot ring out, Felicia's final breath pushing me over the edge as I plummeted toward the city below, screaming at a god I could never to control, or much less become.

Part 3

The War

Chapter XVII
Cain and Abel
(The Ones That Kill, the Ones That Die, and the Ones That Watch)

I was in complete and utter shock, as you can most likely infer. The situation had turned from almost magical to absolutely malicious in a matter of mere seconds, and then it was over - extinguished like a candle in the winter wind. I was completely and utterly blown out in mind as well as body. I had lost perhaps the two and only members of a possible family I had adopted in that mystic world - the ones that made an afterlife a sort of heavenly haven as opposed to a miserable, hellish prison. Like the earth I had been ripped from, they too had passed away into a vast and enticing abyss; Felicia was dead, my former master had betrayed me, and above all, the fact that I was hurtling toward my death was quite alarming, as you can imagine.

I grasped for bearing of myself, senses, and surroundings frantically as I panicked - my stomach hurtling and shaking to match the movement of my limbs as I fell endlessly. I felt the impact of the blast lingering on my chest as the wind whipped my hair around wildly. I was most definitely falling, but it felt as if I was traveling absolutely nowhere simultaneously. I tilted my head downward as I gazed and grazed through the clouds toward the ever-closer ground millions of feet below. The old city had a deep - rather *melancholy* - orange glow to it - that of which I remembered all too well. Patches of flames roared through the desolate and destroyed landscape that I once called home. Smoke billowed past me, a black cloud that baptized me back into the abrupt truth of the real world. It was not until I collided with the ground that I realized what I was witnessing as I tumbled to my death. Perhaps it was the greatest and most opportune time to make any final lifetime realizations; if they were to be unbearable or even as far as to be unlivable, well that quandary would indeed take care of itself in just shy of a heartbeat. *My very first dream.* Everything went black with smoke and unconsciousness.

I awoke against the scalding pavement, nearly singing my skin. By the distance I had fallen, I should have most certainly been dead - either from blunt force trauma or my undying fear of heights. What a sudden and satisfying ending *that* would have been. Contrary to both your belief as well as mine, I felt next to no pain - the burning sensation in my cheek merely an uncomfortability. I managed to roll over and look around me once my world stopped spinning and the stomach-dropping sensation had subsided. I was eye level with the crackling and flaming asphalt. The once magnificently-constructed city then laid in ruins before me.

I climbed to my feet with a heavy breath and a laden stride as I barely heard the mouse-like sound of clinking metal against pavement. I looked down and saw the firelight glinting off of a single bullet casing which rolled beside my feet. I knew that place *all* too well. That was the exact landmark where Jack King had murdered me execution-style as his father had done to my Felicia only moments prior. Memories flooded back to me like a shattered dam in a monsoon. I reached down and turned the bullet over in my fingers, pocketing it. There was no sign of life there - no crowd, no passersby, *nobody.* Not a single soul but myself roamed the streets of the dilapidated metropolis. I feared the worst as I limped away from the gruesome thoughts, unsettling visions, and the crackling flames behind me.

I knew of but one place to go, that being my shell of a house from seemingly eons ago. *Could I bear to call it home?* Certainly not. It was nothing but four walls, but what I searched for was the *roof.* I sought and desperately needed shelter from the smoky atmosphere and the jaded landscape, and I was willing to wage war with the ghosts in that place in order for a moment to think and a safe haven to rest from the poisonous oxygen. I did not know a home that had not fallen; I was then a vagrant in a foreign utopia - an ancient, yellowed picture shattered into a billion minuscule shards. *Had I a heart?* It had been torn from me multiple times over - broken beyond repair and undoubtedly beating for nothing simpler than the necessity of life.

I dusted the ash off of my clothes and made my way out of the town square. The air was filled with thick black smoke like diesel exhaust, making it unbearable to see or breathe. In addition to sensual obstacles, the terrain was nearly unrecognizable. I was relying on mere memory of the city's layout, which was then corrupted with cracks in the concrete, patches of flames, and vast piles of rubble. I passed the vaguely familiar buildings, stores, and houses that I remembered from so long ago. It had all faded into nothing, destroyed by the unknown. *What had happened there?* Reduced to nothing but ash and rubble, the masterpiece of Jack King had most likely been eradicated by none other than the creator himself. I had my thoughts and assumptions, but I silently and solemnly vowed to find out the truth. I swore to provide evidence to my calculations and allegations. Perhaps I would have shed a tear if only I could have seen in front of me.

I passed the once-intact stone sign entrance to my neighborhood; I remembered the elegantly-stacked bricks and how fucking massive they used to stand. They were then nothing but a heap of split concrete boulders - nothing but a product of the city and lifework of Jack King. I stared down at the pile of crushed rubble, all that remained being a tiny green sprout through the thick ash. All of the houses as far as I could see in all directions were either on fire or had been. I thought of the people that once lived there - neighbors and friends - and I felt the steaming flow of tears stream down my dirty cheeks. I could only imagine where they all were. I *hoped* they were dead, for if they were in my position, well, I could not bear to wish that on even my worst enemy. Flashbacks ate me alive as I thought back to so long ago to when life had nearly returned to normal after the start, then again after it came crashing down once more. So much tragedy and change had come between the way things used to be and how they were then. The memories became a blur as I kicked a cracked brick out of my path and continued on before I was overtaken by fiery memories.

I came to the foot of my driveway - the third or fourth I had called the last in my then eighteen years. Had the mailbox not been partially intact, perhaps I would have walked right past it. My family's house was nowhere near recognizable as I stared down the drive at the dilapidated building yards away. No sound or memory of home rang from its depths; instead I heard whispers of shelter as I made my way down the creviced path. I slowly approached the front door past the creaky stairs, each shouting a squall of trespass. The hinges emitted an eerie creak as I slowly turned the knob. The living room was dimly shaded with neglect and the entire house smelled of mildew as if the water pipes had been leaking since the dawn of time. Everything was in shambles - tables were overturned, the furniture was flipped and scattered, and bullet holes had torn through the walls in wild streaks. There was a certain dampness about it, as if the entire house was indeed soaking wet. I could not help but remember the peaceful bliss of the once-calm city home as I finally came to terms with the truth. My middle home - as well as any inkling of my life - had been destroyed.

I passed through the soiled kitchen where my family and I had enjoyed - or at least *gathered* for - many meals together. I let the memories die along with them. I climbed the creaky stairs to my room, and what a mistake that was. Perhaps I only hoped for the bed to be intact; if only I could manage sleep in the slightest confines of comfortability. Once again, I came across disappointment. What was left of my belongings were scattered across the floor, windows were smashed, and the closet doors had been split like wooden logs. My bed had been set on fire. I looked down to the stained carpet beneath my feet as a shimmer of light flashed in the corner of my eye. I reached down and picked up a framed picture, the thin glass pane cracked across the front. I could barely tell who it was as I dusted it off in the dim light, knicking the palm of my hand with sharp drops of blood. The photo was of my family and I when we had first arrived to the city, long before the inevitable trespassing of evil. I was not but ten years old in the photograph, and the dreams had not yet ravaged my reality beyond recognizance and the people I had known had not yet betrayed me and left me to rot in the bittersweet existence all alone. The memories flooded through my veins like a wildfire, pushing against me like a crowd closing in. There was a bottomless grave awaiting my demise, sucking me in with an enticing grip with every step I took. I could look at the picture no longer. It slipped from my grasp into the abyss below, shattering completely as it hit the floor. Much like myself, it did not have far to fall.

There was nothing worth salvaging from the ransacked room; all that remained were torturous photographs, destroyed furniture, and clothes that would no longer fit my muscular frame. I crunched shards of glass beneath my feet as I turned to leave the chamber of past regret in which it had become. I heard the noise as I turned the knob - a crash far more heavy that an unstable foundation. This was another human being, the first I had heard since my return to the city. My reflexes were that of a fox; I ducked into the hallway and behind the corner, ready for anything. I heard the slow and steady footsteps pass in front of the stairway and stop abruptly; my heart pounded as I grew anxious as to who it might be. I saw a shadow in the corner of my eye - a *man's* shadow. I sensed the heavy breathing, the broad shoulders, and the growl of a soldier in a war zone. I prayed it was the undertaker coming to bring me sweet relief; I was ready as I heard the stranger whistle, teasing his prey like an animal. I stepped out to face him, only to find out that it was *no* stranger.

It took me a moment to recognize him. He wore a military uniform identical to that of Jack King. The deep green haunted me like a ghastly fiend molded into my memory. He was six feet tall and rough-looking, with a thick beard stretching across his jawline. The oddly familiar soldier held an assault rifle at the ready position. Perhaps a fox is not the slyest creature afoot; neither was my brother by any means, but I stood face-to-face with him with only a dozen stairs in between us.

"Who the hell are y-", he began, stopping mid-sentence as his pupils widened; he had recognized me as well. "Noah?" he asked in disbelief. I understood; for all he knew, all that remained of me was the blood stains covering Main Street only seven blocks away. It came as a shock, even to the biggest *dickhead* I had ever known. "You're supposed to be dead," he chuckled as I nodded in realization and agreement. "I didn't care for it too much," I replied. I saw a deep look of ponder upon his face as he raised the muzzle of his rifle to aim at my chest. "Let's reason this thing out," he suggested. "Man takes a bullet to the brain in front of the whole city and lives to tell the tale. Now he walks. He talks. My little baby brother, a dead man walking," he laughed once more. I managed a forced smile, even if it was short-lived. "Now how about we come back down to real world U.S.A., shall we?" he muttered. "This bullshittery is just that - unless, of course, you just so happen to be a Dreamer. If that were the case, then I'm afraid I have a different mission than tending to your girlfriend this evening."

I saw his finger move ever-so-slightly toward the trigger. "Where the hell is she?" I said through gritted teeth. *More laughing.* "Dead, dying, or somewhere few and far between. Besides, what's the difference these days?" he asked mockingly. "You're about to find out," I mustered. "That's just like you, kid brother," he raised his voice. "Looking into the barrel of a gun and telling it to go fuck itself. I like that. *Jack* likes that. That's why he recruited me for his army. Too many of them had to be -

well, *handled*, if you will. He needed someone he could trust." Jacob bowed and tipped his military-issue cap in my direction. "He'll love to get a load of you after what happened."

I grew angry and impatient with his Jack-influenced banter. "What did you do to her?" I nearly shouted. He pondered once more in a mocking eye and tone. "It's funny how lonely someone can get until they fall for anyone," he winked. "I took *very* good care of her for you, Noah. "It's just a goddamn shame you'll not live to see her again." It was my turn for a vague, raspy response. "I'm gonna fucking kill you," I uttered, my enthusiastic tone possessed by rage as the words continued. He had long since focused the sight of his gun on my forehead. "All it takes is one shot, brother," he said quite seriously.

"One shot, huh?" I asked, amused at that point. He dropped the gun as I took each step one by one. His hands hung paralyzed in the air. The rifle rose above the stairs once more, this time at *my* command. The hammer cocked as the barrel rested against his forehead as I came face-to-face with my brother for the first time in ages. I knew him no longer as he had evolved; or perhaps *I* had changed so drastically. He reminded me so much of my father as he stood in his uniform and broken scowl, a look of terrified defeat in his eyes. "Yeah," I said. "Go ahead," he smiled. "End my suffering. I never wanted to be on this suicide mission anyway. Jack forced me into it. Every able-bodied man," he said, attempting to distract me. I nodded. "I'll tell you one thing I've learned, big brother," I said cheerfully. I paused as he perked up. "Guns are for pussies," I uttered as I brought my fist across his jaw.

Jacob fell to the floor, unconscious as a pile of nails. I searched the remnants of our old home for rope and settled for some of our father's weed-eater string. I bound his hands and feet as I levitated him onto the couch - the soiled and broken down sofa our father had napped on many a night. I sat against the wall in the corner with my head against my hands, waiting for him to come to. I gazed around the house, taking in long lost memories - broken down and destroyed memories. I remembered family friends and fancy dinners, watching television and feeling accepted, yet never *loved*. Ghosts danced around the kitchen, etches of my family and past. The house was nothing but a tomb - what was left of an ancient ruin. What had made the house a *home* had either died out or vanished beyond recognition, leaving nothing but four walls and a roof - perhaps then even less. Just like every other structure in that city - a whispering graveyard. I remembered Jack King and my father and how I loathed the two men. I thought of my mother and my internal regrets and how I would never get another opportunity to make things right. I looked at Jacob and searched so desperately for even an inkling of the way he was months before, but he - along with the rest of my family - was dead and long forgotten. Images of Sawyer, Topher, and Klaus flickered in my mind and how I had lost each of them in the end. I remembered Valerie's torturous and tortured beauty and regretted that I could save her no more than I could have saved myself. Joshua Peterson and Strauss came across my eyes as I shed tear after tear for their innocent sacrifice. Leroy Hall and Luke had most likely been caught in the crossfire of an empty, fruitless war as my parents had. Stephan and Hugh were most likely dead as well. *Julia.* I bowed my head and prayed to a silent god that she had at least one more breath left in her before the city fell forevermore.

I came out of my deep thought as I heard the grunts and grumbles of a conscious Jacob Willowby several feet away; he was my brother no longer. He had made his choice; he had chosen. He muttered curses and swears as I neared him, this time standing over him. The springs under the furniture squealed as he struggled to get loose. "Sit me up," he demanded, as little in his place as he was. I decided that was the one wish I could fulfill and hoisted him upright. "I ask the questions now," I said sternly. He nodded as he realized his predicament.

"You're going to tell me what happened to this place," I presented. My gun felt frigidly freezing against my hand as I summoned it, even colder as I aimed it at my long lost brother. "No need for that," he said with the slightest shudder of fear in his voice. All I did was cock it with my mind, and I saw the immediate response of control I then had over him. I witnessed him shake with fear - a once arrogant tyrant his own world. "Things only got worse after you were gone," he started. "Jack suspected you of being a Dreamer, so you had to go. Now I see he was *correct*," he sneered at me. I pushed the gun against his forehead. "Keep going," I urged. "He recruited me and every other able-bodied man he could trust that was left - and believe me, it was slim pickings. As time went on, it became harder to find them. We started capturing them and holding them prisoner in his mansion. You know, that place has a lot of damn rooms," he finished. It clicked with me then in that moment - an allusion I had allegated since my first visit to the mansion. The hundreds of doors I remembered were fucking *prison cells*. "Jack tore this city apart searching for even a single Dreamer. He became *destructive* - even more than before. He burned city blocks and demolished his own streets. This place is a goddamn *wasteland* now. We're all dead or dying. And you don't get to pick. *You* don't get to pick, Noah. *Dreamers*. You all have to die. Or he's going to kill all of us." For the second time in my life, I saw a tear in my brother's eye. He was truly scared for his life - shaking in his boots like a child.

Jacob blinked tears down his face and sniffed as he sucked the emotions away. "I have to kill you too, Noah. I have to preserve this place." I pressed the gun further into his skull. "Do it," he urged, half cheerfully. "You're no assassin," he laughed maniacally. "And you're no soldier," I retorted. "Where is Jack now?" I inquired. "Hell if I know. He was never to be found even when things were peaches and cream. I just want somewhere to live. The world can only end so many times. And if I have to kill my prick of a little Dreamer brother to stop it, goddamn it, I will," he said through gritted teeth. "I would do anything to see Marisa again. You people took her from me. You murdered her." There it was - the subtle and silent motive behind my brother's actions. There is *always* a motive behind every single action. That is the dead man's rhetoric.

I had had enough; I had long since reached my breaking point. I wrapped my fingers around his throat, dropping my gun by my side. Contracting my fingers, I saw his ruby red face drop its wide smile. "Where is *Julia*?" I demanded, my turn to speak through a raspy tone. I released, but only enough to where he could utter a sound. "That's the thing," he began. "She was the hardest one to catch. Mainly because she lay right under her father's greasy ass nose this whole time. She was the only one he couldn't kill. Said she reminded him too much of his wife. After all, that's why he's doing all this 'take over the world' bullshit. *His wife was killed by Dreamers.*" And then it all hit me, little by little as the pieces came together. The motive behind all of the charade had been revealed to me, and I had been *lied* to.

"Answer the goddamn question," I ordered gruffly, tightening my grip once more. "I'll give you one thing, brother," he uttered. "You have great taste in women. They put me in charge of guarding her. And of course, as follows." He managed a grin under nearly being strangled. I heard him laugh as I released his entirely and fell back onto my hands in shock. I knew not where Julia was, or what condition she was in. "Dead, dying," Jacob whispered. "*Your* turn to choose," he said as he pointed the gun at my face. He had slipped the knot and grabbed my pistol when I was not looking. My options were simple.

"Doesn't it just irritate you that no matter how much power you have, you still can't conquer reality?" he asked, standing over me then. "You were always pathetic, Noah," he said as he kicked me hard in the side. "Poor little mama's boy. I find it ironic that they were never your parents." Everything stopped. "That's right,

Noah," he pushed. "You were *adopted*. I was four. And so they forgot their own goddamn son and fell in love with you. You are no brother of mine. You never were." It all hit me at once. I knew how words flowed when they were lies, and this was the cold, hard truth. I swallowed it and choked, it killing me as he wished to - as he was about to. "Well, you came into this world hated and you're about to leave it hated as well. Anything you want me to tell Jack? And how about *Julia*?" he sneered. I stood up as well, catching my breath in more ways than one. "Tell Jack I'm coming for him. I'm gonna bury him. And I'm gonna take him straight to hell." Jacob Willowby laughed a frozen, dead laugh - his last.

I lunged at him from behind the gun, knocking his arm sideways. He fired a shot through the front window, shattering the already cracked glass pane to pieces. He lost grip of the handle as I tackled him, rolling us over onto the kitchen tile. He reached out at the kitchen knives, choosing one he could grasp and swinging it from behind. I ducked behind the counter as he got his footing and surroundings in check once more. I rolled out of sight, diving for the gun several feet away. I saw him make his move as I ran my fist into his neck, tripping him to the ground. He hit his head hard on the granite floor, wincing as he rubbed the spot behind his skull. I snatched the handle of the pistol and aimed it at him once more. I knelt down beside him, detaining his flailing punches as I tried to restrain his limbs. I could not kill my brother, even if he *was* telling the truth. We were *brothers*, for Christ's sake. We had grown up together; we would die together. I could not end it for him. As I aimed the gun at his still body, I realized that I would not have to. Jacob had fallen on the butcher knife meant for me when I had knocked him to the ground. I watched the life drain from his eyes as well as the memories we had made - no matter how minuscule and how jaded with division. I thought of how the murderer must have watched Marisa die and what it had done to Jacob, and I was no better. I was a murderer by force at first, but chance caught me in a net of guilt and regret. In that moment, I was without a family as I had perhaps *always* been.

I could not help but blame myself, even if I had not pierced his flesh with my own blade. Everything that had happened raced around me like a tornado - all so fast and overwhelming. I had lost my entire family, all of my friends, and my entire life in such a short amount of time. And in that moment, I knew that a lifetime was an *explosion* - an imploding existence complete with a beginning, a sparking, destructive climax, and leaving a path of wild destruction in its wakeful downfall. I halfway hoped he had managed to overtake me as well, for I had no purpose nor desire to go on. I had lost *everything*; I had been completely and utterly defeated. I felt boiling tears stream down my face as the pool of blood spread across the once-polished white tile. Salty tears seemed to steam as they dissolved into a wet and ruined puddle. I cried for minutes - for *hours* - as I mourned over my brother. He was right, after all. I was no assassin, and I had never meant to kill him. I wanted to *save* him, goddamnit. I hoped he would see my theology and fight alongside me. But Jack King - the infamous dictator of the new world - had enticed him so deeply that my last and final family member had been taken from me like all of the rest. I was relieved in a way that I had not been *forced* to take his life. As cruel and hostile as he had been most times, I knew that my brother had a kind and feeble heart under the rough and abrasive exterior. And then he was gone - snuffed out like a candle in a cyclone.

If I knew one thing out of the thousands circling through my head, I knew that my brother was telling the truth. I saw the honest fear in his eyes through the anger he had displayed. All I had known - all I had known to be *real* - was then a lie. My mother and father - or the strangers filling their shoes - had been a constricted and constructed mistruth. The house had been a lie - the city, the end, the beginning, the room, the good times, had all been nothing but a *charade. A trick. A play. Someone's game.*

This was God - devouring me away from the inside as He had *always* done. Destroying me by my own doing. I had no family left, and I had no family before the family I *thought* was family. I did not *ask* for this. I did not *beg* for this hell - both the literal and the mental one I was held prisoner within. *Prisoner*. My journey was not over yet. Julia was waiting for me somewhere in that vast city. *Maybe*. I felt anger, mourning, and anxiety all tied into one - the three evils. I was *driven*, and I was wrecked at the same time. I had work to do, and upon yet another discovery, I had to continue onward no matter how much I desired and despised my own reflection. I blacked out as I hit the floor, unconscious, sharing the death of my brother. Washed in his blood. For he was free, and I had just been locked away.

My dreams were an epileptic war zone. I had forgotten their wild ferocity over my absence, for however long it had been. They were not *nightmares*, for I did not *fear* what I saw. Yet I ran from it as I tossed and turned on the soaking wet floor. I saw Felicia, smiling and laughing. I saw the grass fold beneath her bare feet as she ran through the field under the cool spring sun. I reached out to chase her but fell flat on my face. She stopped abruptly as a bullet tore through the back of her skull. I cried out in silence as I watched the horrific sequence from behind the barrel of the gun. The soft grass turned to pavement as I heard the crashing of a military vehicle into my father's car. Flames wrapped around the streets, stifling me into pitch blackness once more. I heard Julia shout for help in the abyss as I tried to find her, to no avail. I saw the faces of Mrs. Noy, Sebastian, and Lucious shift around me like shadows. I saw Jack and Peter King coming toward me in the darkness, only memories instead of figures. At one time I believed them to be enemies, but they turned out to be millennial clones of each other. Before I knew it, I was surrounded by ghosts and demons, suffocated and snuffed out like a burning coal.

I sat up quickly in the haunted and dingy kitchen, rubbing the sleep and blood from my eyes. I had a quite bizarre thought come to my head, as if I *knew* what I had to do. The sunset shone through the long shattered windows, losing light with every moment. I knew *what* I had to do. *Where* I had to go. *Who* I had to do it for. It had come to me in my dreams, perhaps as far back as the beginning. I pulled my weak and limp body up onto my feet, catching my balance as I took one last look at my brother before I left him to rot in his home. The only place he had to call *home*. It was what he had wanted, after all. I covered his face with a sheet and folded his hands over his chest like a soldier would have done. Maybe *I* was no soldier. He had died with the memories, and with the memories brought dreams. Dreams brought two things to me - I knew I was responsible for the deaths of everyone around me in some form or fashion, and I knew exactly where the darkness had come from. I limped out the door as the sun set behind a castle a long way in the distance, blanketing the broken city in imminent and eternal darkness. I collected myself and started my journey toward the mansion - the only place in the forgotten world with even the hope of a breath of life left.

The scene was a twisted, demonic masterpiece - a picture of pure, hellish, beautiful destruction as the world *always* was in some shaded and jaded light. I kept to the middle of the cracked asphalt to avoid tripping to a bloody and rather jarring concussive state of immobility. Most of the surrounding buildings were either barely intact or fully demolished, flames snaking through the windows and into the streets. The sidewalks were untravelable and the roadways were nearly caved in, filled with deep canyons and fissures with every mile. Everything becomes so surreal when you are all alone - *truly* alone. Accompanied solely by the sound of crackling embers surrounding me, I made my way toward the home of Jack King. I did not know if it was a mirage or simply a false hope, or even if the house was still standing strong and untouched as it always had before. I could not tell what was real anymore. It was my only hope, for what I had seen was the only truth I knew. It was also quite possible that it was the only place left in the city - a burning, fiery beacon of twisted hope and fulfillment. A place of answers, whether they be satisfying or a suicide mission.

The memories were like *voices* in my head. I recalled the first time I had travelled to the mansion. The feeling of being watched had never dissipated, no matter how far to hell the city had gone. The first time I met Julia in the garden rang through my brain, throbbing into a violent headache. *Sebastian dealing cards.* The sound of the flipping cardboard gave me a monstrous migraine as I looked so far deep into the past. The light and airy manner of his daughter and butler and the vile false hostility of the man himself. And I knew in that moment that the two were father and son. They carried themselves identically in arrogance and superiority. The ability to make you trust them and drive knives through your back in the end. Tall, confident, and cunning. And I wondered in that moment why two men that hated each other so much could be so closely integrated.

My mind was as crowded as a train station. It felt as if I was making no progress whatsoever - walking in place. I saw shadows around me, licking my heels like wolves as I sweated from the heat of the fire. I felt the blistering wind across my brow as I carried on, telling myself that it was all in my head as I *always* had done, for my mind was my worst enemy. The shadows retreated but were far from disappearance. Then the *dog* ran out from the alleyway - the same mangy mutt from my first travels to the mansion. The snarling barking startled me as I mumbled curses at the hideous beast. The dog had grown larger - the quiet howl from before grown into a full growl. The matted fur had grown out and the eyes had yellowed. I backed up in fear with the shadows, for I had become one. *Who was I?* I was no longer someone who could be frightened. I stopped in my tracks, staring the dog down as he kept coming. I was scared of *nothing*. The wolf burst into flames and retreated into the alleyway in which it had come from. I brushed it off as a mere illusion - a hallucination from the heat, a desert mirage. *Testing my composure and response. Breaking old limits and fears. It was all a test.* I focused on the train of thought that was my destination. The mansion glimmered on the hilltop still dozens of miles away, the filthy sunset casting the god of all shadows across the entirety of the city, consuming me and all of my surroundings in imminent darkness.

I passed the town square as I continued onto Main Street. I saw the Perch miles above me, the only building in the vicinity that had not been blacked out with ash and smoke, for it had always been that way. It towered above me, reminding me of what was inside. And with that a theory came to me - Jack King and his military had unleashed the weapons inside upon his own people to find every last Dreamer, taking with it his own very creation. *Creations. His daughter and his city.* He had lost himself as well in the process, and I would find all three; I *vowed* to do it. I was consumed by the shadow of hatred and anger and persistence. I was in control. *All-powerful.*

The train station was as ironic to see then as it is to tell you now - a complete and utter *train wreck*. The underground subway system had crashed along the cobblestone brick-inlaid walls. They had crumbled to dust along the rusty tracks under my feet as I lowered myself down the several foot distance onto the pathway. It appeared to have been struck by a tremor, sending it off the rails and into the ceiling, cracking the asphalt on the city streets above - a tangled mess of steaming concrete and steel. Rats ran from the spreading fire and down into the cool underground tunnels along my feet, tripping over each other. The only way through the train tunnel was to slip through the smashed window and walk through the train to get to the other side of town.

I neared the wreckage, searching for an opening large enough to maneuver through. I climbed onto the window sill and cleared the rest of the glass with the butt of my gun I had long since decided to keep unholstered. I swung my legs over the barrier and ducked inside the train car - the dark and gloomy cave in which it had become. Electrical cords along the roof had shorted out, sending sparks along the floor beneath my feet; water pipes had burst, showering the leather seats with a fine mist. It was a relief from the steaming sweat along my hairline as I got my bearings, my eyes adjusting to the light - or lack thereof.

I hoisted myself across the dozens of torn, ragged seats as I made my way through the long, winding, and destroyed train car. I dodged sparks and gushes of water as I ducked in between suitcases of people that would never reach their destination, not knowing if I ever would either. *People had tried to escape.* Then the question hit me. *Where the fuck was Arnold?* The train station was then dilapidated and collapsed; the train was imploded and folded like a paper napkin. I feared the worst as I had seen come to fruition, and I wept for the old man that I had called my grandfather. I would avenge his death along with the countless others. Come hell or high water. It had, and it would. It *surely* would. I knew all too well that Arnold was hard of hearing, but in that moment he was void of memory as well. And it saddened me. I had lost my way and my guide, and I was truly lost. I finally came to the last window on the opposite side of the car and leapt with a rolling thud onto the other side of the tunnel. I climbed the stairs of the South Side Station and out into the sliver of sunlight left. The moon was conceived and birthed before my eyes as the smoke smudged out the golden star for the final time that day. The only light that remained was that of the driveway path through the forest and up to the castle on the hill. Darkness was the home of all dreams, and I readied myself for what lay ahead. *Was I imagining these things or had my dreams become reality?*

The forest was as can be imagined. I had never feared the dark itself, but what lay inside it had terrified me for all of my life. The feeling of being watched had not subsided since I had found my way back to the city, and that combined with the feeling of being burned alive or ambushed was quite an unsettling thought. The mild distance that I remembered had seemed to expand for miles through the torn tree roots and dead branches. Dew had settled onto the limbs, dripping sappy mist into my hair as I hurried along as quickly as I could manage with my frail and limp body. I had not come all that way to be mauled to death by wolves, for ghosts did a much more proficient job.

It was not shy of an hour's haunted walk along the mangled memory of the yellow-brick road before I stood at the foot of the driveway of the mansion - the long, winding expanse of concrete that strangled the mountaintop above. Two heavily-armed military guards stood at the foot of the security gate, along with countless others perched up in crevices along the rocky cliffside. My mind unconsciously guided my steps, putting myself directly in their line of sight. "Freeze!" the first shouted. Both frontmen raised their weapons. "Down on your knees!" the second followed. I felt my knees grow weak as I fell hard onto them, my hands floating behind my head in unison. They stepped away from the iron gate and proceeded to creep toward me, closing in like lions. These were the wolves, and this was an execution. *Dinnertime.*

Their feet had not left the cobblestone stairs before I waved my hands in their direction. The machine guns raised upward and broke their noses, shoving them into their skulls, both of the men collapsing to the ground. Sniper bullets tore up the gravel around me as I climbed to my feet once more. I took note of three snipers atop the watchtowers as I thought of a way to get up there. I would not have to, of course, for they had already taken their own lives. I slowed their firing and snatched a trio of metal casings, turning them over in my fingers. I curved one into the temple of the first, watching as his body drifted to the ground at least a hundred feet down. Everything moved in slow motion as I drove another bullet into the brain of the second, watching as he hit the ground several feet away from me. I had one last target, and he searched for cover as he realized his defeat. There was no *cover* on the side of a mountain. However, I *needed* something from him. I smiled as he jumped over a large rock, taking the careful opportunity to put the last bullet into his right kneecap. He lost his balance - which was planned and expected - and fell hard right in front of me. I left him alive, for he had not fired at me. He was the one who *watched*. I knelt down beside him, returning to my knees once more. "Unlock the gate," I nearly whispered to him. "Go to hell," he spat at me. I managed a slow laugh as I turned his head up to the mansion above. "Where are we?" I asked rhetorically as I stuck my forefinger into the hole in his kneecap. He screamed as I pulled it out. "Okay, okay, okay," he heaved. "Thanks, brother," I said as I stood up. After he pressed two buttons on his watch, I put my foot in the side of his head, knocking him unconscious. Those who had done no wrong did not deserve to die. I had decided that was the difference between Jack and I.

I passed through the retracting metal bars and started up the driveway. Gazing around the property, I was utterly convinced that that place was the *only* place that had been left untouched. I could only guess and be further assured of who was behind all of the monstrosity before me. I had grown accustomed to rough and rocky destroyed pathways along my journey through the city; a clear path was a much anticipated relief. I rounded the several curves and up onto the plateau, surrounded by the many gardens. *That was where I had first met Julia.* I was minutes, hours, days away from finding her. My heart dropped as I looked around at the once captivating landscaping. *All of the flowers were dead.* The once beautiful roses and marigolds had long since been withered and blackened, void of color and untended to. The house was covered in thick vines and overgrown shrubbery, covering the rest of the path to the house. The shutters were all bolted shut with bulletproof engineered metal, I could only imagine. The mansion was closed tight and locked up, fortified into a solitary compound. There had to be much more than a single coward hiding or being held beneath those walls. Something worth being *protected.*

I had no intention of going through the front door; no, I was much too smart for that. I remembered a back door behind the kitchen that led to the back gardens from my short stay in the home before the incident. The layout came back to me rather quickly the more I pondered it. I stepped over the overgrown weeds and crossed around to the other side of the grounds. The double doors around back were closed up with iron blinds, matching the windows in the front of the house. I shook the handle silently, and it was locked. Jack was not careless. He had left the back door unbolted, but I knew he was too bright to leave it wide open. He had the only key, and rightfully so. *An important man should have keys.* After all, he *was* the key. I tightened my grip on the steel handle, strengthening my grip. When I pulled a second time, the knob came off in my hand. I turned around and smashed the nearest flowerpot I could find with it. The garden was dead, along with the rest of the house - and more importantly - the rest of the city.

As I slipped inside, I checked all quarters for guards; there were none. The house was *dead.* I could have heard a mouse drop a pen if they had not all been down at the subway station getting their tails finely roasted. The kitchen counter was cold as ice, as curled and mangled as the rest of the world outside. I had flashbacks to my last meal in that place, then my escort to my death a near hour later. The kitchen table was immaculate, as if Jack, Julia, and Sebastian still ate there every night since I had been gone. It had been so goddamn long ago, yet seemingly only a day prior. I peeked around the corner, keeping silent as a fox as I scaled the staircase. There were no squeaky stairs; all that lay within the confines of the castle was finely oiled and painted to perfection. Just as I *remembered.* It was a place of elegance as well as arrogance, incapable of being destroyed. It was *above* the city, just as Jack believed himself to be. There had to be a balance for everything, and also an answer. Perhaps even an *end*.

I ducked into my awarded and allotted bedroom and closed the door quickly and quietly, as if I had ever slept there anyway. I sat my gun down on the dresser as I looked around. The same exact manner in which I had left it that morning so long ago - everything in its place and function. It had not been touched. I sniffed the air as I looked up at the edge of the ceiling fan. *There was no dust*. Someone had been in there. *Preserving* it. That room was meant for me to come back to. I swallowed hardly and locked the door before returning to the hallway, leaving my gun inside the prison cell I would never return to.

I turned the corner carefully and locked myself in Julia's room. What I found was much different than mine. The room was torn to shreds from top to bottom. The bed sheets were tattered and hanging off of the frame. The mirror was shattered and splattered with blood. The once pink walls were painted with crimson blood - the dripping red, thick, pitch liquid curved into violent and cruel lettering:

TOO LATE. WE ENJOYED IT. ALL HAIL JACK KING.

It was truly sickening. Someone had done this out of joy. I felt boiling tears in my eyes as I looked away, pounding on her cracked dresser in anger. Julia was either dead, dying, or someone was playing a sick game. I held on to the latter as my only hope. I neared the puddle of blood on the floor under the bed and knelt down. Putting two fingers into it and raising it to my nose, I found that it was *not* blood. *Beets. She had grown them in her gardens.* I had had teeth knocked out and lips busted - I knew the taste and smell of blood quite well. Julia was alive, somewhere. I knew not of her wellness or mortality, but I gripped onto the fact that she was still breathing for even a moment longer.

I turned toward the window to see a pair of black military boots crash through the glass feet away from my face. The soldier had descended from the roof and spotted me in Julia's room. *The second button the man had pressed*. It was an *alert*. He landed on his feet and tackled me across the room, aiming his gun at me threateningly. *Mine was in the other room*. I saw a set of keys dangling on his belt as he wrapped his hand around my throat. I struggled to breathe as I pounded his hand away; I had no weapon to use against him - at least *physically*. His weight was crushing as he put his finger to the trigger. Julia was not there to give me strength, but her spirit was a *steroid*. I could see the writing on the walls as my blood pressure rose higher and higher. My veins pumped as I growled in anger as the man laughed. He grabbed a radio from his belt beside the keys. "Got another one down. About to go back in his box," he said. I heard Jack's voice on the other end. He pressed the gun to my head. "Another one down," I repeated. I snatched the keys from his belt and put the longest one I could grasp through his neck. His blood spilled over me like the unrecognizable walls above me. I hoisted the mass of a man off of me, pocketed his gun, and got my bearings in the destroyed bedroom. A breeze whispered through the broken glass as I wiped off most of the blood from my face. I bent down and collected the radio as well - although it was ruined, saturated, and useless to me. I slammed the door to the endless hell that was meant to trick me, trap me, and hold me prisoner once more. I had to find Jack - and more importantly - Julia.

I left the room quietly and carefully, checking for security once again around each and every corner. For all I knew, there was an army on its way or not a single soul. Down the stairwell and into the main hallway I went, approaching the many dozens and hundreds of rooms - or *prison cells* as I then knew them to be. Perhaps I *always* had. I lay behind each and every door, each one holding a Dreamer exactly like me. *Kill what you cannot use, capture what you can*. I had no clue as to what I was getting into, or how many innocent people were being held captive behind each door. I was either a high-price target or a silent surprise. I was about to find out which one. *To choose.*

I slid the key into the first of possibly thousands of locked doors smoothly and turned the knob, and I was surprised at what I saw. Unlike the upstairs room, these cells were immaculate. *Just like my room.* I was meant for one of them, if not *all* of them. The rooms were fit for *royalty*, it seemed; that was the horror of it all. The prisoners inside had food, water, and shelter - yet they were isolated and helpless in their own power behind a guarded door, left with nothing to use to their aid. The silverware was plastic, and the walls were bare. These were the *boxes*, as the dead soldier had referred to them as. Each one lay on a bed, tucked in tightly and soundly, a bag of suppressants flowing through their veins. Each room held the same thing, the same unconscious captive. *Ones who knew not how to harness their power.* I knew not how to wake them, nor did I want to disturb them. I had a key to every door in the house, and yet I still knew not how to set my people truly free. Men, women, and children lay unconscious before me - a silent army. I began to *recognize* them - the people that had been murdered in cold blood so many momental eons ago within the city. The *bags*. The *bodies*. The *mission*.

And then I remembered what Peter had taught me. *Make them do your will. When the time is right. We are all the same, connected. Like a puzzle.* The answer came to me as I called out to it. I did not need to disturb my people as they lay in sleep. *One is not to wake the lion.* I left the first room and proceeded to the next, only opening the doors and moving on. *They needed to hear me.* There were hundreds of doors along the winding hallways, each floor going deeper and deeper into the center of the mountain - an isolated prison. *Buried alive.* I had no time to slide the same key through each and every door. As I neared the bottom of the mansion, I could no longer breathe clearly; I was so deep inside the cliffside that the air was too thick to inhale. I began kicking in the doors left and right in a fit of rage. *I* would not be held down. They flew off their hinges as I saw the same unconscious person lying in bed under the needles and bags of drugs. They were all *me*, dying as I gasped for air.

I had destroyed the final door as the last wall faded into solid rock. My people could breathe now, even if I could not. I knew what I had to do. I reached my arms out and touched both sides of the solid stone walls, pushing against them as I felt their frozen depth. I felt each and every soul in the house under my fingertips; I felt their breath breathe into me as I took in their spirit. I felt their minds open with mine as I began to speak. *Be free, my people. Come back to me when the time is right. Roar like the lions you are.* The walls shook with such ferocity that I stumbled and broke my grip. I felt the dust settle into my hair as I tripped over the vibrating ground beneath my feet. I had to get out; I broke into a full sprint through the way out of the collapsing tunnel. *Up.* I felt my breath return to normal as I ran around corner after corner of cells. I looked around me as concrete rocks and stone boulders fell around me, blocking the then empty rooms. As I collapsed back on the main floor, the house ceased its violent shaking. I lay outside the first row of rooms as the dust settled - I could not believe it upon the first, though the second, third, and hundredth convinced me. I was *sure* of it. Each and every room was vacant, empty as a tomb. The prisoners had vanished into thin air, waiting until the time was right. *I had freed an army of Dreamers.*

I followed the hallway until I came to the other end, turning the corner to face the staircase that led to the loft, bar, and porch that I recalled so vividly in memorial and memoriam of Jack King. I stepped onto the first stair and heard the same creak in the wood that I remembered, calling out like a muffled squeal. The floorboard lifted as a subtle light caught my eye; perhaps I would have missed it had I not been forced into extraneous detail. I lifted the first stair up and tossed it aside, revealing a handle and latch. I pulled the cellar door open to see another flight of stairs descending into the dimly-lit unknown. The dry-rotted stairs were illuminated by only a few cloudy, yellow light bulbs. The basement smelled and reeked of musty, damp mold - water trickling down the walls into a disintegratory ruin. The wooden steps creaked louder and louder as they echoed under my footsteps as I peeked around the corner and into the open, secret, and hidden room. The dilapidated cellar seemed to belong to another house, nowhere near the elegance of the mansion. The basement did not even hold a candle to the castle above - a prison all its own.

The bottom of the stairs opened up into a destroyed laboratory of sorts. Metal pieces and tools were thrown around like toys across the solid rock floor. Tables were overturned and blueprints were tattered and ripped to shreds just as the suit of the man sitting against the wall was. As I peered closer into the dingy basement, I saw that it was *Sebastian*. I hurried over to him and knelt down beside him. His suit was full of rips and holes, his face was dirty with grime and sweat, and his hands bled slightly from small cuts along his fingers. His eyes opened as I shook him awake, muttering meaningless drool until his pupils focused on me. "Who are y-," he started. "Noah?" he asked, exasperated. I nodded and sat him up further. "My god, boy, I thought you were dead," he said, wiping his face with a tattered cloth. I nodded again - empty of words, yet full to the brim with questions. "So did I," I answered.

"What is this place?" I asked. "Welcome to my humble abode," he smiled through unbrushed, yellow teeth stained with grime. "This place was once my workshop. It was a beautiful collection of simplicity. I'm an inventor, my boy," he answered with a solemn grin. "What happened here?" I continued. "Jack saw my work as a threat to his power. I kept it hidden from him all this time. When he found out, he destroyed my work as well as my sense of self and locked me down here. I once called him a friend as well as my boss, but he truly is an evil man. He told me to stay put and not get in his way or he would kill me. Especially if I let slip -," he stopped. My ears and eyes perked up in his direction. "Let what slip," I asked. "He'll kill me," he added. "Not as long as I'm around, Sebastian. You're a good man who's been done wrong. Like so many others in this place. And I'm sorry for that. I need your help. I need to find him," I asked him desperately.

He pondered for a moment, scratching his head as he paced the filthy floor before me. "I trust you, Noah," he started. "So I'll make you a deal, my boy." I looked at the man, the only friend who had not been torn from me or formed against me. "What is that?" I asked, my turn to smile. "Jack is not here, and nowhere near. He hasn't been here for weeks. I've been locked down here with rations, piecing my creations back together." I could hear the excitement in his voice, but I had no time for it. "What is this deal?" I pushed. He smiled a dark, yellow smile. "If you let me get cleaned up, I've got a surprise for you. We'll find Julia *together*. She is here, after all."

Chapter XVIII
The Crumbling Kingdom
(A Sealed Deal, A Tricked Trapping, and No Way Out)

I paced the hallway in front of the master bathroom, waiting on Sebastian to emerge a cleaner and more determined man. For someone who had been in hiding for weeks and riddled with obsessive compulsions for being clean, he took well over half an hour. Each minute dragged on as steam escaped the bathroom, forming sweat across my hairline. 'Master' was an understatement; that was a mansion, after all. Jack King's own personal bathroom was equipped with every grooming tool known to man, a massive shower stall, and elegant anti-slip tiles. I imagine he was dancing in his idea of paradise, a land free of uncleanliness. Jack King had tortured him in the only way he could - locking him in a filthy room and destroying his belongings. Sebastian deserved a good clean up, or perhaps even *two*. I tried so valiantly to be patient as I awaited the search for Julia. *She was alive.* I was riddled with sheer excitement, wonder, and worry. Perhaps Sebastian and I shared the same cognitive, obsessive mindset. I was perplexed that the jack-of-all-trades butler was alive; I finally had a friend to shake the hand of and fight alongside in both body and mind. Perhaps my greatest fear was being left to fight against an impossible enemy - *myself.*

Before *too* much longer - which seemed like ages to me - the door opened and from the steam emerged the Sebastian that I knew and remembered. His goatee was neatly trimmed and cleanly shaven. His hair was greased behind his ears and tucked away like grass in the wind. His pants were pressed and his shirt was free of wrinkles as well as a tie and coat. Times had changed along with his attire; he *served* no longer. I smelled Spanish cologne as he dusted his pockets off. "It feels good to be back," he smiled. I returned the smile and clapped him on the back, unworthy to touch such an immaculate person. "You held up your end, now let me," he followed as we retreated into the dingy basement.

Pacing the hallway had become so full of anxiety that I could take it no longer. While he was busy finding his former self, I had decided to help him. I had slipped down to the basement and turned his tables back over on their feet, taped his blueprints back together, and laid his metal pieces in rows across the tabletops. I had swept the dust into the corner and replaced the light bulbs. Before I knew it, the makeshift dungeon began to look more like a cozy laboratory once again. It was the least I could do for a true friend like Sebastian, and he was *grateful*. His hands hit his head in disbelief as he ran around the room in joy. He wrapped his arms around me in a hug, hopping around rather flamboyantly. "My humblest thanks to you, Noah," he said excitedly. "We have work to do," I followed. "Indeed."

Sebastian settled back into a serious stature with refocus on the matter at hand. "Jack grew restless as the city's population began to shrink - at his own hand, of course. He almost became as paranoid as me, trying to find all of the Dreamers. He gathered all of the ones left and trained them to search for and destroy the Dreamers. He could cover more ground that way from the inside. Your brother was one of the soldiers. He was infuriated when I told him I wanted no part of it. I signed up to serve him, but never in *that* way. I won't kill for a fight I have no business or cause to. He told me to watch over Julia as I had always done and not get in his way. To keep my use or he would dispose of me. Then he found this place. Locked me down here and threatened my life. I heard him take Julia one night. She screamed and woke me up in the night. I heard Jack and his men drag her down the hallway of rooms. I climbed to the top of the stairs and listened as it happened. I heard bits and pieces of where she was. She's here. '*At the bottom of the mountain*,' they said. There's an iron box built for something down there, and that's where she is. It's impenetrable. The soldiers would take turns guarding it. I felt tremors in the night as the mountain shifted plates. Whatever is holding her, it means there's a reason. That's all I know. I'm sorry I don't know much more, Noah. I know you love her. Please don't be upset with me."

Back in his box. The iron prison was meant for me. I leaned against the table with a smile on my face as he explained. "Why would I be upset with you, Sebastian?" I asked. "You've just solved the whole thing." He looked shocked and surprised. "I did?" he wondered. "I've been down there already," I said. "And?" he asked, not following me. "The rooms end at the bottom of the mountain. Stone wall," I smirked. "Stone," he questioned. "Iron. I must have triggered something down there; the whole bottom of the mansion collapsed. We can find a way down there." He then looked bewildered. "It's impossible to get in there," Sebastian reminded me. I laughed. "There's a reason Jack came after me," I reminded him. He matched my sideways grin. "I have no quarrel with the Dreamers," he said. "And I have no fight with those not like me. Only Jack."

"How can I help you?" he asked. "I serve *you* now." I pondered it for a moment. "Work with me. Fight with me. As *equals*," I said as he smiled in return. "There's only one thing," I thought of. "The air is so thick, you can't breathe down there." Sebastian paced around the tables, fumbling through drawers and across the tops for parts and pieces. "I told you, I'm an inventor." He pulled two odd looking contraptions from a drawer under the back table. "The one thing Jack didn't destroy. These are masks designed to help you breathe better on top of the mountain. I'll bet my ass and *yours* it works the same for thick air as it does thin." I took one of the masks he handed me. "The two thin strips go into your nostrils and push your breathing passages open further, allowing more air to pass through. We used them when we first built this place." I turned the steel mask over in my fingers and looked the inventor in the eye. "How do we get in there?"

The air duct system, of course. At first I thought it to be impossible, but as I watched Sebastian pull the grate off of the wall, I saw it come to fruition before my eyes. "There's only room for one of us," he said. "I'll tell you what. You get in the vault through the air duct, and I'll see if I can't make a hole in it," he followed. "I thought you said it was impossible," I asked. He shook his head. "You doubt me, my boy. You take the safe way down and I'll meet you at Stanley's in the town square." I clapped him on the back. "Don't blow yourself up," I joked, hoisting myself into the narrow and dark air duct system.

I crawled down the first stretch - a horizontal tunnel of steel only lit by a few grates. I slithered around the corner as I mentally laid out the blueprint of the house and where I needed to go. The tunnels began splitting off into separate directions, each leading opposite ways. I slid down the the first downward spiral and landed hard on another flat patch. The metal siding circled around and around as the stairs did. The chilly air soon became thick and heavy as I slowed my pace, wrapping the aluminum arms around my head and strapping them to my ears. I pressed the button on the side of mask and took a large, gasping breath of fresh, clean air, ignoring the possible idea of being buried alive. The air system came to an abrupt stop with only one way left to go - *straight down.* I braced myself against the narrow sides and dropped down the first few feet, catching myself on the frigid metal. My shoes skidded against the steel as I broke my fall every few feet, shimmying down the shaft like a creature of the night. I could see the bright, blinding white lights of the room below, the interior of the supposedly *impenetrable* vault that held Julia that was meant for me. *Was I being led to my trap? Sebastian was a good man. My friend. I trusted him.* I put these thoughts aside as I landed on my feet on the inside of the vault. The pure iron prison was brightly lit and was full of clean, crisp air - the polar opposite of the narrow passageway leading to it. I looked around at the blank and empty room; the walls were a brilliant blinding white.

There was *nothing* in the room; it *was* a goddamn trap. Then I saw the shadow - a light, airy shadow cast across the blank slate of a room. I looked up and saw her; she was not hanging from the ceiling, but she was *floating*. She was *flying*. It came to me all at once. *Julia was a Dreamer.* I had known it all along, but only realized it in that moment. That was *her* dark and hidden secret.

I lifted myself weightlessly into the air and drifted over to her. Her eyes were closed and her limbs were limp; she was unconscious, suspended in a state of imprisonment. I wrapped my arms around her waist and descended back to the glowing floor, which for all I knew was just another wall. I lay her gently to the ground and knelt down next to her, checking for a pulse. Her breathing was healthy and steady; I waited impatiently and worriedly for her to come to, and as her eyes opened, I could tell that she did not recognize me. "Who are you?" she asked in dazed confusion. "Noah," I asked, ecstatic in hopes that she would leap into my arms once more. However, her eyes remained cloudy and unfocused. "Did my father send you to look in on me?" she asked, a sense of irritation in her voice. *This was her father's doing. She did not remember a thing.* "No," I answered coldly. "I'm here to get you out." She rejected it immediately. "I've tried before; it's impossible to get out of here. Who the hell are you, anyway?" *The mind-wiping serum. Jack had used it on Julia.* Tears formed in my eyes as I struggled to speak. "I'm going to get you out of here," I said persistently. "We'll see about that," she scoffed. To her, I was just another *spy*. I could not hope to free her from *that* prison.

The explosion shook the vault like an earthquake. The walls shifted and cracked like dirt as thick, heavy smoke filled the air. As the dust cleared and I could see once more, Sebastian strolled through the gaping hole in the wall adjacent to the air duct. "It appears to be possible, my dear," he said. But I did not hear him, nor did Julia. I heard the spider-like crackling of the concrete above the entryway, as well as all of the others around us. Panic filled the air along with the dusty haze of an oncoming avalanche. "GET OUT OF THERE, SEBASTIAN!" I shouted over the splitting cracks growing larger and larger as we were frozen in place. But he was too late. I saw the terror in Julia's eyes as we watched as the first massive slab of concrete fell on top of Sebastian. I screamed as Julia stood still, knowing that a man had just been crushed in front of her, but unaware that it was the man that had cared for her since she had been born. Smoky tears filled her eyes as well as mine as I pulled the mask over her face and grabbed her hand. The cracks had spread to the ceiling of the vault, only moments away from toppling down on top of us and crushing us as it had Sebastian.

The entire ceiling collapsed as we flew into the narrow hatch of the air duct once more, barely escaping death as we dodged large pieces of concrete and rock. I had no time to answer her questions as she shouted over the sound of bending steel and falling rock. The entire mountain was going to come down and bury us alive. I guided her waist around the sharp bends and curves of the passageway. Thick, cloudy smoke had crept through the openings in the grates as we passed along, matching the color of the daze in her eyes. I pulled my shirt over my face as we glided and smashed across the chilled metal, listening to the deafening screech of the supports of the air duct fall apart behind us. I could see the main panel above us as we came to the final slant in the pathway. The entire air duct system behind us had fallen away into the avalanche, leaving a pitch black, smoky abyss in its wake. I saw the fear on Julia's face as I pulled her through the grate as the last stretch of metal fell away into the darkness.

She threw the mask across the hallway so she could speak clearly. "That poor man," she said. "Did you know him?" she asked blankly as I blinked back tears. "Yeah," I said through gritted teeth. "We both did." She looked puzzled as I dismissed the conversation. The floor shook as the foundation itself cracked and split, unbalancing the entire house. "What do we do now?" she shouted over the rumbling and crashing of the fine China in the kitchen only two rooms away. "Where is the garage?" I yelled back over the noise. "I - I don't *remember*," she muttered. I pondered it for a moment, not frustrated at her, but so fumingly angry at her father. I was filled with rage as I bit my tongue in a painful and reserved exorcism. "We have to get off the mountain."

Shelves toppled over and paintings fell off of the walls as I turned doorknobs and threw open doors. I could barely keep my balance as I searched the kitchen corners and stairwells for a hidden door. *Outside.* I stopped in my tracks and grabbed Julia. I sprinted out the front door with her by my side. I turned back to see why she had stopped; she stared blankly at what used to be her beautiful gardens. Nothing was left but dead leaves and broken stems. "My flowers," she whispered. *A fragment of a memory. There was hope.* I pulled her hand along as the ground shook with a violent, ever-threatening tremor. I heard the windows shatter as the roof cracked open. The uppermost level of the house collapsed. I could nearly hear Jack's bottles shatter into a million soaked pieces.

I could see the garage from across the courtyard - a massive building that held at least a dozen heavily protected vehicles. I had remembered the building from my first visit - hidden in plain view. The perfect spot. I bolted toward the garage doors with Julia on my heels. The garden walls cracked and crumbled into sawdust as we hopped over the wooden curbs. The wind whistled off of the metal siding as we pulled open the doors and hurried inside. The garage lights flickered as the electricity shuttered with the quakes. I searched the row of vehicles through the dim light, searching for something I was familiar with. *I had learned to drive in my father's military-issued Escalade.* I found what I was searching for in the fourth vehicle from the end in front of the second door. I pulled the door open and helped Julia inside; I imagined she had been riding in those vehicles for her entirety of her life, yet she only remembered an hour of it. The keys fell into my lap, and as I started the massive tank of a vehicle, the headlights reflected against the garage door only two feet away from the front bumper.

"Hold on," I said, looking over at her in the passenger seat. I reached for her hand but she pulled away. The tremor shook the garage and the Escalade as one; the roof threatened to cave in on us. I floored the gas pedal as we crashed through the white steel door. I put the vehicle in between the gardens and down the driveway as the earthquake pulled us to a hard right. The ground shook uncontrollably as I gripped the steering wheel with both hands. I rounded the first curve as I saw the mansion collapse in the rearview mirror. The stone pathway cracked and splintered as the heavy car sped and drifted around each corner, struggling to keep traction on dust and smoke. Crevices became small ravines as the mountain slowly crumbled into dust, clouding my view with a thick, foggy haze. The entire mountain was coming down dangerously quickly. I heard Julia screaming beside me as everything went black. The mountainside came down with the avalanche - the house, gardens, and all of the cobblestone brickwork. I felt boulders and rubble smash into the side of the car as I struggled to keep the wheel straight. The vehicle was bulletproof but not rock-proof, and a massive chunk of the cliffside smashed the top of the Escalade inward several inches. I could barely see the gate in front of us, but I did not have to. I knew it was a straightaway - even if a wrought-iron gate stood in the way. I mashed the accelerator and watched the speedometer glass crack as the broken sand-like pieces poked and stabbed at my face. We were off of the mountain - or what was left of it - and I was coming for the man that had killed Sebastian and taken his daughter's memory with such a vengeance that could have very well bent steel and caused the quakes all in itself. I forgot all about Julia in the passenger seat as I gripped the wheel and sped out of the pitch black cloud of smoke, dust, and destruction behind me. The last safe place in the city had then became one with the hell above and below as we drove away from nothing but yet another memory - one in which only *I* possessed.

Chapter IXX
Signs of the Times
(Life's Love, Laughter, and Lies)

"I'm an inventor, my boy." I thought about Sebastian the entire way through the wooded path back to the city. Every dark, corner shadow possessed his face and spirit. The butler was my friend, and he was an extraordinary man. He had given his life to save ours - to aid our escape - and he had done so willingly. *Unnecessarily.* We could have just as easily gone through the air duct without the explosion. Perhaps he wanted to see the downfall of the prison he had been held in since the beginning of the city. Whatever his reasoning was, it had gotten him killed; he was gone as quickly as he had faded into the light.

"I'll meet you at Stanley's in the town square." Stanley's was a corner bar Jack had named after my father. Stanley was his middle name, but that was the name on his dog tags from the military time he had served. That plan had long since expired as he had, but I knew not of anywhere else to go. I stopped on the side of the road outside Main Street as I looked over at Julia. "What's the last thing you remember before they put that stuff in you?" I asked her directly. She thought for a moment. "My father would send his men in to check on me. There was this one in particular that gave me that stuff. He was tall and blonde and rough-looking - as a matter of fact, he looked a lot like *you*." I thought for a moment. *Jacob had done this.* "What did he do to you?" I pressed. I saw tears form in her eyes as she stuttered. "He - he touched me and beat me - I looked at him as he injected me with that liquid. Then I forgot everything. I forgot who he was and who I was, where I was, and what I was doing. That's all I remember. Being violated and tortured until you came for me." She smiled. "I wonder if he is still out there," she said out of fear.

"He's not," I reassured her quickly. "How do you know?" she asked anxiously. I paused for a moment. "Because I killed him."

There was an immeasurable silence for the longest time. "Look, I'm sorry I don't know you like you know me, I really am, but I'm trying to trust you," she said. "I just need some time to process all of this." I looked out the driver's side window. "I have to do something," I said. "Alone." She looked at me intently. "I'm gonna drop you off about a block away. I'll come back for you when I'm done. I won't be but about an hour." I put the Escalade in gear and rolled into the city once more. I turned the corner, dodging potholes and ravines alike. I could barely make out the sign above the door as I stopped abruptly, almost passing it. "Wait inside this building. I'll be back soon." I hated to leave her alone again, but I trusted Sebastian's judgment of a safe hiding place. She hopped out, shut the door, and I drove away as she ducked inside the broken-down doorway of *Stanley's*. The neon lights buzzed and flickered in my rearview mirror as I turned the corner and faced the Perch building. I was alone, and I was going to seek revenge on the man that had ruined his world as well as mine.

I parked outside of the Perch building and stepped out to face the tallest building in the city. Hidden by its plainness among once shining structures, it was right under my nose. *He thought he could hide from me. That was my territory.* I walked briskly inside and pulled the iron doors shut behind me. I remembered the interior of the arsenal, filled to the brim with vehicles lined bumper to bumper, boxes of weaponry stacked to the ceiling, floor after floor. I looked around each and every corner of every floor I crossed as I climbed each flight of stairs, searching for any sign of the warmonger cache I had so recalled. Yes, the Perch building was *empty*. A war had *already* begun and been waged without my participation.

Jack was there. I could sense the smell of the cigars and the whiskey getting stronger as I climbed higher and higher - the scent of pure, premeditated evil. At one time I had wondered if I was chasing wild geese, but in that moment I was sure of it. It frightened me just how much devastating power had once lied in that building, and then it was gone - most definitely in the *wrong hands*. I could not imagine what I could possibly be facing there, whether there would be guards surrounding him or if he would be standing alone. Both possibilities were alright by me. I knew who and what I was, and nothing would stand in my way of killing Jack King nice and slow in a ragged and brutal fashion.

I came to the uppermost floor of the Perch building and stared at the ladder ahead of me. The floor was littered with beer bottles and empty whiskey flasks. Half-smoked cigars wisped into the air as I saw the faint light through the hatch above my head. I put my hands and feet to the rungs as I silently opened the hatch and pulled myself up onto the rooftop. His back turned to me, the hulking shadow of Jack King was propped up against the railing with a drink in his hand, overlooking his city as it laid in ruins.

"You know what I told you would happen if you left your post, Sebastian," he growled, blowing thick smoke over the rooftop. I pulled my coat tighter as I walked closer to him. "There is no more post, Jack," I said blatantly as he spun around, spilling whiskey onto the ground. "Fucking Christ," he whispered, his breath taken away. "This isn't possible." I smiled, *amused* at his response. "That's the same thing I thought when you pulled a gun on me that day," I shot back. I was no longer afraid of that man. I *despised* him. He had brought the downfall of all I had ever loved. "That's the same thing I said when I found your best friend Sebastian living in the fucking rubble. I said it when I found your daughter locked up in a cell meant for me with no goddamn memory of who I am and even less of who *you* are. I didn't think it was possible when I found out you had my parents killed. You were behind the fucking wheel, Jack." I wrapped my arm around his shoulder and spun him around, directing his attention to the avalanche where his home used to stand so valiantly and royally in all of its honor and majesty. I whispered in his ear so the man could understand me, pointing to where he used to lay his head at night. "This is *very* possible."

Jack sat his drink down softly as I raised mine to my lips. He walked over to the railing, his eyes wide in disbelief. "Extraordinary," he mumbled. "It is," I smiled. "It is so incredibly extraordinary that you fought so hard to wipe out something you couldn't be - something you were so terrified of - that your testicle-size brain couldn't consider the fact that your own daughter is a Dreamer. When you found out, you turned your men loose on her. Guess what, Jack? She remembers being beat and raped by your men. She remembers who you are. She knows who she is. And even if she doesn't know me, she knows herself, and that's all that matters. She knows she's a Dreamer, and that's what kills you. You can't change that. And it tears you apart. You are weak. And you are nothing. You've already lost everything. And I'm still going to find a way to take everything from you the way you did me. *An eye for a motherfucking eye.*"

Jack King growled like an angry creature in the night. "Where the fuck is my daughter, you little bastard?" he said through gritted teeth. "You killed her. She's gone, Jack." His anger heightened. "You're lying," he retorted. "She's like me, Jack," I opened. "She is *everywhere.*" With that statement, I felt myself dissolve into a million crystals, materializing behind Jack once more. "*I* am everywhere, Jack," I said in a voice not my own. *"Are you a Dreamer, Jack King?"* I asked in a million shattered voices. He stood frozen for the longest time, petrified in either fear or reverence. I knew not which.

My body came back to fruition as he caught me off guard, head-butting me from behind. It knocked me back several feet, busting my nose. I felt a trickle of blood drip down my lips as I got my bearings once more. When I turned back around, he grabbed ahold of my legs and threw me across the patio table adjacent to the roof ledge. I rolled across it hard and landed on my side. I heard him draw his gun as I rose up to my knees, but before

460

I could get up, he already had the barrel to my forehead. I shook off the pain as I focused on the fight at hand, a knife slipping into my fingers. "Remember the last time you pointed a gun at me, Jack?" I taunted. There was not a trace of fear left in me. I brought the knife across his arm, tearing the sleeve and the skin beneath the pistol as it trailed off and misfired, taking a chunk out of the brick outer layer of the rooftop.

He growled angrily as he lost his grip on the firearm, a blade of his own drawn from his side. The two pieces of metal clashed in midair as he struck at me like a viper, sparks flying in every direction. He put his weight into the knife and forced me to my back again against the concrete ground of the rooftop, pinning me down. I kicked myself to my feet, catching him off guard that time. I dodged another strike as I hoisted myself up onto the table, boot against glass. I raised my leg and kicked him square in the chest, knocking him into the row of lawn chairs and patio furniture beside the table. He had brought his knife across my leg, striking the tendon and rendering my right leg excruciatingly weak. I knew the cut was deep as I felt the blood soak my torn pants leg with a fiery heat. I could hardly move as I kept my balance on the tabletop. Jack rolled over and crawled toward his gun, reaching for it as I kicked it away. I slowly retreated onto the rooftop ledge and balanced on my one good leg as he spoke.

"After all this time, the great Noah Willowby is going to *opt out*?" he spat bloodily. I laughed as I felt the rounded object slide into my grasp. "Something I should have done a long time ago when I had the chance. Maybe I could have spared the damage you caused. Because at the end of the day, you did it all to get to me. You killed your own daughter. Your own best friend. All for this moment right here. So now, it ends for both of us. Because that's the only way you can truly die." Before he could speak, I pulled the pin and tossed the grenade as it rolled across the rooftop. I watched him rear back into the corner as he kicked it away. I counted one second, two seconds, three, and I gathered all the strength I had in my one good leg and leapt off of the rooftop into the city below, disappearing into a million icy crystals as the highest point and the highest man in the city came down with me.

I remembered everything going black with smoke and dust and ash. I saw flashes through the darkness of falling debris smashing into the streets below, the feeling of sinking deep within my stomach. I focused on where I wanted to be and closed my eyes in fear of what would come. And it came to be. *Painfully.* Adrenaline had shrouded the pain of the gash in my leg, but it returned as I stepped onto the pavement, dripping a trail of blood in my wake as I limped away from my final completed dream and wish in the world. Perhaps I could then die in a peaceful, painful bliss. I was never that *lucky*, however.

The roof of the Escalade had been demolished by falling chunks of split concrete to the point of incapacitation. I envisioned the front of the bar, the *Stanley's* sign, and Julia awaiting me inside as I walked up to the door out of the thin, crisp air of creation. I had escaped death for only the umpteenth time in the past few however-the-hell many months had passed since I had begun my search for imminent danger. I had bested the man who had brought me so much misfortune since the beginning of that reborn life, and I was *satisfied.* I had just blown a man to a painted pile of bloody bricks, and I was *satisfied.* And I was satisfied with that *satisfaction.*

The door was cracked and clouded; I could not see inside. I pulled the heavy handle and winced at the sound of the creaking metal. Limping inside, I shut the door and looked around the cold and smoky bar room. The ceiling was falling in, the walls were cracked, and the floor was littered with broken glass and spilled alcohol. I smelled smoke and burnt ashes as I stepped inside; I could barely see in the dim lamplight. "Julia," I groaned, not able to shout. No answer. I worried as my head spun; I could not focus on one particular thing for more than a few moments. "Julia," I moaned again. I heard *nothing*. I began to panic as I collapsed onto a bar stool and laid my head down on the dusty counter. Julia was gone again, and I had no strength left to find her. Perhaps I had to join her father in death in order to truly set her free, and I was content with the idea of my fate. My work was done, my wrongs had been avenged, and my mind was nothing but a haze.

I drifted in and out of consciousness as I heard a scraping noise beside me. I dismissed it at first, brushing it off either because I was far too exhausted to raise my head up or I was far too determined to die to care what the undertaker looked like. "Um - I know the business hours used to be around the clock, so I guess that still stands after there's no one around to run it," the man said. I grunted in response, not hearing in full. I closed my eyes once more, but I stirred awake in realization and recognition of the voice. I had heard that voice many times before. It was a voice I had respected, I had known, but it was *gone*. That voice had been shattered, snuffed out, and *crushed*. I pushed myself up off of the bar counter and looked over at Sebastian sitting beside me. I was either hallucinating or he had escaped the avalanche somehow. *Somehow.*

"Are you here to take me?" my voice shook. "You're a ghost." He laughed slightly and walked over to me, patting my shoulder. "I am very much alive, my boy. I - I can't say the same for you. You are in fact… white as a *ghost*. Red as a river too, my boy. You're dripping blood all over this chapel floor. What in the blazes happened to you?" he wondered out loud. I had no strength to answer, although he would have been satisfied as I was. "Let me see what I can do," he said. My vision blurred as he rolled up his sleeves and lifted me up onto the bar counter. For a relatively smaller-built man, he surely carried a bit of strength with his trades. He tore my pants leg in half and revealed my ghastly wound. I began to sweat as I went into shock, though Sebastian remained calm. He was unbothered about his soiled clothes as he reached behind the counter and returned with a bottle of a clear liquid. He poured it over the gnarly and mangled cut, spilling bloody pools across the bar floor. The searing pain was so incredibly intense, but I could not utter a sound. I fell unconscious as sweat beaded across my brow, blood dripped from my leg, and the shadow of a ghost went to work on me.

I awoke some time later unknown to me. Sometimes sleep can be a dose of heaven or a shot of hell. This was *neither*. This was a colorless, dreamless sleep. I imagine it was as close to death as you could get while still breathing - timeless, figureless, and without form or any sort of entity. I awoke some time later, unaware of where I was. I sat up quickly - *too* quickly. I soon got dizzy and hit the counter hard once more.

"Easy there, my boy," I heard Sebastian say. He looked over at me from a bar stool across the room. "Sebastian," I said. "At your service, sir," he replied. "How did you get out?" I asked. It was the only thing I knew how to ask, for it had been burning in the back of my mind the entire time I had been unconscious. Sebastian put down his newspaper and walked over to the makeshift operating table. He had cleaned my leg, cauterized the bleeding, and stitched the skin back together along with my pants leg with neat and simple stitching. The style of a *perfectionist* - just as Sebastian would have it. The *only* way he would have it. I felt the subtle but sharp pain as I sat up slowly as he had instructed. His clothes were spotted with blood and sweat as he reached into his coat pocket and pulled out a slip of paper. He handed it to me and sat down next to me as I leaned against the back of a chair for support.

"I never told you how I met Jack, or your father, for that matter," he began. I thumbed over the photo he had handed to me. I saw a younger trio of uniformed soldiers posed against a destroyed and smoking building. A stranger riddled with curious questions stood to the left, Jack King in the middle, and yes, a smaller and hardly recognizable Sebastian to the very right. "We all met in a military base over in Turkey about five years before all of this," he continued. "I was a medic in our squadron, your father was an infantryman, and Jack was of course Commander. We were carrying out a mission in Bangkok with our sniper, Vulture, and our ground scout, Pigeon. We were a Special Ops unit tasked with securing and stealing valuable items of international interest. We found what we came for and secured it. Vulture was spotted and taken out by an enemy gunman, and Pigeon triggered an IED on the front lines. Jack led us all to safety. By the time I got to our boys, there was nothing I could do. It was just the three of us. Your father and Jack got us out of there. I never forgot about that, the fact that I couldn't save our own men. Jack always told me that it wasn't my fault, that it was his for leading us into such a hot area. He claimed he lost the item in the blast, but I believe he kept it. Hidden in a safe up in the mansion. He would always talk about its power and what it could do if we could harness it. He believes it created the Dreamers. That's why he led us where he did. We lost men for that piece. I believe that's what brought about the end of world and the creation of the Dreamers. Opened a goddamn window between reality and dreams. If what I believe is true, he'll go to no ends to get it back. He believed your father stole it and had him killed. I think he went after the Dreamers to keep the power contained until he could find the item again. Whatever it is, let you find it before he does. Let it fall in the right hands this time. Jack and your father saved my life, and now I save yours, my boy, for I am capable. I am eternally sorry I could not save him, but his spirit lives on in you. I cannot forget, and I cannot be forgiven. I thank you, my boy, for setting my conscience free. I am not longer guilted by the past, for you have lived. And if I may say, there is a lot of your father in you. You are a survivor, Noah." He wiped tears from his eyes as I flipped over the picture in my fingers. In tiny handwriting, it read: *"Courtesy of the eagle, the hawk, and the sparrow.*" He had not answered my question, but then again, perhaps he had. He was a survivor too.

"I wanted to be the last one to relay this to you, Noah, but the time has come. I have grown so fond of you and I care for you as a godson. As a matter of fact, I am your godfather," he began in a troubled and bothered shake of a voice. "What do you mean?" I wondered out loud. "Who you know as your father is in fact your stepfather," he added, pointing to the image of him in the photograph below. "This man," he pointed, "is your father. Scarlett Willoughby. You're the spitting image of him." I heard Sebastian no longer. I was lost in wonder and thought, sadness and frustration. Anger and angst. Jacob was telling the truth. I was no wanted son. I had seen the man in the picture before. Somewhere. I could not place him, but I had seen him before. But where, goddamnit? "What happened?" I spat in half anger and half curiosity.

"Your father was a Dreamer, as you are. As Julia is. Jack, your stepfather, and myself were not. Jack took notice of this and slaughtered him in private. I studied complex mental engineering in the Army and I had blueprints written up for a certain serum - a particular medication that could erase mental anguish such as abuse and PTSD. Essentially, the creation would switch the sides of the brain and restart the mental processors. Therefore, Jack stole my notes and produced the liquid on a mass scale. With your father dead, he administered the serum to your stepfather and myself, putting him in your father's place and myself as his eternal servant. An endless *slave.* Upon the construction of this city, it became the foundation of this place. To *forget.* To *restart.* To *rebuild.* To *block out.* And I was the proctor of evil." His head hit his hands as tears streamed down his face in blame. In fact, he was the only one who had done right by me in truth.

"You're quite an incredible man, Sebastian," I had to tell him. "What else can you do?" I asked. "I can fly an airplane and drive a boat, save you from choking to death, and oh, I can also marry two consenting individuals in case they still find a god to answer to," he smiled. "I'm a *jackass* of all trades." I tucked this bit of information in the back of my mind. I shook the man's hand and clapped him on the back as he reshuffled the cards. "Will you marry Julia and I one day, Sebastian?" I asked him quietly. "Why of course, my boy," he smiled.

"Thank you, Sebastian. For everything. And I'm sorry about your clothes." He raised his hand in appreciation as we both wiped our tears and sat up. "Well, I wasn't alone…" I raised an eyebrow in his direction. "I had ample help," he grinned. Julia stepped out from the room in the back with a cool rag she wiped my forehead with. I hugged her quickly and suddenly, perhaps catching us both off guard. "Oh, okay," she laughed. There was no trace of me in her mind. I lay back against the counter in disgrace and disgust as I thought of the eagle that I had plucked from the sky, the hawk I had been running from, and the sparrow before me. Sebastian knelt down and whispered in my ear. "I've been talking to her about things - filling her in on what is going on and who you are. Who *we* are. I believe she will come around. There's a look in her eye every once in a while. Try not to give up hope so easy, my boy." I smiled at his reassuring and uplifting words, appreciating the fire he had started in my heart once more - one I had thought to have been eternally extinguished.

"The sun is going down," Julia said as she peeked through the blinds in the corner. I could not help but remember us watching the sunset from the Perch rooftop and her bedroom window before falling asleep. Those times were dead and gone along with the city, and the sun was going down for the last time as long as I was concerned or cared about. "We'll be safe here," Sebastian said. "Apart from that vault under the mansion, this is one of the safest places in the city." I pondered that. "How's that?" I asked. "It's cozy," he said. "Guns and blazes can destroy a house, but it can't touch a home. It can't destroy family. And even though times are tough, we can hold up here. There's food in the back, enough for a week or more, and we're in good company. I already made pallets to sleep on across the room, and I've got a deck of cards ready to put a whooping on both of your asses. Noah needs time to rest, and he's in the care of a decorated medic and a beautiful young woman, if I do say so myself." He winked in my direction. "It's like an apocalyptic hotel, compete with a full bar, night club, and hospital wing." Julia paced the floor, checking the windows. "Are we hiding from someone?" she wondered out loud. "I haven't seen any people since Noah found me. As far as we're concerned, we're the last ones left in this city. The city is ours." She thought for a moment, a look of fear in her eyes. I wanted to comfort her, for I knew exactly what was on her mind - what she was terrified of. *Who* she was looking for. But I was a stranger. And I would watch over her like an *eagle*.

As the night drew to a close, the three of us drew into our makeshift beds - some of us easier and less painfully than others. Sebastian elevated my leg to keep the blood flowing and the stitches tight, and soon he was fast asleep. Perhaps he was more exhausted than I was. I was grateful for him, even if I was not entirely convinced that he was *real* yet. I *knew* Julia was real; I had known that since the beginning. I was the last one to fall asleep that night by far - Sebastian was fast asleep and snoring after a few minutes of rest and Julia drifted off after him. But not I; I lay there for hours, staring at Julia as she slept across the room, the covers pulled up to her neck. I wanted so desperately to wrap my arms around her and tell her it was all going to be alright, but those days had passed. As far as she was concerned, they had never even happened in the first place. I fell asleep in tears as she had, and in just as much pain if not more so.

I slept long after the others the following morning, perhaps even half the day. The hazy sunshine shone through the few cracks in the blinds, giving the room a comfortable daylight feel to it. I rolled over and hoisted myself up with the help of

Sebastian and Julia. They had pulled several boxes of cereal and dry foods for breakfast that morning, and I washed it down with warm water, as unpleasant and unquenching as it was. Sebastian told me I needed to keep my strength up as he guided me through minor physical therapy each morning, beginning with leg lifts to walking on both legs slowly but surely. *One leg at a time*, I suppose.

The old bartender's name was Mike Hardy, a crotchety, grumpy old man whose wife had died in the early stages of the city. Jack King had given him *Stanley's* as a gift which came with a room and bathroom above the actual bar. The stairs were cracked and squeaky as all get out, but the remainder of the second floor was relatively clean and in good manner. There was still running water in the shower, and we made ourselves at home with Mike's belongings. Sebastian told me he had been caught in the crossfire whenever the killings had first started, but that conversation did not last long. He just sifted through the old man's newspapers and fumbled through a new one every morning over dry corn flakes. Mike had left about a dozen T-shirts and pairs of pants in the upstairs drawers, both of which Sebastian and I helped ourselves to. Mrs. Hardy had a drawer of her own just for Julia, and in her opinion, the old woman had great taste. It brought about a blissful morale to feel fresh and clean once again - no matter how much blood and despair stained the human soul.

I took every opportunity I could to talk and get close to Julia, as expected. I waited for her to get up each morning, to come down the stairs from the shower, and to go to sleep each night. We carried on light conversations at first, which blossomed into deep, infatuating talks which lasted long into the midnight hours. I soon began to fall in love with her all over again. It is quite funny because I had never fallen *out*, only *away*. We had nothing but time to grow closer and let her know me once again, and I was grateful for that. It was worth the pain, both physical and emotional.

"You know, you never told me what happened to your leg," she said to me one morning after I finished my exercises. My heart stopped as I knew I could not tell her the truth. Although she did not remember a thing about her father except how he had locked her away, I could not tell her he had died by my hands. She would never forgive me. I was *not* the monster. "When we were getting off the mountain, I cut it on the sharp metal as the air duct split. We were in such a rush, the adrenaline got us here. If not for you and Sebastian, I would be dead. Thank you for what you did," I said, shifting the focus to her for multiple reasons. She nodded shyly as she always did and smiled slightly. She knew I was lying; I could see it in her eyes. I *knew* those eyes. I wondered if Sebastian knew as well, for I had not told him either. It was my own little secret. I was *not* the monster. "Where did you go when you brought me here?" she followed. "I went back for Sebastian," I said without a thought. But it had not even crossed my mind at the time. I had abandoned a man - a *brother* - who had helped me so much. Someone who would have done it for me without a second thought. I had put Julia in danger once again. Perhaps I *was* a monster, if not a miserable lying devil to say the least.

Sebastian was *surely* a devil at poker - he was simply the greatest card man I had ever come across. If we had been putting bets on the table, I would surely lose everything I owned and the stitches too. He would have the cards set up each morning after breakfast and drink instant coffee as he won one hand after another. Julia would eventually quit out of frustration, leaving Sebastian and I to hash it out until he pinned me down for the last time. "How did you get so good at poker, Sebastian?" I asked him one time. "Well, you see, my boy, when the world ended, I had nothing better to do." We all shared a clouded laugh as we all grew comfortable in our little house. I had thought at one time that long after the city's days were over, Julia and I would live together in our own city somewhere across the vast planet, with

Sebastian as a friend and butler. But those days had passed away quickly, and they were no more.

"What do we do now?" I whispered to Sebastian. "Where do we go from here?" Sebastian thought for a moment. "If what you say is true, then war is imminent," he finally said, careful to avoid Julia's keen ear. "Jack will rally his men and his artillery and search the city high and low for us. It's only a matter of time before this place isn't safe anymore. We are going to have to fight." He nervously stacked the cards in rows of three, stacks of ten, and hid two cards behind each of his ears. Julia walked over and sat down next to us once more. "The war is already here. My father has easily a hundred men behind him, and we have the three of us. We're all gonna die." Sebastian laughed. "I certainly miss your more *positive* attitude," he chuckled. I smiled too at her look of confusion. "I wish I knew what all of this is about," Julia sighed, turning away from us and facing the wall.

I reasoned that it was as appropriate of a time as any to lay all of the cards on the table, so to speak. "Your father wiped your mind with the serum Sebastian created, intended for the Dreamers. Your father didn't know you were a Dreamer until after he thought he had killed me that day at the gathering. You see, when you die in this life, you end up in the dream world, which is ruled by your grandfather. A crazy, evil old crock just like your father. I've been there. When you end up in that place, you have to find your 'twin' - the person who shares your dreams, the same unconscious path. You're connected with them. You have to kill them, take their ability to dream, and that's how you get back to the real world. That's how you get back here. In case you were ever worried about your mortality chances. And if you want to blame someone for your loss of memory, blame your father for stealing Sebastian's serum in the first place. It all lands in your father's lap. He built this city to rid the world of people like *his* father. That's what all of this is about. And as for your father, he's already dead. I killed him. That's where I went. There is no more fighting here." I got up and stormed up the stairs. I stopped at the banister as I heard the two of them continue talking. "Why did you make that poison?" Julia asked, tears in her eyes. Sebastian paused. "I was going to use it on myself. To forget the things I had to do." Julia spoke once more. "Why does he care so much about how I feel?" she cried. "You were his goddamn girlfriend," Sebastian muttered. I slammed the door. There was only silence that followed.

I must have collapsed on the bed and fallen asleep soon after because that was where I awoke as the sun sunk below the surface of the earth that evening. I wiped the sleep and frustration from my eyes as my feet hit the floor. I went downstairs as Sebastian fiddled with metal parts on the bar counter and Julia was nose-deep in a book across the room. I poured myself a glass of ginger ale and sat down on a stool, away from my friends - the only people I had left in the world. I sipped the drink until the glass was empty and slid it off of the counter, listening as it smashed against the hard floor. I heard Julia close her book and walk over to me, taking the seat beside me. "You know, I knew my father better than anybody. Before I lost my memory, of course. But I never met my grandfather. That serum couldn't affect that." I stared at her blankly. "What do you want from me?" I asked her flatly. "Tell me about him," she said softly. I sighed and turned around to face her.

"He runs the place like a goddamn king. The entire city is made of emerald. He has this entire building as a safe house. It's like a penthouse crossed with a fucking apartment crossed with a training facility. He knows anything and everything about the real world and the dream world. I want to say that he has the home-court advantage, but he has every fucking advantage." She turned to look at me once more, almost frustrated. "Tell me about *him*, not *what* he is, *who* he is." I thought deeply. "He is so much like your father. At first I placed them as polar opposites, but toward the end, they were mirror images of each other. I understand the conflict based on the dreams, but I never understood how two people so alike could have so much hatred for each other. Your father told me how abusive he was toward him whenever he was a kid, and I didn't believe it at first, but I saw it firsthand. There's a good reason why your father was the way he was, and I'm sorry for what I had to do. The city was nothing but a dream itself, even though your father could never hope to be a Dreamer. I believe that your grandfather hated your father because he couldn't be a Dreamer, but I also believe that your father hated your grandfather because he could never live up to his standards. That's what all of this is about. The cities, the dreams, you and I. All this is is a dream. All it ever will be is a dream. And I'm perfectly content with that. Even if I never get to wake up. All anything is is someone else's dream. Read it how you want to. This city was a prison designed by your father. To keep your grandfather and everyone like him out. We both know it has to end. So the ones like us can be free. As for your grandfather, you didn't miss anything. As a matter of fact, you were saved a shitload of trouble. If I had to guess, your childhood would've been a lot worse than what it was if you had to pick a side. That's what it's all about. The freedom to pick a side instead of it being chosen for you. I also take it upon myself to tell you this - please don't remember your father after the serum. If there's any hope for you to ever get your memory back, remember your father the way he was before. Before this city, back when your mother was alive, and back when everything was okay. And if you never get your memory back, and your grandfather ever finds his way here, we're going to have to fight. And it's going to be hard. And yes, we're going to die. But I would rather be dead any day than be held prisoner here. And I know damn well you know how that feels. Your grandfather is like a god, and there's next to nothing we can do with our numbers. He's going to take over this place. Over everything your father ever dreamed of, and everything mankind ever dreamed of. This is the end, and it's coming very soon, I would imagine. But I want you to know one more thing. It's been a fucking privilege knowing you. And besides having your memory taken away, I wouldn't change a goddamn thing."

I wiped tears from my eyes as I saw some of her own drip down her face. She grabbed my arm and spoke to me from the heart. "I don't blame you for what you had to do to my father. It's probably better that I don't remember much about him besides the bad. Same for my grandfather. Maybe I was just curious out of the void. But I don't blame you. I don't think of you any differently. If I was in your shoes with a full memory, I probably would've done the same thing."

She stood up as I heard the door open and the bell ding. I smelled the cigar smoke and the impossibility before I could even register to breeze and the throat-clearing. "You got everything right except for one tiny detail. I *am* God, you ignorant little fuck." My feet hit the ground and I was off of the barstool before I could think. My fist connected with his face, but he transported and dissolved an inch backward. He grabbed my shirt collar and forced me up against the wall. I saw several throwing knives appear in his hands; Julia winced out of the corner of my eye. He bolted my shirt to the wall; I was not going anywhere. "Let's not get off on the wrong foot," he said, directed at both me as well as Julia and Sebastian.

Peter crept slowly toward me. He stopped at nose length, staring straight into my eyes. "I thought we had an agreement," he whispered. "I told you that Jack was mine. Did I not make that extremely fucking clear? You see, my boy, your generation has a hard fucking time following fucking directions. And that is a problem that is going to surely change. You know who you remind me of? Felicia Noy. I'll be completely honest. That's the first time I ever heard of someone banging their twin. Must have something to do with the whole 'same dream' thing. What do you think?" I gathered up a glob of spit and put it in his one good eye.

"You fucking killed her." Peter looked at me for a moment. "I knew you would never be able to do it. Don't make me out to be the monster. You and I both know who the monster is. Or *was*, thanks to you. You might think that the outcome was the same, but that's not the case. You see, being the one to kill my son would have held a lot of sentimental value to me. And you went and ruined that. So I'm going to be the one to ruin you. And everything you want. That's what you get for crossing me."

Julia and Sebastian had not heard Peter whispering to me. He then turned to face the other two in the room. "I am Peter King, Jack's father. I'm assuming Noah has told you all about me - some truth, some a little twisted." He looked at Julia. "I'm your grandfather. I haven't seen you since you were a little baby. I know you don't know me, but that's about to change. I'm deeply sorry I didn't get the privilege to watch you grow up like a normal grandfather. But I assure you, along my side, I can make up for that." Julia looked down at the ground. He then reached out to shake Sebastian's hand. "I've heard a lot about you, my good sir. Noah speaks of you as an honorable man. I like honorable men on my side. I'm not entirely sure if you are one of us, but I'm sure we can find a place for you." He put all of us in his sight. "I would like for all of you to fight for me and take back this world and restore it to what it was meant to be. A land free of dictation, a land free of guideline, a land free of people like my son - people that want to control what they have no business being a part of or in existence in the presence of. You will fight for me. Or you will surely die."

My anger had reached its climax. The knives holding me in place loosened and zipped into the back wall behind the bar counter, smashing several bottles of liquor. My gun slid into my hand, threatening the old man as he backed up. "Put it away, Noah. You know good and damn well you can't kill me. Why would you want to, anyhow? Look what I've done for you. I've literally turned your world upside down. I trained you to be something you never thought you could be. I'm not asking for appreciation. I'm asking for your understanding. I'm asking for your help. I'm asking for your choice. Unlike my son, I don't plan to make it for you. I only see specialty in you. I never saw that in Jack." Peter then took the form of my father. His face and clothes shifted to match that of my father. His voice matched my father's. An image of my father then stood before me, looking me straight in my eyes. Who I *knew* to be my father. "You have been a son to me, Noah. You gave me what Jack could never provide. An *apprentice*. What did Jack ever do for you? He killed your parents and locked my granddaughter in a prison cell. There are no other feasible options for you. You see, I'm not making the decision for you. I'm simply providing you with no other way out. This is the *only* way. The only way you can earn back what you want. The only way you keep what little family you have left. You already know I can restore her memories, don't you, my boy? I can give you everything. Or I can take it all from you. What do you say?"

"Go to hell," I spat at him once more. "You've lost your mind, kid. Look at you. You're a mess, Noah. This war has confused you beyond belief. You can't tell reality from dreams anymore. You've lost your marbles." He then pointed to Julia and Sebastian. Turning back to look at me, he spoke once more. "You will all fight for me. One way or another." With that, the old man pulled his coat tight, looked out the window, and shivered with a shockwave, splitting into a million particles. Peter was gone as quickly as he had come, as empty as his threats. However, his promises were quite full. All of the glass panes and liquor bottles had smashed with his exit, and the three of us stood amidst the shattered room we had called home for weeks.

Together, we swept glass and boarded up every opening that had been left vacant by Peter King. No one spoke as we cleaned up the mess; the air was dead silent and cold as the winter wind swept through the then-penetrated bar room. It was only a matter of time before Peter came back; I knew that. We could not stay in that place much longer. "We have to leave this place," I muttered as we dumped the rest of the glass in the back trash can. "Where will we go?" Sebastian questioned. "I don't know of any place that isn't ransacked; all I know is that this place is no longer safe," I stated. Julia raised the last board to nail it in place, but Sebastian stopped her and motioned me over. "Look at this, my boy. There are soldiers on every street, ready to carry out Jack's command from the grave. They'll kill anyone in their path on sight. I've seen it happen. Everyone left in this place is either dead or laying low as we have done for the past weeks' time. That's the only reason we're still here. Staying quiet, falling in line, and nobody gets hurt." Julia pushed us aside and nailed the final board in place. "We've all already been hurt," she said. She looked away in pain as I followed her.

"Sometimes the memories come back to me at night. I can remember the beginning of this war. You weren't here for it, Noah. We all thought you were dead. The Dreamers rose up and began to take on my father's men. He found out about me about a month after you were gone. After you were carried to the mansion, I couldn't take it anymore. Me and Sebastian were going to run away one night and hide out on the outskirts of the city, but he caught us and trashed his lab. He found the serum and locked Sebastian and I up down below. He began using it on the captured Dreamers and holding them prisoner in the mansion. I - I can't remember anything more." I had stopped listening long before she stopped talking. I knew this. I also knew that there was hope for her memories to slowly return without having to strike a deal with Peter. I put my hands in my pockets and looked at her intently. "This war started long before I was shot."

When the explosion from the grenade took the life of Jack King, it took with it the top three floors of the Perch building as well. The surrounding city block was covered with rubble and settling dust for at least three days before any of his men would even touch the scene. Groups of soldiers came through and rummaged through the cracked brick and piled wreckage. We watched from the shadows as they pulled his limp and lifeless body from under the heavy rooftop that had been reduced to ashes, just as he had been.

Following the disaster, the once empty streets became patrolled by armed officers hour-by-hour. They knew they were the only ones with enough power to cause something of that magnitude, and perhaps they were searching for us the entire time. But we were right under their noses. Along with the destruction of the mansion on the hilltop and without the guidance of their leader, Jack King's men felt truly threatened for the first time since the beginning of the city.

Stanley's was tucked into a lower-traffic area of Main Street - you had to know it was there and look for it to know it was on the radar. With the windows and doors boarded up, it blended in perfectly with the dilapidated aura of the entire city, and so it was overlooked by the passing soldiers each and every time. Julia spent every night reading a book under a flashlight in the corner before falling asleep on the pallet next to me long into the morning. The beam from the flashlight was the only source of light we had during the night. Its rays spread far throughout the tiny bar room, poured into the city streets, and into the watching eyes that threatened to snuff us out like a candle.

Tensions in our little house rose higher and higher after Peter's visit. The fact that he was in the city somewhere unknown terrified me beyond words. Knowing that we were being watched was eerie enough, and the threats and promises of Peter King stayed fresh on my mind. Sebastian was a nervous wreck, always peeking between the wooden boards and looking over his shoulder. Julia kept to her books when she was not prying me for details about her father. The death had not seemed to affect her the way it would have with her memories, but as she found out more about him, a look of melancholy settled onto her lips.

Details brought about conversations about Peter as well, and as much as I would have liked to make it up as I went, I was forced to tell her the stone cold truth. I would love to tell her that I had fished and hunted with her grandfather and talked over coffee on the front porch of his farm house, but that simply was not the case. Her father and grandfather were evil men who hated each other so deeply that it had torn them from her forever, and that could never be restored or covered up by blatant lies.

I told Julia about how I had met her, all about her gardens and the fancy invitations and the Perch building. I told her about the color of the sky and the depth of our conversations on that rooftop - the same rooftop I had killed her father on. I told her about the walks we used to take around the city back when times were hardly simple and we had a place to call home. I told her about the people we would follow and the strange happenings which always ended brutal and bloody on the city streets. After all, that is when the war had really, *truly* started. I relived it as I fought my own in that moment.

As Julia got closer to me and learned of how things used to be, it seemed more and more like the new and old Julia were two different people. And it *frustrated* me within my own selfish desires. I was trying the absolute best I could to earn her trust and trigger even the slightest tremor of a memory inside her, but to no avail. I began to resent even telling her the stories of *my* Julia, and I kept to myself during the final days of our stay in that bar room. She became the one who watched me sleep as I curled up in the corner out of her sight and slept a dreamless sleep. We had switched places in our stay in that cozy little mansion of our own on the street corner, yet we were just as far apart as we were in the beginning.

I knew not the date nor the time in that place any longer; the pleasure of knowing those things had been whisked away as the winter washed into every crevice of the dead carcass of the city. Each day grew colder as we struggled to stay warm in the empty bar room. We knew we would have to move sooner or later, yet not one of us could accept that as we pushed it off a day and another day later. The days were spent burning odds and ends of the old couple's belongings as we spread blankets around the floor to bury ourselves in. The nights were sleepless and frigid as I huddled close to Julia, though there was no affection in return. I would end up giving her all of my blankets as they slept, lying awake in the ice-cold corner. The fire could only burn for so long, and I felt my own flame begin to die out. We would not make it through the winter, whether our fate be fulfilled by the element or the men who would stumble upon our stronghold sooner or later. I lay awake, keeping steady watch as a winter of another kind inched its way into my mind. It was in a bird's nature to migrate, and for us, it was far too late.

They came in the dead of night - the demons we had been running and hiding from. I saw no indication of their forthcoming; we were taken by surprise, ambushed against the frozen corner we had allowed ourselves to become imprisoned in. *The lion roars from a mile away while the vulture circles overhead; the serpent strikes violently as the cold turns to numb, empty death.* My eyes had been void of sleep for well over a few days, yet I felt no fatigue. I only felt the stiff coldness of the December air through the frigid nightfall in the bar room. Julia lay bundled up in at least three blankets and Sebastian huddled under several coats, none of which were fully intact. I sat in the corner in not nearly enough warmth to suffice the night's brutally decrepit temperature. Our fire had long burned out, quenched by icy crystals and the thin lingering of smoke on our breath and blankets. We had simply run out of books and old newspapers to burn, and I imagined that burning the wooden rafters would have given away our little hole in the wall far too soon, making that option severely obsolete. But the building was already in flames of another origin, and the drifters would come to warm their hands on our lifeline sooner than any of us could have *ever* dreamed of.

I had long since grown used to the sound of my own teeth chattering away into the night, and I mistook the rumbling for another shiver at first thought. Then it seemed to grow *closer*. I could feel the rattling in my hands and my legs as I stood up in wonder of what was the matter. The noise had not yet woken the others, and I intended to preserve that simple pleasure. I needed not disturb my family if not absolutely necessary. I stood up painfully as I worked through the sore stiffness in my joints and hobbled over to the boarded window. Peeking through the thin crack above, I felt the wood vibrate against the numbness in my face. *What could it be? An earthquake? Yes, after all this time, we would die of natural causes.* As much as I would have loved being shaken to a frozen and empty death, that was simply not the end nor the beginning of the violent rumbling out in the city.

Whatever it was, it continued for seemingly hours as dawn broke across the pitch black sky. I knew morning would bring warmth to the bar room - no matter how little - and that in turn gave me hope. I could see more and more of the broken city streets as the sun peeked over the cracked skyscrapers and collapsed buildings of the town square. Yet the noise continued like a *buzzing* - a swarm of bees on their way to sting themselves to their own deaths. I knew in that moment that we get to choose our own demise, whether it be survival or suicide, and I chose neither. I chose to find the source of the everlast vibration and crush it like an insect and take control once again.

I saw shadows round the street corner several blocks away - massive, *metal* shadows. The infantry turned the corner slowly. I counted a dozen tanks, ten heavily-armored Hummers escorted by three tinted Escalades like the one wrecked on the city streets outside, followed by fifty armed machine gunners marching behind the convoy. I turned my view to the rooftops and counted at least twenty snipers at the ready. "Jesus fucking Christ," I mumbled. We were surrounded and more than outrageously outgunned. The war parade came to a halt in the middle of Main

Street, and the rumbling soon followed. I looked behind me nervously; Julia and Sebastian tossed and turned as they began to feel the violent shaking. I kept a close and careful eye on the militia outside as they gathered outside their vehicles. I watched a few of the men rummage in the back of the Escalades and pull out long and narrow strips of metal with an arrowhead attachment on the end. "God - fuck," I stuttered. *Grenade launchers.*

I could not see the man's face as he stood up on top of the first tank, but I could hear what he shouted across the town square. "Come out, come out, wherever you are!" The voice was raspy and commanding. I recognized it, though I was preoccupied sweating and swearing at what *could* happen in mere seconds. The man waved a signal at the row of armed soldiers, each facing a different direction. "I love a good game of roulette," he laughed coldly through the cracked and frozen wood. "Fire!" he shouted. I counted five men armed with RPGs as they each pulled the trigger. The first exploded inside the town hall, one of the oldest buildings in the city. The second hit the street corner adjacent to the bar room, blowing away stop signs and cracking the pavement even further. The third diminished several shops to the left of our little house in the middle of the city, shaking the floors and sending whiskey bottles to the floor. The fourth shattered the top floor of the bar room, shaking Julia awake as Sebastian snored away behind the counter. The fifth came through the door of the corner pub and everything went black.

Chapter XX
This Little Wolf of Mine
(The Burial, the Resurrection, and the Third Day)

I remember blurry vision and extreme disorientation. I remember doors being kicked in, shouting and yelling by armed guards. I remember being kicked in the ribs and dragged across broken glass out the door and onto the city street. I remember mumbling Julia's name as she was jerked to her knees and thrown beside me in front of the line of tanks and vehicles. I remember going unconscious once more, not knowing if it was my time to go or merely another brief stay in another life. No, I would not leave without Julia. I simply could not. Not that time.

I heard the voice before I heard the words. I felt the gun in the back of my head before I felt the hot pavement under my knees. I saw Julia's tears before I saw the man's lips speaking. "It is Judgement Day indeed," he said. "In more ways than one. For starters, you're standing before your maker. That's always an anxious feeling. And secondly, I have to choose which part of my job I want to perform today. Judge, jury, or executioner. Hook, line, or sinker. I guess that's up to you. In my head the choice is obvious, more Dreamers, which the truth is inevitable. You've all gotta go. It's been an established virtue in this city for a long time."

The blindfold was torn from my eyes and I looked around. The man speaking was nowhere to be seen. Julia and Sebastian sat on either side of me, tied and bound just as I was. We were surrounded by the small militia of machine gunners, three of which were pressed against the backs of our heads. I knew the voice but it was that of a ghost, a demon that no longer possessed that world. It was nowhere to be found, and I thought it to be in my head. It *fueled* me, and I feared death no longer.

"You're a fucking pussy," I spat as I stared down at the cracked city street tearing into my skin. "Show yourself. Look us in the eye before you have someone *else* pull the trigger." I heard the cold laugh before I heard the footsteps. "You see, I've been forced to believe in a half-blind jury, those which surround you. So plead your case, I understand my men are a fair-minded group of gentlemen. I've been the executioner for far too long; I can't watch it any longer. That decision was made for me." I scoffed. "Coward."

The weight of the boots was heavy and wounded. I saw the dusty soles as my face was pushed into the gravel underneath. The black pants were free of holes and the belt buckle shone like the clouded sun above. The leather coat was slick and pressed, and the white shirt underneath was clean and free of blood stains. His beard was shaved bare, and his smile was cracked and hidden behind a dominating smirk. His face was split in half by a nasty scar cut down the right nostril that ran up onto his forehead. The left side of his face was sandy and scarred, the right left untouched. He wore a pair of sunglasses at first until he hung them in his coat pocket. I could see his damaged face as I looked him in his one good eye for the first time as I did his father some time ago. I was taken aback at the appearance and existence of Jack King before my very equipped pair of eyes. My mind was questionable and questioning the reality of it all. I was correct, the voice was *very* familiar, and for the first time in a very long time, I was *scared*. I had no answers and nothing was real to me anymore. I knew I was looking at the executioner in that moment.

"I'll be goddamned," he said, his reaction matching mine word for word, thought for thought. "You just won't die, will you, kid?" he laughed. "I could say the same for you," I retorted, but he was not looking at me anymore. I traced his one-eyed stare to the girl sitting beside me. "You - you fucking lied to me," he spat at me. "After what you did to her, your daughter is dead. She doesn't remember anything I didn't tell her. My lie for your transgressions are no fucking match. So do what you came to do, Jack. We've both lost her, and I'm ready to die. I just hope you are too," I said through gritted teeth.

Jack seemed to ignore me as he knelt down in front of Julia. "Cut her loose, goddamnit!" he shouted at the soldier behind her. She rolled her wrists as she breathed heavily, looking him in the eye. "It's me, honey. Do you remember me?" he asked hopefully. "I remember enough," she replied. "You're no father to me," she said, spitting in his distorted face. He stood up and wiped the line of saliva from his eye and thought for a moment.

"Go ahead, Jack, kill your daughter the way any Dreamer deserves. Do it. Face what you fear the most in who you love the most. You can't do it," I threw at him. He pulled a gun from his belt and put it to my temple. I was surrounded on two sides by weapons of one kind and on the other two by a much different kind. I laughed, the fear draining from my body. "I would give it a second look, Jack," I taunted him. I felt the barrel of the machine gun in the back of my head release and bend backward to face the terrified soldier in the face. "Do it, Jack," I continued. "End the Dreamer race as well as the rest of your family," I laughed. "I guess cowardice runs in your bloodline. She hated you. Just as your father hated you. Kill your daughter like you killed your father, like you did your wife, and like you did to your precious city. Do it, Jack. This should be familiar to you." I spoke the words as the weapons filled the air, lines of barrels and sights aimed at Jack this time. My mind left my body as I felt my spirit possess the city street below and fill out the broken buildings around us. I heard the echo as I spoke. "I'm the executioner today," I said. I rose to my feet as the array of flying weaponry clattered to the ground around us. I then held Jack's gun and pointed it at his head this time. "This is the end of an *explosive* bloodline, Jack." I was God in that moment, and I felt the power of the city within me. This was the end.

"I wouldn't advise breaking a deal with me," I heard another voice behind me. I turned around as I saw the icy crystals materialize into the solid shapes of a grey suit and a silver ponytail. The eyepatch was freshly strapped and clean across the old man's face. The two men were one in both features and presence. "I told you he was mine," he reminded me. "I would think twice about pulling that trigger, no matter how satisfying it might be. You do that, and your troubles only *begin*. Don't let me influence your decision. You remember what happened when someone you loved crossed me."

I lowered the gun and stepped back as the two men stood face-to-face in what I made out to be at least fifteen years. "Father," Jack muttered in disbelief. "This is impossible." Peter laughed. "It's very possible, son," he replied. "You knew that all those years ago, you knew that when you built this place, and you know that now. I never left you, son." Jack stepped closer to his father. "You're right. You've haunted me for two decades. Every move I make, you're there. Every person I cross is you." Peter widened his arms like wings. "Kind of a twisted guardian angel?" he asked mimically. Jack kept a straight, hard face - or *half* of one, if you will. "Why did you come here, father?" he asked. "I missed my son," he shot. "Wanted a chance to meet my granddaughter for the first time." I knew he was lying; I knew the truth. Jack's face relaxed as his ears opened. "Bullshit," he spat. "What?" Peter argued sarcastically. "A dead grandfather can't come back to see his family every couple of years?Collect his missed Father's Day gifts? Make sure his son doesn't wreck the whole goddamn world?" He laughed and put his hands down. "Okay, you're right, I didn't come here for a family reunion. I came here to put you in check." Jack tensed up. "You came here to kill me." Peter chuckled in awe of his son. "I didn't say that," Peter fought. "You came here to take over this place. To take over me. Like you tried to do when I was a child," Jack said with weakness. It was rare to see. Peter said nothing, but I knew the *truth*.

"I will be no slave to you," Jack spat at his father, the way Jacob often spat at ours. The way Lucious spoke to Felicia. To way Jack spoke to me. Peter simply laughed. "Speaking of the help, I think yours has chosen a different path." He pointed to Sebastian, distracting Jack. "Why don't you ask how they found you? How they found the prisoners you were holding in that little house? How they knew to hide in the only blind spot in the city? What does your butler have to say for himself?" he asked. Sebastian swallowed hard and looked around at the beady eyes staring at him. Jack stepped down and looked him in the eye. "You betrayed me, Sebastian. You led them to me. You did this to me. You did this to my people. You're gonna pay for this." Sebastian hardened. "I'm not afraid of you, Jack. I serve a different master now." Jack laughed. "And who is that?" he chuckled. "Noah Willowby, the heir to the city," he smiled. Jack smiled too, but a far viler and nasty one. He pulled the gun from his holster and put a bullet straight through Sebastian's chin and into his brain. Blood and whiskers exploded as the world took on a ringing sound deep within my ears.

"NO!!!" I shouted through the silence. I felt the cold grip of my gun slide into my hand as I aimed it at Jack's head in the vast and rapid change of events. "OPEN FIRE!" Jack shouted to his men, and they obeyed. Fifty machine guns erupted with a spray of bullets toward Julia and I, Peter stepping behind us as they grew ever closer. I had taken a bullet to the skull before, and I welcomed it. I had lost yet another friend - a *brother*. I knew when Julia would go I would be forced to follow suit, and I was ready for it. I stared at the seventeenth soldier from the right who had his gun aimed directly at me as well as the three bullets that darted for the center of my forehead, and I urged them forward. I begged them to take me.

But it all went black like a blindfold from behind. I could not see a thing, but I could hear the sounds of shouting and guns firing as I felt my feet leave the ground. *Was this the executioner Jack had warned about?* It was surely a dark place. My stomach sunk as it would in an elevator and dove downward like I was on a rollercoaster of some kind, traveling through a pitch black cave. I searched so desperately for the light, and as my feet touched surface again, I found it. I felt gravel against my skin as I rolled across whatever surface I had found. The light blinded me as I opened my eyes once more, the sun climbing over the horizon. I climbed to my feet on the rooftop as I searched around for Julia. I rushed over to her as she lay several feet away from the railing across the way. I heard footsteps behind me and turned around frantically. "Have you changed your mind?" Peter asked as he strolled up to us. "This doesn't change anything," I said through gritted teeth. Peter backed up. "You two go your own way. I only want my son. But if you get in my way, you'll have to fight for yourselves. If you help me, she can come back with us. You can live with her forever. If you help me, I can give her back her memories." I collapsed onto the railing overlooking the city street below. "Do I have a choice?" I asked with exasperated tears in my eyes and throat, knowing the answer already. I had no choice. He knew I would have to help him. "I'm sorry about your friend," Peter offered. "It's hard to find good help these days," he joked. I glared at him. If he had made that remark only a sentence earlier, I would have thrown him off of the rooftop as I did his son only a short month before. "Good friends too," he said subtly and solemnly like a sad, old hound dog.

"Why do you need my help?" I looked up at him. "I need a distraction, of course," he replied matter-of-factly. "If you are who you pretend to be, then you don't need shit from us. What's the real reason you want us?" I pressed him. Peter seemed to think for a moment, pondering the question, possibly surprised at the doubt I had. "To tell you the truth, kid, I'm damn near fond of you. I enjoyed your stay with me. I'm sorry it had to end the way it did. It had to be done. You're the only people I plan to take back with me. I want you to *earn your keep. Your place at the table."* I stood up and walked over to him. "I don't need shit from you," I pushed my finger to his chest. "And you're gonna pay for what you did to her. And if Julia ever finds out about Felicia, I'll fucking kill you myself," I was then whispering through gritted teeth and frozen breath. Peter smiled once again. "It's not like she remembers anyway," he mumbled. I turned around and brought my fist across his nose. Blood trickled down his lips and onto the rooftop below. "You better deliver on your promise, or *mine* still stands," I said to him, looking into his eyes for the first time without respect.

"What kind of distraction?" Julia asked from behind. I had not seen her get to her feet and walk up behind me. Startled, I turned around and grabbed her shoulder; she shrugged away. "I need to get Jack alone," Peter started. "I need you guys to take out his guards. He's got about five of the real big ones close to him; they never leave his side. The other however many are just his footsoldiers. They keep watch on every corner, every street, every building on Main Street. All they are are *guns*," I looked at him. "How do you know this?" I asked. "Where do you think I've been all this time?" he laughed. "That's right," he continued. "I've got his shits planned before he takes them," he smiled. That grin ran in the family. I hope I never had to see Julia wear it. Peter took my shoulder and walked me over to the railing overlooking the city street below. "Look at them down there," he pointed. I could hear Jack shouting commands and his soldiers dispersing throughout the town square. "They're halfway gone already," Peter smiled. "Pigs for slaughter. Remember what they did to your family. Your friends. Your *home*." I could not see anything but Sebastian's lifeless body on the street below. "Do something for me and I'll return the favor," Peter said. "I'll get your friend out of the street down there. When this is all over, we'll have a proper burial for him."

"What do you have in mind?" Julia asked again. Peter thought again. "Find the uniforms his soldiers wear. Disguise yourselves as his own. Then turn on them from the inside." I looked at him cock-eyed. "Friendly fire?" I asked. "Aren't you a veteran?" Peter laughed. "The game has changed, my boy." My slight grin returned to a solemn grimace. "And what do you do in the meantime?" I asked him, curious to what he would be up to while we were doing his dirty work. "I'll got to find something," he said, his eyes drifting to the sky. "I'll watch over you two. Make sure nothing goes wrong." I did not ask what he was searching for; perhaps it was not important at the time. I looked at Julia and saw the look of distrust in her eyes and matched it. When I looked back, Peter King was gone.

Julia looked at me in confusion. "Where is he trying to take us?" she asked, almost scared. I thought of a way to say it. "It's a place...where you never age. Your wildest dreams are reality. It's the dream world. It's different for everyone, though they all coexist. That's where I ended up when your father shot me. Peter found me and took me in and trained me to use the Dreamer abilities. Then you have to find your 'twin', the person who has the same dream path as you do, and kill them. It upsets the balance or something and you end up back in the real world. It's like a second chance at life. There is no time in that place. It's horrifying and beautiful at the same time. Once Peter finds your father and kills him, there will be no more reality. Whatever he is looking for will bring destruction upon this world. I don't know what it is. I don't know where to go from here," I said, almost sorry I did not have the answers she was looking for.

"We find the uniforms," she said. "Do as he says. Maybe there is some truth to what he's saying." I nodded in agreement, still not trusting Peter in the slightest. Not after what he had done - after he had betrayed me and then turned around to shake my hand. *Fool me once, that's on you. Fool me twice, that's on me.* We leaned against the railing and crouched down to observe the city below. "MOVE OUT!" Jack shouted from a distance. The four dozen soldiers raised their rifles in one hand and flashlights in the other as they searched each building along the perimeter of the square. "Where would they be?" she asked, her memory still nothing but clouds and dark shadows. I pointed to what was once the tallest building in the city, the only building not being searched. "There," I said. "Getting the uniforms is easy. Getting there is the hard part."

I could not help but recall the first time Julia and I visited the Perch building together. Quite a happy time it was indeed, but that was a distant and faded memory that only one of us possessed, and its meaning had drained out of it like a hole in a barrel. Electricity had been a luxury lost some time ago, and the only light that entered the building was that of the rays of sun that penetrated through the shattered windows. Expended bullet casings littered the floor, and the entire weapons cache was damn near empty. Finding the uniforms would be like finding a single box in a crowded storage unit, and it was nearly the complete opposite.

We made our careful and cautious way down the ladder and stairs of the silent building from top to bottom. Peter had been cruel enough to put us on top of one of the tallest buildings in the city, but courteous enough for one of the most unoccupied. Although we checked around every corner, there was no sign of any resistance as we descended one flight of stairs after another. "Wait here," I said, holding my arm out in front of her. I poked my head around the corner and looked out into the city street. Beams of light shone around the morning shadows like ghosts. The nearest soldiers were four buildings to our northeast, out of sight and out of earshot. We waited quietly as they climbed over the rubble and searched the building, leaving the sidewalk and fading from view. I took Julia's arm and pulled her along, halfway rushing her and halfway protecting her as we darted across the street and into the doorway of the Perch building. The sidewalk was cracked heavily, a thin ravine tripping my stride. My shoe slipped off of my foot as I ran and pushed Julia inside and into the shadows once more. I pulled my other shoe off and tossed it out into the street in the opposite direction we were headed. As the evidence would tell and as far as anyone else was concerned, we had just left the Perch building.

We hurried inside as the freezing air in the dilapidated building rushed us along. I remembered how full the armory used to be, how the vehicles were lined up like a new car lot, and how many wooden crates and boxes full of weaponry of all kinds were stacked shelf after shelf, aisle after aisle, and floor after floor. I pulled my coat tight as I looked around at the empty shelves. It was as barren as a grocery store in a snowstorm. There were less than ten boxes on a shelf, and empty and splintered crates lay kicked around on the floor. Julia slipped and nearly fell on empty bullet casings if I would not have caught her. She thanked me and nodded as I released her shoulders out of instinct, and she turned away silently.

"Where would the uniforms be?" she asked. I wracked my brain as to where they were kept. Vehicles were kept on the bottom floor, explosives and anti-tank equipment on the second, guns of all kinds and ammunition to match on the third, and body armor on the top floor. "On the top floor," I replied, not so sure of myself. "Whatever is left of it." And with that, we carefully evaded falling as we climbed the stairs for three empty and skeletal floors. The stairs had not even a creak in them as we rushed upward. The fourth flight had not a creak either; in fact, there were not enough boards there to make a sound. Both sides had been collapsed in the blast, leaving only about two feet of space to climb. I let Julia go first so I could catch her if she were to fall. I followed her up and was amazed at what I saw. The ceiling was completely gone and cascaded in. Some areas of the floor sunk down under the heavy weight of the shelving units, and the ground was cracked heavily, resembling a frozen pond. Everywhere was weak and ready to fall, and nowhere was safe.

"This floor isn't gonna hold," she said to me as she looked back. "Let me go grab the uniforms. I'm lighter." I replied quicker than I thought. "No," I said bluntly. "I can't let you take that risk." She looked at me blankly. "I wasn't asking," she said, stepping out onto the creaky floor. I looked around the vacant and destroyed storeroom, a nervous wreck, hoping she did not have too far to venture out. There were only six boxes I could see in the room, and all were fairly dispersed throughout the wreckage. I could hear the floor creak louder and louder as she searched the first and second boxes, throwing them aside as they were empty. The third contained helmets and gas masks, and the fourth held mildewed patches and buttons. She held up two uniforms from the fifth box and smiled slightly as she walked slowly back toward me, much to my relief.

I had watch Julia fall asleep many times, and I had watched her slip from my grasp even more. My heart stopped as she fell through the floor and disappeared from my view. I ran out to the edge of the weak ceiling as I shouted in fear. She had dropped the uniforms on the edge as she fell, and as I stared down into the hole in the floor, she held on with one hand as she dangled twenty feet up in the air. I grabbed her hand and pulled her up with ease to avoid pulling her arm out of socket. I carried her to the thicker, safer part of the floor as we collapsed in fear and with gratitude.

"Thank you," she said, her head buried in my shoulder. She hugged me and flinched as the rest of the dilapidated floor and shelving fell through the ceiling to the floor below. I heard the crash and perked up as she flinched at the thundering sound and rising dust. "We have to get out of here now," I said sternly. "In the uniforms." I reached out and unbuttoned the coat and pulled it around me, the uniform fitting somewhat tight, but not uncomfortable. My socks were coated with dust and damp with sweat, but the thick boots were a significant replacement for my regular shoes. I pulled the cap on, tucking my hair back into the ring of the band and positioning it over my eyes. I had promised myself I would never wear that uniform, but it was the only way we would make it out alive.

"They're going to know it's me," Julia said as she put on her cap. Her blonde hair was gone from view but her face still resembled that of her outgoing female demeanor. There was no denying her face; she was going to shine no matter what. I felt my coat pocket and pulled out a thick stick of grey chalk. I rubbed the dusty material over her face and around her eyes, darkening her brows and covering her lips. She did the same to me as we took on an impossible task, becoming what we swore we never would. But times were different then; whims had turned to worries, and priorities had turned to problems.

We carefully hurried down the stairs and around the countless corners until we came to the bottom floor. "Where do we go from here?" Julia asked. I really did not know. "We have to follow Jack." I could see the look in her eyes. "On foot?" she asked. I looked at the armored Hummer to our left in the dim-lit building. The bottom floor was a parking garage, and an empty one at that. The three vehicles that remained matched those of the rest of Jack King's military force, and from behind deeply tinted windows, we would blend in flawlessly.

"Do you want me to drive this time?" she asked with a smirk. I laughed. "Too fast for you?" I teased. "Too fast for anyone." I accepted that. "We might need to get away quick. And if you wreck us and that hat comes off, well, we'd be a *dead* giveaway." That made her smile - her *old* smile. But it faded as quickly as it had come. We climbed inside the iron giant and started the engine as the keys to the beast fell into my lap. "What are you waiting for?" she looked at me immediately. I looked back at her, puzzled. "A crash like that had to be distraction enough."

And she was right. As I pulled the roaring car out of the echoey garage, I brought it to a heavy halt in the passageway to observe the roadways. "I saw a group of them head across town towards the mansion, or whatever's left of it. We should head there and tell them to report to the town square. If we can get them all in one place, we can -," she stopped abruptly as something - *someone* - rapped on my window. I nearly leapt from my seat, strangled by the seat belt. I dared not roll down the window. I could hear the muffled shouting from outside. "You nearly ran over my goddamn foot! Get it out of here before I drag you behind the fucking thing."

I pondered for a moment on what to do as I made a decision entirely on my own. I pressed the side button once and listened as the window rolled down slowly, revealing a highly-agitated soldier, his face as red as a beet. I took my cap off and smiled as his mouth dropped, struggling for words. He reached for his radio but I grabbed his hand. "Jack wants everyone to report to the town square immediately," I said. I took his hand and wrapped it around the pistol on his right hip. "You killed my friends, my neighbors, and my family. You're lucky I don't have time to make it right," I spoke coldly. I lifted his hand to his chin and pressed in on the trigger, rolling the window back up just in time to block the spray of brain matter from entering the car. I looked over at Julia with a heavy breath. "I like that plan."

I pulled the truck out into the devilishly bumpy, ravenous street and sped toward the outskirts of the city once more, one hand on the wheel and one hand free to tremble and worry about what could possibly come next. Needless to say, Julia kept a tight hold on the off-road braces on the roof of the car. I was not *that* bad of a driver, although I am sure she was shaken up. I had grown accustomed to killing and the savage destruction of the city, but she was just taking her morning gazes at it. It was a lot to take in and process; I remembered that all too well. It was so much to grow used to and accept so quickly. It could make you sick - something so beautiful reduced to nothing but smoke and ashes, somewhere supposed to be peaceful turned to hell, and someone supposed to keep you safe transformed into a stranger. That was the way of everything. *It could change you like a newborn child.*

I caught sight of the mangled, wrecked train as we neared a decent-sized group of the battalion. I saw two Hummers and nine soldiers grouped outside of the wreckage, standing guard. When I thought about it, it made sense - it was one of the only ways to and from the mansion. Perhaps it had been *designed* that way. But who in their right mind would venture up there at that time? Very little of the house was still standing, and almost none of the landscape was still intact. Then I thought again; there was not much of a *right* mind together either.

The militants saw us approaching slowly and stood guard, guns raised. I stopped the vehicle as my heart began to beat again inside of my chest like a thousand bulls. I felt a cold hand in mine and looked over at Julia. "Please don't do that again," she said quietly. I had *traumatized* her. "Wait here," I replied. I squeezed the door handle and put the toe of my boot to the dusty road below. "Get to the town square immediately," I boomed, surprising even myself. I had heard the gruff tone of the soldiers for years, and I had it mastered in a moment, it seemed and sounded. "Jack King's orders." The group of footsoldiers were apprehensive at first, tightening their faces and questioning me under their breath, but slowly lowering their guns and walking around me back to their vehicles. I kept a straight grimace as they stared me down and kept a close watch as they in turn stared through the black glass at Julia, knowing she was terrified in the passenger seat. I wondered if they knew she was inside - and more horrifyingly - what they would have given to get to her.

The outpost of soldiers sped toward the town square in the opposite direction as my heart returned to a normal pace as I returned to the car. I heard a whistle behind me and spun around to find the source, yet I saw none at first. I looked atop the destroyed train inside the shattered ground and saw the homeless stranger I had called a dear friend saluting me, whistling the strange anthem I had heard for years. "A leader indeed," he said through a straight-toothed grin. Before I could answer, he was gone. I shook it off and rejoined Julia in the car. "Thank you," she said with a smile. "What were you looking at?" I looked down at the steering wheel. "My parents were killed here."

The streets were clear for quite some time. There was no way the armored car was getting across the train wreckage, so I made the conscious decision to make a perimeter around the city, send all the soldiers inward, and proceed to the town square ourselves. I made sure to avoid the rather deadly potholes and craters in the asphalt, and the ravaged city was not exactly a sight for sore eyes as we passed the shattered windows and cracked doorways. Shadows faded into bodies along the broken sidewalks. If the soldiers were not in vehicles on patrol, they were kicking in doors and searching buildings looking for us. I would roll the window down and tell them to report to the town square immediately. Out of the rear-view mirror, I could see them retreat and do exactly as I - or rather *Jack* - commanded. Even after everything he had done, he had not lost all of his followers. There were *always* those as savage and desperate as he was, and perhaps that was what was most terrifying.

"Why would your father go back to the mansion?" I asked Julia, not knowing if she could remember anything or not. She paused for a moment before speaking. "He always kept something in a safe in his office. Told me never to go in there. I would say that's what he went back for," she said. Her memory was *returning*. Perhaps I did not need Peter as much as he needed to find what he was looking for. We passed several clusters of insurgents along the way, those fleeing the chaos and destruction of the city's anarchy. As the soldiers filed in the opposite direction, it was safe for Julia to do what she was destined to do - to *save* people. She would get out of the car as the civilians cowered in fear, reveal herself as they gaped at her being alive and well, and Julia would speak the three impossible, unthinkable words. "Leave the city," she would say. But there was no escaping. All life and memory would die with the city, along with all possible ounces of hope.

I gripped the steering wheel and accelerated quickly as I became lost in thought. I was driven by vengeance and hallucinations of my family and my friends that I had lost. I could see someone in front of me as I hit eighty on the dashboard. I could hear Julia screaming at me to slow down as it faded to silence, only a vast ringing in my ears. Her words whispered through my mind like a drop of water in the ocean. The speedometer crept up to a hundred down the narrow and empty road as I slammed into the single soldier, his body crashing through the windshield, bouncing off of the back seat and into the trunk with a heavy thud. Julia and I lurched forward as we came to a stop, dust rising all around us.

My hearing returned, deafening me. "Holy shit!" Julia screamed. "What the hell was that?" she shouted. I remained silent, for I did not know. I could not see around the car, but I heard the tapping on my window. I rolled it down, not knowing what I was doing anymore. "What the fuck happened here?" the soldier asked, almost impressed. "A Dreamer," I replied coldly. "The fucker came through the windshield." The man clapped and smiled. "I was either gonna guess that or a big ass deer." I was silent in fear of discovery or even worse - confrontation. Perhaps some fears we never can hope to lose. "Jack says to report to the town square immediately," Julia said beside me, half-deepening her voice, echoing off of the large soundproof vehicle. The dust had cleared, revealing another two soldiers on either side of the vehicle. "That's great," the man said. "Give us a lift?" he asked. Before I could refuse, they had piled into the backseat, stepping over the broken glass and blood on the floorboard. As I put the car in reverse, I looked through the rear-view once more. The man I had hit was not there.

"So who made you King's messenger, Boy Scout?" one of the soldiers asked me from behind. I was nerve-wracked and anxious as all hell, and I tried not to stutter or anger them. "Merit," I replied. They laughed. "Remind me to get you a golden star when this is all over," he said. That was the last thing he said directly to me, but I listened closely to their conversation. "Talk about a golden star, alright," one started. "Take a gander at his daughter. What a ravishing young sight she is." They all punched each other in the arm and exchanged gestures. "Yeah, if only she was a little older and her father wasn't the head bounty around here." More laughing. "What I wouldn't give to be the lucky bastard guarding *her* cell," another added. I was animalistically furious as I saw grey tears drip onto Julia's pants as she listened. "Not many women left in this place, I'm sure Jack wouldn't mind as long as we treated her right. Kept a close watch on her." I had had enough. "Have a little fun time and wipe the bitch's memory."

I felt the wheels connect with the sidewalk and crash into one of the old grocery store buildings. Julia gripped the handle and held on as I spun the car around and reversed back into the building, cracking the wall and shattering the taillights on the brick. The trio of soldiers were disoriented and cursing as I leapt from the front seat and jerked their door open. I pulled them out one-by-one and hurled them hard onto the pavement. They cursed and tried to get their footing but I already had my gun in hand. "I wouldn't worry too much about Jack," I said. "You should worry about me," Julia said. I had not seen her get out of the car. She put a bullet in each one of their heads before I could pull the trigger.

Whatever Jack had done to her, it had split her into half of her old *self* and half of a new *soldier*, and she struggled with it inside every waking moment. I had to hold on to the hope that one side would overcome the other, and I hoped it would be *my* Julia instead of the cold-hearted killer that stood before me then.

I knew Jack wanted me dead. I had challenged him man-to-man, and I was a Dreamer. It is only natural to seek vengeance on what you do not understand and cannot be. Could I blame him? Of course not. He hated me with all he had as I did him, and there was fuel adding to the fire with every burning minute. I also knew Peter was watching us, making sure we did not stray off of the path of what he wanted. I was never one to follow orders, but I had my mind on two things - I wanted to escape the city with Julia, and I wanted to bury Sebastian. After all that had happened and the sudden change of plans, we needed to get away from the middle of the city as soon as possible. And I knew just the place.

The once immaculate military vehicle was then a crumpled sheet of metal before us, but it would still run and it had enough power to get us where we needed to go. I put the wheels in the direction of the other side of the city and sped away from the growing crowd. They would be impatiently waiting on Jack, and impatience leads to doubt, doubt leads to fear, and fear leads to discovery. The best thing for Julia and I in that moment was to get away, clear our heads, and rethink what to do next. Perhaps we could escape the city and leave it all behind, but that was *fool's* thinking. If Jack could not find us, Peter surely would. He had a hold on us far tighter than any chain, and he *knew* that he did. He truly *was* God, and there was no permanent escape - only a temporary one.

I knew of a private place we could clear our heads for a while, as well as keep a higher ground advantage. Above my old neighborhood, there was a hillside crested about two miles outside the gates. I vaguely remember my family having picnics up there in the beginning of that place and how beautiful it used to be. I passed the entrance to my old home and remembered the vast array of memories I possessed from that place. I drove on and put it aside me. I needed no distraction - at least of that kind. We crested the hilltop and parked atop the large plateau that overlooked the city. The massive willow trees swayed in the wind just as I recalled, and I looked across the city and saw the shadow of the mansion smoking in the morning sun. The grass was soft and the shrubbery was fresh. Some things never changed, no matter how much destruction carried on around them. Felicia would have *loved* that place.

I saw it before Julia spoke a word of it as we climbed out of the car and strolled briskly toward the edge of the cliff. I saw a shimmer across the toes of shiny shoes in the dim sunlight as I neared the bushes. I pushed the branches out of the way and gasped at what I saw. Sebastian's body lay limp in the soft dirt with a note tucked inside his jacket. I unfolded it and glanced at it. I recognized Peter's handwriting immediately, yet I could not process what it said. I could not face it, understand it, nor come to grips with it. It was the spreading of lies that had brought the downfall of everything, and I refused to face it as I tucked the note into my coat pocket. The sunlight gleamed off of a silver shovel leaned against the trees. I unbuttoned my coat and took it off, the winter air frigid against the sweaty and soiled white t-shirt underneath. But I faced the cold as I did the death of another friend, and I buried him six feet under the ground beneath the bushes where flowers would bloom upon his decomposition. An *honorable* burial. A proper goodbye. I would burn the rest, for those who stood against me deserved no peace.

Julia and I sat on the edge of the cliff for a while, legs crossed and minds open. I could see and hear the faint rustling of the vast crowd in the town square below, and I could sense the tensions rising everywhere in the city below us. I had wiped the dirt and sweat from my brow on the uniform coat, for I had no respect for it. I could see my old house from the ledge, the place I had called home in the city after everything had changed, and I thought back to how things were before the city. I became lost in thought and memories once more. As I looked over at Julia as she stared across the city at *her* past, I knew she was just as lost as I was.

"I remember more and more every day," she said, her eyes cloudy and distant. I looked over at her silently, listening. "I try to forget more and more every day," I smiled. "Wanna trade?" she asked. I nodded and looked down once more. "What do you remember?" I asked. "I remember coming here with my dad after my mom died, I remember watching this place grow and believing in it, and I remember believing in my dad. I remember watching him grow more and more insane, how he built this place for my mom, and how it fell eventually. He was so driven to fight the Dreamers. For no reason. I guess he needed someone to blame. He always blamed my grandfather. He didn't talk about it much. All he talked about was what was in that safe. How someone close to him stole it. That's when he really became who he is now. It came back to that same scapegoat. Whatever it is, it must be important. He told me one time that my mother didn't even know what it is. It's long gone now, and so is he. I know I should be against this whole thing; maybe it's just an unreal dream. I never knew my grandfather and us being his ransom for a better life is insane. If I could rescue my father and bring him back to how he used to be, I wouldn't think twice. But I think it's too late. Maybe he's fighting a hopeless cause because he wants to die. I think he wants to be with my my mom again. I don't think he sees her in me, I think he sees his father in me. He did what he had to do. He's got to be too far gone. I understand what we have to do, but I won't enjoy it. I've lost just as much as you have, Noah. But I remember you. I remember falling in love with you on that rooftop, and I remember falling asleep with you many nights when you lived with us. I remember how horrified I was the day you were murdered. I remember screaming at my father and the swirling of emotions I felt. That's when he found out I was a Dreamer. I nearly killed him that night. He locked me up and wiped my memory and had me guarded all the time. I pleaded with him to let me go, but he told me it was for the best. That he had to protect me. I've got this anger inside me for him that comes out sometimes in waves. Then it fades and I'm myself again. But I remember, Noah. I remember that I love you and that I don't want to lose you again. I remember now. And I thank you for saving me. For making this city worth living and fighting for. When this is over, promise me we'll leave this place."

I listened as tears rolled down her face and as mine followed suit, putting piece after piece together as to what had happened to start the puzzle of destruction. I remembered the story of Sebastian's telling and his theory on the stolen item. I believed it, and it made sense as I pondered it. Jack was driven to find it, and so was Peter, and both would stop at nothing to get to it. If it had truly brought about the end of the world by the creation of Dreamers, I could only imagine what it could do in another set of hands - whether they be right *or* wrong. That is what started the city, that life, and that war. I would be goddamned if it could not end it as well. We had to find it before either Jack or Peter did, for *both* of those hands were stained and tainted with wrongdoing. I was so entirely and completely relieved that she remembered even *half* of who she was; it was good enough for me, and I was contently satisfied. But I could tell as I looked into her eyes that she remembered it in that moment, but she did not feel it. Whatever Jack had done to her had taken away her ability to feel emotions, and that could not be undone. That was not something I could tell her; she would have to discover that on her own. And so I kept it inside of me, as gut-wrenching and difficult as it was. "I promise. You'll never lose me again." She smiled and wiped her eyes as we stared down into the city of loss below, ghosts and shadows drifting through the streets and empty carcasses of the past, whispering to us from the vast depths of the unknown. She took my hand as we joined them.

The last place I wanted to go was that shattered, broken old house, but after putting everything together like I had done, I was left with no choice. If Sebastian was right and my father had stolen the talisman from Jack, it would be in his office - I was sure of it. I remembered how trashed the house was and how I was internally and morally forced to leave my own brother to rot on the kitchen floor, and the traumatic memories and stories from that place continued to haunt me. But I had to go. Perhaps I would gain some closure about my parents' deaths in the process.

I helped Julia into the beat-up car and rolled down the hill toward the neighborhood I had reluctantly called home for years. If I could only slip inside and retrieve whatever was so important, Julia and I could evade the city quickly and quietly. If I had learned one thing, it is that things of that matter are never cut and dry. They are *always* one or the other. The neighborhood was gated on all four sides, so going in the back way was strictly out of the question. As we neared the entrance - as tangled and gnarled as the gate was - I could see the entryway blocked by two Escalades and several soldiers. Although they were *different*. These were the special guards Peter had warned about. *Jack King was there.* If only I could have seen the entrance from the hilltop above. We were utterly and completely stuck and fucked then. *Cannot go over the abyss, cannot go under it. We would have to go straight through it.*

Smoke through the neighborhood was thick and rising; I could hardly see as I rolled up in front of the guards. I could not make out their faces nor their weapons, and I had a terrifying, haunting feeling deep within my stomach. "Climb in the backseat and hide under the seat," I whispered to Julia. "Why?" she asked. "Do it now," I said. She hoisted herself into the back and lowered herself beneath the open leather space, hidden from view. I struggled to see in the thick air, and I revved the engine so he knew I was there.

A crowbar came through the driver's side window and caught me in my left cheek, splintering glass across the wound. Disoriented, the door opened and I felt thick hands take ahold of me and jerk me out of the vehicle. I rolled across the cold pavement and turned to look him. Jack King stood above me with the steel bar in his hand and a satisfied look in his one untouched eye. My cap hat rolled off my head and my hair was free, blood washing the chalk from my face. "You know something?" he asked. "Your father had the same look you do now when he thought he was going to steal from me," he spat, swinging the crowbar around again, bringing it down hard on my chest. He knelt down beside me. "Yeah, I know what you're looking for. I'm looking for it too. But you see, your father never stole it from me. *You* did. When you came to visit me that night for dinner. I want to know where it is." I laughed, as hard as it was to do. My chest exploded with pain, but it was worth it to taunt Jack. "You blame the Dreamers. I get it. But you can't face the fact that *you* killed your wife, Jack. Your father didn't. And my father didn't steal your precious *artifact*. I didn't steal it either. Your father did. You pinned the death of your wife on your father because it was *easy*, and you built this place around revenge on him. Around revenge on people *like* him. You wanted the power of that talisman but couldn't erase what it had already done. This war is personal for you, and now you've made it personal for me. I'm gonna kill you, you son of a bitch. I'm gonna let you watch your precious city fall and then cut your goddamn heart out like you did mine." Jack laughed as he turned his gravelly, contorted face toward me. "An eye for an eye," he spoke quietly. He raised the crowbar above his head as I winced in preparation to go blind.

Jack shouted in pain as the dented front bumper of the armored car slammed into his right side, sending him flying into the vehicle he had arrived in. His men shouted curses in confusion as they too struggled to see in the smoky haze. Julia shouted at me to get in the passenger side seat as I painfully climbed to my feet. My chest ached so excruciatingly as I gasped for breath, each one feeling like my last. I slammed the door and Julia stepped on the gas pedal, bullets bouncing off of the rear bumper.

I heard tires squeal and smelled burning rubber as we were chased by Jack's elite team of guards. Both military vehicles raced toward us as Julia swerved in and out of alleyways, struggling to see in the dense, hazy fog. The first car rammed ours from the right side, and the second driver emptied a pistol clip into our back left tire. The vehicle dragged to the left as we sideswiped a building and slid out onto the next road as Julia floored the gas pedal. We spun around and lost the two assailants. The road in front of us was clear as we sped away through the city, and we thought we had gotten away. We were cut as well as dry, and I saw the third Hummer roll out from the alleyway and hit us head on. All I remember is the car leaving the city street and flipping into the air until we crashed and rolled into the town square. A perfect ambush plan. The perfect distraction - only used in our opposite favor. Then everything went dizzy, fuzzy - and eventually - black.

I heard the rumbling once more as my body lay limp, the roaring of a thousand people swimming in my ears. I heard chants and shouts and screams. I shook awake, but my vision was still blinded. *Had Jack cut my eyes out?* No, I felt no pain within my sockets. They were *covered* with some sort of soft cloth. My body ached and my hands were bound around a pole of some sort. My eyes were *blindfolded.* I could feel the rope on my wrists as I dug them into the metal pole in which I was tied to. I writhed around in place, showing my captors I was awake. My mouth was not covered, and I took advantage of that simple, powerful freedom.

"Where the fuck am I?" I shouted. I could hear cheering and laughter. My breath was cold in the winter air as I gasped heavily, my ribs still morbidly sore from taking a crowbar to the abdomen. I could feel the frozen blood against my forehead as my temple throbbed. "He's awake now, too," I heard someone say. I pair of rough fingers pulled the blindfold from my eyes as I took in my surroundings. I was on my knees in the town square, on the stage, and surrounded by hundreds of people. A fist came across my face, busting my lip and reopening my head wound. I collapsed against the rope, the thick string digging into my wrists even further. I hung there on my knees, weak and bleeding. "Sit him up!" I heard the voice order - the voice I had long since come to despise. The vocal cords I wished so *desperately* to cut out. I pair of gruff hands raised me up onto my feet again, and I wobbled around in place. Julia stood bound beside me, her helmet still intact and pulled down over her eyes. *Jack did not know it was his daughter yet.* I had been there before. It was an *execution*. The army gathered at the foot of the stage around Jack as he spoke, guns drawn, feet apart, laughing and cheering as my head pounded.

Jack paced the stage as he would *always* do, a rich showboy and a brilliant spokesman. The crowd fell silent as he began to speak. "The last of the Dreamers!" he shouted. "And I certainly saved the best for last," he added. "Noah Willowby, everybody!" The army cheered and spat in mockery. "The son of Joseph and Karen Willowby. My great brother in arms and secretary of this city. You see, my boy Noah here killed them in cold blood. It's the way of the Dreamers. They wish to take over us. To rule us. To eradicate us!" he shouted, spitting hateful lies and vulgarity. "He did this to my face," he shouted, running his hand across his sandy expression. "Tried to blow me up. He stole from me the very thing that brought the Dreamer race into this world, the very bane of the city's existence! This city will not fall. Not today, not ever. We rebuild on the blood of the final Dreamers!" More cheering. "As you can see, the snake and his friend disguised themselves as two of our own. I wouldn't be surprised if he wasn't wearing his brother's uniform, which he also murdered in cold blood. He cut the poor boy's heart out. One of our own!" The crowd went ballistic. "ONE OF OUR OWN! GUT HIM!" I heard them shout. It was all jumbled together as I struggled to stay conscious and see straight. "But I would recognize Noah Willowby anywhere." He laughed a long, raspy, mocking chuckle.

He turned to look at Julia, whom he did not know was his daughter. "And who is this?" he teased. Julia did not make a sound. I knew she had to be terrified, but she was brave. If this was how it was to end, come whatever may. Jack kicked her in the back of the knee and she keeled over, her helmet sliding to the ground. Her blonde hair dropped with her head, and the crowd fell silent once again for a much different reason. "What in the name of fuck-," he stopped. I stood up, as hard as it was. "Go ahead, Jack," I said through gritted teeth. "Kill your own daughter in front of your people. Tell them how you used her and wiped her memory. How you kept her chained up for months. How your men abused her and hurt her. Tell them, goddamnit!" The crowd remained silent, surely doubting the truth as they *always* had. "Tell them how you killed your wife, how you killed your father, and how you killed my parents. Tell them how you betrayed your country and your people for personal reasons. How many families and lives you ripped apart for your own personal gain." I felt weak at the knees though I was already on them, for I had faced my own greatest fear and conquered it. Jack stepped back as the army raised their weapons. Jack pulled his gun from his coat pocket and aimed it at me. The ropes that bound me melted into a pile of ash and twine as I stood up, opening my arms. "Tell them, Jack. You wanted this war. Now you've got it." Before he could pull the trigger, the gun left his hand and clattered to the ground. Julia stood up and flipped her hair back, wiping the rest of the chalk from her face. "Things are *never* as they seem, Jack King.

So let me ask you, are you a *Dreamer*?" He growled like an angry animal, and he was.

I turned my attention out to the crowd as the army of hundreds shifted in image, their weapons and uniforms disintegrating into ash, leaving behind nothing but the army of Dreamers I had set free from his prison under the mansion. None of Jack's men had gathered in that city street at all, for they were too large of cowards to follow orders. Jack backed up slowly as he looked at me with a deadly smile. "Are we really gonna compare dick size today, Noah?" he laughed. "Not today, son," a voice said from the crowd. I was even surprised as I turned to see Peter King emerge from the crowd, his one good eye shining and his silver ponytail glistening in the mid-morning sun. "But I assure you, mine is bigger," he spat. With that, he pulled a gun and shot his son in the right leg, echoing throughout the town square. A calling of *all* arms, for Jack King's men had hidden and waited for the right time as ours had. As I saw heads and weapons emerge from shop windows and rooftops, I knew the war had only *just* begun.

Chapter XXI
The Stars Will Fly
(The Ones That Shoot, The Ones That Fall, and the Ones Left Behind)

Bullets cracked the sky like stones through glass windows, the sound deafening as men fell from two-story windows and keeled over on the sidewalks. Muzzles flashed and explosives were triggered as all hell broke loose in the town square. Everything went silent as I looked at Julia and the terrified look in her eyes. She looked at me for guidance, although I had none. All I could hear was the everlast ringing of armageddon around me. All I could think of was protecting Julia. The onslaught shattered the city into a million pieces, parting ways like oil in water - what was moments prior an organized gathering turned anarchic chaos. I threw my body over Julia, shielding her from the spray of bullets flying in every direction. Jack's guards rushed from the nearby doorway and split off, half rushing to his side and half tackling Peter. I watched the old man put the pistol in one guard's mouth and put a knife in the throat of the other, climbing to his feet from being pinned to the pavement. The other two guards pulled Jack upward and carried him off into the building they had come from. I grabbed ahold of Julia and rolled the both of us off behind the stage and into the street below. I lifted the tarp and rushed Julia under the stage, following her crawl close behind.

I could see bodies fall and blood spill onto the pavement, images of Sebastian's grisly murder running through my head. Jack had been taken to safety and Peter was fighting for his life, but I could not put Julia in danger. Not again. If we were to leave the bottom of the stage, we would surely he hit by stray bullets and ricochet. If we were to stay, we would surely be discovered or crushed by the weight of the massive wooden boards only inches above our heads. *We could not go above or through it; we would have to go under it.*

The manhole cover caught my eye as it presented the only way out. I pried my fingers under the steel disc and pulled upward - it was *loose*. The five-foot wide gap was just enough for us to slip into, and I looked at Julia to go first. She looked horrified at the thought of climbing down into the sewer, but compared against the threat of imminent death, she hoisted her legs onto the ladder rungs and disappeared down into the darkness as I followed her down, pulling the manhole cover back over the hole to cover our tracks. The dark tunnel was saturated and smelled as expected, at least three inches of water across the stone floor. The only light illuminating the path was from the cracked asphalt ceiling above us. We stepped off of the ladder and winced as the filthy sewer water filled our shoes and soaked our socks. Our voices echoed as vehicles drove by overhead, rumbling like thunder as pebbles and dust fell from the sky. We had been in the city and looked down upon it, but now we looked up at the hell from *under* the beast.

I motioned for Julia to crouch down as I climbed up to the crevasse in the road and peered out into the city. Jack King's men took shots at the Dreamer legion as some were killed and others disappeared into the air. Lights flashed and explosions commenced throughout the square. The Dreamer army had no measurable numbers against the soldiers as they fired from higher ground, but I watched as *my* people - *our* people - rose into the air and found cover outside of Main Street. If the battle was to spread throughout the city, we would never be able to find Jack and Peter, which were nowhere to be found. They could not kill one another; it would be the end of everything. We had to keep the war contained and escape the madness.

I had felt earthquakes and I had seen cyclones rip houses from their foundations, but I had never experienced both at once. I felt the ground shake as we were one with it, vibrating our bones and rattling our teeth. Wind whistled through the crack in the asphalt as I struggled to see what was going on. *Had a storm spun up at the most inopportune time?* Of some sort, I imagined so. I had heard the noise and felt the shaking before. It was *impossible.* But of course, the impossible was sure to become reality in due time. I saw the shadow creep across the sky like an eclipse. The massive aircraft carrier came into fruition over the city as soldiers of both sides ventured out into the cityscape.

The carrier touched down in the town square, nearly taking up the entire perimeter. Questions ran through my mind as to how it could be, but I had not the time to ask. We needed more reinforcements, and this could be exactly it. *Higher ground.* I watched through the foot-wide vein in the ground as the hatch dropped on the craft and the platoon stepped foot on the city street, led by none other than Commander Logan Aaron. He stepped out onto the pavement, his gruff beard trimmed to his face and his assault rifle at arm's length. "What a day to die, gentlemen," he said to his men behind him. They remained silent as he looked down and saw me.

"Noah, what are you doing down there?" he asked. "It's not time to get buried yet," he laughed. He bent down and extended his free hand out, pulling me through the crevasse with ease. I helped Julia up as we faced the group of soldiers, this time the infantry being in *our* favor. "How did you get here?" I asked. "We're Peter's protection. He pulled all the stops to get here." I nodded. "What's going on here?" he followed. I knew Peter was secretive, but I thought he would at least have informed his men on what they were fighting for. I knew not where to start. "His son. He wants him dead. He wants to take over this place. He used me to get back here. Now we have to fight for him or we'll die with this place." Logan looked back at his squadron. "Sounds like a good day to die, right, men?" They all shouted in unison and gathered around us.

"What's your plan?" Aaron asked me. "Aren't you supposed to call the shots?" I smiled. "Not in this world," he replied. I nodded and took it as I inherited the earth. "We need to keep the fighting within the town square. We can't find Jack and Peter in a warzone. I need you guys to take position on the rooftops and take out any of Jack's soldiers that try to leave this perimeter. There are twelve of you; I need each one of you to take a rooftop and make sure nothing gets past you. Julia and I will go in and find them," I said, confident in myself, hoping I was not putting Julia in danger. "Julia?" Logan asked her. "You're Peter's granddaughter right?" he asked. "By rights, yes. By actions, no," she said strictly. "He talked about you once. I never thought I would get the chance to meet you. You remind me a lot of him," he smiled. "If your father is anything like him, then this place is a ticking time bomb."

"You might want to change out of those uniforms," one of his men interrupted. "Right," I muttered. "Wouldn't wanna pop you shits on accident," the Mexican soldier spoke up from the back with a giggle. Logan turned to his men and dismissed them, each one dispersing in a different direction and disappearing into their assigned location. Julia and I pulled off our suits and tossed them to the side. I had grown to *like* the boots, so I kept them. The gigantic metal aircraft had disappeared along with the soldiers, leaving Julia and I alone with the sound of gunshots close by once more.

I turned my eyes to the sky as the platoon of soldiers popped up across the city skyline, guns propped up on the brick outer layers. The occasional popping of silencers brought bodies sailing to the ground as a patrol was set along with a boundary. "Where would my father go?" Julia asked me. It occurred to me that I knew him better than she did at that time. "He would go to the nearest place where medical supplies are kept. He can't afford to be wounded now. I used to think we were after him to kill him, but now we have to *protect* him. We have to get to him before

Peter does." She nodded in agreement. "Where would those supplies be kept?" she asked. I thought and smiled, deep in the past. "The first place I came to when I got to this city."

I remembered the doctor's office quite well - how it started as a small house and was converted into an infirmary when the massive hospital was built across the street. All of the medical supplies were kept in there, and from my understanding, the building was still standing. I knew Jack quite well *indeed*, and we headed in the direction of the only place he could be. His father, on the other hand, could be *anywhere. He was everywhere.* The hospital stood three blocks away from the Perch building, and it was just outside the perimeter of the Dreamer army on the rooftops. It made perfect sense for the guards to take Jack there to patch him up, which meant two things - Jack King was going to see another day, and all of the soldiers were trained by army medics. Gunshot wounds were like paper cuts to them, and we had a fight on our hands. The fighting had migrated outward from the town square, leaving Main Street virtually clear. I could hear gunshots echo off of the street corners as we darted across the shattered concrete, careful to avoid the craters and potholes left by the many explosions the city had seen. We ran across the stage and down the stairs as we rounded the corner, sprinting toward the hospital. I could hear footsteps behind us as I took Julia's arm, pulling her in front of me to shield her from view. I heard a gunshot behind me and watched the bullet ricochet off of the sidewalk beside us. I turned to face him, pulling my gun from my belt and pointing it behind me. I heard another gunshot, but it was not my own. I waved to the sniper above me as he whistled, signaling the path to be clear.

We rounded the final corner as the hospital came into view, towering high above the town square - a beacon of hope for many. I turned head first into someone, and I raised my gun to his chin. The man shouted as I realized it was a Dreamer soldier and pushed him aside. I took Julia's hand as we ran across the street and fell quiet outside of the hospital doors. I raised my gun and pulled the hammer back, the only noise as we stepped inside the hollow and silent building. The hospital was dark - the only light being the sunlight through the torn and tattered curtains. I pulled a flashlight from my back pocket and shone it around the walls. Blood was smeared across the floors and on the blue paint, creating an eerie picture of the abandoned hospital and what had happened in that place. The stairwell to the basement was caved in; I imagine Jack wanted no one *meddling* down there. He had kept records of everyone that had died in the city, some of which I could feel roaming the streets just outside the doors. They called *my* name. Shouting turned to whispers, whispers turned to footsteps, and I spun around into a metal bar as I shoved Julia into the nearest room.

I fell to my knees as I rubbed my head - the steel pipe had knocked the wind out of me and stunned me into a frozen state. The soldier stepped into the beam of my flashlight as I tried to climb to my feet. He kicked my legs out from under me with the pipe as my face collided with the cold tile. My fingers closed around the handle of my gun as I rolled over, the pipe crushing my wrist and numbing all feeling in my right arm. I looked at his face and into his eyes as I was sure of it - he was one of Jack's guards, one of which had carried him away. He had me pinned against the tile floor as he rose the pipe above my head one last time.

The ceiling above him caved in, a pile of dusty rubble and light fixtures showering over him. The wires wrapped around his neck and chest, cutting off his air supply. They tightened and sparked, lifting him into the air as they retracted back into the ceiling. Before his feet disappeared from view, he was electrocuted and fell back through the hole, hanging from the ceiling like a sick, twisted, and gruesome chandelier. His pipe clanked to the floor as I picked it up. There were two guards that took Jack to safety, and one was still roaming the abandoned hospital.

I got to my feet and staggered as my vision blurred, dizzy from the concussion I most probably had acquired somewhere along the line. I turned around and opened the door to the room I had pushed Julia into, startled at what I found. The second officer had Julia in a headlock, gun to her head. *I had done this.* "We can work this out," I said, hands in the air. "Just let her go." I began to panic. "I'm sure we can," he laughed sarcastically. "I'm sure we can bring my family back from the dead and rebuild this place and pretend like it's all alright," he followed. "You killed *my* family," I said through gritted teeth. The man chuckled as I clutched the pipe in my left hand, the only one with feeling left in it. He pointed the gun at me as a tear ran down Julia's face. Blood dripped onto her hair as the scalpel pierced the back of his neck and severed his throat. He released the horrified Julia as he fell to the ground in a pool of his own blood.

"Are you alright?" I asked, knowing she was scarred and terrified. "Did he hurt you?" I asked. "No," she answered blankly. "But you're hurt. Your arm," she pointed. My right arm was lost all feeling and fell limp against my side. "Sit down," she ordered, going back to that dark place she become so familiar with. I sat down on the gurney as she tore my jacket sleeve and wrapped it in the fabric. My makeshift sling would have to do; it was all she had to work with. The nerves have been severed, and I had a minuscule amount of movement left in it - but it was dying nonetheless. "You've got a broken wrist and a fractured shoulder," she said. "Great," I muttered. "You have a remarkable pain tolerance," she said. "I know the timing is horrible, but try to rest it," she smiled. I shook my head. "I can rest when I'm dead," I replied. "The day's not over yet."

I stood up and walked toward the door. "Your father will be here alone," I said. She looked away. "When we find him, let me talk to him alone. I have to convince him to leave with us. To leave all of this behind. It won't be easy and he will he hostile. I can't put you in danger." She looked at me with a broken gaze. "He's my father," she said. "Not anymore," I said. "Perhaps he's forgotten that," I said, my heart breaking at the truth for her. "I know," she accepted. She stepped over the body of her attacker and joined me in the silent hallway. All of the doors were open except for one at the end of the hall, and I knew just who lay inside.

"I need you to stay out here," I told her. "Please," she asked. "I can't let you go in there. I've caused you enough pain," I stuttered. "You've done nothing but try to help me," she argued. I looked back at her and handed her my gun. "That's what I'm trying to do now," I left her. I turned the knob slowly and cracked the door open, a knife sliding into my left sleeve in caution. Jack lay on the hospital bed, unconscious. His leg was wrapped in bloody gauze and a cold compress was applied to his head, his sunglasses sitting on the bedside table. His coat was unbuttoned, his chest floating up and down again with unsteady breathing. I closed the door behind me quietly as I sat down in the chair beside the bed, cradling the knife in my hand, awaiting his awakening.

I stared at the man that had caused me so much pain and anger - the source of all my loss - and realized that I had complete power over him in that moment. I could have so very easily driven the blade into his other eye, or perhaps through his ear to puncture his brain. I could have very well made him suffer. I could have marked him for the rest of his life, never to forget how much he had taken from me. I could have murdered Julia in front of him if things were any different, just as he had done all I had ever loved. But out of all of these things I could have acted upon, I chose to *save* him. For that was the only way to save Julia, and the only way to save myself.

I snapped out of it as Jack stirred awake, muttering curses as he saw me beside him. "I'm no fool, Noah," he said raspily. "You've come here to kill me," he muttered, laying his head back once again. I laughed. "Not today, Jack. As much as I would love to and as much as you deserve it, I've actually come here to help you." He returned a painful and deep laugh. "How are you going to help me?" he spat. "Peter is after you. He's going to kill you. Whatever was stolen from you, he's looking for it. If he finds it, he has no use for you. When you die and when he finds it, this world will be destroyed. I can't let that happen. Not for Julia. I have to keep you alive for this world, the place you believe to be yours. We have to escape this place before Peter finds that thing and finds you. You have to leave with us." I begged and pleaded with the man that had ruined everything, in hopes of gluing the pieces back together once more. I watched as he grimaced and sat up, awaiting a grim response as only he could return.

"I've lost everything, Noah Willowby," he said. "My wife, my daughter, my home. My city. The place I built to protect and restore order. And you and your people tore it apart. I owe you nothing," he gritted his teeth. "You've taken everything from me," I returned. "But we have to look past that at the bigger picture. We have to get away from Peter to save this place, a place for you to grow old and die in, a place for your daughter to have a life in. A world for you to want me out of. This isn't about Dreamers anymore. This is about preserving this world, or you'll be lost forever. I want nothing more than to bury you, but I don't want to watch you die like that. I can't let Julia die like that. You have to come with us," I said firmly. Jack remained silent. *Had I convinced him?*

I wrapped my arms around Jack and felt the hospital room, the bed, and the air disappear from reality. We hurled through an endless dream - *my* endless dream - and the ground hardened and the air was numb and frigid as we looked around. We were *exactly* where I wanted to take him. He was able to walk in the twisted reality I was about to show him, and more importantly, he was able to *drive*. I looked over at him through two windows as the engines revved and the exhaust filled the open country air. He gripped the wheel and the gear shift in his two hands as I pressed the brake and gas at the same time. My vehicle was nearly fifty years newer than his, but they sounded just as angry as two *brothers*. "We race for it, Jack," I said to him as he looked ahead and let off of the clutch pedal. We sped ahead together, pulling ahead of each other at different points along the open country road. The path was straight and flat for hundreds of miles in front of us, and we *raced*. As *brothers*. Two *angry* brothers. We drove into oblivion - a smoky and heated truth that drifted into a dream-filled reality, and I showed Jack King the world in which he could not touch. I released his arms as he turned over in the hospital bed once more.

"Go fuck yourself," he spat at me one last time, followed by a lengthy, anticipatory silence. I stood up to leave, frustrated and as angry as he was. Julia burst through the door, startling me as I stood back against the bed. "Please, Dad," she pleaded. "We can leave this place. We can be safe." Jack sat up, wincing as he stared as the young woman before him. "You are no daughter of mine," he pronounced every word. "Get out," he muttered. He lay down once again as I motioned Julia out, following her and slamming the door behind us.

Julia collapsed in tears in the hallway, her cries surely loud enough for Jack to hear. I knelt down next to her and held her as her tears dripped onto my arms, her chest rising and lowering as she bawled. I knew the memories had begun to come back to her, but I had no idea how quickly they had revealed themselves. As I saw her break down before me, I knew that she remembered everything. She lay there for the longest time, sniffing between sobs and wiping her eyes on my sleeve. I kissed her forehead as she pulled away from me. The city was dying as the world before it had done. I had watched the world die from the basement in my old home as it fell, and now I watched the city crumble before my own eyes. The war had spread out into the city on all sides, and the soldiers' efforts to suppress it from the rooftops were exhausted as rooftops exploded and bodies dropped to the littered streets below.

Days drifted by as Julia and I hid from the battle atop the Perch building. Logan Aaron and his men had taken on lower levels of the buildings and worked their way down to the ground levels and secured city blocks minute by minute. I overheard their conversations, and their plan was to make their way to the hospital and capture Jack. It was the inevitable, and a close and careful watch made sure that the leader of the city had not left the hospital several blocks away. He was still there - whether he be dead or dying - and fate was coming for him in finality. One city block at a time. I remember his judgement day quite vividly - the day it all came to an end. It started with a reminiscent conversation and ended with fire and brimstone as the ever-approaching hell inherited the earth, tearing it from Jack King's fingers like a vicious animal.

The air was windy and the rooftop was a boulder against my spine as I awoke into the frigid morning stars beside Julia. She was still fast asleep against the railing as I sat up and climbed to my feet, standing over the icy rail and looking out into the frozen figure of a city that had taken on so very many faces in its time. I watched Julia toss and turn as crystals formed on her nose in the winter night. I could only imagine what she was dreaming about under the warmth of my coat. I shivered as I stared out into the barren wasteland of falling snow and fiery streets. I gazed into the glimmer of snowflakes for hours or moments; I lost grip of time as the winter crept into my bones and made dams of my blood. I went numb as I became one with the city, absent of warmth and life as I lost myself in it.

Julia stirred awake and wiped the frozen tears from her eyes as she wrapped my jacket around her shoulders and joined me on top of the world. We could not help but stutter our words as our teeth chattered away as the sun climbed above the horizon.

"Do y-you remember the f-first time we came here?" I asked her. "Yes," she said. "They were throwing a *p-party*. How the times have changed," she smiled through the numbness.

She followed me down the ladder inside the top floor and tore more pages out of the books that were left, tossing them into the fire. Commander Aaron had left us with a box of matches and a few days worth of rations - those of which were dwindling quickly. I let Julia have over half of mine each day, and she was skeptical at first, but she ate. And I went hungry. I was losing strength with each day, but as long as Julia had a full stomach and a warm place to sleep, I was alive enough. At first she had turned the things down, but as I curled up without my coat and ate only half of my food, she saw it as a waste to let it go unused. Even in her mental absence, she was not selfish. She had been made a survivalist - a *warrior*.

We would watch each day as Logan and his men advanced across city streets and set up perimeters to move along the sidewalks and into the buildings. Every day they drew closer to the hospital, and we watched on the day that they disappeared inside the deep and dark shadow of a building. We heard pops and shots echo across the city block as lights flashed in the morning darkness. More guards had filed into the hospital on days prior, and they were no more as the squadron of elite soldiers overcame another. They would not kill Jack. No, Peter would be the one to do that. If he had anything as severe as a hair disturbed on him, the old man would surely eradicate them from eternal existence. We watched in silence as the hospital went silent, as the city went silent, and as the world went silent. A single tear dripped down Julia's face as Jack King was dragged out of the doorway by two soldiers, one on either arm. Three men followed behind and Commander Aaron kept watch in the front, leading the group of men in retreat to the town square.

The city had kept a silent aura forever in that moment, but as Jack King was pulled along in arrest, it took on a much darker and emptier chill. The winter air was frigid as our breath clouded through the shattered window and as the heat from the fire warmed our backs. It was the only source of warmth in the city in that moment. It was *ours*, and it was mine. We watched the silent parade for hours it seemed, and as they reached the town square below us, the soldiers themselves retreated. Our eyes had followed the army along the way as they urged Jack along, but as they stepped back in shock and alarm, we saw that there were indeed *two* men standing in the town square.

Aaron and his men raised their weapons at the second man, the man who I had become so familiar with - so *conflicted* with - and the man I stood before and answered to. Peter turned to the men and waved his arms to them, their weapons pulled from their grasp, and pointed at their heads several feet above them. They backed up and stood on the sidewalks, turning to face the wall and kneeling. I turned to Julia as my heart began to beat quickly. "You have to stay here. Please," I begged her. I turned to run out the door before she could argue and darted down the stairs two steps at a time. I wrapped around the walls and slid, nearly falling as my shoes lost traction against the frozen concrete. I slid behind the doorway on the bottom garage floor and looked out through the crack in the door, listening to what was said and thinking about what I could possibly do to protect Julia.

"Father," Jack muttered. "We meet again at the doors of death. Your men have killed my soldiers, and now you've captured me and are here to kill me before your slaves. What a brilliant display of leadership. I learned from the best." He had accepted his death and was toying with his father, his final reprieve and enjoyment in the world. He had indeed lost everything. I had watched it be taken from him like a thief in the night. After all, I had learned from the best. "Give it to me," Peter replied, ignoring his son's remarks. I saw Jack raise his one eyebrow. "Give *what* to you?" he asked. "You stole it from me. I blamed many others before, but as I lay unconscious in that hospital room, it came to me in a *dream*," he mocked. "It was you. It was always you. Take off the goddamn eyepatch and show your men what you came for."

Peter looked at his son with disdain and disappointment. "No more fighting, Jack," he said. "You will lose. You will always lose against me. You have lost. Against what you cannot have. Never able to live in the *real* world." Jack hobbled closer to his father. "You're a crazy old bastard. You cannot exist here as I cannot exist in the dreams. Take off the fucking patch." Peter cackled. "We're actually very different, son. You see, I'm willing to risk my child's life for my power. Something you've never been able to do. Something you'll *never* be able to do." Jack grunted a charred grimace. "You leave her out of this!" he shouted raspily. Peter pointed to the top of the Perch building, where Julia lay. "She's right up there, son," he said happily. "She can watch you die." Peter raised his arms and looked around. "Come out, come out, wherever you are, Noah," he said cheerfully. He looked directly at me through the crack in which I stood and has trusted to conceal me. *One does not hide from God.*

Jack took his chance and brought his fist across his father's jaw. Peter turned slowly to look at his son, exhausted from the one hit. The man was brutally and bitterly *weak*. The man I had once looked at as the epitome of strength was a *child*. "Have you ever wondered why you've never been able to dream, son?" Peter asked manically. "No clue?" he taunted. "Because I *took it*," he said, reaching behind his head and letting the eyepatch drop to the ground below. The black fabric burst into flames and dispersed into nothing as the silver orb shone where his eye once lay. It fell from his socket and rolled across the pavement toward Jack. Jack fell to his knees and waited, mesmerized as the ball of pure silver rolled toward him ever-so-slowly.

The two men stood on opposite sides of a sewer grate, and one falls deaf to the sounds of the city depths when distractions arise. Neither of the two men nor myself heard the slithering or saw the serpent emerge from the grate and out onto the city street, moving in between chipped concrete and pothole crevices. Jack knelt down, hypnotized by the glow of the orb as it moved within his grasp. As he was about to wrap his fingers around what he had searched for and lost for so long, the snake swallowed the ball and slithered into plain sight for all to see. Jack shouted and Peter stood back as the serpent curled and curved around in the middle of the street before them, digesting the orb of light and glowing a slimy, shimmering black. Jack dove at the snake as it turned and reared its head, its fangs dripping venom, both men distracted by the snake.

I took my chance and ran out from behind the door, my gun sliding into my hand. I pointed my gun at both of them and cleared my throat, making them aware of my presence. "Kill him, Noah," Peter said. I should have killed Jack. I should have killed Peter. Perhaps I should have killed myself. "He killed your parents," he said. "And you're surely an *angry* orphan." Jack turned and spat at his father. "I know all about that." He turned to look at me then. "We can rebuild this place, Noah. Your home." I cocked the pistol softly, the only noise left in the city. I pointed the gun at Jack. He had killed my parents and taken everything from me. He had destroyed the world for his own gain and he deserved to drown time and time again with a weight tied to his ankles. The dreams were solid and peaceful - and above all - *powerful*. That world was dead and weak, and the choice was obvious. I made my decision, pointed the gun at Peter, and pulled the trigger.

The old man faded into nothing as the bullet stopped in his chest, reappearing and plucking the piece of metal out of the air. He turned it over in his fingers as the world stopped. It was only him and I. "Time and time again you make the wrong decision. It's gonna cost you, my son," he said sadly. He threw the bullet toward the Perch building. I turned and looked up at Julia, her terrified look glued to her face as she witnessed the scene. I watched the bullet sail through the air and near her, penetrating her skull. She lost her balance and fell from the thirty-sixth story, collapsing on the street below in a puddle of blood. My ears rang and my vision blurred as I struggled to process what had just happened before my eye, but I knew.

I tried to scream but no words would animate from my lips; I tried to cry but no tears would form. I tried so desperately to take her place in that moment and bring her back, but it simply could not be. Jack shouted and lunged at his father before attempting to run to his daughter's side, but he did not deserve to mourn her. He had *abandoned* her as he had been abandoned - as much as he had ran from it. The sewer grate flew into my hands as I brought it across his head, leaving a nasty gash in his forehead and knocking him nearly unconscious. "When are you going to learn, Noah? You're as bad as *Lucious Noy*," he said, the name hanging on his tongue and in my ears forevermore. My heart stopped at the mention of his name and what he had just done. I could not accept it, although I knew it. I lunged at him, but he drew his coat across his body and disappeared from view once more, that time for good. I was alone in the silent city street, devoid of answers and emotions. I ran over to Julia, but I stopped in my tracks as I heard the voice.

"What is an artist to a blind man?" I heard in Lucious's creepy, raspy tone. I looked around for him, but he was nowhere to be found. "What is a musician to a deaf man?" I heard him say. I saw nothing amid the destruction. "What is a philosopher to a dumb man?" he said finally. *Could it be in my head?* It had to be. The voice grew louder and louder. "You're a fool, Noah Willowby. You are nothing." I spun around. "SHOW YOURSELF, YOU FUCKING *COWARD!*" I shouted into the empty city. I heard his maniacal laugh echo throughout the entire town square. The snake uncurled and chased itself around a five foot radius, circling faster and faster as it slithered in place. I could feel the wind from the creature before me as I heard the voice and saw the fangs drip poison onto the concrete as the animal took on another form. The black scales shed into pale skin, the white teeth into blonde hair, and the blue eyes matching those of Lucious Noy before me. He had finally revealed himself to be the *snake* I had always known him to be. He had *always* been there. *Tempting* me. *Pushing* me.

"You're a long way from home," I said through gritted teeth. I raised my gun, pointing it into his oceans of eyes he so possessed. "You're going to point that at me like you pointed it at my sister before you killed her?" he spat, tears in his eyes. "I -," I started. But he interrupted me. "SHE WAS ALL I HAD LEFT AND YOU TOOK HER FROM ME!" he shouted. He got quiet and stood very still, staring at the hole in the street where the manhole cover used to be. "Peter killed your sister, not me," I said. "You're a lying prick," he spat at me. "Peter took me in and took care of my family. He would never hurt Felicia," the name stung in my memory. "Peter killed your family, just as Jack killed mine, just as he - ," I stopped and looked back at Julia's limp and lifeless body. "How does it feel?" Lucious asked with tears of anger in his eyes. "How does it feel?" he asked again. "Lucio -," I started. "No!" he shouted. "I'm the one talking now!" I backed up. "I'm telling you the truth, Lucious," I said. "Just calm down," I said, another bullet sliding into the chamber behind my back. "You're gonna feel my wrath, Noah Willowby," he said through slow, gritted teeth, pronouncing every word like a speech. I pointed my gun at him and put a round in his chest. The blonde, frail teenager fell into the sewer grate under him and splashed into the filthy water below.

I stood back and struggled to turn and look at Julia behind me. For an instant I hoped that she would be standing beside me once more, but that was reality. There were dreams there no longer. I walked toward her slowly, not wanting to face the truth and brutal reality of what had happened. I knelt down beside her and wiped the blood from her face with my shirt tail. I cradled her in my arms and hoped for a moment that I might feel a breath, but I knew there would be none. The thought only prolonged the shock and ripping sensation within me. My tears washed the blood from her broken neck down onto the pavement and into the city depths. The entire city mourned her death, and this was what I had inherited -a *burial ground* for the dead I had lost - that had been *taken* from me.

The guns had long since clattered to the ground, and Commander Aaron's squadron watched the scene silently from the sidewalk behind. He signaled for two of his men to come to me, and they progressed slowly with respect. "We will take her. Keep her safe while you figure this out. She is with us now," the soldier said. I had long since forgotten his name. *Had I ever known it?* I thanked him silently and shook his hand as he clapped me on the back and embraced me in a hug. I was sure that the soldier had known loss quite well. I was *empty*. The two men picked Julia up and sat her down on a bench, wrapping her in sheets from a nearby shop and cleaning her wounds. I looked away as a feeling of anxiety came over me. It was much deeper than loss or fear. I turned to face the manhole as I heard the sound.

I saw a slimy hand reach out onto the street as I heard the gurgling bubble of water beneath the street. The other hand pulled his body up out of the sewer as he stood up once more, a smile on his face. His shirt was ripped open and green slime dripped down his chest. "This is why you can't be a Dreamer, Noah," he said, rather serpent-like. "I am a Dreamer," I argued. "You were one of Peter's experiments. Training someone like you to be a Dreamer. Felicia and I brought you back only for him to fail. You can't have both worlds, Noah," he shot, grinning a yellow grin. "How do you know he failed?" I asked, a serrated knife sliding into my hand. "Because he failed with me," he said, his tongue slithering out of his mouth and back inside. I brought the blade across and slit his throat, green blood dripping from the opening. I stood back, horrified at what I saw.

"Didn't your mother ever tell you not to cut off the head of a snake? Two grow back, right?" he cackled, his tongue forked and bloody, his eyes yellow, and his skin peeling into scales. He spat slime in my face that tasted of motor oil and pineapple juice, and I wiped my eyes to see his true form. His wound was sealed by the deep green blood, his hair falling out and to the ground. His head shone bright and grew scales to match the rest of his body. His limbs retracted as he fell to his knees, his skin fading to black as he convulsed on the concrete below. The snake grew and thickened from a corn snake to a constrictor, its fangs baring and dripping green venom. Lucious Noy had become a serpent before me, as I knew he *always* was. The snake dove back into the sewer and the city fell silent once more. I heard the slithering and splashing from the street above, and I felt the vibrations and tremors through the shattered concrete under my feet. I stood back and looked around; there was no movement or sound in the town square, yet it was *alive*. Echoes bounced off of the buildings and reverted to shaking dusty smoke off of window sills and doorways. The city was alive under my feet, yet the power was not mine. Then it all fell silent. I stepped toward the sewer, an inch at a time. I peered over the edge and stared into the darkness. My heart skipped a beat as the snake - now at least ten times its size - cracked the concrete around the manhole and emerged from the crater in the pavement, its slimy body knocking me into the air and rolling across the sidewalk. I turned around quickly as the tail - at least a hundred feet long - wrapped around a massive chunk of asphalt and hurled it toward me. I dodged it barely with an inch to spare as the tail smacked the concrete, shaking my bones violently and separating the city street even further. The serpent hissed and sprayed venom across the sidewalk as I got to my feet and backed up against the building. I could have gone either way, and I moved slightly in both directions in indecision. I had to get the snake away from Julia, and Aaron's men stood at the ready. The soldiers aimed their weapons at the snake's head and took petty shots before opening fire. Lucious hissed once more and reared his head before diving into the row of men, sending them sprawling into the wall and cracking the concrete mural behind me. Julia lay on the bench still, untouched, and I could not get to her. I had to *tear* Lucious away from her.

As the snake expanded and grew as it became angrier, I turned and sprinted as he wiped out the line of soldiers. His tail was growing an inch every second, and his body became thicker and meatier with each passing minute. I ran out into the street behind him as he turned to look for me, hissing and showering venom as he spat in anger. He dove back into the sewer hole and tore up the concrete under my feet and sent me flying as he emerged back onto the street. The middle of the town square had been made an unstable crater, a massive abyss into the sewer below. I nearly tripped as the asphalt was torn from underneath my feet and changed direction as the serpent's head chased me into an alleyway. He could not fit through the narrow passageway as he slammed his head into the two buildings with force, shaking dust and debris from the rooftops on top of me. I remembered Julia and I running through this alley from the soldiers long ago, and I was still running. And she was gone. She could *not* be.

I could hear the angry hissing of the massive serpent as I darted through the dumpsters and over trash cans. I came to the other side of the alley and glanced behind me; the snake was *gone*. I looked around for him, but I could not hear or see it. I was thrown into the air as the serpent burst through the ground beneath my feet, tossing me a dozen feet in the air and whipping me into the wall once again. I rolled to my feet as his tail - the size of a tree trunk - smacked my legs out from under me again. I moved to one side and faked to the other as he dove head first into the dilapidated building, becoming lodged in the concrete. I climbed to my feet as they wobbled in weakness and ran for the bar room I had called home for weeks when I had returned to the city. The explosion had blackened the walls and lowered the ceiling, broken glass littering the floor. Our pillows were still on the floor, covered in blood. The room was silent, and the snake was gone once more.

I knelt down behind the counter and lifted an open bottle of liquor to my lips. I poured the remainder of the liquid on my wounds and did not wince as it stung; I had become *accustomed* to pain. I could not beat Lucious, I could only hope to escape his grip. I heard nothing through the open bar room as I dreaded poking my head above the counter ever-so-slightly. I saw no sign of the snake out of the shattered windows and broken doorway, and for a moment I hoped he had lost my trail. But that could not be. He was *above* this world, and he would not rest until he constricted the final breath from my lungs.

I lifted my head an inch or two above the cracked and stained wood, and the bar room was empty. I stood up and leaned against the counter as I crushed glass under my boots - the boots of a drained army. There were no more *armies* - only the dead and the dying. The serpent came through the ceiling above me as I dove behind the counter once more, dodging him as he leapt from the window and back through the door, taking massive chunks out of the building as it threatened to fall. The ceiling caved in as Lucious barely escaped; the bar room fell in on me as I covered my head with the blood-stained pillow I had rested on with hopes that had been crushed, hoping my bones would not follow suit.

My body was weighed down by countless pounds of force; I could not move at all in the slightest. I would suffocate before I could budge an inch, and I accepted a slightly less honorable death. I waited, and I *urged* it. I *begged* for it. The air was knocked out of me from above and below as the serpent pushed me up and out of the rubble, holding me in his teeth as I was thrown from the wreckage. I shouted in agony as he dug his poisonous fangs into my chest. I felt them pierce my bones as the venom spread into my blood, my body going numb and weak as I screamed. I heard the hissing as my vision blurred, giving in to death and feeling its grip. A feeling of relief spread over me as I recognized death and welcomed it; I was released from his grasp. I fell from his mouth, covered in slime and rolling nearly unconscious across the town square, my skin scraping against the torn pavement. I breathed heavily and struggled to see straight as the venom pumped through my veins. I could see the serpent growing and growing and wrapping around the buildings and taverns, witnessing my struggle as he prepared to finish me off. To *swallow* me whole. The snake disappeared behind the town hall and wrapped around the side; I had to escape while he had his head turned. I pushed myself up and saw stars as I shook with dizziness and nausea. The Perch building was on the opposite side of the town square, and I had to put distance between Lucious and I. I pulled all of the minuscule amount of strength I had left and ran toward the Perch building across the way, barely missing potholes and crevices, which were then massive ravines that the serpent had torn further apart. I tore through the doorway and around the corner as Lucious spotted me and hissed violently. He was coming for me, and I had nowhere else to run.

The poison in my body flowed through my blood and into my mind, causing violent hallucinations and surreal visions. I saw the garage in pristine condition and full of freshly-shined vehicles, even though I knew in my heart that it was cracked and empty. I climbed up the stairs as the snake nipped at my heels. I saw the armory full of weapons and armor as I shook it off and ran faster to escape the bite of the serpent. I ran around another corner as he slammed into the wall, shattering the brick and insulation, shaking the entire building. He tore through windows and doorways, destroying the foundation and supports of the building. The floors shook and the walls rattled as Lucious taunted me through his angry hissing. I was sweating in the freezing winter air as I pushed my body further and further beyond its limits. The snake moved faster and faster as he shattered ceilings and the floors began to cave in as I climbed set after set of stairs. Everything around me was falling as I threw myself onto the ladder and pulled myself onto the rooftop.

The rooftop cracked, shook, and shattered as the snake threw himself into the ceiling and exited through a window to wrap himself around the top of the building and take me. I slipped and regained my balance as the ground beneath me became uneven. There was only one way off of the rooftop, and I struggled to come to grips with it. If I were to perish from the consequences, come whatever may. I saw the head of the snake and its deep yellow eyes and I *knew* them. I ran up the slanted chunk of rooftop and knew in my mind what I had to do. My feet ran across the concrete as the lawn chairs fell down into the abyss below, the place where Julia and I had fallen in love. She had fallen with the chairs to a broken and crushed fate. My feet connected with the railing and leapt into the air, the metal handle of the sword materializing in my hands. He watched me and seemed to tease me, to urge me to try my best against his forces. It was all I had.

I felt the sword slide through the gelatin-like material of the snake's left eye as I slid across his massive back, slipping on the slimy scales. He reared back, threatening to throw me off forty-stories above the town square. I held on to the sword as I buried it deep within his eye socket, listening to the screams of agony from the serpent. His head began to fall as his tail whipped around the Perch building, bringing the final supports below to a crumble. The Perch building fell, covering the town square in a layer of dust and debris. There was nowhere to go but down, and I would surely perish if I were to let go.

The tail of the snake brought about the downfall of several other skyscrapers as I brought about his own destruction. I watched as buildings crumbled to the ground just as I had watched them climb to the sky many years before. I shouted as I struggled to hold on as the sword shook within his eye, the creature shaking violently and destroying everything in his wake. We lowered closer to the ground with each tremor, the snake shriveling and shrinking back to his original state inch by inch. The sword wrinkled free of his socket as I dug it into his back, holding on for dear life. Lucious screamed with each time I stabbed the blade into his skin, green blood oozing from his spine. We neared the pile of rubble which was then the city street, the once all-powerful town square where Jack King led his people in a broken world he had mistaken to be his. The world belonged to no one. It was *destined* to be destroyed, and I was a *witness*. I had *inherited* the earth, and Jack King was crushed underneath layer upon layer of wreckage hundreds of feet below.

As the black skin of the serpent shrunk and took on yet another form, I pierced the sword into the head of the snake. We hovered above the square as his shaking grew more violent. I could hold on no longer. I lost my grip and slid further and further down the spine, dragging the blade down the body as I fell. He spun around as I gripped his tail, losing my grasp as he circled, finally throwing me off. I sailed through a window and rolled across a falling floor, holding my head as the building crashed toward the ground. If it be death, I welcomed it. I had done what I came to do, lost all I had, and become responsible for a great amount of evil surpassing any reasonable amount of guilt. It was my time, and the earth had no heir. The world would surely die with me.

I braced myself for the collision and grimaced as my body slammed into wooden boards and piles of bricks. My body was cut and bruised beyond recognition, and I became numb from the venom in my blood. The roof above me had been disintegrated into dust, and I could move freely. I had fallen in the middle of an insulated wall, and I was no longer pinned down. I gripped the wooden supports and pulled myself out of the rubble and struggled to gain footing on the unstable wreckage. I ducked out of the broken doorway and searched around for the snake for a final time, and it was no more. I caught sight of a limp figure several yards away. I hobbled over to him, hallucinations creating a false truth in front of me. I saw the city as it once was, as I remembered it, and as it was then. The visions blurred and smeared together like paint across my memory as I staggered toward the bloody and unconscious teenager.

Lucious lay sprawled across a section of untouched pavement, one of the only places in the town square not harmed from weeks of destruction. He coughed and spat blood as he came to, not having the strength to sit up. I knelt down beside him as he opened his eyes. He spoke two simple words as he pointed at the two tooth-shaped tears in my shirt. "You lose," he muttered, managing a sly grin through his painful grimace. I looked down at the blood dripping a yellow infected tint, soaking through my shirt I was freezing with sweat, chills running down my spine and a shiver in my bones.

"You're wrong," I said. He looked at me. "The *only* way to deal with a snake it to cut the goddamn head off," I sneered before bringing the sword completely through his neck, severing his head from his body as it rolled down the cracked concrete of the town square and into what was once the sewer manhole. The sword dropped from my hands as the tint silver orb rolled into my foot. I knelt down, picked it up, and pocketed it as I turned to leave the body of Lucious Noy. Julia's body lay on the bench as the soldiers had left it, and they were nowhere to be found. Whether they had been crushed or fled, I knew not. I was only sure that she was safe - even though she was most definitely deceased. The horrible hallucinations cast ghastly shadows across the scene as I saw her sitting on the bench, alive and well. I knew in my heart that it was not true. I limped over to her as quickly as I could and bent down beside her, lifting her body into my arms, one hand under her head and one under her legs. I knew not whether it was mine or her blood on my body, only that we had both perished by the hands of another. I had killed her, and I had been crucified by the city.

I knew not where to go or what to do, only that I needed to escape the wrath of the city, for it would not stop, even after every structure had fallen and every heart had been torn from its body. I carried Julia past the town square and past my old home which carried the ghosts of my family under the shadow of the hill where Sebastian was buried. My heart was heavy with the burdens of the city, and I turned for a moment to look at the shattered image of the mansion on the hill above the city. It shone through the destruction of the city, a broken dream and clouded memory of the past. My body was weak and my will to go on was urged by nothing more than the promises of the doors of death waiting on the other side. As I turned around to face the city gate leading into the vast unknown - an infinite dream of the outside world - I saw the blurred figures of a man carrying his son outside of the gates as I carried Julia into a world we had once vowed to escape to. Perhaps it was a mere mirage - another hallucinatory hoax - but I had a promise to keep, and it came with a vast knowledge and understanding. I have learned that you get to choose your path, and I had chosen that of the Dreamer race - the *inheritors* of the earth - for it is the *only* choice. The *only* way to see the world is through an unclouded eye, and I possessed it in that moment as I broke free from the city that had held me prisoner for years. I am a Dreamer, and your choice is your own. So allow me to ask you, my friend - are *you* a Dreamer?

CPSIA information can be obtained
at www.ICGtesting.com
Printed in the USA
LVHW030320171218
600716LV00003B/775/P